FAIRHAVEN RISING

TOR BOOKS BY L. E. MODESITT, JR.

L. E. MODESITT, JR.

FAIRHAVEN RISING

TOR

A Tom Doherty Associates Book

NEW YORK

FAIRHAVEN RISING

Edited by Jen Gunnels

A Tor Book
Published by Tom Doherty Associates
120 Broadway
New York, NY 10271

www.tor-forge.com

Tor® is a registered trademark of Macmillan Publishing Group, LLC.

The Library of Congress Cataloging-in-Publication Data is available upon request.

ISBN 978-1-250-26519-7 (hardcover)
ISBN 978-1-250-26518-0 (ebook)

Our books may be purchased in bulk for promotional, educational, or business use. Please contact your local bookseller or the Macmillan Corporate and Premium Sales Department at 1-800-221-7945, extension 5442, or by email at MacmillanSpecialMarkets@macmillan.com.

First Edition: February 2021

Printed in the United States of America

0 9 8 7 6 5 4 3 2 1

For Jen Gunnels, with appreciation

CHARACTERS

Beltur   *Head councilor of Fairhaven; majer, Fairhaven Guard; black mage and healer*

Jessyla   *Councilor and chief healer of Fairhaven, black mage, Beltur's consort*

Kaeryla   *Apprentice healer, daughter of Beltur and Jessyla*

Arthaal   *Beginning black mage, apprentice smith, son of Beltur and Jessyla*

Tulya   *Councilor and justicer of Fairhaven*

Taelya   *White mage, guard undercaptain, daughter of Tulya*

Dorylt   *Beginning black mage, cabinet maker's apprentice, son of Tulya*

Margrena   *Healer, mother of Jessyla*

Meldryn   *Black mage, baker*

Jorhan   *Coppersmith*

Johlana   *Sister of Jorhan*

Gustaan   *Captain, Fairhaven Guard*

Therran   *Senior undercaptain, Fairhaven Guard*

Graluur   *Chief, Fairhaven Town Patrol*

Dussef   *Assistant chief, Fairhaven Town Patrol*

Korlyssa   *Duchess of Montgren*

Koralya   *Heir and daughter of Korlyssa*

Korsaen   *Protector of Montgren*

Maeyora   *Trader and consort of Korsaen*

Korwaen   *Son of Korsaen and Maeyora*

Maenya   *Daughter of Korsaen and Maeyora*

Raelf   *Commander, Montgren*

Zekkarat   *Majer, Montgren*

Halacut   *Duke of Lydiar*

Maastyn   *Duke of Hydlen*

Rystyn   *Viscount of Certis*

OCEAN

Gulf of Austra

AUSTRA

Brysta

Valmurl

NORDLA

WESTERN OCEAN

Swartheld

Luba

Cigoerne

Atla

AFRIT

Swartk River

MEROWEY

HAMOR

GANDAR

Devalonia
Armat
Diev ruins
Bleyans
Rulyarth
SUTHYA
West Cliffs
HIGH STEPPES
Dosai
RIVER SARRON
carpa
West Horns
SARRONNYN
Jera
Bornt
Sarron
Lornth
Middlevale
JERYNA R.
NORTH BRANCH
Rohrn
the Ironwoods
WEST-WIND
Biehl
Berlitos
JERANS
RIVER SARRON
Roof of the World
GALLO
Fenar
DELAPRA
the Stone Hills
SOUTH BRANCH
Clynya
Kyphri
Summerdock
CERLYN
West Horns
Dellash (Esalia)
SOUTHWIND
Stone Hills
COPPER MINES
MILDR R.
Southport
Stone Hills
NACLOS
The Great Forest
GRASSLANDS
PHROM
the Empty Lands
Rybatta
HIGH DESERT
Fen

Diehl

GREAT WESTERN OCEAN

NORTHERN OCEAN

Gulf of Murr

Land's
End

Black Holding

Alberth   Extina

Reflin

Cape Devalin

Spidlaria   Lydkler

Quend

SPIDLAR   Alaren

Kleth

East
Elparta Horus   Maltra Feyn

Rytel   Wandernaught
Lavah   Clarion   Enstronn
SLIGO   Sigil
Tyrhawen   Nylan
CERTIS   Southpoint
Jellico   MONTGREN
Passera   Vergren
Yrinja   Weevett Fiven Freetown
Tellura   Freetown
Meltosta   Hydolar   FREETOWN
OHYDE   RIVER   (LYDIAR)
KYPHROS   HYDLEN   Renklaar
Dasir   Telsen
ikoya Arastia   Asula   Pyrdya

ythga   Sunta

STURBAL   HIGH
DESERT
Ruzo   Worrak

RECLUCE

Gulf of Candar

Northern Bay

FYTN R.

Fakla River

EASTERN
OCEAN

C.Mitchell 1995

FAIRHAVEN
RISING

I

In the early afternoon of fourday, the three blue-uniformed Road Guards reined up under a spreading oak tree on the south side of the road, in a valley whose western end was roughly ten kays east of Fairhaven.

"There's no sign of the riders that the shepherds reported," offered Lendar, a stocky black-haired man, who was neither old nor young.

Taelya guessed that he was about ten years older than she was. Her eyes went to Hassett, one of the most recently trained guards, roughly four years younger than Taelya herself, before she replied, "Not within two kays of the road."

Lendar eased back the visor cap that all guards wore—including Taelya—and blotted his forehead with the back of his hand. "It's hot for this early in spring."

"You think summer will be even hotter, or that today's just an exception?" asked Taelya.

Lendar shrugged. "Could be either." He looked eastward along the road that eventually led to Lydiar, but that curved slightly to the north around a low hill roughly two kays farther east at the end of the valley. "There's a hint of dust beyond the hill, ser," said Lendar to Taelya, deferentially.

"Wagons, you think?" asked Taelya. "Or guards and wagons?"

"Most likely both. It rained yesterday morning."

Taelya concentrated, then nodded to Lendar. "Two large wagons and four mounted guards. There's likely a guard riding with the teamster of each wagon, although it's hard to tell."

Hassett looked from Taelya to the senior Road Guard.

"All of the mage-guards can sense that far," said Lendar.

"Majer Beltur can sense farther," added Taelya. She didn't mention that some mages couldn't sense nearly that far, which was one reason she was a Road Guard with the rank of undercaptain, a rank partly because of her actual abilities and partly because mages had to be officers, although Beltur had strongly advised her to listen to senior Road Guards such as Lendar.

She took out a water bottle, filled with slightly watered ale, and took a swallow. She would have preferred unwatered ale, but, given her size, she worried that enough ale to keep her going would also hamper her magery.

Almost a half a glass passed before the two traders' wagons neared the three guards and Taelya led the Road Guards out to meet the wagons, then turned her mount to ride alongside the two men in the seat of the lead wagon. Lendar rode beside her, while Hassett rode on the other side of the wagon.

The man with the crossbow looked to the three Road Guards, his eyes lingering on Taelya just a moment longer. "You Road Guards are farther east than usual."

"That's because we had reports of possible brigands," replied Taelya. "We'd prefer that traders arrive in Fairhaven safely."

The man looked to Lendar quizzically.

"The undercaptain's in charge," the senior Road Guard replied cheerfully to the unspoken question.

"I beg your pardon, ser," the trader said flatly to Taelya, looking directly at her, not quite leering.

Taelya wanted to make him swallow his words, which were scarcely apologetic. Instead, she gathered a small ball of free chaos and placed it in midair perhaps a yard from his face, letting the heat radiate toward him. "Women mages have always fought for Fairhaven. We're also good at removing brigands." Smiling, she let the chaos disperse. "We'll escort you back to town, just to make sure you arrive safely."

The trader tried not to swallow . . . and failed. "Ah . . . we appreciate that."

The teamster sitting beside the trader on the wagon seat managed to keep from smiling, as he kept the two big dray horses moving down the road.

"You're coming directly from Lydiar?" offered Taelya conversationally.

"We are."

"The last traders were talking about Duke Halacut's health. Do you know if he's any better?"

"He was when we left. For now, anyway." The trader paused. "Have you any word on the Prefect . . ."

"Traders coming from the west have said that he's talking about raising tariffs again." Taelya didn't mention that the reason that several successful traders had built warehouses and started working out of Fairhaven was because the town only charged the tariffs required by Montgren and didn't put the additional squeeze on traders the way most cities in Hydlen and Certis did, but then a large portion of the Montgren trade tariff was retained by the town, and traders who built warehouses or factorages also paid property tariffs. Even so, Fairhaven's finances were still chancy, as Taelya's mother—the town treasurer—had mentioned more than once.

"He just raised them a little over a year ago."

"We've heard that he's had trouble paying off the moneylenders he borrowed from to pay the mercenaries who held off the Viscount's troopers."

The teamster looked quickly at Taelya, then away, as if he hadn't expected something that she'd said.

"And we're supposed to pay for his foolishness?" The trader spat, but carefully away from Taelya.

"Only if you want to trade in Gallos," replied Taelya.

"Getting so it doesn't make much sense to go to Certis and Gallos, not with the tariffs getting higher and higher. Hydlen's almost as bad."

Taelya just nodded and kept riding, still trying to sense if there might be brigands anywhere along the road ahead.

More than a glass later, the trader frowned as they approached the stone indicating that the edge of Fairhaven proper was five kays ahead. "Road's different, since last fall."

"It's metaled," said Taelya. "Packed gravel. That way it won't rut and get as muddy. The main street's stone-paved now, too, from one end of town to the other."

"Your Council raise tariffs to pay for that?"

"No. It was paid from past tariffs."

"And your Council didn't make us traders pay for it?"

"Only with past tariffs. It took years to set aside the golds to do it."

"Begging your pardon," said the teamster, "but how does an undercaptain know as much as you do?"

Taelya smiled pleasantly. "It might be because Majer Beltur likes his Road Guards to be well-informed. That way people are less likely to pass along false rumors. We wouldn't want traders to get the idea that we're raising tariffs, for example."

"I can see that," said the trader. "Is there anything new we should know?"

"The distillery still has some kegs of pearapple brandy for a decent price."

"What about apple brandy?" asked the teamster.

"The East Inn might have some at the public room. This year's kegs won't be ready until late summer or early fall."

Taelya wondered if one would ask why the pearapple brandy was available when the apple brandy was not, but since neither did it was clear that they knew the pearapple brandy cost more.

When Taelya and the two other guards reined up on the main street in front of the East Inn, where the trader guided his two wagons and guards into the stable yard, it was half past third glass.

"Undercaptain . . . ?" said Lendar.

"I don't see there's much sense in riding halfway to the edge of Fairhaven and turning around," replied Taelya. "So we can ride to headquarters, and we'll all spar until fourth glass."

Taelya didn't even have to look at Hassett's face to sense the junior guard's dismay. "We both need the practice, and Lendar needs to stay in shape."

"Ser . . . I can't even touch you," protested Hassett.

"That's true," replied Taelya. "That's why we use wooden blades." *And also because iron blades striking my shields hurt a lot more than wooden wands.* "But I need to get better with the blade for the times when I'm too tired to hold shields, and you definitely need to get better."

"The undercaptain has a point." Lendar grinned. "Better now than in summer."

Taelya smiled at Hassett. "I won't pick on you." *Not at first.* "I'll spar against Lendar to begin with. Then against you. And the time spent unsaddling and grooming doesn't count." Taelya added that because those times weren't counted as duty glasses, but it made more sense to unsaddle and groom first, then spar, and they'd all be finished sooner that way, without stinting duty time.

Lendar nodded at her last words, as if to emphasize the point.

The three rode past the town square, where several women were gathered around the fountain, talking more than filling their water buckets or jugs, and where a few carts with goods remained. Taelya glanced to the south side of the square and toward the new Council House and Healing House. Although people called them new, they were both over fourteen years old, rebuilt after the Hydlenese had burned the originals.

She had no doubt that her mother was still at the Council House, either working with the land tariff records or dealing with some aspect of her duties as town justicer. In the Healing House next door, Aunt Jessyla and Great-Aunt Margrena held sway, and on the south side of the square was the chandlery.

The three guards turned off the main street into the buildings that served as the headquarters for the town patrollers and the Road Guards, as well as quarters for those Road Guards who had no consorts or families. Taelya could remember when it had been a rather run-down inn before the innkeeper had been exiled to Certis for failing to pay his town tariffs. *And a few other things.*

Outside the stables, she dismounted and led her horse inside, where she unsaddled him, then checked his hooves, before beginning to groom him.

Lendar finished with his mount before Taelya did and stopped by the end of the stall. "I'll get the wands and meet you outside."

"Thank you."

Hassett was still brushing his mount when Taelya left the stable and walked from there to the courtyard that served as an exercise yard.

Lendar was waiting. "I brought the wand you usually use, and a practice jacket." The senior Road Guard already wore such a padded jacket.

"Thank you."

"And a heavier wand," added Lendar. "The majer suggested it."

Taelya said nothing for a moment, because her initial feeling was to reject the heavier wand. Instead, she said, "I'll try it." After pulling on the heavily padded practice jacket, which she needed when she kept her shields close to her skin, she took the heavier wand. The grip was about the same.

"It's slightly heavier than your sabre, the majer said." Lendar's words were offered almost apologetically.

Taelya understood the reason for Beltur's suggestion, but there were definite disadvantages to being under the command of the man who'd been her uncle for almost as long as she could remember. *Most of those disadvantages being that you can't get away with anything.* Not that Taelya really wanted to do anything that Beltur or Jessyla didn't think was a good idea, but . . .

"It's probably better," she admitted, knowing that, until she got used to the additional weight, Lendar would get more hits on her shields, some of which might result in bruises, despite the padded jacket. But bruises were nothing new, since Taelya hadn't had a natural talent with blades, and it had taken her a good year to learn to even hold her own against the other junior guards. Unfortunately, once Taelya had finally reached that level, her uncle had insisted that she start working with those who were better, like Lendar, who was better than most Road Guards, except perhaps Gustaan and one or two others.

The two stepped into the large brick-paved circle, and Taelya reduced the extent of her mage-shields close to her body, because, otherwise, Lendar would simply be striking at a wall, and Taelya wouldn't be learning anything.

She began with a feint that Lendar ignored, then had to slip a slash-cut. But she didn't counter quickly enough, and Lendar blocked that.

For the next set of exchanges, neither scored a hit on the other.

Then, one of his thrusts slammed under her guard, and the impact on her shields was definitely unpleasant, but not nearly so unpleasant as a thrust with a sharp iron blade would have been.

"You've been working on that," she said, moving to the side.

"I had to. You're shorter than me. It's work to get lower."

After a quint, during which Taelya had hit Lendar perhaps once, and he'd definitely landed thrusts or cuts on her shields, the senior Road Guard stepped back. "Perhaps you should do a time with Hassett."

Taelya nodded and took a deep breath. She was sweating heavily, both from the padded jacket and from the exertion, but she stepped forward into the circle and raised her wand.

Hassett held his wand too high. So Taelya feint-attacked high and came in low, tapping Hassett just below his ribs before darting back.

After that, the sparring was more even, possibly because Taelya had already sparred, and the heat and long day were taking a toll. She couldn't help remembering that Beltur had made her practice magery when she was tired, even when she was much, much younger, saying that it strengthened her over time.

Less than a quint later, Lendar spoke up. "It might be time to stop. You're both getting sloppy."

Taelya stepped back.

So did Hassett, blotting his forehead with an already damp cloth, then saying, "You and the other younger mages spar. The majer doesn't."

"He and Mage-Healer Jessyla were never taught blade skills when they were young," replied Taelya. "That's why he's insisted that all the younger mages and healers learn them. That way we can defend ourselves some when we can't use magery."

"You can do better than just defend yourself some, ser. I'll have bruises to show for that."

Taelya smiled wryly. "So will I."

"You've said you hold those shields close to you when you spar, and that means you can get bruised or hurt. Why do you do it that way?"

"Because that way I can learn how to use a sabre better for when I'm too tired to hold shields." Taelya also suspected that Beltur wanted all the mages to understand a little about how fighting felt to those without magely shields.

Hassett shook his head.

After the junior guard left the exercise yard, Lendar turned to Taelya. "Someday, he'll understand." After a hesitation, he said, "You learned young, didn't you?"

"I can remember being told to shield my mother when the Hydlenese attacked. I was seven. It didn't come to that, but I still remember. That was still easier than what you went through, though."

"I was a little older," replied Lendar, "but . . . you don't forget."

No . . . you don't. Taelya smiled pleasantly. "I'll see you tomorrow." Then she retrieved the second wand, the one she hadn't used.

"Until then, ser."

Taelya carried the two sparring wands to the armory and racked them. Then she took off the practice jacket and hung it up. As she turned, she saw Beltur standing in the doorway. With his bright silver hair, and his jet-black forehead—the result of excessive magery during the war against Hydlen—he was an imposing figure and likely would be for years to come.

Her uncle—also the head councilor of Fairhaven as well as the majer who commanded the Road Guards—was smiling. "You're getting much better with blades. Much better. I was watching."

"Thank you, ser."

"It might be best if you practiced with Gustaan occasionally. I'll mention it to him."

"What about my starting to practice with Kaeryla?"

Beltur shook his head. "Right now, you're a much better mage, and you're far better with wands or blades. Also, neither of you is likely to ever fight another woman. That's why you don't practice with Varais, either."

"She's also better than Gustaan," said Taelya. "I've watched them."

"That's not surprising. She's from Westwind. How else have they held their own? In any case, it's better for both you and Kaeryla to practice against men." He smiled again. "You've accomplished so much already."

"But it's not enough . . . is it?"

"It would be more than enough if you were an undercaptain anywhere else. With all the squabbling and bad blood between Gallos and Certis, the sad state of Lydiar, and with Montgren caught between Certis and Lydiar, I'm afraid we'll be in another war before long. I hope not. We're trying everything we can to avoid it, but that's why we've begun to train another squad of Road Guards."

Taelya had wondered about that since there were already three fully-trained squads. She also wondered how the town could pay for them.

"That's also why I'd rather have you, Dorylt, and Kaeryla as prepared as possible . . . even Arthaal as soon as he's able."

Taelya noticed that he didn't mention either Sheralt or Valchar. So she decided to. "What about Sheralt and Valchar?"

"What do you think?"

"They're both older than the three of us, and much older than Arthaal."

Beltur raised his eyebrows. "What does that have to do with ability?"

"Sheralt's almost as strong a mage as I am, and he's a white. Valchar has strong shields."

Beltur nodded. "And?"

"Sheralt's shields aren't as strong as mine or Dorylt's. They're about as strong as Kaeryla's, but shields are really all she has so far. I mean, for fighting or battle."

"So . . . you're saying that together, Valchar and Sheralt might be as strong as you are."

"Yes, ser."

"And you're younger."

Taelya understood her uncle's point. She just didn't like it. So she said, "Sheralt's physically stronger than I am. Why aren't his shields stronger?"

"Because he didn't want to learn how to make them stronger. He tried for a few days and said it made him feel strange. He also suggested that he'd rather go elsewhere than be treated like he was fourteen again."

"So you didn't push him?"

"I've had more than a few things to do over the years, Taelya, and you can't make someone do what they don't want to unless you're willing to risk destroying them."

"You made me do things."

"You wanted to learn. Sheralt didn't."

Taelya was still thinking that over when Beltur added, "You don't like the idea that I'm expecting more out of the three of you than mages who are older and more experienced. Do you think I'm being unfair?"

"It doesn't seem right . . . somehow."

"It isn't," Beltur agreed, a certain weariness in his voice. "It isn't right that healers have to fight. It isn't right that Fairhaven has to fight when we've never attacked anyone else. You know that better than almost anyone."

"Why don't they leave us alone?"

"Because we're getting prosperous, and they have troubles, and it's easier to blame us . . . and if they can take what we have, then they think that will get rid of their troubles."

"Why can't they see that it won't?"

"Can't . . . or won't?"

"You're saying that they're choosing not to see the real problems."

"Isn't that true of most of us?"

"You see the real problems. Why can't they?"

"I didn't always see the real problems, and then I didn't have any choice. You haven't had much choice, either. The rulers of larger lands have more ways to deceive themselves." Beltur smiled again. "You're off-duty. You ought to head on home."

Taelya abruptly remembered. "I do need to go. I promised to take a ride with Kaeryla."

"She'll appreciate that."

While Taelya sometimes wondered about that, a promise was a promise.

With a quick nod to her uncle, she turned and hurried out of the patrol building. She had to walk home, because she had ridden a Guard horse for the day's road patrol, rather than Bounder, although Bounder was better trained, but she preferred to alternate riding Bounder and another horse, so that she could choose to use Bounder for the more demanding Road-Guard duties. She'd barely walked a hundred yards when she saw a courier in the pale blue of Montgren riding toward headquarters, and she wondered what the message he carried might be.

II

"It's time to head back." Taelya glanced at the wall of dark clouds to the north-east, sensing the interplay of order and chaos behind the darkness, then turned in the saddle to look at the not-quite-gangly redheaded young woman in the light green tunic and trousers of an apprentice healer riding beside her.

"Do we have to?" asked Kaeryla. "We're only halfway to the kaystone. Can't we go a little farther?"

"Not with that storm coming. You ought to be able to sense the strength of the order and chaos."

"I can't sense as far as you can."

Taelya managed not to wince at the hint of bitterness behind the words. "You'll be able to when you're older. Your sensing is beginning to improve every eightday."

"You could sense that far when you were my age. I can't."

"Your parents have told you that you take after them." Taelya knew she'd pointed this out before, but Kaeryla needed to keep hearing it. "Uncle Beltur couldn't do anything at all until he was eleven, and your mother was a healer who didn't become a mage until she was twenty. You're fourteen, and you can do more than either of them could at your age. You have strong shields, solid concealments, some containments, and you can already do healing."

"That's not enough, and I'm nearly fifteen."

"You're an acting junior undercaptain Road Guard." *And that's more than Dorylt can do, and he's a year older than you are.*

"That's just for my shields, and because there aren't enough full mages."

"It's also to give you experience."

Kaeryla snorted. "You're just trying to make me feel better."

"Is that so awful? Besides, what I said was true, and you know it. Every mage is different."

"That's easy enough for you to say."

"In time, you'll likely end up as strong as your mother is, if not stronger." Taelya managed a pleasant smile, something she'd been getting more practice with in the past season.

"You can throw chaos bolts, and she can't."

"But her shields are stronger than mine," *if only a little,* "and she can throw back any chaos thrown at her." Taelya paused, then said, "We do need to head back." She turned her gelding toward the center of Fairhaven.

Kaeryla guided her mare to follow Taelya, not without a slight grimace.

The two rode back along the tree-lined road, past some of the newer houses built on each side of the road in the last few years. Less than quarter glass later, they passed the two brick posts, one on each side of the road, that marked what had once been the edge of Fairhaven, back when it had just been known as Haven, and the hooves of their mounts clattered on the stone paving of the main street.

The rain had already begun to pelt down in large drops when the two rode up to the small barn behind Kaeryla's house, or rather, her parents' house, where they dismounted and led their horses into the barn. Taelya glanced at Kaeryla, now more than a head taller, despite the fact that Kaeryla was eight years younger and might grow even more.

Taelya didn't speak as she groomed Bounder, her thoughts once again on the messenger in the pale blue uniform of Montgren that she'd seen enter headquarters as she had left to walk home just after she'd finished sparring.

When they finished grooming and watering their mounts, Kaeryla looked to Taelya. "I'll close up the stable. You've had a longer day."

"Thank you. Dinner's at our house tonight."

"Then I'll see you when Father gets home."

"He might be late. I saw a Montgren dispatch rider going into headquarters just after I left."

"That's not good."

"Probably not," agreed Taelya. "I'm sure your father will let us know." *Sooner or later.*

Then she hurried out of the stable, through the rain and across the street to the house she shared with her mother and brother. After she closed the kitchen door behind her, she stood in the alcove and straightened the sleeves of her uniform tunic, glad that they were only damp. She could smell the burhka immediately . . . and smiled.

Tulya looked up from the stove, where several large pots rested. "You didn't get too wet, I see."

"We cut the ride short."

"How was your patrol today?"

"We didn't find any brigands. We ended up escorting two traders' wagons from the north valley all the way into town. The trader was surprised to find a woman mage-guard in charge. You'd think that after the war with Hydlen, people wouldn't be surprised, especially a trader from Lydiar."

"Fairhaven is the only land in Candar with women mages who serve as fighters, except Sarronnyn, and it does take time for word to get around. Then, he might not really be a trader from Lydiar. Or he might have moved there recently."

"He didn't seem to be lying when he said that. There weren't any swirls of chaos." Taelya paused. "Where's Dorylt?"

"He's in his room reading a history of Candar. He borrowed it from Johlana. He already set the table and laid out the dishes."

Taelya glanced to the far end of the kitchen at the closed door leading to the small bedroom that was her brother's, a room added almost ten years earlier when the front parlor and kitchen had been extended, and when Tulya had decided that Taelya should have her own room as a young woman. "What can I do?"

"Sit, and we can talk until the others arrive."

Taelya took the end chair closest to the stove, turning it to face her mother. "Uncle Beltur might be late. There was a messenger from Montgren."

Tulya smiled wryly. "He's often late. He has to deal with the orchards and the distillery, and everyone wants something from the head councilor."

"They usually don't get it."

"That's because they want special favors, and your uncle isn't about to grant them." Tulya's eyes twinkled. "He'll grant exceptions, but the exceptions require even more work or golds, if not both. That's something you've known all along."

"Dorylt has trouble with that."

"He'll learn."

"Learn what?" The slender blond youth who walked into the kitchen was more than a head taller than his mother and a few digits more than that taller than his sister.

"That Uncle Beltur doesn't grant special favors," replied Taelya.

"I know that. Everyone knows that. That's why I can't ride as a Road Guard yet."

"Do you want to practice shielding later?"

"You won't have time tonight," interjected Tulya.

"What are you working on with Jaegyr?" asked Taelya.

"A dining room table and chairs and a sideboard for Trader Waaltar, for the house he's building on the north side of town, on the new lane just north of Julli and Jaegyr's house."

"I saw that the other day," said Tulya.

Dorylt frowned. "Only the foundations are done."

"His assistant brought in the plans for me to see. He doesn't want there to be any misunderstandings when we assess the house for tariff purposes."

Taelya and Dorylt exchanged puzzled glances.

"The house is just a dwelling. There's only one small study in it, and no storage space for goods, and the stable doesn't have a loading dock. He doesn't want it tariffed like a factorage or a warehouse. He's being very careful." Tulya laughed softly. "It won't be just a house, though. It's a small mansion."

The three looked up at the sound of knocking, but before any of them could reach the kitchen door, it opened, and Kaeryla stepped in, followed by her mother, the silver-haired and green-eyed Jessyla. Arthaal was the last one into the kitchen. He carefully shut the door behind him, and shook off rain from his oilskin jacket, before walking to the pegboard on the wall by the front door, where he removed the oilskin and hung it up. Then he returned to the kitchen, his reddish-brown hair plastered to his skull by the rain.

"Beltur's washing up," said Jessyla. "He'll be here shortly."

Tulya nodded to Taelya. "If you and Dorylt will get everyone ale . . ."

Taelya immediately picked up two beakers and moved to the keg of ale on the wooden stand next to the kitchen cistern, where she filled the two deftly, one after the other, handing them to her brother to pass out while she filled two more beakers, and then two more, setting a last beaker by the keg for when her uncle arrived.

The six settled around the long table, leaving the chair at the head vacant for Beltur.

"What did you do today, Arthaal?" asked Tulya.

"I'm working at the smithy with Jorhan. Father can't spend that much time there these days. So I'm learning everything. Jorhan says someone else here ought to learn how to forge cupridium before he can't."

"He's not that old," said Kaeryla.

"He's not that young," replied Jessyla. "He's old enough to have children as old as Beltur and I are."

"Do you like it?" asked Tulya.

"I've only been doing it less than a year, Aunt Tulya, but I think I do. Jorhan's showing me how to make molds, and I can sense the order and the chaos in the forge and the metal and how Father places an order/chaos net in the molten bronze." Arthaal shook his head. "I can do shields, and even concealments for a little while, but I can't even put the weakest order/chaos net into metal."

"That will come in time," said Jessyla.

The kitchen door opened once more, and Beltur stepped into the kitchen, accompanied by a gust of wind and rain. The band of black skin that covered his forehead, and, in fact, the top of his entire skull, if under his silver hair, glistened with the rain that had obviously blown under his visor cap, a cap that he immediately took off.

"It's really coming down," he announced, quickly closing the door behind himself and setting the cap on the nearest window ledge.

Taelya immediately filled his beaker and carried it to his place at the head of the table, then took his oilskin and hung it on the front pegboard.

"Thank you. I can use that . . . and the excellent fare it goes with." Beltur settled into the chair and took a healthy swallow.

Tulya nodded to her children. "If you'd get the bread, Dorylt? I'm just going to serve the burhka from the stove. So if you'd hand me the bowls one at a time, Taelya, and then put them on the table . . ."

Taelya immediately moved to get the bowls. In just a few moments, everyone was seated with a full bowl. Beltur sat at the head of the table, with Tulya on his left and Jessyla on his right. Taelya sat beside Jessyla and Kaeryla beside Tulya, with the two young men at the end across from each other and not seated beside their sisters.

"What was in the message from Montgren?" asked Arthaal, looking toward his father.

"It was a dispatch from Lord Korsaen," replied Beltur, after swallowing a mouthful of burhka.

"Father . . ." protested Kaeryla.

"Duchess Korlyssa is in ill health, and her daughter Koralya is effectively acting in her stead. This isn't exactly unexpected. We've talked about it before."

"Then there was more in the dispatch," pressed Kaeryla.

Taelya noticed that both her mother and Jessyla tried to conceal smiles.

"Yes, there was," admitted Beltur, his tone pleasant. He took another swallow of ale, and then broke off a chunk of warm bread and dipped it in the burhka.

"What did it say?" Kaeryla's voice was mild.

Even so, Taelya could sense the younger woman's exasperation.

"Lord Korsaen, Maeyora, and Lady Koralya met with an envoy from the Prefect of Gallos . . ." Beltur paused, looking at his daughter for a long moment with a smile on his face before continuing. "The Prefect wants an alliance with Montgren and Hydolar against the Viscount. Korsaen and the others aren't pleased with the idea, but they told the envoy they'd consider it, depending on what Duke Maastyn does."

"An alliance with the Prefect?" Tulya's tone was half horrified, half astounded. "He tried to invade Spidlar and then Certis. And Duke Maastyn's father tried to destroy Fairhaven."

"The problem is that the Viscount has rebuilt his forces and the Prefect hasn't had the golds to do the same," replied Beltur. "He's also getting along in age and doesn't want to fight Certis alone."

"He should have thought of that ten years ago," said Tulya. "None of his neighbors should trust him."

"That's exactly why he's approaching Montgren and Hydolar." Jessyla turned to Beltur. "What are you going to tell Korsaen?"

"To listen, but not to commit to anything, either way. There's nothing to be gained by offending the Prefect."

"You'd say that after what he did to you and your uncle?" asked Dorylt. "And what the old Duke of Hydlen did to Father?"

"That was in the past. I can't change that. What's important now is what's best for Fairhaven. Our tariff receipts are up, but . . . without help from the Duchess . . ." Beltur paused, then went on: "I thought the Council could meet first thing tomorrow morning, and we could talk it over. I sent word to Taarna and Claerk."

"And not to us?" Tulya smiled as she spoke.

Beltur grinned back at her. "You're getting your notice now." He paused and added, "I made it early because I need to talk to Taarna about buying more land for the orchards. We're selling out of the apple brandy earlier every year. And I promised Jorhan I'd work at the smithy tomorrow."

"Another special piece for Waltaar to sell somewhere else at an exorbitant price?" asked Kaeryla, her tone only mildly sarcastic.

"He pays as well as we were paid in Elparta, and no one else is buying right now. We do well, and so does he."

"Did Lord Korsaen say anything about the garrison in Weevett?" asked Taelya. "Whether he was sending another company there or not?" She couldn't help but remember how long it had taken the Duchess to send troopers to Fairhaven when the Hydlenese had attacked.

"The dispatch didn't mention that."

Of course not. But Taelya didn't say that. It was better that she didn't. Just asking the question had made her point.

Kaeryla looked as though she might say something, until Jessyla shot her a sharp glance.

"The burhka's excellent, as always," Beltur said cheerfully.

"You're kind, as always," returned Tulya, with an amused smile.

Taelya could tell that nothing else of import or of great interest would be discussed at dinner, and she turned her attention to the burhka . . . which was good . . . as always.

III

On fiveday morning, Taelya had to struggle to get out of bed, possibly because it was cloudy and there was no direct morning sunlight to ooze around and through the inside shutters in her room. She was the last one to the kitchen, where she immediately poured half a beaker of ale and began to eat the oatmeal porridge left on the table in a bowl for her.

Dorylt was wiping off the stove, and he said. "You're late. You'll have to clean up after yourself."

"I cleaned up after you yesterday."

"I didn't sleep late yesterday."

"You could have rapped on my door."

"Both Mother and I did."

"Next time . . . knock louder."

"The last time I knocked louder, you threatened to throw a chaos bolt at me."

Taelya vaguely recalled that, but she'd been so tired, and she'd had cramps, something that she wasn't about to share with Dorylt, especially after her mother had told her that it was all part of being a woman, and not to complain about it because, while other women might care, it was something they didn't talk about, and men didn't understand. "I'm sorry I was cross, but I didn't feel well then."

"Mother told you that was no excuse."

Taelya winced at the superior tone in her brother's voice, but decided not to say more. She'd get him back when she worked with him on shielding exercises.

At that moment, Tulya peered into the kitchen. "I'm leaving for the Council meeting. Make sure you clean up after yourselves." Without waiting for a response, their mother was gone.

"I told you so," murmured Dorylt.

Taelya didn't bother replying, but finished the porridge and the ale as quickly as she could.

By the time she finished, Dorylt was standing by the front door and called out, "I'm leaving for Jaegyr's! I'll see you tonight."

Taelya washed the bowl, beaker, and spoon quickly, and set them on the drying rack. Then she filled her water bottle with a mixture of ale and water before hurrying from the house, making sure to lock everything before departing. Since she hadn't ridden Bounder that far on fourday, Taelya decided to saddle him and ride to patrol headquarters.

She had to unlock the stable because Jessyla and Kaeryla had already left, Kaeryla likely for the Healing House, and Jessyla for the early Council meeting. *It would have been nice for Dorylt to help a little.* Except she knew it was her own fault, and that didn't help with her worry that she'd be late for the morning briefing . . . and she had to take time to close and lock the stable as well. She would have liked to make up the time by having Bounder at least canter, but that wouldn't have been fair to the gelding, especially on the stone paving that wasn't as smooth as it could have been.

When she reached the headquarters building, just before seventh glass, Taelya glanced to the far end of the paved yard, where the twenty or so new recruits stood in formation, waiting as Undercaptain Therran strode up. Taelya turned her attention back to Bounder, reining him up at the railing outside the stables. After tying him to the rail, she hurried inside to the conference room to join the senior Road Guards and other officers.

Valchar and Sheralt were already there, standing on one side of the conference table, while Lendar, Nardaak, and Dhulaar stood on the other side. As Taelya neared the two other mages, Sheralt nodded politely, and Valchar smiled briefly. But Taelya didn't have time even to offer a greeting before Captain Gustaan arrived and stood at the end of the table.

"No need to sit down. I'll be brief," began the captain. "Mage-Undercaptain Taelya will accompany Nardaak on the west road, Mage-Undercaptain Valchar will accompany Lendar on the south road, and Mage-Undercaptain Sheralt will accompany Dhulaar on the east road. Since there are no reports of brigands, the east and west patrols should not ride more than five kays beyond the kaystones. The southern patrol will begin where the south road intersects the east road and proceed as usual to the Hydolar road and thence to the west road, and then return by the same route."

"There was a messenger from Montgren last night," said Sheralt before Gustaan could say more. "Is that indicative of something we should know?"

"The Council is meeting about that right now," replied Gustaan. "I'm certain Majer Beltur will let you all know by the time you return from your patrols or at tomorrow's briefing. That's all I have for now. You're dismissed to your patrols." Gustaan turned and left the conference room.

Even before the captain was through the door, Sheralt sidled up to Taelya. "What are they meeting about? Surely, you know something."

Taelya smiled pleasantly. "I knew there was a meeting, but Mother didn't tell me anything about the subject. She left the house very early this morning." Every word Taelya said was true.

"You aren't answering the question."

"That's something you'll have to ask the majer about."

"It's got to be something about Certis or Gallos," pressed Sheralt.

"Not necessarily," replied Taelya. "Remember that Duke Halacut isn't in the best of health."

"I'd forgotten about that," said Sheralt.

Taelya could sense that Sheralt had done no such thing, but she just added as she began to walk toward the door, "Also, anything new about what's happening in Worrak would come to Lydiar and then to Montgren first. Didn't you say that one of the reasons you left Worrak was because the pirate lords were getting so strong?"

"No one in Montgren would think that was a threat," Sheralt pointed out, hurrying to keep up with her.

"Not to Montgren, but it might cause problems for Fairhaven, and Lord Korsaen doesn't want any problems for us." Taelya kept moving down the short hallway toward the stable yard.

"Do you think he really cares that much?"

"He might care a lot if Uncle Beltur decided to deal with a problem in a way that he thought wasn't in Montgren's interests." As she stepped outside, she adjusted her visor cap.

"Do you really think he would?"

"If he had to. You've seen him. Do you think he wouldn't?"

Sheralt paused. "I suppose he would."

Taelya untied Bounder, then mounted before she replied. "We can talk about that later."

Then she turned the gelding toward Nardaak and Breslan, the junior Road Guard, both of whom were already mounted.

"Did Mage-Guard Sheralt have anything of import to say?" asked the dark-haired Nardaak with a smile as he urged his mount forward and toward the main street.

"Not a thing. He was hoping I had information."

"Given your family and friends, he might think that's not an unjustified hope."

"Given them, it's totally unjustified," replied Taelya, easing Bounder up alongside Nardaak's mount.

Nardaak grinned. "He'll learn."

He should have learned by now. Especially since, handsome as Sheralt was, with his hazel eyes and light brown hair, he was a good five years older than Taelya. *But then, being so handsome just might be the problem.* "Someday, but don't hold your breath."

The senior Road Guard just shook his head, then glanced back at Breslan.

While Nardaak said nothing, Taelya suspected she knew the gist of the unspoken message . . . and she immediately regretted her last words. *You know better than to offer public judgments of other mages.*

She said nothing until they had ridden several hundred yards farther. "Have any of the other patrols seen signs of brigands or heard anything?"

"Not recently."

"What about traders?"

"The only ones in the last few days were those that you and Lendar escorted in yesterday."

"You've been with the Road Guards . . . what? Ten years?"

"Nine."

"I've always had the impression that by the third or fourth eightday of spring, we had more traders than we're seeing from the west and the south. You've much more time watching the roads than I have. Am I mistaken about that?"

Nardaak shook his head. "I can't recall any traders from Gallos and Certis, and only a few from Hydlen. There have been more than a few from Lydiar, and even one from Spidlar and another from Axalt."

Taelya knew all about the last two, because they'd come looking for fine cupridium objects from Jorhan's forge. "Harvests were good everywhere last fall so we should be seeing more traders. I'd like to hear what happened at the Council meeting."

"So would we all," said Nardaak dryly.

By shortly before eighth glass, the three had reached the west kaystone, without any sight of traders, although they had passed several carts and wagons, all of which Taelya recognized as being from Fairhaven or nearby. She reined up and took a long swallow of watered ale from the bottle she extracted from its leather holder.

"I don't see anyone on the road west," said Nardaak.

"There's no one near the road except some people working the fields on the south side of the road about half a kay ahead," replied Taelya. "I can't sense clearly as far as the Weevett road, but there's a feeling that there's no one near the junction."

"I've never known your feelings about whether people were there or not to be wrong."

"Ser . . ." ventured Breslan, "is it true that the majer can sense almost five kays?"

"That would likely be a stretch for him, even on a day like today," replied Taelya. "It all depends on the weather. In a heavy rain, any of us might only be able to sense half a kay, if that." She wasn't about to disclose exactly how far any mage-guard might sense, especially given that Sheralt was fortunate to be able to sense order and chaos for a kay at most, and that Valchar wasn't that much better. But then, they hadn't been trained by Beltur from the time they were seven.

After a brief rest, the three resumed riding westward, and before long, Taelya was certain that no one was on the Weevett road, at least not for a kay north of where it intersected the road that the three traveled, a road that led first to Certis and, eventually, to Gallos. On the other hand, she had a feeling that there were travelers due west of them heading toward Fairhaven, but that was only a feeling that likely wouldn't become a certainty for a time.

When they reached the junction with the Weevett road, the three reined up, and Nardaak and Taelya studied the road itself.

"No new tracks from the north," said the senior Road Guard.

"We still need to see if there's anyone on the Hydolar road," said Taelya. "It'll be another glass or so before the southern patrol gets close."

"If then," said Nardaak.

The three had covered a little more than a kay and were nearing the Hydolar road, which remained empty of travelers, both to sight and Taelya's senses, when she was finally able to sense the travelers farther to the west.

"There's a whole group of wagons headed this way on the road from Certis," said Taelya. "They're just beyond that curve in the road around the hill ahead on the north side of the road."

"What about riders?" asked Nardaak immediately.

"There might be one or two. There are people on foot, too."

"How many?"

Taelya understood what he wanted to know. "I don't think it's a group of arms-men. Some of those walking might be children."

"Who would be doing that at this time of year, when it's still planting time?" asked Breslan.

"We'll see before long. What if we wait at the junction with the Hydolar road?" Taelya didn't want to make that an order, just in case Nardaak had a better idea.

"That's probably the best place. There's a small grove of trees on the north side of the road." Nardaak paused. "They aren't coming from that hamlet to the north, are they?"

"No. They're on the main road west of the lane that leads to the hamlet."

Before long the three had reined up under the trees and dismounted, letting their horses graze on the spring grass that would get sparser by mid-summer. A half a glass passed before the first wagon came into view, not quite a kay to the west, followed by several others. The later wagons raised enough low dust that Taelya found it hard to make out more than general shapes of those walking beside them, but some of those shapes were definitely children.

"They're farm wagons," observed Nardaak. "Not a merchant's wagon among 'em."

"And there are children. That means they're fleeing something . . . or some-one. We might as well mount up and see what we can find out. I'll lead, just in case someone thinks we'll do something to hurt them."

In moments, Taelya was mounted and riding toward the oncoming wagons.

As they neared the first wagon, a single man, with gray hair and wearing a leather jacket over faded brown trousers and shirt, rode to meet them.

Taelya reined up and waited.

The older man halted his horse a good five yards from Taelya. "Young . . . ser . . ." He looked puzzled.

"Yes, I'm a woman, a mage, and a Road Guard undercaptain of Fairhaven. Where are you headed . . . and why?"

"You're from Fairhaven? Then we're almost there."

"A little less than eight kays east of here. Why are you headed there?"

"We heard that the Council there would accept any who were willing to work. We're willing to work, and we are skilled in certain trades."

"Where did you come from, and why did you leave?" Taelya rephrased the question that still hadn't been answered.

"We came from Erkham. We had to leave. The Viscount is taking everything from anyone who is a Kaordist."

Taelya managed not to frown. She'd heard of the order-chaos believers, whose god had two faces—one of order and one of chaos—but she hadn't heard of any in Certis or any conflict between the Kaordists and the Viscount.

"Or anyone his officers accuse of being one," added the white-haired man driving the wagon that had pulled up behind the rider, a wagon with stained and sagging sideboards. He also wore faded brown trousers and shirt.

"Why?" asked Taelya.

"No one's saying. They're just taking. We managed to get out of town before the first troopers rode in. The folks in Kaskcar weren't so fortunate. They killed the men and boys and took the women and girls. We had to circle west into the Easthorns and then take the river road until we neared Hydolar. We barely avoided Duke Maastyn's men." The white-haired man's eyes narrowed as he studied Taelya. "Never seen no woman armsman before."

"I'm not an armsman. I'm a mage-guard undercaptain of Fairhaven."

The driver looked to Nardaak. "You let her command you?"

"Besides the fact that she's an officer, and I'm not," replied Nardaak, "she is a white mage, and can throw enough chaos bolts to turn all of us into cinders. She's also not bad with the sabre."

"I told you Fairhaven had woman mages," said the rider, a certain exasperation in his voice.

"There's lots you told us, Storch. Too much for a body to remember."

Taelya looked past the first wagon, then decided she'd learn more by sensing. So far as she could tell, there were nine wagons. "Besides the nine wagons, how many people do you have with you?" she asked Storch.

"We had ten wagons. One family stayed in Hydolar."

"They might have been right," interjected the white-haired driver.

"How many people?" Taelya's tone turned cold and icy.

"Offhand, I don't know. Nine families, forty, maybe fifty men, women, and children."

Taelya turned to Nardaak. "I think we'd better send Breslan back with a message to the Council to expect nine wagons with as many as fifty people looking for a place to settle."

Nardaak turned to the junior Road Guard. "Did you get that?"

"Yes, sers."

"Then off with you."

As Breslan turned his mount, Taelya focused her attention on Storch. "We'll escort you into town." She just hoped that the Council would be amenable to having the refugees use the way station on the east side of Fairhaven, because she couldn't think of another place that would hold that many people.

"Will that be necessary?"

"If you expect help in getting settled."

"What if we don't like Fairhaven?"

Taelya shrugged. "Then you can keep going. There aren't any sizable towns east of Fairhaven until you get to Lydiar and the Great North Bay, not by road. You'll have to take the Hydolar road there"—she gestured over her shoulder—"if you want to get to Renklaar or any of the coastal towns in Hydlen."

"What about other places in Montgren?"

"In a kay or so, we'll ride by the road north to Weevett. If you take it, you'll get to Vergren in a couple of days. Most of what people do in the rest of Montgren is raise sheep and grow things." She paused and extended her senses as far as she could to the west, then looked to Nardaak. "There's no one following them. Not within two or three kays."

"Good." The senior Road Guard nodded.

Taelya returned her scrutiny to Storch. "Now . . . we'd better get started." She turned Bounder and gestured, then urged her mount forward.

After several moments, Storch caught up with her.

She turned in the saddle. "Are you interested in seeing if you want to settle down here? If you are, you can help with that by talking to me as we ride. It will be very useful to the Council to know what sort of skills the men and women in your group have. Are there men who've worked with orchards? Any smiths? Possibly any fletchers? Or fullers? And young men with an interest in becoming armsmen?"

"Armsmen?"

"Fairhaven has always had to take on more than its share of defending itself. That hasn't changed. We have three squads of Road Guards and a squad of town patrollers." That wasn't totally accurate, as far as the patrollers went, but it was close enough, especially for someone like Storch, about whom Taelya knew almost nothing. "We do train and pay Road Guards and patrollers, if they can meet our standards."

The leader of the group from Erkham looked as if he might be about to speak, then closed his mouth for several moments before finally replying, "One of the men is a mason. He does good work. Another was a cooper. He even has his tools."

"If the cooper is good, I know someone who'd be more than happy to pay him, and there's always a need for masons." *These days.* Taelya recalled clearly when that had not been so.

"How many mages are there in Fairhaven?"

"Enough," replied Taelya. "We also have several very good healers."

"I'd think you'd more likely be a healer."

"White mages are more suited to being mage-guards. We do have two women healers who are also black mages. Now . . . you were telling me about what skills some of your people have."

"We're mostly growers, except for Fernaam and Barrelan . . . and, I guess you could include Varsyn. He was an apprentice wainwright before he became a grower . . ."

Taelya listened, prompting Storch with gentle questions until they were about a kay from the stone posts that marked what had been the edge of town, when Storch looked ahead and pointed. "Those look to be new houses."

"Most of the houses between here and the stone posts ahead have been built in the past five or six years. We've had several traders move to Fairhaven. They're the ones with warehouses and stone lanes to the main road."

"You let traders move here?"

"We let anyone move here who is willing to work and pay his or her tariffs."

"Women work in trades here?"

"Some do. The brewery and the distillery are owned and run by a woman. The town justicer is a woman." Taelya decided not to mention that her uncle was half owner of the distillery or that her mother owned a tenth part.

Storch frowned, but lapsed into silence.

Taelya couldn't help but wonder if the Kaordists were so traditional that they wouldn't want to stay in Fairhaven because a few women were in positions of power. *That's their choice.*

Just before they reached the stone posts that had marked the west end of the town proper when Taelya had come to Fairhaven, they neared the West Inn, an expansive two-story structure with large stables and even a shed that could be locked and held two wagons. The inn had only been finished little more than a year before by Claerk, who had taken over the East Inn after the death of his stepfather five years earlier.

"Mighty fine-looking inn," said Storch.

"The traders with large wagons and guards mostly stay there," replied Jessyla. "The East Inn is just as good, but it's a bit smaller."

"Erkham wasn't big enough for an inn, just a hostel."

Although Taelya had never heard of a hostel, she gathered that hostels were much more modest.

When Taelya and Nardaak reined up outside the headquarters building, Beltur walked out and stopped short of her mount. He wore the same blue uniform as Taelya did, except the two bands on the ends of his tunic sleeves were black, while Taelya's were white.

Taelya gestured to Storch. "Majer, this is Storch. He's the leader of this group. He told me that they're Kaordists who had to flee Certis because the Viscount was seizing everything that they had . . . and worse." She paused, then added, "There was no one following them closely."

Storch just stared at the silver-haired majer with the black forehead for a long moment before speaking. "They killed all the boys and men in the neighboring hamlet," said Storch. "We left before they did that to us."

Beltur nodded. "We need to talk and see if we can be of help." He turned to Taelya. "Thank you, Undercaptain, Senior Road Guard. You can return to your patrols. Road Guard Breslan is waiting for you in the stable yard."

"Yes, ser," replied Taelya.

Once she and Nardaak met up with Breslan, the three rode back out along the west road, this time just to the Weevett road, before returning. They arrived back at headquarters slightly after fourth glass.

After signing out, from headquarters Taelya rode Bounder back to the stable behind Beltur and Jessyla's house, where she groomed, watered, and fed Bounder before returning to her own house.

Dorylt was in the kitchen, sitting at the table drinking a beaker of ale. "I heard you brought in nine wagons of people fleeing from Certis."

"I didn't bring them in. We escorted them so Uncle Beltur could talk to them. They're not used to women armsmen, or women who work outside the home or stead."

"Most people in Candar aren't. That's what Aunt Jessyla and Uncle Beltur are always saying. Even I know Fairhaven's different from most small towns." He paused, then added, "Don't tell me it's not a small town, either. We're still not half the size of Weevett."

Taelya took a beaker from the cupboard and filled it only half full, then sat down opposite her brother. "You're right. But the way the town is growing, it won't be that way long."

"You think so?"

"I don't think that Waltaar would be building that enormous house or the warehouse on the west side of town if he didn't think Fairhaven would grow. He wants to be here before others discover what he has."

"That may be, but every time he sees you, he watches you. At least, when I've been around."

"That's because I'm a white mage."

"I don't think so." Dorylt smiled. "Both Valchar and Sheralt look at you the same way."

"You're imagining things."

"Am I? Then why are you blushing?"

"You're impossible."

"Taelya. You're good-looking. Men look at good-looking women. Especially women who aren't consorted. Some of them still look at Mother or Aunt Jessyla. You don't think they'd look at you?"

Taelya was more than aware of that. She just didn't want to discuss it with her fifteen-year-old brother, even if he was more than a head taller than she was. "I can't stop them from looking."

"Then don't get upset if I tell you that Waltaar's looking. I only said it because he's . . . well, he sort of feels like axle grease, dark and slimy. I know we need traders, and I know he's paying Jaegyr well for the cabinetry and furniture. But I don't like him, and I don't like him looking at you like that."

Taelya looked at Dorylt. "Thank you. Those are the nicest words I've heard from you in quite a while. I'm sorry if I've been a little short with you. I've been worried . . . and I don't even know quite why."

"Is it Sheralt or Valchar?"

"Valchar's nice, but . . . he's more like you."

"Is that because he's younger than you?"

"No. It's more a feeling."

"And Sheralt?"

"He's polite, but he's always trying to get close to me. I really don't want to cause trouble, especially now. We might need every mage we can find."

"Before long—"

"You're not ready yet. Your concealments are good, but your shields won't take more than a handful of chaos bolts, and Gustaan says you need a lot more work with blades. And Arthaal definitely isn't ready. Kaeryla has containments, concealments, and shields, and her shields are stronger than yours, but none of the three of you can return chaos bolts. Whether I like it or not, we need both Sheralt and Valchar."

"They can't throw back chaos bolts, either, you said."

"But Sheralt can throw his own chaos bolts, and Valchar's shields are strong enough to hold off most whites." When she heard the front door open and sensed her mother, she immediately asked, "Would you like me to get you an ale?"

"Just half a beaker," replied Tulya. "Remember . . . we're going to Jessyla's for dinner."

Taelya moved to the cupboard, then to the keg of ale, and had the half-filled beaker in hand by the time Tulya reached the kitchen.

"Thank you." Tulya took the beaker and sat at the end of the table. "I heard you had an eventful patrol today."

"Some Kaordists from Certis. They're . . ." Taelya couldn't find a word to describe exactly how Storch had struck her.

"Very traditional, I imagine," suggested Tulya after taking a sip of the ale. "Women stay on the stead or mostly in the home."

Taelya nodded. "That's it."

"They'll change after a while."

"If they stay," said Dorylt.

"Where else can they go? The only other place they'd be welcome is Worrak, and there's no easy way to get there . . . and that's if they wanted to live in a city run by pirate lords."

Left unspoken was the fact that Tulya and Taelya's father had come to Fairhaven for very similar reasons.

"You're a little dusty, Taelya. We should wash up before we leave. You, too, Dorylt. Especially you. You're carrying more than a little sawdust. And you need to spend some time working on your shields with Taelya."

Taelya washed up quickly, then waited in the front room for Dorylt. As soon as he appeared, she said, "You're not carrying your shields, and you weren't when I came home."

"It was a long day. I'm tired."

"Put them up, or I'll start thumping you with tiny firebolts."

Dorylt's shields appeared. "Why can't you use order instead of chaos, like Uncle Beltur."

"Because I'm a white. He's a black."

"He uses both. You should, too. That's if you want to get stronger."

Taelya started to speak, then paused. Finally, she said, "You might be right." Then she smiled. "I'll use both." With that, she probed Dorylt's shields with order, thinly dusted with chaos, because it wasn't as uncomfortable.

He backed up.

"You stand still and let your shields take the blow."

"All right."

After another order probe, she switched to one of chaos, then followed it with one of order.

After three more sets of probes, Dorylt's forehead was damp, and Taelya could tell that he was straining. She switched to using straight order, ignoring the slight discomfort, realizing that she could press him harder without worrying about burning him.

Less than a third of a quint later, his shields collapsed.

"Ohh . . . that hurt."

"It was just order," she said. "You can catch your breath, and we'll do it again."

Dorylt looked to the archway where Tulya stood. "Do I have to?"

"No," replied Tulya, "not if you don't mind dying young."

Dorylt rebuilt his shields.

After another quint, Tulya said, "We need to go before long. Dorylt, you need to wash your face."

As Dorylt headed to the washroom, Tulya moved closer to Taelya and said quietly, "You're pushing him harder."

"He needs it. He was right, though, about my using order."

"Was it harder?"

"A little, but not that much."

"Then you ought to keep drilling him that way."

Half a glass later, the three walked across the narrow street to a house almost identical to their own, one that had been expanded in the same fashion nearly ten years earlier.

Kaeryla met them at the door. "Good. You're here. I'm starving."

From behind his daughter, Beltur said genially, "You only think you're starving."

"Father . . ."

"You can allow your father a few pleasantries, dear. Just head to the kitchen." Beltur beckoned to Taelya. "I need a few moments with you."

Taelya stiffened. When Beltur wanted a few moments, it was seldom for praise. "Of course."

Kaeryla, Tulya, and Dorylt immediately headed for the kitchen, leaving the two alone just inside the front of the parlor.

"Taelya, Sheralt suggested that you weren't exactly as pleasant as you might have been with him this morning."

"I was very pleasant with him. I just didn't tell him what he wanted to hear. He wanted to know what the Council was discussing. I told him that Mother had left the house early and told me nothing. He kept pushing, but all I said was that we could talk about it later."

"So you told him a partial truth in a misleading way. It might have been better just to say that it was a matter for me to announce."

"It might have been, ser, but I was almost late, and he was being sneaky."

"Why didn't you just say that he should ask me?"

"I did. That was when he said it had to be about Gallos and Certis, and I pointed out that it didn't have to be, that Duke Halacut had health problems and . . ." Taelya stopped as she saw Beltur's expression.

"Taelya . . . you need just to say 'no.' Don't talk around the problem or offer what else it might have been. As a matter of fact, one of your guess-excuses was right. Duke Halacut is failing, and that was also in the dispatch. Just what will Sheralt think when he finds that out? Especially after you reported yesterday that the trader said he was improving?"

Taelya tried not to swallow.

"Just keep it simple from now on," said her uncle. "Either say you don't know—but only if you don't honestly know—or say that any information has to come from me or from Gustaan. And . . . since your shields are more than strong enough to stand against any chaos he could throw, or against any physical attack, you shouldn't be worrying about that, either. And Sheralt knows that I can tell who's telling the truth and who isn't." He smiled sympathetically.

"It's not just that . . ."

"You can tell him you're not interested in him, that being friendly is all you're interested in. If he doesn't like that, there's nothing to keep him from going elsewhere."

"But . . . we need mages."

"We don't need mages who don't follow the rules of common courtesy or who can't be trusted. We've done without untrustworthy mages before."

"That was a long time ago, ser. And Sheralt isn't untrustworthy. He's just . . . stubborn."

"That's why he's still here. Stubborn or not, he is trustworthy." Beltur smiled. "Just be firm and pleasant. We'll stand behind you. Completely." He paused. "That's all I had to say. We ought to join the others."

Taelya didn't even shake her head as she walked toward the kitchen.

IV

Taelya woke well before the white sun rose over the horizon into the clear green-blue sky, and she washed and dressed quickly, making it into the kitchen well before Dorylt.

Taelya looked at Tulya, standing by the stove. "Mother, you sit down. I can cook the scramble."

"Thank you." Tulya moved from the stove, but took three beakers from the cupboard and filled each with ale before settling herself at the table.

Taelya sliced off a bit of fat, then let it melt to cover the bottom of the heavy copper skillet while she sliced the cold leftover mutton into small chunks with the sharp cupridium kitchen knife that Beltur and Jorhan had forged for her. Then she sliced the mushrooms and minced the small piece of ginger root. While she could handle iron blades, they made her feel uncomfortable, and she'd always appreciated the cupridium kitchen knife, which had been in the kitchen before she was eight, as well as the cupridium belt knife and sabre that her uncle had forged for her as soon as she was old enough to begin weapons training. Beltur and Jorhan had also forged cupridium blades for Sheralt, which was more important for him because he had more trouble with order and iron.

When the fat just began to sizzle, she added the mushrooms, followed by the mutton chunks, and then the eggs from the bowl that Tulya had already frothed. When the eggs were soft-cooked, she lifted the skillet off the stove quickly used the big wooden spoon to ladle out the scramble onto the platters, beginning with her mother and serving herself last, after which she set the still-hot skillet on the wooden trivet that Dorylt had crafted to replace the old one, then took her place at the table.

At that moment, Dorylt stepped into the kitchen and sat down at the table, looking slightly sheepish.

Taelya refrained from grinning.

"Very nicely done," said Tulya, breaking off a chunk of bread and then handing the basket to Taelya.

"Thank you."

"I'll clean up," Dorylt offered. "You helped make breakfast, and you need to get to headquarters early today."

Taelya gave her brother an inquiring glance.

"Uncle Beltur took you aside last night, and you were really quiet at supper. You were up early this morning . . ."

Abruptly, Taelya laughed, then said, "You know me too well."

"You don't exactly hide your feelings," Dorylt replied.

"No," interjected Tulya, her voice even but firm. "What you saw, Dorylt, wouldn't be enough for most people to draw that conclusion. How much additional chaos did you sense?"

"Some."

"More than some, I'd wager," replied Tulya.

As Taelya listened, she realized, again, what an advantage she and Dorylt had in reading people. *And yet, even without that advantage, Mother can discern what she can't order/chaos-sense.* And, most likely, so could others.

"She was pretty upset last night," admitted Dorylt.

"How long have you been able to really sense the order and chaos around Taelya?"

"Really sense it? The last season or so."

"People who aren't family and who aren't mages won't sense all that, Dorylt. So it might be best when you're with others if you don't say things that reveal, even indirectly, what you sense." Tulya paused, then added, "Unless it's to family or to prevent physical harm. And if you're not sure, then don't say anything others can overhear."

"But I was just talking to family," protested Dorylt.

Tulya smiled warmly. "That's why I was so gentle with you. Beltur or Jessyla wouldn't have been. You saw your sister's reactions to what Beltur said. Would you have wanted to hear what he said?"

"No, ser," said Dorylt quickly.

"Good." Tulya turned to Taelya. "The scramble is quite good, but you don't have that much time to eat it if you want to get to headquarters early enough not to hurry whatever you have in mind."

Taelya nodded and turned her attention to eating, realizing as she did that the scramble had turned out well.

A quint later she was saddling Bounder, after checking him over and grooming him quickly. She'd just finished and was leading the gelding out of the stable when Kaeryla appeared.

"You're early this morning," said the girl who was effectively her cousin.

"I need to do some things at headquarters before muster. I'll see you later. You'll be at the Healing House?"

"I will. Is something happening? Father left early as well."

"I don't know of anything new. I just have to take care of some things, and I won't have time for them after muster. We can talk about it later."

"Do you promise?"

"I promise," replied Taelya as she mounted Bounder and turned him toward the main street, her thoughts returning to how she could deal with Sheralt, preferably without getting him too upset. *Although he was the one pushing for information that wasn't yours to provide.*

She had no more than turned Bounder east on the main street, heading toward headquarters, than she saw Taarna's brewery wagon just ahead, with Buskar in the driver's seat, unmistakable because only he and his mother had the same white-blond hair. Buskar was most likely heading for the East Inn, and probably after having delivered a keg or even two to the West Inn first.

As she rode up along the left side of the wagon, he glanced back, then smiled. "Taelya! You're out a bit earlier than usual."

"So are you." Once Taelya had ridden up even with Buskar, she slowed Bounder so that they kept pace with the wagon. "How come?"

"Claerk's running low on ale, and he thinks he'll be getting more traders from Certis."

"From Certis? How does he know?"

"That's what he said. He didn't say any more. Ma said some might be leaving Jellico for good. That's because the Viscount keeps increasing tariffs on everyone."

"Thank you for letting me know. I need to get moving, though." She eased Bounder forward.

"You're always in a hurry, Taelya."

"Not always."

"Every time I see you, you are."

Taelya just smiled and kept riding.

When she reached headquarters, she noticed that she was early enough that the recruits were just beginning to form up. She dismounted and tied Bounder at the hitching rail in the shade, or where it would be shady for the next glass, then hurried inside and made her way toward the duty and briefing room—the space that had once been a small public room.

Lendar, Nardaak, and Varais stood at one side, quietly talking, while Sheralt stood alone at the far side of the table.

Taelya nodded to the three and then made her way to Sheralt. She wanted to take a deep breath. She didn't. Instead, she smiled warmly. "Good morning."

"Aren't you cheerful."

"It is a pleasant morning, but I owe you an apology for yesterday morning. I was trying to be gentle, and I might have misled you. After I left, I realized that firm directness would have been much better. Anything I hear at home stays at home until the majer or Captain Gustaan announces it. That is what I should have told you."

"I appreciate the apology, Taelya, but you still ended up misleading me. You said we'd talk later, and then you avoided me."

Taelya wanted to shake her head in disbelief. Instead, she smiled and said, "I didn't avoid you. I was tied up dealing with the refugees from Certis. Now is as soon as I could have talked to you, and that's what I'm doing. Also, the other matters that I mentioned are still concerns that face Fairhaven. Even though they are, I shouldn't have mentioned them because you might have thought I was letting you know what was in the dispatch, when I was just guessing. But it's not a good idea for me to share guesses, not when my mother and uncle are on the Council."

"No . . . it's not. How are you going to make it up to me?"

Taelya had a very good idea what Sheralt had in mind, but she smiled pleasantly. "By being pleasantly firm when I can't say anything and by being nice to you even when you don't deserve it."

Sheralt's face clouded.

Taelya could sense the swirls of chaos around Sheralt that suggested anger and strengthened her shields.

"Just because the majer is your uncle . . ."

"If he weren't, you wouldn't be trying to get information you shouldn't have from me, and you wouldn't even be angry." *Not about that, anyway.*

"She's right about that, you know," added Valchar, who had eased up as the two had been speaking.

"Of course, you'd say something like that," replied Sheralt, turning toward the other mage.

Even though Valchar was carrying full shields, something that Beltur insisted upon all the time, Taelya could sense at least a swirl of chaotic anger.

But Valchar smiled politely before replying. "I understand your skepticism. You spent far too much time in Worrak, where everything is based on immediate self-interest."

"Please don't tell me you have no self-interest."

"Black angels, no. I have a very healthy self-interest, especially in not being blinded by appetites and greed of the moment."

Sheralt snorted, then started to speak, but stopped as someone stepped through the archway into the briefing room.

Rather than Gustaan, Guard Undercaptain Therran entered, followed by Beltur. Therran only said, "The majer has a few words for all of you."

Beltur smiled wryly before speaking. "As most of you know, yesterday, several families arrived from Certis. They're Kaordists who fled from the Viscount because his men have been taking the golds and property of at least some of the Kaordists, as well as killing the men and boys and enslaving the women and girls. It's likely the Viscount is doing that, at least in part, to blame the Kaordists for all the unpleasantness in Certis and to raise more golds than he can get from tariffs. That suggests that he's making more preparations for war. We've also learned that there was at least one white mage with the force that destroyed the neighboring Kaordist village."

After a brief pause, the majer continued. "The Prefect of Gallos has sent an envoy to Vergren to talk with Lord Korsaen . . . and the Duchess, and later possibly to approach Duke Maastyn. The Prefect is likely to propose an alliance with Montgren against the Viscount. There's no word about whether the Prefect's envoy will also attempt to engage Duke Halacut after he leaves Vergren, but I doubt that will happen."

As if in response to Sheralt's skeptical expression, Beltur added, "Duke Halacut's forces were less than impressive in the defense of Fairhaven, and there's every reason to believe that they are even less impressive today. In addition, Lydiar does not share a border with Certis. That provides Duke Halacut with even less reason to fear an attack by the Prefect. Does anyone have any questions?" The majer glanced around the briefing room.

Sheralt looked squarely at Beltur. "Why would the Duchess even consider an alliance that included Duke Maastyn?"

"That decision is for the Duchess to make, not the Council of Fairhaven," replied Beltur. "I can only guess that she and Lord Korsaen will listen to the Prefect's envoy and then make what they believe to be the proper decision."

"Wouldn't it be better to reject such an alliance and just let the Prefect attack Certis?" pressed Sheralt. "Because Gallos and Certis have been fighting for years, if Montgren becomes an ally of Gallos, wouldn't that just give the Viscount another excuse to attack Montgren and especially Fairhaven?"

"That's one possibility," said Beltur agreeably. "There's also the possibility, if Montgren and Hydlen don't ally with Gallos against Certis, that Hydlen will throw in with Certis and persuade the Viscount to attack Montgren so that they can split Montgren between the two of them. Then, the Viscount could turn his attention to Gallos without any worry of attacks from the east. I've sent a dispatch to Lord Korsaen pointing out both possibilities."

"That sounds as though you favor an alliance with Gallos and Hydlen," returned Sheralt.

"Those are the possibilities as I see them," declared Beltur. "Do you have another likely possibility, Sheralt?" Beltur looked around the briefing room. "Does anyone? I'm scarcely infallible. If there's something I've overlooked, I'd like to hear it."

For a moment, no one spoke. Then Valchar asked, "What if the envoys from the Prefect are just a stratagem to distract the Viscount from attacking Gallos . . . or at least to delay such an attack?"

"That's also a possibility, and it's likely that Lord Korsaen has considered that as well, but I'll send a dispatch to Vergren suggesting that, just in case he hasn't. Since neither Montgren nor Hydlen had any idea that envoys were coming, all that the Duchess can do is react as she thinks best." Beltur surveyed the room again. "I wanted all of you to know that so that you can keep your eyes open for any more signs of trouble. That's all I have, but I'll keep you posted when I know more." He nodded to Therran. "Carry on."

"Yes, ser."

Taelya barely listened as Therran assigned patrols, except to note that she had the south patrol with Varais as the senior Road Guard. Her feelings hadn't changed—the idea of an alliance with either Hydlen or Gallos didn't appeal to her at all. At the same time, she thought that Valchar had a very good point. And as soon as the senior undercaptain left the room, she turned to Valchar. "I think you're right. That sort of devious stratagem is exactly something that would appeal to the Prefect."

"But don't you think the Viscount would see that?" questioned Sheralt, almost testily.

"He probably does," interjected Taelya, "but it might give him a pretext to attack Montgren and Fairhaven, and Duke Maastyn would like nothing better. You've pointed out that Maastyn has had more troubles with his own people, especially in Worrak and Renklaar. So he's very unlikely to get involved directly."

"That means we stand a good chance of being in another war before long," said Valchar.

Another war? You weren't involved in the last one. But Taelya just nodded and said, "It's looking that way."

"We'd better get moving," suggested Valchar. "The senior guards already left for the courtyard."

"You still owe me," Sheralt murmured to Taelya as Valchar started to leave the briefing room."

"I've already paid that debt," replied Taelya quietly, turning away from him and walking from the briefing room.

When she reached Bounder, she immediately untied him, mounted, and rode to where Varais waited with Chaslar. Unlike the other senior guards, who carried sabres in waist scabbards, Varais wore shorter twin blades in crossed shoulder sheaths, since those were the weapons with which she, as a former Westwind guard, had been trained and with which she excelled. She was also the most recently promoted senior guard, at the end of harvest, having come to Fairhaven only a little more than five years earlier.

"Ready to ride, ser," declared Varais crisply.

"Routine patrol. No special instructions. You can lead, Chaslar," replied Taelya.

"I heard you brought in a bunch of Kaordists yesterday," offered Varais as the three rode eastward toward the square. "How did that go?"

"There were something like nine families. One of their teamsters couldn't believe that Fairhaven had women officers."

"I'd have liked to have seen his face if I'd been riding with you."

"He'll see soon enough if they decide to stay."

"They'll stay. Where else would accept them as they are?"

"True enough, but we get more good people than bad that way . . . like a certain recently promoted senior guard. That's one reason why we've grown so much." Taelya glanced to her right at the nearly empty square, where the only figures near the fountain were two girls filling buckets seemingly too large for them to carry.

"It's also another reason why the Viscount might want to attack us. Fairhaven's prosperous now, and getting more so."

Taelya nodded. "Have you been able to find more junior guards?"

"More volunteers, but not enough that Gustaan and the majer are likely to accept."

"Maybe they'll get some from the Kaordists."

"They don't have much of a tradition with arms."

Unlike Westwind. But Taelya merely said, "I don't come from that tradition, and neither did the majer." Her eyes and senses went to the two older men standing to one side of the front entrance to the East Inn, but neither even looked up at the passing Road Guards.

"No . . . but none of you had any choice, from what I've heard. That tends to make you a quick and passionate learner . . . if you want to survive, and all of you clearly did."

Taelya laughed at Varais's dry tone of voice, even while she winced slightly inside, because not all of them had survived, and one of those had been her father.

When the three passed the East Inn, Taelya could see the east patrol ahead—Sheralt, Nardaak, and a junior guard she couldn't absolutely recognize from behind, but suspected was Sheppyl, who glanced back, then spoke to Sheralt. Sheralt did not look back.

"You once mentioned that all the Westwind guards had other skills . . ."

"And you wonder why I've never mentioned mine?"

"I have thought about it a few times."

Varais reined in her mount slightly, slowing and letting Chaslar move farther ahead. Taelya did the same.

After a short time, Varais spoke again, keeping her voice low. "I was a scrivener. I wrote up all the reports, all the tariff receipts, all the discipline reports, anything that needed to be documented in our part of the border."

The flat statement, along with a certain amount of free chaos, told Taelya that Varais either hadn't been pleased with those duties or was unhappy mentioning them. For a moment, she wondered why. Then she nodded. "I won't ever mention it. I never asked, and you never told me."

Varais's laugh was sardonic. Then her voice softened slightly. "I never liked it. This is what I enjoy. It's what I always wanted, except in someplace warmer than Westwind."

"And you thought . . . ?"

"I was very good at scrivening where many weren't. But here, in a place where few women bear arms . . ."

"You didn't want to be a clerk, ever again." *But you needed to tell someone.* For a moment, Taelya wondered why Varais had chosen her as the one, but realized that there was no one else, given her own mother's hardheaded practicality and the fact that Tulya really needed a clerk and that Jessyla would likely support anything that would make Beltur's life less demanding, even if it happened to be the last thing that Varais wanted . . . or needed.

The senior guard nodded.

"Have you thought about trying to recruit women for patrollers or Road Guards?"

"I would, if I'd seen any likely to want this kind of life and who'd be good at it."

"Some of the girls who run sheep are strong enough."

"They're happy with the sheep."

Taelya had the feeling that the word "sheep" referred to more than the ovine quadrupeds.

By the time the three passed the stone posts on the east side of town, which, as in the west, no longer marked where the houses ended, the two had closed the gap with Chaslar and were nearing the side road to the left which formed an irregular semicircle around the south side of Fairhaven, and which had been one of the sites of a major battle during the war with Hydlen—and the place where her father had died in destroying most of that part of the invading army.

The first time she had ridden through the battle site as an undercaptain, she'd choked up, and she still felt a certain sadness each time she passed, despite the fact that his bravery and sense of duty had likely saved her and all of Fairhaven. Past the site of the battle, where the once-shredded trees and bushes had long since recovered with no trace of the carnage, the road slowly curved to the southwest, then straightened out heading due west.

As they neared the low red sandstone bluffs that stood just north of the border with Hydlen, Taelya concentrated on sensing whether there were other riders nearby, but all she could discern were sheep and their herders, and they were well to the east of the road and north of the border. But, as they neared the midpoint road that ran from the southern road north and into Fairhaven proper, she had a vague feeling, but the road only showed recent wagon tracks, and not separate hoofprints.

"I feel that there are riders ahead to the west, maybe a little to the south," she told Varais and Chaslar.

"How far, ser?" asked Varais.

"More than two kays."

A quint later, when they had passed through the narrower gap between the bluffs and the small dense woodland just north of the road, where the woodland gave way to rocky grassland, with but a narrow winding path that eventually led to Fairhaven, Taelya could clearly sense four riders.

"There are four them, definitely on the Hydlenese side of the border, a little more than a kay ahead. At the moment, they're not moving. None of them are mages. Four riders are likely troopers."

"That's more than usual," said Varais. "Most times, they travel as a single pair. Too bad they're not on our side of the border."

Taelya sensed that the four riders were on the side road that led into Hydlen just off the southern road—and seemed just barely on their side of the border. "The few we've sensed or seen before don't usually get as close as they are. We'll just have to see if they move as we get nearer."

The moment that the three Fairhaven guards cleared a stand of trees on the left so that they could see the green uniforms of the four Hydlenese troopers, all four turned their horses and withdrew at a gallop, although Taelya could sense that they slowed their mounts once they were out of sight.

"They moved quick-like," observed Varais wryly. "Then, they always do."

"They know there's usually a mage with each patrol." Taelya frowned. "But I've never seen a patrol that close, not in the eight years I've been riding patrols."

"Haven't seen four scouts at once, either," added Varais.

Taelya wondered about that as well. *Why were there four scouts? Is Duke Maastyn scouting to see about allying himself with the Viscount?*

She'd certainly report it when they finished for the day.

V

Once Taelya finished reporting to Gustaan, and then to Beltur, she was about to leave the headquarters building when she sensed her uncle following her. For a mage it was impossible not to sense his unshielded presence, although she knew he could conceal himself so well that he could neither be seen nor sensed.

She stopped and turned. "What is it?"

"I've been thinking. We should go to the small rear courtyard."

The small courtyard was the one where she and Sheralt practiced throwing chaos bolts. "Do you have something in mind?"

"Actually, I do. I had Jorhan and Jaegyr make something for me. That is, a training aid for you and Sheralt. After what you reported today, the sooner we see if it works, the better."

A training aid?

A few moments later, when they stepped into the stone-walled training courtyard, Beltur pointed. "There it is."

Taelya looked at the square box that stood atop a masonry base a yard on a side and not quite two yards high, with a front and sides that were clearly cupridium. There were five openings in the cupridium front, except behind five of the openings was more cupridium, perhaps two digits back. Each opening was roughly the size of her palm.

"What is it supposed to train?" asked Taelya.

"Your speed and accuracy," said Beltur. "One of the things that I've noticed is that most white mages just throw chaos bolts at a formation, or at a rider. And after a fairly short time, they have trouble throwing more chaos."

"That's why you've always wanted me to keep my chaos tight and directed."

"Exactly. This device should help you and Sheralt to become even more accurate . . . even if it doesn't work perfectly. By becoming more accurate, you should be able to use less chaos on any one target. That should make you more effective for longer."

If it works, and I can do it. Taelya looked at the cupridium box once more. "What am I supposed to do?"

"To begin with, I want you to stand at the back of the courtyard and put a strong chaos bolt through the open hole without touching the cupridium around the hole," said Beltur. "A bolt strong enough to kill a trooper."

"Now?"

"Now."

Taelya walked to the back of the courtyard, some ten yards from the device, then aimed the chaos bolt.

The edge of the chaos caught the cupridium, and part of it sprayed across the metal. The remainder weakly splatted on the stone wall behind the device.

"That's harder than it looks," said Taelya.

"This is only the first step," replied Beltur. "Try again."

Taelya concentrated.

Her second bolt barely touched the edge of the opening, but that was enough to weaken it. The third bolt went through cleanly.

"Good!" Beltur smiled. "Now, it gets harder. I'm going to spin the disk in the box, slowly. Watch it. Just watch it." He moved to the device, then stepped back, and reached behind the cupridium-fronted box, doing something that Taelya could not make out. Then he quickly moved several yards to the side.

The first opening closed, and another one of the five opened, and then, after a moment, it too closed, and a third opened . . . and closed.

Beltur looked at Taelya. "You need to put a targeted bolt in each opening, one after another."

Taelya swallowed. She'd never been required to do something like that.

"Go ahead," Beltur ordered.

Her next bolt went through an opening, not quite cleanly, but mostly, as did the next one, but her third attempt splattered on the cupridium to one side of the opening and into the opening at an angle. That brought the rotating disk to a halt.

"You need to be more precise," said Beltur. "Make the chaos bolt narrower, but with the same amount of chaos. That way it will go deeper. Now, hold off for a moment, while I restart the disk." He stepped forward and restarted the disk.

"I can see why the front and the disk are cupridium," Taelya said as Beltur stepped away from the device. Then she aimed another chaos bolt, making it narrower. It went through the opening cleanly, as did the next two, before she again missed on the lowest opening on the device. "Frig!"

As Beltur walked back to the device, he looked to Taelya and said, "I'm going to spin it a little faster now that you know what to expect."

"Faster?"

"Things happen quickly in a fight. You need to be able to switch from one target to another. And you need to be as precise as possible."

"You think we'll be fighting soon?"

"I don't know. Not for certain, but if I waited to see before trying to make your chaos bolts more accurate, we'd both be sorry. I just wish I'd thought of this earlier." He shook his head. "They say regrets are a waste of time, but I still have trouble accepting that. Sometimes they're useful. Now, get ready for the faster openings and closings." He spun the disk again and quickly stepped back.

Taelya narrowed her next chaos bolt even more and arrowed it through the opening, then managed another one through the next opening, and a third . . . before being late on the fourth and missing entirely.

"Get ready," called Beltur, moving to restart the disk once more.

Taelya took a deep breath, waiting.

Then she fired the chaos bolt cleanly through the opening, wondering how long she could keep doing it.

Half a glass later, Beltur called an end to the exercise. "You're too tired to aim straight any longer . . . and your order/chaos levels are too low for you to continue."

Taelya was more than tired. She was actually shaking as well as sweating. "Do you have any ale left in your water bottle?"

"A little."

"Drink it all before you ride home, then have some more when you get there." He smiled. "You did very well, even at the end. That's also very much the way you'll feel after a fight where you have to use a lot of order and chaos."

"Have you tried it with Sheralt?"

Beltur shook his head. "I wanted to see if you could do what I had in mind before I asked him."

Taelya smiled wanly. "So you could tell him that I could do it?"

"Of course." Beltur grinned.

Taelya shook her head, then turned and walked slowly back to the stable. Tired as she was, she could definitely see the purpose behind the device, and she worried about Beltur's seriousness and insistence on her being as precise as possible.

VI

After breakfast on sevenday and taking care of Bounder, Taelya walked the distance to headquarters, still thinking about the chaos-bolt practice of the afternoon before. Town Patrol chief Graalur was waiting for her in the front hall when she arrived just before seventh glass.

"Good morning, ser," offered Taelya, wondering why the graying chief was there instead of the patroller with whom she'd be patrolling the square on foot.

"Good morning, Undercaptain." Graalur paused. "I've detailed two patrollers to accompany you for the day, rather than just Marrak. The other is Zenyt."

"Two?"

"With all the Kaordists who just arrived, I felt a little prudence might be in order, at least until we know how things shake out. The majer thought we should provide a strong impression for their first market day . . . if any even show up."

"Some will. They've been on the road for days. They'll need some things. Are they still all at the way station?"

"So far. It's pretty small to hold the lot of them."

The way station wasn't really a way station so much as a place just outside the town proper for those who sought refuge in Fairhaven and didn't have the coins for an inn. It did have a fountain and a public jakes, and several large sheds that were just walls and a roof against the weather.

Graalur went on. "The majer went out there yesterday and laid out the rules. Scared the darkness out of them from what Dussef said."

That scarcely surprised Taelya. Her uncle's reputation alone set most people back, and his appearance reinforced that history. "What else do I need to know?"

"Just patrol as usual. Maybe a little more obviously. According to Dussef, the place they come from was barely bigger than a hamlet, and they're Kaordists. I'd think they'd be cautious, but you never know. I already told Marrak and Zenyt that. They're already on the square." Graalur grinned. "So . . . patrol as usual."

"I can do that."

"Then I likely won't see you later." With that, Graalur turned in the direction of his study.

Taelya adjusted her visor cap and made her way from headquarters. Once outside, as she walked the few score yards to the square, she checked her personal shields, then looked east and then to the north. While the green-blue sky was hazy, suggesting that the day would be warm and muggy, she couldn't see any clouds.

When she reached the northwest corner of the square, she looked toward the fountain in the center, where she spied two older women in the faded brown long dresses seemingly favored by the Kaordist women and girls. While both men and women appeared to wear brown, only men and boys wore shirts and trousers. The two, and a younger girl who had moved from the other side of the fountain, filled water jugs and fastened them onto a harness of sorts worn by a slightly swaybacked horse.

Taelya frowned. There was a fountain at the way station. Were the three just getting water while they waited for the various vendors to set up their carts and tables for market day? Or weren't they staying at the way station?

She surveyed the square, locating Zenyt on edge of the square, roughly in the middle of the east end, while Marrak was opposite him on the west side. Then she headed south along the west side toward Marrak.

"Good morning, Taelya," called out a voice.

Taelya turned and smiled at Julli, who stood beside her already-arranged produce cart, as she had almost every market day that Taelya could remember. "Good morning."

"Will your mother be here?"

"Sooner or later."

"Then I'll save her some of the chard greens, and some radishes, but I've got plenty of those."

"Thank you. She'll appreciate that." Taelya kept moving, her eyes taking in the fifteen or so vendors already setting up. Except for the Kaordist women, nothing seemed any different from any other sevenday market.

"Good morning, ser," offered Marrak as Taelya neared him.

"Good morning to you. When did the Kaordist women get here?"

"Half a quint ago, just after I did," replied the older patroller. "I asked why they were here. They said they heard the water was better here, and they wanted to see what might be available. They haven't left the fountain yet."

"I think I'll walk over and talk to them."

"They're pretty shy. They wouldn't even look in my direction. You might do better."

"We'll see." Taelya walked toward the fountain. As she neared it, she saw that one of the Kaordist women had white hair, and the younger woman was likely the mother of the girl.

All three stopped and looked askance at Taelya.

She smiled. "Yes . . . I'm a mage-guard undercaptain and a woman. Are you with the group I escorted in on fiveday?"

"Yes, ser," replied the older woman. "We told the patroller why we were here."

"I know. He told me. I just wanted to know if you could tell me any more about what's been happening in Certis. We've heard that the Viscount might be preparing for war."

"We don't know anything about that," replied the apparent matriarch of the group. "We just know that his men would have taken anything of ours they could . . . and a lot worse." She shook her head. "We got out. The folks in Kask-car didn't, not the menfolk . . . and the women . . . especially the girls . . ." She glanced at the girl, who was likely only nine or ten, and let her words trail off.

"Did you see any armsmen on your way here?"

"We kept away from anywhere they might be," said the girl's mother. "The first soldiers we saw were you and your men. We took back trails and paths to cross the border from Certis."

Taelya could tell that there wasn't much more that she was going to learn from the three. She smiled. "Is there anything you'd like to know about Fairhaven that I might be able to tell you?"

The Kaordist matriarch immediately asked, "Is it true that there are more women than men on the town Council here?"

"That's definitely true. There are three women and two men."

"Are they all mages?"

"Two are mages; three are not."

The two women looked surprised, but after a moment the younger of the women asked, "What . . . do the women . . . do?"

"One is a mage-healer; one is the town justicer; and one owns the brewery and distillery . . . well, all of the brewery and a little less than half the distillery."

There was a moment of silence, and Taelya noticed the girl looking at her. "You had a question?"

The girl dropped her eyes.

"I don't bite or scratch," replied Taelya gently. "What did you want to know?"

The girl gingerly pointed to the end of Taelya's uniform sleeve. "The stripes . . . the majer had black ones. Why are yours white?"

Taelya inadvertently glanced at the two white sleeve bands before replying. "That's because he's a black mage, and I'm a white. Some of the mage-guard officers are blacks, and some are whites."

"Never heard of a place with both blacks and whites," said the older woman.

"You'll find that many things are different here." *Better, in most cases.* But Taelya didn't say that because that was just her opinion, and she hadn't lived anywhere else in the last sixteen years.

"Different's not always better."

"You'll have a chance to see whether Fairhaven suits you," replied Taelya. "As long as you obey the laws." She looked at the girl and smiled. "You're a little older than I was when I came here. Fairhaven was much smaller then."

Then she turned and walked across the rest of the square to where Zenyt stood.

"Good morning, ser."

"Good morning. Have you seen anything I need to keep an eye on?"

"Not yet, ser. Bannet saw some boys eying the square on threeday, but they slunk off before he could talk to them. He didn't recognize them. They might not come back today, seeing as there's always a mage here on sevenday."

That was another reminder, at least to Taelya, that, despite what her uncle had said, Fairhaven needed more mages, especially the way it was growing.

By two quints past eighth glass, more than a hundred people were in the square, although half were those selling produce—mostly early vegetables and spring berries—as well as other goods, while the other vendors hawked a variety of other items. At times, as much for practice as anything, she cloaked herself in a concealment and used her senses to guide her, since the concealment bent light around her and kept her from seeing. On her trips across and around the square, those not under a concealment, Taelya had seen herbs, baskets, and pots, even fowl and several puppies, as well as an assortment of knives and tools.

She kept looking for shimmersilk scarves like the one Jessyla occasionally wore, although it wouldn't have been right for Taelya herself, but only because the color was healer green. So far, over the years, she'd never seen any shimmersilk. *But with Fairhaven growing . . . maybe before long . . .*

She pushed that thought out of her mind and concentrated on sensing any untoward chaos as she walked through the square yet again.

She'd almost reached the fountain, noting that, crowded as the square was, no one was even trying to get water, when she sensed the smallest flash of chaos. Immediately, she concentrated, but it took several moments to locate a small figure on the far side of one wagon. Another moment passed before she recognized the wagon as belonging to young Farlaan, obviously selling the last of his father's potatoes from the late harvest.

Slipping a concealment around herself, she moved closer, hearing, as she did, someone murmur.

"Trouble . . . the mage-guard vanished . . ."

Moving as quietly as she could, since concealments didn't block sounds, she circled around the back of the wagon, where she could sense clearly that less than two yards in front of her, the small figure was quietly lifting potatoes from the wagon bed while Farlaan was talking to someone, most likely Bryella.

Taelya clapped a containment around the figure, then dropped the concealment to discover that her captive was a scrawny boy garbed in the faded brown that all the Kaordists seemed to wear, but there were holes in his trousers, and his bare feet were callused, scarred, and dusty.

After a moment, he stopped struggling against the containment and just looked at Taelya, his teeth chattering.

"Why were you trying to steal the potatoes?"

"He . . . they . . . wouldn't be missed . . . I had to do it."

"You had to steal?"

"Da said I had to get us something to eat. He didn't care how." The boy shuddered. "Don't take me back. He'll kill me. He really will."

Taelya could sense both truth and fear emanating from the boy. Rather than immediately address his plea, she asked, "How old are you?"

"Ten . . . I think. Da never said. My ma died when I was born. Jamya's his consort now. He beats her, too."

"What's your name?"

"He calls me Trashboy."

Taelya's lips tightened for a moment. "You're coming with me."

"Don't take me back . . . Please . . ."

Taelya could not only sense, but hear the sheer terror. "We're not taking you back. Not yet. I'm going to loosen the containment around you. Put down the sack."

The moment she widened the containment, the boy tried to run, but only took two steps before hitting the containment.

"Put the sack down. Now."

He did, glaring at her. "He'll kill me."

"No one's killing anyone." She shifted the containment so that the sack was outside of it.

At that moment, Farlaan came around the end of the wagon, floppy brown hair drifting down over his forehead, almost in his eyes. He stopped with a start. "Taelya! I mean, Undercaptain. What . . . ?"

"This young fellow was lifting your potatoes while you . . . were otherwise occupied." Taelya didn't bother to smile at Bryella, who had stopped behind Farlaan. "Your potatoes are in that sack." Then she looked at the boy. "We're walking to the west side of the square."

Zenyt hurried to join Taelya as she reached the edge of the square closest to headquarters.

"Zenyt, we're going to need the majer. Please find him, immediately."

The patroller's eyebrows rose. "For a thieving boy?"

"No. For why the boy tried to steal. I need to stay here and see if anyone else is trying the same thing."

A momentary puzzled frown crossed the junior patroller's forehead, then vanished. "Yes, ser."

In moments, Zenyt was out of sight.

"The majer? He's the one who's black and silver?" asked the boy.

"He is."

The boy shuddered again. "Both of them . . . gonna kill me."

Taelya didn't feel like telling him, again, that no one was going to kill him. *Besides, he needs to fear and respect the patrollers more than his rotten father.*

At that moment, Marrak joined Taelya and the boy. "Something I should know about?"

"I caught the boy stealing potatoes. His father made him do it. I sent Zenyt for the majer. Boys stealing is one thing; being sent is another."

"Especially when they just got here." Marrak shook his head.

In less than a third of a quint, Zenyt and Beltur joined Marrak and Taelya, who quickly related what had happened.

When she finished, Beltur looked at the boy. "Is what she said what happened?"

"Yes, ser . . . pretty much, ser . . . excepting . . . we're all so hungry . . ."

"No one mentioned that," Beltur said mildly.

"Da says we can't be beggars."

Beltur nodded, as if the boy's statement made perfect sense, then said, "Taelya, if you'd ask Worrfan to join us?"

"The tinker?"

"He's a Kaordist, and he's never acted like that. Frydika would never put up with that. I'd like to hear what he has to say. I'll take over confining the young man."

"Yes, ser." Taelya released the containment.

As soon as Taelya released the containment, once again, the boy tried to escape, but he slammed against Beltur's containment.

"Not so fast, young man," said Beltur firmly.

He's really terrified. As Taelya hurried toward where the tinker was set up, along with his consort, she realized that she'd never known that Worrfan was a Kaordist, only that he'd come from Worrak and had later consorted Samwyth's widow.

The tinker looked up from the small foot-pedal grindstone as Taelya approached.

"Worrfan, the majer would appreciate a few words with you. He needs some information you might have."

"The majer needs me?"

"He does."

Worrfan looked to the young woman who was waiting for him to finish sharpening a cleaver. "I'll be back in just a moment."

The two walked back to where Beltur and Zenyt waited. Taelya had the feeling that half the square was watching what was going on, although she only saw a few people looking in their direction.

Once she and Worrfan reached Beltur, the majer said, "Taelya, tell Worrfan everything you told me."

She did so, faithfully repeating what the boy had said.

When she finished, Worrfan frowned, then said, "Knew a few men like that, but most in Worrak treated their consorts better than the fellows I've seen in Certis or Lydiar. I once heard tell of a group like that. Never believed it, though."

Beltur nodded. "I thought as much, but I wanted your thoughts. Thank you. We won't take any more of your time."

"My pleasure, Majer." Worrfan nodded to Beltur, then to Taelya, before turning and walking back to his grindstone and the young woman waiting for him to finish sharpening her knives.

"We need to pay a visit to the way station and see Storch," said Beltur, turning to Marrak. "If you and Zenyt need a mage, you can call on the head healer."

"Yes, ser."

Beltur looked to Taelya. "We'll take the duty mounts and the standby half squad."

From Beltur's expression, it was clear to Taelya that he either thought there would be trouble or wanted to prevent it.

In less than a quint, Taelya, Beltur, and the boy had walked back to head-quarters, mounted up, and were riding eastward past the square. Behind them rode ten fully armed guards, and Squad Leader Moshart. The boy rode in front of Taelya's saddle, held in place by a loose containment, which did nothing to reduce the various odors emanating from him.

Beltur turned to Taelya. "Put a shield around the entire group and make it large enough to include a full squad. That's something that you should be able to hold for at least half a glass."

"Do you think we'll be fighting before long?"

"You'll be called on to do it sooner or later. You might as well work on it now, rather than discover you can't hold a large shield long enough when you really have to."

Taelya couldn't argue with that, although the boy looked at Beltur curiously, and she created the larger shield, expanding it enough to cover at least a full squad.

"Good," said Beltur. "Hold it until we get to the way station."

Taelya knew that Beltur did nothing without a solid reason, and she under-stood why he wanted her to raise a large shield, but what was it about a poor boy's theft of potatoes that had required two mages and eleven armed guards? *It has to be something he learned from when he met with Storch.* At least, she thought it had to be, because she couldn't think of any other reason.

When they neared the way station, Taelya immediately tried to sense who and what was where. The wagon horses, not really dray horses, all seemed to be in the corral adjoining the way station, little more than a building some twenty-five yards long and eight wide, divided on the inside into three rooms, each with a door on one side and two windows on the other, a hearth, and a sleeping platform high enough to sit on. She didn't sense any children outside or near the corral, but several men were working on replacing a wagon wheel.

Beltur reined his mount to a halt several yards short of the group working on the wagon. He said nothing, but waited.

At that moment, Taelya dropped the large shield, but kept her personal shields.

After several long moments, one of the men turned and walked toward Bel-tur and the guards. Taelya recognized Storch.

"Majer . . . is there a problem? Or are you stopping by on your way some-where else?"

Beltur eased back his visor cap slightly and looked at Storch. "One of your boys was caught stealing in the market square." He gestured to Taelya and the boy. "The undercaptain caught him in the act with a sack of potatoes."

"You've brought a lot of men for the supposed theft of a sack of potatoes."

"It's better to deal with little problems before they become bigger. We're learned that the hard way. The boy was ordered to steal."

Storch looked at the boy dismissively, then said, "He's not mine."

"He's from one of your families."

"He might be Durwaad's."

"Then fetch Durwaad," said Beltur.

"I'm not someone to be ordered around—" Storch's words were choked off by the containment around his neck, and his face began to turn red.

Abruptly, Beltur released the containment. "We've provided a place for you to rest. We've offered to help you settle here. You've been here less than two days, and one of your men sends his boy out to steal. That's not smart, and it's a poor way to repay hospitality."

"What hospitality . . ." Storch clearly saw the expression on Beltur's face. "I'll get Durwaad."

"And come back with him," ordered Beltur.

Storch turned and headed toward the way station building.

Taelya was beginning to wish that she hadn't been quite so welcoming when she'd met the Kaordists. If all the men were like Storch and the driver she'd met, there might be a few other reasons why the Certans had attacked their towns. On the other hand, murdering people . . .

A beefy man accompanied Storch back from the building.

"This is Durwaad," Storch declared. "If you have no further need for me . . ."

"It might be best if you stayed for a bit," said Beltur evenly. Turning his eyes on Durwaad, and gesturing toward the boy, he asked, "Is he yours?"

"He is. But he's always been a troublemaker," declared Durwaad. "Always getting into things. Never minds."

"He minded very well," said Taelya. "He did exactly what you told him to do."

"Are you calling me a liar?"

"Only if you're denying that you sent him out to steal," replied Taelya.

Durwaad turned to Storch and then to Beltur. "No . . . woman can call me a liar!"

"The undercaptain's telling the truth," declared Beltur.

"No woman can judge me," snapped Durwaad.

"You judged the boy," replied Beltur evenly. "Both the boy and the under-captain are telling the truth. Why did you send him out to steal?"

"He must have misunderstood. I just told him to see if he could make himself useful and find some food for the rest of the family."

"Is that what he said?" Beltur asked the boy.

"He said something like that—"

"I told you so!" declared Durwaad.

"What else did he say?" asked Beltur.

The boy looked down.

"Did he say more?"

"Yes, ser."

Beltur waited.

Taelya murmured, "Go ahead. Tell the majer what else he said."

"He'll kill me," replied the boy in a murmur so low she could barely hear it.

"He will anyway," Taelya replied quietly. "We're the only ones who can save you."

The boy swallowed. "My da told me to get some food. He didn't care none how I did it, even if I had to steal it."

"He's lying again," snapped Durwaad.

"So you're saying that he's a thief and a liar?" said Beltur.

"No . . . he's worse than that. He's an ungrateful thief and liar."

"Since you have no use for the boy, and find him a liar, and since he is a thief, we'll deal with him in our own fashion."

The boy stiffened and started to cry out, but Taelya covered his mouth with a secondary containment and whispered, "You're going to be safe, and you'll be fed. Don't say a word until we leave."

"Before we do, I'd like to hear what your consort has to say about him."

"She's not his ma."

"Then she's likely to tell the truth. Storch, please bring her out."

"Why do you want to talk to her?" asked the Kaordist leader.

"Because the boy is charged with theft, and he may be a liar—"

"I'm no liar!" The boy's words were almost screamed.

"So we need to know more to determine what to do with him," Beltur finished calmly. "Get the woman, or we'll get her."

Storch snorted. "You can talk to Jamya. That's all." He turned and walked back to the building.

Before that long, he returned. The woman who appeared was thin and worn-looking, although her mahogany hair was neatly woven into a single braid that extended just to the top of her thin shoulder blades. Her long-sleeved and faded brown dress almost touched the packed clay, and her leather sandals looked to be held together with thin leather thongs. Taelya doubted that she was much more than a few years older than Taelya herself.

"You've been taking care of this boy?" asked Beltur.

"Yes, ser. When he's not with his da, that is."

"Do you have other children?" asked Beltur. "Is that why he spends time with his father?"

"No, ser. I can't have no children. That's what the healer woman said. That's why Durwaad has Chyla. She's given him two. I help her much as I can."

"But you're Durwaad's consort?"

"One of them, ser."

Taelya stiffened at that, her eyes going to Beltur.

Her uncle nodded slowly, as if that revelation didn't particularly surprise him. "Have you had any trouble with the boy?"

"Not . . . much, ser."

"Excellent!" said Beltur cheerfully. "Then, since Durwaad already has a consort, and since you can obviously manage the child, you can come with us and work full-time at making sure he behaves."

"You can't—" began Durwaad.

"The majer has the power to do what he will," said Storch coldly. "Whether it is right or wise is another question."

"Do you have a better solution?" asked Beltur. "If the boy is not a liar, then remaining with his father is not good for him. If the boy is a liar and a thief, his behavior will not improve if he remains where he obviously cannot be controlled."

"That much I grant you," replied Storch. "Do what you will with the boy. We're well rid of him. But taking a man's consort is another matter."

"Even if he has two, and the boy needs her more than Durwaad does?" replied Beltur.

"You would break up a family for a worthless youth? And you call yourself an honorable councilor?"

"Is not a family composed of a both a man and a woman who are consorted and any children they may have until those children are old enough and able enough to support themselves? By letting a woman go to support and guide a boy who needs guidance, how will that break the family of Durwaad and Chyla?"

"In our families a man may have two consorts," intoned Storch sanctimoniously. "And that family stays together. Otherwise, every unhappy consort or ungrateful child would be telling tales and sowing misery, and there would be no order at all."

"How does one woman leaving create disorder? It would appear to me that having two women for each man is a form of disorder. It leaves other men without the possibility of consorts, and that is disorder. Unless you drive off some of the young men . . . and that also creates disorder."

"Men and women each partake of some of the attributes of Kaorda," replied Storch. "Men embody the beauty and strength of order. Women display the chaos of creativity. Men's order would overwhelm a single woman's creativity. Only with two women together with one man can a family unite in the wholeness that is Kaorda. As you must know as a black mage, order must rule over chaos."

Taelya thought that Storch's expression verged on smugness, and she wanted to turn him to ashes on the spot. *Not that you will.* After a moment, she added, *Not yet anyway.* She waited to see what Beltur would say.

After a long moment, Beltur smiled, except the expression was that of a mountain cat about to attack.

"That sort of order is not welcome here. You *will* depart within a glass. You may depart in peace, but only under one condition. Every single member of your group must stand outside the way station and hear what I have to say. Then each of them can decide whether they will stay under our ways or depart under yours."

"You can't make us choose to forsake our ways," declared Storch.

Beltur laughed. "We aren't making you do anything. Each person in your group has the choice of staying under our ways or leaving under yours. But they must choose freely right here and now. And you will not stand in their way."

"You offer only tyranny here," declared Storch. "You're no better than the Viscount."

"We're not killing anyone. We're offering each one of them a free choice. Now . . . get your people out here."

"You can't make me—" Storch's words were cut off by the containment that Beltur placed around him.

Slowly, Storch turned red. Then his face turned blue. As Beltur released the containment, the Kaordist leader pitched forward onto the packed clay.

Beltur gestured to one of the guards. "Tie him up and gag him." Then he turned to Durwaad. "Get everyone else out here."

Almost a third of a quint passed before men, women, and children stood outside the way station. Several of the men looked defiant. Most of the women looked at the ground, or avoided looking in the direction of Beltur, Taelya, and the guards.

Beltur glanced at Taelya, then addressed the Kaordists.

"Fairhaven is named the way it is because it is a haven, and neither men nor women rule the other. If any of you wish to remain here in Fairhaven, you may do so, but no man may have more than one consort, and no woman may have more than one, either. Any men or women who do not wish to remain with the Kaordist group may also remain here. Anyone who does not wish to remain here under the laws and customs of Fairhaven has one glass to pack up and depart." Beltur surveyed the line of men and women. "In a moment, I will ask any of those who wish to remain to walk past the guards and stand by the fence behind those guards. Anyone who tries to stop another person will be restrained and will also be required to leave Fairhaven."

Taelya looked down the line.

Several of the women had looked up. Two were looking at her, and one was Jamya, except she was likely looking at the boy.

"Jamya!" the boy called. "You can stay here!"

Durwaad grabbed Jamya by the arm.

"Let go of her," Beltur commanded.

Durwaad looked up, but did not release the woman.

Taelya created a small ball of chaos less than a yard from Durwaad, but well above his head. "Let go! Or you'll never see to harm another woman."

The Kaordist looked from Beltur to Taelya, then threw Jamya toward the chaos ball. She staggered and then fell awkwardly.

Taelya hurled the tiniest point of chaos into Durwaad's forehead. At the moment it struck him, Durwaad yelled, then pitched forward. Taelya could sense that he was still alive, and both his order and chaos were strong enough that he should recover.

"You killed him!" cried the boy.

"No. He'll be fine in a while, but he's going to have a scar in the middle of his forehead." Taelya looked back at the line of Kaordists.

Jamya was walking away from the way station and directly toward Taelya and the boy.

"Any of you who wish to stay," called Beltur, "walk past the guards to the fence." He turned to Taelya and said loudly, "Mark any man who tries to hold a woman."

"Yes, ser!"

"He's getting up," murmured the boy.

Taelya shifted her eyes to Durwaad, who slowly stood, putting his hand to the burned scar in the middle of his forehead. The man glared at her, then turned toward a blond woman who held the hands of two children. The blond woman turned and walked back into the way station building, followed by Durwaad.

Taelya blinked. *She's staying with them?* Then she looked at Jamya, who had stopped a yard short of Taelya's mount.

"I can really stay here?"

"You can. We'll find a good place for you."

Jamya half turned and spit in the direction of the trussed-up Storch, then kept walking toward the fence.

Taelya kept watching, trying to make sure than no man hampered any woman, but, surprisingly, at least to Taelya, out of the nearly fifty Kaordists, only a few women chose to stay in Fairhaven. There was one couple, both young. Taelya thought the woman, if she could be called that, was only a year or two older than Kaeryla. In the end there were four women besides Jamya, all seemingly close to the age of Taelya's mother, and three young men, who looked to be close to Dorylt's age.

Taelya frowned at that, then nodded as she realized that the young men likely saw no future, and no consorts, with the Kaordists. *But why didn't more of the younger women leave? Because they don't have any idea that they could be more? Or because they fear what they don't know?*

When it was clear that all of the Kaordists had chosen, one way or the other, Beltur turned to Moshart, the squad leader. "Take two guards and escort the ones who wish to stay to the Healing House. Tell the head healer about what happened and have the healers deal with any health problems they may have. Then inform Justicer Tulya of the situation." Beltur paused, then added, "And send a courier to inform the eastern road patrol that the Kaordists are leaving Fairhaven and are not permitted to return."

"Yes, ser."

Taelya released the loose containment from the boy and lifted him off the horse.

"Stay with Jamya. Otherwise, you'll be leaving Fairhaven as well."

"Yes, ser." The boy hurried toward Jamya.

Once the three guards escorted the nine Kaordists away from the way station, Beltur gestured to the nearest man. "Untie Storch."

When the Kaordist leader stood up, he immediately looked to Beltur. "The Duchess of Montgren will hear of this."

"Oh, we'll make sure of that," Beltur said. "The Duchess doesn't much care for men who abuse women. You might be better received in Lydiar or even Renklaar. But I wouldn't make any threats. Now . . . you have one glass."

Taelya eased her mount closer to Beltur and waited to speak until it was clear that the Kaordists were packing up. Then she said, "Did you expect something like this?"

"I didn't think most of them would fit in here, and if we forced it, we'd just have had problems. This way, we get the ones who really want to leave the Kaordists and who are more likely to fit in."

"And you brought a half squad so that we wouldn't have to use magery against all of them?"

Her uncle nodded.

Taelya could see that. Even her uncle could only handle four containments at once, in addition to his personal shields, and it was a strain for Taelya to handle three for long. So dealing with ten angry men might have required enough force to kill some of them in order to keep control. The half squad of armed Road Guards had kept matters from going that far. *Not that Storch or Durwaad would ever appreciate Beltur's concerns for their health. Still . . .*

"Do you think that most of the women really wanted to stay with the Kaordists?"

"Most likely not, but we can't save people who don't want to be saved, or who won't take a few steps toward being saved."

Taelya was still thinking about that after the nine wagons rolled away from the way station, heading eastward in the direction of Lydiar.

VII

Once the Kaordist wagons were out of sight, Beltur took charge of Jamya and the boy, whose name turned out to be Teshkat, as well as the other Kaordists who had decided to stay in Fairhaven. Then he turned to Taelya. "You need to get back to the square, because Jessyla and Margrena will need to look over Teshkat and the others. Just tie your mount in front of the Healing House. I'll have one of the guards lead it back to the stable after we get finished here and the healers are done with those who are staying."

"Kaeryla's not at the Healing House?"

"She visits Khresso on sevenday mornings. I doubt she'll be back from the hamlet for some time."

Taelya recalled that Kaeryla had mentioned something about traveling to the outlying hamlets, but she hadn't mentioned when. "No, that's more than a ten-kay ride. She didn't go alone, did she?"

"She can handle herself, but the guards make it easier."

Like here. Taelya nodded and turned her mount, riding the few yards to the main road and then heading west into town, first past the newer dwellings built beyond the old stone road posts, and then through the east part of Fairhaven on the smooth stone-paved main street, past Julli and Jaegyr's house—and the woodworking shop where Dorylt was doubtless working, at least until noon, although it might be longer with all the commissions that Jaegyr had recently received.

While the white spring sun was bright, the air was pleasant and not muggy, the way it would be by summer, and the older trees shading the road kept it from being uncomfortable, unlike the square, which would definitely be much warmer. When she passed the East Inn and reached the north side of the square, she could see that the area around the fountain was crowded, at least for Fairhaven, with well over a hundred would-be buyers wandering among the carts and tables.

As Taelya guided her mount along the west edge of the square, she immediately noted that Marrak was posted at the west side of the square, nearer the carts and tables selling tools, some few pieces of jewelry, and other items that could be light-fingered, while Zenyt was just north of the fountain. While she sensed for chaos or anything untoward as she rode, even by the time she reined up at the hitching rail fronting the Healing House, she hadn't discerned anything amiss.

She quickly dismounted and tied the horse, then walked swiftly to where Marrak stood.

"Any problems?"

"Nothing yet, but it's barely noon. What happened at the way station?"

"The majer forced them into admitting that one of them had sent the boy out to steal and that they were allowing men to have two consorts—"

"I wondered about that. Some of the women came to the fountain in pairs, early-like, before most were selling."

"He offered any who wanted to live by our customs and laws the chance to stay. One couple, five women, including the one who's been caring for Teshkat—"

"That the boy you caught stealing?"

Taelya nodded. ". . . Teshkat, and three other boys, all a few years older than him, they decided to stay. The majer gave the others a glass to leave."

"Just a glass?" Marrak shook his head. "They must have pissed him off good."

"They lied a lot, were disrespectful, and then had the nerve to talk in sanctimonious tones. He's going to have the healers look at the ones who decided to stay." At a flash of chaos between her and the fountain, Taelya turned. "Something . . . just stay here and keep watching." She quickly moved in the direction of the chaos.

Taelya had taken a score of steps before she saw Julli gesturing to her and pointing in the direction of Worrfan's small cart, but she couldn't tell what it was all about until she got closer and saw Worrfan holding his consort. As she drew nearer, she could sense the orangish red of wound chaos inside Frydika's skull.

She turned and shouted, "Marrak! Get Healer Jessyla!"

Taelya could sense the chaos in Frydika's skull, and she knew that even Kaeryla could have done something, but Taelya herself wasn't about to try working with small bits of order inside a woman's skull.

It seemed like a glass passed, but it was likely less than a fifth of a glass before Jessyla hurried up beside Taelya, immediately looking at the unconscious Frydika. After a moment, she looked at Taelya. "There's wound chaos there, and I think it's spreading. Can you sense that?"

Taelya forced herself to focus. "There are little points moving."

"I can't sense that small. Can you sense the boundaries of that chaos? Clearly?"

"I can." Taelya frowned.

"Good. It's fuzzy to me. Can you put a containment around those points? One with order on the outside?"

Taelya managed not to wince. "For a while."

"Then do it. Just hold that. I'll send for Beltur."

"He's still likely at the way station, with a half squad of guards. You might have to take over for him there. Take my horse. It's tied in front of the Healing House."

"Just hold that containment."

Worrfan looked at Jessyla, his expression half worried, half aghast.

"I can't do what has to be done. The only one who can is Beltur. Taelya can keep it from getting worse. You can lay Frydika down, but only if her head is higher than her feet."

"But . . . you're the healer."

"Believe me, Worrfan. Whatever I could do would only make matters worse. I'll hurry."

True to her word, Jessyla ran back toward the Healing House, where she quickly untied the horse and rode toward the main street.

Less than a third of a glass later, Taelya could sense the concentration of order and chaos that was Beltur nearing the square. He rode through the crowd, which parted at his approach, directly to where Taelya stood beside Frydika. He dismounted and handed the horse's reins to Julli, then immediately stepped up beside Taelya. "Can you feel pressure against the containment?"

"Not as much as when I put it in place."

"That's good." For several moments, he stood there, his eyes on Frydika.

Taelya could sense the tiny bits of order-bounded chaos that he inserted inside the containment. With each bit, the orangish-red wound chaos shrank . . . until there was none.

Then Beltur said, "Remove your containment."

Taelya eased it out. From what she could tell, none of the orange-shaded chaos remained, but there was an area of dull red, which she knew was the color of a healing wound.

Beltur took a deep breath, then turned to Worrfan. "There was a nasty chaos spot in a small part of her brain. What Taelya did kept it from getting worse and would likely have done what I did, if much more slowly. I can't tell you what will happen now. She'll likely not wake for a little while, but it's all right to move her to the Healing House now. We'll need a cart. Then we'll put her in a bed there, where one of the healers can watch her. You can stay there with her."

"I'll get a cart," said Julli to Worrfan. "You just stay with her."

After Julli tied Taelya's mount to Frydika's wagon and moved away, Beltur murmured to Taelya, "You know, you could actually do some healing if you had to." He held up a hand to forestall anything Taelya might say. "I didn't say you should be a healer. Over time, balancing order with your chaos would be a strain, but you have great control and you can sense the tiniest bits of order and chaos. You ought to spend a little time with Margrena and Jessyla just so you know a few basics beyond what you know about wound dressing and bone setting."

For a moment, Taelya wondered why it mattered. Then she understood. "You think we're going to have to fight?"

"I don't know that. Matters aren't looking good. I just have a feeling about it."

The fact that he'd said the same thing the night before worried at Taelya, but she said nothing.

It took longer for Julli to find a small cart than it had taken Jessyla to find Beltur and for him to return, but Julli and Beltur lifted Frydika onto the cart.

Worrfan looked at Frydika and then at the wagon, almost helplessly.

"I can watch your wagon," said Julli. "You just worry about her."

"Thank you."

Taelya led Beltur's horse behind the others while the two men wheeled the cart to the southwest side of the square where the Healing House stood. While they carried Frydika inside, Taelya tied the mount to the hitching rail and then went inside, where Margrena was settling Frydika onto one of the pallet beds in a back room.

Once Frydika was settled, with Worrfan on a stool beside her, and Beltur had left to relieve Jessyla, Margrena motioned to Taelya.

"Yes?"

"Beltur said you could have handled that brain chaos by yourself if you'd known what to do."

"I just did what Aunt Jessyla told me to do."

Margrena laughed harshly, if softly. "That's what all healers do—do what older healers tell us and learn from that and experience, and then pass it on. Healing takes more order than you'd be comfortable with all the time, but you'll be a better mage and a better officer if you learn a bit more than what you already know."

"Especially if we get into a war."

"Even if you don't. Your being there likely limited the damage to Frydika's brain. In healing, time often makes a difference. Why don't you stop by here after your patrols for the next few eightdays."

Taelya could tell that the words weren't a question, not after what Beltur had said. "As I can."

"As you can. We know duties sometimes take longer than you think."

When Taelya left the Healing House to resume her patrol duties in the square, she realized that she had the slightest of headaches . . . and she never had headaches. *Except for the first day of your cycle.* Was the headache from using order to heal, and the imbalance it created?

She immediately found Marrak. "There hasn't been any trouble, has there?"

"Not any sign. Not so far, anyway."

Over the next three glasses, Taelya's headache subsided, first into a barely noticeable dull ache, and then it gradually faded so that by fourth glass there wasn't even the hint of an ache.

Still . . . as she walked home from headquarters after her patrol duty was over, she wondered.

When Taelya stepped inside the house, an aroma of cooking surrounded her, but the scent was unfamiliar, and she hurried toward the kitchen.

"Good!" said Tulya, from where she stood before the stove. "You're home. I could use some help. Dorylt's going to be a little late."

"What are we having?"

"I wanted to fix something different. We're having fowl, two of them fixed with a cumin sauce. The other day, Taarna came by with Buskar when he delivered the new keg of ale, and we got to talking . . . she told me the way to fix it. It's actually a Hamorian dish. Let's just hope it turns out the way she said it would. We're having cheesed potatoes as well. I would have liked to have tried something called biastras, but there wasn't time, and, besides, one new dish at a time is safer." Tulya paused, then added with a smile, "We also have an early mixed-fruit pie from Meldryn. He said he could just scrape together enough for it, and that it's a little tart."

"Tart or not, it'll be good." Even a small slice of one of Meldryn's pies was likely to be mouthwatering. "What do you need me to do?"

"I put the quilla in the old pot to marinate in ale overnight. If you'd dry it and put it on an old platter, by then I'll have the potatoes in the oven, and I can spice the slices and then flour them."

"Fried quilla?"

"Why not? Everyone's tired of it boiled or baked."

Taelya couldn't help but smile at her mother's tart tone of voice.

Before all that long, or so it seemed to Taelya, the two finished all the preparations, aided slightly by Dorylt, who didn't arrive home until after fifth glass. After they finished, Taelya once again worked with Dorylt on his shields for a little more than a quint. While she made an effort to use more order, using order in pressing Dorylt's shields didn't bring on a headache, and she wondered what the difference was.

While Dorylt cleaned up, Taelya settled in the front room and began to read, trying to keep her mind on the copy of *The Wisdom of Relyn* that her mother had borrowed from Beltur. She had just barely read a handful of pages when there was a rap on the front door.

She sensed it had to be Beltur, Jessyla, Kaeryla, and Arthaal, and immediately hurried to greet them. As soon as they were all in the front room and moving toward the kitchen, Taelya looked to Jessyla and said, "Could I have just a moment?"

"Of course." The silver-haired healer moved back to near the front door, waiting for Taelya to join her before asking, "What is it?"

"After I helped with Frydika, your mother said she agreed with Uncle Beltur's suggestion that I learn some healing . . . but she said doing too much wouldn't be good for me. I had a headache after I did what I did for Frydika, and I almost never get them, but when I used more order in working on shields with Dorylt, I didn't get a headache."

"You're asking if you think the headache was because you did some healing? That's possible, but it's more likely because you're not used to using order and chaos in that particular way. I had some headaches when Beltur was first showing me uses of chaos surrounded by order. It's something you should let us know, though, if it continues when you're learning battle healing. The parts that involve order and chaos, that is." Jessyla smiled warmly. "You'll do well, I suspect."

"What if I don't?"

"You've already proved you can do it. The only question is how much better you can be and how often you'll be able to do healing. You shouldn't worry about that. You're an accomplished mage." She gestured. "We should join the others."

Taelya trailed her aunt toward the kitchen, only to be stopped by Kaeryla.

"I hear you're going to be a healer now, too," said Kaeryla, with a slight edge to her voice.

Taelya shook her head. "I'm going to learn a little more so that I can do battle-field healing. Both your father and mother . . . and your grandmother . . . told me that anything more wouldn't work. There's too much order involved for me to be a regular healer. I had to do just a little to keep the chaos in Frydika's skull from spreading until your father got there. That little bit was a strain, and I ended up with a headache."

"A headache? I never get headaches from healing."

Taelya thought she sensed a slight smugness in Kaeryla's words, but she merely said, "It wasn't a bad headache, but I never get headaches, except . . ."

Kaeryla nodded.

Taelya could sense a certain relief and relaxation from Kaeryla, and that saddened her. She'd never wanted to compete with her cousin, and she kept hoping that Kaeryla's order abilities would strengthen soon. "What do you do when you visit the hamlets?"

"I can set bones, and lessen wound chaos, but mostly, I clean out cuts or boils that are festering and make sure that ailing children don't have the red or green flux. Sometimes, I sense women who are carrying to make sure there's no chaos . . ."

Taelya just listened for what might have been half a quint, until her mother spoke up. "It's time for dinner."

That caught Taelya by surprise, because usually she was the one who filled the beakers with ale for when they had others for dinner, but then she caught sight of Dorylt filling a pitcher for refills. She had barely seated herself next to her mother, who sat at one end of the table, opposite Beltur at the other end, when Beltur cleared his throat, loudly, then waited for the few words being spoken to stop.

"Now that we're all seated," said Beltur, "I have two pieces of news. First, the Gallosian envoy and his party will be arriving on oneday. The Council will meet with him in the afternoon, and then the Council and all full mages and healers, including Kaeryla, will have dinner with the envoy and his party at the West Inn. That's all I've told anyone." Beltur held up his hand to forestall objections by the two youngest males. "The reason Arthaal and Dorylt aren't attending is because the envoy is attended by two white mages, and Lord Korsaen specified that only full mages capable of immediately fighting be included, and only practicing healers. I'd prefer that no mages attend besides those on the Council, but I'd also rather not disregard a request from Vergren, especially since Lord Korsaen will be accompanying the envoy."

Taelya nodded. While her uncle had never directly flouted a request from the Duchess, he'd ignored certain aspects of a few requests, but Korsaen's presence made that impractical, especially since Fairhaven would need support from the Duchess in the event of an actual war.

"The better news is that we're all invited for eightday dinner tomorrow at Johlana and Jorhan's place at fourth glass. Meldryn and Margrena will also be there." Beltur looked to the end of the table and lifted his beaker. "To Tulya, for the latest in a long series of excellent meals."

"Thank you . . . again," replied Tulya.

Taelya couldn't help smiling. Even after all the years of shared meals, her uncle seldom failed to offer some sort of compliment about her mother's cooking, even though he wasn't a bad cook himself, and a better than fair baker, although, when he was complimented, he always pointed out that he'd learned it all from Meldryn, who was far better.

She turned to her mother. "When did you find out about the Gallosian envoy?"

"Sometime in midafternoon. Beltur told me right after the courier found him. He was at the distillery at the time. I would have told you when you came home, but I was trying to get the dinner right. Then, when I remembered I hadn't told you, it was when everyone arrived. I would have told you after everyone left if Beltur hadn't said something."

Taelya nodded. She could easily believe that. She took a small swallow of the good ale that Beltur had provided for them the whole time they'd lived in Fairhaven.

Dinner would be good. That, she knew.

VIII

On eightday morning, Taelya slept late, since she didn't have eightday duty as a Road Guard, although late in her mother's house was seventh glass. But she could and did eat breakfast without rushing, then spent two glasses working with Tulya to scrub the kitchen and front room, after which she did the same to her own room. Then she walked over to the stable with Dorylt, and the four younger members of the two families cleaned out the stable and thoroughly groomed all of the horses. After that, Taelya saddled Bounder and set out on a ride.

Near the end of that ride, roughly a glass later, as she neared the West Inn, she saw Sheralt, with Lendar and Sheppyl, riding toward her. Having no polite way to avoid Sheralt, she reined up and waited for him.

"How far west did you go?" asked the white mage, reining up close to her, closer than Taelya would have preferred.

"Just to the kaystone. Bounder needed the exercise. I didn't sense anyone out there but our local people. There wasn't any road dust farther out, either."

"What do you know about the Gallosian envoy that the majer didn't tell us?"

"Likely not much. You probably heard about it before I did. I didn't find out until dinner last night."

"What *do* you know?" pressed Sheralt.

"Just that the envoy, two white mages, and Lord Korsaen are arriving tomorrow and that the Council and the Road Guard mages and healers are to have dinner with them."

"That's all? You're sure?"

"Very sure." Taelya paused briefly. "That's all he told us."

"What else did he tell your mother?"

"If he told her more, she didn't tell me. Even if she had, you know I couldn't tell you." She smiled brightly. "But since I don't know . . ."

"Why are you so difficult?"

"I'm not. The reason you think I'm difficult is because I'm following the majer's orders. You'd do the same if you were in my position . . . and please don't tell me you wouldn't."

Abruptly, Sheralt grinned. "You're right, but you can't blame me for trying."

"I don't." *Not much, anyway.*

"Why do you think we're invited to dinner?"

"What do you think?" countered Taelya gently.

"Perhaps to show the Gallosians that we still have capable mages." Sheralt frowned. "Or maybe the majer doesn't trust the Gallosian mages. Or it could be that he wants us to sense what other mages are like."

"I don't *know* the reason," Taelya said, "but the last reason sounds very much like him."

"Do you think he'll tell us why later?"

"I don't know. He might think it should be obvious, or . . ." Taelya shrugged.

Sheralt paused, then said, "How are you doing with that awful training device?"

"I've only done it once. I was exhausted after half a glass."

The older mage just nodded. "Well . . . we'd better get on with the patrol. I'll see you at dinner tomorrow."

"You have tomorrow off?"

"Your cousin has my duty tomorrow."

Taelya nodded. Kaeryla always rode a patrol on oneday to fill in for whoever had drawn eightday duty. Her shields were as strong as Sheralt's, which was acceptable for routine patrols.

"When will your brother start riding patrols? He's older than Kaeryla, isn't he?"

"He's a year older, but you know that mages don't develop all the same way. He'll ride patrols when his shields are as strong as Kaeryla's. It probably won't be too long."

Sheralt frowned. "Have you been doing something different?"

"Different? What do you mean?"

"Your shields are . . . grayer. That's the only way I can describe it."

"That's not new. I've always had a gray shade to my shields. That's because I link order and chaos in them. Maybe you should try something like that. It might strengthen yours."

"Order mixed with chaos?" Sheralt didn't quite shudder.

"Aren't my uncle's shields stronger than anyone's? Aren't they a mixture of order and chaos?"

"They are. But . . . he's paid quite a price for that strength."

"The blackness across his forehead and head was from battle, not from the shields."

"How can you separate the two?"

"Fine. Don't expect me to shed too many tears over your scattered ashes."

Sheralt didn't or couldn't conceal his expression of bewilderment. After a moment, he said, "Isn't that a bit harsh?"

"If you still need an explanation in a season or so, I just might give you one. If you're pleasant in the meantime. For now, I need to get back to the house, and you need to get on with your patrol." Taelya managed a smile. That was the best she could do.

As she continued toward the stable, she knew she'd been short with Sheralt. *But how can you possibly explain? How could he understand?* Taelya didn't even want to think about it herself, even as she knew why her uncle had been so insistent on her learning to incorporate chaos into her shields, even though Beltur had never mentioned the underlying reason—the one besides the fact that doing so increased the strength of her shields considerably.

Why couldn't you learn from him, Father? She blinked back tears, the ones that almost always came the few times when she was reminded in unexpected ways of her father's death. A second thought occurred to her as well. Had her father been like Sheralt, unwilling to change because it was uncomfortable . . . or strange?

She shook her head. That was something she'd never know. But she did know that men often were stubborn when they shouldn't be. *And women aren't?*

She smiled wryly.

By the time she reached the stable she was fully in control, and she even felt the smile she offered Jessyla, who was using her healing skills on the old mare that was now seldom ridden, but for whom the healer had great affection. "How is she doing, Aunt Jessyla?"

"Well for her age. I'd like to see her make it through the summer. She deserves a last pleasant summer. How was your ride?"

"Short. I just felt Bounder needed to get out a little."

"I'm sure he appreciated it."

"I think we both enjoyed it," said Taelya as she dismounted and led the gelding into the stable, where she unsaddled him and let him drink. Once he'd had his immediate fill, she went to the water tap outside Jessyla and Beltur's house and filled a bucket, then lugged it back to the stable, where she used an old towel dipped in the water to get the dust off his coat and help him cool off.

When she finished with Bounder, she walked back to her own house to get ready for dinner.

At two quints before fourth glass, Tulya, Taelya, and Dorylt left the house, walking toward the square, since Jorhan and Johlana's house and Jorhan's forge were at the east end of town. Given how long the dinner would last, and the fact that the late afternoon was warm and muggy, Tulya had declared that riding the horses and then leaving them outside and tied up was neither fair nor good for them if they were needed on oneday. At that pronouncement, both Dorylt and Taelya had managed not to smile, since neither of them had even thought about riding.

As the three neared the spacious house, Taelya remembered when Johlana and Jorhan had first come to Fairhaven, just eightdays after the last battle with Hydlen, and Jorhan had set about rebuilding the burned-out trader's house across the main street and slightly east of Julli and Jaegyr's house. Although the coppersmith hadn't been a young man, he had worked the same long glasses as Beltur and Jessyla and Taelya's mother, and before winter not only had the house been rebuilt, but Jorhan had rebuilt a shed into a working smithy. More than a few times, Taelya had spent the day with Johlana, who'd always been glad to see her, and later Kaeryla and both Dorylt and Arthaal—if for reasons Taelya hadn't fully realized for several years.

For all practical purposes, Johlana, Jorhan, and Margrena were the closest to grandparents either Taelya or Dorylt had, and Margrena, of course, was Kaeryla and Arthaal's grandmother. Meldryn was more like a kindly great-uncle, although Taelya couldn't have said exactly why.

Jorhan was the one to greet them at the doorway. For all of his broad shoulders, and full gray but neatly trimmed beard, Jorhan was only half a head taller than Taelya, but his gray eyes were smiling. "Come on in! You're the first, except for Margrena, but I expect the others won't be long."

The smell of roasting lamb alternated with that of fresh-baked bread and other scents, none of which surprised Taelya given that, when Johlana invited what amounted to her extended family for eightday dinner, the food was always outstanding.

"Margrena's in the kitchen, I take it?" said Tulya.

"Where else?" replied the smith.

"I'll see if they need help," replied Tulya. "You two keep Jorhan company." Without looking back she headed for the kitchen, past the large dining room with a table already set for eleven.

Taelya immediately turned to Jorhan. "What are you forging right now? Besides blades?"

"From what you say, Taelya, you'd think that's all Beltur, Arthaal, and I forge." The smith's eyes twinkled in amusement.

"No. It's all I know about because Arthaal never says much, and Uncle Beltur somehow never answers the question." Belatedly, she thought about the cupridium-fronted training device, but decided not to mention it.

"Yes, he does," said Dorylt. "It's just when you're not there or not listening. They're working on—"

"Enough said," rumbled Jorhan. "The less said the better. We've also just finished a set of candelabra for a wealthy trader in Lydiar . . ."

At the knock on the door, the smith stopped. "That sounds like Meldryn. He always knocks twice, like a courier."

"I'll get it," said Dorylt, turning back toward the door.

Taelya never did get to hear what Jorhan might have said, because Beltur and his family arrived just behind Meldryn, and everyone crowded into the front parlor, all except Margrena and Johlana, to hear the latest that Beltur had to say about the arrival of the Gallosian envoy and the mages who would be accompanying him.

Beltur just stood before the cold hearth and waited until the murmurs died away. Then he grinned. "I don't know any more than what I've already said. The envoy, Lord Korsaen, Maeyora, and the rest of the envoy's party will arrive tomorrow."

"You didn't mention Maeyora before," said Tulya.

"I thought I did," replied Beltur. "I didn't mean to deceive anyone."

"That makes sense," added Jessyla. "She can tell when someone's being deceptive."

"Doesn't that mean that the envoy can only tell the truth?" asked Kaeryla.

"No," replied Taelya, almost without thinking. "He has to say what he believes is the truth, but the Prefect didn't necessarily tell him the truth."

"That could be a problem," added Jessyla. "We'll just have to see."

"What did you do with the Kaordists who wanted to stay here?" asked Meldryn.

"We found homes for them. Some are just for now."

"What about Teshkat and Jamya?" asked Taelya.

"Julli and Jaegyr took them. Jamya turns out to have some talent in stitchery," said Beltur.

Taelya could see that. Julli could have used help for years in making uniforms for patrollers and Road Guards, and both Julli and Jaegyr were at least ten years older than her own mother, and they'd never had children.

"As for Teshkat, he seems to like the idea of learning to be a cabinet maker." Beltur looked to Dorylt. "He'll start in the shop tomorrow. We're counting on you to help him and Jaegyr."

"Once he learns something, he should be a help," admitted Dorylt. "There's so much to do right now."

Left unsaid, Taelya knew, was the fact that a war with Certis or Hydlen, or both, could change that quickly, and Dorylt might be needed elsewhere.

Beltur turned as Johlana appeared in the archway to the kitchen.

"Dinner's ready. Everyone take your places."

Taelya smiled. Whatever might occur on oneday would not be discussed at dinner or thereafter, and that was fine with her.

IX

At muster on oneday morning, Gustaan announced, "Undercaptain Taelya will take the southern patrol, Valchar the western patrol, and Healer-Undercaptain Kaeryla the eastern patrol."

Taelya waited for the captain to finish his announcements before she moved closer and said, quietly, "If I might ask, did the majer make the assignments for today?"

"In fact, he did," replied Gustaan.

"Did he say why?"

"Just that it would become obvious in time."

Taelya couldn't help a momentary frown.

Gustaan added, "He just told me not to change those assignments or to let anyone switch. Oh, and the envoy and his party will be staying at the West Inn, but they'll be coming to headquarters first."

"Thank you." Taelya kept her voice pleasant and even offered a smile she didn't feel as she left the headquarters building. She'd known about the envoy staying at the West Inn, but not the patrol assignments. While she was certain the assignments reflected the expected arrival of the Gallosian envoy and Lord Korsaen, she was still considering the reasons for them as she, Dhulaar, and Sheppyl rode east on the main street, out to where the southern road joined the east road that eventually led to Lydiar. She was riding a Road Guard horse, not Bounder, just on a feeling that it might be better to save Bounder for twoday, although she couldn't have said exactly why she felt that way.

Given Beltur's earlier words about shielding squads, and the implication that she might even be required to shield as many Road Guards as a full company, Taelya created a second shield around her small patrol, but one big enough to protect a full squad.

Of the three mages riding patrols, Taelya knew that she was the strongest, but Valchar had been assigned the patrol most likely to be the one that would end up leading the envoy's party into town. Then a second thought struck her. The patrol that Kaeryla was leading was the one least likely to meet that party, and, in fact, given the timing of the patrols, either Taelya or Valchar might be the undercaptain meeting the arrivals.

Which means that he really didn't want Kaeryla to be the one meeting them. And that made definite sense, given that she was only fourteen going on fifteen. *And that Beltur didn't want to take her off patrol duty.*

Still . . . Taelya had the feeling that either she was missing something or there was something she didn't know. *But you'll likely find out.*

"When do you think this envoy will arrive?" asked Dhulaar.

"Most likely between third and fourth glass, but it could be a bit earlier or later."

"Earlier, I'd wager, if Lord Korsaen has anything to say about it."

"He won't say much," replied Taelya. "It will just be arranged so that it works out the way he wants."

"You've met Lord Korsaen before, haven't you?"

"I was seven when I met him the first time. It's been a good five years since he last came to Fairhaven. And I've only been to Vergren once."

"What's he like?"

"You were here then. Didn't you see him?"

"All of us saw him, but I never talked to him."

"He's always seemed fair. He's devoted to his consort and children. He's likely the closest advisor to the Duchess and her daughter, who will be the next duchess."

"She will?" asked Dhulaar.

"The Duchess didn't have any sons, and women can rule in Montgren."

"Is that why there are more women on the Council here?"

Taelya shook her head. "There have been times when there were as many men as women. It's just a question of who's more able."

Dhulaar frowned.

"Do you want to live in Westwind or Sarronnyn?"

"You have to ask?" The senior guard's words were close to indignant.

"So . . . I feel the same way about living in Gallos or Certis. In Fairhaven, or Montgren, whoever's better for the job has a chance."

"But . . . ser . . . you're a mage."

"So far as I know, there aren't any women who are white mages in Certis or Gallos, and there aren't any women black mages, either, or in Spidlar. And for that matter, Frydika likely would have died on sevenday if Beltur hadn't been her healer."

"I heard you helped with that."

"I did, but Beltur was the one who trained me enough to be able to help. Another thing . . . if Jessyla hadn't learned to be a war mage in addition to being a healer, everyone who lived in Fairhaven would have been killed."

"I heard that . . ."

"I saw her kill Hydlenese troopers."

"She doesn't carry a blade."

"She turns her shields into knives and cuts men and mounts down."

"Can you do that?"

"If I have to." Taelya looked directly at the older guard.

Dhulaar didn't quite meet her eyes. "What about the young healer, Undercaptain Kaeryla?"

"She can use her shields like that, but only close to her mount. In a few years, she should be able to do everything her mother can." *Possibly more.*

"So why does the Viscount want to risk fighting Fairhaven?"

Because there are so few of us. "You'd have to ask him. It might be because he wants to build an empire, like Cyador was."

Dhulaar shook his head. "What for? He's got a fancy palace and lots of golds, and no one's going to attack him."

"Some people always want more. Just like Duke Maastyn's father."

Dhulaar fell silent.

As they neared the stone posts that had once marked the eastern edge of town, Taelya let her senses range as far as she could, but all she could discern to the east was a one-horse wagon and a cart being drawn by a donkey, with the grower leading the way. There were two people, likely youths, and a large dog herding sheep on the grassland south of the main road and east of the road that ran around Fairhaven to the south.

Taelya wondered if they'd see more Hydlenese troopers, as they had on six-day, or if they'd stay farther from the border, the way they usually did.

By the time the three Road Guards had turned onto the southern road and covered about a kay, with the white sun pouring down on her out of the green-blue sky, Taelya was definitely aware that it was the fifth oneday of spring and that for the next two seasons patrolling would be hot, muggy, and usually dusty.

Through the course of the day, she kept sensing and looking for traders, but they didn't come across any. She usually wouldn't have seen any on the southern patrol, except on the section of road that paralleled the road from Hydolar, just before it joined the main road west from Fairhaven, but the comparative lack of traders bothered her.

At just after third glass, as she and the others reached the main east-west road for the second time, she could sense two white mages amid a party of riders, which included Valchar, all headed toward Fairhaven from the Weevett road.

"The Gallosians are headed into town with Valchar," she said. "They've got two whites, which is what the majer said."

Much as Taelya would have liked to have seen the group, by the time that she, Dhulaar, and Sheppyl had finished their patrol, reported in, and taken care of their mounts, everyone in the group had departed for the West Inn, where they would be staying. Then Taelya had to walk home.

She was still thinking about the white mages when she stepped into the front parlor of the house.

"I've laid out your good uniform," Tulya announced as soon as Taelya had closed the door behind herself. "Also, Beltur said that none of you are to wear sabres."

"Did he say why?"

"It's a peaceful dinner. I think he doesn't want the Gallosians to know how well-trained any of you are."

Taelya didn't care for the implications of that, much as she understood her uncle's reasoning.

"Dorylt is readying the horses for us. So we can leave as soon as you're ready."

"Dinner won't be that soon, will it?"

"Dinner won't, but Lord Korsaen arranged for refreshments and what he calls a reception before the dinner. Beltur and Jessyla have already left. Kaeryla will be going with us."

"A reception?"

"Lord Korsaen feels people should have a chance to meet the envoy and his mages, and Beltur wants you to see the Gallosians. He told me to tell you to observe them very carefully, and to be courteous and polite, but no more and no less. Jessyla told me something similar."

"Why?"

"I'm sure they have their reasons. Remember, the Prefect tried to have Beltur killed, and they both had to flee Gallos. So it's not a surprise that they want us to be careful."

"I knew that, but we're in Fairhaven, and there likely aren't any mages as powerful as either of them."

"We don't know that, and there might be mages that could give you trouble."

They'd have to be almost as strong as Beltur to give me trouble. But Taelya only said, "I'll be very polite and very careful." Then she headed for the washroom to remove a day's worth of road dust before changing into her clean good uniform.

Not quite a quint later, Taelya left her room in her uniform, and she and Tulya walked across the street toward the stable. Taelya looked at her mother, who wore a pale blue shirt, with dark blue trousers and jacket, as well as polished black riding boots. "You're wearing your justicer garb."

"Beltur suggested it. He said it was definitely an official occasion."

Taelya glanced ahead. Arthaal and Dorylt held the reins to the three horses, lined up outside the stable. As Taelya watched, Kaeryla, wearing apprentice healer greens, mounted, and Arthaal stepped back.

When Tulya and Taelya reached Dorylt, with a smile, he handed the reins of Tulya's mount to her, then Bounder's reins to his sister. "Good luck."

"Let's hope it's not that bad," replied Tulya. "And would you and Arthaal keep a close watch on things?"

"We can do that."

Once the three were on the main street headed west, Taelya asked Tulya, "Do you know anything more about who came from Gallos and Vergren?"

Tulya shook her head. "No one came by the Council House, and Beltur didn't know any more when he stopped by around noon. He's worried, though."

Kaeryla nodded. "He said that it would be interesting to see which white mages the Prefect sent. He didn't sound happy when he said that."

"Did he say more?" asked Taelya.

"No. And Mother gave me that look that told me not to ask."

Taelya was familiar with that look, either from her own mother or Jessyla.

"It's possible that whoever the Prefect sent might be one of the mages who tried to kill him," Tulya pointed out.

"Would the Prefect even know Uncle Beltur was still alive?"

"I'm sure that, after more than sixteen years, both the Prefect and the Viscount know who he is," said Tulya dryly.

"Then why would the Prefect send someone who tried to kill Beltur? There must be a newer white who doesn't know Beltur."

"I'm sure the Prefect has considered that, but he might still have sent someone who knew Beltur in order to get better information," said Tulya. "We'll just have to see."

When they reached the West Inn, Taelya's eyes quickly passed over the handsome two-story brick structure and turned to the long stable building on the west side of the brick-paved courtyard. There three uniformed Road Guards stood waiting, clearly there to help stable their mounts.

Taelya managed not to smile as she saw that the three were Hassett, Breslan, and Chaslar . . . the most junior of the Road Guards. She reined in Bounder slightly, to allow her mother to be the first to dismount.

Once all three were dismounted, Tulya led the way into the inn, past the two patrollers at the side entrance and directly to the public room, which, Taelya knew, Beltur had essentially commandeered for the reception and dinner, not that Claerk would have opposed its use in any case, since he was councilor and was also being paid to house the visitors.

The moment Tulya stepped through the wide arch from the hallway into the public room, Beltur appeared and nodded to the three. "I need to introduce our justicer and councilor to Envoy Faelsham." Looking at Kaeryla and then Taelya, he added, "You two are to sit at the smaller round table with most of the other mages. In the meantime, feel free to talk to anyone. The refreshments are on the table to the left." Then he escorted Tulya to a small group in the middle of the room, which had been cleared of tables, and introduced her to a dark-haired man who wore what appeared to be a black uniform with silver-gray piping, except without insignia.

Taelya immediately surveyed the room, taking in the two mages in white, one of whom had his back to her, but was talking to Jessyla, who listened intently, without smiling, and three other Gallosians in black-and-gray uniforms, presumably officers. All the others were either councilors, mages, or officers in the Road Guards or the Town Patrol. Then she looked to the refreshment table, where Sheralt and Valchar stood talking to the second Gallosian mage. As she watched, the mage walked away. Taelya looked to Kaeryla. "We might as well get some ale and join Valchar and Sheralt."

"I'd rather talk to Therran or Gustaan," replied Kaeryla. "We'll have to sit with the other mages at dinner, anyway."

"Then you should," said Taelya, with a smile.

The two walked to the table, where one of Claerk's servers immediately poured each a beaker of ale.

Kaeryla slipped away and joined Therran and Gustaan, while Taelya joined Valchar and Sheralt.

". . . looks as though the majer might know the older white mage," Sheralt was saying to Valchar.

"The healer doesn't look all that impressed with him," replied Valchar.

"Why would she?" said Taelya. "They both had to flee Gallos, and the whites tried to kill Beltur."

"That was war," said Sheralt. "War's often not personal."

Taelya's eyes fixed on Sheralt. "They tried to kill him in Fenard. That was long *before* the war with Spidlar."

"Well . . . you'd know that better than I would." Sheralt's words were almost dismissive.

Valchar's eyes narrowed, but Taelya spoke before the younger black mage could. "They also killed his uncle, and his uncle was loyally serving the Prefect. That was just because his uncle told the Prefect something he didn't want to hear."

Sheralt shrugged. "That's always a danger with rulers."

"Not here," retorted Taelya. "You can disagree with the Council without being in danger of your life."

"But . . . if you don't follow the rules, you have to leave. Just ask the Kaordists."

"That's different. They could choose to follow the rules, or they could leave."

"It's not as different as you think," replied Sheralt. "If people break the rules badly, and steal a lot or kill someone, they'll be killed in turn."

Taelya was about to reply when she saw Beltur walking toward Kaeryla, accompanied by the older and taller white mage.

"What do you say to that, Taelya?" pressed Sheralt, smiling.

She turned her attention back to Sheralt and forced a shrug. "You can still leave if you disagree. That's if you don't steal or hurt someone."

"Other lands have different rules."

"I know. That's why we left Spidlar and Axalt. That's also why we're better than they are."

"The thousand or so Hydlenese troopers you killed to keep your rules might disagree."

"They invaded. They tried to impose their rules. Their duke didn't have to invade lands that weren't his. And they're your rules, too, now."

"They are," agreed Sheralt. "And I agree that they're better rules. But others think their rules are better." He stopped and turned.

So did Taelya, because Beltur was now escorting the older white mage toward them.

Chaos swirled around him and the white tunic, trousers, and boots that he wore. He was also taller than Beltur, with smooth black hair, and piercing blue eyes, although the lines running from his eyes and the creases in his forehead suggested that he was considerably older than her uncle.

Taelya thought he'd probably been incredibly handsome when he was her age, but he was definitely showing his years.

"Sydon, here are some of our Road Guard mages. The young black on the end is Valchar. You might have met him on the way in. Beside him is Sheralt, and this is my niece Taelya."

After an almost perfunctory nod to the two young men, Sydon turned to Taelya as he said to Beltur, "You mean Jessyla's niece?"

"She's our niece," Beltur said firmly, clearly ignoring Sydon's warm but definitely condescending tone.

Sydon smiled winningly at Taelya. "I'm pleased to meet you. Your uncle and I go back a long ways."

"We were both assistants to my uncle Kaerylt," said Beltur.

"Back when Beltur was a white mage," added Sydon.

Taelya distrusted Sydon almost immediately, although she couldn't have said why. "You mean back when he thought he was a white, before he discovered that he was much stronger as a black?"

"More a gray, I'd say." Sydon offered a warm smile. "You're incredibly powerful for someone your size."

And you're incredibly condescending. "I've had very good training. That helps." Taelya managed a pleasant smile.

"Still . . . this is the first place I've been where there are women mages . . . and I've never even read about a woman who was a white. You're clearly very special."

"That's because we let women do what they do best," Beltur said, gesturing toward the center table and adding, "Dinner's about ready. I just wanted to give you a chance to meet some of those here." He looked back to the three junior mages. "The other Gallosian mage is Klosyl, and he'll be sitting with you."

Sydon smiled again at Taelya. "Perhaps we can talk more later."

"Perhaps we can." *But not if I can help it.*

Taelya immediately turned back to Sheralt and Valchar.

"He's pretty strong," said Sheralt.

"Not near as strong as the majer," said Valchar.

Sheralt laughed softly. "I doubt that there's anyone in Candar as strong as he is. And not many are as strong as the healer." He turned to Taelya. "I still can't believe she fought as a war mage."

"She did. I told you that earlier." Taelya could still remember that . . . and her mother telling her that sometimes even healers needed to fight. "I think sometimes it hurt her a lot, but that didn't stop her."

"Then there's Varais," said Valchar.

"But she's from Westwind. All the women there are . . ." Sheralt looked at Taelya and stopped.

"Were you going to say that they're all crazy?"

"They're different."

Taelya could tell that wasn't what he might have said.

"Did you know that besides the pair of blades she wears in that shoulder harness, she carries two more in knee scabbards?"

"I know," replied Taelya. "That's so that she can throw two and still have two left."

At that moment, a bell rang—loudly.

"If you'd all sit at your tables!" Beltur said.

In moments, except for the servers, everyone was seated. The large circular table held the five Council members—Beltur, Jessyla, Tulya, Taarna, and Claerk—Lord Korsaen and Lady Maeyora, Envoy Faelsham, a Gallosian majer, and Sydon. Taelya, Kaeryla, Sheralt, and Valchar were seated at the smaller round table with Klosyl, the other Gallosian mage. The third, oblong table contained Gustaan, Therran, Patrol Captain Graalur, Patrol Undercaptain Dussef, a Gallosian captain—a narrow-faced older officer who likely had made his way up through the ranks—and a younger Gallosian undercaptain.

Once everyone was seated and quiet, Beltur stood and said, "This dinner is to welcome Envoy Faelsham and his party to Fairhaven. Please enjoy yourselves. Councilor Claerk went to considerable lengths to provide this dinner, and it would be a shame not to enjoy it." With a smile, Beltur sat down.

Taelya found herself with Sheralt on her left and Valchar on her right. Kaeryla sat between Valchar and Klosyl, who looked to be about Sheralt's age. Since no one was saying anything, she did. "Since we didn't meet earlier, I'm Taelya, and I'm an undercaptain in the Fairhaven Road Guard, but then, all of us are."

"I'm Sheralt, and I'm originally from Worrak."

"I'm Valchar, and I grew up in Lydiar in a hamlet so small that no one elsewhere knew its name."

"Kaeryla. I'm also a healer, and I was born here."

The dark-haired and brown-eyed Gallosian smiled politely. "I'm Klosyl, and I'm from Portalya. It's the largest port town on the River Gallos."

Taelya surreptitiously used her senses to try to determine just how strong a mage Klosyl might be. There was a fair amount of chaos swirling about the Gallosian, but not so much as around Sydon, and his comparatively small amount of free order was almost randomly mixed among the free chaos. Klosyl was carrying shields, but they seemed weak compared even to Sheralt's. *But then he might be able to muster stronger shields if he wanted.* But the fact that he wasn't carrying stronger shields suggested that doing so was an effort . . . and that suggested that she well might be able to overpower him. With Sydon, she wasn't so sure, although she had no doubt that Beltur could destroy either of the Gallosians.

Sheralt lifted the pitcher of ale and looked to Taelya.

"No, thank you. Not yet." Taelya had barely sipped from the beaker she held, and she was glad to notice that Kaeryla had been equally careful.

Sheralt refilled his own beaker and passed the pitcher to Klosyl, who poured a slight bit into his beaker before passing the pitcher to Kaeryla, who in turn passed it to Valchar, without adding any ale to her beaker.

"How did you end up in the Prefect's service?" asked Taelya, knowing full well that it was unlikely that Klosyl had had any choice.

Klosyl offered a humorous smile. "There aren't many opportunities for white mages in Gallos except in serving the Prefect. I don't imagine it's that much different here, though, is it?"

"There are a few mages and healers here who don't serve the Council," replied Taelya, "but the Council pays better than most other jobs here, at least for mages."

"Not all mages serve the Council?" Klosyl lifted his eyebrows.

"No. There's a black who works as an apprentice smith, another who's an apprentice cabinet maker, and an older black who's a baker." Taelya was shading matters somewhat given the ages of Arthaal and Dorylt, but she wanted to see Klosyl's reaction.

"But no whites who don't serve the Council?"

"At present, Sheralt and I are the only whites here in Fairhaven. There are several others elsewhere in Montgren."

"Women white mages are . . . rare, and it's not that usual to have both blacks and whites working together . . . these days."

"In these days," agreed Sheralt, "but in the time of Cyador, both whites and blacks worked together, and they founded a mighty empire."

Sheralt's words totally surprised Taelya, because he'd never spoken of Cyador before, not around her, at least.

"That was a long time ago," Klosyl pointed out, leaning back slightly as servers approached the table and placed platters in front of each of the five, then added two small baskets of bread.

Taelya glanced down at her platter, taking in the small rack of lamb, the cheese-lace potatoes, and the early peas and wondering who was paying for the fare, not that she was about to complain.

Klosyl looked down at his platter. "Not bad for a small town."

"And you're not paying for it," said Valchar cheerfully.

Kaeryla didn't bother to hide her grin. "Montgren is known for its lamb. I doubt you could get better anywhere in Gallos." After the slightest pause, she asked, "What is your favorite Gallosian dish? Perhaps some type of burhka?"

"I'm partial to river trout with pearapples and new potatoes. Fresh river trout."

"Well . . . we can't give you trout here," said Sheralt. "We don't have any rivers big enough to hold trout."

"You said you were from Worrak. Why would you ever leave a city for a small town like Fairhaven?"

"You obviously don't know much about Worrak, then. The pirate lords run the town and pay tribute that they call tariffs to the Duke so that he'll leave them alone. The only law is what a man can obtain by force or golds, or the force and golds of his friends. A white mage from a poor family either must work for one of the pirate lords or leave."

"More like sneak away, I'd imagine," said Klosyl with a sneering laugh.

"It's really not that much different in Gallos, is it?" asked Kaeryla with an innocence that Taelya knew was feigned. "I mean . . . don't all the mages work for the Prefect? And if they wanted to leave, wouldn't they have to sneak away?"

"It's a great honor working for the Arms-Mage and the Prefect. Why would any of us want to forgo that honor?"

"I'm most certain you wouldn't wish that," said Taelya. "You clearly respect the Prefect and the Arms-Mage. You didn't serve in the battles between Gallos and Spidlar, did you?"

For an instant, Klosyl looked puzzled, before he replied, "That was before my time. Why do you ask?"

"I just wondered. Are there any women mages that serve the Prefect?"

"I'm not aware of any. Most women who have talent with order are healers, if they practice magery at all. Women white mages . . . I don't know of any."

"In Gallos, you mean?" asked Kaeryla, seemingly guilelessly. "Women are mages here, and in Sarronnyn, I've heard."

"I imagine every land is different," Klosyl said smoothly.

"That's definitely true," said Valchar cheerfully. "Some rulers value women more."

"Some women are worth valuing more," said Klosyl.

"As opposed to men, where all with magely abilities are of worth? Is that what you mean?" asked Taelya.

Klosyl offered a lazy smile. "You're very good with words . . . Undercaptain."

"I fear not, Mage Klosyl. Words are by far the least of my abilities." As soon as she'd spoken, Taelya regretted the words, fearing that they might have undermined the impression Beltur had wanted to create by not having the undercaptains wear weapons.

"Oh . . . so you sew and do other things?" Klosyl's voice oozed condescension.

Taelya noticed that even Sheralt winced slightly, but she replied mildly,

"Among many other things. As I'm sure you have other talents besides magery. Perhaps you have some skill with a sabre or a bow?" Rather than say more, she cut off a slice of the lamb and ate it, followed by some of the lace potatoes. The lamb was good, the potatoes not as good as her mother's.

Klosyl shook his head, as if the question were ludicrous. "Why would the Prefect have us bother with such? He has thousands of armsmen and hundreds of archers."

"But not so many as the Viscount, it appears," suggested Sheralt, after swallowing a mouthful of lamb.

For several moments, Klosyl busied himself with eating.

After a bit of silence, Valchar asked, "What has the Viscount done recently that suggests he wants to attack Gallos . . . or anyone else, for that matter?"

"He threatened the Prefect with war if he did not reduce the tariffs on Certan merchants and traders passing through Gallos. He claimed that they should not pay tariffs if they sold no goods in Gallos, but he tariffs Gallosian traders who pass through Certis."

Taelya nodded, not in agreement, but because she'd heard of the tariff disputes ever since she'd been a small girl.

"Why doesn't the Prefect just tell the Viscount that he'll treat Certan traders in the same fashion as the Viscount treats Gallosian traders?"

"The Viscount claims that the Prefect has overtariffed Certan traders for years." Klosyl shrugged. "That's all I really know about it."

Taelya suspected that Klosyl's last sentence was the most accurate statement he'd made so far.

From that moment on, Taelya was as polite and charming as she could be, as was Kaeryla, and that was likely for the best, especially as condescending as Klosyl had turned out to be.

After the last toast and various professions of hope and the need to maintain peace in Candar, Jessyla and Tulya surrounded the two younger women, and the four walked back to the stable. While Taelya had wanted a few moments with Kaeryla, that appeared unlikely until twoday, possibly later.

Beltur was the last to join the group. Just before he mounted, he turned to Taelya. "I need a few words with you on the ride back."

Once they were on the main street Taelya obligingly eased Bounder alongside her uncle's horse. "You wanted to talk to me about your friend?"

Even in the dark, Taelya could see and sense the expression of chagrin on Beltur's face.

"He was never my friend, and he very well may have betrayed my uncle. But I'd prefer not to antagonize him or Faelsham. At least for the present. There's nothing to be gained by it, and we don't need to upset anyone else."

Upset anyone else? Besides Gallos, Certis, or Hydlen? Weren't those enemies enough? Or was there some other land that was unhappy with Fairhaven? She decided not to ask. Sooner or later it would come out. "That was why Aunt Jessyla was so polite to him." Taelya paused, then asked, gently, "Is there something else I should know . . . besides not to trust him?"

"Not really . . . except he can be very charming, and he's always liked younger women."

"I'm not interested. There's something . . . about him." Taelya paused, then asked, "Were you ever close?"

"We had to work together, but we weren't that close, even if he was only a few years older."

"A few years?" Taelya's words were involuntary. "I mean, he looks at least ten years older than you."

"He's just three years older. But he never really bothered with separating his order and chaos, the way I taught you."

"Oh . . ." Taelya shivered just a little, thinking again about how much older Sydon looked. She also wondered if Klosyl happened to be younger than he looked.

"What did you learn from Klosyl?" asked Beltur.

"He's sloppy about the way he handles chaos, and he really doesn't have much free order. He hasn't been trained to handle arms, and he doesn't think much of women. He's also arrogant."

"That description would apply to most whites in either Certis or Gallos." Beltur laughed softly, but ironically. "What else?"

"He's from Portalya, and he doesn't seem to know much about trade. He said the reason why there was trouble between Certis and Gallos was that the Viscount wanted the Prefect to stop tariffing Certan traders entering Gallos."

"Sydon and Faelsham said the same thing, almost word for word. That means that something else is afoot."

"Because they've all been told to say exactly the same thing, even when it doesn't make sense? The Prefect and the Viscount have been squabbling over tariffs for years. They even fought some skirmishes over tariffs, didn't they?"

Beltur nodded. "Right after we took care of Hydlen . . . and intermittently even after that."

"What do you think is really happening?" asked Taelya.

"Some form of attack on Fairhaven and Montgren. I can't explain what form it will take. It may be that the Viscount, the Prefect, and Duke Maastyn haven't figured out how they intend to deal with us, but they definitely aren't happy."

"So why is an envoy from Gallos here? As a spy?"

"What better way to get a look at us and get a sense of what's changed?"

"So Sydon's here to see how many mages there are and how strong we are?"

"And ostensibly to protect the envoy from any magely attack, as if we'd be stupid enough to provide the provocation for the Prefect to ally himself with the Viscount in an attack on Montgren."

"So why doesn't Montgren send an envoy to Jellico to discuss a possible alliance between the Duchess and the Viscount?" Taelya's words weren't quite flippant, but close. "Wouldn't that give the Prefect something to think about? He can't very well attack Montgren without going through Certis, or possibly Hydlen, and even a temporary alliance with Montgren would allow Certis greater certainty in dealing with the Prefect."

"Korsaen and I have been discussing it," Beltur replied quietly. "The problem is that Certis doesn't really gain anything by that. We'd likely have to send troops, and mages, to support an attack on Passera."

"Passera?"

"That would give the Viscount control of the Passa River, and it would give his traders direct access to Spidlar without paying tariffs to the Prefect or having to travel twice as far by wagon."

Taelya frowned. "But doesn't it join the River Gallos south of the border with Spidlar?"

"At the Junction Rapids, but the canyons there are impassable to large forces, and the lands between the two rivers are rugged with few good roads. For the Prefect to dislodge Certan forces once they have taken Passera would be far more costly to Gallos than to Certis." Beltur's voice turned ironic. "Of course, actually taking Passera could also be costly."

"But fighting off Certis would be even more costly, wouldn't it?"

"In all likelihood," said Beltur. "Right now, nothing has been decided. After Faelsham leaves, then we'll be talking with Korsaen about what we should do."

"None of the possibilities sound good," said Taelya quietly.

"None of them are. The only question is which one costs us less."

"Thank you for being honest," said Taelya. But then, her aunt and uncle had always been honest, even when it hurt.

She kept riding through the darkness, her thoughts going back to what both Klosyl and Sydon had said about her being unusual . . . and possibly the only white woman mage, at least since the time of Cyador. Saryn had been a mage, but a black . . .

X

When she woke early on twoday morning, Taelya was still thinking about her conversation with Beltur. She hadn't shared it with her mother the night before because she wanted to think it over. But, because she didn't want to keep it from Tulya, and because Dorylt had left even earlier to spend more time working on some furniture with Jaegyr, she related what Beltur had said as she ate breakfast. When she finished, she asked, "What do you think?"

"I don't like any of it," replied Tulya tartly. "If we ally ourselves with Gallos, or don't work out something with the Viscount, we'll end up fighting Certis, and a war with Certis would be far worse than what happened with Hydlen."

Taelya didn't ask about whether Lydiar would support Montgren because she already knew that, in all likelihood, even Fairhaven alone could likely defeat what was left of the Lydian forces, especially given that several of the best officers and squad leaders had left Lydiar—or been driven out by the Duke's incompetence—and joined the forces of Montgren or Fairhaven. As a result, Lydiar was essentially protected by the existence of Montgren and by the success of Fairhaven.

"Then what should we do?"

"The Council is meeting this morning to discuss the matter—before Lord Korsaen and Maeyora return to Vergren."

"What about the envoy and his party?"

"They're headed to Hydolar. That way they can return to Gallos without going through Certis."

"That's rather convenient." Taelya finished the last mouthfuls of the egg scramble and then her ale. "For playing Duke Maastyn, that is."

"We all thought so."

"When will Lord Korsaen go to Jellico, then?" asked Taelya.

"You're assuming that we'll propose an alliance with Certis. That hasn't been decided."

"I won't say anything. Anything at all. But nothing else makes sense."

"Except for one thing. If we ally ourselves with the Viscount, then what happens to us when the Prefect allies himself with Hydlen and sends some troops to help Maastyn to take over Fairhaven?"

"Maastyn would jump at that chance." Taelya paused. "But he still doesn't have all that many mages."

"If our mages, or most of them, are fighting with the Certans in Passera, he won't need many, and what the Viscount will want most are mages. He has troopers." Tulya offered a wry smile. "The situation's . . . delicate."

Taelya nodded. "I won't say a word."

"Don't even offer guesses this time."

Taelya couldn't help wincing. "You're not going to let me forget that, are you?"

Tulya laughed. "Not for a while. Not until it's clear that you learned from it."

Which is another way of reminding you. Except Taelya really couldn't blame her mother . . . or Beltur. Especially now, when matters were getting even more complicated. She stood, then picked up her platter and beaker and washed and racked them. "I'm going to try to get to headquarters early this morning."

"So you can see what Sheralt and Valchar thought about last night?"

Taelya smiled. "Of course." Then she hurried off and finished getting ready, after which she walked to the stable, where she checked Bounder and saddled him.

Kaeryla and Jessyla were leaving their house as Taelya rode away from the stable. She waved, but didn't stop.

When she reined up outside the stables at headquarters, she was surprised to find Sheralt outside, as if he'd been waiting for her. Valchar stood several paces back, clearly watching the older mage.

"I'm glad you're early," he said as she dismounted and then tied Bounder to the hitching rail. "I have a favor to ask."

"What sort of favor?" she asked cautiously.

"Put a containment around me," said Sheralt. Before Taelya could say anything, he went on. "I still can't figure out how you do it from watching you. Maybe, if I'm inside it, it will feel different."

"You never wanted me to do that before," said Taelya. "Why now?"

"Maybe if I can learn to do containments, I can use that to strengthen my shields."

From where he stood, Valchar shook his head. "I've got stronger shields than you do, and I can't do containments, either."

"Our shields aren't as strong as Taelya's or the majer's or the head healer's, and they can all do containments." Sheralt looked to Taelya. "Will you do it?"

Taelya had never thought that doing containments was particularly special for a mage. Her father had been able to do them, and so had Beltur and Jessyla, and Beltur had taught her containments from the time she'd shown the first traces of magely abilities. She'd thought that her early training might have been the difference, but that didn't seem to follow because Jessyla had learned late, and Taelya had found out later that Beltur himself hadn't learned containments until after he was fully grown.

After a moment, she said, "I will, but I won't make it tight."

"I'd appreciate that."

Taelya placed a containment around Sheralt, just holding it.

After several moments, he said, "It feels just like your shields."

"Look at me with your senses," said Taelya. "You should be able to sense bands of order and chaos."

"I've always sensed that. Your uncle said I'd do better if I'd separate order and chaos."

"Did you try?"

"It made me feel . . . strange. So I stopped doing it."

"You're an idiot, Sheralt," said Taelya tiredly as she released the containment.

"My shields work fine."

Taelya clamped a new and tighter containment around his shields and immediately began to contract it.

"What are you doing?"

"I'm showing you why you're an idiot. Just try to stop me." Taelya squeezed in on his shields slowly, feeling them slowly crumple.

"Stop!"

Taelya stopped, but only after Sheralt's shields collapsed.

Valchar's mouth dropped open.

"Do you see why you're an idiot?" demanded Taelya. "You're a head and a half taller than me. If I let you, you could pick me up and probably hold me overhead . . . and you can't even hold shields against me."

"What does that have to do—"

"It's part of the technique. Do you want to die because doing it right makes you feel uncomfortable?"

"What do you mean . . . die?"

"Why do you think we were at dinner last night? Why were Lord Korsaen and Lady Maeyora here with a Gallosian envoy and two Gallosian whites? Why are there now more Hydlenese troopers riding close to the border? Do you think any of that's good?"

Sheralt just looked at Taelya.

"Well?" she pressed.

"You could have killed me, couldn't you?" Sheralt said slowly.

"Why would I want to do that?"

"But you could have."

"A strong white's chaos bolts could do the same thing," Taelya pointed out.

Sheralt shivered just slightly, as if he couldn't believe what had just happened.

"Sheralt," Taelya said, kindly, "I was trying to get your attention. Chaos and order together are stronger than either by itself. Whites and blacks have to combine them differently for that strength, but it's just like our bodies. We'll die if we don't have both."

"So what should I do?" Sheralt's voice was subdued.

"Start by doing what I do. First, you have to study yourself. There's natural order and natural chaos. That's what's in our bodies. You just keep sensing, until you can sense the differences. Then, because you're a white, you use your natural order as barrier between you and the free chaos. In turn, you keep the free order outside the free chaos. Once you can do that, I'll show you how to build shields that are stronger."

"Your uncle said he would help with that . . ."

"Except you didn't keep your free order and chaos separate, did you?"

Sheralt looked down. Finally, he said, "Not really."

"It's up to you. I'll help you, but only if you work at it."

"Ah . . ." Valchar cleared his throat. "Does it work for blacks?"

"It's a little different. You keep your natural order around your natural chaos. Then you have free order outside of that, and free chaos beyond that. That's the way the majer and the head healer do it." *And Kaeryla, Dorylt, and Arthaal.*

"You could do magery really young, couldn't you?" asked Valchar.

Taelya didn't want to get into that, but she didn't want to be deceptive, either. "I almost died because there was too much order in the wrong places in my body. The majer fixed that, but it's likely that's why I could do things earlier than most. It's also why I'm much shorter than my parents." Taelya could remember, hazily, when she had been so tired she could hardly move.

"Too much order?" asked Sheralt.

"Too much order or too much natural chaos can kill you. So can too little. It's all about balance." Hoping to get back to shielding, she added, "The same is true of shields. The right balance between order and chaos makes shields stronger, and that balance is a little different for every mage." At least it was for all the mages she'd observed, not that she'd seen many more than a double handful, if that. She glanced to the south end of the yard, where the recruits were lining up. "We'd better get to muster."

Valchar glanced toward the new squad. "I'm glad I didn't have to go through that."

Recalling the years of training under her uncle, Taelya just nodded.

As the three walked across the paved stable yard, Sheralt eased closer to Taelya. "You will help me?"

"If you work on keeping your order and chaos levels separate. All the time. Not just when I'm around. I can tell the difference. So could the majer. Once you've got that under control, then we'll work on shields."

"What about containments?"

Taelya looked at Sheralt. "If you can't get stronger shields, you won't last long enough to worry about containments."

The older mage actually swallowed.

The three made it to the briefing room before Gustaan or Therran appeared, but Varais, Dhulaar, Nardaak, Lendar, and Khaspar were all there. Within moments, both Beltur and Gustaan appeared.

"The majer has a few words," said Gustaan.

"As I'm sure all of you know, yesterday Lord Korsaen, Lady Maeyora, and the Gallosian envoy and his party visited Fairhaven to meet with the Council. Gallos and Certis are likely on the brink of another war. We may be dragged into it whether we like it or not. This is something the Council has been concerned about for some time. I know some of you wondered why we began training another squad of Road Guards at the end of winter. We did so because it became apparent that we would need more guards whatever occurred. There will likely be other changes. One of those I am happy to announce this morning." Beltur gestured to Varais. "Senior Guard Varais has been promoted to squad leader. Some of the other changes will depend on what the Duchess decides. We will let you know once those decisions are made, and the Council has decided on what actions we need to take." Beltur looked around. "Are there any questions?"

"How soon will we likely know?" asked Valchar.

"It will likely be at least an eightday. It could be even longer. We don't control how long it will take the various rulers to decide on their course of action. Or how long before we get word."

"Will you keep training the recruits even if we escape being in a war?" asked Gustaan.

"Yes. The Council has decided that we need more control over our future. We couldn't have done it much sooner, because we didn't have the golds until recently."

"Will the Lydians offer help?" asked Khaspar.

"The Lydians are in no condition to help anyone."

The briefing room grew silent.

Finally, Beltur said, "Then, since there are no more questions, I'll turn you over to Captain Gustaan."

Once Beltur had left, Gustaan made the patrol assignments, and Taelya got the western patrol with Khaspar.

Before she left the duty room, she made her way to Varais. "Congratulations . . . but I will miss patrolling with you."

"You haven't needed me for years, ser." Varais grinned briefly.

"That doesn't mean I won't miss patrolling with you."

"Thank you, ser."

After leaving the duty room, as she and the other two undercaptains headed for their mounts, Sheralt asked, "How much of that did you know?"

"Only that matters were getting serious. I did know that the Council felt we didn't have enough Road Guards, but not why. I didn't know about Varais's promotion, but it didn't surprise me."

"You like her," said Sheralt.

"That doesn't have anything to do with it. She's better than anyone with blades, including Captain Gustaan, and she's got more fighting experience than all but a few of the Road Guards."

"I've never seen you spar with her."

"First, she's too good for me. Second, the majer told me that there wasn't any point to it, because I'd likely never fight against another woman. That's why Kaeryla and I never spar, either."

"That makes sense. But . . . some of the rest . . . you must have guessed . . ."

"I was thoroughly reprimanded for sharing my guesses." Taelya's words came out more tartly than she meant, and she immediately added, "I'm sorry. I didn't mean to be quite so sharp."

"The majer's harder on you, isn't he?"

"He's harder on himself than on anyone." While that didn't answer the question, it was also true.

Sheralt grinned. "That's an answer of sorts. I'll see what I can do about arranging my order and chaos on patrol. We're not likely to see that many traders coming from the east. You might get some, though."

"We'll have to see." She made her way to Bounder, untied the gelding and mounted, then guided him to where Khaspar and Harrad waited.

"Good morning, ser," offered the red-haired Harrad.

"Good morning. Let's head out and see if the situation has scared off any traders."

"If they have any sense, they'll come here," replied Khaspar.

"All those with sense likely already have," replied Taelya.

Khaspar smiled. "We'll see, ser. Some are always late to their senses."

"You're right about that." *And some never do come to their senses.*

Once the three were on the main street, Taelya added the larger, squad-sized shield around the group. She *thought* that it was getting easier and not tiring her so much, but that also might have been in her mind.

During the entire patrol, they encountered exactly one trader, a sorry sort with a narrow wagon pulled by a single horse. The trader claimed he was headed for Lydiar. While the man wasn't lying, he wasn't totally certain, Taelya sensed. What was certain was that he was definitely heading east.

As she neared the end of her patrol, and the three rode in past the West Inn, Taelya dropped the larger shield with relief, before realizing that she needed to go to the Healing House for her "instruction." At least she was riding Bounder, so that she could get home without walking. She'd spend more time grooming him than walking would have taken, but she also would have had to groom a Road Guard mount.

After reaching headquarters and signing off duty, Taelya walked back to where she'd tied Bounder, thinking that she hadn't practiced as much as she should have with blades.

Beltur appeared almost from nowhere. "Where are you headed?"

"To the Healing House."

"You can take a quint to practice with the chaos-bolt device."

Taelya managed not to sigh. "Yes, ser."

"It's even more important now," Beltur pointed out as they walked toward the small courtyard.

Exactly a quint later, Taelya mounted Bounder and rode toward the Healing House, because she'd also promised to learn about healing as well, and she hadn't yet shown up there. She took a deep breath. She'd likely have to alternate practice at both blade and chaos bolts . . . and healing in the glasses after duty and before dinner.

When Taelya reined up in front of the Healing House, she couldn't help thinking about Frydika, and the fact that she should have thought more about the older woman sooner. So, after tying Bounder outside, as soon as she entered the building, she looked to Jessyla, who was writing an entry in the daily journal.

"Aunt Jessyla . . . do you know how Frydika is doing? I should have asked—"

"She's at home. She's walking with a limp. She likely always will. Her words are a little slurred, but she's better. She'll likely never be as strong as she once was."

Taelya hadn't realized she was holding her breath until she released it.

"You couldn't have done more than you did." Jessyla closed the journal and rose from the table desk. "I just splinted a young man's arm. I'd like you to take a look at it . . . with your senses."

Taelya followed her aunt back to the second room, where a boy who looked to be perhaps ten sat in a chair. His splinted right arm rested on a large pillow on his lap positioned so that the arm was supported without any strain. Just from the streaks running down his cheeks, Taelya could tell that the process of bone-setting and splinting had been painful. His eyes widened as he took in Taelya and her uniform.

"Undercaptain Taelya is just here to look at you," said Jessyla. "She's also a mage with some healing skills. She's helped us occasionally."

Taelya let her senses range over the boy's arm, then looked to Jessyla, inquiringly.

"I know you're better with tiny bits of order and chaos. Do you sense any?"

"There are two small points on each side of the wound healing chaos where the bone is injured. That's where it broke, isn't it?"

Jessyla nodded. "Are the points orangish/white/red?"

Taelya concentrated again. "More orange than white or red. That's the way it seems."

"Can you put the tiniest bit of free order into one of those points?"

"I think so."

"Do it, then."

The boy tightened up.

"This might feel a little warm," said Jessyla.

Taelya eased the smallest bit of order into the one of the chaos points. Half of the chaos vanished. "It's half gone in one of the chaos points." She looked to the boy. "Did that hurt?"

"I didn't feel anything. It hurts a lot anyway."

Taelya added three more tiny points of order, and the ugly orangish chaos subsided into the dull red of a healing wound. "Now it's just all the dull red that's normal healing."

"That should help." Jessyla turned to the boy. "What she did will help your arm heal faster. I'll be back in a moment after I talk more with the under-captain."

Once the two left the room and walked back to the front of the Healing House, Jessyla said quietly, "Thank you."

"The chaos was very small."

"Even if he most likely would have healed anyway, it's better when it's more than likely." The healer paused, then said, "I splinted his arm for now. Why do you think I didn't put a cast on it?"

Taelya had to think for a moment. "There was too much swelling?"

Jessyla nodded. "That might happen in battlefield healing, especially if it's been a while since the injury or if there's been other damage to an arm or leg. The boy's father didn't realize his arm was broken until this afternoon. The boy's mother died several years ago."

"The father was telling the truth?"

"He was. He's a journeyman mason." Jessyla turned to the floor-to-ceiling cabinet at the side of the room. "I'm going to go over the herbs you ought to carry if you're in a battle situation. It wouldn't hurt to carry them all the time now, either. They're light enough that it won't put any real extra weight on your mount . . ."

As her aunt began to explain, Taelya concealed the wry smile she felt. Jessyla hadn't pointed out the obvious—that Taelya was far lighter than any other Road Guard officer and that the herbs wouldn't be any real burden on Bounder or any Road Guard mount.

When Jessyla finished perhaps half a quint later, she said, "I've kept you long enough, and I need to get home and help Kaeryla with dinner, since you three are joining us this evening. Just stop by after your duty when you can. You don't have to be here every afternoon, but the more often you can, the better it will be. I'll have a small duffel of herbs ready for you the next time you come."

Taelya understood that message as well. "Thank you. I'll be here except when duty drags out." *Which includes blade and chaos practice.*

"Good."

Taelya nodded, then made her way out to where Bounder waited. The gelding gave a low "chuff-whuff," signifying that he was tired of being tied up, and would like to get back to the stable. "And you probably want a carrot or something as well."

Bounder nuzzled her.

"I understand."

She untied him and mounted, then turned him toward the main street.

After Taelya reached the stable, she had just finished unsaddling Bounder when Jessyla arrived. Taelya immediately said, "After you unsaddle her, I'll groom, water, and feed her."

"You've had a long day, too," protested Jessyla. "I can tell. Both your order and chaos levels are lower."

"I've been doing more with them, but grooming your mare won't strain me that way. Besides, you're cooking dinner, and this way, everyone will get fed sooner."

"Perhaps," replied Jessyla, "but both Beltur and Arthaal are at the smithy."

"Dorylt's still at Jaegyr's." Taelya gestured. "I'll groom her."

"Thank you."

After Taelya finished grooming, watering, and feeding Bounder and the mare, she hurried across the street to her own house. Neither her mother nor Dorylt had arrived home, late as Taelya herself was, so she could take a little time washing up and thinking about the day.

Sheralt had been stunned when she'd crumpled his shields, and that had surprised Taelya. Why hadn't Beltur done something like that to Sheralt? He'd certainly done similar things to make a point to Taelya, Dorylt, Kaeryla, and Arthaal. Was the difference because the four of them were family?

That raised another question. Why hadn't Beltur tried to instruct her father? Or had he, and had her father been either unwilling or unable to do what Beltur suggested? Or had Beltur deferred to the older mage?

She had barely stepped out of the washroom when Tulya and Dorylt hurried into the house.

"I thought you'd already be at Jessyla's helping with dinner," said Tulya, her voice slightly on edge.

Sensing that her mother was upset, Taelya explained, "I had to go to the Healing House after duty because Beltur and Jessyla strongly suggested I needed some basic training as a healer. Then I took care of Jessyla's mare so that she wouldn't have to."

"At least you did something." Tulya hurried into the washroom.

Taelya quickly brushed off her uniform, then turned to Dorylt. "Tell Mother I've gone to help Jessyla and Kaeryla."

Dorylt grinned. "Coward."

"Cautious. She's upset about something. I don't want her any more upset." With that, Taelya left the house for Jessyla's. Once there, she knocked quickly on the kitchen door, and let herself in, saying immediately, "What can I do?"

Kaeryla quickly said, "Set the table. Arthaal's supposed to do that, but he's late again. Jorhan needed both him and father at the smithy."

Taelya headed for the cupboard. "Just the seven of us?"

"That's more than enough," replied Kaeryla.

By the time Taelya had everything laid out, her mother and Dorylt had arrived, and Taelya, seeing that there was little else she could do, slipped back into the front room, where she was soon joined by Dorylt and Kaeryla.

"Mother said you were at the Healing House today," offered Kaeryla, her voice casual, but with a hint of tension.

"Just for a glass or so, after I finished my patrol. She wanted to show me how she'd set a broken arm and what the swelling could do. Then she went over the herbs I should carry for battlefield healing. She said she'd make up a pack of them for me. She thinks I ought to carry them anyway when I'm on patrol."

"She said you can sense tiny bits of order and chaos."

"You can do that, too."

"I can sense them, but not as well as Father, and it's hard for me to do anything with them." A touch of bitterness clouded Kaeryla's words.

"You two are lucky," said Dorylt. "I can't sense the smaller bits. They're just dark or white blobs."

"You can't?" asked Kaeryla.

"Can Arthaal?" questioned Dorylt.

"He can sense them," replied Kaeryla, "but he can't do anything with them."

"He's only thirteen," pointed out Taelya.

"I'm getting close to fourteen," declared Arthaal as he came through the front door. "Why are you all talking about how old I am?"

"We were talking about when we could sense small bits of order and chaos," explained Dorylt.

"That doesn't mean anything," stated Beltur as he closed the front door. "Every mage develops and learns differently. I couldn't discern the small bits until I was nearly twenty."

"But you didn't have the training you've given us," said Kaeryla.

"That's true enough, but training can only do so much until you grow into your body. That's just the way it is, and sometimes, some people just have to wait until their body's ready. You have no idea how frustrating it was for me for the longest time."

Kaeryla began in a bored tone, "You've told us that—"

Beltur looked hard at his daughter.

Kaeryla shut her mouth abruptly, then said, "I'm sorry, ser."

Taelya was just glad he hadn't looked at her in that way, although she could remember a few times that he had.

At that moment, Jessyla appeared in the archway between the kitchen and the front room.

"Good. You're both here. As soon as you wash up, we'll have dinner. Kaeryla and Taelya . . . if you'd come and give us a hand . . ."

Less than half a quint later, everyone was seated at the long table and serving themselves from the platter of sliced roasted fowl, as well as the boiled new potatoes, both of which were improved, Taelya thought, by the lightly peppered brown gravy . . . and, of course, by the good ale that was always a feature in both houses.

"Can you tell us if anything more happened with the Council?" asked Kaeryla.

"The Council doesn't know anything more than we did yesterday," said Beltur. "We have decided on a few other matters. You know we're training another squad of Road Guards. We decided that we will need more mages doing Road-Guard duty before too long. So . . . Dorylt, Arthaal . . . the two of you will start accompanying the Road Guards on their patrols, beginning shortly. Just one or two days out of each eightday, to begin with. Which mage you accompany will alternate."

Taelya could sense that none of the three adults was happy with what Beltur said, including Beltur himself.

After a moment of silence, Beltur went on. "You both have basic shields. We'd all be happier if you had stronger shields, but for now, it doesn't appear that we'll be getting any more mages from any other land."

"Is this because of the problems with Certis and Gallos?" asked Arthaal.

"It's because, before too long, some of the older mages may have to join the Duchess's forces."

"The way . . . it happened in the fight against Hydlen?" asked Dorylt.

"Not in quite the same way," replied Jessyla. "Right now, we don't know how this is going to turn out. We're just trying to prepare you for what you might have to do so that you won't have to learn everything all at once. You two are going to have to work more on your shields. Once you've improved them, we'll work on your containments. Neither of you can hold more than a small containment for more than a few moments."

"But . . . Valchar and Sheralt can't do containments at all," said Arthaal.

Taelya said nothing about what she'd promised to the two other junior mage officers, just hoping that they'd both do what she suggested.

"No, they can't, but Sheralt can throw chaos bolts, and Valchar's shields are stronger than yours." Beltur paused, then added, "They also might decide to work harder on their shields when they realize that, before all that long, they just might have to face other mages in skirmishes or battles."

"It's that bad?" questioned Arthaal.

"It's very likely we'll be attacked by someone," said Jessyla. "If Montgren allies with Gallos, Certis will attack. If we ally with Certis, Hydlen will attack because Certis will be occupied with Gallos."

"And if we don't ally with either, then both Certis and Hydlen will likely attack," added Beltur dryly.

"Why can they just leave us alone?" asked Dorylt. "We're not bothering anyone."

"They think we are," said Tulya. "More and more traders are coming through Fairhaven or building warehouses here to avoid the higher tariffs in Hydlen, Certis, and Gallos. We have the distillery and Jorhan's smithy, and both are doing quite well. The new woolen mill in Weevett can produce cloth cheaper than anything in Certis and Hydlen."

"So it's all about golds?" Arthaal snorted.

"Most things are about gold and power," replied Tulya, "one way or another."

Especially power, thought Taelya, thinking about Sheralt's reaction to her crumpling his shields.

"There's nothing more to be said about it," declared Beltur. "But you all wanted to know. Now . . . can we enjoy the fowl?"

After Beltur's words, Taelya knew the rest of what was said would be pleasant, but not terribly interesting. She cut a morsel off the fowl slice she'd taken and ate it, deciding that it was moist, but that the brown gravy helped even more.

XI

On threeday morning, when she stepped into the headquarters briefing room, Taelya wasn't in the least surprised to sense that Sheralt had managed a rough order between his levels of natural chaos and natural order, and even a slight separation between natural order and free chaos, but the comparatively small amount of free order was hopelessly entangled amid the free chaos.

"That's better," she said. "But you've got free order and chaos all mixed together on the outside."

"But separating the free chaos and free order makes me feel more like a black," replied Sheralt.

"I'm sure that will be a great comfort to any friends you have after the whites of Certis, Hydlen, or Gallos have turned you into ashes."

Valchar, standing beside Sheralt, tried not to smirk.

"The same's true for you, Valchar," said Taelya quietly. "Sheralt at least has some chance of fending off other whites with his own chaos. You're a black. Your shields need to be stronger, and they could be if you worked some chaos into their pattern."

"Pattern?" Valchar looked surprised.

"You don't build a strong stone wall by just piling up stones. You organize the stones, shape them, and then strengthen the wall with mortar. If you're a black, the mortar is chaos. If you're a white, the mortar is order."

"How do you shape order or chaos?" asked Sheralt.

"By the amount you put in each place." Taelya saw that Gustaan was entering the briefing room and said, "I'll show you tomorrow morning, before muster . . . if you're still interested. And if you've made more progress in organizing your order and chaos." With that, she turned her attention to the captain.

Gustaan had no new information to provide, except for the patrol assignments, one of which had Taelya and Thrakyl taking the southern patrol.

When Taelya mounted, this time riding a Guard horse, she joined Thrakyl and Breslan, and the three headed east on the main street. Taelya again raised a larger additional shield, trying to make it a habit.

"How soon do you think we'll know whether we'll be fighting, ser?" asked Thrakyl as they passed the older East Inn.

"That depends on what Lord Korsaen and the Gallosian envoy discover and decide. I'd guess that we won't hear anything for around an eightday, and more likely two, but that's just a guess. I doubt if it will be sooner because the envoy can't take the most direct route back to Fenard." Taelya suspected that Korsaen would use that time to talk to the Viscount or someone close to him, given that Jellico was an eightday nearer in travel time, and the Gallosian envoy would likely spend some time in Hydolar. But she wasn't about to mention that possibility, even to other undercaptains, let alone to a Road Guard.

"Then things might be quiet for a while?"

Taelya shook her head. "Even before the envoy arrived were things quiet?"

Breslan grinned.

"A fellow can hope, ser," replied Thrakyl.

"We all hope," said Taelya cheerfully.

Between the stone posts that marked the old town limits and the beginning of the road that skirted Fairhaven to the south, the three passed several carts heading for the square, since threeday was the other market day in Fairhaven besides sevenday, but the road east to Lydiar was empty when they turned south.

The three continued all the way past the crumbling redstone bluffs and south to where the southern road paralleled the one to Hydolar and from there onto the main road as far as the junction with the way north to Weevett, before retracing their route. They took a break under the trees north of Fairhaven, where Taelya took time to sense in detail for travelers and traders, but found none. After a break of a quint, they headed back south.

When they reached the end of the rocky grasslands west of the redstone cliffs, Taelya began to sense something ahead, but they covered another kay or so before her senses could vaguely discern five riders. "I'm sensing riders on the Hydolar road."

"Which way are they headed, ser?"

"Right now, they don't seem to be moving either north or south."

The three kept heading west for the next two quints, and Taelya could sense that the riders had moved north until they were close to the border. After the Road Guards turned north toward the road west to Certis and the Weevett road, they passed the last of the low hills blocking their view of the Hydolar road, and Taelya could not only sense but see the riders.

"There's five greenies, ser," announced Breslan. "They've reined up just short of the stone border posts."

Taelya studied the riders. There were definitely five green-uniformed troopers, although they were far enough away that Taelya couldn't make out much more than their uniforms and mounts. After several moments, all five turned their horses and began to ride south.

Five Hydlenese troopers. *Why five?*

"They didn't want to stay around us, it looks like," offered Thrakyl.

"They were scouting something," said Taelya. "Maybe they were watching the Certis road." *But why?*

The rest of the patrol was as uneventful as the first part had been, but Taelya was still wondering about the troopers when she entered headquarters to sign out of her duty. She noted the five Hydlenese troopers in the log, then signed it and straightened up, only to see Beltur standing in the doorway of the duty room.

"You made a longer entry in the log. Did you see anything unusual today?"

"We didn't see any traders coming from the east or from Hydlen. We did see five Hydlenese troopers around second glass on the Hydolar road, but on their side. As soon as they saw us, they withdrew farther back into Hydlen. We've often seen two, sometimes four, but I can't remember ever seeing five. That seemed strange."

Beltur frowned. "It sounds that way. I can't say that I can recall a group of five, either. If they have more than four, it's usually half a squad or a full squad. Could you tell if any of the five happened to be officers?"

Taelya shook her head. "They were too far away to see insignia. None of them were mages, though. I could sense that they were just troopers."

"That's not surprising. From what we've heard, Maastyn only has three or four mages. I'd be surprised if he'd send any that far from Hydolar. Not now, anyway." He paused. "I'll let Gustaan and Therran know, and we'll ask the other mages to watch even more carefully on the southern patrol. I'll meet you in the small courtyard after you groom your mount."

After leaving the headquarters building, Taelya returned to the stable and groomed her mount, then stepped back out into the stable yard.

"Undercaptain!"

At the commanding sound of a woman's voice, one that could only have been that of Senior Guard Varais—Squad Leader, Taelya mentally corrected herself—she immediately turned.

"Yes, Squad Leader?"

Varais walked swiftly toward Taelya, then stopped. "I have a favor to ask of you. Would you mind sparring with one of the recruits?"

Taelya frowned. "I'm not nearly as good as you are."

"You're better than you think, and you're small, and you're a woman, and you're not from Westwind."

Taelya could only think of one reason. She smiled. *And I'll cheat if I have to, but let's hope it's not necessary.* Because it would be so much better if she could pull it off just by skill. "Of course."

"You can use my jacket. It might be a little big." Varais eased off the padded jacket and handed it to Taelya.

In turn, Taelya eased it on over her uniform, then rolled up the sleeves several turns. The jacket was a little loose, but not enough to hamper her movements.

Varais handed over a wooden wand. "It might be heavier than you use."

Taelya took it, then shook her head. "The majer insisted on my using heavier wands. This will be fine."

"Kavnah. He's the one holding the wand at the edge of the circle."

The recruit was more than a head taller than Taelya, with a broad face and reddish-brown hair. He appeared puzzled as the squad leader and undercaptain approached.

"Kavnah, the undercaptain was born in Elparta and has lived here most of her life. Since you seem to think that Westwind has imparted some mystical strength and skill to me, you'll spar with the undercaptain."

"Yes, ser." The recruit's voice wasn't quite sullen, but Taelya got a certain feeling of arrogance, although that was more a feeling on her part than anything she gained from her order/chaos senses.

Kavnah held his wand in a fashion that suggested he was somewhat familiar with it, but whether that was because of four eightdays of training or for some other reason she had no idea. Most likely, Varais could have told instantly, but Taelya couldn't.

Not yet. Taelya narrowed her shields to just above her skin, stepped into the circle, then asked, "Are you ready, Kavnah?"

"Yes, ser." Kavnah took a position opposite Taelya, holding his wand in a defensive position, but one too high for dealing with a shorter opponent.

Taelya studied him and, realizing that he was waiting for her, feinted to her left.

Kavnah shifted his weight and moved to block her cut.

Taelya whipped her wand around, darted right and undercut his wand, striking the top of his hip, and then stepped back, avoiding his counter, then again darting inside his wand and bringing her wand down on his wrist with enough force to knock it out of his hand.

Then she stepped back.

"That was an accident," declared Kavnah. "Besides, that wouldn't have cut through wrist guards."

Wrist guards? Where did he come up with that? Hydlen? Fairhaven patrollers and guards had never used wrist guards.

Rather than shake her head, Taelya simply raised her wand and eased forward back into the circle. "Then you should try again."

Kavnah immediately moved forward and attacked, with a full-strength thrust straight at Taelya.

She darted both forward and to his right, so that he'd have to backhand any counter, except Taelya never gave him the chance, slamming her wand into the underside of his upper arm, hard enough that he dropped his wand. Then, in that moment when he was trying to recover, she jammed the blunt tip into his gut, hard enough that the recruit doubled up. "If this were real, you'd be dying painfully of a gut wound. It might take you several days. It gets very painful, I'm told." She stepped back and handed the wand to Varais. "Do you need anything else from me?"

"Thank you, Undercaptain." There was a hint of a smile in the squad leader's eyes, but nowhere else.

Taelya eased off the padded jacket and returned it to Varais. She could see the glances of surprise in the eyes of several of the recruits. As she walked away, she could hear Varais addressing them.

"The undercaptain is good with blades, but not outstanding. That little demonstration should have told you that good technique will almost always win over poorer technique and greater strength. Also, Kavnah, don't even think about getting even. First, if you were even lucky enough to actually hit her, striking a superior officer could get you executed. Second, since she's a white mage, if she got angry enough, she could turn you to ashes."

"Then, Squad Leader, why does she carry a blade at all?" asked one of the recruits.

"Sometimes, mages need all their ability to deal with other mages. When that's the case, they can use their sabre to defend themselves against ordinary armsmen."

That wasn't quite true, Taelya knew, but close enough, and more useful than admitting that too much magery could leave a mage without any shields, a situation in which Taelya fervently hoped never to find herself.

She still wondered about why Kavnah had mentioned wrist guards. Had he been a deserter from Hydlen? Or was he a spy?

She took a deep breath as she saw Beltur walking toward her.

"You looked good sparring against Kavnah. Let's see how you do against the infernal or awful device, as Sheralt calls it, depending on his mood." Her uncle grinned.

Taelya walked with him to the small rear courtyard, where she waited for Beltur to set the device moving. She fired three chaos bolts before missing the first time.

When she finished a long quint firing chaos bolts through the various openings, she was again sweating, but at least she wasn't shaking.

"You're definitely getting better," observed Beltur.

"How is Sheralt doing?"

"He's improving . . . if slowly. You've been working with him, haven't you?" Beltur offered a hint of a smile.

"A little, just about how to order levels of order and chaos." Taelya did not return the smile.

"It shows. I'll see you later. There are some things I need to take care of." With that, Beltur hurried off.

He didn't want to talk much about Sheralt. Taelya wondered why.

XII

On fourday, Taelya was up earlier than she would have liked, and she was out of the house well before either Dorylt or her mother, all because she had promised to go over shields with Valchar and Sheralt. Even with the time it took to saddle and ready Bounder, she still reached headquarters two quints before the morning briefing and muster.

The other two mages were waiting for her just outside the stable.

"I told you she'd be here early," said Valchar.

"Not this early, you didn't," replied the older mage.

Even before Taelya dismounted, she ran her senses over Sheralt. "Your separations are better, but they're still sloppy." She could sense his probing her shields, but said nothing as she dismounted and tied Bounder to the hitching rail.

"How do you keep everything in place?" asked Sheralt.

"Practice—like everything else that has to be good."

"You said you'd show us how to hold stronger shields."

"I will." Taelya turned to face Sheralt directly. "I'm going to create a small shield, with very little order in it. Once I've created it, I want you to hit it squarely with a small chaos bolt."

Sheralt frowned. "What's the point of that?"

"You'll see. Just do it."

Sheralt flung a tiny chaos bolt at the small shield, which collapsed.

"Now, I'm going to create an interlocked shield of order and chaos." Taelya did just that. "Notice. It doesn't have any more links than the other shield, but there's more order and less chaos, but it's still mostly chaos. This time, throw another chaos bolt the same size as the last one."

Sheralt did so.

The chaos bolt struck the shield and flared into pieces, but the shield held.

"It's not just the amount of order or chaos, but the way you put them together."

"You created a shield separate from your own as if it were the easiest thing," said Sheralt. "How many mages can do that?"

"Everyone in my family. Most of the black mages in Elparta. I'm sure there are others."

"I don't know of any others," said Sheralt.

"I don't, either," added Valchar.

"Then we need to get you two added to those who can," said Taelya cheerfully. "It might even save your lives. Now . . . look at that shield, with your senses."

Valchar was the first to respond. "You've got order linking all that chaos. All that chaos wouldn't work for me."

"You're right. If you look at the majer's shields or the head healer's, you'll see it the other way around. They have much more order and less chaos."

"I'll have to see about that. I need to take care of some things before muster." Abruptly, Valchar turned and walked toward the headquarters building. He did not look back as he trudged away.

Taelya looked at Sheralt, waiting.

He finally said, "You're a white. Not even a gray. Any mage sensing you wouldn't have the slightest doubt. How can you use that much order and be a white?"

"Because there's more chaos, and I've made some of the free order part of my shields and containments. By linking the free order to free chaos, the order structures and strengthens the shields, but the chaos dominates." Taelya's lips curled in a slightly ironic smile because she realized that she was basically repeating what Beltur had told her more than once. *Far more than once.*

"But how do you do that? You make it sound simple, but I don't have any idea what you mean."

For a moment, that stopped Taelya. "How did you learn to create shields?"

"I just watched other mages."

That unfortunately made sense. Taelya nodded. "Then watch what I'm doing." Recalling how she'd begun to make her first shield, she moved five small blocks of chaos into a circle, then placed a sixth and smaller piece of free order in the middle, linking it to the other five. "See? You could do four or six, but that's the idea."

Sheralt looked at her. "You make that look so easy."

"I've had a lot of practice. That's what it takes. Try it. Just take two small pieces of free chaos and link them with a tiny bit of order. You can do that." She looked at Sheralt encouragingly.

After a moment, he did so.

"Do the same thing again, with two other pieces of chaos and another little bit of order. Then link the two remaining blocks together."

Sheralt concentrated.

Taelya watched, then smiled. "You did it. That's the beginning of a containment. You'll need to work on it, but you just proved that there's no reason why you can't work up to doing containments. And if you structure your shields with more tiny bits of order, they'll be stronger."

Sheralt blotted his forehead. "That's hard."

"I didn't say it was easy, but the more you do it, the easier it gets." She glanced toward the headquarters building, where she saw Varais standing, waiting. "I promised to show you how, and it's mostly up to you. If you have problems after working with larger blocks, let me know. I need to talk to Varais right now."

"You'd better do that, then." Sheralt frowned slightly. "You've given me a lot to think about."

"It's not that much to think about, but it will be a lot of work." *That's your choice.* She smiled pleasantly and strode across the paving stones toward Varais. *Did he think it was going to be easy?*

Varais half turned as she saw Taelya heading directly toward her. An expression of puzzlement momentarily crossed her face as she waited.

Taelya stopped a yard away and said, "There's something I wanted to ask you about Kavnah. He mentioned wrist guards. We've never used them . . ."

"Oh . . . that. He escaped from a pirate galley that foundered off the point of the Great North Bay. If you look closely, you can see the scars from the shackles on his right ankle."

"What did he do to end up on a galley? He's not that old."

"He said that his father had angered an important pirate, someone called Lepaget. Lepaget killed his father, took his sister, and put him on the galley."

Taelya could believe that part. "If he was shackled . . ."

"He claims that the slavemaster unlocked the chains after the crew took the boats and left him behind." Varais paused, then said, "The head healer believes he was telling the truth."

While Taelya had had her doubts, Jessyla was almost never wrong about whether something someone said to her was truthful, but that raised another question. "Why didn't he stay in Lydiar?"

"Would you? The Lydians tried to conscript him, and he figured that the one place that he could be safe was here."

"So long as Montgren is ruled by the Duchess or her heirs," Taelya said dryly. "How are your recruits coming? Was the demonstration useful . . . or did it cause more problems?"

Varais smiled. "It helped. It likely didn't hurt you, either. Several of them were murmuring about how small you were . . . and that you were obviously tough."

"Anyone the majer's trained is tough."

"Anyone the majer's trained from the time they were seven years old is tough."

Taelya frowned. "I don't think I ever mentioned that."

"I asked Undercaptain Kaeryla. She's tough, too, especially at her age. Even the Westwind arms-commander wouldn't complain about your toughness."

"They might fault our blade skills."

"They're adequate, and for a mage, that's something."

"Thank you," replied Taelya. From Varais, "adequate" was a compliment.

"You were trying to show the other undercaptains something?"

"How to strengthen their shields. It might prove useful." Taelya glanced toward the doorway. "I'd best be heading into the muster and briefing."

"I won't keep you, ser." Varais nodded.

"I said it before, but congratulations on your promotion. I will miss patrolling with you."

"We'll likely be working together again, ser. The guard's too small for us not to be."

"True enough." Taelya smiled and headed inside the building.

XIII

On fourday, Taelya patrolled the west road, along with Nardaak and Wustyff, another junior guard. Outside of locals and a courier from Vergren, they only encountered a Brystan spice merchant coming from Hydolar and headed to Lydiar, clearly wanting to catch a trading vessel back to Nordla before any fighting broke out. That afternoon, she had another practice session with the awful device, followed by a glass at the Healing House.

On fiveday morning, both Sheralt and Valchar were pleasant at the briefing, but hardly voluble, as if neither wished to say much. Taelya did notice a slight improvement in the separations of order and chaos around Sheralt, but no discernible change in Valchar's aura or shields.

You'll just have to see what they do. She tried to put that thought out of her mind as she headed out to the stable yard to meet up with Khaspar and Hassett.

After an uneventful morning, slightly after noon, the three reined up under an oak just short of the five-kay marker east of Fairhaven under a warm haze that washed out the green-blue sky. Distant clouds to the northeast suggested that Fairhaven might receive a late-afternoon or early-evening shower.

"There was a courier who rode in from Weevett or Montgren yesterday," ventured Nardaak.

"We saw him headed into town, but no one has said anything to me." She smiled pleasantly. "That means that it's very important, or that it's routine."

"Routine?" asked Wustyff.

"It could just be reminders about tariffs, or a change in the laws, or a message confirming that something the Council sent was received. My mother gets more than a few messages like that."

The younger guard offered a puzzled expression.

Nardaak laughed and said, "The undercaptain doesn't like to talk about it much, but her mother is the Council treasurer and the justicer for Fairhaven."

"That's exactly why I prefer not to say much, because people think I know more than I do, and even a guess on my part is taken as possibly true."

"Your guesses might be better than others' could be," Nardaak pointed out.

"I've been wrong enough to learn to keep guesses to myself." Taelya was about to suggest that they turn back toward Fairhaven when she had a feeling that someone might be approaching from the east. "There might be someone headed our way. We'll wait just a bit."

"That's one kind of guess I won't wager against," said Nardaak.

Taelya looked farther east where the road to Lydiar curved around a low hill on which a flock of sheep grazed. Before that long, she nodded. "We've got a pair of riders headed our way. They're likely couriers, but that's strange. Who would send couriers from Lydiar to Fairhaven? Any messages to the Duchess would take the north cutoff directly to Vergren." *And Duke Halacut doesn't much care for Fairhaven.* Not that Taelya was about to say that anyplace but at home.

"Can you sense any more, ser?" asked Nardaak.

"Just the two riders. They should clear the hill to the east in half a quint or so. We'll wait and let them come to us."

While the riders appeared in the distance in slightly less than a half quint, almost two quints passed before they approached the three Road Guards. At that point, Taelya removed the larger shield, and, in a way, she felt lighter.

The dusty maroon uniforms indicated that the riders were indeed Lydian couriers.

"Welcome to Fairhaven," Taelya said cheerfully.

The lead rider looked warily at the three and slowed his mount, but the second and more weathered-looking courier called out, "They're Fairhaven Road Guards." He eased his horse forward toward Taelya. "You're Undercaptain Taelya, as I recall. We have a dispatch for the majer and the Council."

"I am, and we'll escort you in. You'll pardon me if I don't recall your name."

The older courier laughed softly. "You couldn't know. I saw you several years ago when I carried a dispatch through Fairhaven on my way to Duke Maastyn. I wondered what such a small young officer was doing in charge of a road patrol. Your uncle told me you were almost as old as he was when they fought off the Hydlenese."

"You meant, what was a slip of a girl doing in an undercaptain's uniform?" Taelya smiled. "Even now, I'm not quite that old."

"But you're also a white mage."

Taelya understood the courier had said that to make sure that the younger man knew. "Most of the Road Guard officers are mages, except for Captain Gustaan and the senior undercaptain." She turned her mount and eased the mare alongside the older courier, then said, "We don't often get dispatches from Lydiar. Usually they go to Vergren." She managed not to sigh as she once more created the larger shield.

"We don't know what's in the dispatches, but I'd wager it has something to do with the pirate attack on the waterfront in Lydiar."

"Pirates? From Worrak? Did they attack beyond the port?"

"In this part of Candar, do they come from any other place but Worrak?" The courier's tone was dryly sardonic.

Taelya laughed at his tone of voice.

"They didn't go much farther than the piers, but they burned most of the warehouses. I suspect that the dispatch is so that your Council can tell your traders about that. With the summer rains coming on . . ." The courier shook his head.

"That's not good at all." *And that's an understatement.*

Taelya didn't say anything more for a time, but then asked, "Did you have to ride through any rain earlier?" The dust on their uniforms meant that they couldn't have been in the rain recently.

"The rain squalls were coming across the bay when we left the post. You'll likely get some tonight or early tomorrow."

"Then you should stay at headquarters until they pass . . . if you can."

"We'll at least have to wait to see if your Council has a response."

They rode another stretch before the courier asked, "If it's not asking too much, how did you end up as a mage Road Guard?"

"My father was a mage-captain in the war with Hydlen. My uncle was already training me then, and . . . after my father's death, I just . . . it seemed that was what I was meant for." Taelya managed a wry smile. "Black mages can do a lot of things other than magery. Whites are usually more suited to what I do."

"Are there others like you in Fairhaven?"

"Women, you mean? The majer's consort fought against Hydlen, and his daughter is a junior undercaptain, but they're blacks and also healers."

"Can blacks fight that way?"

"It hurts some, but the majer's a black, and he and his consort each wiped out companies of Hydlenese. If we don't fight, we'll lose the only home we have."

The courier nodded.

Neither said much on the remainder of the ride to Fairhaven.

Once they reached the outskirts of town, Taelya released the larger containment, then turned in the saddle and said to Hassett, "Ride ahead and go find the majer. Tell him that there are two Lydian couriers with an urgent dispatch for the Council. We'll meet him at the Council House."

"Yes, ser." With that, the junior guard cantered off toward the center of Fairhaven.

"The town's grown a lot in in the last few years," observed the older courier.

"Especially in the last three or four," replied Taelya.

When they reached the market square, Taelya led the group along the west side to the Council House, which stood just east of the Healing House. As they neared the hitching rail to one side, Beltur stepped outside. He inclined his head to Taelya. "Thank you for the notice, Undercaptain."

"You're welcome, ser."

"You can return to your patrol."

The courier looked to Taelya. "We thank you as well, Undercaptain."

"I hope your stay here is pleasant, even if it's short."

The rest of the patrol was without incident and without encountering any traders, either coming or departing.

Once her duty was over and Taelya had signed out, she groomed her mount as usual, then watered her, and checked the manger. With a last pat to the mare, she left the stall, closing it, and then stepped out of the stable, turning to head toward the Healing House, except that Sheralt was standing outside the stable, clearly waiting for her.

"I heard that you escorted some Lydian couriers to see the Council."

"Whoever was patrolling the east road would have done the same." She could tell that he'd at least made some more of an effort at trying to keep his levels of order and chaos separate.

"I don't know that we've ever gotten couriers from Lydiar before."

"I don't recall any, either, not for us. There might have been one or two on the way somewhere else."

"Did they tell you anything? Anything you can share, that is?"

"The only thing the senior courier said was that pirates had attacked the waterfront in Lydiar and burned the warehouses."

Sheralt shook his head. "That means we definitely won't get any help from Duke Halacut."

"We wouldn't anyway. That just gives him a better excuse," Taelya pointed out. When Sheralt didn't immediately say more, she added, "You've been working on keeping your levels separate."

"You can tell?"

She nodded. "Can you can tell that mine are?"

"Well . . . sort of."

"Look. Now that you know what I meant . . ."

Sheralt frowned, clearly concentrating. "You're right." He paused. "It's not as easy as you made it sound."

"I'm sorry about that. I didn't mean to say it was easy. I just meant that you could do it."

"You and the majer are very much alike, you know?"

Taelya hadn't the faintest idea of what he meant.

Her face must have shown that because Sheralt shook his head and said, "You both make things look so easy when they're not."

Taelya laughed. "You have no idea how many nights I cried because I couldn't get things right. And I knew I had to, because when my father and Beltur and Jessyla went out to fight I was the only one who could protect my mother."

Sheralt was silent for a moment. "How old were you?"

"Seven."

He winced. "Things make a lot more sense, now. You've never said anything about that."

"There wasn't any reason to. That was just the way things were."

He nodded. "If you have just a moment, would you build one of those little shields again so that I can watch closely? I think I must have missed something."

"The part where I used the tiny bit of order to link the bigger pieces of chaos?"

"Yes. That part."

"I didn't mention it, but I think of order as having little hooks all over it because it wants to hold things together. Maybe that will help." Taelya concentrated on constructing the tiny shield very slowly and deliberately. When she finished, she held the shield so that Sheralt could examine it.

"Let me see if I can even do part of that."

Taelya sensed as he gathered two pieces of chaos and then tried to link them with a tiny piece of order, but the linkage only held for a moment.

"Frig!"

"Sheralt, you might try either smaller pieces of chaos or a little larger bit of order. Or you might think of the order piece with lots more hooks. You've got the right idea."

The second time the older mage tried to link the three pieces, they stuck.

"Good. Now you'll have to make another linked chaos piece and combine the two linked pieces. That might take a little more time."

"Let's hope I have that time."

Taelya frowned. "You're doing better."

"I didn't mention it, but a Hydlenese patrol started riding toward us. I threw a chaos bolt, and they turned back, but . . . I was thinking that it might not be so easy the next time . . . or if there were more of them."

"You've got the right basic technique. You may have to try different sizes of each until you find what works for you. Now that they know we have mages who are willing to use chaos, you should have some more time to work on your techniques."

"That might be . . . Are you practicing with the infernal device?"

"Not this afternoon. I have to go to the Healing House so I can learn a bit more about field healing."

"You're learning that? I thought whites couldn't do healing."

"Some whites can do a little healing. The strain of being a full-time healer would likely having me dying young. This is just for healing when no one else is around."

"Have you actually done any healing?"

"Just a few times. Whites shouldn't do a whole lot of healing." It wasn't that simple, but Taelya didn't want to spend more time explaining. "I'll see you tomorrow."

Then she turned and walked swiftly from the stable yard.

XIV

Somehow, sixday and sevenday both passed relatively uneventfully, except for the rain that drenched Fairhaven on fiveday night and lasted until noon on sixday. Both were long days, since she had to spar with Gustaan on sixday, and he'd used a blunted blade against her wand, something that Beltur had suggested to get her used to actual battle. Then, she'd had to work on chaos-bolt accuracy with the infernal device. On sevenday, she'd had to spend time at the Healing House, even after market was over.

On eightday, Taelya could have done without getting up early, but since it was her turn to take the endday patrol duty, she didn't have much choice. She almost forgot to fill her two water bottles with ale and water, but she still ended up leaving the house before Dorylt had even awakened.

When she reached the stable, she found Arthaal saddling one of the geldings . . . and wearing a Road Guard uniform, albeit without rank insignia or mage stripes on the sleeves. Even before she could speak a word, Arthaal said, "I'm supposed to ride with the patrol this eightday because Jorhan needs as much help as possible on the other days. Father said it would be better with you the first time. I can ride with any undercaptain except Kaeryla."

Even if they hadn't been siblings, given their ages, Taelya knew that was for the best, although Kaeryla, at least in uniform, looked considerably older than her age, but few would have said the same of the gangly Arthaal, physically strong as he was. "You can use some of the time to practice your shields, and we can see about starting you on containments."

"Father said you'd say something like that." Arthaal's words were not quite doleful.

"You'll need them when you ride patrols without other mages. Now, let me get Bounder saddled. We don't want to be late."

In less than half a quint, the two were riding through the misty early morning on the main street toward headquarters.

Since Arthaal remained disinclined to talk, Taelya used her senses to examine Arthaal's shields. As she expected and had noted in passing before, they were methodically constructed, like his sister's and Dorylt's and unlike those of either Valchar or Sheralt. "Have you ever really tried to do containments?"

"Father's worked with me on them."

"Project a containment in front of your mount. Show me the best that you can do."

The containment was little more than a cubit on a side, from what Taelya could sense before it vanished.

"That's a start." *And not much more than that.* "Now . . . do it again."

"Now?"

"Now," affirmed Taelya.

Once more, Arthaal concentrated, and the containment appeared, if only to Taelya's and Arthaal's senses.

"Now . . . hold it as long as you can . . . and then hold it longer."

The containment vanished sooner than the previous one had.

Taelya turned to Arthaal. "You can do better than that."

Arthaal looked down at the saddle pommel.

"I'd hate to have to tell your father that you're lazy."

"It hurt."

Taelya managed not to blurt out something she'd regret. Magery didn't hurt. It exhausted. It wore a mage out, but the only time it hurt was when another mage's shields or chaos struck. Instead of disputing Arthaal, which would lead nowhere, she just said, "Getting better takes concentration and work. It might just hurt. There's no getting around it." *Besides, you don't even know what hurt is. Every woman hurts more than that every time she has her cycle.* And that didn't even count the aches and bruises she'd gotten from sparring. "Take some deep breaths." Taelya waited a few moments. "Now do it again, and hold it longer." Taelya smiled pleasantly. "And don't tense up and clench your jaw. That just makes it even harder. Take a couple more deep breaths and shake your shoulders." She waited a bit, then said, "Now, do it."

Arthaal concentrated.

Taelya counted mentally.

The containment vanished.

"That was almost three times as long as the last one, and likely twice as long as the first one. You can rest for a little bit."

Arthaal took a long deep breath.

"It wasn't that bad," Taelya said mildly. "Just wait until someone slams your shields with an iron blade, rather than with a wooden wand." *Except iron won't hurt you as much because you're a black.*

"You've done that in sparring?"

"Only occasionally. Just to let me know what it feels like."

"You're a white. Doesn't iron hurt, even against your shields?"

"It does. Not so much for me as for Sheralt. He has trouble including order in his shields, and that reduces the hurt. Some whites are so filled with chaos that a deep cut with an iron blade will kill them. That's another advantage for a black with strong shields. You can actually use iron weapons to kill."

"Could you do that?"

"With what your father taught me, I could . . . but it would be really dangerous and painful. My cupridium sabre's just as effective against anyone, including another white." She paused. "You should know that."

"Father told me that, but I wasn't sure."

Taelya looked hard at Arthaal. "Your father *never* lies, especially not to anyone in the family. Don't you ever forget that."

Arthaal had to look away. "Sometimes, you're scary."

"Only when you do or say something stupid."

"You're more like an aunt than a cousin."

"That's because I'm a lot older."

"Not that much."

"Enough that I can crush your shields." Taelya said the words lightly. "Unless you do more work on strengthening them."

"Put more little bits of chaos in them?"

"That would help." She looked to the headquarters building just ahead. "When we get to headquarters, we'll ride to the stable and tie the horses outside. Then we'll go to the duty room and sign on. On any day but eightday, we'd be assigned a patrol by Captain Gustaan or Senior Undercaptain Therran. On eightday, we're the only patrol, and we combine all three patrol routes and do shorter versions. So we just report in to the squad leader on duty and then head out with the two Road Guards assigned eightday duty. We'll start by heading east, but just to the first kaystone."

Once they reached the stable and tied the horses, Taelya led the way to the duty room, where Squad Leader Kuchar sat behind the duty table desk.

"Good morning, Kuchar."

"Good morning, ser. I see you've got one of the trainee undercaptains."

"I do. I think you may have seen Arthaal around. Arthaal, this is Squad Leader Kuchar."

"I'm pleased to meet you, Squad Leader."

"It's good to meet you."

Taelya bent over and signed the duty book, then said, "Sign beneath my name, and add, 'Trainee Undercaptain.'"

"Yes, ser."

"Is anything happening we should know about?"

"The town patrollers haven't seen anything in town." Kuchar smiled. "You'll let us know if anything's happening on the roads."

"That we will. Who's on duty with us?"

"Lendar and Sheppyl. They've already reported in."

"Then we'll see you later."

Taelya led the way back to the stable where the two Road Guards were leading their mounts out into the courtyard. "Arthaal is one of the trainee undercaptains." She gestured to the stocky black-haired guard. "This is Lendar. He's a senior guard, and Sheppyl's a junior guard." Then she untied Bounder and mounted.

In moments, the four were headed out of the stable yard and onto the main street, heading eastward, Taelya and Lendar in front, and Sheppyl and Arthaal following. Taelya again raised an additional company-sized containment.

"Why did you do that?" asked Arthaal.

"What, the large containment? I did it to get in practice for when I have to. Even if I don't, it's making me a stronger and better mage."

Arthaal looked away.

After a time, Lendar asked, "Have you heard anything about Gallos or Certis, ser?"

"The only thing I've heard about anything in the last few days is what the majer told us about Lydiar."

"I wouldn't care that much about Duke Halacut's problems, except they make ours worse," replied Lendar. "There won't be as many traders coming our way, and we'll lose men whether we stand alone or have to fight battles for Certis or Gallos. Makes more sense to ally with Certis, but . . ." He shook his head.

"From what I've heard about the Prefect," replied Taelya, "it's hard to believe that the Viscount could be worse. But the Kaordists didn't have much good to say about him."

"Moshart didn't have much good to say about the Kaordists." Lendar laughed sardonically. "You were the one who brought them in. What do you think about them?"

"The same as Moshart, most likely. Some of the children and women are all right, but the men believe women ought to be their slaves."

"Worse than the Prefect, then?"

Taelya shrugged. "How can you tell? We'd be better off if we could avoid dealing with any of them. We don't have that choice." She just hoped that Korsaen would make the least bad choice. "I understand you and your consort are building a cottage."

"Rebuilding one of the last ones that was abandoned years ago. It's almost like building it from scratch, but it'll be ours. Your mother gave us a deed, conditional on our rebuilding it and living there for at least a year." Lendar smiled. "There's no annual tariff until a year after it's finished, and then it's only five coppers a year for the next two years."

By midmorning, the four had ridden out to the kaystone and then back to the southern road as far as the crumbling redstone bluffs south of Fairhaven. The bright white sun had burned off the mist, and the afternoon promised to be warm and muggy, something that Taelya wasn't looking forward to, since, unlike her mother, she preferred cold to heat.

She'd had Lendar move back to ride with Sheppyl and was working with Arthaal on containments when she sensed riders ahead to the southwest. "Can you sense anything ahead?"

"There's a mountain cat in brush on top of the bluff, maybe half a kay ahead on the left."

"I sensed the cat, but what about farther ahead and closer to the road?"

"No, ser . . . except . . . I don't know . . ."

"You're feeling something? Or do you feel you should feel something because I asked?"

"Both, I guess."

"Create another containment. Now."

Arthaal tried not to sigh. "Yes, ser."

Taelya watched as the containment appeared, sensing its strength and size . . . and duration. When Arthaal could no longer hold it, and it vanished, she said, "They're larger, and you're holding them quite a bit longer, aren't you?"

"Yes. But it's work."

"Arthaal . . . everything good is work. Now . . . tell me what you sense that's as large as the mountain cat . . . or larger."

The young mage frowned. "There's something . . . a haze of order and chaos."

"Order and chaos together, what does that tell you?"

"It's almost always living."

"How big is that haze?"

Abruptly, Arthaal nodded. "It has to be at least two horses, and usually that means riders."

"You're right, and the hazy feeling is what you'll sense when you're not close enough to discern clearly how many riders there are." Taelya turned in the saddle and said, "There are riders on the side road to the burned-out stead that the Hydlenese once used."

"How many?" returned Lendar.

"I'll let you know when Arthaal can tell us." Taelya already knew that there were three, and that likely meant troopers.

After the four had ridden another three hundred yards or so, Arthaal said, "It feels like three riders. They're not moving. I'd say they'd have to be troopers."

"They likely are. Once we reach the end of the bluffs, we might be able to see them. That's if they don't withdraw. They're actually on our side of the border, but not by much."

Just about a quint passed before Taelya could see the three riders, who immediately turned their mounts and withdrew.

"They're out on an eightday," said Lendar. "Could be they're checking to see if we patrol on eightdays."

"They should know that we do. It's more likely that they're trying to see when we cover the area south of Fairhaven."

"Are they still withdrawing?"

"So far."

"Do you sense any others?" asked Lendar.

Taelya looked to Arthaal. "Do you?"

"No, ser. I don't sense hazy order and chaos anywhere near the road. I mean, on the south side. There's some farther north on our side."

"That's likely the herder who lives in the cottage in the midst of the rocky grasslands."

There were no other signs of Hydlenese troopers anywhere along the rough arc of the southern road, even on the stretch paralleling the Hydolar road, and by midafternoon, the four were again headed out east toward the kaystone on the road to Lydiar.

Even before they quite reached the stone that marked five kays from the original boundaries of Fairhaven, Taelya could sense a hazy mass of order and chaos to the east, enough that it had to represent far more than a handful of riders or a few traders' wagons.

"There are a lot of people headed this way," she said quietly.

"Armsmen?" asked Lendar.

"I can't tell, but I don't think so. But if they are armsmen, Sheppyl, you'll ride back to inform the duty squad leader and the majer immediately." With the number of people Taelya felt she would be sensing more clearly before long, she had no doubt that they would be dispatching Sheppyl. The only question was what information he'd be relaying.

They covered the last hundred yards to the kaystone and then reined up in the shade of the trees just west of the stone marker. Taelya took out her water bottle and had several swallows. Only half a quint passed before she could more clearly discern what moved toward them from beyond the curve in the road to the east.

"They aren't armsmen, or at least not all armsmen. There are wagons, riders, and people, and the wagons aren't at the rear, but in the middle."

"That's not a military formation," said Lendar. "Supply wagons would be in the rear."

Almost three quints passed before Taelya and the others could make out those approaching. While the outriders wore maroon uniforms, several of those walking beside the wagons were women and older children.

"Some of those wagons are supply wagons," said Lendar. "Not all of them, though."

"Something went very wrong in Lydiar," added Taelya.

When the Lydian contingent neared the waiting Road Guards, two uniformed troopers moved well ahead and trotted forward. As the two neared, Taelya could make out the insignia and sleeve markings, showing that one was an undercaptain and the other a squad leader. Even before they reined up and Taelya released the larger containment, she could see that both the undercaptain and the squad leader were older, suggesting that the undercaptain had come up through the ranks.

"Welcome to Fairhaven," said Taelya, easing Bounder forward slightly.

The undercaptain studied her for a moment, then said, "You're a white mage-undercaptain?"

"Undercaptain Taelya. All of the mage-undercaptains do road patrols. We'd heard that there had been a pirate raid on the port at Lydiar. From your presence, it appears that matters did not go well."

"Begging your pardon, Mage-Undercaptain, but that's like saying camma bark burns hotter than oak. You must have heard about the first attack. There was a second one two days later. The bastards brought in camma bark and catapulted it into the city. The fires got out of hand. The Duke holed up in his citadel. Some of the merchants got tired of the Duke's incompetence and bought off a couple of companies to storm the citadel. It didn't work. Then the Duke offered golds to the raiders to kill any troopers in maroon. The idiot bastard said that we were all traitors. Frig! Our company was posted just west of town, and we barely got away, those of us who did."

Taelya listened intently, looking for any signs of untruth. She didn't sense any. Then she turned to the squad leader. "Is the undercaptain exaggerating anything?"

The undercaptain flushed, likely with anger, and stiffened, but did not speak.

"He isn't. He didn't tell the worst of it."

"Thank you both." Taelya looked back to Arthaal.

He nodded.

"I apologize," said Taelya, as contritely as she could, "but that was the fastest way to assure that you were both telling the truth. Now . . . how can we help you?"

Abruptly, the undercaptain laughed. He laughed for several long moments, then shook his head, and finally said, "A woman mage-undercaptain . . . figures out what's happening and who's telling the truth in a couple of moments, when a frigging Lydian majer gets himself killed because he didn't believe us."

Somehow, from what Taelya had seen and heard as a child, that didn't surprise her. But she just nodded.

"We need shelter, a place to stay, maybe call home. We can't go back, and we wouldn't be welcome in Hydlen. No man in his right mind would want to live in Certis. We heard that Fairhaven needed folks and might welcome troopers for the Town Patrol. Just hope we can work something out here."

"We have a large way station where you can stop. It has clean water and several buildings. You'll have to talk to the Council about permanent arrangements, but I'll send word to the majer, and he'll meet us there."

"The majer? The black mage with the silver and black face?"

Taelya nodded again.

"How do you know he'll meet us?"

"Because he's head of the Council."

"He's also the undercaptain's uncle," added Lendar.

"And you're patrolling on eightday?"

"All the Road Guard mages alternate patrols, including on eightday. This eightday, it was my duty. The trainee Road Guard mage with us is the majer's son."

The Lydian undercaptain glanced at the squad leader, then back at Taelya. "We're in your hands, Undercaptain."

"How many of you are there? How many wagons?"

"A little more than two squads of troopers, and some fifty women and children. Eight wagons. All the troopers have mounts."

"Thank you." Taelya turned to Sheppyl. "You heard all of this?"

"Yes, ser."

"Inform the duty squad leader and the majer personally. Tell the majer that I recommend he meet us at the way station immediately. Make it quick, but don't strain your mount."

"Yes, ser."

Once Sheppyl was on his way, Taelya turned to the Lydian undercaptain. "As I said before, I'm Undercaptain Taelya. And you are?"

"I'm sorry. Gheldryn, and Vhoman is the senior squad leader."

"I'm pleased to meet you both. The way station is a little less than five kays ahead. While we're riding, it might be helpful if you tell me a little more about what happened in Lydiar and how many others we should expect, if any."

"I can't say whether many will come the way we did. Some might go through the hills to Hrisbarg and that way to Montgren. Most folks will just stay put, but with the pirates and the Duke after us . . ."

"You weren't part of the troopers that attacked the Duke, then?"

"We didn't even know about that until the Worrak bastards started attacking us. We fought them off, but it cost us maybe half the company, and when we heard about the Duke putting a price on everyone who'd attacked him or the pirates . . ."

Taelya managed to keep her mouth closed as Gheldryn continued to provide details.

Just about a glass passed, and it was nearing fourth glass before Taelya and the others reined up at the edge of the way station where Beltur, Jessyla, and several Road Guards waited on their mounts.

"Majer, this is Undercaptain Gheldryn. He's in command of what's left of the Third Lydian Mounted Foot. His senior squad leader is Vhoman. They have about fifty women and children and eight wagons with some provisions and equipment."

"Thank you, Undercaptain," replied Beltur. "Since you're duty is about up, you and your patrol can head back to headquarters and sign out."

"We can stay if there's anything else you need."

Beltur smiled. "I appreciate the offer, but there's nothing else you can do right now, and you've already had a long day. Jorhan said that you and Arthaal can ride there after you sign out. He has space in the stable and feed. We'll be there when we can be."

"Yes, ser."

Gheldryn cleared his throat, then said, "Thank you, Undercaptain."

"You're very welcome. I hope you can work out matters so that you feel comfortable staying in Fairhaven." Taelya nodded, then turned Bounder and led her patrol toward headquarters.

XV

By the time Taelya had filled Kuchar in on what had happened, finished the log entries for her patrol, ridden to Jorhan's, and taken care of Bounder, it was almost fifth glass when she and Arthaal walked into the front room. Then Margrena, Johlana, and Meldryn immediately wanted to know the details, and another quint passed before she even got to more than sip the beaker of ale that her mother had passed her.

She forced herself not to gulp it and listened closely as Kaeryla questioned her brother.

"How was your patrol?"

"Long." Arthaal yawned.

"Did you see or sense anything?"

"Taelya made me use my senses to track three Hydlenese troopers. Oh, and I sensed a mountain cat up on the redstone bluffs."

"What else besides the Lydian troopers?"

"Nothing. We rode and watched, rode and watched." Arthaal yawned again.

"That's what happens on most patrols. If that's all you did, why are you so tired?"

"Because she made me do containments the whole time we were riding." A yawn punctuated Arthaal's words.

Kaeryla shook her head and looked at Taelya. "How did he do with the containments?"

"At the end he could hold a containment a yard on a side for a ten-count."

"Arthaal," said Kaeryla, "you said you couldn't hold containments for any time."

"I couldn't. She made me. It hurt a lot at first."

Kaeryla shook her head. "Go to sleep."

"I just might."

Kaeryla turned to Taelya and lowered her voice. "I thought it was something like that, but Father just thought he was slow to develop." She grinned. "I can't wait to tell Mother."

Arthaal stifled another yawn, then said, "I get to tell them first." Then he leaned back into the corner of the settee and closed his eyes.

"You really did wear him out."

"If he doesn't get a lot better soon . . ." Taelya shook her head.

"You think it's that bad?"

No. It's worse. But Taelya only nodded, before adding, "Arthaal just needs to be pushed a little."

"That's why Father has him working for both Meldryn and Jorhan."

"He's strong, and physical work is easy for him. Magery takes more than physical strength. I'd wager he has more trouble with the baking."

"He does," Kaeryla admitted. "I'll find a way to get that across to Mother."

"If Uncle Beltur asks, I'll tell him."

"I'll take care of that," said Kaeryla quietly.

Taelya just sat quietly, sipping her ale, and listened as Meldryn talked about the fact that he could now actually sell fruit pies and fancy breads, if mostly to the inns and to traders.

Then Jorhan called out, "Beltur and Jessyla just rode up."

The various conversations all died away when the two stepped into the front room.

"Did we interrupt something?" asked Beltur, taking off his visor cap and hanging it on one of the wall pegs.

"Well . . . don't keep us guessing," said Meldryn cheerfully. "Are they staying . . . or just passing through."

"I need an ale," replied Beltur, his voice good-humored. "I usually don't have to talk that much . . . although I'd probably have had to talk longer if it hadn't been for Taelya."

Taelya suddenly felt as though everyone was looking at her, possibly because most of those in the front room were. "I just did my duty."

Beltur nodded, then accepted a beaker of ale from Johlana and took a long swallow, then cleared his throat. "You did your duty, but you did it so effectively that it impressed some very experienced and skeptical troopers. Anyway . . . we made an agreement. It's the best we can do." He took a deep breath. "In return for help in settling here, the armsmen will serve as Road Guards, but they won't have to fight anywhere but around Fairhaven."

"While some of our Road Guards will have to fight with the Montgren forces elsewhere?" asked Johlana. "That's not exactly fair. Folks may not like that."

"It's not as unfair to us as it seems," Beltur said dryly. "Duke Maastyn has been looking to attack us for years. The Lydian troopers number more than two full squads, and they have their own mounts. That many troopers will help a great deal. The Council has an agreement from the Duchess—"

"Lord Korsaen and Maeyora, really," interjected Jessyla.

"—to post at least two full companies here to defend Montgren's southern border with Certis. Maastyn only has a few mages, and he can't raise much more than a battalion, possibly a company or two more at the outside, unless he uses inexperienced levies, and even then he'd struggle to get two battalions. He might not even attack, unless he's convinced that we're weaker. It may well be that he's the one who paid the pirates of Worrak to attack Lydiar, thinking that would stop Duke Halacut from providing troopers."

"In short," cut in Jessyla, "the situation is just slightly better than the last time."

"Has there been any word from Lord Korsaen?" asked Jorhan.

"Not yet," replied Beltur. "The soonest we could possibly hear anything would likely be late on twoday, and more likely it would be fourday or fiveday. I do worry a bit about Korsaen. He's looking worried, more than I've ever seen him, and his order/chaos levels are much lower than they should be, but neither Jessyla nor I could sense anything obviously wrong with him."

"It could be that dealing with the Duchess-to-be has been more difficult than he expected," added Jessyla.

Taelya noticed that Beltur frowned as Jessyla spoke, and wondered if Korsaen might be sicker than either had indicated.

"Is there any other news?" asked Margrena.

"Not that I know of," replied Beltur with a smile. "Except that one of Johlana's meals would really taste good at the moment."

"Then . . . everyone into the dining room," declared Johlana.

Once at the table, Taelya sat where she usually did, between the younger mages and the older adults, feeling, as she sometimes did, that she didn't quite belong to either group, since her brother was the closest to her in age of the younger ones, and he was eight years younger, while Jessyla was the youngest of the older group, and she was twelve years older than Taelya.

But at least the dinner was excellent, as were all dinners at Johlana's house—this time roast lamb, accompanied by bread-apple stuffing and cheesed potatoes on the side, with early asparagus, which Taelya carefully avoided. The dessert was a redberry cake that Meldryn brought.

By habit and long-standing and now-unspoken rules, there was no discussion about worrisome topics during dinner, worrisome meaning those dealing with the Council and other lands. There was a great deal of discussion about how soon Beltur and Jessyla's newer apple orchard would start bearing, which would allow greater production of the already successful apple brandy from the distillery.

After dinner, as Tulya, Taelya, and Dorylt left the house, Taelya turned to her mother. "You ride Bounder. Dorylt and I can walk alongside."

"I can walk," retorted Tulya. "I'm not exactly an old woman."

"I'd rather walk," said Taelya. "I spent most of the day in the saddle, and Dorylt likely did very little except read."

"I did scrub the floor in my room."

"And then you read."

"I'd rather walk, too."

Taelya smiled.

XVI

Taelya would have liked to have slept late on oneday, since she didn't have patrol duty, a duty that Kaeryla would be taking—but Jessyla had been firm about Taelya spending the day at the Healing House, especially since there would likely be more than a few ailments from the Lydian troopers and their families, and that would give Taelya some much-needed experience. Since she really didn't have any clothes that suggested healing, after washing up she put on one of her older Road Guard uniforms.

She didn't quite drag herself to the breakfast table, where Dorylt was already sitting and finishing his porridge. While porridge was about Taelya's least favorite breakfast, she had to admit that her mother's version of it was more than edible, unlike Jessyla's, which was just barely so.

Once Taelya was seated and had eaten several bites, Dorylt said enthusiastically, "Taelya . . . take a look at this."

"Take a look at what?"

"With your senses. It's a containment."

Taelya studied the containment, a good yard and a half on a side. Then she probed it with a tiny bit of chaos. The containment held. "I thought you said you couldn't do them."

"I can't do big ones, not enough to put around people."

"That's almost big enough to put around someone. Why did you say you couldn't do one?"

"Because I couldn't, not until the other day. I was watching Jaegyr put together a chest. Somehow, it reminded me of containments. I did something like that, and it worked. Then, last night, Arthaal was moaning about how hard you made him work at containments. He was so tired he could barely keep his eyes open. That made me think that I'd better work even harder."

"You're afraid I'd do that to you?"

Dorylt shook his head. "You wouldn't do that just to be mean. Even Arthaal understands that. You did it because you think we don't have much time to learn. What happened to the Lydians is scary. That could happen to us if we're not ready. And I'm not really ready, either."

"Have you changed your shields the same way you did your containment?"

"I put a little more chaos in the containment."

"Try the same thing with your shields. Just make sure that you link order on each end of the chaos. The chaos makes a black's shields both stronger and more flexible."

"What about your shields?"

"Order is what strengthens and stiffens mine," replied Taelya before taking another mouthful of porridge, and then some ale.

"You don't have patrol today," said Dorylt. "Why are you up so early?"

"Because I'm wanted at the Healing House."

Her brother shook his head. "It's weird that they're teaching a white healing skills."

"Not any white," interjected Tulya from where she sat at the end of the table. "She's one of the few whites, maybe the only one, who can handle large amounts of order and chaos without endangering herself."

"Still seems strange."

"Because she's a white or your sister?" asked Tulya.

"Both, I guess." Dorylt took a final mouthful of porridge, gulped the last of his ale, and then stood, quickly taking his bowl and beaker and washing and racking them. "I need to hurry. Jaegyr wanted me there earlier today. Thank you for the ideas about shields. I'll work on them." After those words, he headed for the front door.

Once the door closed, Tulya turned to her daughter. "That was a good conversation. He's growing up, and you were kind."

"Working with Jaegyr's been good for him."

"Work is good for everyone," replied Tulya. "Don't you feel better as a Road Guard? Or what about when you have patrol duty in the square on market days?"

"Better? I don't know. I feel like I'm doing something that needs to be done. But it's not like healing or even crafting a chair or a table."

"Taelya . . . there are many kinds of worth. I'm the justicer and the tariff inspector and collector. Without justice and tariffs to pay for roads and water pipes, towns don't hold together. Without patrollers and Road Guards, there isn't law and justice, and good and honest traders wouldn't come to Fairhaven. In fact, you might recall that they didn't."

"And without troopers and mages—"

"There wouldn't be any Fairhaven," Tulya finished.

"You have said that before," said Taelya, with a smile.

"I have. Sometimes, even grown daughters need reminding. We all do. Now . . . you'd better finish up if you want to get to the Healing House. And take a water bottle of ale and some bread with you."

Taelya nodded. She ate the last of the porridge, knowing that she wouldn't have much of a chance to eat until dinner, except for the ale and bread.

A quint later, she was walking along the west side of the square toward the Healing House, past the chandlery and the quarters building for the patrollers who didn't have consorts, just as the unattached Road Guards were housed in the rear part of the headquarters building. Ahead, she could see Margrena sweeping the narrow front porch.

The older healer looked up. "Good morning, Taelya. Jessyla said you'd be coming. She's inside."

"Thank you. How are you this morning?"

"As well as might be expected. It's good you're here." Margrena gestured toward the door. "You might as well go in."

Wondering why it was good for her to be there, Taelya entered the Healing House.

Jessyla turned from where she stood before the open cabinet against the wall and looked at Taelya. "We don't have any apprentice green tunics. I should have thought about that, but a guard uniform will do."

"For what?"

"There are a lot of injuries among the Lydians, according to what Beltur saw. He told them to come here today. We're likely to have a lot of sores and boils, and possibly more than that. Some of those can be handled by an infusion of order and chaos. I'll show you how, and it will help if you can handle some of those. I'll also be asking you to sense for small bits of wound chaos if I think it's likely . . . or there's a fuzziness . . ."

"Like when I can sense someone in the distance, but not clearly."

Jessyla nodded. "Exactly. I wish I could discern the tiny bits the way you and Beltur can. Kaeryla can do it better than I can, but not so well as you two."

"Not yet. She's still learning and growing."

"I couldn't sense the small bits when I was her age, and that didn't change."

"But Beltur said it took him until he was older."

"I suspect he had the ability all along, just not how to use it."

"You learned strong shields and containments later." After a moment, Taelya said, "Is that why you thought I could do healing?"

"I'm not sure I follow that."

"What I meant was that if you could be a healer and still fight, then did you think that I could be a white and do some healing?"

"It was more of a feeling," admitted Jessyla, "but if any white could, it would be you."

"You were right, but the idea still makes me uneasy."

"I'm not saying it would be good for you to be a healer all the time, but knowing more about healing could be very useful for you upon occasion. You might not have too many opportunities to learn more."

Although the certainty in Jessyla's words chilled Taelya, she replied, "Then it's been decided that I'll be one of the mages to go with the Montgren troopers?"

"I would have suggested you learn some healing in any event. Right now, nothing's been decided. We don't know what agreements Korsaen has been forced to make."

While Taelya could sense that Jessyla was telling the truth, she also knew that if Montgren allied with Certis, she would be one of those sent, along with Sheralt and Valchar. With help from Arthaal, Kaeryla, and Dorylt, and a few companies of Montgren troopers, Beltur and Jessyla could defend Fairhaven. *And Korsaen could claim he had provided three mages, one of whom was a white.* But there was no point in saying so bluntly, even though she felt a certain anger at the unfairness of the situation. "I see."

"I'm sure you do," replied Jessyla gently. "Sometimes there aren't any other choices."

No there aren't. Yet because Taelya could sense the caring in her aunt's tone, she didn't snap back those words.

Jessyla gestured to the supply cabinet. "You know where everything is. All we can do is wait for the Lydians . . . and anyone else . . . to arrive."

"I'd rather not be waiting for the Certans or the Hydlenese," said Margrena as she stepped back into the Healing House, still holding the broom, which she carried toward the back of the building, returning moments later.

Little more than a quint later, there was a knock on the door, and then a woman and a young girl entered. The woman looked to be more Margrena's age than Jessyla's, and her eyes went to Jessyla and Margrena, then halted as she took in Taelya.

"Undercaptain Taelya is also a field healer for the Road Guards," said Jessyla. "She spends part of her off-duty time helping us several days an eightday."

"Were you the one who escorted us in? Vhoman said there was a woman officer . . ."

"I was. There are two women undercaptains." Taelya offered a pleasant smile while she concentrated on the redheaded girl, who looked to be eight or nine and seemed to be favoring her left leg, although it was hard to tell exactly, since she wore baggy trousers that only came down to the top of her calves. Taelya concentrated on the right leg, sensing both wound chaos and additional free chaos there, seemingly centered on the knee.

"You're worried about the girl's leg?" asked Jessyla.

"She was hurt in fighting before we left Lydiar. Her mother died last year."

"You're her grandmother . . . or aunt?"

"Her aunt. My sister was much younger."

"Come with us." Jessyla gestured toward the doorway in the center of the front room, also beckoning to Taelya. "We need to take a look at that leg."

"There are others coming . . ."

"Healer Margrena can see to whoever arrives next," replied Jessyla.

Taelya followed the three into the first room.

"Can you get up on the table?" Jessyla asked the girl, who slowly shook her head. "Then would you like me to put you on the table or your aunt?"

The girl looked to her aunt.

The older woman lifted the child onto the table.

"There's a problem around her knee," said Jessyla, easing the baggy trousers up on the girl's right leg.

Taelya almost winced at the bruising above the knee, which was yellow and purple in places.

"How did this happen?" Jessyla asked the aunt.

"We were running from the pirates. One of them threw something at us." The woman pulled back her right sleeve. From shoulder to elbow, her arm was a mass of purple and yellow.

"I don't know what it was. Maybe several things. We couldn't stop to worry about it."

"Whatever it was, it knocked her kneecap out of place." Jessyla turned to Taelya. "The swelling from the bruises is going to make it a little harder to put it back in place. We'll also need to splint her leg afterward." The she looked back to the girl and pointed to the lump on the side of her knee. "That has to go back in front of your knee, and it will hurt more when I do it. But after that it will slowly get better. We'll need to stretch you out on your back first."

The girl nodded solemnly.

"Taelya, can you use a containment to hold her thigh and leg in place, but leave the area around the kneecap, and where it should be, in place?"

Taelya studied the girl's leg, then nodded.

"I need to get some things before we do this," said Jessyla. "I'll be back in a moment."

It was more than just a moment before Jessyla returned with several items, which looked to be two palm-width strips of wood, each about a cubit long, with notches in various places, and several long canvas strips, all of which she set at the end of the table.

Jessyla gently eased the child onto her back, then waited for Taelya to create the containment—essentially two linked by a rod of order. Then she deftly did . . . something.

"OHHH!"

"It's all over," said Jessyla. "Just stay on your back. We need to splint the knee so that she doesn't twist it. There's one other thing as well, but it shouldn't hurt." She looked to Taelya.

"You can remove the containment. Would you check for any nasty wound chaos?"

Taelya concentrated. Most of the bruises looked worse than they were, and seemed to be healing, but there was one small area . . . She eased tiny bits of free order into the reddish-orange chaos. "There was a small place. I took care of it."

"Thank you."

Jessyla turned to the aunt. "We're going to put this splint around her knee so that the kneecap will heal in place. Watch how we do this so that you can do it as well."

Taelya ended up slipping a flat containment under the girl's leg and knee to keep it straight while Jessyla splinted the knee.

After they finished, Jessyla said, "She'll need to wear the splint for at least an eightday. Leave it in place until tomorrow night. Then you can take it off when she goes to bed, but she should keep it on the rest of the time. The swelling should go down in an eightday. If it doesn't, or it gets worse, bring her back to see us."

Then they helped the girl off the table.

"It still hurts."

"It will hurt for a while," agreed Jessyla.

"Now . . . let's take a look at your arm," Jessyla said to the aunt, adding, "Taelya."

Taelya immediately sensed the aunt's arm, taking in the areas of bruising and trying to see if there was any underlying chaos. She didn't see anything out of the ordinary, and the bruises seemed to be healing. "There's only normal healing there."

"I thought so, but you can sense more deeply." Jessyla turned back to the aunt. "We've done what we can."

"Thank you, Healers. I wish—"

"Don't worry about it," replied Jessyla. "That's what we're here for."

By the time they finished with the two and sent them on their way, there were four more people waiting in the front room, and Margrena was dealing with a young woman with a suppurating boil.

It was past the second glass of the afternoon before the last of the injured Lydians left, and Taelya just sat on the bench.

At that moment, Beltur walked in. "Do you have a moment, Taelya?"

"She does," replied Jessyla. "She's been quite a help, and she's done more than she probably should have."

Beltur gestured toward the door. "If you'd join me . . ."

Taelya immediately wondered if she'd done something wrong.

"No, you haven't done anything wrong," said Beltur with a smile, clearly reading her reaction.

Once the two stood on the narrow porch, he said, "I heard that you wore out Arthaal when you were on patrol."

"I was just following what you had me do," replied Taelya.

"He said that doing a containment hurt at first."

"He *thought* it hurt, and most likely because he thought it did, it hurt. That's one reason why I kept him at it. I kept a close watch on his order/chaos levels, and neither changed much at all. They were just a little bit lower when we finished the patrol, but so were mine and so were Lendar's."

Beltur smiled. "I told him if he didn't keep improving that he'd have to work with you every day after he finished at either the smithy or the bakery. He also admits that containments don't hurt anymore."

"You were more effective with me than my father was," Taelya replied. "Sometimes, children just don't listen as much to their own parents. Sometimes, they do. Kaeryla seems to."

"Mostly. It helps that she has you to talk to, though. She worries too much."

Taelya looked at Beltur. "With what you and Aunt Jessyla have done, how can she not worry about disappointing you? Or failing to live up to your expectations?"

"We've thought about that." Beltur offered a wry smile. "If we say it doesn't matter, she'll know we're lying. It does matter, unfortunately. It matters very much how all four of you turn out because in another few years you'll have to do what Jessyla and I and your mother are doing now."

"Not that soon," replied Taelya.

"I hope not, but you're older now than Jessyla was when we came to Fairhaven. We'd prefer that you won't have to take over any time soon, but we never thought we'd be trying to rebuild a town when we were just about your age. Life is uncertain. That's one of the few certainties in life."

Taelya really didn't want to discuss that much more. She definitely knew how uncertain life could be. "What are the other certainties?"

"The only two others I can think of are that everyone dies, sooner or later, and that everything has to be paid for, one way or another. Usually, trying to avoid or postpone the payment means you pay more later." Beltur looked as though he might say more, but instead shook his head as if he'd decided not to.

But what if you can't pay now? As soon as she thought that, Taelya reconsidered Beltur's words. After a moment, she only said, "One way or another?"

Beltur just nodded. "I've never known anyone to escape paying. Maybe a few do, but that's not a good wager, not from what I've seen." He paused, then said, "I just wanted to know about whether Arthaal actually hurt. Thank you. I won't keep you from whatever Jessyla needs you to do." With a smile, he turned and walked in the direction of headquarters.

In turn, Taelya reentered the Healing House.

XVII

Patrolling on twoday was uneventful, although Taelya thought she sensed some riders to the southeast, but if there were riders, they never came close enough for her to be sure. She ended up tired, though, because after her duty, Beltur put her and Sheralt through a practice session with the infernal device. Threeday was also equally uneventful, although she did notice several of the Lydians setting out with a wagon filled with tools, and she wondered if they were going to clear land somewhere for a dwelling . . . and from whom they might have purchased the land . . . or obtained permission to rent the ground.

Fourday morning, Gustaan assigned her to patrol the southern road, along with Thrakyl and Wustyff, while Dorylt got his first Road Guard assignment riding with Valchar on the western patrol. Taelya couldn't help but worry a little about Dorylt, even though she knew his time as a Road Guard had to come. But his shields were strong enough to hold against brigands, and he wasn't likely to run across anything hostile in greater numbers. *In the seasons ahead, that will likely change.*

Since Taelya had ridden a Road Guard mount on threeday, she rode Bounder. As the three in her patrol left headquarters riding eastward on the main street, and Taelya had again raised the company-sized additional shield, Thrakyl cleared his throat, then asked, "Ser . . . some of the others have been saying we might have to fight with the Certans against the Gallosians . . ."

"The way things are going now, it's likely we'll have to fight someone. Who that might be, I don't know, and no one's told me anything that would make it clearer." While Taelya had her own ideas, expressing them definitely wasn't a good idea.

"I can't believe Duke Maastyn would attack after what happened to his father," Thrakyl continued.

"Greed and the desire for power can blind anyone," replied Taelya. "So can hatred. Maastyn likely hates us for killing his father and his older brother. He's likely been looking for a way to destroy Fairhaven for years. If he sees an opportunity, he just might take it."

"Even if he might lose?"

"We'll just have to see what happens." Taelya saw Julli working on her garden with another woman and realized that the woman was Jamya. When Julli looked up, Taelya waved.

Julli waved in return and then returned her attention to the garden.

Half a quint later, as the three passed the way station, Taelya noticed that there were only four wagons in the yard, and she wondered whether the others were being used for some sort of work or if the families involved had found other and better lodgings. Turning back to the road ahead, she couldn't sense any travelers, not in the more than two kays that her senses reached, although she did discern two flocks of sheep, each with a herder and a dog.

Before that long the three were on the south road, which made a rough arc around the town and which, at one point to the southwest past the redstone bluffs and the small thick forest, came within a few hundred yards of the border with Hydlen. That point was one where Taelya had often sensed Hydlenese troopers, but none had so far made any moves to cross into Montgren territory. *Really it's Fairhaven's territory.* But that was something else that Taelya wasn't about to say out loud.

They rode almost two quints before the road finished curving so that it headed mostly west, if still just slightly to the south. Then, just after they rode past the lane on the right that led north to Frydika and Worrfan's holding, Taelya began to feel that there were riders ahead somewhat to the southwest, but she couldn't really discern them until they passed the small thick forest on the right and were riding past the rocky grasslands.

"There are ten riders ahead, on that side road that leads into Hydlen," she told Thrakyl and Wustyff.

"Are they on our side of the border or theirs?"

"So far as I can sense, they're just about on the border."

"Ten of them—that's not good."

"At least none of them are mages," replied Taelya. "We'll keep riding. In years, none of them have actually crossed the border." *But there's always a first time.* She just hoped this wasn't the first time. *Still . . . half a squad? Why that many?*

Taelya kept a close watch on the riders, who were definitely moving, if slowly, along the side road toward the southern road traveled by the three Road Guards.

"They seem to be crossing the border," she said quietly. "We'll keep moving until we see them."

"Ten is half a squad," replied Thrakyl.

"We need to see what they have in mind."

"Yes, ser," replied Thrakyl, who did not sound particularly happy.

"They definitely don't have any mages," said Taelya, knowing that she'd said that before, but wanting to reassure the two guards, even as she sensed that the riders were definitely across the border and would be within sight within moments.

When she caught sight of the green uniforms, the Hydlenese were riding in a two-abreast column, headed north on the side lane, less than a hundred yards from where it joined the south road. Although the troopers could clearly see the Road Guards, they just kept riding.

"They're not stopping, ser."

"No . . . they're not. You two drop back, directly behind me, and as close together as you can manage. Stirrup to stirrup, if you can. That way, you'll be shielded." Taelya judged that the Hydlenese were still some two hundred yards away. She extended her senses, but found no traces, or even hints, of other riders anywhere near. "We'll just keep riding."

Neither guard spoke, but from the slight increase in chaos swirling around Thrakyl, Taelya could sense that he was agitated.

When the Hydlenese were little more than a hundred yards away, Taelya saw and sensed that the troopers had brought out bows, and she immediately contracted the larger shield, which would allow greater strength.

"They're mounted archers," declared Thrakyl, "and they're nocking shafts."

"Just stay close behind me, stirrup to stirrup!"

"Ser . . . there's a half squad," said Thrakyl.

"None of them are mages," repeated Taelya. "My shields will hold."

The moment the first volley arched toward Taelya, she angled her shields into a wedge, a tactic Beltur had taught her years earlier, and when the shafts reached her shields, they broke on the shield or skittered off it to the side. The same happened with the second volley. Then the Hydlenese stowed their bows, drew sabres, and charged.

"I'm reining up," said Taelya, stopping Bounder, and concentrating on the charging troopers, waiting until they were closer.

When the lead trooper, with his sabre in hand, was some fifteen yards away, she began to loose narrow-targeted chaos bolts. The first trooper went down with a chaos bolt to his head, as did the second trooper. The third and fourth bolts grazed troopers because both ducked.

Taelya lowered her aim to the troopers' chests, methodically aiming and releasing chaos bolts, dropping three more with charred holes in their upper bodies. A hint of black misty chill seemed to drift from somewhere . . . or perhaps it had been there for a while. The trailing Hydlenese turned their mounts, and Taelya managed to take out another two, but the remaining three troopers had galloped too far away for Taelya to be sure of hitting them with tightly-focused chaos bolts . . . and she was feeling a little tired.

"Frig . . ." Taelya's single word was muttered. Then she said, "Let's see if we can gather in some of those mounts."

"You . . . killed seven of them," said Thrakyl.

"They were going to kill all of us if they could. What was I supposed to do? Tell them to turn around and go home?"

Wustyff emitted a sound that might have been a snigger.

"Wustyff!" snapped Taelya. "We need to catch as many of the mounts as we can. We'll need them." *And a lot more.*

Between her use of containments and the efforts of the two Road Guards, the three managed to collect five of the Hydlenese mounts. The entire time, Taelya kept sensing for other riders, but even the three who fled were well beyond her ability to discern by the time they'd gathered the five horses. Then she had Thrakyl and Wustyff quickly strip the seven dead troopers, collecting uniforms and weapons, and turning over the belt wallets to her, before the three began their ride back to headquarters, taking the winding lane through the rocky grasslands.

"Do all mages use such small bits of chaos?" asked Thrakyl as they continued north on the narrow lane.

"I don't know. According to the majer, most don't. He thought that we'd be effective longer if we used smaller amounts that were well placed when we could. He'll be pleased to learn that it worked."

"It happened so fast," said Wustyff.

"Most fights do," replied Thrakyl.

Taelya didn't say anything. She kept sensing, but she still could find no trace of any Hydlenese. *What was the point of the attack? And if they wanted to attack Fairhaven, why aren't there other troopers nearby?*

She was still pondering the whole engagement when the lane turned into one of the back streets on the south side of Fairhaven and they kept riding toward headquarters. She saw more than a few people look at the three riders and the five extra mounts, all five of which were carrying Hydlenese weapons and gear.

She supposed that some of the coins in the wallets should go to Thrakyl and Wustyff.

They had barely reined up in the stable yard when Beltur appeared, an expression between disapproval and concern. "What happened?"

"A half squad of Hydlenese attacked us," replied Taelya. "We took out seven, and the other three fled before I could get to them."

With an inquiring look, Beltur turned to Thrakyl.

"The undercaptain did it all, ser. Shielded us against their shafts and used little bits of chaos, sort of like arrows or crossbow bolts. Don't think she missed a one."

"I missed two. That's likely why the others got away. Two of their mounts ran off, but we corralled five of the seven. The gear on the captured mounts belonged to the dead troopers." She leaned forward and handed the captured belt wallets to Beltur. "I don't know the custom with spoils."

"The Road Guards involved split half. The remainder goes into the Guard treasury. You three will get your shares when you sign out." Beltur paused, then said, "You just left the bodies there?"

"For now, ser. I thought you'd like to know about an attack by half a squad on Road Guards. I kept sensing, but none of the Hydlenese stayed on our side of the border or even close on their side."

Beltur nodded, almost reluctantly.

"I thought we'd report and return to patrolling that area, ser."

"Take a short break and then return to patrol. If I could have a moment with you, Undercaptain?"

"Yes, ser." Taelya dismounted and tied Bounder, then followed Beltur to a shady spot under the overhanging stable roof.

"Taelya . . . how did they attack?"

"They were on their side of the border, on the narrow road that leads to the burned-out stead . . ." Taelya went on to relate exactly what had happened.

When she had finished, Beltur looked even more worried than before, but he only said, "I don't see that you could have done anything else. What do you think about it?"

"I think it was to see how we'd react, possibly to determine whether we really had mages riding patrol. What I don't understand was why they didn't have a squad or company to take advantage of the situation if they'd been successful."

"It's likely that they weren't meant to be successful. It would have been a pleasant surprise if they had been, but I suspect the idea was to show that we're bloodthirsty killers, and that we wiped out most of a peaceful scouting party."

Taelya could see that, unfortunately, but felt she had to say something. "Even if they fired two volleys of arrows? We collected some of those as well. Then they charged with drawn sabres."

Beltur smiled sadly. "It doesn't matter what really happened. The Duke or the Prefect will tell the story they want, and everyone in their lands will believe it. If they'd known you were a woman, they'd even say that we'd recruited some bitches from Westwind. But from the way you described the skirmish, all the survivors will know is that seven out of ten troopers were killed by a white mage of Fairhaven. That will suffice for the Prefect's purposes."

"How do you know his purposes?" Taelya managed to keep her words even.

"I don't. What I do know is that he knows we cannot afford to ally ourselves with anyone but Certis. Since Certis is his enemy, anything that weakens us helps him. If Fairhaven and Montgren have to fight Hydlen, then we cannot offer as much support to the Viscount. Also, if we're successful against Hydlen, then that weakens Hydlen, and that's to the Prefect's advantage as well."

"And, once again, everything's about power."

"Is anything ever about anything else?" returned Beltur dryly. "Now . . . you need to get back there. Just patrol the area from the lane that Frydika's stead is on out to the Hydolar road."

"Yes, ser."

"You did well," replied Beltur, "and that's seven troopers we won't have to face."

"Thank you." *Both for the appreciation and the message.*

Beltur smiled again, then turned to the squad leader who stood waiting outside the main building. "Kuchar . . . have someone check over the captured mounts before they're stabled and groomed, and bring all the gear into the briefing room. Not the tack, though. Then send half the duty squad to deal with the bodies."

"Yes, ser."

Taelya walked back to where Bounder was tied and where the two Road Guards stood. "We need to get back out there to make sure there isn't another force coming." She went on to relay Beltur's orders as to where they would patrol.

Half a quint later, they reached the beginning of the winding lane that they'd ridden the other direction.

Taelya didn't sense anything ahead, except a few fieldworkers and two separate flocks of sheep. She had the feeling that there wouldn't be any other Hydlenese, but she still worried.

By half past the third glass of the afternoon, she'd still sensed no one near the border on either side, except for the duty squad collecting the bodies and a few scattered individuals. So the three took the south road where it ran parallel to the Hydolar road and rode north until they reached the west road, where they turned east and headed back into Fairhaven.

As Beltur had promised, a small cloth bag was waiting for each of them at the duty desk. Taelya didn't even open it, but slipped it into her belt wallet, and went outside to wait for Dorylt, who was sparring with Lendar. She didn't want to practice with the infernal device, and she definitely wasn't in the mood to go to the Healing House.

When Dorylt finished and walked to where Taelya waited with their horses, his first excited words were, "Is it true? Did you actually fight Hydlenese troopers?"

Taelya sensed the combination of amazed disbelief and concern, and replied in a matter-of-fact tone, "Not exactly. They attacked, first with arrows, then with sabres. I used chaos bolts, the way I told you about, and killed seven of them. The three survivors fled. It wasn't a fight. It was more like a slaughter."

"But they attacked you, didn't they?"

"They did. That's what makes it seem so pointless. If we win, then we're not that much better off, and they'll have lost a whole lot of troopers. If they win, they'll still have lost a lot of troopers, and they'll destroy Fairhaven, and they won't be any better off."

"You should sound happier than that," said Dorylt as he untied his mount.

Taelya untied Bounder and then mounted. "Maybe I will be later." She had her doubts about that, but it could happen.

XVIII

When Taelya woke on fiveday morning, early, she finally took the small cloth bag out of her belt wallet, untied it, and eased the coins out into her palm—a Hydlenese half silver and two coppers. *Seven coppers . . . a copper for each life.*

She shook her head, knowing at the same time that, without her, neither Thrakyl nor Wustyff would have stood a chance. And while Valchar and Dorylt could have stood off half a squad, they wouldn't have been able to do much damage to the attackers, since Valchar could barely use his shields as a weapon, and Dorylt wasn't much better. Those thoughts didn't make her feel that much better.

With those thoughts in mind, she washed and dressed quickly and hurried to the kitchen.

"You're up early," said Tulya.

"I had a lot on my mind."

"Don't fret over the Hydlenese. They don't deserve it. No one forced them to attack you." Tulya's voice was tart as she set a platter of lamb and egg scramble in front of her daughter, accompanied by a chunk of bread.

"That wasn't all of it. I was worrying about Dorylt. He still can't shape his shields, and he's going to need to do that before much longer."

"Do what before much longer?" asked her brother as he stepped into the kitchen.

"Learn to shape the edges of your shields into blades."

A wary expression crossed Dorylt's face. "Did you talk to Valchar yesterday after patrol?"

"No. I wasn't in the mood to talk to anyone but you. Why?"

"When he heard that you'd fought the Hydlenese, he asked me if I could do what Uncle Beltur does with shields. All he can do with them is run into people. He was really worried."

"He ought to be. So should you," said Tulya.

"Did you talk to Sheralt?" asked Taelya.

"I didn't see him. Valchar said he was practicing with that device."

That was one good sign, Taelya thought, as she took a mouthful of the warm scramble, followed by a bite of the bread.

"You need to work on shaping your shields," Tulya said to Dorylt.

"I did work on it . . . while I was on patrol. It's hard, but I can hold an edge maybe a yard out for a little while."

"For how long?" asked Taelya.

"A ten-count."

"You might take out one Hydlenese . . . if you're fortunate."

"How far can you extend shields?" countered Dorylt.

"Two yards on a side . . . but I can hold them there for a quint at a time." But then, Taelya realized that perhaps she could do more for longer now that she'd been carrying an additional large shield. She hadn't practiced the edged shields recently.

"That's not much farther than Kaeryla can," Dorylt pointed out.

Her mouth full, Taelya just nodded.

"The shields are the only weapon you, Kaeryla, and Arthaal have," said Tulya. "Your sister also has chaos bolts. That means you have to turn your shields and containments into weapons."

"I wish I could handle chaos," replied Dorylt.

"You can," said Taelya, "and you know it. Once you get better with containments, you'll be able to throw chaos bolts back at white mages." *If you work harder on containments.* She quickly finished her breakfast, swallowed the last of her ale, and stood. "I need to get to headquarters, and I'm walking this morning." She quickly washed her platter and beaker, then racked them to dry.

In less than half a quint, she was walking quickly toward headquarters.

As she neared the headquarters building, Squad Leader Varais stepped toward her, saying, "Good work. It won't stop them, but it's a start."

"Do you know something I don't?" asked Taelya.

Varais shook her head. "It has to be the Prefect's doing. If he can get Hydlen to attack Montgren, then Montgren can't support Certis as much. That gives him a better chance of hanging on to Passera."

"Do you think Maastyn's that stupid?"

"He has to be desperate. He can't control the pirates operating out of Worrak. With what they took from Lydiar, they could take Renklaar. After that, how long before they'd move on Hydlen? The Prefect has a fleet, enough of one to pose a problem for the pirates."

Taelya could see that . . . unfortunately, but she didn't recall Beltur or her mother talking about that possibility. "How did you come up with that?"

"The Prefect threatened to use his fleet against Suthya if the Suthyans traded with Westwind. They laughed at him, but no one's going to stop the Gallosians if they attack pirate ships."

"Did you mention that to the majer?"

"I told the captain. He said he'd pass it on."

Taelya nodded. Knowing Gustaan, she had no doubt he would. "If you'll excuse me, I need to find Valchar."

"He and Sheralt are in the stable, readying their mounts."

"Thank you."

Since the two were still saddling up their horses, Taelya did the same with the gelding that she liked to ride. She finished only a few moments later than the other two undercaptains, who stood by the stable door, waiting for her.

Taelya didn't sense any difference in Valchar's shields, but the order and chaos levels in Sheralt's were definitely separated, and she said, "You've been working on keeping your levels separated."

"It's made throwing those small chaos bolts easier."

Taelya raised her eyebrows. "Just the chaos bolts?"

"Pretty much everything, but you don't have to rub it in."

"You deserve it," said Valchar, with a laugh.

"He's trying to get better," said Taelya quietly. "From what I can sense, you aren't. You were patrolling with my brother yesterday. Just what would you have done if those Hydlenese had attacked you?"

"I'd have used my shields to unhorse as many as I could."

"Dorylt doesn't have large enough shields to protect the two Road Guards. How would you have handled that? Let the guards fend for themselves?"

"You're not the captain or the majer," said Valchar.

"No . . . but I am Dorylt's sister, and I don't like him being put in an awkward position because you're uncomfortable with the idea of changing your shields to make them stronger . . . and turning them into weapons." Taelya smiled coldly.

Valchar stepped back.

"You might want to think about it." Taelya turned to Sheralt and said more warmly, "I heard you were working with the device last night."

"After what happened to you, I thought it was a good idea."

She nodded. "You might try modifying your shields, too, just a little."

"Into blades, the way your family does?" Sheralt frowned.

"Not all the time," Taelya said. "But you ought to practice doing that so that you could if you really had to. It would allow you to cut your way through other riders." She looked meaningfully at Valchar, then back to Sheralt.

Sheralt turned to Valchar and grinned. "I think that message is for both of us."

Valchar grimaced.

Taelya managed a shrug. "We're always going to be outnumbered." Then she smiled at Valchar. "I don't bite." *Much.* "We probably ought to head to the duty room."

"As if we have much choice," murmured Valchar.

All the Road Guard squad leaders were already in the room as well as the duty senior Road Guards when the three undercaptains entered the duty room, and several looked intently at Taelya, if only momentarily.

Squad leaders as well? Taelya had the feeling that there was a change in the works.

Gustaan walked in, followed by Beltur. After a moment, he said, "The majer has a few words."

Beltur stepped forward and surveyed those present. After a moment, he said, "For those few of you who may not have heard, yesterday one of our patrols was attacked by a half squad of Hydlenese troopers. While the attack was repulsed and the majority of the attackers were killed, it could have turned out differently. So, for the present, we will be changing patrols. All patrols will include one mage, one squad leader, and half a squad. This should discourage attacks in the near future and will also provide more training for Road Guards.

"If you are attacked, you are to give no quarter, and you are to kill any Hydlenese trooper who does not immediately surrender. The reason for that order is simple. We may be in a war before long, if we're not already. Any dead Hydlenese trooper is one you don't have to fight again. The same is true of any trooper who surrenders. A surrender is just as valuable as a death. At the same time, do not pursue anyone who flees. That only risks your men with little gain. Is that clear?"

Most of those in the room nodded.

Beltur turned to Gustaan. "Captain."

Gustaan cleared his throat, then said, "Undercaptain Taelya, you'll have the west patrol, with Squad Leader Barkhan and half of First Squad, Undercaptain Valchar, the east patrol . . ."

Taelya walked out of the duty room with Barkhan, considering how the larger group could affect how she used order and chaos.

As they walked toward the stables where the half squad's riders were mounting up, Barkhan spoke: "Ser, might I ask just how you took out seven greenies?"

"I used very small targeted chaos bolts at close range . . . less than thirty yards. That works well against smaller groups. It would be much less effective against an entire company." That was a calculated guess on Taelya's part, since she'd never faced a company. In fact, the ten Hydlenese were the largest group of troopers or brigands she'd ever faced. *But it looks like that will change.* After a moment, she added, "I can still likely protect a full squad against archery attacks, but I doubt I could hold shields against a charge of ten horses." *And I really don't want to try.*

"Thank you, ser."

Taelya almost stopped in her tracks as she realized that now that she could handle a larger containment, that meant she could also put a concealment over a squad. "There's one other thing we're going to try."

"Ser?"

"When no one else is around, we're going to work on having you and the men ride under a concealment."

"Yes, ser."

"Barkhan . . . it won't be easy. None of you will be able to see. It's like moving in total darkness, but if we had to face an entire company, it might make all the difference."

"Then we'll need some line or some rope, ser," replied the squad leader. "At least, that was the way the majer did it. Gustaan told me that."

Taelya could feel herself flushing, but she managed to say, "I'm glad you know that. I was wondering . . ."

"I don't know much more than that, ser, but we can work it out."

As a result of getting some rope, the patrol was more than half a quint late in leaving headquarters.

For all of the concern expressed by Beltur, throughout the glasses of the patrol Taelya could discern absolutely no trace of Hydlenese riders, or any other riders or wagons coming from the west, and her patrol was without any incidents with the Hydlenese. Trying to travel under a concealment was another question. Even with ropes being used as guides, Taelya all too often had to call out directions, and that would destroy the whole purpose of the concealment in facing a larger force.

She consoled herself with the thought that at least she'd realized it while there was still time to get the squad used to it. She did test her ability with bladed shields, and found that she could hold shields with bladed edges about two and a half yards out without strain for about a quint while also holding a company-sized shield.

Once she and her patrol had returned to headquarters and she had signed out and then groomed the mare, she walked to the Healing House, because she hadn't been there in several days.

Margrena and Kaeryla were inside, but without anyone seeking healing.

"Mother's over at the Council House with the other councilors," Kaeryla volunteered.

"Did she say why?"

"Does she ever?" replied Kaeryla with muted sarcasm.

Margrena gave her granddaughter a sharp glance.

Kaeryla offered an apologetic expression, then said, "But it's true. She never says anything."

"Until the Council decides, that's as it should be," replied Margrena, before turning to Taelya and asking, "Have you ever splinted an arm or a leg?"

"No. I've watched you and Jessyla, but I've never done it."

"I thought as much. You can practice on Kaeryla. Until someone needs healing, anyway."

Kaeryla tried to conceal a wince.

Taelya ignored the expression and smiled pleasantly.

Since no one did come to the Healing House, over the next glass Margrena instructed Taelya in applying various kinds of splints, something that Taelya hoped wouldn't be necessary and feared would be all too likely.

After that, Margrena left the Healing House, headed to her small dwelling, and by two quints after fifth glass Jessyla returned, accompanied by Beltur.

"What happened with the Council?" Kaeryla immediately asked. "What did you decide?"

"We didn't decide anything," replied Jessyla, "because, right now, there's nothing to decide."

"When will you find out? When we're abandoned . . . or attacked?" replied Kaeryla.

Jessyla looked hard at her daughter, while Beltur said firmly, "We need to head home. That is, if you want to eat."

Kaeryla didn't quite meet her father's eyes, but Beltur said nothing.

Nor did anyone else, for a time, as Jessyla and Kaeryla closed up the Healing House.

A little later, as the four walked westward from the square toward their houses, Beltur fell in beside Taelya, not exactly accidentally, she thought.

"I understand you're training troopers to ride under a concealment." His voice was bland.

"I thought it might come in useful. Is that a problem?"

"Not at all, but you might have asked me, rather than having squad leaders ask about it." Beltur smiled. "I was about to ask if you'd do something like that, since you're the only one who can handle a large concealment besides Jessyla and me, but since you'd already started, I just told Gustaan and the squad leaders that I'd neglected to mention it with everything that's happened. I also told them to make sure that the men didn't talk about it except among themselves because it would be helpful if we could surprise the Hydlenese."

"I'm sorry. You're right, but it just came to me, and I decided to do it when I had the chance."

"Your instincts were right, but you should have at least told me after the first time when you began teaching the men."

Taelya could see that.

"There is one other thing," added Beltur.

Taelya tried not to tense up. "Yes?"

"Valchar came to see me right after he finished his patrol today."

"Oh?"

"He said you made a veiled threat this morning."

"I told him that his shields needed work. He told me I wasn't either you or Gustaan. I told him that I was Dorylt's sister, and that I didn't like my brother being put in an awkward position because Valchar merely felt uncomfortable with the idea of changing his shields. That was all I said. Well, I also said to both of them that being able to form blades on the edge of their shields would help if they were surrounded."

Beltur nodded. "I thought it might be something like that."

"Were you beating up on them again?" asked Kaeryla cheerfully.

"I just want them both to get better before it's too late. Sheralt is trying. Valchar's stubborn."

"And you're not?" returned Kaeryla.

Taelya couldn't help but laugh at Kaeryla's warmly sarcastic reply.

Even Beltur and Jessyla smiled, if only briefly, as though they had other thoughts on their minds.

XIX

On sixday, Taelya commanded the eastern patrol, and all the patrol encountered were locals heading in and out of town and a cart with a family of five who had fled from Lydiar and were joining a cousin in Fairhaven. She also had the half squad practice riding under a concealment. Sevenday found Taelya once more in charge of the southern road patrol, this time with Moshart as the squad leader.

On the very first sweep of the road, the patrol had just finished riding under a concealment after passing the redstone bluffs and was riding past the rocky grasslands when Taelya thought she discerned something to the west-southwest, near the border.

"There might be Hydlenese ahead near the border. We aren't close enough to tell for certain, though."

"How long before you can tell?" asked Moshart.

For a moment, the squad leader's question surprised Taelya, before she realized that she'd usually ridden with senior guards, not squad leaders, except for Varais, who'd just recently been promoted. "I don't know yet, but that means that they're more than two kays away."

"Can the other mages sense that far?"

"The majer and the head healer can, and all of the others can sense at least a kay away."

Moshart nodded thoughtfully.

Even when they passed the side road from which the Hydlenese had attacked her patrol on fiveday, Taelya still couldn't discern any riders, but after riding another few hundred yards, she finally discovered what she'd only felt before. "There are two riders ahead. They're not on the road, but on the northern edge of the top of the northernmost of the hills just east of the Hydolar road."

"Then they must be there to watch our scouting patterns."

"Once I'm absolutely sure that they're Hydlenese," said Taelya, "we'll need to dispatch a guard to carry that message to the majer."

Even before the patrol reached the point where the narrow southern road turned back north, Taelya could make out the green uniforms of the two troopers—or scouts—standing on a rocky ledge on the north side of the hill. From there, the pair could survey the southern road on which the patrol rode, the Hydolar road, the Weevett road, and much of the road from Fairhaven that led to Certis and eventually to Gallos.

"You can dispatch the messenger now. There are two Hydlenese scouts, but no other troopers within a kay of them, and they're positioned where they can watch all four roads."

"Yes, ser."

Taelya watched as the messenger galloped off, wondering what Beltur would do, then returned her attention to the scouts.

The two Hydlenese troopers did not move as the patrol passed the hill, the closest distance between the patrol and the scouts being slightly more than a kay, and rode to the main road. After a rest of half a quint, the patrol headed back south on the side road and retraced their path eastward. They were just approaching the lane that led north from the redstone bluffs toward Frydika's stead when Taelya sensed a single rider headed down the lane toward them.

"There's a rider coming from Fairhaven down the lane. We'll wait where it joins the road, just in case the majer wants us to change our patrol."

The patrol didn't have to wait long for the same guard who had carried the message to headquarters. He rode directly to Taelya and extended an envelope. "Ser, a dispatch from the majer."

"Thank you." Taelya took the envelope, opened it, and began to read.

> Undercaptain Taelya—
>   You are to continue normal patrols. Headquarters is posting scouts on a continuing basis. Report any other contacts or encounters with Hydlenese troopers.

The signature and the seal were Beltur's.

Taelya handed the orders to Moshart, who read them and handed the single sheet back to her. Then she turned. "The majer has posted additional scouts. We're ordered to continue regular patrols."

For the rest of the day, Taelya sensed no other Hydlenese except the two scouts, but she did sense two riders coming down the road from Weevett and proceeding into town. While she suspected they were couriers from Vergren, and likely from Korsaen or the Duchess, since she did not see them, she could only surmise. In the meantime, she ordered another session of riding under a concealment.

At the end of her duty, when she went to sign out, she asked Varais, the duty squad leader, "Were the two riders coming from Weevett couriers from Vergren?"

"They were Montgren couriers with a dispatch for the majer. That's all anyone knows, but the majer summoned all the concilors."

Taelya nodded. "Thank you."

"Were the Hydlenese you found just scouts, ser?"

"So far as we could tell, and there weren't any others anywhere near."

"I don't like the sound of that."

"I'm not sure we'll like the sound of anything right now," said Taelya dryly.

Varais shook her head, then asked, "Are you going to have every patrol spend time riding under a concealment?"

"Unless there's some reason not to. It could prove useful if we have to fight."

"More likely *when* we have to fight," replied Varais. "Thank you, ser."

"Thank you. I'll likely see you in the morning." Taelya headed out to where Bounder waited.

Sheralt had just ridden up and dismounted. "I asked the scouts on the west road why they were there. They said you ran into Hydlenese scouts."

"We did." Taelya quickly explained.

"If you didn't sense anyone else, it's likely to be a little while before anything happens . . . don't you think?"

Taelya smiled wryly. "I'm not about to guess, first because I've been ordered not to, and, second, because I don't know enough to even do that."

"But . . ." Sheralt shook his head. "I'm not thinking. You've been on patrol. You wouldn't know any more than I do." He glanced toward the headquarters building. "I need to sign out."

"Then I'll see you in the morning." Taelya wasn't about to practice more with the device or to go to the Healing House. She just wanted to go home.

After she got there, even when she finished taking care of Bounder, neither her mother nor Dorylt had arrived. So she took stock of what was in the kitchen and decided to use the last scraps of lamb to put together a dish that was similar to burhka, but was creamier and also included some diced boiled new potatoes. Then she made the batter for skillet bread, because she doubted she'd have time to bake regular bread.

Half a glass later, as she was fiddling with the seasoning, Dorylt walked in.

"What are you cooking? It doesn't smell bad, even."

"Thank you for the encouraging words. You'll see when you taste it."

"Where's Mother?"

"Two Montgren couriers brought a dispatch for Uncle Beltur. He called a meeting of all the councilors. They must still be meeting. After you wash up, you can set the table."

Taelya tried not to think about what was in the dispatch, but she was afraid she already knew the gist of the message, simply because she couldn't see what else it could be. *You could be wrong.*

Shortly after Dorylt finished setting the table, Tulya entered the kitchen from the rear door. "Whatever you fixed, dear, it smells good. I'm starving."

"It will be a few moments. I didn't want to do the skillet bread until you came home. It's much better warm."

"That it is. I'll wash up while you're fixing it."

Taelya turned to Dorylt. "If you'd fill the beakers."

"I can do that."

Dorylt was back in his chair, waiting impatiently, by the time Tulya sat down, just before Taelya began serving.

"What did the dispatch say?" asked Dorylt. "Was it from the Duchess?"

Tulya took a small swallow of ale before replying. "It was from Lord Korsaen and Duchess Koralya."

"Duchess Koralya?" asked Taelya. "Did Korlyssa die?"

"She stepped down in favor of her daughter because of her health," replied Tulya. "That was an eightday ago, according to the dispatch."

"What did it say?" asked Dorylt again, his voice impatient.

"What do you think it said?" replied Tulya.

"I don't know," replied Dorylt, not quite sullenly. "That we're allied with either Gallos or Certis, or that they've made peace, or that everyone's against us. It could be anything."

"Stop being difficult," said Tulya calmly. "Start thinking. There's no way everyone would be against us. Why not?"

"I don't know."

"Taelya?"

"Because we'd fight, and they'd lose men and mages, and they wouldn't gain anything." She paused. "Also because we have mages, none of them could bargain to use any of our mages to their advantage."

"Exactly. Given how long Gallos and Certis have been fighting, is it likely that they'd suddenly make peace?"

"No, ser," answered Dorylt grudgingly.

"So Montgren has allied itself with Certis?" said Taelya. "What's the price?"

"Mages and squads to support them. In turn, Duchess Koralya will send two companies of troopers here."

"How many of our mages?"

"Two, or possibly four."

"Me, Sheralt, and Valchar. Who else?"

"The question of which mages will be required to do what hasn't been worked out."

"Does that mean I might have to go?" asked Dorylt.

"Neither you nor Arthaal are strong enough yet to do anything in a large battle but get yourselves killed," replied Tulya.

Taelya considered the situation, but before she could speak, Tulya went on, her voice falsely cheerful. "It's out of my hands now, and we might as well enjoy a good dinner." Then she added, "This stays between us. Always."

At that, Taelya swallowed, because there was only one possibility for the fourth mage if that many were required. *If Fairhaven were to survive.*

XX

While Taelya slept well enough, she woke early on eightday morning, her thoughts still on what her mother had revealed. She washed and dressed quietly, then sat down at the kitchen table, still thinking.

Half a glass later, when Tulya joined her, she was still thinking.

"You can't change things by endless pondering," said Tulya gently. "Would you like some cheesed eggs?"

"I can fix them." Taelya started to stand up.

Tulya gestured for Taelya to remain at the table. "You fixed dinner. By the way, I should have told you how much I appreciated that and how good it was."

"You had a lot on your mind."

"So did you," replied Tulya, her tone wry but warm. "Breakfast won't take long, and you'll need it if you're going to work in the stable. I'll do the house, and Dorylt can help me with the floors."

For a moment, Taelya wondered why she wanted Dorylt to help in the house, but then understood that it would give Taelya a chance to talk to Kaeryla without Dorylt being around. She smiled and asked, "Is Arthaal going to the orchard or the distillery with Uncle Beltur?"

"That's what I understand."

Still smiling, Taelya did get up, but only to get two beakers, which she half filled with ale before reseating herself at the table.

A half glass later, she took a last swallow of ale and then walked out the front door and headed for the stable. From what she could see, Kaeryla wasn't there yet, but that would give Taelya a little time with Bounder. She actually finished grooming Bounder and had cleaned out his stall and the adjoining one when Kaeryla joined her.

"Where's Dorylt?" asked Kaeryla.

"He slept late, and Mother decided that he could scrub floors."

"Serves him right for being lazy, but that means it's just the two of us."

"It's not too bad. I've already mucked out two stalls. We are running low on hay and grain, though."

"I told Father that on fiveday."

"He's been pretty occupied."

"Well . . . in less than an eightday, maybe sooner, he won't need so much," said Kaeryla. "I'll be riding with you and Sheralt and Valchar."

Although Taelya had already suspected that, she said, "You shouldn't have to do that. You're not even fifteen."

"I will be by the time we get to Jellico. Besides, I'm taller than you, and I look older than I am." A faint hint of defiance colored Kaeryla's words.

"You shouldn't have—"

"I *have* to go," said Kaeryla. "There's no real choice. The Viscount won't agree to an alliance unless he gets the two strongest mages or four lesser mages. Even with two companies of Montgren troopers, you, Sheralt, Valchar, and I can't do what Mother and Father can do in defending Fairhaven. If the Viscount knew about Dorylt and Arthaal, it would be worse."

"Dorylt's older than you," Taelya pointed out.

"Less than a year older, and my shields are stronger. I'm also a healer."

"But—"

"Father wouldn't *ever* let both you and Dorylt go." Kaeryla looked directly at Taelya. "We both know why."

Taelya did, and that bothered her as well, even if Kaeryla was making sense. With Taelya already going to Certis and Dorylt and Taelya's father's death in the last war, there was no way that Beltur and Jessyla would allow both Taelya and Dorylt to leave Fairhaven to fight the Gallosians. Not only that, but both Arthaal and Dorylt stood a better chance of surviving, as did Fairhaven, if Beltur and Jessyla were in charge of defending the town, particularly since Beltur was likely to be a far better and far more experienced commander than anyone else. "I understand all that. I don't have to like it."

"You're going to have to help me get stronger with shields," said Kaeryla. "It's not something—"

"—that you planned for?"

Kaeryla shook her head, then said, "Well, not until the last two eightdays, anyway. I've spent more time practicing blades and wands with Lendar, and Father's been working more on shields with me. I insisted." She looked to Taelya. "I'm having Mother cut my hair short like yours, and Julli's working on a Road Guard uniform for me and a spare set of trousers as well. I'd need them no matter what happens."

Taelya couldn't argue with that.

"But you're not to tell anyone my age. No one. And don't mention my birthday."

"I won't. Have your parents said when we might leave?"

"Within a few days. Most likely not more than an eightday, but not until the companies from Montgren arrive. Father was very specific about that. He sent a dispatch back to the Duchess, the new Duchess, I mean. He said there had already been one attempted attack on Fairhaven's Road Guards by Hydlenese troopers, and he wasn't about to remove the mages and their support squads until Montgren troopers arrived."

"It might be longer than an eightday," said Taelya, "unless they've already mustered the troopers in Vergren. Some of the companies have to come from the north."

"Father thinks some of the companies were already in Vergren."

Taelya still doubted that they'd leave in less than close to an eightday, not when it would take close to two days for the message to reach the Duchess and two solid days for troopers to ride to Fairhaven. "Since we're not leaving soon, we might as well get back to work."

"I think Arthaal got off easy by going to the orchard," said Kaeryla.

"Dorylt didn't," replied Taelya with a smile, knowing all too well how her mother wanted the floors scrubbed.

XXI

The next four days passed, and little changed. The Hydlenese scouts remained, usually on the west end of the same low hill, and Taelya caught hints that more Hydlenese might be posted well south of the border, but they never came close enough for her to clearly discern and confirm their presence. She continued to train guards and their mounts to ride under a concealment, and with each patrol, she had a different half squad, something doubtless arranged by Gustaan or Therran at Beltur's direction, although it was never mentioned.

Following the decision to make Kaeryla a full undercaptain road mage, a fourth daily patrol was added, and the southern patrol route was split into two separate patrols in order to be able to respond more quickly should the Hydlenese appear to be mounting another attack. So far, Beltur had only announced that a contingent of mages and Road Guards would be required to support the Viscount's forces, without providing any details.

Gustaan continued to work with the Lydian troopers, who, with the newer recruits, formed an additional three complete squads of Road Guards, which, even with the squads likely to accompany the mages to Certis, would result in almost a full company remaining in Fairhaven. Taelya had the feeling that Beltur had carefully failed to mention the Lydian refugees to Korsaen or the Duchess, and that made sense to Taelya, given that most were troopers of a sort.

Fiveday afternoon, just before third glass, Taelya's western patrol had stopped in the shade on the south side of the main road where the Weevett road joined it when she sensed a pair of riders heading south toward them.

"We've likely got Montgren couriers headed our way," she announced.

"How far away, ser?" asked Moshart, the squad leader assigned to the half squad.

"Around three kays," replied Taelya.

Moshart offered a questioning look. "I thought you couldn't sense more than two kays. That's what I heard, anyway."

"Lately, it's been closer to three. It could be that trying to find out where the greencoats are has stretched my range. Or maybe it's easier to sense farther in warmer weather."

"The farther, the better for all of us."

Almost two quints passed before the couriers came into view, during which time Taelya sensed the area to the south and west, but found no other travelers.

Another quint went by before the Montgren troopers rode up to the patrol. Then Taelya released the larger shield.

"Welcome to Fairhaven," she called out.

"You haven't had any more attacks by the greencoats, have you?" asked the weathered older courier.

"Not since the first one," replied Taelya. "Do you know what's happened with the Viscount and the Prefect?"

The courier shrugged. "No one tells us anything. Where would we find the majer?"

"At headquarters. We'll accompany you as far as the edge of town." Taelya eased Bounder up beside the older courier, who glanced at the white bands on the end of her tunic sleeves, but said nothing.

She and the two couriers rode at the head of the group, followed by Moshart and the ten rankers. Once more she created a shield and expanded it enough to cover possibly a full company.

Finally, the courier said, "Have there been any folks coming from Certis?"

"Not in the last eightday. Earlier, there were some Kaordists. Only a few chose to stay in Fairhaven."

"Why were they leaving Certis?"

"The Viscount wasn't happy with them, apparently, and he destroyed one small town and killed a lot of the people."

"His own people?" The courier shook his head.

"The Prefect's no better, from what I've heard. How many companies have mustered in Weevett?"

"Three so far. One more is on the way from Vergren. Word is that some are coming here, and some are going to help the Viscount. Doesn't make much sense to me. The Viscount doesn't need any more troopers. He needs mages."

"It's a threat. If Montgren doesn't support him, he'll regard us an enemy." What Taelya didn't say was that there was a second factor, that Korsaen and the Duchess would be far less likely to support Fairhaven unless Fairhaven supplied the heart of the forces going to assist the Viscount—and Fairhaven wasn't strong enough to refuse. *Not yet.*

"Both the Prefect and the Viscount are bastards."

"Don't forget Duke Maastyn," replied Taelya.

The courier snorted.

Once they reached the edge of town, Taelya quietly removed the larger shield and then reined up and turned to Moshart. "If you'd have one of the men escort the couriers to headquarters to see the majer."

"Yes, ser."

Taelya didn't immediately recognize the man assigned, but once the three were on their way, she and Moshart and the rest of the troopers turned back west to continue their patrol. The guard assigned to escort the couriers, who turned out to be Praevyt, a guard Taelya barely knew, rejoined them just after they'd turned south on the narrow road paralleling the Hydolar road.

"Did the majer say anything?" Moshart asked Praevyt.

"He just thanked me and told me to rejoin my patrol."

Taelya nodded.

As the patrol neared the hill from which the Hydlenese scouts had been observing the patrols and the roads, she sensed not two troopers, but four, two on the north side of the hill, and two on the southwest side. For a moment, she frowned. Then she realized that the troopers to the southwest were nearing the Hydolar road and heading away from the hill. *They've just been relieved and are heading back to their encampment or post.*

She knew that the scouts had to have reliefs, but she'd never been close enough to sense the change of duty . . . especially since she'd alternated patrol routes. As the half squad continued south, Taelya kept track of both groups of Hydlenese, but the two southernmost troopers kept heading south until Taelya could no longer sense them.

Nor did she sense any other Hydlenese along the southern road, and the patrol returned to headquarters by the lane that led by Frydika and Worrfan's stead.

Once Taelya logged in her patrol report, signed out, and determined that Beltur was nowhere in headquarters, she returned to the stable yard, where Valchar and Kaeryla immediately stopped her. Taelya didn't see or sense Sheralt anywhere.

"I sensed riders coming to headquarters," said Kaeryla. "They had to be couriers. What did they tell you?"

"Not a single thing except the Duchess is massing troopers in Weevett and that some are supposed to come to Fairhaven . . . and that they had a dispatch for the majer. They didn't know anything else."

"That sounds like we're going to be fighting someone," said Valchar glumly.

"We'll just have to see," said Taelya evenly, while looking sharply at Kaeryla.

"If the Duchess is gathering troopers," added Kaeryla, "it won't be long before we find out."

"Go sign out," Taelya said to Kaeryla. "We can ride back home together . . . although it might be better if we stopped by the Healing House first."

"Why . . . Oh, you think that there's Council meeting?"

"The majer's not here, and couriers arrived."

"Wait for me. We'll go to the Healing House together."

Taelya watched the two hurry into headquarters, then turned as Sheralt and his patrol rode into the stable yard. After turning the half squad over to Varais for dismissal, he rode over to where Tulya stood beside Bounder and reined up.

"You're a little late," she said. "Did you have any trouble?"

"I think they've posted scouts back on the east end of the redstone hills. I can't sense anything clearly, and there's no way to get there from our side of the border without actually climbing up there and crossing the border."

"Why would they post anyone there?"

"It would tell them how long it takes us to go from there to the lane that leads to town or the lane that they used to attack you."

Taelya nodded. "That sounds like someone is planning an attack. Or considering it, at least."

"That's what I'll suggest in my log report. I'd better get to it. What do you know?"

"Two couriers from the Duchess rode in. They didn't know anything except that the Duchess is moving troopers to Weevett and that some may be coming here."

Sheralt winced. "That means some of us will likely be leaving."

"Leaving or staying," replied Taelya, "it's not looking good."

He shook his head. "What are you doing now?"

"Kaeryla and I are going to the Healing House. Jessyla is likely at a Council meeting."

"Of course. Then I'll see you in the morning." He turned his mount toward the stable doors.

A few moments later, Kaeryla reappeared, and the two mounted and rode toward the square. After they reined up, dismounted, and tied their mounts outside the Healing House, Taelya noticed a single horse tied to a corner post of the narrow front porch with blood across the horse's neck. "Someone's been hurt."

The two hurried inside, where they found Margrena in the midst of dealing with a woman with a slash-like wound across her left arm, underneath which was a broken bone.

More than a glass later, between the three of them, they'd cleaned the wound, stitched up the slash, and splinted the arm. Then they sent her off with her consort, one of the Lydian armsmen, with instructions to bring her back the following afternoon.

"How did all that happen?" asked Kaeryla, as she and Taelya cleaned up while Margrena put the supply cabinet back in order.

"They were repairing an old shed and trying to turn it into a small cot. Some sort of timber broke loose and slammed into her arm and the splintered wood slashed her arm and broke it." Margrena shook her head. "I had just stopped the worst of the bleeding when you two showed up. Made dealing with the rest of it a lot easier, thank you."

"I suspect that we just might have to deal with similar wounds before long," said Taelya.

Kaeryla looked at her questioningly.

"Sabre slashes delivered from a charging horse can break bones." Taelya had seen that once, from the window, back when she was seven.

Margrena nodded knowingly, then said, "As soon as you finish here, you two need to head home. You've already had a longer day than you planned."

Neither of the two argued with her, and a quint later they were riding west toward their homes.

"Dinner's supposed to be at our house," offered Taelya, "but if there's been a Council meeting . . ."

"They're still in the Council House," added Kaeryla.

"Then we'll have to see what we can do . . . if you wouldn't mind helping."

As soon as the two reached the stable, they quickly groomed and settled the two horses and then hurried to Taelya's home. On the kitchen table was a short note.

> The burhka's already made. If you get home before I do, you know
> what to do. Use the dough in the green bowl. Punch it down once and
> wait half a quint before you put it in the oven.

Taelya shook her head and handed the note to Kaeryla. "We'll need to put more wood in the stove. I'll take care of that, if you'll set the table."

A quint later, the burhka was gently bubbling, the bread baking, the table set, and Dorylt was home and washing up when Tulya entered the kitchen, her hair slightly disarrayed. "Thank you. I'm glad someone knows what they're doing."

Taelya managed not to wince and said warmly, "With what you'd already done, you didn't leave us too much. Why don't you just sit down?"

Tulya shook her head almost violently. "I can't. I need to move around. I thought better of Korsaen. Or maybe he did the best he could with the new Duchess. Whatever it was . . ." She shook her head again.

"What happened?" asked Kaeryla.

"I'll let your father tell it when he gets here. He might be more objective. Or maybe not." Tulya walked back to the stove and inspected the burhka, after which she poured herself a completely full beaker of ale, something Taelya didn't recall her mother ever doing. Then Tulya took a long swallow, still standing.

Kaeryla looked at Taelya, raising her eyebrows, and Taelya nodded just slightly before saying, "We weren't sure we'd get everything done here. We were later than we expected because we had to help Margrena at the Healing House." She could tell her mother was furious, but wasn't going to talk about it, at least not until Beltur and Jessyla arrived.

"That's not surprising. Everything waits on the Duchess or her dispatches."

Taelya was struggling with what else she might say when there was a rap on the front door, and then Jessyla stepped inside. "It smells so good in here."

"That's because the girls were here to put it together, rather than at a demeaning meeting," replied Tulya bitingly.

Beltur had followed his consort, and Taelya saw him wince and halt, if momentarily, as he stepped into the front room and heard Tulya's words.

Even Jessyla raised her eyebrows, but she replied, "I'm sure that they just got ready what you prepared, and we're all looking forward to it."

"It might be hot enough to get the taste of that dispatch out of my mouth . . . maybe," returned Tulya.

In moments, everyone was in the kitchen, and Dorylt was filling beakers with ale, and handing them out.

As soon as everyone had a beaker, Kaeryla turned to her father and asked, "Just what was in that dispatch?"

"I'll tell you . . . if all of you keep it completely among yourselves and don't mention it while others are around." Beltur surveyed the group.

No one spoke.

After several moments of silence, during which Beltur took a small swallow of ale, he finally said, "The Viscount and the Duchess agreed, rather reluctantly, that four lesser mages are acceptable—"

"You practically had to say that you'd overthrow the Duchess if she didn't accept four mages," said Tulya sourly.

"No," replied Beltur sardonically, "I just told Korsaen that we might as well remove the Duchess and turn Montgren over to Certis if she insisted on agreeing to any proposals by the Viscount that would result in the destruction of Fairhaven."

"He had to know that without you and Jessyla here," snapped Tulya, "there would be no way to defend Fairhaven against Hydlen, now that Duke Maastyn has refused to ally himself formally with either Certis or Gallos."

"Ally formally?" asked Taelya sarcastically.

"That purported neutrality gives Certis no reason to engage in hostilities with Hydlen, but it allows the Prefect to use his ships against the pirates," replied Beltur.

"It also means that the Prefect can't be blamed if Maastyn attacks Montgren," added Jessyla. "Fairhaven, in particular."

"Why is the Duchess opposed to letting us defend ourselves?" asked Dorylt.

"She's afraid that we'll eventually take over Montgren," said Jessyla. "So she'd rather have Certis swallow her land now rather than risk that in the future."

"Fairhaven's a fraction of the size of Vergren," protested Arthaal.

"She wants to make sure we stay that size," said Tulya.

Beltur held up his free hand. "We can't fight them all. We can only bargain for the best terms. Do you want to hear the rest?"

All the others stopped talking.

"In the end, we got about what we expected, as well as a commitment for Montgren to pay not only all our expenses but to provide more golds in years to come."

"When will Montgren troopers arrive?" asked Taelya.

"The first company will be here on eightday, the second on oneday. Our detachment is requested to leave no later than threeday. You and Kaeryla and the other two mages will ride to Weevett to join the two companies headed to Jellico."

"Just two companies?" asked Arthaal.

"Montgren only has five, and two are coming here, and two are going to Certis. If it appears that Maastyn has a much larger force, the reserve company, which likely is understrength and undertrained, will move to Fairhaven."

"Only because the fall of Fairhaven would leave Montgren totally undefended," offered Kaeryla in a sarcastic murmur.

"That's true enough, and likely Korsaen had to point that out to Koralya," Beltur acknowledged.

"How can you be sure of that?" asked Tulya.

Beltur offered a smile both bitter and wry. "Because Maeyora wrote me a personal note saying that."

"Maeyora?" asked Kaeryla.

"Of course," replied Beltur.

Taelya understood immediately. That way, Korsaen could honestly deny that he'd said or written anything to Fairhaven. *And Korsaen probably didn't have to even suggest it.*

At that moment, Taelya saw her mother nod just slightly.

Then Tulya said, "I think we've heard enough, and there's no point in letting the bread or the burhka get cold. If you'd help me serve, Taelya."

Taelya moved to her mother's side near the stove.

XXII

Taelya and Kaeryla arrived at headquarters early on sixday. Taelya wasn't in the slightest surprised to see Valchar and Sheralt walking from the junior officers' quarters almost as soon as they stepped into the stable yard. All four under-captains first turned to their mounts, and, as usual, Taelya and Kaeryla had their horses saddled and ready before either Valchar or Sheralt. The two women stood in the shade to one side of the doors, waiting.

Sheralt joined them after perhaps a tenth of a quint. "You two are here early. That means the majer is going to announce something."

"That's no surprise," said Kaeryla. "We all knew that Montgren couriers arrived yesterday, and that the Council met right after that."

"And you can't tell me anything?"

"We can't tell you what the majer will say," replied Taelya. "He hasn't told us what that will be, but if he had we still couldn't."

"You know the subject, though."

"So do you. It has to be what was in the dispatch for the majer. That's what everyone wants to know," said Taelya.

Valchar laughed as he approached. "I don't know why you bother, Sheralt. They won't tell you."

Sheralt grinned. "I know that, but it's interesting to hear how they avoid answering without lying."

"You're easily amused, then," said Valchar.

"Unlike some," said Taelya, "who seem so bored that they don't work even to stay alive."

"If drudgery be the height of life, why toil on, most elevated muse of magery?" replied Valchar in a tone of lofty dismissal.

"Everything good requires some drudgery, Valchar," interjected Kaeryla, adding gently, "and you ought to know that."

"I don't like condescension," muttered Valchar.

"Taelya's not condescending," replied Kaeryla. "She's trying to get you to do what you need to in order to stay alive . . . and she's the only one of us younger undercaptains who's lived through a real mage war." After a pause, she continued, "It would be nice if you lived through what's coming."

Valchar seemed about to reply, but with Kaeryla's last words, he abruptly shut his mouth.

"Some of the squad leaders are heading into the duty room," said Sheralt. "We probably ought to start heading that way."

When the four entered the duty briefing room, Taelya saw immediately that every officer was there, except for Beltur, as was every squad leader and all the senior guards.

"Must be important," said Sheralt dryly.

"You think so? That maybe we're invading Lydiar?" replied Valchar sarcastically.

"That's a better idea than some," said Sheralt agreeably. "At least it would give us a port."

Conversation stopped as Beltur stepped into the room.

He looked over the assembled Road Guards and mages, then offered an amused smile. "Is there anyone here who doesn't know that the Council received a dispatch from Lord Korsaen yesterday and that the Council spent some considerable time discussing it?" After a momentary pause, he went on. "I thought not. There's been a great deal of gossip about what's happening between Certis, Gallos, Hydlen, and Montgren . . . and how it will affect Fairhaven. As all of you *should* know, Certis and Gallos have been fighting over the Passa River for more than fifteen years. As some of you also know, the Prefect of Gallos sent an envoy to explore alliances with Hydlen and Montgren. And as most of you may not know, the Viscount of Certis has declared in no uncertain terms that if Montgren does not reject that proposal and support Certis, he will attack Montgren. For the past several eightdays, the terms of that support have been hammered out. If Fairhaven does not support those terms, then Montgren will disavow its claim to Fairhaven. That would allow either Certis or Hydlen to attack us without any support from Montgren. We are not in a position to fight Certis by ourselves. Neither is Montgren, with or without Fairhaven. The price for assuring that Certis does not attack us is that we are to supply two squads of Road Guards and four mages, as support for two companies of Montgren troopers who will be part of the Certan force moving on the city of Passera. That control will allow our traders and those of Certis and Montgren to use the Passa River and the lower River Gallos without paying tariffs to Gallos. In return for our guards and mages, Montgren will move two companies of troopers to Fairhaven and will pay and supply them as well as pay and supply our forces that are supporting the Montgren companies."

Two squads? Taelya tried not to wince. That only left one fully trained Road Guard squad, plus the squad of recruits . . . and the Lydian troopers, whose abilities were more than a little suspect. But then, Beltur and Jessyla had managed under worse conditions. *And barely survived . . . while Father did not.*

"Captain Gustaan will be in command of the two squads going to Certis. Those squads are mainly Second and Third Squads, but the captain and I have made some changes in the guards in those squads. The squad listings will be posted after this meeting. The two squad leaders are Barkhan for Squad Two and Varais for Squad Three. The four mages accompanying the squads are Undercaptain Sheralt, Undercaptain Taelya, Undercaptain Valchar, and Undercaptain Kaeryla. The Fairhaven squads will be considered as a company, although no two mages may be detailed to support the Montgren companies without their squads as support—and only to support the Montgren companies. The Fairhaven company will depart for Weevett after the second Montgren company arrives. That departure is to be no later than threeday." Beltur paused, then asked, "Are there any questions?"

After a moment, Sheralt spoke. "What do we do if the Viscount wants to fight beyond taking and defending Passera?"

"The agreement is that this effort must be concluded by the first day of harvest, and that, in the event that Certan forces proceed west beyond Passera, Captain Gustaan will withdraw the Fairhaven company and its mages. Lord Korsaen and the Duchess are well aware of that stipulation. So is the Viscount."

"Ser . . ." ventured Therran, "this doesn't seem like the best . . . for Fairhaven. We fought off Hydlen . . ."

"We fought off Hydlen with three mages and six full companies from Montgren and Lydiar. Lydiar has collapsed. The Prefect will likely quietly support Hydlen, and that leaves Montgren with four solid companies, and a training and reserve company, and us with less than one. Three additional mages aren't likely to make up the difference, not if Certis decides to attack Montgren."

"I see . . . ser."

"Why didn't we build up more troopers? Or why didn't Montgren?" Beltur shook his head. "We can barely pay for the troopers we have, and without the traders who've come to town in the last few years, we'd have a hard time supporting barely two squads. Montgren has a hard time supporting four full companies and a training company." He paused. "If . . . if we can get through this mess without losing too many guards or mages . . . things could get better, possibly much better." He paused, then finally said, "That's all I have for you." With that he turned and left the duty room.

"The changes to Squads Two and Three are being posted right now," said Gustaan. "Those of you staying here won't have any easier a time than those going to Certis. It might even be worse. The majer and I made the changes to make sure that all three squads had about the same capabilities. Undercaptains Sheralt and Valchar are assigned to Squad Two with Senior Squad Leader Barkhan. Undercaptains Taelya and Kaeryla are assigned to Squad Three with Squad Leader Varais. Now . . . for today's patrols . . ."

Taelya was assigned to the west end of the southern patrol with Squad Leader Kuchar, who walked beside her from the building toward the stables.

"Do you know which squad you'll have here?" she asked.

"The captain said that hadn't been decided yet. They're thinking that they might have enough men with the Lydians for five squads . . ."

"But there are some things that need to be worked out?"

"The captain's been drilling the Lydians. The majer's had a few words with them. Things are . . . better." Kuchar's voice was flat.

Taelya managed not to wince.

"Ser . . . do you think we'll have some time . . ."

"To get them into better shape?" Taelya frowned. "No one's said anything to me. With two Montgren companies here, that might give the Hydlenese some concerns about immediately attacking. But then, they also might attack immediately in order to surprise us." Except she realized right after she said the words that she wouldn't be part of the defenders, so she added, "You've probably already thought about that."

"After what you did to them, they might be cautious. They won't likely know that some of our mages are leaving."

"You might not be able to count on that."

"That's true. There are spies and scouts everywhere," replied Kuchar almost morosely.

Taelya wasn't sure about spies, although, with all of the recent arrivals in Fairhaven, that was a possibility, but there was no doubt about the Hydlenese scouts. "Well . . . we'll see where some of the scouts are today."

While she was correct about that, there was nothing at all unusual about the patrol, except for some difficulties in dealing with riding under a concealment. There were two scouts on the north side of the hill, as before, and they were relieved and replaced by two others around third glass. The relieved scouts hurried away, also as before, far enough to the south that Taelya could not discern where the Hydlenese encampment might be. They also only encountered one trading wagon, which belonged to Waaltar and which was returning from Vergren, not fully laden, but not empty.

Once she finished the patrol, signed out, and then groomed the Road Guard mount, Taelya left the stable to find Kaeryla waiting for her.

"We need to go to the Healing House," offered the younger woman. "Mother's put together healing kits for us, and she wants to explain what's in them."

"She wants to explain to me," said Taelya. "You probably know it all." She paused. "Is this in addition to the small kit she gave me earlier?" The one that Taelya hadn't always carried when she patrolled using a Road Guard mount.

"We're to give those to our brothers. She said she wanted to go over the new kits with each of us. Besides, we'll each have to carry our kit back home."

Taelya nodded.

Kaeryla turned and headed south toward the Healing House, adding, "It's strange to think that we'll be leaving Fairhaven in less than an eightday."

"It's even stranger to think that we'll be in Jellico in less than two eightdays."

"You've been in Certis. What's it like?"

"We didn't go through Jellico. Your father wanted to stay as far from the Viscount as we could. We crossed in the north, from Axalt to Rytel and then to the north of Montgren. Everything up there seemed old and dingy. Jellico should be better, but I don't know if it will be."

"Wasn't any place nice?"

"We stayed a few nights at a trader's compound. That was better. The rest . . . even the inns . . ." Taelya shrugged.

When they reached the Healing House and stepped inside, Jessyla was already standing, although Margrena was seated on a straight-backed chair. The head healer gestured to the small table, on which rested two small duffels, empty. Beside each was an array of items. Taelya immediately recognized the cloth bags that likely held brinn, burnet, and knitbone, as well as the narrow roll of canvas, the bound cloth strips, and some carved wooden splints. There was also something that looked like a large set of pincers. Taelya had seen Jessyla use something similar, but hadn't known the name.

"Did Father and Jorhan make the surgical forceps for us?" asked Kaeryla. "They're out of cupridium."

"Arthaal helped some," replied Jessyla with the hint of a smile. "You just might need them to remove arrowheads or large splinters."

Splinters?

Jessyla saw Taelya's expression. "Sometimes lances splinter, and sometimes they hit a trooper's throat and crush it. There's not much you can do about a crushed throat in a battle, because most will die long before you'll see them."

Crushed throat? "Couldn't we use containments to do that?"

Jessyla frowned. "I suppose so, but using our shields as blades is much more effective. It would also take a great deal of control."

Taelya nodded. That made sense.

"I didn't put in bone saws, because neither of you has the expertise to do amputations. You'll also have to use your cupridium belt knives for any cutting. Remember, you're not there for healing. You're there to defeat the Gallosians as quickly as possible with as little risk to you and your troopers as possible. You're only to do healing *after* the fighting's all over . . . and if you have enough order to do it. Is that clear?"

Both younger women nodded.

"The splints are there more for you to show troopers what size and length of wood you need, rather than to use on the first broken bone you get," said Jessyla.

"And don't let anyone tell you different," added Margrena.

Taelya forced herself to concentrate intently as Jessyla explained each item, discovering that she actually remembered more than she'd thought. At the same time, she kept thinking about the use of containments as a weapon.

They might help Dorylt and Arthaal, at least until they get stronger. She decided to think that over more.

Then Jessyla told them, item by item, the best way to pack everything in the very small duffel, watching intently as they did so. When the duffels were packed, she smiled faintly and looked at Taelya. "Your mother likely will have dinner ready within a quint after we get there." She turned and began to close the inside shutters nearest the table.

Taelya and Kaeryla immediately moved to deal with the other shutters, and in moments the Healing House was closed up and the four were walking home.

The healing kit, which couldn't have weighed even half a stone, felt much heavier than that to Taelya.

XXIII

Sevenday found Taelya once again paired with Arthaal, with Daevoryt as squad leader, while Valchar was dealing with Dorylt as an undercaptain trainee. Before she mounted the Road Guard gelding, Taelya tied a large bag full of small stones she'd gathered earlier to her saddle so that she could work with Arthaal in a fashion similar to what she'd done briefly the night before with Dorylt, not quite surreptitiously.

Arthaal looked at the bag. "What do you have there?"

"Something that might improve your use of containments."

For a moment, Arthaal's face stiffened.

"Your father will have enough on his hands once we leave. This will start another part of your training." With that, Taelya mounted and turned the gelding toward the center of the courtyard where Daevoryt had mustered his men.

In the still air that was almost as warm as a summer morning, although the beginning of summer was more than four eightdays away, she glanced to the northeast. There were no signs of either clouds or a breeze, and that meant the day would definitely be summer-like—warm and muggy.

After several moments, Arthaal mounted and followed her.

In less than a third of a quint, Taelya was leading the half squad south from headquarters toward the lane that ran past Frydika's stead. She turned in the saddle to Arthaal and said, "Let's see a containment."

Arthaal created one hanging in the air between their mounts.

"Show me the largest one you can manage."

The younger mage concentrated before forming an oblong roughly two yards by one and a yard deep.

"That's much better. You can release it." Taelya leaned forward slightly and eased a stone out of the bag that hung from the saddle just in front of her knee. "I'm going to throw a stone into the air out in front of you. You need to capture it with a containment before it strikes the ground. You're not to look at me. You need to react to when the stone comes into view." As she finished speaking, Taelya tossed the stone in an arc over Arthaal.

The stone fell without Arthaal even reacting.

"You just lost a trooper," said Taelya. "Or you would have if you'd been patrolling and an archer fired at your squad." She extracted another two stones from the bag.

"I wasn't ready."

"The Hydlenese—or anyone else—won't care if you're ready." Taelya didn't snap, but her voice was edged. "You'd better be ready all the time from now on." This time, she silently counted to nine before tossing another stone.

Arthaal managed a small containment, but not quickly enough to catch the stone.

"That's two men you could have lost." She immediately arched another stone over Arthaal's head.

He didn't even react.

"Arthaal . . ." Taelya's voice was like cold cupridium. "This is not a game. You will be holding the lives of other men in your hands. You owe it to them, if not to yourself, to improve enough to give them a chance. We are *always* outnumbered. We cannot afford to lose a single trooper because we are careless or unprepared."

"But this isn't real. We can sense—"

"No, you can't. When there's a company of troopers riding at you, you can't sense who's loosing shafts at you. You can only pick out the shafts—or take down whatever trooper is likely to attack the men closest to you. You're not strong enough to hold a wall shield for more than a few moments. You are strong enough to use containments quickly to block weapons or single riders. Also, this exercise will strengthen all your abilities." She paused, extracting two more stones.

"How can I take down a trooper with small containments?" Arthaal's voice contained traces of both irritation and frustration.

"You put a small containment around his neck, then squeeze it shut as fast and as hard as you can. You do it with strength, and you'll crush his throat in moments. But, without practice at seeing a moving target and getting a containment around it, you won't be fast enough to do it. Learning to do this gives you another weapon."

"How did you come up with this?"

"From what your mother taught me at the Healing House. She didn't have the idea, but she said it would work, if you couldn't use your shields the way she and Kaeryla can."

"That doesn't sound like her," said Arthaal dubiously.

"It wasn't her idea. It was mine, based partly on some training your father gave me and Sheralt. You're not strong enough yet to use your shields the way your mother and your sister do. This will give you and Dorylt a weapon you can both use until you are that strong." *And it might just let you survive until you are that strong.*

"Oh . . ."

"Now . . . are you going to try, or do I have to tell your parents, especially your mother, that you're selfish and lazy?"

At the word "mother," Arthaal stiffened slightly. "I'll try."

"And it's 'I'll try, ser,'" said Taelya. She followed her words with another stone.

Arthaal almost contained the stone, but was a moment too late.

"That's better." Taelya followed with another.

Finally, Arthaal actually trapped the stone within a containment.

"Good. I'm going to wait awhile. How long I won't tell you, and after that, you'll get stones intermittently and without warning. Once you get that down, you can work on the squeezing part."

While she rode southward, Taelya extracted several more stones from the bag, but she didn't toss another one until the patrol was nearly to Frydika's stead.

Almost predictably, Arthaal was late in forming his containment.

Taelya tossed another stone within moments, and Arthaal managed to catch that one. Taelya followed with a third one, which Arthaal missed.

"In a fight, nothing's predictable," she said coolly, although there was a slight edge to her voice.

"Why are you being so hard?" he murmured.

"Because I'm trying to save your life."

Arthaal must have sensed the truth behind her words, because he swallowed, then said, "I'll try harder."

After that exchange, Arthaal began to catch more and more of the stones, and after about a glass, Taelya said, "No more stones for a while. You can do it if you concentrate. You need to rest from that. In another quint, we'll work on your ability to sense at a distance."

Then she took out her bottle of watered ale and took a long swallow, looking ahead to where the lane joined the southern road. She didn't yet sense any riders, but she wasn't quite close enough to the border to sense that far, and since her encounter with the Hydlenese, none of the greencoats she'd sensed had crossed into Fairhaven lands.

That could change any time.

Once they turned west on the southern road, Taelya turned to Daevoryt. "Prepare for riding under a concealment."

"Yes, ser." He turned in the saddle. "Prepare concealment lines!"

Taelya turned to Arthaal. "You'll have to use your senses to keep beside me and to stay on the road."

"Yes, ser."

"Squad ready for concealment, ser," reported Daevoryt.

"Beginning concealment."

In the darkness created by the concealment, Taelya always felt warmer although she knew that there was no reason that she should, but when she ended the concealment a quint later and a kay farther west, she was sweating, and to her, the air felt cooler.

At that point, the patrol had just passed the middle of the small thick forest on the north side of the southern road. Taelya rode only a few hundred yards farther before she began to get the feeling of riders to the southwest. She turned to Arthaal. "We'll be approaching the lane to the burned-out stead before long. What do you sense?"

"There's a small flock of sheep on the northern side of the road on the grasslands just west of the woods."

"Is there anyone on the road ahead beyond where you can see?"

"No, ser. Not for about a kay, anyway."

"Do you have any feelings about the road beyond them?"

"Not yet . . ." Arthaal paused, then said, "There might be someone, something off to the south . . . and there's someone in the bluffs up ahead."

"Are you sure about that?" asked Taelya evenly, although she had already sensed both the single man, likely a scout with a flag or some signaling device, and what appeared to be half a squad of troopers.

Arthaal concentrated. "It's clearer now. There are several riders. I can't tell how many. I think they're on that lane into Hydlen, the one to the burned-out stead."

"Good!" Taelya turned in the saddle. "Squad Leader, there's a half squad of riders on the lane into Hydlen up ahead on the left. They're not moving, but they're waiting just about on the border. I'll let you know if they move."

"Thank you, ser."

Taelya turned to Arthaal. "Why is there a single man in the bluffs?"

"He must be a scout."

"You're right. Keep that in mind in the future. Also, if they have scouts out, it's more likely that they don't have a mage. Now . . . tell me if the Hydlenese move and where they seem to be headed."

Arthaal looked as if he might question something, but then just said, "Yes, ser."

Another quint passed before Arthaal said, "They're moving toward us. Not very fast. Maybe a fast walk."

"Tell that to the squad leader."

Arthaal cleared his throat, then said, "Squad Leader, the Hydlenese are moving toward the road at a fast walk."

"Thank you, ser."

The Hydlenese were about a kay away, and if both half squads kept moving, they'd see each other in less than half a quint.

As she rode the next several hundred yards, Taelya kept close track of the Hydlenese, who continued to move north toward the southern road at a steady pace. She could clearly discern eleven riders—suggesting a squad leader and half a squad, rather than an officer, a squad leader, and ten men, but that was only a suggestion. She extended her senses, but as far as she could discern, there were no other Hydlenese near. There was no way of telling whether the Hydlenese were merely scouting or preparing for an attack on the patrol.

Or perhaps probing to see if an attack is feasible. And since there was little point to using so many men for reconnaissance, either a probe or an attack was likely.

Before that long, Taelya could see dust and riders. "Arms ready! Close up behind us."

"Arms ready!" repeated Daevoryt. "Closing up."

The greencoats were less than two hundred yards from the southern road and continued to close the gap.

"Squad halt!" ordered Taelya once she was just over a hundred yards from where the lane joined the south road. She wanted to make certain that the Hydlenese intended to attack before she acted.

The Hydlenese kept coming, then turned onto the road heading toward the patrol. Abruptly, they reined up, then immediately loosed shafts. Taelya extended her shield just enough to cover her troopers, and the first volley of arrows skittered off it, as did the second. Following a third volley, the greencoats stowed their bows and charged. The moment the last arrows slid off her shield, Taelya dropped the larger shield and threw a narrow-targeted bolt at the lead rider, followed by a second. The chaos burned through the first trooper's chest, and the second struck the shoulder of the trooper beside him. Almost immediately, the Hydlenese turned. The turn slowed the greencoats for several moments, and Taelya fired off two more chaos bolts, one of which missed, before she felt that the Hydlenese were too far away for targeting to be effective.

As the dust began to settle, and the black mists that Taelya realized were death mists had dispersed, she confirmed that no other troopers were nearby. Then she studied the road ahead. Two dead troopers lay on the lane, as well as one downed horse and rider. She winced, wishing that she'd been able to get the greencoat without taking out the horse. Then she saw a single riderless horse draw up farther down the road. "Strip the bodies and take the gear and weapons! Let's see if we can catch the extra mount."

"Yes, ser," replied Daevoryt, his voice flat.

Taelya decided not to react to that. *Not now.* Instead, she largely let Daevoryt's men follow her order, although she did use a containment or two to help them catch the Hydlenese mount.

Once the patrol was on its way again, heading farther west, Arthaal turned in the saddle and asked, "Why did you throw chaos after the Hydlenese turned? The skirmish was over."

"The war is just beginning," replied Taelya. "That's three troopers you and the others defending Fairhaven won't have to face. Besides, they were on Montgren territory and attacked us. They were hoping to find a patrol without a mage so that they could destroy or weaken it. They know they have the advantage of numbers. If they'd withdrawn without attacking I wouldn't have used chaos."

Arthaal was silent.

"If I hadn't been here," asked Taelya in return, "what would you have done?"

"I could have raised a shield against the arrows for a few moments with each volley."

"That would have helped. What then?"

"I suppose I could have contracted my shields and blocked the worst of the attack if they charged us."

"You could. What if you'd used small containments to crush the throats of the lead riders?"

"Would that have stopped them?"

"It might have. At the very least it would have given your men better odds." She waited a moment, then added, "Do you sense any more Hydlenese?"

"Only the one behind us in the bluffs. He's moved south and west." Arthaal pointed almost due south. "That way."

"Always check right after a skirmish or battle to see if anyone's crept up on you while you were fighting."

"You sound like Father."

"Where do you think I learned all that?" Taelya didn't mention that she'd heard Beltur say similar things to both Arthaal and Kaeryla. Kaeryla had clearly paid more attention, but that might have been because she was older . . . or more attuned to her father's tone of voice. Then, she reflected, Dorylt was less than two years older than Arthaal, and he'd just recently started paying more attention.

The remainder of the patrol was uneventful, but Beltur was waiting for her, Arthaal, and Daevoryt when they signed off duty.

He looked at Taelya. "You seem to draw Hydlenese attacks. What happened?"

Taelya told him, making sure that she went through the attack step by step.

Then Beltur looked at Daevoryt. "Do you have anything to add . . . anything at all?"

"No, ser . . . well . . . except that the undercaptain was careful to explain all her actions to the trainee undercaptain . . . after it was all over."

"Thank you, Daevoryt. You can go."

Once the squad leader left, Beltur looked at Arthaal. "How do you feel now?"

"They just . . . attacked, ser. They didn't give any warning."

"Why would they? Warning us isn't to their advantage." Beltur smiled sadly. "I wouldn't wish this on anyone your age, but it's better you saw it with Taelya by your side. You two take care of your mounts. We'll talk later."

As Taelya and Arthaal left the building, Arthaal murmured, "He was so calm."

Taelya shook her head. "Underneath he wasn't all that calm. He's worried. Possibly that the Hydlenese might bring up all their forces before the Montgren companies arrive." *And he can't help but be worried about you.* But she didn't say that to Arthaal, because that was the last thing he needed to hear at the moment.

Once they were outside and in full late-afternoon sun, Taelya realized that her uniform was still damp, although she didn't recall sweating that much.

When they reached where they'd tied their mounts, Arthaal blotted his brow with his forearm sleeve, then untied his mount. He looked at Taelya. "Thank you. I don't think . . . I understood . . ."

"You would have, sooner or later. This way, it wasn't quite so brutal as it could have been."

"I worry about that."

"We all do."

"I'll be working more on containments." He turned and led his horse into the stable.

Almost the moment Arthaal was out of sight Daevoryt walked over to where Taelya stood. "You worked him hard, ser, even before the attack."

"You think I was too hard on him?"

"That's not for me to say, ser."

"I think you just did." Taelya smiled wryly. "I wouldn't have pressed him that hard, except that it's likely the last time I'll work with him before I leave for Certis. And there's no way he could have learned that without someone putting him through those exercises time and time again. It's also better that he get pressed that hard before men die because he can't use his magery effectively."

"The Hydlenese may have helped in making that point."

Taelya hoped so.

"Might I ask how . . . those containments . . ."

"The small containments aren't as effective as a chaos bolt, but he's a black, and that gives him a weapon to use. He can also use it to pick off arrows if they're loosed infrequently. Just as important, the next time he tries to use containments, he'll be much stronger."

"I've . . . never heard of anything like . . . that, ser."

Neither had Taelya, but she said, "Is there any difference to a Hydlenese trooper between a blade or a lance crushing his throat or a mage using a containment to do it?"

"It . . . just seems different, ser."

Taelya remembered something Beltur had once said. "Dead is dead, Daevoryt. Does it really matter what weapon is used? Especially if it saves your men?" And since Daevoryt wasn't going to Certis, it would be his men.

"When you put it that way, ser . . ."

After the squad leader left, as Taelya led the Guard horse into the stable, she couldn't help wondering why Daevoryt, or any of them, thought that using magery to kill was somehow less honorable or more suspect than using arrows, sabres, knives, or lances.

XXIV

On eightday morning, Taelya was up early enough to start fixing breakfast before Tulya woke and entered the kitchen, but her mother soon arrived.

"You didn't have to get up early today, especially after yesterday."

"I couldn't sleep any longer. I woke up thinking about it." *And about Dorylt.*

"You were thinking about containments, weren't you? That you didn't come up with the idea of using them as weapons until the other night when you made Dorylt practice with them while you threw stones?"

Taelya nodded as she scooped off a dollop of lard and dropped it into the skillet. "I should have thought of it sooner." Next, she began to chop up the small chunk of ham that she would add to the egg scramble.

"Why is it just your responsibility? Beltur or Jessyla could have thought of it just as well. Or Sheralt or Valchar."

"No. Sheralt and Valchar can't do containments. Or barely," she added.

"Why are you talking about containments?" said Dorylt, walking into the kitchen and then yawning. "I'm getting better every day."

"I just wish I'd thought about how you could use them as a weapon earlier," replied Taelya.

"It wouldn't have made much difference," said Dorylt as he half filled his beaker with ale. "I haven't been able to do containments well enough except in the last eightday or so. Neither has Arthaal." He carried the beaker to the table, where he sat down. "You asked if I'd bring some of the spoiled small green apples from the orchard. There weren't that many, and Taarna told me to make sure I only took the bruised ones or ones that the birds or bugs had spoiled. I didn't have that much time, either, but I managed to come up with almost half a bucket."

"Thank you."

"Why did you want them?"

"So you can make sure that when you shrink your containment it's strong enough to do what it has to."

"I think it's time to stop talking about containments," said Tulya firmly. "It's time for breakfast. Taelya, you can work with Dorylt on containments after breakfast. And I'd appreciate it if you don't talk about them when everyone comes for dinner."

"What are we having?" asked Dorylt.

"Just roasted fowl with cheesed new potatoes and little carrots."

Taelya broke the three eggs into the skillet, where the fat had begun to sizzle, and, using a wooden spatula, scrambled them before adding the ham chunks. Dorylt rose and set out three platters, and Tulya grated some of the rock-hard white cheese into a small bowl that she held for Taelya so that her daughter could add the cheese to the scramble before serving it.

Along with the leftover bread from the night before, breakfast was adequate, although Taelya knew it would have been better if her mother had made it, but it made her feel better to do something for her mother.

Once they cleaned up breakfast and their rooms, Taelya took Dorylt outside with the bucket of spoiled apples.

"What do you want me to do?" asked Dorylt.

"I'll throw an apple into the air. I want you to put a containment around it, one the size that you'd use on a greencoat's neck. Then I want you to immediately squeeze it as small as you can, enough to squish the apple to a pulp."

"So I can do that to a greencoat trooper?"

"That's the point," replied Taelya. "If you can't do something to them, they'll keep attacking and trying to kill our men. The faster and sooner that you can take out some of their men, the better." She set down the bucket by her feet and grabbed several of the apples. "Ready?"

"Any time."

Taelya tossed the first apple in an arc that reached as high as a mounted rider.

Dorylt's containment caught the apple, but both apple and containment remained horse-high. Belatedly, juice squeezed out of the apple, and Dorylt released the containment.

"That's a good start. Can you do it faster?"

"I'll try."

Taelya threw another apple.

Dorylt contained the apple immediately, but it still took a moment for him to squeeze it to a pulp. "That's harder than I thought."

"It'll be even harder with someone riding toward you."

"Thank you so much for the encouraging words."

"You're most welcome." Taelya tossed another apple.

Two quints later, Dorylt was catching and squeezing the apples almost instantly, and that was good, Taelya thought, since they were out of apples and since Dorylt was sweating heavily in the late-morning sunlight and his order levels were slightly but noticeably lower. "That's all for now. You've got it as worked out as we can do now."

"I need to cool off and then wash up . . . again." He paused. "Thank you. This will help."

Taelya just hoped it would help her brother enough that he would survive any Hydlenese attack.

"The Gallosians aren't going to be at all happy with you," Dorylt said cheerfully. "You have a nasty way with order and chaos."

"I'm not happy that I have to have a nasty way," she replied. "If they'd just leave us alone . . ."

"The only way they'll leave us alone is when they have to, just like when Uncle Beltur had to slaughter hundreds of them. Before it's all over, you'll have to do something like that as well . . . if you want them to leave us alone."

Before coming inside, Taelya used the water tap to wash the apple residue out of the bucket, then set it on the kitchen-door stoop to dry before she returned to the kitchen to help her mother fix dinner.

As soon as Taelya closed the kitchen door, Tulya turned from the worktable, where she was chopping spring scallions. "Taelya . . . ?"

"Yes?"

"Thank you. For working with Dorylt."

"I just wish I'd thought of it sooner."

"We all wish that at times. I certainly have. There are so many . . ." Tulya shook her head. "You're barely twenty-three years old. You can't think of everything. And, thinking of that, if you're looking for your riding jacket, you won't find it. I took yours and Kaeryla's to Julli. She's lining them so they'll be better for colder weather."

"But we're heading into summer."

"That's true, but you almost froze riding patrols this winter. The best time to deal with problems is before you have to. I should have thought about that sooner."

Taelya stiffened. "What did you find out?"

"Nothing more. We haven't heard anything new. I'm just trying to think ahead. Now . . . if you'd finish here . . ."

"I can do that." Taelya managed to smile, although she worried about the reasons behind her mother making their riding jackets warmer. *It has to be because the Easthorns in summer are colder than Fairhaven in winter, and she knows you two are going.* That really wasn't surprising, but it was a reminder of reality.

Almost five glasses passed before everything was ready. Seemingly in moments after Taelya took the bread from the oven, there was a rap on the front door.

Kaeryla and Arthaal were the first into the house, and Arthaal immediately asked, "What smells so good."

"Roast fowl," replied Taelya, rising from her chair in the front room, a chair into which she had settled less than half a quint earlier.

"Your mother's fowl is always good," said Kaeryla.

"That it is," added Jessyla as she and Beltur entered the house. "Kaeryla, see if she needs any help."

Kaeryla nodded and headed for the kitchen.

Beltur stopped just inside the door and gestured for Taelya to join him. At that gesture Arthaal hurried toward the kitchen. "I'll help Dorylt."

Taelya moved around the settee in front of the cold hearth, then stopped several steps from her uncle and waited to see what he had to say, although she had a general idea of the subject.

"Yesterday you worked with Arthaal on a particular exercise with stones and containments. This morning I saw you tossing green apples for Dorylt to catch with containments," said Beltur, adding half-humorously, "Spoiled, I hope?"

"He said Taarna was very clear about that," replied Taelya. "He only had a half bucket of spoiled apples."

"Wouldn't stones have done as well? The way you did with Arthaal?"

"Not for what I had Dorylt do today. I needed the apples so he could figure out how much force to use to turn them to pulp quickly. I didn't have time to get apples for Arthaal yesterday, because I only thought of the idea on sixday night."

Beltur winced, if slightly, partly opened his mouth, then closed it and did not speak.

"I wanted to give them a weapon they could use right now, until they're strong enough to use their shields the way you and Aunt Jessyla do."

"That could be dangerous . . . they're both young."

"Dorylt's older than Kaeryla, ser."

"Both of you are older than your age. They're not."

"But they're likely going to have to do their best to protect troopers . . . and without weapons—"

"They're better with blades than most greencoats."

Taelya was having trouble understanding why her uncle was so opposed to what she had done. "You've already said they'll have to fight. Why do you think I'm wrong to help them this way?" She worried as well because she saw Jessyla moving to join them.

"Using containments that way . . . at their age—"

Before Beltur could say any more, Jessyla put her hand on Beltur's shoulder. "I know how you feel, but she's right, dear."

Beltur opened his mouth, as if to protest, then looked at his consort. After a moment, he shook his head and smiled almost sheepishly. "I should know better than to argue with any of the women in this family." He paused. "I don't worry so much about Dorylt, but Arthaal won't even be fourteen until harvest, and that's young to be given a weapon like that." Before either woman could speak, he quickly added, "I think I let my worries get in the way of what he'll have to do. I'm thinking of him as a boy, and he can't be that any longer. Not now. But I have to say that it bothers me."

"You're trying to give him the childhood you never had," said Jessyla, "and he's had more than you did. But . . . now . . ." She shrugged sadly.

For a long moment, Beltur did not speak. Then he shook his head once more. "I'd hoped that we'd have a little more time."

"Almost sixteen years is far more than we could have hoped for," Jessyla pointed out.

"As usual, dear, you're right. I just don't have to like it." Then he forced a smile. "We should enjoy dinner."

The last eightday dinner we'll all likely share for some time. Taelya managed not to swallow at that realization.

XXV

Once dinner was over, the dishes washed and racked to dry, and Dorylt had retreated to his room, Taelya turned to her mother, but before she could speak, Tulya did.

"Something's bothering you, isn't it? You've been looking in my direction for the last quint."

Taelya smiled wryly, thinking that while her mother might not be a mage she still was very perceptive. "I have a question. Maybe several questions . . ."

"Ask them. Don't make me guess. I'm a little tired for that."

"They're about Uncle Beltur. Did Aunt Jessyla tell you about what he said to me just after they arrived?"

"She said that Beltur asked you about how you came up with the idea of using small containments as a weapon for Dorylt and Arthaal. Was there anything else?"

"At first, he seemed worried and upset that I'd done that. Then he said that he was more worried about my teaching Arthaal because he wasn't even fourteen yet. Aunt Jessyla told him that she understood how he wanted Arthaal to have a childhood, but that Arthaal had had much more than Beltur. She said

I was right and that Arthaal needed to know how to defend himself. Those weren't the words, but that that was her message."

"I can believe that. What's your question?"

"There's something I don't understand. He's put himself in danger time after time. He's let Aunt Jessyla do the same. He's pushed me and Kaeryla to do patrols, but he worries about pushing Dorylt and Arthaal?"

Tulya nodded. "You're right about Jessyla. Beltur *let* her take the risks. What you don't know is that she pushed him. From the beginning, she pushed to learn how to become a mage. She insisted on going into battle. I think she was afraid he would do too much and get himself killed."

Taelya managed not to wince at what her mother hadn't said—that she hadn't had the magely ability to do the same for her own consort—Taelya's father. "What about me . . . and Father?"

"Your father knew he had to fight. Beltur never pushed him. I think Beltur felt that it wasn't his place to try to change an older and experienced mage. In some ways, now I wish Beltur had. Your father could have learned from Beltur, but your father never asked, and Beltur doesn't like to impose on people. He will, but he doesn't like it. He'd rather risk himself than risk others. I think that's one reason why he's pushed himself so hard. That way, he doesn't feel quite so bad when he orders others to do things."

"But he pushed me."

"Especially in the beginning. That was because he felt responsible. By healing you, it's quite possible he turned you from a black into a white, and that was his fault, he felt. Part of that might be because you're the only white mage any of us know who is a woman. You had abilities that could kill people by the time you weren't much past seven. That was why he was always watching you after your father died. He pushed you in ways to make sure that you'd always have control of those abilities."

Taelya stood there in the kitchen, her mind going back over the past, trying to remember, bit by bit, each skill that Beltur had taught her and most definitely recalling that he'd worked with her and tutored her on shields at first, almost to the exclusion of everything else. She'd been almost fifteen before he'd seriously worked her in using chaos bolts. Still . . . "He just pushed me to refine how I threw chaos bolts."

"Doesn't that give you more control?" asked Tulya.

After a moment, Taelya nodded. "But that doesn't explain about Arthaal."

"From what I know, Beltur never really was allowed to be a child. His mother died when he was around six, I think, and his father died when he was nine. His uncle loved Beltur and did his best, but I doubt his younger years were all that good. Didn't Beltur play with you as well as teach you?"

"After the war with Hydlen."

"You had your father before that. Beltur would never have wanted to even come close to getting between you."

Taelya continued to stand there, thinking.

"Does that help, dear?"

"I think so . . ."

"Everyone thinks of him as this powerful and calculating mage. In some ways he is. In others, he's like the rest of us. He has his weaknesses. One of them is that, except when he's fighting, he doesn't like to dictate. He can, and he has, but he avoids it when he can. Why do you think there's still a Council, and it's one where everyone's voice is heard? Not only heard, but listened to."

"He's killed people, not just in war."

Tulya shook her head. "Only when someone innocent or someone he cared for was threatened. Remember, in Spidlar, he saved your father and almost died because he did." After several moments, Tulya asked, "Do you have any other questions?"

"Why . . . why didn't Father learn from Beltur?"

"That might have been as much my fault as his. Part of the problem was that your father was very traditional. He didn't like change that much. Neither did I, especially back then." Tulya's voice lowered as she spoke, almost to a trembling whisper. "We had to leave Elparta for two reasons. One was because you were a white, and your father and I suspected that was because of what Beltur had to do to save you. No one else could have done what he did. We were grateful. Overjoyed, truly . . . but bitter that the cost was that we had to leave the only home we knew. The other reason we had to leave was because we were considered friends with Beltur, although at the time we were really little more than acquaintances. Then we were pushed out of Axalt because of what Beltur did. It would have happened later, anyway, but the timing was such that we ended up in Fairhaven in time to be in another war. Let us say that I harbored some reservations about Beltur. No . . . I almost hated him for everything that happened to us. I even wondered how Jessyla could love him . . ." Tulya's voice trailed off, and she swallowed.

"But . . ." Taelya wasn't quite sure what to say to the last.

"When your father died . . . I can't tell you . . . it hurt so much . . . and I wanted to lash out . . . but . . . Beltur and Jessyla both almost died . . . and Beltur just lay there for days . . . and he was so young . . . and I didn't want Jessyla to hurt the way I did . . ." Tulya blotted her tears with her fingertips. "I began to realize how basically good he was and that he was just a young man only a few years older than you are now . . . just doing his best to work things out in an unfair world, and there was no way to change what had happened."

"Have you told him . . . or Aunt Jessyla?"

"What good would that do? They've done everything they can for us . . . I should have talked to you about this sooner . . . but there never seemed to be the right moment."

"I wondered . . . I wondered a lot, but I didn't want to ask. You always are so . . . so in control. But . . . I'm leaving . . . and I wanted to know."

"I'm glad you asked. Your father . . . he would have been so proud of you. I am, too . . . more than I say . . ."

Taelya could feel the tears welling up, and all she could do was swallow for several moments. Finally, she said, "You always showed me that you were, but . . ."

"I never said it, and I should have. That was a mistake."

"You didn't have to tell me. I knew."

"You shouldn't have had to guess, but we all make mistakes, more when we're young. I never wanted to burden you or Dorylt with my faults . . . or Jessyla and Beltur. I'm not about to burden them with my faults. I'm only telling you so that you know, and so that you won't blame Beltur for my mistakes. He has enough trouble dealing with what he regards as his own failures."

"His own?"

"Two men saved him. His uncle sacrificed himself so that Beltur could escape the Prefect's white mages. Athaal—we've talked about him and you might faintly remember him—he and Meldryn took Beltur in when he had nowhere to go, and Athaal trained him to become a black mage . . . but Athaal—"

"He was the other mage who saved Father in Elparta."

"He was, but he died doing it, and Beltur's always blamed himself for not being able to get close enough to save them both. He also blames himself for your father's death, although none of us blame him, and none of us can still figure out any way it could have been avoided without Fairhaven being destroyed and almost everyone being killed."

"All of this is why you never let me say anything bad about Beltur?"

Tulya laughed softly and wryly. "You've always been free to comment on his decisions. I just didn't let you attack his character. There's a difference."

Taelya could see that . . . now.

"Any more questions?"

"Not exactly a question. He's offered to help Valchar and Sheralt to improve their shields. He's even given them the first steps toward doing it. Neither of them tried." Taelya paused. "I pushed Sheralt . . . well, I did more than that. I crushed his shields and told him he was an idiot and that I wouldn't even pay attention to his death if he didn't start working on his shields. Valchar ran off. He's been wary of me ever since. Sheralt's slowly been improving his shields and the way he throws chaos bolts . . ."

"That's not a question. You're looking for a compliment," said Tulya dryly.

After a moment, Taelya replied, "I suppose I am. But was I wrong to press Sheralt?"

"What else have you done with Valchar?"

"Nothing. I offered. He turned away."

"You also offered to Sheralt. Perhaps more forcefully than you should have. But he responded. You did what you thought was right, and you didn't actually force either of them to change their shields." Tulya yawned. "Has any of this helped?"

Taelya immediately nodded. "Yes. I still need to think about it."

"Then you think. I'm going to bed. I'm not as young as you are."

Taelya stepped forward and put her arms around her mother, holding her tightly. "Thank you."

Tulya's arms went around her daughter. "You'll make your own mistakes. Maybe you can learn from mine."

Once her mother left the kitchen, Taelya sat down at the table. She had the feeling she wasn't going to sleep all that soon.

XXVI

Taelya had no more than stepped into the duty room on oneday morning, accompanied by Kaeryla, Dorylt, and Arthaal, than Valchar immediately cornered her. "Wasn't the first Montgren company supposed to arrive yesterday?"

"That was what I heard, but the majer didn't say anything, and I certainly didn't sense any large numbers of riders yesterday."

Valchar looked at the other three mages. "Did you?"

"No more than you," answered Kaeryla, while Dorylt and Arthaal shook their heads.

"Sheralt and I didn't, either. I checked with the duty squad leader. There haven't been any couriers. Do you think the majer will say anything today?"

"I don't know," replied Taelya. "He hasn't said anything to any of us. Not about anything like that."

"Do you think something's happened?"

"Probably, but it's more likely to be a delay because of problems with supplies or wagons or something like that. When the second company comes is what determines when we leave." Taelya was about to say more when Sheralt hurried into the room, followed by Gustaan and Beltur.

Everyone turned toward the majer.

Beltur offered a good-natured grin. "No . . . I haven't heard anything from either Weevett or Vergren. Since I haven't, it's likely that we'll see some troopers today or tomorrow. Then again, I could be wrong. At the same time, I've made it very clear to the Duchess that none of our forces or mages will be leaving until at least two Montgren companies are posted here under my command."

Taelya hadn't heard Beltur mention the last point, although she always assumed that he would be the one in charge of the forces defending Fairhaven.

"In the meantime," Beltur went on, "we'll be continuing regular patrols with undercaptain trainees. We will also be posting scouts to observe the Hydolar road and the lane from the burned-out stead. The reorganized squads remaining in Fairhaven will continue to work on maneuver training until further notice. Captain Gustaan will announce patrol assignments." After his last words, Beltur nodded to the captain, then turned and left the duty room.

Gustaan assigned Sheralt the eastern half of the southern road, along with Dorylt, while Taelya once more was given the western section of the southern road, with Arthaal, and Varais as squad leader.

As Taelya and Arthaal walked toward the stable, Arthaal said quietly, "Father had me bring a sack of small apples. He said you'd know what to do with them."

Taelya managed not to show any surprise. "I do. You'll be doing some of the exercises I had Dorylt doing yesterday."

"Dorylt said they weren't too bad . . . after a while."

"Most exercises that help are hard in the beginning." *Or tedious, if not both.*

Before they mounted up, Dorylt unfastened the bag from his horse and handed it to Taelya, who tied it to the saddle in front of her left knee. Then the two rode to join Varais and her half squad.

"Good morning, sers," offered Varais. "The men are ready to ride."

"Then we should head out," replied Taelya, gesturing for Varais to ride on her right and Arthaal on her left for the moment, although they'd have to go to riding two abreast once they passed Frydika's stead on the way south.

"Squad! Forward!"

Once everyone was moving steadily, Varais turned to Taelya. "Do you think the greencoats will try another attack?"

Taelya smiled wryly. "You'd have to ask them. If I'd been in their position, I wouldn't have tried either one."

"Why do you think they did?"

"If I had to guess, I'd say that someone told Duke Maastyn that some of our mages were going to Certis to be part of an attack on Passera."

The squad leader nodded. "You don't think the Prefect wants Hydlen to take over Fairhaven?"

That's not quite it. Taelya paused, thinking. Finally, she said, "I think the Prefect wants to weaken both Hydlen and Fairhaven." *And he wouldn't be that unhappy if something happened to Beltur.*

"Word is that the Prefect is sending ships against the pirates."

"We don't know that yet, but if he does that will make it harder for them to pay tariffs to the Duke."

"They're pirates, and they pay tariffs?"

"Not what they should, according to the majer, but they'd rather pay that than force the Duke to send troops to Worrak. And the Duke accepts lower tariffs because he doesn't want to fight a civil war. The Duke and the pirates have an uneasy agreement. If the Duke is stupid enough to upset it, it's to the Prefect's advantage."

"The Marshal always worried about the Prefect."

The Marshal? Then Taelya realized that the squad leader was referring to the Marshal of Westwind. "Doesn't every ruler near Gallos worry about him?"

"Gallos invaded Westwind twice. Westwind triumphed both times, but it was costly."

From what Taelya had seen, and that was little enough compared to the older members of her extended family, all war was costly, but she just nodded, then said, "If you'll excuse us, I need to work with Arthaal now, before we reach the southern road. After that, we'll practice riding under a concealment . . . that is, if we don't have to worry about the Hydlenese."

Varais smiled in Arthaal's direction. "She means real work, ser."

Arthaal managed a smile in return. "I've discovered that, Squad Leader."

After Varais slowed her mount slightly and rode behind the two and at the head of the half squad following, Taelya pulled the first apple from the sack. "Did Dorylt tell you what I had him do?"

"Yes, ser. He had to catch the apple in a containment as fast as he could and then squeeze down the containment hard enough and fast enough to squash the apple."

"That's right. I'll toss the first one out to the side. See what you can do." A moment later, she tossed the apple.

Arthaal's containment surrounded the apple quickly, but the containment continued to hang in the air for almost three counts before he began to shrink it, and then it stopped for another moment before he exerted more force and crumpled the fruit. "It's a lot harder than I thought."

"That's why you're practicing. You won't have nearly that much time if someone is charging at your men."

"Taelya . . . I mean, ser . . . what was it like the first time when those green-coats charged you and your squad? How did you feel?"

"I wasn't feeling. I just knew I had to protect the men and take out as many of them as fast as I could."

"You . . . didn't think about killing them?"

Taelya turned and looked directly at her cousin. "Arthaal, I was much younger than you are when the Hydlenese attacked Fairhaven. I saw them killing troopers and others from the window, well . . . from a crack in the shutters. There was even one little boy they dragged from a house. They didn't have any concerns about killing us. You can't think about whether you kill or hurt them. If you have to think, more of your men will die." *And so might you.* "You have to do what I'm training you to do and to do it as quickly as you can."

"They really killed children?"

"They did that and worse. Now . . . back to your containments."

"Yes, ser."

Taelya tossed another apple.

Arthaal missed it.

"Arthaal."

"I'm ready now."

Arthaal caught the third apple, and only took a two-count to squeeze it to a pulp.

"That's better. Much better."

By the time Taelya and Arthaal neared the point where the lane ended and joined the southern road where it paralleled the redstone bluffs, Arthaal was consistently catching and pulping the apples, not quite instantly but in less than a long single count.

"Time to stop for a bit," said Taelya. "We need to concentrate on sensing for Hydlenese now. See if you can sense anyone in the bluffs." She would have been surprised if he had, because she hadn't, not within several kays at least.

"So far I can't sense anyone," Arthaal said after several moments.

"Neither can I, but keep at it."

"Yes, ser."

When Taelya called a halt for a brief rest once they passed the small thick forest, Varais eased up beside her. The squad leader had a quizzical look on her face.

"Yes, Squad Leader?"

"Begging your pardon, ser," offered Varais in a voice barely above a murmur, "but I couldn't help overhearing what you said to the trainee undercaptain. You really saw them killing children?"

"I did. My mother wasn't happy when she found out." Taelya didn't mention the nightmares that had followed for years.

For a long moment, Varais was silent, before finally saying, "Have you sensed any greencoats?"

"Not so far. There aren't any on that next lane that leads south, and it's a bit far for me to tell if their scouts are still on the hill overlooking the Hydolar road."

"After what you did last time, I'd be surprised if they show up for a while."

"I'd think so, but you can never tell." *Then again, it might be better for Arthaal and Dorylt if they showed up now.* That way, there might be more time before the next attack.

After the patrol resumed riding and once Taelya was convinced that there were no Hydlenese around, except for the scouts on the hill, she had the guards spend almost a quint riding under a concealment. After that she resumed working intermittently with Arthaal on his containments . . . until she ran out of apples a little before midday.

While there were sheep grazing here and there, and a few carts heading in or out of Fairhaven, the patrol neither saw nor encountered traders or troopers.

At roughly a quint past second glass, as her patrol turned north on that part of the southern road leading to the main road, Taelya noted that the Hydlenese scouts remained posted on the north end of the crest of the last hill overlooking the scrublands but that, in the time since they first had passed the hill, another scout had joined the two that had usually been posted there. She was still puzzling over that when the patrol reached the west road and stopped for a brief rest.

That was when she had a hazy vague feeling about riders to the northeast, but, given the terrain and the numbers, she was fairly certain that they had to be on the Weevett road coming south, and that was well over three kays away. While she knew that she'd been sensing people and large animals at greater distances, she hadn't realized just how much farther that was.

Could you be mistaken? Or are you just imagining riders there because you think this would be the time when a Montgren company should arrive?

"What is it?" asked Arthaal.

"I'm trying to determine whether there are riders heading south on the Weevett road."

"Where on the Weevett road?"

"Likely several kays north of the crossroads."

"It's more than two kays from here just to the crossroads. That's a long ways from here. Can you really sense that far?"

"We'll see if I can." Taelya turned to Varais. "We're going to ride toward the Weevett road for a bit. I can barely discern some riders there, and I want a better sense before we start back on the southern road."

"Yes, ser. You think they're the Montgren company?"

"Most likely, but I'd like to make sure."

Varais offered an inquisitive expression, but didn't voice the question.

"If there are supply wagons with a full company of riders, they'll definitely be from Weevett. If not, we'll have to wait and see."

Varais nodded. "The greencoats wouldn't take wagons and a full company fifteen kays over the backroads."

"Not and come back down the Weevett road," agreed Taelya. Still, she wanted more confirmation, both of her sensing and the approaching riders. She urged the Road Guard gelding east toward the crossroads.

By the time they had covered little more than a half a kay, Taelya was absolutely certain that the company approaching was from Montgren, if only because of the six heavy wagons that rolled behind the riders. She looked to Arthaal. "What do you sense?"

"I can't sense anyone but us."

"Keep at it." Then Taelya ordered, "Squad! Halt!" She turned to Varais. "It's a full company with six wagons. We'll turn back and resume our patrol."

"You don't want to meet them?"

"Not particularly." *Especially not with Arthaal here.* "If the majer wants us to meet them, he'll let us know. In the meantime, I'd like to see what the Hydlenese scouts on the hill are doing . . . and if more troopers have joined them. Right now, they're the danger."

For an instant, Varais frowned. Then she nodded.

Taelya guided her mount back past the squad, then ordered, "To the rear, ride!"

As the squad rode back to where the southern patrol road joined the east-west road, Taelya kept sensing the oncoming Montgren troopers, although, given the trees and the terrain, she wouldn't be able to actually see them. She also kept sensing the three Hydlenese scouts.

Just about the time that she and the patrol were abreast of the hill that held the scouts, where the southern road was about a kay from the hillcrest, Taelya sensed that the Montgren troopers had reached the crossroads.

"Squad, halt!"

Arthaal looked quizzically to Taelya.

"I need a moment to sense things when I'm not riding." While that was true enough, Taelya knew that the Hydlenese scouts were enough higher than she was that they could see the crossroads, and she wanted to see how the scouts reacted, if they did at all.

Almost half a quint passed before she sensed one of the scouts riding down the south side of the hill and then heading westward on the Hydolar road. She still couldn't sense any Hydlenese troopers to the south or southwest, but she knew they had to be somewhere out there.

Then she nodded to Varais. "We can continue the patrol now." Before Arthaal could say anything, she looked at him and said quietly, "Not a single word until after I report to your father."

Arthaal nodded.

For the rest of the patrol and the return to headquarters, there were no signs of other Hydlenese troopers or scouts. Once Taelya stalled her mount, she immediately headed back to the headquarters building and the duty desk.

"Is the majer in his study?" Taelya asked Moshart, who was seated at the duty desk.

"Yes, ser. He's with the Montgren captain."

"Would you knock on the door and tell him that one of his patrol undercaptains needs a moment to report something to him immediately."

"You could . . ." Moshart saw Taelya's look and said, "Yes, ser."

In moments, Beltur appeared alone. When he saw Taelya's face, his expression turned to one of both surprise and annoyance, but he walked over to her. "Is this important?"

"It might be." She lowered her voice. "Early this afternoon, the Hydlenese added another trooper to their hill scouts. As soon as the scouts saw the Montgren company reach the crossroads—they can do that from the hill—one of the scouts rode off south at a good pace. They've never had three scouts there in the past eightdays, and this one left—"

Beltur held up his hand. "You could have—"

"No, ser. The Montgren captain would hear that, and that limits how you choose to use the information and who knows it. I didn't tell Varais, for the same reason, and I told Arthal not to say a word." The unspoken reason was that information was power, and Taelya felt that Beltur needed every advantage possible.

Beltur nodded. "Thank you." He smiled wryly. "I might as well introduce you. It could be interesting." He turned and walked back toward his study, then waited for Taelya to enter.

The Montgren officer stood. He was blond-haired, green-eyed, muscular, verging on the excessively beefy, and looked to be about ten years older than Taelya. His expression was polite, but his eyes widened as she stepped into the study.

"Captain Karlaak, I'd like you to meet Mage-Undercaptain Taelya. She's the mage officer who killed all the Hydlenese attackers, the ones who didn't flee."

Taelya smiled, also politely, and said, "I'm happy to meet you, Captain."

"And I, you."

"Undercaptain Taelya is one of the mage-undercaptains going to support the Viscount." Beltur turned to Taelya. "Thank you for the report. Unless there's anything else . . ."

"No, ser." Taelya inclined her head, then left the study, closing the door behind herself. She returned to the duty desk, where Arthaal was signing out, and signed out after him. "Go take care of your mount. I'll be there in a moment. I'll fill you in then."

Once Arthaal had left, Taelya asked, "What can you tell me about the Montgren captain?"

Moshart glanced around, then lowered his voice. "He came in here like he owned the place and asked to see the majer. More like a demand, ser. The majer took him into his study and told me to keep the other undercaptains out—unless it was really important." He looked at Taelya.

"Even he thought what I told him was important," Taelya said reassuringly. "But you can tell him that I was very insistent if you need to. He knows I can be like that." She smiled briefly.

"Thank you, ser."

"Is there anything else you can tell me?"

"His boots were polished, and there wasn't any dust on them."

Even after her brief encounter with Karlaak, Taelya wasn't surprised. "Thank you. I appreciate it."

Then she hurried out to the stable, thinking that everything about Karlaak confirmed her decision to report what she'd observed only to Beltur.

Arthaal stopped grooming his mount and walked over to her. "What were you doing?"

"I told your father about the scouts. You're not to talk about it except to me and him." She paused, then asked, "Do you know why?"

Arthaal shook his head.

"The extra scout who left as soon as they saw the Montgren company means that someone told them that the company was expected today. There might have been an extra man there yesterday, but your father should be the one to ask Valchar if he noticed that. He might not have."

"Most of the men knew that," Arthaal pointed out.

"That's true, but who here in Fairhaven would know how to contact the Hydlenese . . . unless they'd made arrangements some time ago? And since most of the mages can tell when someone's lying . . . who here would risk it? And why, since the Hydlenese are likely to kill everyone in Fairhaven if they win? Any trader would risk losing everything, and anyone else would risk their life." Taelya shrugged. "It still could be someone in town, but I'd wager against it."

"When you put it like that . . ." Arthaal nodded.

"Now . . . we need to get the horses groomed and get home for dinner."

Almost two quints passed by the time Taelya and Arthaal, as well as Kaeryla and Dorylt, arrived home. Unsurprisingly, Tulya was fixing dinner for everyone, at her house, helped by Jessyla, who had only arrived less than a quint before the four junior mages. After quickly washing up, the four pitched in in various ways.

Arthaal had barely finished setting the table, and Dorylt was setting out beakers for ale, when Beltur stepped through the front door. For a moment, no one noticed because everyone was in the kitchen.

Then Jessyla called out, "We're all in the kitchen."

Tulya motioned for Dorylt to pour a beaker of ale for Beltur.

Dorylt did so and handed the beaker to his uncle as soon as he entered the kitchen.

"Thank you. I can definitely use this."

"Did you learn anything from Captain Karlaak?" asked Taelya.

"After a while," replied Beltur. "He's rather traditional."

"You mean shortsighted and arrogant? Or that he feels women should only cook and bear children?" asked Jessyla sarcastically.

Beltur frowned.

"Or is Jessyla being too charitable?" interjected Tulya before Beltur could respond.

Beltur looked down the table at Taelya. "Did you say anything?"

"Not a word. We were too busy trying to help with dinner."

"Your use of the word 'traditional' said it all," Jessyla pointed out. "Korsaen knows that we'll likely be sending female mages to work with the Montgren companies going to Certis. He won't want them to have trouble with Montgren officers. That means the most traditional officers, as you put it, will be sent to Montgren, where you're in charge."

"And where you'll also make sure they understand that things are different here," replied Beltur dryly.

"What did you learn?" pressed Taelya.

"Let the man sit down first," said Tulya.

"I'd rather stand for a bit." Beltur took a long swallow of the ale, then set the beaker at his place at the head of the table. "The other company will arrive tomorrow, along with more supplies. The dispatch that Karlaak brought stressed that our force is expected to leave on threeday. One of the wagons that they brought will be turned over to our force for spare equipment and weapons and any special supplies we might have." Beltur smiled wryly. "I think that means I'll have to send a keg or two of brandy with you. That might help with any 'traditional' officers."

"How good are the troopers Captain Karlaak brought?" asked Arthaal.

"They're likely at least adequate," said Beltur. "They might even be better than that. The Duchess doesn't want to send poor troopers because she might lose Fairhaven and a chunk of Montgren while gaining nothing, except a promise from the Viscount not to attack Montgren."

"All of it still sounds like we got the worst of it," said Dorylt.

"Unless we can turn it to our advantage," replied Jessyla.

"How can we do that?" countered Dorylt.

Jessyla laughed sardonically. "We haven't figured that out yet."

"Except," Beltur added, "it starts with doing whatever you can to win battles without any of you doing something to get yourselves killed. I've told Korsaen that our troopers and mages are not to be used for sacrificial or suicidal attacks.

```
*** TRANSIT SLIP ***
*** DISCHARGE ON
ARRIVAL ***

Author: Modesitt, L. E., Jr.,
1943-
Title: Fairhaven rising
Item ID: 4602084420
Transit to: SOTAU
```

I've also let Gustaan know that he's not to allow any such attacks." His eyes went to Taelya. "If anyone tries to issue such an order, Gustaan will delay doing anything until he informs you. If he thinks an order is unwise or suicidal, it is, and you'll have to do something about it."

Taelya understood all too well the unspoken duty that Beltur had laid on her. She managed not to swallow.

Then Beltur turned to Kaeryla. "And you may have to help with that, because no one besides you two should know that anything happened."

"What about us?" asked Arthaal.

"Your job is to protect yourself and your troopers. You're not to lead attacks or the like. We'll have a little more time to work out the details with you and Dorylt. For now, there's nothing more I can add . . . and we should enjoy a good dinner."

"Everyone sit down," said Tulya, "except Taelya and Kaeryla. They'll help serve."

As she took bowls filled with burhka from her mother to the table, Taelya thought about what her mother had said about Beltur the night before. In a strange way, what he'd just said fit.

He wasn't at all happy about matters, and he'd made it very clear that the duty of those from Fairhaven was to find ways to win without sacrificing themselves. *In whatever fashion is required.*

And that was exactly what Taelya intended to do.

XXVII

On twoday, Beltur stopped all Fairhaven patrols, and instead posted scouts at points all along the previous patrol routes, initially with three troopers at each point, one from Fairhaven and two from Montgren. The scouts were positioned so that guards at every posting point could see two other points. Then Taelya, Sheralt, Valchar, and Kaeryla were dismissed and ordered to spend the day readying themselves and their horses and gear for a very early departure on threeday.

By midday Taelya had everything packed and arranged, her spare uniform and smallclothes and other personal items in one small duffel, including a few ointments and salves for her own use, the healing kit in another, plus an even smaller case for various items such as a brush and curry comb for Bounder, and a leather bag for provisions. She'd checked her wallet, and she had five silvers and four coppers, hardly enough for purchasing much, but she'd always given half of her pay as an undercaptain to her mother to help with running the house.

Even her boots were cleaned and polished, and she was standing in the arch-way by the hearth, wondering what she'd forgotten or overlooked, when there was a rap on the kitchen door.

From the balance of order and chaos, and a few other aspects, the person knocking had to be Jessyla.

Why is she here in midday, and not at the Healing House? Taelya walked to the door and opened it.

"I hope I'm not intruding. Do you have a moment?"

"Certainly. Would you like some ale?"

Jessyla looked somewhat surprised, then said, "Actually, I would."

Taelya got out two beakers and filled one two-thirds full and the other half full, then gave the first to Jessyla and gestured to the kitchen table. "How is Kaeryla coming?"

The older woman sat down on one side of the table. "She's just about finished."

Taelya sat across from her and took a sip of the ale, studying Jessyla and get-ting the impression that she wasn't totally at ease. "Your showing up in midday surprised me a bit. I thought you might be helping Kaeryla or at the Healing House."

"I think I was making her a little nervous . . . and there's something I wanted to talk over with you . . . something to do with healing . . . and you."

Taelya could definitely sense the older healer's growing unease. "Did I do something wrong? Or is there something I shouldn't do?"

Jessyla shook her head. "It's nothing like that." She paused. "It's something about fighting . . . and battles we haven't discussed." After another hesitation, she went on. "You know . . . if you're forced to use too much order or chaos, you might end up unconscious . . . where you can't use magery . . . and you're a very attractive young woman . . ."

For a moment, Taelya didn't know what to say.

"You don't want someone else to choose when you have a child, do you?" asked Jessyla gently.

After an instant of shock, Taelya managed not to laugh . . . but she did smile before she spoke. "Oh . . . we went over this several years ago. You can check, if you want, but I've been careful to make sure that . . . well, that that small bit of order-bounded chaos remains in place."

Jessyla actually flushed. "I didn't mean to be intrusive, but Kaeryla . . . she insisted I at least talk to you."

Taelya shook her head. "That was thoughtful of her."

Jessyla smiled wryly. "She also just might have wanted to know that someone else got my instructions. I worry about you both, but if I didn't talk to you now, she'd feel . . ."

"That you were fussing too much over her," said Taelya.

"There's that, but . . ." An embarrassed smile followed. "I'd also worry if I didn't at least talk to you."

Taelya could sense the absolute truth behind those words. "I appreciate that. You and Beltur have always taken great care with me . . . and looked after Mother. I probably haven't always shown how much that's meant to me. I should have said more . . ." She could feel the tears behind her words, but she just swallowed. "I meant to . . . more than once. You've done so much . . ." She just sat there, not knowing what else she could say.

"You didn't have to say much," replied Jessyla. "Everything that you've done over the years . . . all the times that you took care of Kaeryla and Arthaal . . . and how you've pushed Arthaal in the last eightdays." After a moment, she went on. "There's something else I wanted to say. Something that I need to say." Another brief silence followed. "Take good care of yourself. I told Beltur the same thing once . . . and for the same reason. You're the only one strong enough to follow him."

"Kaeryla's strong. She'll likely be a stronger mage than I am."

"She might be . . . but that's not the kind of strength Fairhaven needs the most. You see what needs to be done . . . and you do it, or tell others what they need to do." Another wry smile followed. "Sometimes without letting others know what you've done and why, but you're already learning about that. The way you can foresee isn't easily learned, if it can be learned at all."

"You're making me more than I am," Taelya protested.

"Most likely," agreed Jessyla, "but I'm not making you more than you will be . . . *if* you take care of yourself and Kaeryla and get through this mess with Certis. Don't be kind if it will jeopardize your safety or Fairhaven. By the same token, don't be cruel unless it serves a very good purpose."

"Have you told Kaeryla all this?"

"About the cruelty and kindness and surviving? Yes, I have. I spoke to her even more strongly."

Taelya could see that. Kaeryla was still a healer at heart.

"You see?" said Jessyla. "You understood immediately."

But what does that make me? A calculating, ruthless bitch?

Jessyla must have sensed something of Taelya's reaction because she went on. "I was fortunate not to have come into real magery until after I was consorted to Beltur, and he had much more power than I did. You don't have that shield. You're already powerful and will become even stronger. While there aren't many women in Candar with power, too many of those who do have power use it indirectly. From what little I've seen, you'll be more respected and more effective if you avoid scheming as much as possible. You won't avoid nasty comments whatever you do."

"I still say that you're making me more—"

"No, I'm not," interjected Jessyla. "You're already one of the strongest mages in the east of Candar. You have to realize that because that makes you a target. You need to understand that women who do not know you will fear you, and some will scheme against you. Men who are mages will try to undermine you, and healers who don't know you will suspect that you use healing as a subterfuge to weaken others. Haven't you already seen some of that?"

Taelya thought, then said, "From the Kaordists."

"What about Sheralt? Until he understood you really wanted to help him? Or that Gallosian mage, the younger one?"

Taelya smiled wryly. "You've made your point in more than one way."

For the first time, Jessyla looked surprised.

"With Sheralt," said Taelya. "I didn't scheme. I was direct. Too direct, I thought at the time, but it's much easier and more open with him now. Thank you."

"That won't always work, you know?"

Taelya nodded. *It certainly didn't with Valchar.*

Jessyla stood. "There's not much more that I can say."

Taelya rose, then stepped forward and hugged her aunt. "You don't have to." This time she didn't even try to stem the flow of tears.

"Just take care of yourself." Jessyla barely managed to choke out the words.

Then the two just hung on to each other for a time.

When Jessyla finally stepped back, she said, "This way, it won't be quite so hard at dinner."

Taelya nodded, although she had her doubts, as she suspected Jessyla also did.

After Jessyla left, Taelya washed her face in cold water, then began to ready things for dinner.

Then, just before third glass, Taelya sensed her mother walking up to the house, a good glass earlier than she usually did, not that Taelya had expected otherwise for the last dinner they'd have together for some considerable time. She walked to the door and opened it, noticing that her mother carried several bags. "You've been shopping?"

"Not exactly. Meldryn brought me some fruit pies. They're spring-apple and berry, and enough for a generous piece for everyone. And earlier today, when Julli brought your jackets, she also brought me some fresh chard and a few other things."

"I have the stove warming up."

Tulya smiled. "I thought you would."

The two worked together until slightly after fourth glass, when Dorylt appeared and hurried into his room, then reappeared almost instantly and joined in helping.

By fifth glass everything, including the special version of burhka, was ready, but Taelya noticed that Dorylt was pacing back and forth. "You'd think you were the one leaving for Certis tomorrow."

"Can't I be nervous for you?" he replied cheerfully.

Taelya shook her head, knowing that wasn't it at all, but she didn't have much time to ponder on it because, at that moment, Beltur, Jessyla, Kaeryla, and Arthaal all arrived.

Arthaal slipped ahead of everyone else into the kitchen and right past Taelya without even looking at her, just as Jessyla asked, "What can we do?"

"Just have Dorylt get you an ale and enjoy it," replied Tulya. "Taelya started everything, and the bread just has to cool a little bit."

Taelya glanced around, but neither Arthaal or Dorylt was anywhere to be seen. But before she could call for either, Dorylt hurried into the kitchen and immediately began to fill the beakers with ale.

"Everything smells wonderful," declared Beltur, "but it always does."

Taelya took a beaker from Dorylt and handed it to her uncle. Between the two of them, she and Dorylt had beakers in everyone's hands in little more than moments.

"The other Montgren company arrived before first glass this afternoon," Beltur announced. "That means our force will definitely be leaving before sunrise tomorrow. I'm hoping that will gain us a little extra time before the Hydlenese attack . . ."

Taelya realized that she'd never even sensed the incoming troopers, but then, that had happened around the time she'd been talking to Jessyla, and her thoughts had definitely been elsewhere.

". . . and there's not much else to be said. So we should talk about other things and enjoy this dinner together."

Most likely the last one together for some time. As she thought that, Taelya moved toward the stove to help her mother serve.

"Dorylt and Arthaal are helping tonight," said Tulya.

"They need to get used to it," added Jessyla.

And they'll get very tired of it before long. With that thought, Taelya looked at Kaeryla, and the two exchanged amused smiles.

The burhka, as always, was excellent.

After everyone had finished eating, Beltur cleared his throat loudly, then waited for relative quiet before speaking. "Arthaal has something to say."

"In just a moment." The youngest mage flushed slightly as he stood up and hurried in the direction of Dorylt's room, returning almost instantly. In each hand was a palm-sized leather case. He looked down at the case in his left hand, then extended it to Kaeryla, after which he handed the second one to Taelya. "You can do at least two things with them." Arthaal grinned.

Taelya looked down at the case, which had a single bronze letter—"T"—affixed to the top. She opened it to find what looked like a square but flat cupridium box, no thicker than two digits. She frowned.

"Open them," Arthaal said. "They're not boxes. Not just boxes."

Taelya looked closer and saw a catch on one side and a long narrow hinge on the opposite side. She slipped the catch and lifted the top, only to see her own face reflected in the silvered-bronze cupridium finish. "Oh!"

"You can use them as signal mirrors or," Arthaal grinned again, "for other things."

"It's beautiful," said Taelya.

"Gorgeous," added Kaeryla.

"Father and Jorhan helped me with them a lot . . . a whole lot, and Dorylt, too, but it was my idea."

"And the case is beautiful, too," added Taelya.

"Dorylt did the cases," said Arthaal, "except for the initials. I did those all by myself. They're just bronze, not cupridium."

"Since we're giving things," said Tulya, "here are two other items you two might find useful." She extended two flat oilskin packets, no more than eight digits on a side and less than a digit thick. "The oilskins are to keep dry what's inside."

After taking one of the packets from her mother, Taelya lifted the flap and extracted what looked like folded paper, but was clearly not. As she unfolded it, her mouth opened. "It's a map!"

"Precisely," said Tulya, "it's a map of Certis and the eastern part of Gallos. It's a bit smaller than I'd like, and not as detailed, but they're for your use and only your use. Beltur and Jessyla added a little order-bound chaos to strengthen the leather because it's much thinner than map leather. Gustaan has a larger version, but he doesn't know you have those, and he shouldn't."

"These must have taken . . . forever," said Taelya.

"I didn't have forever, dear, but it felt like forever."

"Much as we'd like this to last longer," added Jessyla, "we need to clean up so that certain undercaptains can attempt to get a decent night's sleep."

Beltur immediately stood, then looked to Tulya. "As always, it was an excellent dinner and a pleasure."

"You always say that." Tulya offered a mischievous smile. "And I always like it when you do."

Dorylt immediately moved to the washtub, and the cleanup began.

Once everything was cleaned up and Jessyla, Beltur, Kaeryla, and Arthaal had left, Tulya and Taelya sat down at the kitchen table.

"I'm going to miss dinners like this," said Taelya.

"Kaeryla will miss them more," said Tulya. "She's never known any place but Fairhaven."

"I'll watch out for her." Taelya smiled. "But you already knew that, and so does Aunt Jessyla."

"Of course, but there will be times when she may need to look after you, and you should let her."

Taelya nodded.

"There is one other thing." Tulya rose. "I'll be right back."

Taelya wondered what her mother had in mind, but she was surprised when Tulya returned carrying what looked to be a leather belt, tastefully but not elaborately tooled with a simple design of recurring diamond-like shapes.

"I haven't worn anything like this in years, but I had this made a while ago, knowing you might need it. You'll wear it in place of your usual belt, not your sword belt." Tulya turned it. "If you look closely there are concealed coin slots. I've taken the liberty of filling most of them. At the end are several golds. Those are to be saved for the most desperate of needs. The silvers are to be used as you see fit. There are some empty slots for most of the silvers in your wallet. Just carry enough silvers in your wallet that it looks as though that's all you have." She handed the belt to her daughter.

Taelya examined it realizing that there had to be at least twenty silvers in the slots, not to mention three golds. "Mother! You can't afford this."

"I could, because we've been very careful, especially with the earnings from our small share of the distillery, but Beltur offered, and I accepted. Kaeryla will also be wearing a similar belt. Obviously, it would be best if you never mentioned anything."

"Of course." That was obvious, but Taelya understood her mother's concern. "Thank you. It's perfect, but I never would have thought of it."

"Mothers occasionally do know a few things, dear."

"More than a few." Taelya stood, setting the belt on the table, and then hugged her mother tightly.

XXVIII

Taelya was up and dressed well before dawn on threeday, of necessity, since Beltur and Gustaan wanted the Fairhaven force out of sight of the possible Hydlenese scouts before there was enough light to see their departure. Even before she was dressed, though, Tulya was in a robe in the kitchen making breakfast.

"You didn't have to make breakfast," said Taelya as she entered the kitchen. "You'll have a long enough day anyway."

"You're not leaving on a long ride without a hot breakfast. Besides, this way I get to see you and talk to you." Tulya pointed to the table. "Sit down. The scramble's almost ready, and I saved a bit of the fruit pie for you."

"Is there any of that for me?" asked Dorylt, still in smallclothes as he yawned his way into the kitchen.

"I should say no, but there's enough for each of you, especially since your sister doesn't eat everything that's not claimed."

"I'm still growing," protested Dorylt.

Tulya just shook her head. "You can get ales for everyone." She turned to Taelya. "Your water bottles are filled with ale, only watered a little. So try not to drink a lot at once."

"Thank you."

All too soon, Taelya finished her breakfast, knowing that she needed to saddle Bounder and load her gear. She stood and said, "It's time."

"I'll carry your stuff to the stable," volunteered Dorylt.

Taelya looked at him.

"It's dark out. No one will see anything except Kaeryla, and she's seen me in these more than a few times." Abruptly, he flushed. "That's not what I meant."

Both Tulya and Taelya laughed.

"I'm not walking over there in this," said Tulya.

And we said what really mattered last night. Taelya gave her mother a last hug, then picked up the healing kit. She let Dorylt carry the rest, not that it was terribly heavy, even with the blanket rolled up inside.

Given how dark it was, Taelya was using her other senses as much as her eyes to make her way across the street to the stable. Kaeryla and Jessyla were already there in the stable when Taelya and Dorylt entered the area lit but dimly by a single lamp.

Before Taelya could speak, Kaeryla said, "Father's already at headquarters with Arthaal." She looked at Dorylt. "Aren't you doing patrols?"

Dorylt set down the gear he'd carried. "I'm not supposed to be there until sixth glass. I'm seeing Taelya off." With that he gave his sister a quick hug, murmuring, "Do whatever it takes to come back safe." Then he was gone.

"He does have more than a glass, almost two glasses," Jessyla pointed out. "Arthaal didn't have to go with your father. But you two don't have that much time."

"We'll hurry," said Kaeryla.

At that moment, Taelya realized that Kaeryla's hair was cut short, possibly even shorter than Taelya's own. *And she looks even better—and older—with short hair.* Still thinking about the difference, Taelya stepped into the stall and began to saddle Bounder. Once she had the gelding saddled and her gear secured behind her saddle, she immediately led him outside to wait for Kaeryla, just in case the younger mage wanted a few last moments with her mother.

Shortly, Kaeryla led her mare out, followed by Jessyla.

Taelya could sense the swirls of chaos around the older healer, far more than she'd ever noticed around her aunt, and she said, "We'll be fine."

"I'm sure you will be," replied Jessyla, the firmness of her voice concealing the worry.

Then Taelya and Kaeryla mounted, and Kaeryla turned to her mother and added, "Really, we will be."

As they rode away, Taelya didn't say anything, not wanting to intrude on Kaeryla at least for a while.

When the two turned east on the main street, Kaeryla finally said, "You know, I've never been farther from Fairhaven than Vergren, and only once beyond Weevett."

"It's been something like sixteen years since I've been farther than Vergren, and I wasn't that old. I think I'm going to be very glad for the signal mirror that Arthaal made . . . and for the map."

"I know I am. I studied the map for a while last night."

"I'm glad you did," replied Taelya. "I didn't have a chance."

"Can you tell me what you and Mother talked about yesterday? If you think it's all right . . . I don't . . . I mean . . ."

Taelya frowned, but doubted Kaeryla noticed in the darkness well before dawn. "She wanted to make sure I'd taken precautions . . . against being taken advantage of . . . she said she'd talked that over with you."

"She was there quite a while."

"She also said that we needed to be careful and to take care of each other, and that when she first came into having magely abilities, no one really noticed at first because Beltur was so much stronger. She said we wouldn't have that cushion, and that it was important for us not to engage in scheming, because that would work against us. It took longer than that, but that was what it was all about."

"What did she say about me?"

"She worries about your being too kind, and she said that neither of us should be kind if it jeopardized us or Fairhaven, and that we should avoid being cruel unless it was absolutely necessary to save us or Fairhaven."

"That sounds just like Mother."

"It should, since that was pretty much what she said."

"You're telling the truth."

Taelya could sense the surprise. "How could I not? You'd know. She also said that we'd be targets once people—I think she meant men—realized that we have power in our own rights."

"Thank you. I worried."

"What? That she came over to tell me to protect you? I told you that she worries about your being too kind. I have to say that I've worried about that as well."

After a long moment, Kaeryla finally said, "I worry about it, too, and then I worry that I'll be too cruel because I'm trying not to have any kindness taken advantage of."

Taelya laughed softly. "I don't think that's just a problem for women who are mages or healers. It's just that people are likely to watch us more closely."

"They'll watch you more. You're a chaos mage, and you're beautiful."

"Beautiful? I'm small and slender. I look more like a boy than a woman. You have that gorgeous red hair, brilliant green eyes, and—"

"Taelya! Just listen to me. You know a lot more than I do, but men look at you. Everyone can see it."

Taelya wanted to protest, but Dorylt had said as much earlier, and Jessyla had come over, worried. After several moments, Taelya said, "I've felt that, and Dorylt's said so, but . . ."

"You don't have to understand it," replied Kaeryla. "You don't have to like it. You just have to accept that's what they feel."

Abruptly, Taelya asked, "Is this something your mother wanted you to talk to me about?"

"Yes. I told her you'd know it wasn't my idea. She said it didn't matter. Are you upset with me?"

Taelya shook her head, then realizing that Kaeryla might not catch the gesture in the darkness, said, "No, I'm not upset with you. I just never thought of myself that way. So . . . it's . . . a little disconcerting . . ."

"You didn't notice it at all?"

"Oh . . . I knew Valchar and Sheralt were a little interested, but that's because they'd rather consort a mage, and I had the feeling that some of the others were interested just because I was . . . exotic . . . a woman who was a white mage."

"That might be true, but it's not the only reason," replied Kaeryla with a tartness that abruptly reminded Taelya of Jessyla.

"I'm sorry."

"What are you sorry for?"

"For your having to remind me of something that I should have seen." *Even if I'm still not sure that it's all that true.* "I just never thought of myself that way."

"I can sense that. But how could you not?" Kaeryla paused.

"I just didn't."

"Oh . . . Taelya . . ."

Taelya could sense both a swirl of chaos and hear a hint of exasperation in her cousin's voice. "Perhaps I should have thought that way, but I just didn't."

"But you're so confident."

"I know I'm a strong mage. Not the strongest, but strong. And I'm a white.

Most men are wary of women who could kill them. So why would I think of myself as being appealing to them?"

Kaeryla was silent for several moments. "I've always thought you were beautiful . . . and caring. I never thought . . . that way."

"Maybe you're right . . ."

". . . and maybe we both are."

Taelya could accept that.

Once the two reached headquarters, Taelya could see guards leading out mounts and that the dray horses for the supply wagon were already hitched in place. Keeping to the west side of the courtyard, the two rode to the stable, where they tied their mounts outside before hurrying between mounts and men across the pavement and inside headquarters to the duty room.

Both Sheralt and Valchar were already there. Even in the dim lamplight, Valchar looked twice at Kaeryla, and the second time Taelya could see that his eyes widened, clearly a reaction to Kaeryla's shorter hair and how it changed her appearance.

Then Varais and Barkhan appeared, followed by Gustaan and Beltur.

Taelya immediately noticed that Beltur was completely shielded, so that while she could see him, every bit of order and chaos around him was blocked from her senses. *In battle, but here?* Then she swallowed, realizing what that meant: that his daughter was leaving to fight—and that he'd made the decisions that required it.

"This won't take long," Beltur declared. "As you already know, you're to join the Montgren forces at the post on the west side of Weevett. Not a single one of you undercaptains is to agree to operate without the support of your squad. If Lord Korsaen or Commander Raelf or Majer Zekkarat insists, and Captain Gustaan agrees, you may support a Montgren company with no less than half a Fairhaven squad behind you. Is that clear?"

While all four nodded, Taelya had the feeling that such refusal would not be taken lightly by senior Montgren officers. "To what extent are the Montgren senior officers aware of this restriction, ser?"

"The three most senior officers are aware that each of you requires the support of your squad. They have not been informed that, under necessary circumstances, you may proceed with half a squad. If a squad is split, the squad leader will lead the half squad commanded by the *junior* undercaptain." Beltur looked to Varais and Barkhan. "Is that clear, Squad Leaders?"

"Yes, ser."

"I also need to remind you of the chain of command among undercaptains. The most senior is Undercaptain Sheralt, then Undercaptain Taelya, followed by Undercaptain Valchar, and Undercaptain Kaeryla."

After a few more mundane instructions dealing with supplies and wagons, Beltur concluded, "That's all I have. I know you all will do your best." He turned to Gustaan. "They're yours, Captain." Then he turned and left the duty room, still totally shielded.

Without looking sideways at Kaeryla, Taelya tried to sense what her cousin was feeling, but could only discern swirls of chaos.

"Form up, ready to ride," ordered Gustaan. "We'll alternate which squad leads, but Squad Two will ride out first. Dismissed to form up."

Varais immediately walked over to where Taelya and Kaeryla stood. "Sers, Squad Three stands ready to mount at the south end of the courtyard."

"Thank you, Squad Leader," replied Taelya. "We'll join you momentarily."

"Yes, ser."

As soon as Varais turned and headed out, Taelya looked to Kaeryla. "Are you ready to mount?"

Kaeryla nodded. "We shared words at home."

Taelya noted the precise choice of words. *Not "parting" or "farewell" or anything hinting that they might not see each other again.* "So did we."

The two walked from the headquarters back across the courtyard to the stable, where they untied their horses, mounted, and then rode to the back of the courtyard, where Varais had Squad Three mounted and waiting. Behind the squad was the supply wagon, with one teamster seated on the wagon and the second mounted alongside the wagon.

A few moments later, Squad Two, formed up in front of Squad Three, began to move.

Taelya waited a few moments, then ordered, "Squad, forward!" Then she urged Bounder ahead through the darkness.

XXIX

By seventh glass on threeday morning, the Fairhaven force, a company only in name, was riding north on the Weevett road more than ten kays north of the junction with the road to Certis. Even that early, the damp air was getting warm enough that Taelya knew it would be uncomfortable well before midday, despite the fact that the first day of summer was still more than three eightdays away. The Weevett road was wide enough—barely—for three riders, and Taelya rode in the middle with Varais on her left and Kaeryla on her right. Squad Two and Gustaan still led the way.

"If you have to split up into half squads," asked Varais, "how do you want to handle that?"

"You decide the half squads, and you lead the one under Kaeryla. I'd prefer Nardaak as the senior guard, and Khaspar as the senior guard under you."

Varais nodded. "That makes sense to me. As for the half squads . . ." She handed a sheet of paper to Taelya. "I worked on these last night, but we didn't have much time, and it was dark this morning. If you and Undercaptain Kaeryla would go over the lists and let me know if you have any changes."

"We can do that." Without looking at the sheet, except to see that it had two columns of names, Taelya handed it to Kaeryla and said, "You look it over first. Then I will."

"I can do that."

Less than a quint later, Gustaan called a halt for a brief rest near a stream where the horses could be watered. Then he passed word for Squad Three to move forward and to let Squad Two take the rear position.

When Taelya and Kaeryla rode to meet the captain, Varais dropped back to ride with Senior Guard Nardaak.

Gustaan rode in the middle, with Taelya on his right and Kaeryla on his left. Two outriders rode several hundred yards ahead.

"You've both been to the post at Weevett before, I know," said Gustaan. "It's going to be a lot more crowded now. I don't know if there will be more than two Montgren companies there. Captain Karlaak said that only the training company was left at Vergren when the second Montgren company left to ride to Fairhaven."

"That's the reserve company that could go to Fairhaven?" asked Kaeryla. "Just a training company?"

"That's the way I understand it. Lord Korsaen may be holding it back a bit so that the Weevett post isn't totally overcrowded. They also support two squads that man the small guard station on the east side of the Montgren Gorge bridge. They alternate the squads every two eightdays."

"Why don't they just maintain a half company at the bridge?" asked Kaeryla.

Gustaan laughed softly, then said, "Because the gorge is almost twenty kays west of Weevett and the last ten kays are rugged drylands where even sheep can have a hard time. But with both the extra companies and the off-duty bridge squad, I can see why Lord Korsaen might want to delay the reserve company's arrival."

"I hope he doesn't hold it back very long," replied Kaeryla.

"That's up to Lord Korsaen and the Duchess, and how well Majer Beltur can persuade them."

Taelya nodded. *Which is another reason why it was better for Beltur to stay and fight from Fairhaven.*

By midday, the white sun was pouring down through the clear green-blue sky, and Taelya was blotting her forehead or adjusting her visor cap almost with every step Bounder took . . . or so it seemed to her. She'd been careful with her lightly watered ale, but she wondered if she should have considered carrying three water bottles, instead of two.

She glanced toward Kaeryla, then smiled wryly as the younger mage blotted her forehead and the back of her neck.

Well before second glass, when Third Squad was again riding in the lead, Taelya could see that they were nearing Weevett, simply because there were more and more steads on each side of the road and they were encountering more local carts and wagons. While most of the dwellings they had passed heading north had been constructed of wood, now the larger and more well-tended homes were built of a dusty yellow brick, although the roofs held wooden shingles, rather than thatch or fired pottery tiles. The flocks of sheep were far larger, and definitely more numerous than around Fairhaven.

After they passed a field holding a small flock tended by two girls and a pair of dogs, Kaeryla said quietly, "They looked like they'd never seen Fairhaven guards before."

"All most of them have seen is the faded or pale blue that the Montgren troopers wear," replied Taelya. "We're wearing much darker blue, like Elpartan troopers."

"Our couriers travel this road all the time," Kaeryla pointed out.

"Seeing half a company of dark-blue-uniform riders is a lot different from two riders in dark blue every so often."

"They still should know," murmured Kaeryla.

After they rode around a gentle curve because of a hill on which grazed several hundred sheep, Taelya saw clusters of houses, suggesting the edge of Weevett proper, and several hundred yards immediately ahead, the beginning of stone pavement, pavement that extended all the way to the central town square and that had been extended south from the square some five years earlier. The street north from the square toward Vergren had been paved for as long as Taelya could remember, as had been most of the street leading west from the square to the walled post on the west side of the town on the road leading to Certis and Jellico, although the last half kay had not been paved until a few years ago.

As they rode into the town, Taelya studied the buildings, but little seemed to have changed since her last visit almost a year earlier. The larger houses and dwellings were largely of the yellow brick, but the window trim and the doors seemed to come in a wealth of colors, including blues that ranged from pale mist blue to full bright blue. The square in the center of the town was filled with vendors and customers, and most turned to watch, if momentarily, the uniformed

Fairhaven guards as they rode along the south edge of the square before turning onto the street heading west.

"They don't look like they were expecting us," said Kaeryla.

"The town officials had to know," replied Gustaan. "But they likely saw no reason to say anything. Fairhaven is part of Montgren and always has been."

Taelya wondered what else hadn't been mentioned, but said nothing.

Before all that long, or so it seemed to Taelya, they neared the Weevett post, a structure surrounded by yellow brick walls, set back no more than fifteen yards from the road, with no other structures near the post on the west side and none closer than fifty yards on the east. The post had been expanded to hold three companies, if on a crowded basis, close to ten years earlier. The slightly brighter yellow shade of the newer bricks was obvious once the Fairhaven squads were within several hundred yards. The walls weren't designed to resist a siege or prolonged attack, since they were barely three yards high. Nor were the iron-bound gates more than a few digits thick.

As Gustaan led the way through the gates, Taelya took in the inner courtyard, brick-paved and spacious enough to contain two large quarters buildings, as well as two large stables and several other structures, all of yellow brick. Almost immediately, a trooper in the faded blue of Montgren appeared.

"Quartermaster Bylltyn, ser. We didn't expect you quite so early, ser. The west end of the far stable is for the Fairhaven mounts, and there are two officers' rooms for you and your . . . officers. They're marked with dark blue chevrons."

Gustaan nodded. "One woman senior squad leader will be billeted with the two women mage-guard undercaptains. I'll share with two male mage-guard undercaptains."

Taelya knew that Gustaan had to point out that two of his officers and one squad leader were women, but it still annoyed her slightly, necessary as it might have been.

"Yes, ser. I'll have that noted. Officers are to be at the mess at half past fifth glass for a dinner."

"Thank you."

Bylltyn hurried off.

Gustaan turned and said, "Go ahead to the stable. I'll pass that on to Second Squad."

"Yes, ser," replied Taelya, urging Bounder forward across the paved courtyard and toward the farthest stable.

When she neared the open door a young ostler in smudged blues without rank insignia hurried out. "Sers . . . your stalls are at the end. You might have to double up in the larger stalls." The young ostler glanced from Taelya to Kaeryla, his eyes widening even more as he took in Varais and the twin blades she wore in the crossed shoulder harness.

"Yes," said the squad leader. "We're women, and between us we've killed more men than any of the other troopers."

"Yes, ser. Sorry, ser." The ostler backed up slightly as the three dismounted and led their mounts into the stable.

Taelya led the way down the middle of the packed clay floor, finding the stable tolerably clean, but not as well-kept as Beltur's or those at Fairhaven headquarters. The comparison didn't surprise her.

She had just finished unsaddling and grooming Bounder when Gustaan appeared at the end of the stall. "All of the Fairhaven officers have been requested to meet with Commander Raelf and Majer Zekkarat at fourth glass in the officers' mess. That will give you a little time to get settled and cleaned up."

"Make sure you tell Valchar about the cleaning-up part," said Kaeryla from the adjoining stall.

"I already made that point to him. The officers' mess is in the same building as the troopers' mess hall, behind the barracks. Officers' quarters are in the square building east of the long building that's the main trooper barracks. Your quarters are the closest to the small rear courtyard with the well and hand pump, and there are chamber pots under the bunks."

Left unsaid was the fact that using the officers' jakes might be awkward, if not unsettling.

"Thank you," said Taelya.

As soon as Gustaan had headed off, Taelya said, "Since I'm done with Bounder, I'll see how Varais and the squad are coming. I'll let her know about quarters, and then I'll be back."

Varais had already taken care of her mount and stood watching Breslan. She turned as Taelya approached. "Ser . . . about what I said to the ostler . . ."

"I take it you've had trouble before, and you wanted to give fair warning?"

"Yes, ser. The stable types aren't so bad here, but in Gallos and Certis . . ." Varais shook her head.

". . . and, besides," said Taelya with a smile, "it works better from a former Westwind guard with twin blades on her back."

Varais offered an amused smile. "Yes, ser."

Taelya relayed the information about quarters, then added, "We're to meet with the commander and majer in about a glass. Is there anything I should know or bring up?"

"The fodder's not that good, but I've seen worse. So far, nothing else obvious."

"If there's anything . . ."

"I'll let you know, ser."

"Good. We'll see you at our quarters."

Varais nodded. "Little strange to share quarters with officers."

"You'll manage, and we'll likely learn more than if you weren't there."

After leaving the squad leader, Taelya rejoined Kaeryla, and the two walked across the courtyard, carrying their personal gear, past several Montgren troopers engaged in various tasks, including replacing a wagon wheel and loading barrels into a supply wagon.

Taelya had the feeling that none of the troopers paid much attention, most likely because, so far as Taelya knew, outside of Westwind, there weren't any women officers. In addition, both undercaptains had hair that, under their visor caps, didn't look that much different from male undercaptains' and were lugging gear. *That lack of notice will change when word gets around.*

The center corridor in the officers' quarters was empty when the two entered, not surprisingly, since most officers would be handling some duty or another between third and fourth glass.

The small room considered appropriate for visiting junior officers consisted of a space barely four yards by three holding a narrow table with one pitcher and washbasin, wall pegs for clothes, and two sets of bunk beds, barely wider than a pallet. All the wood was the dark gold of aged oak. There were no locks, just a sturdy door bar.

Taelya looked at Kaeryla. "It will do. Pick a bunk."

Kaeryla put her duffel on the left upper bunk, and Taelya took the right upper, then said, "I'm going to fill the pitcher for the washbasin. That way, we'll be through, or mostly so, before Varais gets here. We also need to talk over what Varais proposed, if we have to split the squad."

"I'd only like to make one change," said Kaeryla. "I'd like to have Mattark in my half squad. He's shown an interest in healing, and he's got a higher order level than most."

"I don't see any problem with that, but I'd like to ask Varais if she sees any problem with that and who would be best to move from your half squad."

Kaeryla nodded.

Then Taelya hurried out with the pitcher, returning shortly.

Both undercaptains were finished cleaning up, and had emptied the dirty water several times, as well as refilled the pitcher, by the time that Varais knocked on the door.

"Sers?"

"Come on in," answered Taelya.

Varais stepped inside and closed the door. "It's a little strange to be in officers' quarters."

"If anyone asks, tell them you're a temporary undercaptain," said Taelya. "They can check with either of us." *You likely will be at some point.* Taelya wasn't quite sure where that thought came from, but it made a sort of sense. "We took the top bunks. You can have either of the lower bunks. Since there's no one else with us, we can use the one you don't take for gear."

"I'll take the one that's behind the door when it opens."

"We've already washed up, but the basin's clean," said Kaeryla, "and the pitcher is full."

"We're going to have to leave for an officers' meeting in a little bit," explained Taelya, "but we went over the list you recommended." She nodded to Kaeryla.

"Do you see any problem with moving Mattark to my half squad, that is, if the squad has to be split?" asked the younger undercaptain.

Varais thought for a moment, then said, "That shouldn't be a problem."

"Who would you recommend shifting, then?" asked Taelya.

"Breslan. He and Mattark are about the same."

"Then, with those changes, that's the way you'll split the squad if it's necessary."

"Thank you, sers. Now, if you don't mind . . . I think I'll use that basin."

A quint later, Taelya picked up her visor cap, donned it, and said to Kaeryla, "We should leave now."

The younger mage raised her eyebrows.

"I don't want Sheralt and Valchar getting there before us."

"You think they'd do—"

"No. I worry about what the senior Montgren officers would think if we're the last ones there."

Both Kaeryla and Varais nodded.

With that, the two undercaptains set out for the officers' mess and, when they got there, found it consisted of little more than a single long table in a small room off the troopers' mess. Gustaan was already there, standing by the table and talking to another officer, honey-skinned and dark-haired, if with some gray, a majer from his collar insignia, clearly Majer Zekkarat. Taelya remembered his name, and he did look vaguely familiar.

"Undercaptains," began Gustaan, "I'm glad you're here a little early so that you could meet Majer Zekkarat before the meeting begins. He fought against the Hydlenese as a Lydian captain, but he's now a Montgren majer and the field commander for the two Montgren companies." Gustaan gestured to Taelya. "Undercaptain Taelya."

Zekkarat's mouth opened for an instant before he smiled broadly. "You must be Mage-Captain Lhadoraak's daughter. I can recall when you were much smaller, but you were very determined even then." The smile was replaced by a more somber look. "I'm sure that you've heard this before, but I've never said it to you. Your father's bravery, intelligence, and tactical understanding saved all of us. He also saved all the people of Fairhaven as well. I know. I was one of those he saved."

For a moment, Taelya could say nothing. Finally, she managed, "Thank you. I'm very glad to see you again, and I appreciate so much what you said."

"I only spoke the truth," replied Zekkarat.

"And this is Undercaptain Kaeryla. She's the daughter of Majer Beltur."

"Your father is not only a formidable mage, but an excellent field commander."

"Something that Commander Raelf and the majer found it necessary to emphasize," added Gustaan, "although that should remain between us."

"I understand that you're capable of both healing and fighting," Zekkarat continued, intently looking at Kaeryla.

"As a black, I'm likely to be more effective in protecting our guards and troopers in their attacks than in physically leading attacks the way my parents can."

"As I mentioned a few moments ago," said Gustaan, "the various skills of the four undercaptains are why they're assigned as they are, with one white and one black leading each squad. The two whites are also the oldest and most experienced."

"Which white is the oldest and most experienced?"

"Undercaptain Sheralt is the oldest; Undercaptain Taelya is the most experienced. Both are older than either black."

Zekkarat looked as if he were about to ask another question when Gustaan said, "And here come Undercaptain Sheralt and Undercaptain Valchar. Sheralt's the brown-haired one."

"Good afternoon, Undercaptains," offered Zekkarat. "I'm glad you're here a little early. Commander Raelf, Captain Ferek, and Captain Konstyn will be joining us in a few moments." He looked to Sheralt. "I understand you're originally from Worrak. Can you shed any light on why the pirates of Worrak attacked Lydiar?"

"Not really, Majer. They likely attacked because there was a good chance of plunder or because someone paid them well and told them they could keep all they could take."

"Who would have told them or paid them, do you think?"

"It could be anyone. They've always paid for information. They could have attacked in hopes of getting golds enough to challenge Duke Maastyn."

"Or someone could have paid them and pointed out the same?"

"They'd have to have been paid well to take that risk," replied Sheralt.

Zekkarat nodded and fixed his eyes on Valchar. "You're from Lydiar?"

"Barely, ser. I grew up in Fowtyn. It's a hamlet maybe five kays inside Lydiar on the road from Fairhaven. When Duke Halacut started demanding that the mages of Lydiar serve him as arms-mages, I decided to come here. That was four years ago."

"Just like that?"

"My father was also a bit of a mage, but just before he died of the green flux, he told me never to serve as an arms-mage under the Duke. There was only one place to go that I knew had mages and treated them well."

Taelya sensed the approach of three other men and half turned.

As she did, Zekkarat said, "Commander, all the Montgren officers are here."

Taelya studied the three as they neared the table. Raelf's eyes, slightly bloodshot, were sunken into a wrinkled face, and while his carriage was erect, his steps not shuffling, Taelya could sense that the commander's order levels were low, more like those of an ancient man, rather than the strong majer she recalled from sixteen years earlier. He walked to the end of the table, then gestured for the others to sit down. "Just take a seat anywhere."

Despite that statement, Zekkarat ended up in the seat to Raelf's right, with Gustaan across from him. Sheralt sat beside Gustaan, followed by Taelya, Valchar, and then Kaeryla, while on the other side Konstyn flanked Zekkarat, leaving Ferek as the last Montgren officer at the table.

"Lord Korsaen would have preferred to have been here," said the commander, "but his presence is required in Vergren to help Duchess Koralya become more . . . conversant with certain aspects of her duties."

Taelya didn't care for that explanation in the slightest, suggesting, as it did, that Korsaen was required to keep matters under control.

"Likewise . . . my health is not what it once was, and that is why Majer Zekkarat is in command of the Montgren forces." Raelf cleared his throat and swallowed twice before continuing. "Majer Beltur has conveyed that all of the Fairhaven officers have been on patrols where you encountered in one fashion or another Hydlenese patrols. Have you in fact been attacked?"

"Yes, they have," replied Gustaan.

"Which of you?"

"I have, ser." That reply came almost simultaneously from Sheralt and Taelya.

Raelf nodded, then said, "All of you will be departing Weevett tomorrow. You will be riding directly to Jellico. A small force of Certan troopers will join you at the tariff post just inside Certis. They will escort you to Jellico. There you will meet the Certan commander. The Viscount has not indicated whether he will meet any officers personally. In Jellico, you will join with a battalion or more of Certan troopers. The combined force will then take the road through the Easthorns to a point east of Passera. Once there you will prepare for the assault on Passera. The details of that assault will be worked out between Majer Zekkarat and Captain Gustaan and the Certan commander. Our commitment to the Viscount lasts only until Passera is in Certan control, or until the attack is called off by the Certan commander, or until the first day of harvest. Your supply wagons contain enough provisions for your men sufficient to travel to Jellico and return. The Viscount is responsible for provisions from Jellico to Passera and back to Jellico."

Once again, Raelf cleared his throat and swallowed. During that silence, Taelya concentrated her senses on him, finding tiny points of orangish-red chaos all throughout his body. She managed not to swallow. *No wonder he looks so old.*

"Neither Captain Konstyn nor Captain Ferek has any experience in dealing with arms-mages. It might be useful for each of you to give a quick statement of what you can provide to them and their men. Undercaptain Sheralt?"

"Yes, ser. I can shield a squad from arrows for possibly half a quint. I can shield a larger force for less time. I can throw a moderate number of large chaos bolts roughly a hundred yards, but quite a few more smaller and narrower chaos bolts at nearer targets. I can also shield myself against occasional arrows, blades, and lances."

"What do you mean by a moderate number?"

"That depends on how large the chaos bolt and how far I have to throw it. It's an estimate on my part, but I think it would be difficult to throw more than three to four large chaos bolts—ones with enough chaos to destroy a squad—in a quint. After that, I'd likely need rest and ale immediately."

"Useful, but not decisive. Undercaptain Taelya?"

"I can shield a company for half a quint against arrows. I also can conceal a company from the eyesight of anyone for about the same time, but not from the senses of another mage. My ability to throw large chaos bolts is similar to Sheralt's. I can also use small chaos bolts effectively at close range, and I can shield myself against attacks, as well as use my shields as a defensive weapon."

"Undercaptain Valchar?"

"I am strictly a black mage, ser. I can shield troopers in the way the others can, and I can conceal perhaps a squad of troopers for a quint. I can also shield myself, and use those shields defensively."

"Undercaptain Kaeryla?"

"I'm a black mage and a healer. I can shield a squad easily for as long as a glass, a company for less time. I can also conceal both. Like the others, I can withstand most attacks on me personally if they don't go on for more than several quints. I have a limited ability to use my shields to cut through riders trying to surround me."

Raelf suddenly looked back to Sheralt. "I'm curious. If it came to conflict between you and Undercaptain Taelya . . . ?"

"There's no question, ser. She could kill me and most mages in moments."

Taelya could see that Gustaan had trouble hiding a smile.

Raelf looked slightly disconcerted, but turned to Valchar. "Could any of the rest of you stand up to her?"

"No, ser. Kaeryla would last the longest. She has the next-strongest shields."

"I believe that answers your questions, ser," said Zekkarat smoothly. "You might recall that Undercaptain Taelya has been trained by Majer Beltur extensively since she was seven, and that she played a role in the Fairhaven victory even at that age by protecting some of the families with her shields."

Although the last was definitely an overstatement, and one that Gustaan had to have supplied, Taelya couldn't help liking the majer.

"It's rather different . . . having two women officers," offered Raelf.

"Majer Beltur and Healer Jessyla were quite effective in destroying a goodly number of Hydlenese," Zekkarat pointed out.

"But she was his consort."

"Undercaptain Taelya is their niece and Undercaptain Kaeryla their daughter," said Gustaan.

Abruptly, Raelf nodded. "Good enough." He looked to the two Montgren captains. "Do you have any questions?"

"Yes, ser," replied Konstyn. "Undercaptain Taelya, have you ever fought hand-to-hand with the Hydlenese . . . or anyone else?"

"I have adequate skills with a sabre. On the two occasions where my patrol was attacked, I used tightly focused chaos bolts and killed seven attackers in the first attack and three in the second before they turned and fled."

"Adequate sabre skills?"

"I've watched her disarm and take down troopers twice her size," said Gustaan dryly. "She's comparing herself to the best, like her squad leader, who was a Westwind guard before she came to Fairhaven."

Even Raelf smiled for a brief moment. "Do you have any more questions? Good. Then I'll see you all here for dinner." With that, he stood.

Immediately, all the other officers rose.

Raelf nodded, then turned and walked out of the mess.

Once the commander had left, Zekkarat looked to the two Montgren captains. "Now . . . what questions do you have that you didn't want to ask with the commander present?"

Konstyn and Ferek exchanged glances.

Finally, Konstyn spoke. "I've never heard of mages who were trained in blades. It seems almost an admission . . ."

"That our magery will fail at some point?" replied Taelya. "In every prolonged conflict in which Majer Beltur was engaged, every single mage either ended up exhausted and without magery . . . or dead. Mages can retain enough strength to protect themselves, but no one else. Ability with a sabre gives them a weapon. The other reason is one that most commanders don't consider. When we practice blades, we're required to hold shields only against our skin. We're trained so that part of the time, we have wooden wands, and our opponents have blunted blades. Every time we fail and are hit, it's painful. It's especially painful for Sheralt and me. It's like being burned with a hot iron. The majer wanted us to understand what our men felt. Or as close as we could."

"Anything else?" asked Zekkarat.

"Couldn't you have just used your shields to stop the Hydlenese who attacked you?" asked Ferek.

"That would have been stupid," replied Taelya. "First, they'd crossed into Montgren territory. Second, the attack showed that they'd attack again. We're always outnumbered. Why would I let anyone escape who was going to attack again? Every man they lose is one we don't have to fight again." She smiled politely, even though she could tell that she'd disconcerted the black-haired Ferek.

"You've had to explain that before, haven't you?" asked Zekkarat.

"More than once," replied Taelya.

"That's all I have for the Fairhaven officers," said the majer. "I look forward to learning more at dinner. I'll need a word with you two captains, now."

The four undercaptains rose, as did Gustaan, and Taelya moved toward Kaeryla and murmured, "Go ahead. I'll be along shortly." Then she let the four others lead the way from the officers' mess. Once she sensed that Zekkarat and the captains weren't looking, she raised a concealment and began to move slowly and quietly back to the three officers who still stood beside the table. She stopped as soon as she could hear.

"You still have concerns, don't you?" asked Zekkarat.

"Even the two senior captains are so young," said the swarthy Ferek.

"Taelya lived through the attacks on Fairhaven at age seven. She's likely killed more men than either of you, and she's been riding patrols for years. What else do you need?" asked Zekkarat, his tone sardonically humorous.

"She's a woman."

"Her aunt, who isn't even a white mage, killed more than a company's worth of men."

"But among all the troopers . . ."

"Ferek . . . all you have to tell your men is that even touching a white mage without permission could get them killed on the spot. They carry those shields all the time, even when they sleep, I understand."

"I could spar with her . . ."

"Why? What would that prove? She doesn't need a blade to kill you, and if it turns out that she's better than you, you'll look like a fool. I knew Gustaan years ago. He was a Hydlenese squad leader that Beltur captured. He's forgotten more about blades than you know. If he says she's adequate, the odds are that she's at least as good as you are."

"These are their weaker mages?" asked Konstyn.

"Of course. The two strongest are Beltur and Jessyla. Lord Korsaen would have been an idiot to insist they come. We'll need the strongest mages against Hydlen because that's likely where the greatest danger is. Our job is to support the Certans in their greedy push to take Passera. We need to do it in a way that costs us the least in men and mages, because we get nothing from it except a certain forbearance from the Viscount. The Fairhaven officers all know that as well. So we need to work together. Also, remember that the younger woman mage is an accomplished healer. That could be most useful." After a moment, Zekkarat said, "You two can go. I need a moment here to think."

Taelya eased back against the wall and waited for Konstyn and Ferek to leave, but once they had left the mess and before she could move, Zekkarat turned in her direction and spoke.

"You can remove the concealment, Taelya."

She did. "How did you know?"

The majer smiled. "I didn't, not exactly. What I did see was four officers in blue leaving the mess, not five, and I've seen your uncle and aunt do concealments. You mentioned that ability. If I'd been in your position, I'd have done what you did."

"So how much of what you said to them was because you thought I might overhear it?"

"Very little. I suspect you might not be quite as good with a sabre as I said. Have you sparred against Gustaan?"

"Only occasionally. He's still better than I am. But I can usually keep from getting hit most of the time."

"Given his size and strength, that means you're likely better than you say." Zekkarat smiled again. "I'll keep your secret about overhearing us. I might call on that ability in the future, though. I would like your assessment of your other undercaptains. Your honest assessment."

Taelya considered the matter, then said, "Sheralt's likely almost as good as I am with narrow chaos bolts. He's probably a bit stronger in throwing a large chaos bolt at an entire squad or company. His shields aren't as strong, but he's working on strengthening them with some techniques that Beltur suggested. So far he can't do concealments, except around himself."

"Valchar is the weakest, then?"

Taelya raised her eyebrows. "Why do you think that?"

"Because Beltur wouldn't send his daughter if she didn't have strong shields."

He's right about that. "I don't know for certain, but I'd tend to agree, since Kaeryla can do concealments and Valchar can't."

"How is Sheralt's judgment?"

"I've never seen him make a bad judgment, but I don't know. He managed to escape from Worrak to avoid serving any of the pirate lords, so . . ."

"Fair enough." Zekkarat glanced toward the door. "You better leave here under a concealment because Konstyn and Ferek just might be waiting outside somewhere."

"I'd planned to, but I appreciate the suggestion."

Zekkarat smiled. "You first."

Taelya was both heartened and a little chagrined as she left the mess under a concealment—heartened by Zekkarat's open frankness and perception and chagrined at her own inability to avoid being detected. *You're going to have to be much more careful about using concealments if you intend to prowl around.*

She remained under a concealment until she stepped into the shaded entry into the officers' quarters and she sensed no one near. Then she entered and made her way into the room she shared with the other two.

"What did you find out?" asked Kaeryla as soon as Taelya shut the door. "Varais is working with the squad."

"Ferek isn't all that happy that we're women, but Zekkarat is more interested in what we can do. Zekkarat is also very sharp."

"I could have told you all that."

"Zekkarat also said that it was really important that your parents were the ones who stayed in Fairhaven because that was where the most important battles would be fought. He also told the captains that their job and ours was to support the Certans in the ways that cost us the least in men and mages."

"You're leaving things out," said Kaeryla a trace testily.

Taelya sighed. "Ferek wanted to spar with me. Zekkarat told him it was stupid, because mages aren't supposed to fight that way, and if he won, it didn't add anything, and if he lost, he'd look foolish. He also said he'd known Gustaan since he was a Hydlenese squad leader Beltur had captured and that Gustaan had forgotten more about blades than Ferek had ever learned."

"I like him even better," said Kaeryla.

"Just keep that between us."

"Everything except Ferek not liking women. I'd figured that out already."

"Only talk to Varais about that. She should know."

"I never thought of telling anyone else, except you, but you already knew."

Before all that long, Taelya, Kaeryla, Sheralt, and Valchar were walking back to the officers' mess for dinner. At the entry to the mess stood Gustaan, who motioned them over.

"The seating will be, as usual for the evening meal, in order of rank. As a courtesy, each of us is presumed senior to our Montgren counterparts of the same rank. For the most part, that's likely true in fact, with one exception. To make it easier though, for this one meal, there are place cards."

All that meant that the commander was at the head of the table, with Zekkarat at his right, and Gustaan at his left. Taelya had Ferek on her right and Kaeryla on her left, and the two Montgren undercaptains, Drakyn and Maakym, were seated at the foot of the table opposite each other. Taelya couldn't help but wonder why the two undercaptains hadn't been at the earlier meeting, but suspected that meeting had been designed to let Konstyn and

Ferek meet and gauge the Fairhaven officers, without their subordinates being present.

Just from Maakym's age and appearance, clearly older than all of the junior officers except Gustaan, Taelya decided that he was a former squad leader who'd come up through the ranks and who had possibly been assigned under Ferek because of his experience.

As soon as everyone was seated, Raelf immediately said, "Although the seating is by rank, there is no agenda to be discussed. It's just a hearty meal at which you all have another chance to talk and meet each other before you leave tomorrow." With that he lifted his beaker of ale and said, "To a successful campaign."

"To a successful campaign!"

Taelya took but a small swallow of the ale, which was considerably more bitter than the ale at home. That hardly surprised her, since she had experienced the poorer ale at the East Inn.

The main fare, to no one's surprise, was roasted lamb with a heavy pepper gravy, accompanied by boiled new potatoes and bread. The lamb was good, but Taelya used the gravy sparingly.

After a little time of general comments about the hope for clear weather and other innocuous topics, Konstyn looked across the table at Taelya and said, "A thought occurred to me. You're a white mage, yet you are able to use blades. Doesn't iron . . . affect you?"

"I can use an iron blade," replied Taelya, "but my personal blades are cupridium. They're as strong as black iron." She didn't mention that Kaeryla also had cupridium blades, just for their strength.

"Then . . . isn't cupridium . . . hard to come by?" asked Ferek, seated to her right.

"You mean costly?" Taelya nodded. "I'm fortunate that my uncle is also able, with the help of another smith, to forge cupridium blades."

"You mean Majer Beltur?" Konstyn looked surprised.

"My father has many talents," interjected Kaeryla. "He's not only a mage, but a smith and a healer, and has orchards and a distillery."

"How did a healer like you," asked Maakym, seated to Kaeryla's left, "get to be an arms-mage?"

"I'm like my parents, who are both healers and arms-mages."

"That's unusual . . ."

"Everything about Fairhaven," said Zekkarat cheerfully, "is different. Some aspects, I wish we had, but we will be enjoying one of them at the conclusion of dinner. Majer Beltur was kind enough to send us a keg of his superb apple brandy for the mess. We'll be served some after the meal. What's left, which should be considerable, will accompany us to Certis and then to Gallos. We will save it for special occasions, of course."

Taelya couldn't help but wonder what those special occasions might be. *Heading back to Fairhaven without many casualties and without angering the Viscount, perhaps?*

Clearly taking his cue from the majer, Konstyn then asked, "Are there other special goods or beverages that Fairhaven is known for?"

"There is a special dark ale that's better than almost any I've tasted," said Sheralt, adding with a wry smile, "and since I've been forced to travel more than many, I've tasted a number of brews that left a great deal to be desired . . ."

From there, the conversation was much lighter, although Taelya could see that Zekkarat was ready to divert it from anything controversial if any officer was unwise enough to offer such a topic.

None was, and slightly before eighth glass, Taelya and the others headed back to their temporary quarters.

XXX

Given the length of the ride to Jellico, the combined Fairhaven/Montgren force did not attempt a predawn departure from the Weevett post, but neither did Majer Zekkarat delay. At almost precisely seventh glass, the outrider scouts rode out through the gate, followed in order by Gustaan and Squad Two, then by Konstyn's company, Ferek's company, the supply wagons, and finally Squad Three, acting as rear guard.

Taelya had thought that she might have difficulty in refilling her water bottles with ale, but the orderly in the officers' mess had been clearly briefed about the needs of mages and quickly filled both of Taelya's water bottles, as well as those of the other three undercaptains.

Once the column was moving and the horses settled into a rhythm, Taelya eased the squad back slightly in order to let some of the dust from the wagons and the main body of the force settle so that Squad Three wouldn't be breathing or wearing it.

Since Weevett lay some five kays from the beginning of the hills that separated Montgren from Certis and since those hills stretched almost another fifteen kays west, the Montgren force would not reach the far side of the hills and the Montgren Gorge that separated Certis from the lands of Montgren until at least midafternoon, and they would end the first day's ride at Orduna, some five kays to the west of the gorge, which scarcely seemed like a long or hard ride, at least not in good weather.

As Taelya studied the green slopes of the first hills, she found it hard to believe that the hills beyond were as barren as Gustaan had described them. *But they must be. He doesn't exaggerate.*

A glass and a half later, Third Squad rode up the curving road toward the crest of what amounted to a pass between two hills that looked more like the ends of low mountains. The mountain-like hills showed much more black rock than grass, and what trees there were seemed low and stunted. When they reached the crest of the road, Taelya looked westward across what looked like a jumble of black and red rock with infrequent and scattered small patches of green.

"That's a chaos land," said Varais. "There's a story that the ancient giants of chaos were stopped here by the forces of order and they ripped up the land in frustration and created the Montgren Gorge. Some of that black rock is like black glass, and the edges can cut cleaner and deeper than a blade."

"I can see why they rotate the garrison at the gorge bridge," said Kaeryla.

"From what I've heard, you'll see why even more when we reach it," replied the squad leader.

The descent on the west side was more gradual, if with more sweeping turns, and the road wound through outcroppings of rock, some of reddish sandstone and some of the black rock, most of which was dull and not glassy in the way Varais had described it, but Taelya did see a few glossy black surfaces, although not where she could have reached them easily. She also could see that the terrain would be far easier to defend than to attack, which partly explained why Certis had not attempted to conquer Montgren, especially given that Montgren offered little wealth to pay for such a conquest—except sheep and wool.

She also wondered why the Duchess's ancestor had built the road and the bridge across the gorge. *Was the increase in trade worth it?* Then she thought about how much Fairhaven had benefited from increased trade. *But we didn't have to spend fifteen years building a road and bridge.*

The rocky wasteland seemed to last forever, but winding through it took only a little more than three glasses before the road rose over another kay to what looked to be a level and grassy plain. Unlike Gustaan, Zekkarat did not alternate Second and Third Squads, but Taelya had to admit that doing so would have been awkward and time-consuming. Several kays ahead, Taelya could see, on the south side of the road, several buildings apparently built of the red sandstone and roofed in fired tiles that had to have been carted from Weevett. Just beyond the buildings were two stone towers flanking the road. Beyond the towers the road narrowed so that it could barely accommodate a wagon.

Belatedly, Taelya realized that the "narrow road" was actually the timbered bridge that extended possibly twenty yards over what she had taken to be a stream, but had to be the Montgren Gorge.

"It doesn't look that wide," observed Kaeryla.

"It's wider in most places," declared Varais. "They built the bridge at the narrowest point. It's a lot deeper than it is wide."

Taelya tried to sense more about the gorge, but there wasn't much to sense because all any mage could sense was order and chaos levels, whether of people or animals, or even plants . . . or structures created with order. She could sense the bridge, but only the faintest trace of order and chaos beneath it, except for what she thought might be nesting birds beneath the bridge.

When the outriders reached the buildings, which meant that Taelya and Squad Three were still almost half a kay from the bridge, the column slowed and almost stopped, then resumed at a crawl. For a moment, Taelya wondered why, until she saw that the lead riders were crossing single file separated by a good yard.

Slowly, Taelya and her squad crawled toward the bridge and the red sandstone buildings. Just about the time that they reached the buildings, the column came to a complete halt. Taelya couldn't see why, but then she sensed that the first wagon was crossing—by itself. Each wagon crossed the same way, with no riders or other wagons on the bridge at the same time. A glass passed before the last wagon crossed and only Squad Three remained.

One of the Montgren troopers stood next to the left bridge pillar, positioned so that he could see both the riders and the last wagon. When the wagon was off the bridge on the west end, he called out, "One rider at a time, and two yards between riders."

Varais moved to the side. "I'll bring up the rear, ser."

Taelya had thought about doing that, but only nodded, then urged Bounder forward.

As she rode between the red sandstone pillars and onto the timbered roadway of the bridge, she couldn't help but look to the side, over the timber railing and posts that were little more than a yard and a half high. She almost wished she hadn't. Stretching to her right was the narrow gorge, its lower depths so far down that they were cloaked in shadows, even in midafternoon. The view to the left wasn't that different, except she did see the glint of sun on water at the bottom of the gorge in the distance to the south. But then, a river at the bottom of the gorge made a certain sort of sense.

Bounder's hooves thudded on the heavy timbers, and while Taelya didn't feel any give in the bridge, she felt more than a little uneasy suspended by just timber over what looked to be a gorge close to two hundred yards deep. She was careful to keep Bounder in the middle of the bridge. She also couldn't help but take a deep breath once she passed the pair of Certan troopers in their green-and-brown uniforms standing beside the far smaller support pillars on the west end and as Bounder's hooves clattered on the stone of the west end approach.

When she glanced ahead, she saw another set of buildings some fifty yards away, alongside which and farther westward the column was halted. When she reined up well short of the last supply wagon, she found Gustaan still mounted and waiting for her.

"We're taking a bit of a rest stop here. We have half a squad of Certan troopers—and an undercaptain—as an escort from here to Jellico, but we only have a ride of about a glass before we get to Orduna, where we'll spend the night."

"That's quite a gorge," Taelya admitted. "I didn't realize it was that deep."

"It's a good defense for this part of Montgren," said Gustaan. "It gets shallow some thirty kays north of here and about twenty south, and the hills north of here are just as rugged. To the south . . . not so much."

After seeing the gorge and hearing Gustaan's explanation, Taelya definitely understood why all the traders had taken the older road through Fairhaven before the Duchess's ancestor had built the more direct road and the bridge.

"We'll be resuming the ride after all the horses are watered," the captain continued. "Just follow the wagons to the watering troughs."

"Yes, ser. Thank you."

Gustaan nodded and turned his horse back toward the front of the column.

"That was amazing!" declared Kaeryla as she joined Taelya, her voice carrying clearly an unfeigned enthusiasm that Taelya did not share.

"That's one word for it," Taelya replied.

"Out in the middle of the bridge, with that breeze, I could almost have been a bird."

Taelya managed not to shake her head. Instead she retrieved her water bottle and took a long swallow of ale, leaving very little in the bottle. Then she relayed what Gustaan had said to Kaeryla, and then, after the last rankers and Varais had crossed the bridge, to the squad leader as well.

Varais nodded, then glanced back at the bridge. "That's another reason why Fairhaven is important."

"Because it's easier to get into Montgren that way, you mean?" replied Taelya. "It would take more time, though."

Varais shook her head. "Think about how long it would take to get an army across that bridge, and that's if the guards didn't burn it or destroy it. If you think about it, Fairhaven guards the access to both Montgren and Lydiar."

"If Fairhaven's so important," said Kaeryla, "then why did the Duchess and her predecessor let it go to ruin?"

"Most likely because they didn't have the mages, golds, and troopers to maintain it," said Taelya. "Even with all the newer merchants and more trade, we can barely afford a single company of Road Guards." *And it's why we're being forced to do the bidding of the Viscount.* She wished, not for the first time, that Fairhaven were strong enough to stop having to bend to the needs of the Duchess.

"They're troopers by any other name," said Varais sardonically, "and the Duchess, the Viscount, and the Prefect all know it."

Taelya knew that as well, but she'd been raised to think of herself as a Road Guard.

Although Gustaan had said the stop would be short, more than two quints passed before the column resumed the ride, and it was well past fifth glass when Orduna came into view, a ramshackle assemblage of houses, cots, and a few scattered warehouses clustered around the road. A small stream bordered the town on the south side, then that meandered toward the southeast, presumably eventually ending up by joining the narrow river at the bottom of the gorge tens of kays to the southeast. Orduna looked to be even smaller than Fairhaven had been when Taelya had first seen it, and was even more compact, with perhaps a hundred homes, although from her position near the end of the column she could only catch glimpses.

Before they reached the town proper, the riders turned in to what appeared to be a way station of sorts at the east end of the town, an area close to twice the size of the way station in Fairhaven, flanked on the north and the south by two modest one-story inns.

The Fairhaven "company" got the stable and three rooms at the smaller inn, partly because, Taelya suspected, Zekkarat wanted to stay in the good graces of the mages, but as Taelya was grooming Bounder after she'd unsaddled him, she noticed a Certan undercaptain dealing with his mount two stalls away.

After she finished with Bounder, making sure he had water and grain, as she stood outside the stall, waiting for Kaeryla to finish grooming her mare, the undercaptain closed the stall and stepped toward Taelya. He was barely a head taller than her, with black stubble, and a scar across the bottom of his cheek and his jaw. With his visor cap eased back slightly, she could also see that he was balding and a good ten years older than she was, suggesting that he'd come up through the ranks, because it was highly unlikely that anyone would remain an undercaptain for fifteen years.

"You're one of those mage-undercaptains, aren't you? One of the ones who are women."

Brilliant conclusion. But Taelya smiled politely and said, "There are two who are men, and two of us who are women."

"I'm Bradoch."

"You're in command of the escort squad, then?"

"Yes . . . ser."

Taelya ignored the slight hesitation, and said, "I'm Taelya. Mage-guard undercaptain from Fairhaven. Are you from Jellico?"

"These days. I was born in Rytel."

Taelya nodded. "I've been there. I was surprised at how high the river walls were." The river walls were among the few things she did remember about Rytel, that and the merchant compound where they'd stayed for several days.

"But you're from Fairhaven?"

"I've lived there for sixteen years. How long have you been in Jellico?"

"I've been with the battalion for seventeen years. Only spent the last year in Jellico. We'll be posted somewhere else before long." Bradoch's eyes went past Taelya, obviously centering on Kaeryla, whose presence Taelya sensed approaching.

"You're looking at Undercaptain Kaeryla. She's my cousin."

Bradoch's eyes came back to Taelya, then went to her sleeve. "She's got black bands, and you have white."

"I'm a chaos mage. She's a black mage and a healer."

"And she's going to fight?"

"Blacks can fight as well as whites, sometimes better. Spidlar's black mages defeated he Prefect's whites."

"That was years ago," said Bradoch before turning to Kaeryla. "I'm Bradoch. I understand you're Undercaptain Kaeryla."

Kaeryla nodded.

"He's in command of the Viscount's escort squad," said Taelya.

"Are you staying here?" asked Bradoch, still looking at Kaeryla.

"Just the four Fairhaven undercaptains and our captain and our . . . troopers," replied Taelya.

"Then we'll be eating together." Bradoch inclined his head. "I look forward to seeing you both then." With a satisfied smile, he turned and walked toward the stable door.

"He's definitely interested in you," said Taelya.

"Who is?" asked Valchar as he hurried toward the cousins.

"The Certan undercaptain who commands the escort group," said Taelya.

"He seems full of himself," replied Valchar.

"Aren't we all?" said Sheralt, a trace sardonically.

"We'll likely find out more at dinner," suggested Taelya. "We should let him talk . . . as much as he wants."

After carting their gear to the small chamber that, again, they shared with Varais, and washing up the best they could, the two cousins made their way to the small chamber off the public room that they'd been told would serve the officers. Gustaan was already there, as was Bradoch, and, in moments, Sheralt and Valchar appeared.

"We'll be getting just about what the men are being fed," said Gustaan, "except we can have another ale or lager—if you want to pay two coppers each for it. The men are eating in shifts in the public room. We can eat less hurriedly."

He moved to the head of the table, then gestured. "Sit where you want. You're all undercaptains, and I'm not about to sort out seniority."

"Who is the most senior of yours?" pressed Bradoch.

"Both Sheralt and Taelya have been undercaptains longer than you have, if you must know," replied Gustaan.

Bradoch looked puzzled as to how Gustaan might know.

"I asked around," replied Gustaan with a smile.

Taelya knew, and doubtless so did Bradoch, that Gustaan had asked the squad leader serving under Bradoch.

In the end, Bradoch seated himself to the left of Gustaan, and Taelya sat across from the Certan undercaptain, while Valchar sat beside the Certan, and Sheralt sat between Taelya and Kaeryla.

Shortly, a younger serving woman likely not even as old as Kaeryla appeared with platters, quickly setting four down before Gustaan, Taelya, Bradoch, and Valchar. She returned twice more, once with the last three platters, and then with a large basket of bread and a capacious pitcher, from which she filled all six beakers. Then she vanished.

Gustaan lifted his beaker. "To a hearty dinner and a safe journey to Jellico." The others raised their beakers and drank.

Gustaan then turned to Bradoch. "We appreciate your taking on the tiresome duty of escorting us to Jellico." He laughed softly and added, "Might I ask how you received such a dubious honor?"

Bradoch actually laughed. "I had the choice of training new recruits for four eightdays or escorting you. It was an easy choice. I've trained more recruits than I could possibly count. I thought someone else should have that honor."

As the Certan undercaptain answered, Taelya took a chunk of the rough-cut bread and surveyed what was on her platter—small pieces of unknown meat covered in a reddish sauce dumped over some sort of square noodles. She took a small bite. The sauce wasn't quite as spicy hot as she feared, and it actually had an acceptable taste. The meat was something she didn't recognize, but wasn't especially gamy. She'd still be alternating bites of sauce and noodles.

Gustaan laughed sympathetically at Bradoch's reply. "I understand. I've done a fair amount of training myself."

Bradoch took a large mouthful of the fare, swallowed it, and nodded. "Not a bad coney burhka."

Although Taelya wouldn't have considered the dish a true burhka, there was a definite similarity to the types of burhka she'd eaten over the years, and the rabbit meat wasn't bad.

"What do you find the hardest skill to teach recruits?" asked Gustaan.

"When to think and when not to. Some junior officers don't ever learn it, though."

The first part of Bradoch's response surprised Taelya. She hadn't considered him that thoughtful. She decided to address the barb of the second part, if in a cheerful tone. "Those undercaptains with less experience or those who haven't come up through the ranks, you mean?"

"More those whose fathers bought them their commissions."

"Exactly," agreed Gustaan warmly. "We're fortunate not to have that problem in Fairhaven."

"Oh?"

"Commissions aren't for sale. It also helps that there aren't any easy billets in Fairhaven. Everyone either patrols or has patrolled, and there's a long training period before undercaptains are confirmed."

Bradoch looked at Taelya. "Then you must be older than you look."

"I've been an undercaptain for almost seven years, and I had ten years of mage training before that."

Bradoch's eyes widened slightly.

Before he could say more, Taelya spoke. "You said you were part of a battalion. What battalion is that?"

"The Eleventh Battalion."

"It sounds like the Viscount has quite a few battalions," said Kaeryla ingenuously.

"More than a score. Certis is a large land. It stretches from the Northern Ocean almost to the Ohyde River. Even making good time, it will take us almost another eightday to reach Jellico, and it will take you an eightday beyond that to reach the end of Certan lands near Passera."

"You won't be accompanying us that far?" asked Taelya.

"Oh, no, the Eleventh is to be deployed elsewhere."

"Do you always get dispatched to where there's trouble?" asked Kaeryla.

"Not always. What about you?" Bradoch looked at Taelya, rather than Kaeryla.

"We usually patrol south of Fairhaven. If there's any trouble, that's where it will be."

"The border with Hydlen?"

Taelya nodded. "Is your border with Hydlen where there's sometimes trouble?"

"The Dukes of Hydlen have always been a problem. That's for everyone around them. You know that."

"So Duke Maastyn is just like his ancestors?" asked Valchar. "Not giving the Viscount his due?"

"It's true that he does nothing to deal with pirates and smugglers, but he hasn't ever raised arms against Certis."

"Not yet, anyway," suggested Sheralt, with an amused smile.

"He knows better," replied the Certan officer.

"What was the most difficult assignment you've had?" asked Kaeryla.

"They're all about the same, part difficult and part routine."

"Have you had to deal with brigands in the Easthorns?" asked Taelya.

"Certis doesn't have brigands in its lands."

Taelya was tempted to mention the ones that her family had encountered after leaving Axalt, but refrained, instead saying, "Have you had to fight brigands and smugglers from other lands?"

"Not often. I'd think Fairhaven might have that problem. Since Duke Maastyn doesn't seem to control either, that is."

"Not in years," replied Gustaan. "It helps that the mages can usually tell when someone is not telling the truth."

Bradoch stiffened for just an instant before offering an easy smile. "I can see where that could be useful."

"You seem to have seen most of Certis," said Kaeryla. "What part is the most beautiful of those parts that you've seen?"

"There's much of Certis I haven't seen, but there's a part of the River Jellicor upstream and west of Jellico that is most striking . . ."

For the remainder of dinner, the conversation dealt with geography and lands in some form or another, ranging from places Bradoch thought they should see to places that Gustaan never wanted to see again, and even to the varieties of sheep that grazed in different places in Montgren and Certis.

When dinner was over, as Taelya left the mess and she and Kaeryla walked back toward their small room, she realized that something felt different about Sheralt . . . but that she couldn't have said what exactly it was.

XXXI

On fiveday morning, Taelya woke early and couldn't sleep. While she tried to get back to sleep, she couldn't, even after Varais quietly dressed and departed, with her thoughts flitting from one thing to another, especially that the Viscount had far more battalions than Montgren had companies. Once Taelya knew it was close enough to the time the inn would be serving, she got up and dressed, trying not to disturb Kaeryla.

Kaeryla opened her eyes and glared at Taelya. "Just go. I'll be there shortly."

"I'll wait . . ."

"Go!" snapped the younger mage. "I don't want you looking at me every moment as if I need to hurry."

"I'll make sure they save some breakfast for you." With that, Taelya left and walked toward the small room that served as an officers' mess.

Just ahead, she saw Sheralt and was reminded that she'd noticed something different about him the night before. From behind, he didn't look any different, but when she extended her senses, studying his order and chaos patterns . . .

Abruptly, he stopped and turned, waiting for her to approach. "You were sensing me. Why? Is something wrong?"

She offered an amused smile. "No. Not at all. You've really gotten your order and chaos well separated. Your shields even look stronger."

"Someone told me that I should. Long rides without much really to do gave me a chance to really work. My shields are stronger. From what I can tell, anyway." He smiled wryly, adding lightly, "Are you happy now?"

"I'm happy for you. Where's Valchar?"

"He's not the most cheerful in the morning. It was better to leave."

Taelya just nodded.

"And Kaeryla?"

Taelya couldn't help grinning for a moment. "Pretty much the same."

"Well, we'd better uphold the reputation of senior undercaptains, then." Sheralt gestured in the direction of the "mess."

When they entered the room, Gustaan was seated across from Bradoch and looked to be finishing whatever was on his platter.

Bradoch had no platter but had a beaker of ale in front of him. "Where are the other two undercaptains?"

"They'll be along shortly," replied Sheralt.

"Together?"

"Possibly," said Taelya, "but not in the way you're implying. They're just a little more deliberate this morning."

"Just so they don't slow our departure."

"They won't," declared Gustaan as he downed the last of his beaker of ale and stood. He said to Taelya and Sheralt, "All of you fill your water bottles here. I've told the serving girl."

"Thank you, ser."

As Gustaan departed, Bradoch looked quizzically at the two.

"We just follow the captain's orders," replied Sheralt cheerfully, seating himself at the table.

For a moment, Bradoch didn't speak. Then he said, "He's been around, hasn't he?"

"He came up the same way you did," replied Taelya.

"It shows. All you mages wear blades. I've never seen mages do that."

"The majer and the captain insisted that we all be able to defend ourselves," said Taelya. "The captain is in charge of making sure we can."

"But you two are whites."

"Our blades are cupridium." Taelya didn't feel like explaining more.

"Oh . . . like the old Magi'i of Cyador?"

That the Cyadoran mages had used cupridium blades was new to Taelya, but she simply replied, "Something like that."

At that moment, the serving girl arrived with three platters, each of them containing a flatbread round on which were piled two fried eggs topped with cheese and a glob of a greenish sauce. Taelya hadn't quite recovered from the sight when the server returned with three beakers and a pitcher, set the beakers in front of the three, and then filled them.

Taelya tasted the green sauce. Her first feeling was that of cool blandness, followed by spice-fire. Then she tried the eggs. They were greasy. She looked across at Bradoch, who had rolled the whole mess into a cylinder and was eating the cylinder from one end. She followed his example, discovering in the process that the combination of less than appealing individual ingredients turned out to be slightly more than marginally palatable.

As Taelya finished her breakfast cylinder and was drinking the last of the ale in her beaker, Kaeryla arrived and sat down beside Sheralt, who had insisted on eating his breakfast piece by piece. Moments later, Valchar hurried in and sat across the table from Kaeryla, leaving an empty chair between him and Bradoch, who rose almost as soon as Valchar seated himself.

"Seventh glass we head out," Bradoch announced before leaving the small chamber.

"What's for breakfast?" asked Valchar.

"You don't want to know," replied Sheralt sourly.

"It's not that bad if you roll it up and eat it from one end," added Taelya. "The flatbread and the sauce make it palatable."

"Next time, if there is a next time," said Sheralt, "I'll try that. It couldn't be any worse that way."

"I'll see you in the stable," Taelya said to Kaeryla. "You need to hurry."

Kaeryla nodded, not quite sullenly.

Taelya finished the last of her ale and then stood as the serving girl reappeared with two more platters containing the same ingredients that she'd served the others.

Looking at the platter that had appeared before her, Kaeryla replied, "Hurrying won't be hard."

Taelya returned to the room, finished getting ready, then lifted her gear and made her way back down to the small room, where she had her water bottles filled with ale, then hurried to the stable. Even before she began to saddle Bounder, Gustaan appeared.

"Squad Three will take the lead today. I've already told Varais."

"Should I have been here earlier?"

"A little, but it doesn't matter today."

Taelya understood. "Yes, ser." She also saddled Bounder quickly and led him outside into the open area, then mounted and rode to where Varais was mustering Squad Three directly behind the Certan escort squad. She noticed that Bradoch barely looked in her direction.

"Good morning, ser," offered Varais.

"The same to you. Is there anything I need to know? Are all the horses sound?"

"They're all sound. No problems that I know of, except Chaslar's coughing. It doesn't sound too bad."

"I can look at him. If it's serious, I'll have Undercaptain Kaeryla look at him as well. She should be here any moment."

"If you wouldn't mind, ser."

Taelya turned Bounder and rode alongside the squad. Chaslar was in the next-to-last rank, and Taelya reined up beside him.

"Ser?"

"As you were. I'm just here to check on that cough." Taelya ran her senses over the junior guard, or trooper now, she supposed. There was the faintest hint of dull reddish chaos in his chest. "How long have you had that cough?"

"Three . . . maybe four days, ser."

"So far, it doesn't seem bad, but if you feel a lot worse, let the squad leader know."

"Yes, ser."

When Taelya reached the front of the squad, Kaeryla had just arrived, and she shot Taelya a sharp glance.

Taelya smiled politely and said, "Varais wanted one of us to take a look at Chaslar. He's got a cough. There's a touch of chaos in his chest, but it doesn't seem that bad. When we get to the first rest stop, you might want to take a look at him. You'd have a better idea about that than I do."

"You could have waked me earlier."

"I did. You told me to go, and that you'd be along shortly. I took you at your word."

"In the morning . . . please don't." Kaeryla's voice softened slightly on the last two words.

"Then don't snap at me when I do."

"I'll try to be better." Kaeryla's tone was contrite.

At that moment, a series of trumpet calls echoed across the open area, and immediately the escort squad started forward.

"Squad Three," ordered Taelya, "forward!"

In less than a fifth of a quint, the escort squad and Squad Three were riding through Orduna, heading west. In the early-morning light, the town appeared even less welcoming than it had the afternoon before, with most of the few buildings and warehouses still shuttered.

Even before they reached the end of Orduna, and they neared the open lands that seemed to consist mostly of rocky hummocks and scattered patches of ragged grasses, Taelya noticed that Bradoch had looked back at Kaeryla several times.

XXXII

By threeday, after six straight days of riding, both Taelya and Kaeryla were ready for a change. The first two days had largely taken them through the same sort of land as that around Orduna. By sevenday, they had reached stretches of comparatively flat lands separated by rolling and wooded hills from just more flat lands, on which scores and scores of small steads seemed to grow mostly grains. That had made a certain sense to Taelya, although she couldn't have exactly said why.

By oneday they had finally ridden into the lower and more fertile lands that bordered the River Jellicor, where seemingly all sorts of crops and trees flourished, from orchards containing apples, pears, figs, and even pearapples to fields with beans, potatoes, and melons, and good-sized towns.

Along the way, a day's ride apart, were military way stations, all of which were empty except for a squad to maintain each. The number of such way stations bothered Taelya, for more than a few reasons, chief among them being the fact that they were in good repair and that, once they had left the rocky lands around Orduna, the road, narrow as it was, was either paved or gravel-packed. That made travel much faster, but it also meant the Viscount had the ability to move troopers in most kinds of weather.

But if he has all those troopers and roads, why does he need us?

That was the question that Taelya kept pondering as she and Kaeryla rode with Third Squad at the front of the column, as they had for every other day.

Kaeryla gestured to the small orchard on the north side of the road with trees that looked to be close to twenty yards high. "Do you know what kind of trees those are?"

"I've never seen them before," admitted Taelya.

"They're black walnuts," offered Varais, from where she rode in front of them with Gustaan. "They're a good hardwood. You can eat the nuts, but they're a pain to hull."

"How do you harvest the nuts?"

"You don't have to. When they're ripe they fall off. Very messy, and they'll stain your hands almost black."

"That's why they make a black stain out of the hulls," interjected Gustaan, before adding, "Bradoch and Zekkarat are gesturing for me to join them."

As the captain rode forward, Kaeryla asked Varais, "How do you know so much about black walnuts?"

"I worked for an old woman who grew them for a time after I left Westwind. Never again."

"You've never talked much about how you got from Westwind to Fairhaven," said Kaeryla.

"No, I haven't. I'd rather not, ser."

While Varais's tone was pleasant, it was also firm.

"Do you know anything else about the black walnuts?" asked Kaeryla.

"They taste better than groundnuts or acorns, but not as good as almonds. She said the healers used the husks, but she didn't know much about that."

"Thank you," replied Kaeryla. "I hadn't heard that. I'll keep it in mind." She lowered her voice and murmured to Taelya, "I wonder if they might cure wandering eyes."

"You seem to have made a conquest," replied Taelya quietly, but with an amused smile.

"The good Certan undercaptain is far too old for me, even if I were interested. Which I'm not."

Taelya doubted that Bradoch was interested in Kaeryla in any way that the younger undercaptain would find in the slightest appealing, but so long as all he did was look and behave politely, there wasn't any point in antagonizing him.

After what appeared to be a brief discussion between Zekkarat, Bradoch, and Gustaan, the captain turned his mount and rode back to rejoin Taelya, Kaeryla, and Varais.

"We'll reach the bridge over the Jellicor in about two glasses. Jellico is slightly north of the bridge on the far side," said Gustaan. "I'm going to ride back and tell Sheralt and Valchar."

"Did they tell you anything else?"

"Not much, except that we won't know where we'll be lodged until we reach Jellico. There are apparently several army posts in and around the city."

"How long will we be staying in Jellico?" asked Taelya. "Just overnight, or longer?"

"Bradoch doesn't know that. He thinks it's likely to be more than one night, just in order to rest the horses, but he wasn't told. He just dispatched a messenger to the marshal, advising him of our arrival." With a nod, the captain urged his mount toward the rear of the column.

Once Gustaan had left, Taelya said, "We've seen lots of prosperous steads, but nothing that suggests we're close to a city. I wonder how far north of the bridge Jellico really is." She looked toward Varais. "Do you know?"

The squad leader shook her head. "I stayed well away from both Fenard and Jellico."

"For a former Westwind guard, that was a good idea," said Taelya. "From what I've heard about the Viscount and the Prefect, I'm not all that comfortable with the idea of riding into Jellico."

"Right now, we're likely fairly safe," returned Varais. "Once we've done what the Viscount wants, that's another question."

Almost a quint passed before Gustaan rejoined Squad Three.

In less than another quint, Taelya saw the first sign that they were indeed nearing a city. The comparatively narrow stone-paved road widened to the point where it could easily accommodate two large wagons side by side with more than enough room to spare. There was also a well-chiseled kaystone that read JELLICOR BRIDGE 10K. In another quint, the road became completely level on the top of a wide berm that stretched directly west, and kays to the northwest, Taelya could see a long wall, presumably on the west side of the river that she couldn't yet see.

More than two glasses passed before Bradoch and the escort rankers reached the causeway to the wide stone bridge, a bridge with two spans that met on what looked to be a small rocky islet in the middle of the grayish blue waters of the fast-moving river. The stone roadbed was a good five yards above the water.

As she began to ride across the bridge, Taelya looked to the south, which was upstream, and from what she could tell, the river was much wider there. Then she glanced north and realized that the bridge had been built on what amounted to a rocky shelf where the river was much narrower and that farther to the north, opposite the city walls, there were rocky and swirling rapids. Also, Jellico was closer to the bridge than Taelya expected, more than a kay to the north, possibly close to two kays, and the granite ramparts looked to rise more than twenty yards above the pavement just in front of the southern gate to the city, not to mention that they seemed to extend more than a kay, possibly two, to the north and at least that far west.

Perhaps a hundred yards west of the bridge was a crossroads, and the escort riders turned north on the wide stone-paved road that ran straight toward the city walls.

A quint or so later, after the escort riders started through the open and un-guarded city gates, Taelya could see that they were made of iron-bound oak and slid back on oiled iron grooves into stone recesses, leaving an open archway high enough for riders to pass under with more than enough space overhead. Inside the city walls, the street narrowed, being barely wide enough for four horses or a single large wagon. Although the majority of dwellings outside the walls were built largely or completely of timber, the buildings and dwellings in the city itself all appeared to be constructed of fired brick with tile roofs, and all were comparatively narrow and tall, rising two to three stories, sometimes more.

And there were people everywhere, or so it appeared to Taelya, talking, walking, bargaining with street peddlers, and very few seemed to look at the passing riders, except occasionally with expressions of annoyance. After following the street from the gate for almost a kay, the escort riders reached a large square filled with vendors and even more people. They followed the edge of the square west before again heading north, then turning west on a broader avenue. After riding several hundred yards, Taelya could make out yet another set of walls rising from a low hill near the western end of the city. In the center of those walls was a multistoried structure that filled most of the space within the walls.

"That has to be the Viscount's palace," said Kaeryla.

"It's as big as all the buildings in Westwind," observed Varais.

"It's much bigger than the palace of Duke Maastyn," added Gustaan, "unless he's added more in the years since I was in Hydolar."

As they rode even closer to the palace, Taelya saw that the walls were perhaps only ten yards high and that the granite had been smoothed and polished so that the stone shone in the afternoon sunlight.

The column halted outside the gates, and, within a few moments, an officer in a brilliant green uniform rode out through the open and well-polished bronze gates, escorted by troopers in what looked like green-and-brown dress uniforms. The escort riders edged their mounts to the side so that the officer could ride up to where Majer Zekkarat and Captain Gustaan had reined up.

"On behalf of Viscount Rystyn, I welcome all of you to Jellico. Capacious as the palace is, it cannot accommodate three full companies. Therefore, Majer Zekkarat and the Fairhaven officers and troopers will be quartered in the north quarters building of the palace. The Montgren companies proper and their company officers will be quartered in the main quarters building adjoining and to the north of the palace, but all the officers will eat at the palace officers' mess. Again . . . welcome to Jellico."

Taelya noticed that Bradoch and the escort troopers did not enter the palace but moved to the left as if to guide the Montgren forces toward the main quarters building.

Then the welcoming officer turned his mount and led the way into the palace complex.

Despite the elaborate bronze gates, the actual entry to the palace was narrower than the city gates, and the archway entry was more like a stone-walled tunnel that extended at least twenty yards. The stones forming the ceiling were low enough that the taller riders in front of Taelya could have bumped their heads had the stones above been even a cubit lower. The courtyard into which she and the others rode was paved in smooth granite, but clearly could not have handled more than a single mounted company.

Once everyone was in the courtyard, the green-clad officer again spoke. "The officers' mounts go in the guest stables through the west archway. The troopers' mounts go in the lancers' stables behind the guest stables."

Surprisingly to Taelya, after she had ridden through the west archway, she found herself in yet another courtyard, this one roughly fifty yards on a side with walls five stories high on all sides, although there were windows everywhere in the walls above the courtyard level. With the others, she dismounted, and then led Bounder into the stables. While the stables weren't filthy, neither were they as clean as either the Road Guard stables or even those in Weevett.

When she finished unsaddling and grooming Bounder, as well as checking on his manger and grain basket, she picked up her gear and closed the stall, wondering where exactly the junior officers' quarters might be. Then she walked to what appeared to be an archway from the stables and waited for the others to join her.

Gustaan appeared about the same time that Kaeryla and Sheralt had dealt with their mounts. Pointing past Taelya, he said, "There's an orderly just beyond that archway. He'll direct you to your quarters."

Moments later, Valchar joined the other undercaptains as they walked from the stables into what might have been called an antechamber. There stood another Certan trooper in a green-and-brown dress uniform.

"Sers, even undercaptains here in the palace have their own quarters. They're small but private. If you would please follow me."

The orderly led the four up a narrow staircase and then along another corridor for some twenty yards before stopping at the junction to another seemingly identical corridor. "The four chambers on the left side are for you. You can decide among yourselves who has which. There are wash facilities at the end of the corridor, and the small chamber on the left is where wash water and chamber pots need to be emptied . . ."

After providing information about the quarters and the location of the officers' mess and other matters, all of which Taelya hoped she could remember, the orderly departed.

Taelya took the first chamber and Kaeryla the second. In moments, Taelya was standing inside her temporary chamber, seeing just how small it really was, holding a narrow pallet bed, a straight-backed chair, and a built-in writing desk, with a brass lamp in a holder above it, along with a narrow wash table and wall pegs for uniforms, and a head-high shelf above the bed for gear. There was also a heavy door bar that fit into sturdy iron brackets.

By the time she cleaned up and checked and reorganized her gear, it was almost time for the evening meal, and she decided to make her way in the direction of the officers' mess. She had no more than stepped out of her quarters when Sheralt appeared.

"You were waiting for me, weren't you?"

He smiled sheepishly, then said, "I thought it might not be too long before you got hungry." He gestured toward the corner where the corridors joined, and the two began to walk.

"Before I got too hungry, or before you got too hungry to wait for me?"

"Does it matter? They aren't going to feed me any sooner. At least the quarters are better than the inns or the way stations. We can hope the food will be."

"In the Viscount's palace, it might be a little better," she replied.

"So long as it's not worse." Sheralt gestured to an archway ahead. "I think we take the steps through there."

"It might be the next archway," suggested Taelya.

"I think it's this one."

"Why don't you go up and see?" suggested Taelya, since all she could sense beyond the upper end of the steps was a corridor that seemed to end abruptly.

Sheralt frowned, then said, "All right." He hurried up the steps and vanished down the corridor, returning shortly. "It just ends with a locked door. How did you know?"

"I didn't sense anyone up there, and if it led to the mess there should have been someone there."

"Remind me not to wager against you."

She smiled cheerfully. "I thought I had."

Sheralt shook his head.

Beyond the next archway was a much wider staircase lit by several narrow slit windows. The two walked up to a wider corridor, one where the lower section of the wall was painted a rich brown below the dark brown chair rail and a cream above it. A series of paintings were hung at intervals, all of which appeared to depict various battles, suggesting to Taelya that they were at least headed in the right direction. Ahead was a small square hall, but some ten yards before reaching the hall, the corridor down which they walked intersected another corridor.

"The officers' mess must be off that hall ahead," said Sheralt.

As they crossed the other corridor, Taelya looked to her left, noting doors a good thirty yards away, and a pair of guards posted there. "That must lead to the palace proper."

"You think the other way is for senior officers?"

"I'm not about to guess," replied Taelya.

There were two closed doors, one on each side of the small square hall, but a trooper in a plain green-and-brown uniform stood outside the closed door on the right, the door that Taelya thought might be the entrance to the mess. He frowned for a moment as he looked at Taelya, but then his face cleared, as if he recalled something.

That we have women as mage-undercaptains?

"Sers," the orderly said politely, "the mess will open in a little less than a quint. Tonight is informal. The larger table is for junior officers, captains and undercaptains. You may sit anywhere except at the head. Nothing but ale or lager will be served until the senior officer appears and is seated at the head of the smaller table."

"Thank you," replied Taelya. "We'll look around until the mess is open."

The orderly nodded.

Taelya walked to the windows and looked out, seeing a courtyard below, one containing a formal garden, with stone walks amid the flowers, small trees, and greenery, but she neither saw nor sensed anyone in the garden. *For the Viscount's family perhaps?*

"It must take quite an effort to keep that garden," mused Sheralt.

Before long, Kaeryla and Valchar joined them outside the mess door, and then Gustaan, Konstyn, and Ferek showed up, along with Zekkarat.

Moments later a sole Certan undercaptain appeared, younger-looking than Valchar, his eyes first going to the older Montgren officers, and then to the four Fairhaven undercaptains. After a moment, he walked toward Taelya and Sheralt, but more toward Taelya, possibly, she thought, because she looked more like a very young male officer.

With a smile, he said, "I'm Naastyrn, one of the more junior Certan undercaptains."

"I'm Sheralt."

"Taelya."

Naastyrn paused, clearly surprised by her voice, then said, "I didn't know . . ."

"The only undercaptains who are women in Montgren are mages," replied Taelya.

The young undercaptain glanced from Konstyn's light blue uniform to Sheralt's darker blue one and then to the white bands on Taelya's sleeves.

"The Fairhaven uniforms are darker than the other Montgren uniforms, and the sleeve bands mean we're mage-undercaptains," she added.

"So all of you in the darker blue are from Fairhaven?"

"That's right."

"Why do you have different uniforms?"

"We started out as Road Guards for the town against the Hydlenese," said Taelya, "and we never changed the uniforms." That wasn't exactly the whole explanation, but it was basically accurate, and she didn't feel like giving the whole explanation.

"We've had trouble with the Hydlenese. I guess everyone who shares borders with them does."

"It does seem that way," said Taelya. "Are you from the southern part of Certis?"

Naastyrn shook his head. "I'm from Podcarr. Forty some kays south of here on the river."

"How did you end up as an undercaptain here in Jellico?"

Naastyrn offered a crooked smile. "I just finished training. I'll be leaving to join my company at Tyrhaad on sevenday."

"I have to say," replied Taelya, "I have no idea where Tyrhaad might be."

"Oh, it's the last town in Certis on the river before it enters Sligo. The company there deals mostly with smugglers and brigands."

"Why did you choose to be an undercaptain?"

"I'm the fourth son, and I have a black thumb when it comes to trees, and I'm all thumbs when it comes to dealing with wagons, mills, and the like. I'm not bad with blades or a bow, and my father said a commission would cost us all less." Naastyrn offered an open smile. "So it seems to be working out for the best for everyone. I do know enough about trade to be useful in Tyrhaad."

"They've opened the mess," said Valchar, standing to Taelya's left.

"Would you like to sit with us?" Taelya asked Naastyrn.

"If you wouldn't mind. I barely know most of the officers here at the palace. I'm just here to study the tariff laws before I leave."

Taelya and Sheralt sat near the end of the longer table, with Naastyrn between them and across from Kaeryla and Valchar.

Dinner consisted of sliced pork covered in a light brown gravy, accompanied by boiled potatoes, and thin-sliced boiled turnips, with generous baskets of warm bread.

"I haven't seen any mages here," said Sheralt cheerfully, once a commander had taken his place at the head of the senior officers' table and everyone had been served.

"Oh, there aren't that many mages in Certis, and most of those serve the Viscount. The few arms-mages are on the marshal's staff. Usually, we don't need them in most duties and operations. That's what one of the captains told me."

"I wouldn't think so," replied Taelya, "not when you have twenty battalions of troopers."

"I'm sure the marshal would love to have twenty, but right now it's around fifteen. He can call up local town troopers, and they might amount to ten battalions, but they're not all that good except for dealing with Kaordist rebels or brigands in the northern Easthorns."

"Like the ones east of Rytel?" asked Taelya in a tone she hoped was guileless.

"We haven't had that much trouble with them in more than ten years," replied Naastyrn. "Even I knew that."

Every word the young Certan officer said rang true, but as Taelya well knew, that only proved that he believed them to be true. Still . . . she suspected most of what he said was probably close to accurate.

"What about for smuggling?" asked Valchar.

Naastyrn shook his head. "The local troopers would keep most of what they found and not report it."

"We don't know much about the Viscount," offered Kaeryla. "Have you ever met him?"

"No. He only meets with senior officers. You know, commanders, submarshals, or the marshal. I've heard that he's very pleasant in demeanor, but he doesn't like it when officers do stupid things."

"Most rulers don't," said Sheralt dryly.

"Have any officers said much about the Prefect or the Gallosians?" asked Taelya.

"Why do you . . ." Abruptly, Naastyrn shook his head. "Of course, you're part of the force that's going to Passera. No one's said much to me. They wouldn't because I'm being posted almost as far from Passera as I could be."

Kaeryla smiled warmly. "You probably know a lot more than we do."

"Just the usual things. The Prefect wants to tariff everyone, but he doesn't want his traders and merchants to pay anything. He uses white mages to burn traders who try to avoid paying their tariffs. His troopers have white mages to support them at times. That's why we have to have engineer companies. To build berms against chaos bolts."

"And the Viscount doesn't send his own mages?" asked Valchar.

"I don't know about that," Naastyrn confessed.

Kaeryla gave the faintest of nods.

"Do you know if the Prefect has ever talked or sent an envoy to talk about giving Certan traders access to the Passa River?" asked Taelya.

"Several years ago, the Viscount sent an envoy," replied Naastyrn. "The Prefect sent his head back in a basket. He might not wish to risk an envoy."

"And any possible envoy might not want to be risked," said Sheralt sardonically. "I can't imagine why."

"That's really all I know," said Naastyrn. "No one talks much about the Prefect. No one thinks much of him, either."

"There's a garden courtyard just below. Is that for the Viscount's family?" asked Taelya.

"It might be. I don't know. I've only been here a few days."

In the end, while the remaining conversation was pleasant and Naastyrn willing to offer what he knew, Taelya couldn't say that they'd learned much more about the Viscount and the Prefect.

Once the meal was over, as they were leaving, Gustaan motioned for the four undercaptains to join him.

"Tomorrow morning, after breakfast, some of the Certan senior officers are giving all of us, as well as their field officers, a briefing on the situation in and around Passera and what we can expect there. I just wanted all of you to know." Gustaan paused. "Did you find out much from that undercaptain?"

"Very little, except that the Viscount doesn't actually have twenty battalions, more like fifteen, and that he has a pleasant demeanor but isn't terribly forgiving of stupidity," said Taelya. "And that they actually try to put undercaptains where they can be useful, even if their parents pay for their commissions."

Gustaan nodded. "We can compare what we've learned on the ride to Passera. I'm sure we'll have plenty of time."

With something like an eightday more of riding ahead of them, Taelya had no doubts of that. *If we even learn that much.*

XXXIII

Breakfast on fourday was even less structured than dinner the night before, the only apparent requirement being that officers sit at the table appropriate to their rank. Although Taelya was the first one out of her room, she first went to the stable to check on Bounder, since she didn't know how much time she might have during the remainder of the day. By the time she reached the mess, the other three undercaptains were already there, but Kaeryla had kept a seat beside her for Taelya.

Platters arrived shortly, along with a large pitcher of a rather bitter dark lager. The fare consisted of fried ham strips and scrambled and cheesed eggs, along with warm bread. Taelya had no trouble eating it all. She did notice that very few Certan senior officers appeared, nor did she see Naastyrn anywhere.

Since Taelya had already dealt with Bounder, she just remained in the mess, along with Gustaan, when the other undercaptains hurried off to check on their mounts.

"I didn't see many senior officers here. Zekkarat was almost alone at the other table."

"Some of the senior officers likely have families and don't always eat at the mess. It's hard for junior officers to have consorts and especially families."

"Except in Fairhaven?"

Gustaan smiled happily. "In Fairhaven, I'm treated like a senior officer."

Before long, the uniformed servers cleared all the platters and beakers, and the three Fairhaven undercaptains returned, so that all of the Montgren officers were present, along with three Certan majers. Two troopers carried in an overlarge easel that displayed a map, one that appeared to portray mountainous terrain on one side and a town located on both sides of a river, presumably the area around Passera and the Passa River.

Then a tall blond man in a solid green uniform stepped into the room, and all the Certan majers immediately stood. After a moment, so did all the Montgren and Fairhaven officers.

"As you were . . . as you were," declared the officer, who, Taelya decided, must be a submarshal, since his insignia were two linked stars, unlike those of the commander from the evening meal, which had been single stars.

"I'm Submarshal Akkyld, and I'd like to welcome all of you to Jellico, including the Certan and Montgren majers who command the battalions and units included in the campaign to free Passera and the Passa River from the clutches of the Prefect of Gallos.

"Those of you from Montgren, and particularly from Fairhaven, are doubtless wondering why the Viscount has requested your assistance in this campaign. It's no secret that the Viscount has a score of battalions. So why do we need your assistance? It's embarrassing, but simple. Certis only has a few mages, and most of them are either not . . . equipped to deal with the Prefect's white mages or are past their prime in terms of magely strength . . ."

Taelya was vaguely surprised by the clear truthfulness of the submarshal's statements about Certis having few mages.

". . . We need your mages to allow our troopers to do their duty to take Passera. In the last campaign, we lost troopers even before they could engage the Gallosians. It's that simple. Now . . . before we begin the briefing proper, I would also like to invite, on behalf of the Viscount, all of you to a reception this afternoon at fourth glass. The Viscount is hosting this reception especially to show his appreciation for the Montgren and Fairhaven officers for your assistance in dealing with the most recalcitrant Prefect of Gallos. Instead of a dinner, there will also be hearty refreshments and food at the reception."

Then the submarshal moved to stand beside the map. He picked up a long thin wooden pointer and placed the tip on the town. "This is Passera. Most of the town lies on the west side of the river. The only bridge is in the center of the eastern half of the town. Here! There is one fortified Certan post on the east side of the river, guarding the bridge and its approaches, and a much larger post on the west side within two hundred yards of the bridge. The bridge is of solid stone blocks reinforced with order magery . . ."

While the submarshal's voice was pleasant enough, Taelya had to force herself to concentrate on his words and on the map, trying to commit important facts and figures to memory . . .

". . . three battalions posted there at all times . . . number of white mages varies, from as few as three to as many as six . . . black iron gate in the middle of the bridge . . . river fast-flowing but narrow . . . too deep to ford . . . but easy boat crossing . . . general plan . . . overwhelm the outlying earthworks, then move forward to take the two posts on the east side . . ."

More than a glass passed before Submarshal Akkyld set down the pointer and concluded, "And that is the general plan for the operation. It will, of necessity, be changed as necessary as circumstances require." He smiled broadly. "That is all for now. I look forward to seeing you at the reception this afternoon. In the meantime, feel free to explore the open areas of the palace. The guards will tell you if they're not open. Oh . . . and a last reminder, we leave the palace at sixth glass tomorrow morning."

Once the submarshal left and everyone stood, Gustaan looked to Taelya. "How truthful was he?"

"He was a little chaos-fuzzy on the number of battalions—"

"Chaos-fuzzy?"

"Not quite fully truthful," supplied Kaeryla.

"And he was mostly truthful about the general plan," continued Taelya, "but there was some fuzziness. He was quite truthful when he described Passera and the river and when he said that the plan might need to be changed if circumstances changed."

"In short, he talked like most senior officers when they don't want to reveal everything," said Gustaan dryly.

Taelya couldn't help but smile. Then she asked, "Do you need us for anything?"

"Just be back here before fourth glass. Explore carefully."

"I'd like to see if we can get into that courtyard garden," said Kaeryla.

"Then let's see if we can," replied Taelya.

The two hurried out of the officers' palace mess and headed for the nearest staircase. After more than half a quint, the two finally reached the courtyard level and a locked door, one beyond which both could sense the courtyard, largely because of the differing levels and concentrations of order manifested by the various types of plants.

"Now what?" asked Kaeryla.

"We find a guard and ask politely if we could look into the garden."

It took another half quint to find a second door to the courtyard garden, where a graying guard stood. "Yes . . . sers?"

"We wondered if we could see the garden," said Taelya. "We looked at it from above, from the officers' mess."

"Well . . ." The guard frowned. "It is the ladies' garden, and the consorts of senior officers can use it when the Viscount's family isn't."

"We are women and officers," said Kaeryla cheerfully.

After a moment, the guard smiled. "No one's using it now. You *are* ladies as well as officers. If you just want to take a quick look, I don't see that it could hurt. But best you make it quick."

"Thank you so much."

After the two entered the garden, Taelya sensed that the guard had largely closed the door, leaving it barely ajar. The two turned to the right and immediately passed a lacquered dark green bench set in the shade of a broad-leafed plant that Taelya did not recognize. The moist air was filled with scents that changed with each step, most of which Taelya could not identify. As they followed the patterned path of the walkway, they encountered even more of the lacquered benches, all placed so that they were isolated from each other by various foliage and flowers.

"It is beautiful," murmured Kaeryla.

"In a way that's not at all like nature."

Then as they neared the door through which they had entered the courtyard, Taelya heard a loud and strident voice.

"The door's ajar. Who did you let in there?"

"Ser—"

"Don't deny it. I'll see for myself!" With that the speaker, presumably some functionary or another, strode past the guard and into the courtyard, headed along the path that the undercaptains had taken.

"Concealments," murmured Taelya. "Let him get farther along, and we'll leave before he can see us."

The two did just that, then reached the half-open door and eased past the guard before dropping their concealments.

The guard turned, and his mouth opened.

"Don't say a thing," said Taelya. "We'll take care of it."

The clearly puzzled and worried guard finally nodded.

Taelya waited until she sensed the functionary returning, but she didn't speak until he was within earshot, but not sight, saying loudly, "Isn't there any way we can see the courtyard garden?"

"It looks so lovely," added Kaeryla. "Are you sure we can't see it?"

The guard smothered a smile and said loudly, "I'm sorry, but it's only for the family of the Viscount and for the lady consorts of senior officers. I already had to turn down some other officers."

The round-faced functionary, who wore a green-and-brown uniform without insignia, stopped in the doorway and declared firmly, "That's correct."

Taelya offered what she hoped was a warm and winning smile. "We'd heard that it was a ladies' courtyard garden . . . and being women officers . . ."

The functionary opened his mouth, taking in the uniforms, then finally said, in tones much more measured, "I'm sorry, but that is the way it is."

"We understand," replied Taelya before turning to the guard and saying, "Thank you for at least giving us a peek at the garden. It would have been nice to walk through it, but if the Viscount has said that it's only for senior officers' consorts, we wouldn't have wanted to get you into any trouble." Then she turned back to the functionary. "Thank you. We hope our wanting to look at the garden isn't a problem, but we had hoped . . ."

"You're really officers?"

"Oh, yes," said Kaeryla. "We're mage-undercaptains."

For just a moment, the functionary stiffened. "Well . . . I suppose you could come to the door here and take a good look. There's nothing against looking."

"Thank you," returned Kaeryla. "That would be lovely."

The functionary stepped aside, and the two moved forward.

"That large flowering plant at the first corner in the path to the left," asked Kaeryla, "do you know what it is?"

"It's a beamflower from the Great Accursed Forest of Naclos. It's likely the only one in the east of Candar."

"That's amazing." After several moments of looking, Taelya stepped back and turned. "Thank you both. We do appreciate getting a closer look at the courtyard."

"Our pleasure, sers," offered the functionary.

As the two moved away, Taelya listened closely, but all the superior said to the guard was, "Don't let me catch you leaving the door ajar again. We're both fortunate that Haarak wasn't near."

"No, ser. I won't, ser."

Once they turned the corner, Kaeryla looked at Taelya with a broad grin.

Smiling, Taelya just shook her head.

Over the next glass or so, the two explored what they could, including the long statuary hall that led to the Viscount's throne room, which was locked and guarded when they reached the oversized gilt doors.

Then the two returned to their quarters.

Taelya debated using a concealment to explore some of the guarded areas. From what she could sense, there weren't any mages anywhere nearby, although she thought she could sense two concentrations near the rear of the sprawling structure, possibly on the fourth level.

That suggests that there aren't many mages here, but they could be in the other building where the Montgren troopers and officers might be.

With that thought in mind, Taelya slipped out of her small chamber and made her way to the nearest guard. "Could you tell me the quickest way to get to the main quarters building?"

The guard looked at her uniform, as if almost puzzled.

"I'm a mage-undercaptain from Fairhaven, and I need to meet a Montgren officer in the main quarters building. I'm quartered here."

"Oh . . . go to the end of the corridor. Turn left, and take the staircase on the right down one level. When you come out on the next level, go to the first corridor on the left. You'll have to take that quite a ways, more than a hundred yards. That connects to the main corridor on the second level of the main quarters building."

After following those directions, Taelya reached the doors to the main quarters building, where the Certan guard looked at her for several moments.

"Yes?" said Taelya, not quite imperiously.

"Ah . . . these are officers' quarters."

"These are officers' quarters, ser," said Taelya coolly. "Thank you. I do know that."

Then she stepped past him and opened the door into a hallway that didn't look much different from the one where her own quarters were located. She kept sensing the guard for several moments, but he didn't attempt to follow her or to raise an alarm, and she turned her senses to seek out any possible concentrations of either order or chaos that signified an order or chaos mage.

She'd almost reached the end of the corridor when a tall and broad-shouldered Certan captain appeared, taking a stance that almost blocked the hallway.

"I don't recognize the uniform."

"I'm a mage-guard undercaptain from Montgren, Fairhaven, actually."

"Likely story." He reached for her.

Taelya stiffened her shields, and his hand slid away from her.

His mouth opened.

"I'm being polite," she said. "I'm a white mage. Now, if you could tell me where the Montgren officers are quartered . . ."

"The visiting officers are quartered on the first level, the one below this."

"Thank you." When he didn't move, she expanded her shields slightly and pushed him out of the way, then walked to the nearest staircase.

The captain didn't follow.

Rather than descending, however, she took the staircase to the upper levels, where she hoped to discern whether there were any mages there . . . or whether there had been, because most chaos mages would have left traces in the form of additional chaos swirls. She found neither mages nor traces. Nor did she encounter any more officers, not that she expected to run across many at midday. Then she descended to the first level, where she located the officers' stable, which had its own gate off the boulevard fronting the palace.

After more explorations, she then returned to the palace roughly the same way she had come. Along the way, she finally encountered a painting of the Viscount. At least, the bronze plate under the picture stated: VISCOUNT RYSTYN OF CERTIS, LORD OF THE FERTILE LANDS, and the frame and plate looked recent. For a long time, she studied the image, taking in the reddish-blond hair, the pale green eyes, and the slightly lopsided but squared-off chin and the thick neck. She might not ever run across the Viscount, but now, at least, she had a chance of recognizing him.

When she returned to her quarters, she sat in the chair and thought. While Submarshal Akkyld had been clear about the need for Montgren mages and hadn't been obviously lying, Undercaptain Naastyrn had said there were mages on the marshal's staff, and he definitely hadn't been lying. Both had said that there weren't that many mages in Certis. She was still thinking about it when there was a knock on her door. Even before she opened the door, she could sense two people outside, one of whom was Kaeryla. The other was Gustaan.

"I'm sorry to bother you, but an older man asked the majer if there were any officers from Fairhaven. The majer summoned me . . ." Gustaan shrugged. "The man—he looks like a rather wealthy merchant, and he must have connections to be in the palace. He asked me if I knew of two mages and a healer who had traveled through Certis to Montgren more than fifteen years ago. I told him I had two undercaptains who might be able to tell him something."

Kaeryla looked to Taelya.

"We did travel with some traders," Taelya admitted. "I don't see that it could hurt to talk to him."

"He's waiting in the hall outside the mess."

As the three made their way up to the hall, Taelya wondered whether the man who awaited them could be the fur trader. There had only been three traders, and one had been from Sligo, the second had been Lord Korsaen under another name, and the third had been the fur trader from Jellico, who had been gathering pelts for coats for the Viscount's family.

The man who stood waiting in the hall outside the officer's mess was of average height, with white hair and a square-cut white beard. His dark green trousers and jacket were well-cut and his brown boots were well-polished. His eyes went first to Kaeryla and then to Taelya. "You aren't Taelya, by chance? I'm Jhotyl. The last time I saw you was in Rytel. You asked me what I was going to do with all the ermine pelts."

Taelya managed not to gape at how the once black-bearded trader had aged. "I remember that. Did they like them?"

"One of the Viscount's daughters still occasionally wears her coat, but only in winter." Jhotyl looked to Kaeryla. "I'm guessing, but you look like you could be Jessyla's daughter—same flame-red hair and green eyes, and I'd guess you're a healer as well as a mage."

"You guess well . . . if indeed you're guessing," replied Kaeryla.

"When the majer said that there were mage-undercaptains from Fairhaven, and that they were the only mages in Montgren who fought, I thought there might be a connection. I didn't know. I asked because I've wondered for years what happened to your parents."

Taelya could sense the absolute truth in Jhotyl's words.

"They made it to Fairhaven and became the town council."

"And pretty much everything else," added Gustaan. "Taelya's father died in the last part of the last battle against the Hydlenese, but he destroyed several companies with his death and saved everyone else. Beltur is the area commander and head of the town council. Jessyla is the head healer."

Taelya was momentarily annoyed at Gustaan's words, but then realized that the captain had been trying to save her from explaining. She could also sense Jhotyl's unfeigned surprise.

"I'm sorry. I had no idea. I only knew that some mages had turned back the Duke's attack and had rebuilt Fairhaven afterward. I'd thought that it had to be your parents, but I didn't know. When the chance came, with your being hosted at the palace, I just couldn't not take advantage of the opportunity to find out more. Meeting both of you has been a great and happy surprise." Jhotyl smiled broadly.

Taelya could again sense that the man was truly happy, almost more so than she could believe.

Jhotyl turned back to Taelya. "You were very determined even then. How is your mother?"

"She's fine. She's the town treasurer and justicer."

"Might we ask how you are in the palace?" asked Kaeryla.

"You might. I'm still the one who supplies furs and fabrics to the Viscount and his family. More really to the palace seneschal, although once in a great while, I might see the Viscount, usually at a distance. He's always pleasant in person, even to those whom he later . . . has no use for." Jhotyl's voice dropped in volume almost to a murmur after observation that the Viscount was always pleasant in person.

"You've done this for a while, then?" asked Kaeryla.

"Oh, yes, for years, but that's why I wanted to find out about your parents. Without them, well, matters might not have gone so well for me. The year before brigands stole everything, and the Viscount was not pleased. But the pelts your parents saved for me were superb, and the Viscount was most pleased." Jhotyl smiled again.

This time, Taelya could sense a certain unease, and she said, "It was so kind of you to seek us out. I can't tell you how much I appreciate the effort you made, both years ago and this afternoon. But we certainly don't wish to detain you if you must be elsewhere."

Jhotyl nodded. "You are kind . . . most understanding, and I should take my leave before the seneschal remarks on the amount of time I've spent in the palace."

"Then we won't keep you." Taelya smiled warmly.

Jhotyl stepped back, smiled nervously, and then hurried away. He did not look back as he headed for the nearest stairway.

"Was that about what I think it was?" asked Gustaan in a low voice.

Taelya and Kaeryla both nodded.

"So this Jhotyl actually did know you and your family?" Gustaan asked Taelya.

"He did. He hired Father and Beltur to protect him on the trip from Axalt to Rytel. He was how we were able to leave Axalt. And he was pleasant and kind to me and to Mother. His hair and beard were black then, though."

"We all get older," said Gustaan. "But why . . . ?"

"If I sensed him correctly, our parents saved his life and possibly his family by preserving those pelts. He's never forgotten it, and it's preyed on him. He's obviously heard something . . ." Taelya paused. "Either that or it's just the Viscount's habit of turning on people when they're no longer useful, and he wanted us to be aware of it."

"Either way, he wanted to warn us not to trust the Viscount, especially after we do what he wants," added Kaeryla.

"That's good to keep in mind," said Gustaan, "but I'm not certain what we can do, except keep it in mind. For now, anyway."

Taelya thought about going back to her quarters, but since it was less than a quint before the Viscount's reception began, eased over to the window overlooking the courtyard garden.

Kaeryla immediately joined her, saying quietly, "That was strange."

"More than a little, but he was really happy to see us."

"I think mostly to see you."

"You're right, but I don't know why."

"Maybe you remind him of someone. A daughter he lost . . . or his consort when she was young?"

"I don't know that we'll ever know, but he was risking something to talk to us. I never thought that agreeing to support the Viscount was the best idea . . . and now . . ."

"Did the Duchess or the Council really have much choice?" Kaeryla's voice was lower, and bitter. "Did we, given Arthaal and Dorylt? And our parents?"

Taelya didn't have to answer the question. Kaeryla hadn't been asking for a reply.

The two just stood there, looking down into the courtyard garden, which seemed to be empty, as it had been every time they'd observed it.

Then a hearty voice called out, "Undercaptains!"

The two turned to see a group of Montgren officers moving toward them, with Konstyn in the lead. He grinned at Taelya. "I heard you were looking for me."

"Or me, possibly," added Ferek.

"That was an excuse. I was really exploring, and the guard was being obnoxious," replied Taelya.

"Exploring the officers' quarters?" Ferek raised his eyebrows.

"We'd finished exploring all the other areas that were open to look at," said Taelya. "I like to be thorough." She smiled sweetly. "And I wouldn't make any comments about that, either."

"But I like—" Ferek found he couldn't speak, not surprisingly, since Taelya had clamped a containment across his mouth.

"I did say there would be no more comments about my being thorough." Taelya released the containment.

Ferek swallowed. "I'm sorry."

"Your apology is accepted, Captain. I'd prefer not to make that point again."

Konstyn looked to Ferek in confusion.

"I couldn't talk. I couldn't breathe."

"He's your superior officer," Konstyn said to Taelya.

"I didn't hurt him, nor did I lay hands on him," replied Taelya. "I just stopped him from making an inappropriate comment before he could. Isn't that better? Or do you think the majer would like to have heard about disparaging comments to officers who stand between you and the Prefect's chaos mages?" Taelya turned to Kaeryla. "I do believe they've opened the mess for the reception."

"Then we should all enjoy the Viscount's hospitality," said Kaeryla.

"That's a good idea," said Ferek, leveling a hard gaze at Konstyn.

Abruptly, Konstyn nodded.

"We'll follow you two," said Taelya warmly, not that she felt quite that way, but it couldn't hurt. She knew it would have been better if she were wittier, but she wasn't going to put up with being put down.

She and Kaeryla followed the others to the sideboard where uniformed servers offered pale ale, lager, and red or white wine. Taelya took the pale ale, Kaeryla the lager.

As Taelya sipped the ale, knowing she was drinking on an empty stomach, she slowly surveyed the room, noticing that Submarshal Akkyld was surrounded by majers, three of them Certan, and then Zekkarat. Konstyn and Ferek eased toward one of the groups of Certan captains, since there likely had to be fifteen of them, unless some of the companies were commanded by senior undercaptains. She also noticed that there were far fewer undercaptains than captains.

Because they were discouraged from coming . . . or because not all companies have undercaptains? "Shall we join the nearer group of undercaptains, the ones from Certis?"

"They couldn't be any worse than some captains," returned Kaeryla.

Belatedly, as the two eased toward the edge of the group, Taelya saw that among the Certan undercaptains was Maakym, Ferek's undercaptain.

Surprisingly, at least to Taelya, Maakym grinned cheerfully and murmured, "I've wanted to do something like that to Ferek, whatever it was, for most of the last year." Then he added, in a normal tone of voice, "The ale's not bad, but some of these fellows like the lager better."

The Certan undercaptain standing beside Maakym said, "You weren't the one who walked into the main quarters earlier this afternoon, were you?"

Taelya managed an amused smile. "It wasn't Kaeryla, and there are only two women undercaptains from Montgren."

"I wish I'd been there," continued the Certan undercaptain. "Olaafsyn tried to put his hands on her, and she just pushed him aside and left him there."

"I'd like to have seen that, too," said another Certan, if in a lower voice.

"You did that?" asked Maakym.

"I used my shields. Then I just walked away."

"Olaafsyn was saying he was glad he wouldn't have to deal with mages after this campaign."

"He still might have to deal with the Gallosian mages," Kaeryla pointed out.

As the conversation turned to speculations about what the Gallosians might do, Taelya tried to keep an eye on the part of the room where the majers were gathered with the submarshal, although two seemed more interested in Zekkarat than in their superior.

Then she spied a table with platters of food, and said, "I'm hungry enough that I'm going to try some of the fare they've laid out." As she moved toward the table, she found Kaeryla on her right and a young Certan undercaptain on her left.

"I'm Dhoraat, submarshal's staff."

"Taelya, Fairhaven company."

"There's just one company from Fairhaven?"

"That's all that there's ever been, from Fairhaven itself. Montgren has other companies."

Since most of the officers in the room were, so far, at least, more interested in drinking, almost no one was near the table filled with platters of small bits of various foods, and Taelya picked up what looked to be a small sausage in a pastry crust and quickly ate it. She needed food if she wanted to drink any more ale and remain fully in control. *One of the problems with being small and slender.*

After a single bite of the sausage, she immediately looked for either bread or biscuits, because the sausage made any burhka she'd ever tasted seem mild by comparison. The best she could do was a square of dark bread covered with something white, which turned out to be a sour-tasting cheese. The combination did cool the sausage.

"I can't believe you ate that parika," said Dhoraat. "They're too hot for me."

"They're too hot for another," admitted Taelya. "What would you suggest?"

"The amber-looking crescents aren't bad. The filling is mint and cucumbers."

The crescents weren't bad, but they weren't that good, either. The third item that Taelya sampled was a piece of fowl surrounded by a soft cheese inside a golden pastry crust, tasty enough that she ate three, one after another, even though she couldn't identify either the cheese or the spices in which the fowl had been marinated before it had been baked.

After perhaps half a quint of sampling the various delicacies, although she would have hesitated to call some of them, like the parika, anything close to delicate, she moved away from the table, accompanied by Maakym, Dhoraat, and Kaeryla.

"How did you come to be an undercaptain?" Dhoraat asked Taelya.

"My father was a mage-captain, and my uncle is a mage and a majer. I'm a white, and Fairhaven has always needed mages to deal with the Hydlenese. Also, I get paid, and being a mage-undercaptain is really one of the few jobs that pays whites." *Especially women.*

"I never knew that there were women mages," admitted the Certan.

"There never have been many, but Saryn of the black blades—she's the one who founded Sarronnyn—she was a war mage. So is my aunt, along with being a healer. What about you?"

"My father was a majer. He was killed in the fighting against Gallos years ago. They consider sons of officers who die in service for commissions . . . if we pass certain tests."

"Not many pass those tests, do they?" asked Kaeryla.

Dhoraat offered an embarrassed smile. "No . . . not many."

"Then you must be very good with weapons and riding."

"I'm good with those, but I'm best at handling numbers and organizing supplies. I'm the junior quartermaster for the submarshal."

"Then you must have been very busy in getting ready for this campaign," said Taelya. "Arranging supplies for all those battalions must have taken a great deal of effort."

"Getting supplies together for the traveling to Passera was a challenge. Keeping all of you supplied for however long it takes to capture and fortify the town and river will be even more of a challenge. Especially fortifying the town against a Gallosian counterattack. No one wants to think much about that. They tell me to worry about that later, but if I don't worry about it now . . ." Dhoraat shook his head.

Taelya could see that, although it hadn't happened in Fairhaven yet, possibly because her mother, uncle, and aunt all thought about those kinds of possibilities. "Do you deal with merchants and traders to purchase those supplies?"

"Dark angels, no. Majer Kinnwyn and the submarshal do that, even determining the cloth for uniforms or tents. Sometimes, they include me, just so I'll learn, but I keep the ledgers and make sure that vendors deliver when they're supposed to. And if a majer or a commander complains to the submarshal, then I have to brief him on the details."

"That must keep you busy," said Kaeryla.

"Most of the time. Commanders always need something, and when they don't, they still think they do." Dhoraat smiled almost shyly. "It was a pleasure to meet you, but I can see that the majer is looking for me." He turned and headed toward a balding and graying majer, who immediately began talking.

"I'm not sure I'd want his billet," said Maakym, "even if he sees less action. That's a thankless job. I'd wager no one's ever happy."

As Taelya considered Maakym's words, she realized that what her mother did was a great deal like what Dhoraat did, except what Tulya did was often even more thankless, given that everyone thought tariffs were too high and what the town and the Road Guards could pay for goods was too little.

At that moment, she would have preferred to leave the reception, but she knew that wouldn't be wise. So she smiled politely and said, "How did you get to be an undercaptain, Maakym?"

While she wasn't exactly looking forward to the next glass, she might as well find out what she could.

XXXIV

Mindful of Gustaan's earlier comments, Tulya was up early on fiveday, and had Bounder groomed and saddled and ready even before she went to the officers' mess for a hurried breakfast. Kaeryla wasn't that far behind, and was only a fraction of a quint later in seating herself across the table from her cousin.

"Do you really think they'll leave at sixth glass?" asked Kaeryla.

"Close enough," mumbled Taelya through a mouthful of egg scramble that was slightly underdone and filled with overdone bits of ham, possibly left over from the reception the night before. Even the bread tasted somewhat stale.

Just before she left, she motioned to one of the mess stewards and had him bring a large pitcher of ale, which she then poured into the two water bottles she'd brought to the mess. She did smile and thank the confused steward.

From across the table, Sheralt shook his head. "We're supposed to go to the kitchen for that."

"No one mentioned it to me."

"That might be because you left the reception early."

"I left after Majer Zekkarat and the others did."

"They had a meeting."

"What else did I miss, then?"

"Not much besides that."

Taelya wanted to shake her head. *Were you just supposed to stand around and wait until some senior officer said something?* She got the feeling that was exactly what she was supposed to have done. "Are you sure?"

"Well . . ." Sheralt drawled, "there was something about women undercaptains assaulting their superiors . . ."

Even though Taelya knew that he was jesting, she still winced. "How many know about that?"

"By now, probably every junior officer in Jellico," said Valchar cheerfully.

"Most likely because you made sure of it," said Kaeryla.

"Then it's probably better that we're leaving this morning," replied Taelya. "Even if I didn't assault anyone. I just kept a Certan captain from assaulting me." She took the water bottles and headed out of the officers' mess, and from there back down to the stable, where she began to lead Bounder toward the courtyard.

That was when Gustaan appeared. "You know that everyone has heard you were insubordinate to two Montgren officers and one Certan officer?" The captain's voice was mild.

"I wasn't insubordinate," replied Taelya. "I just stopped Ferek from insulting me, and the Certan officer from grabbing me in a more than lecherous fashion. I didn't refuse any legitimate orders or inflict any harm on anyone."

"Since that's what I told Majer Zekkarat, I'm glad that was what happened. But why were you roaming through the main officers' quarters?"

"Because I didn't believe the submarshal, and I was trying to discover if there were any mages in the palace or the main quarters."

"I don't believe him, either, but do you think the submarshal or the Viscount would risk having any around while we're here?"

"I'm pretty sure there is at least one in the area around the Viscount's apartments."

"That would certainly be understandable. He would want some protection. He has to know what Fairhaven mages can do."

"Why would we risk that now?"

"He also has more than a few other enemies, Taelya."

Despite her feeling that she was justified in scouting the palace, Taelya saw no point in saying more about it. "Is Majer Zekkarat that unhappy?"

Gustaan smiled wryly. "I don't think he's all that displeased, for several reasons. He doesn't much care for Submarshal Akkyld, and he's even less fond of the second-in-command. That's Commander Laklaan. Zekkarat also won't have to admonish his officers to behave around you and Kaeryla. That means he won't have to worry about you two." Gustaan paused. "But you might consider that the position of women isn't the same in Certis, or even the rest of Montgren, as it is in Fairhaven. Nowhere else east of the Westhorns are there any women under arms, let alone as officers."

Taelya said nothing for a moment, thinking how best to reply. "I was aware of that. I didn't expect an officer to grab at me with no provocation. That was uncalled-for anywhere."

"I also made that point to the majer, but it might not hurt to avoid the Certan officers for at least a while. That shouldn't be a problem, given our order of march."

"We're in the rear . . . or the front?"

"The front, for now. The scouts will be mixed, a half squad from Montgren and a half squad from Certis. Then Second Squad followed by Third, for half a day. We'll change at midday. Then the first Montgren company, followed by supply wagons, and then the second Montgren company, then the Certans."

"Almost like two separate commands. It's also an arrangement that would make our deciding not to go to Gallos . . . rather difficult."

"Majer Zekkarat and I noticed that, but there's a risk for Certis in that as well. We could conceivably just ride into Gallos and throw in with the Prefect."

"Except that wouldn't serve us well for very long."

"I'm sure that's obvious to both Akkyld and the Viscount. We can talk about it later. Nothing's going to happen at the moment in Jellico. You need to get to your squad, and we need to be ready."

"Yes, ser."

Varais had Third Squad mustered, and less than a fifth of a quint later Kaeryla appeared. Then Sheralt and Valchar rode by, heading for Second Squad, mustered just at the edge of the courtyard archway leading to the larger entry courtyard.

At sixth glass, a trumpet call echoed across the courtyards, and Squad Two rode out, followed by Squad Three. The rest of the companies were already formed up on the avenue in front of the palace, stretching as far to the north as Taelya could see. She had to admit that they were leaving on time.

Even so, it was close to a glass later before the Fairhaven squads were actually out of the city and on the road heading southwest from Jellico, a road that, according to the map Tulya had created for Taelya, would swing southwest before heading due west toward the Easthorns . . . and Passera. Even with all the companies riding three abreast on the wider roads of Certis, Taelya could sense that the rear guard was roughly two kays behind the van.

Taelya turned to Varais. "Was the road you traveled through the Westhorns this wide?"

The squad leader shook her head. "I traveled a trading road well to the south. It was so narrow in places that two wagons couldn't pass, except at turnouts. But there weren't as many Certan troopers patrolling it, either."

"What about Gallosian troopers—on the part in Gallos?"

"Except for the post at Vryna, I never saw any. There's no easy way into Gallos except Vryna or Passera. So the Prefect doesn't need troopers anywhere else. Traders pretty much have to take one road or the other."

"Is there any road between Vryna and Passera?"

"Not a chance. The Easthorns are rugged there, and there's no bridge across the Passa except at Passera. Why do you think that the Prefect and the Viscount are fighting over Passera?"

"Well . . . I wondered if it might be because they're both men."

Both Kaeryla and Varais laughed.

XXXV

The next three days were very similar to the last three days of the trip to Jellico, if in reverse, as the combined force traveled first through the lusher lands in the wide river valley, and then through lands somewhat higher and drier. By the fourth day—which was oneday—the road began to wind more between hills that seemed to get slightly more rocky with each kay that Taelya rode. As the hills became more rugged, the towns along the road got smaller and much farther apart. One thing Taelya had noticed, though, was that the way stations where they stopped were not manned by even the smallest of trooper contingents, unlike those east of Jellico, where a squad of local troopers maintained each way station.

Gustaan had already passed on the information that there was only one substantial and manned way station remaining along the way, in a town called Relugh. From there, it was a four-day ride to the Certan border post in the low hills east of Passera.

Not quite surreptitiously, she studied the map her mother had created for her. If what Gustaan said happened to be correct, they had at least a two-day ride to Relugh, and overall, they would be bivouacking three of the next five days.

Behind Taelya stretched out the bulk of the force that would attack, and hopefully take Passera. Ahead, between the low points in the hills, she could see the snow-covered heights of the Easthorns. As she looked at them, she couldn't help recalling how cold she had been when she had ridden with her parents from Axalt through just half of the Easthorns. *But it was earlier in the year.* Then she smiled, if sadly, thinking about her mother's making sure that her riding jacket would be warmer, even if she would only need the added warmth for perhaps an eightday. *Then again, you can freeze to death in far less than a day.*

After blotting away the perspiration oozing from under her visor cap, she uncorked her water bottle, which now contained only water she'd cleansed with both order and chaos, because the limited amount of ale in the supply wagon was being reserved for use during and after fighting.

She looked again toward the Easthorns, knowing that the heat from the early summer sun would give way to mountain chill then cold within days.

XXXVI

Just before fourth glass of the afternoon on threeday, Third Squad, following the scouts, emerged from a narrow passage between two rocky hills sporting irregular clumps of scrub oak and scattered ponderosa pines and began to ride down a long gentle slope toward Relugh. From what Taelya could see and sense, there were perhaps a hundred dwellings scattered almost haphazardly around the walled enclosure in the middle of the valley. Six long and low buildings with steeply pitched roofs stood within the walls.

"Relugh doesn't look like much," said Varais in a matter-of-fact tone. "I've seen steads abandoned for decades that looked better."

"I'd rather not sleep on rocks any more than I have to," said Kaeryla.

"You're thinking that now, ser," replied Varais. "If it looks this way from here . . ."

"It's not likely to look that much better close up?" said Taelya.

Before Varais could reply, one of Akkyld's adjutants, an older undercaptain with green braid on his shoulders, rode up beside Gustaan. "Captain, the Montgren and Fairhaven troopers will be in the first building. Officers' quarters are at the east end. Stables are only available for officers' mounts. Each company has an assigned corral for mounts . . ." The adjutant's voice was definitely loud enough so that all nearby could hear him.

Taelya doubted that was by accident.

When the adjutant finished and rode back toward the Certan forces, Gustaan turned in the saddle. "Did you three hear that?"

"Yes, ser."

"Good. I'm going to relay that to Second Squad."

The descent into Relugh took longer than Taelya had thought. That was because, when the road flattened and they reached a point only several hundred yards from the east wall of the way station, she realized that each of the four walls was a good quarter kay in length. As she rode closer, she also could see that the way station was less than impressive except in size. The walls were barely three yards high, if that, and the iron-bound main gates looked worn, and as if they hadn't been closed in years. The wall bricks scarcely looked that durable, each an unglazed muddy brown, as if they'd hardly been fired at all, and brick dust lay in sporadic piles here and there at the base of the walls.

Two guards, posted at one side of the gate, seemed indifferent to the new arrivals, as if the appearance of almost two thousand troopers and officers was nothing new or surprising.

And perhaps it isn't . . . or they just don't care one way or the other.

Taelya suspected it was mostly the latter as she guided Bounder to the stable for officers' mounts, essentially the west end of the first long barracks building. The floor was packed clay, swept carelessly and not recently, and the stall walls were of the same muddy bricks as the building walls, most likely because there didn't seem to be that many trees suitable for timber close to the valley, and the few available were likely used for roof timbers. There was hay in the mangers and a small basket of mixed grains for Bounder, more than Taelya expected and less than she would have liked for the big gelding, although she had made extra efforts to find good grass for him all along.

After stabling their mounts, Taelya and Kaeryla went to find their quarters—a small room containing two platforms without pallets and some wall pegs, as well as a tin pitcher and basin, a chipped chamber pot . . . and nothing else.

"I hadn't thought I'd need the second blanket inside," said Kaeryla, "if only for padding."

Taelya glanced at the unglazed window with its inner wooden shutters. "This inside is more like outside. I wouldn't want to be here in winter. At least we have a room. The troopers just have rows and rows of platforms side by side."

"The Viscount wouldn't send troopers here in winter, would he?"

"Although we've never met the Viscount, if he's like most rulers, he'll do whatever he thinks is necessary. The real question is whether it's for his personal gain or whims or for the best interests of the people he rules."

"You're sounding like Father," said Kaeryla, smiling.

"Who do you think told me that?" returned Taelya dryly, adding, "We should hurry so that we're not the last ones to dinner. Especially if the submarshal is going to be the senior officer at whatever passes for an officers' mess."

"I'll get the water. I saw where the hand pump is."

"They actually have one?"

Kaeryla nodded and picked up the pitcher before hurrying out of the room, while Taelya checked and reorganized her gear, somewhat disarrayed from bivouacking. Then, after Kaeryla returned with the water, Taelya washed up and fetched more water, while Kaeryla cleaned up her gear.

When Taelya, Kaeryla, and the other Fairhaven undercaptains arrived at the chamber designated for the officers' mess, Taelya could see that the designation was an overstatement. Two trestle tables sat on an uneven brick floor, with backless benches on each side. The shutters swung open on the unglazed windows in the walls. More than a few flies circled around the room, dimly illuminated by the open windows, because the valley itself was in shadows.

The majers stood by the small table, while the captains circled the upper end of the long table. Taelya posted herself opposite the middle of the table.

"How long do you think we'll stand around?" asked Valchar.

"Only until the submarshal arrives," replied Sheralt. "It shouldn't be long. All the other officers are here. But he'll want to make everyone wait for a little bit. He seems to be one who wants to remind others who's in charge."

When Akkyld did arrive, flanked by Commander Laklaan, all the officers fell silent and stiffened to attention. After only a moment, if a rather long one, the submarshal declared, "As you were. Informal seating."

Almost as soon as everyone was seated, troopers appeared. The first group placed a tin beaker in front of each officer, followed by a second who filled the beakers with ale. Then the troopers placed a large tin bowl filled with a steaming stew-like mixture before each officer. Last came baskets of bread.

Taelya and Kaeryla found themselves surrounded, with Sheralt seated on Taelya's left and Valchar on Kaeryla's right. Across from them were Drakyn and Maakym, with the Certan undercaptains farther down the table on both sides, and the Certan captains and Gustaan taking over the part of the table close to the small table holding the senior officers, all of whom were majers except for the submarshal and Commander Laklaan.

Taelya's first and small mouthful of the meal, for she'd decided that it couldn't be called dinner, tasted mainly like a crude, excessively salty version of some bastard version of burhka, with a faint aftertaste of moldy cheese. The stringy chunks of meat could have been anything. The second mouthful didn't taste even that good.

"This tastes worse than brinn bitters," murmured Kaeryla.

"At least it's hot," said Sheralt, adding, "I have tasted worse."

"Not in a long time, I'd wager," countered Valchar.

Valchar's reply surprised Taelya, because the hubbub of various conversations made it hard for her to hear him, and Sheralt was even farther away, but then, maybe he'd been looking at Sheralt and concentrating.

"That's true," admitted Sheralt.

"When was that?" asked Taelya.

"Back when I was working as a cargo hand on the ship that brought me to Lydiar. Most of the biscuits had weevils. They were tastier than the biscuits."

Taelya winced, even though she knew how spoiled she had been by her mother's cooking.

"Some of the hardtack will be like that if it takes through the summer to defeat the Prefect's forces," said Valchar.

Taelya had no doubts of that. She tried not to dwell on the taste of whatever the stuff in the bowl was as she slogged through it, just glad that the bread was merely hard and stale.

"We might be able to have fresh meat in Gallos," added Valchar, "if we can bring down some mountain goats or some Gallosian sheep."

"I'd rather not be there that long," replied Sheralt, "even close to that long."

"I'm just saying . . ." protested Valchar.

"We know," said Kaeryla warmly.

By the time the meal was over and the submarshal and commander had left, a cool and chill breeze blew through the open windows, one strong enough to keep the flies at bay, but one cold enough that Taelya knew that she'd need a blanket to be even halfway close to comfortable in the drafty quarters where she'd be sleeping, and given the gaps and cracks in the wooden shutters, even with them closed, there would be drafts.

XXXVII

To the west of Relugh the road steepened and narrowed so that it could barely hold a wagon and a mount side by side and with shoulders less than a yard on each edge. The packed clay and gravel surface was often uneven, and rutted in places where rain runoff had cut across the road proper. After ten glasses of riding on fourday, the combined force finally reached an encampment site some twenty-five kays closer to Passera. That night, Taelya was definitely grateful for the warmer riding jacket and two blankets, but she was tired enough that she slept, if less than comfortably.

By noon on sixday, the combined force reached the top of Middle Pass, only a few hundred yards lower than where the still snow-covered upper slopes began and stretched upward for thousands of yards. As a low point between the mountains and the only pass across in the Easthorns for more than two hundred kays to the north and close to a hundred to the south, the crest of the road was also what amounted to a wind funnel, and Taelya was more than happy when, several glasses later, they had descended below the worst of the winds. She was less happy when they reached the next encampment site, a boulder-strewn valley on the north side of the road.

"At least there's no snow on the ground," she said to Varais.

"There's never that much snow in Gallos," replied the squad leader. "There's not that much rain, either. The Easthorns stop most of the storms coming from the east or northeast, and the Westhorns do the same on the west side. That's also why there's so much snow on the Roof of the World."

"Didn't you ever get tired of the snow in Westwind?"

"I grew up with it. It was part of life." Varais's voice was matter-of-fact. "Just like magery is a part of your life."

"But snow affects everyone."

"And, sooner or later, magery doesn't, ser?"

The quietly voiced question took Taelya aback, and she didn't speak for several moments. "I never thought of it that way, but you're right. I've always thought of magery as affecting a very few people a great deal, either by healing them or . . . even killing them, but . . . what happens to those few affects even more people."

"The magery of your family is why I came to Fairhaven, and it's why we're riding to Gallos to take a town from one bastard ruler to give to another. If we're successful, the first bastard, sooner or later, will try to take it back. And, if we're not successful, both bastards will be unhappy with us."

Cynical as Varais was, Taelya definitely agreed.

The evening meal was little more than hard bread and cheese with cold mutton slices and water. Taelya was more than careful to make certain she used enough order and chaos to clean the water.

Not all that much after the full darkness of night fell across the encampment, Taelya was asleep, tired not just from riding, but also from quietly practicing multiple containments and carrying heavy shields, as she had every day since leaving Fairhaven, knowing that the more she could do with her magery, the better her chances.

In the darkness . . . something touched Taelya's shields, and she was instantly awake, her senses reaching out through the blackness to find four figures standing less than a yard from her. "There's something stopping my blade . . ." murmured one figure, a voice Taelya's sleep-fogged senses didn't know whether she should recognize.

She cleared her throat and sat up. "My shields are stopping your blade. Who are you, and what are you doing here?" Easing the blanket back, she stood, if barefoot, anchoring her shields to the rock below.

"I beg your pardon," replied a taller figure standing back slightly. "We were just following orders."

"Whose orders?" snapped Taelya.

"The commander's orders, Undercaptain."

Taelya finally could make out that the second speaker was a captain, if one not that much older than she was, at least from what she sensed of his order/ chaos flows. "And why does the commander need to know how I sleep?"

"I wouldn't know, Undercaptain. I don't question his orders." The captain turned to go, then stopped, halted in place.

"I do," said a second voice, that of Kaeryla. "And you should too." She released the containment.

The captain stumbled. "I don't question him, and you don't, either."

Taelya pulled on her boots and said quietly, "You're very fortunate that you didn't end up as a pile of ashes, trying to wake a sleeping mage. But that just might be why the submarshal chose a relatively junior captain. Good night, Captain."

As the four retreated, Taelya bent down and murmured to Kaeryla, "Stay here. I'm going to follow them under a concealment." With that she raised a concealment and moved through that darkness after the four, slowly closing the gap between them.

". . . how were you to know that you can't touch them, ser, even when they're sleeping?"

". . . uppity little bitch . . . we'll see how she does when she faces real Gallosian mages."

"Yes, ser."

Taelya had to concentrate intently to follow the four as they moved through the rows of sleeping troopers toward the single tent in the encampment—that of the submarshal.

When the captain neared the outer ring of sentries around the tent, he stopped for a moment and said to the three troopers, "Wait here."

"Yes, ser."

Knowing where the captain was headed, Taelya eased around and between the sentries and was standing close to the front of the tent, still under her concealment, when the captain neared the sentries directly before the tent.

"Captain Rulfaast, reporting as ordered."

"I'll tell the commander, ser."

In moments, another man stepped outside. "Join the other sentries for the moment, troopers."

"Yes, ser."

Once the pair had moved away, one coming within cubits of Taelya, the commander asked quietly, "What did you find out, Captain?"

"You can't touch them even when they're asleep . . . and it wakes them quickly. She knew I was a captain in moments."

"But she didn't wake until when?"

"When Boddkyr hit her shields with his blade."

"She didn't seem to be in pain? There wasn't any trace of fire when his blade touched her shields?"

"No, ser. She was angry, though."

"That's not surprising, from what I've heard. But she didn't wake up until your man touched her shield?"

"No, ser."

"That means we don't have to worry about anyone molesting them, or Gallosian assassins creeping around. Thank you, Captain."

"Yes, ser. My pleasure and duty, ser."

Despite the commander's words, with a element of truth in them, but a certain amount of chaos as well, Taelya had the feeling that he wasn't really all that concerned about either molestation or assassination of sleeping mages.

By the time the captain returned to his men, Commander Laklaan had reentered the tent, and the pair of guards had returned to their previous post. Taelya listened intently, but Laklaan said nothing that she could hear, and after a short time she made her way back to where Kaeryla waited.

"What was that all about?"

"The commander wanted to know if anyone could touch us and what it took to wake us. He didn't tell the captain why."

"I don't like that. What does it mean?"

"It could mean that he wanted to make sure that no one could force himself on either of us, or that we can't be killed in our sleep. He did say something like that."

"Why did the commander send out a captain in the dark? There's more to it than that. There has to be," insisted Kaeryla.

"But what?" At the moment, Taelya couldn't think of what it might be . . . and she was still tired. "All we can do is sleep on it, and tell Gustaan about it in the morning."

"If we can get back to sleep," retorted Kaeryla quietly.

Somehow, after a time, Taelya drifted back into slumber, if restlessly.

XXXVIII

Late on eightday afternoon, the force that was to attack Passera neared the fortified Certan border post, situated on the east side of a narrow stream, opposite and across the water from the blackened ruins of what had likely been the Gallosian border post in less contentious times. Those ruins were considerably smaller than the Certan post, although what remained of the walls suggested they had been thick and more than five yards high. From the earlier briefing by Akkyld, Taelya knew that the Gallosians had thrown up a long line of earthworks less than a kay east of that part of Passera that occupied the east bank of the Passa River . . . and that the earthworks were less than five kays west of the stream that marked the border between the two lands.

The Certan border post itself was half the size of the enclosure at Relugh, but the walls were solid stone and looked to be a good six yards high. Even from where she rode some two kays away and thirty yards higher, Taelya could see that the enclosure and the buildings within it could easily hold the close to four battalions riding downhill toward it. She also could sense no recent chaos that was out of the ordinary.

"That's a large post," said Varais. "A lot went into building and supplying it, and they've destroyed the Gallosian post. The Gallosian post was much smaller. So why haven't they been more successful?"

"They've pushed the Gallosians back into the town," replied Taelya, adding dryly, "They just haven't been as successful as the Prefect would like. He doesn't control the river, and that's what he wants."

"They do have the better position here," admitted Varais, "but I'd like to see the approaches to the town."

"We'll see them soon enough," said Kaeryla.

As they drew nearer to the post, Taelya noted the simple timber bridge over the stream, a span of perhaps seven yards across a narrow gorge than dropped some four yards to the water below. The bridge was wide enough for two wagons, if barely, and had timber guardrails that looked as though they could easily break if a strong horse could careen into them.

Unlike the gates at Relugh, the post gates were closed and only swung open after the guards confirmed that the approaching force was from Jellico. Once they were inside the stone walls, troopers directed Second and Third Squads, and those who followed, past the first stone buildings and into a spacious and stone-paved rear courtyard. Taelya was reluctantly impressed by the courtyard, not only with the three stone-walled barracks buildings of two stories, but by the stables, sufficient to hold all the mounts.

The Certan cadre at the post, clearly having been briefed, swiftly directed the Fairhaven squads, then the Montgren companies, and finally the Certan battalions to predetermined stables, barracks, and quarters. In less than a glass, Taelya and Kaeryla stood inside a neat but spare and small chamber with two narrow pallet beds.

They'd barely stepped inside when Gustaan rapped on the door.

Kaeryla opened it.

The captain didn't enter, but said, "I thought all of you should know that the submarshal has called a meeting of all the majers—and me—for fifth glass to discuss tomorrow's evolutions. I suspect everyone will get to rest except for some of you."

"And we'll be doing some sort of reconnaissance?" asked Taelya.

"That's my best guess. Either that or everyone gets to rest tomorrow, and you do recon on twoday."

"That makes more sense," declared Kaeryla. "The horses need rest, more like two days' worth."

"That's all I have. I've already told Sheralt and Valchar. If the meeting's over before dinner, I'll be outside, and I'll let you know."

"Thank you," replied Taelya.

Gustaan nodded, then turned.

Kaeryla closed the door and shook her head. "Someone's in a hurry."

"Not necessarily. They just might be organized. If they are, we'll actually get rest tomorrow and recon duty on twoday. Anyway, there's nothing we can do now but clean up a little and hope that what they serve is better than field rations or the slop we got at Relugh. I suspect it will be."

"Optimist," snorted Kaeryla.

"Realist. There's a submarshal here, and this is a more important post. Most of the officers posted here won't want him reporting badly on them. The ones at Relugh are just putting in time before getting a stipend. They looked sloppy, as though they couldn't have cared less."

"I still say you're an optimist, especially after what happened in that valley. Gustaan should have done something when you told him."

"What? Laklaan would have just said that the captain was checking and went a bit too far. It's just another reason not to trust the Certans. Right now, we just have to be careful." Taelya paused, then added, "I'll get the water."

A little less than a glass later, after cleaning themselves up as well as they could, the two walked across the courtyard to the officers' mess, once more a single room with two tables and benches in the same building and adjoining the troopers' mess hall.

Gustaan, Sheralt, and Valchar were waiting just outside.

"Now that you're all here," said Gustaan, "the submarshal has ordered two full days of rest and preparation. That's if the Gallosians don't attack, of course, but Akkyld thinks that's unlikely, given that the Gallosians would have to attack uphill and over a narrow bridge. He'd actually welcome that because he has a full company of archers and plenty of shafts, as well as you four to deflect any mage firebolts that might get over the walls. We're scheduled to begin reconnaissance on threeday. I'll know more later. Now . . . let's go and enjoy a hot meal."

As Gustaan turned, Kaeryla looked at Taelya with a glance that suggested that her cousin not say a word.

Taelya just smiled and turned to follow the captain.

XXXIX

By twoday afternoon, even after several long briefings by the Certan post commander on the terrain and tactics used by the Gallosians, tactics that boiled down to only attacking under the protection of white mages, Taelya was feeling restless. After checking on Bounder for the third time that day, she climbed the narrow stone staircase to the top of the west wall and looked out over the parapet toward Passera. The sentry posted at the corner tower glanced in her direction for a long moment, then looked away.

Taelya saw no sign of any Gallosian troopers, and while she sensed a few individuals here and there in the area beyond the stream and short of Passera itself, she sensed no riders and no groups that could possibly be Gallosian troopers. Not only that, but she hadn't sensed or heard any Certan riders or scouts entering or leaving the post, except for two couriers, riding together, heading east out of the post gates, which closed quickly behind them.

For at least a quint, from behind the fort parapets, she continued to study the terrain, noting that the uneven ground around the post seemed to be composed more of red sand and rock than real soil. In places, scrub pines grew, as well as scattered bushes with small greenish-gray leaves almost the same color as false olive trees. She couldn't see trees of any great size except near the Passa River, and that was at least five kays to the west and several hundred yards lower. On the other side of the bridge crossing the narrow gorge and the stream below, the road ran downhill in a straight line toward the river, although the scattered trees around the houses and shops flanking the road made it difficult to see if the road turned before it reached the river. There were reddish-brown berms on each side of the road just before the first houses, most likely the Gallosian earthworks. She could also see a tower near the river, presumably part of the Gallosian defenses.

When Taelya sensed someone coming up the staircase that she had used, she turned and watched as a Certan officer walked toward her. As he neared, she could see that he was lanky, with a lined but unwrinkled face that suggested he was likely fifteen years older than she was, and the undercaptain's insignia strongly suggested that he'd come up through the ranks. She thought she'd seen him at the officers' mess, but he hadn't been one of the undercaptains seated near her.

"You must be one of the Fairhaven mage-undercaptains," he offered as he stopped a yard away.

"Undercaptain Taelya. And you are?"

"Sondhyn, also an undercaptain." The Certan's smile was easy and pleasant. "As you know."

"And you're posted here?"

"For the last two years, and one to go." Sondhyn paused, then said, "What about you? You don't look like you're up here for a scenic view, since there isn't one."

"It's good enough to keep track of anyone heading this way, especially from Passera. I'm trying to get a feel for the terrain." Taelya gestured toward the gutted Gallosian post across the narrow stream. "How many years ago did that happen?"

"Five, maybe six years back. That was when the Prefect demanded double tariffs on all traders who weren't Gallosians. Back then, we were also a tariff post. I suppose we still are, but there's no one to tariff these days. Anyway, we took out their post and pushed them back across the river. The Prefect sent a bunch of white mages, but they hid and didn't throw chaos until we crossed the river. They burned three battalions to the last man, and pushed us back to the fort here. The walls held. Then the Viscount sent a couple of mages. Their mages and ours made it hard for any trooper to move outside the walls or their earthworks without getting turned to ashes. So, it's a standoff. At least, it was, until their mages killed our two."

"How did they do that?"

"They attacked. Our mages started throwing firebolts. Then they both exploded in white flashes and turned to ashes. So did some of the troopers near them. That's what I heard, anyway. They haven't attacked since then."

"When was that?"

"About a year ago."

"And no one's done anything since then?"

The Certan undercaptain offered a sardonic smile before saying, "The walls'll hold against anything but siege engines. From here our archers can kill scores of troopers before they can get close. The gorge is deep enough and the bridge narrow enough that they can't bring up a siege engine without losing hundreds of men, if not more. We could burn the bridge if we had to." Sondhyn shrugged. "If they took the post, what would they have? Just a pile of rocks."

"So there aren't any traders coming this way?"

He shook his head. "They all take the south road. It's longer, and they have to pay tariffs, but it's safer."

And it goes through Fairhaven.

Taelya could see why the Viscount wanted to take Passera and gain control of the river. She could also see why the Prefect didn't want to lose Passera, but under the present conditions, it seemed to her that they were both losing, especially the Viscount. It made a kind of sense for him to press for mages to deal with the Prefect's mages, but only . . . *Only if you're able to kill them.* Because, otherwise, as soon as the Fairhaven mages left, the situation would return to what it had been.

She wanted to shake her head, but she just nodded.

"You got four mages . . . three besides you?" asked Sondhyn.

"Two whites and two blacks."

"Seems like you'd need more whites."

"Not necessarily. Blacks usually have stronger shields than whites."

"The white bands on your sleeves mean you're a white?"

"They do."

"Never knew there were white women mages."

"There never have been many. There are more women mages who are blacks than whites." Taelya had thought about it, more than once, but so far as she could tell, she was the only woman white mage she knew about, though that wasn't something she was about to mention. Besides which, doing so was not only presumptuous, but might well be dangerous.

"Does magery run in your family?"

"It seems to."

Sondhyn laughed wryly. "Only thing that runs in my family is being troopers. Been at least one in every generation as far back as we remember."

"Magery isn't that dependable in running in families." Even as Taelya said the words, she wondered. Jessyla and Beltur were both mages, and so were both their children. While Taelya's mother wasn't a mage, she was almost black enough to be a healer. It could be simply that most mages hadn't consorted with either healers or other mages. That they hadn't was scarcely surprising, given how rare mages and true healers happened to be.

"Most things folks think of as dependable aren't, especially people." The undercaptain shook his head. "I have to take that back. Some things about people you can count on. Most folks will do what fattens their wallets, even when they're talking about the need to do good. They'd also always rather gossip about other folks' problems than what they did right."

"What about rulers?"

"They'll do anything to keep power or get more. You can count on that. Why else are the two of us here?"

"It seems that way, but wouldn't all of us be better off if the Prefect and the Viscount came to an agreement so that both could use the river?"

"That'd mean that the Prefect would have to give up power over who uses the river. No ruler ever does that unless forced. That's why you're here, isn't it? To use your magery to force him out of Passera?"

"That seems to be the plan."

"That's another thing you can count on. Plans never turn out as planned." Sondhyn inclined his head. "Enjoyed talking with you, Undercaptain Taelya, but I need to get back to duties." With that he turned and headed down the narrow staircase.

Somehow, Taelya doubted the encounter or conversation was coincidental. But what did he really want? To see if she was indeed a mage? Or just to meet her as a prelude to something else? Or just because it was an excuse to talk to her without anyone else being near, unlike at the officers' mess?

While Taelya didn't know his reasons for talking to her, one way or the other, what he'd said suggested that she be extremely careful.

XL

Both Taelya and Kaeryla were at breakfast early on threeday, not because they were enthusiastic about the fare, but because Gustaan had informed them that one of the squads would be riding out on the first reconnaissance mission at sixth glass.

After following a reluctant bite of nearly burned mutton-egg scramble with a small swallow of bitter ale, Taelya nudged Kaeryla with her elbow, murmuring, "The older undercaptain near the end of the table. He's the one I told you about."

"He's not the one who tried to talk to me in the stable," replied Kaeryla in an equally low voice. "He's the one with the sandy hair two up the table from the one who talked to you."

Taelya frowned. Neither undercaptain had been overtly forward. Nor had either been intrusive or pressed questions about the Montgren or Fairhaven forces . . . or magery. *But it still seems odd.* "What do you think?"

"Either they haven't talked to a woman in seasons or someone put them up to it. Most likely both."

Taelya paused. "We'll talk about this later."

Kaeryla nodded.

"What are you two whispering about?" Valchar, seated beside Kaeryla, leaned forward and kept his voice low.

"About how long we'll have to endure nearly burned scrambles," replied Taelya pleasantly.

"You expect me to believe that?" asked Valchar.

"No," said Kaeryla pleasantly.

"That's all you're going to say?"

"That's right." Kaeryla's words were cheerful.

Valchar frowned, but Sheralt just shook his head.

"Do you know who will be taking the first recon patrol?" asked Taelya.

"The captain hasn't told us," replied Sheralt. "Just what he said last night— that we're to meet him outside the mess before sixth glass."

As soon as the four finished eating and left the mess, they found Gustaan waiting in the hallway outside. "I just met with the majer. Third Squad will do the first reconnaissance patrol." Gustaan's voice was level. "You'll be accompanied by two Certan troopers from the post who can point out the Gallosian earthworks and other local features."

"Was Third Squad a decision you or Majer Zekkarat made, ser?" asked Taelya.

"The majer told me. I don't know whether that was his decision or the submarshal's." Gustaan paused. "Do you think that's a problem?"

"I don't know, ser. I do know that there were no scouts sent out yesterday, and only two riders left the post, a pair of couriers heading east. One of the post undercaptains told me that the Gallosian mages killed the two Certan mages who were posted here about a year ago. He believed he was telling the truth, and he's been posted here for two years. He also said that it was dangerous for troopers who weren't protected by a mage."

"That would seem to back up why the Viscount wanted mages," Gustaan pointed out.

"It could, but I thought you should know."

"No other troopers?" asked Valchar.

"It's a recon patrol, and the Gallosians are several kays to the west. All of you mage-undercaptains can tell if they move closer. If they appear likely to attack in force, then you return to the post. I'm sure that neither the Viscount nor the submarshal wants to have spent all the time and golds to get you here and then lose you to a Gallosian attack because you aren't adequately supported. Your first task is to find out how many troopers and mages there are and where. After that, the submarshal and the majers will determine the best plan of attack. Is that clear?"

"Yes, ser." The four responses were close to simultaneous.

"We may need a second patrol this afternoon, or tomorrow, depending on what Squad Three determines," said Gustaan, looking to Sheralt.

The oldest undercaptain nodded.

Gustaan turned back to Taelya. "Get your squad ready. The Certan troopers will meet you at the front gates."

"Yes, ser."

As Taelya and Kaeryla walked swiftly toward the stables, the younger mage asked quietly, "Why do I think that those two undercaptains were put up to talking to us?"

"You know as well as I do that they were." *The real question is why.*

"Because they think we're the weakest of the mage-undercaptains? Why would the post commander care?"

"He likely doesn't. Akkyld does. The only way to find out why"—*short of doing things that would make matters far worse*—"is to get through the patrol and see what happens."

Kaeryla frowned, but said nothing.

That was fine with Taelya.

Varais was waiting at the stable doors.

"Squad Three gets the first recon," said Taelya. "We'll have two Certan troopers as guides of sorts."

"That's about what I'd expect," said the squad leader dryly.

Less than half a quint later, Squad Three was formed up just inside the main gates, and Taelya had already sensed that, outside of a few scattered growers and herders, there was no one within a kay of the post, and there were few beyond that, and certainly no riders.

Two troopers in faded green-and-brown uniforms rode up, reining up their mounts short of Taelya and Kaeryla.

"Troopers Gurdash and Jaavyn reporting for guide duty . . . sers."

"Good. I'm Undercaptain Taelya, and this is Undercaptain Kaeryla. Our squad leader is Varais." Taelya gestured.

Both troopers' eyes widened slightly, most likely in surprise at seeing an all-woman command.

"You're the two who are here to point out local features."

"Yes, ser," replied Jaavyn.

"Then we should head out." Taelya gestured to the troopers manning the gates, then said to the troopers, "Fall in behind Undercaptain Kaeryla and me. Keep close enough so that we can hear what you have to say."

A few moments later, the gates opened, and Taelya led Third Squad out, turning west on the road that led to the narrow bridge. "Will it take two mounts abreast?"

"Yes, ser." After several moments, Jaavyn added, "Ah . . . begging your pardon, Undercaptains . . . ah . . . is it true that you know where the graycoats are, even when they can't be seen? And mages?"

"In good weather, we can usually sense either within a kay, sometimes farther," replied Taelya.

Because the Certan trooper's relief was almost palpable, Taelya said, "I take it that you worry about being surprised by their troopers and mages?"

"Yes, ser."

"I thought they didn't venture that far from their two forts or their earthworks," said Kaeryla.

"They only use the earthworks if we try an attack. Just scouts there otherwise. Most of their troopers are in the river forts."

"How far are the earthworks from the river?"

"A little more than a kay, ser, just outside the town. They can see the earthworks from the tower on their east river fort. They can also see our post."

"Do they attack everyone who rides toward the town?"

"Not always, but mostly. You never know."

"Are mages always with the attackers?"

"No, ser. Not always."

From Jaavyn's tone, Taelya had the definite feeling that mages were present more often than not.

"How do they attack?" asked Kaeryla.

"As soon as they come close enough, they loose shafts."

"Don't you loose shafts first?" asked Varais from behind the two Certans. "The road slopes so your shafts should travel a little farther."

"Sometimes. But if they have a mage, he just burns them out of the air or blocks them."

"We'll just have to see," replied Taelya. From what she'd heard so far, she wasn't all that impressed with the Certan troopers. *But you haven't encountered the Gallosian mages yet, either.* She couldn't help worrying that some of them might have techniques or tactics that Beltur had not prepared her for.

As she rode onto the causeway leading to the bridge, Taelya could sense no one nearby, except for what felt like an older man working in a small vineyard about half a kay north of the road on the west side of the stream.

Once past the burned-out ruins of the Gallosian post, Third Squad rode for almost half a kay through fallow lands, although Taelya wasn't certain what could have been grown on the sandy and rocky soil, even if a grower had been able to get water from the narrow stream running through the small gorge. Before long they passed an orchard. Taelya did not recognize the trees, which appeared neglected. "What are those?"

"Olive trees, they say. You can't eat the olives right from the tree. They're almost poison. They have to do things to them before you can eat them. I don't know what."

Beyond the orchard was an abandoned cot. In fact, most of the fields, as well as the scattered olive orchards, looked to have been abandoned, even as Third Squad rode closer to the edge of Passera and neared the reddish-brown berms that angled eastward from the end closest to the road. For a moment, Taelya wondered about the angle, then realized that the angling would allow archers to concentrate their shafts on anyone using the road.

As they drew closer to the earthworks, Taelya sensed several men posted at points behind the berms. Then, one after another, the three sprinted from the rear of the earthen barriers that flanked the road and mounted horses shielded by an earthen wall. They immediately rode west into the town and toward the river and the fortified post that guarded it on the west side.

"They always do that," offered Gurdash. "Next thing you know, there'll be a couple of squads or a company riding out with one of those white mages."

"We'll keep riding," said Taelya. "I'd like a better look at those earthworks." She also wanted to see what the Gallosians might do.

"They're just earthworks, ser," replied Gurdash almost plaintively.

"Is there anything dangerous about them? When no one's defending them?"

"I suppose not, ser. But it won't be long before the graycoats show up."

Taelya didn't doubt that, but it was already clear that Third Squad was only discovering, so far, at least, what the Certan troopers already knew. Once she was just past the end of the earthworks, she called out, "Third Squad! Halt!"

Then she rode to the south side of the road and took a closer look at the earthworks, finding that it was little more than a berm raised above the ground east of it by about a yard, with a stepped trench behind it so that archers could drop into the lower front of the trench to avoid chaos bolts and arrows or step up to the higher rear from which they could loose shafts.

As soon as Taelya had finished inspecting the earthworks, she returned her attention to the Gallosian post a little more than two kays away, waiting.

Within half a quint of the time that the three Gallosian riders had entered the gates of the river fort, the gates opened again and riders poured out, quickly moving eastward toward Third Squad. Taelya could only sense a single white mage, a mage who didn't seem to hold that much chaos. "They've dispatched a company to deal with us."

"I told you so, ser," said Gurdash.

"Yes, you did. Thank you." Taelya looked to Kaeryla. "Do you sense anything beyond the one mage?"

"Just the one. And there's no . . . sense of emptiness, either."

"So there's likely not another who's fully shielded."

"I don't think so. I can sense the emptiness when Fa— . . . the majer is fully shielded."

"Then there's just one." Taelya looked back to Varais. "Once they get closer, we'll withdraw, but slowly . . . so that we're close to the stream bridge . . . but not within the range of archers from the Certan post."

"*Not* within range?"

"I want them to think they can attack, or at least push us back." Taelya smiled wryly. "And if I've miscalculated, we'll be in a position to withdraw to the post before we're overwhelmed."

"Ser . . . reconnaissance missions aren't . . ." As Taelya looked at him, Gurdash's words died away.

"Reconnaissance missions are about finding out about the enemy." Taelya turned to Varais. "We'll start back now, at a fast walk. They're not moving that much faster . . . so far."

Within moments, Third Squad was headed back toward the border, with Taelya and Kaeryla effectively being the rear guard.

"Are we going to take out the white mage . . . if we can?" asked Kaeryla.

"I'd like to see what he can do, and what we can. If he throws chaos bolts at us, I'd like to turn them against his troopers, hopefully in a way that suggests we're just plain white mages."

"The way Father and Mother did, you mean?"

"Something like that, but we know nothing about this white, and anything could happen. And we were told not to do anything especially risky."

"I believe the idea was to avoid any risk," said Kaeryla, with the hint of a smile in her words.

"We're withdrawing in the face of a larger force. How can we be faulted for that?" Taelya smiled sweetly.

The approaching Gallosian force was less than three hundred yards west of Third Squad when Taelya re-formed her troopers slightly farther than that from the narrow bridge over the border stream. She and Kaeryla positioned themselves on the south shoulder of the road and waited. From what Taelya could sense, the Gallosian white was similar to most whites Taelya had encountered, surrounded by undisciplined free chaos, enough so that he might not even be able to sense either her or Kaeryla until the two forces were closer together.

The Gallosians halted when they reached a point some two hundred yards from the squad.

Varais asked quietly, "What do you want me to do if they charge?"

"They can only charge four or five abreast on this road," replied Taelya. "Trying to attack through the rocky ground on either side of the road will cost them more than a few mounts. If they attack, they'll need to use their mage unless they want to lose more troopers than I suspect they do."

At Varais's long-suffering look, Taelya added, "If we fail, get everyone across the bridge. If we prevail, keep them here in position. We'll lose men if we pursue, and that's not why we're here. We're here to keep white mages from destroying Montgren and Certan troopers. There's a white mage in that force. We'd like him to attack so that we can do just that."

"Do you think they'll attack two mages?"

"They may not know there are two of us, and they likely know that some of us are only women, or very young men. I'd wager they'll attack." *This time, anyway.* "We'll just have to wait and see."

After another half quint, the Gallosians began to move forward, slowly, at a moderate walk. As they did, arrows flew from what looked to be the second squad.

Taelya extended her shields and let the shafts drop short of Third Squad. A second volley struck her shields and dropped, but the Gallosians kept moving forward.

"At a hundred yards or less, they'll charge at a full gallop," said Varais.

"Then, at fifty yards or so, we'll take down their front line," replied Taelya. "Have the men ready arms in case one or two get through."

"Squad! Ready! Arms!"

The Gallosians were perhaps eighty yards from Third Squad when they charged, leaving one squad containing the mage, and likely the archers, behind.

Given the speed of the charge, Taelya fired off her first chaos bolt at sixty yards. Although it would have been hard to miss, close as the oncoming mounts were, her first bolt struck the center horse full in the chest, and in moments, all five lead riders and mounts were down.

The riders behind tried to avoid the carnage, and Taelya took out the two that avoided the downed men and mounts.

At that moment, a chaos bolt arced from the Gallosian mage toward Taelya.

"I have it!" snapped Kaeryla, immediately redirecting it into the milling riders behind the fallen men and mounts. A second chaos bolt followed the first, and Kaeryla threw that one farther back.

Something about the Gallosian response bothered Taelya, although she couldn't have said what at that moment. Then, abruptly, a trumpet call echoed across the road, and the Gallosians turned and immediately began to withdraw, beginning with the squad surrounding the white mage. In less than half a quint, the kay or so of road west of the bridge was empty except for Third Squad and fallen Gallosians and mounts.

"See if there are any wounded," ordered Taelya. "But be careful. We don't need to lose men in getting captives."

Jaavyn looked to Gurdash, who just shook his head.

As she watched Varais direct the squad, Taelya realized what had bothered her. She'd sensed the Gallosian mage and his shields, but the mage had made no effort to shield his troopers.

Why? Because he'd been surprised to run into mages tied up with the Certan forces . . . or because he didn't want to extend himself . . . or couldn't extend shields that far? He also had to have known that she or Kaeryla had shields, even if he couldn't have sensed them, by the fact that all the shafts dropped short. Whatever the reason, she doubted matters would go that smoothly with the next encounter.

Little more than a quint later, Third Squad re-formed, with two prisoners, one with a broken arm, the other with a broken leg, both with cuts and bruises, and Varais had taken charge of what spoils and arms there had been. Then the squad rode back over the bridge to the Certan post. The gates were open even before the squad reached them.

As they neared the gates, Taelya turned in the saddle to the two Certan rankers. "Thank you for the information about the Gallosians. It was very useful." *If not in the way that Akkyld or the post commander likely intended.*

"Our pleasure, ser," replied Jaavyn.

Gurdash just nodded.

"Do you require anything else?" asked Jaavyn.

"Not at the moment," replied Taelya as she guided Bounder through the gates and toward the stable.

Taelya had just started to unsaddle Bounder when Gustaan arrived.

"Wasn't that a little dangerous? Just to have the squad stand there?"

"No. It would have been more dangerous to charge them. They were coming uphill, and they couldn't bring more than four or five mounts at once. Either one of us could have stopped five mounts. It would have taken Kaeryla a little longer." Taelya sensed Kaeryla moving closer in the stable under a concealment.

"The submarshal wanted to know why you didn't follow up and mount an attack on them."

"You know as well as I do, ser. That would have gotten some of our men killed once we left what was a protected position."

Gustaan smiled wryly. "I told him the same thing, and, if you hadn't told me that, I would have told you to tell him just that if he asked."

"You need to tell Zekkarat that both of the ranker guides knew what would happen. Once we neared the earthworks, the Gallosian sentries took to their mounts and galloped back to the river fort. It took less than a quint for them to send a company with a white mage out to engage us."

"And you withdrew to an advantageous position and killed close to half a company in perhaps a third of a quint. They won't fall for that again."

"I'd hoped that the white mage would be closer to the fighting, or that he'd throw another chaos bolt, but he didn't. He just backed off."

"Sensible man, unfortunately." Gustaan frowned. "Was he one of the whites you met in Fairhaven?"

"It wasn't Sydon. I couldn't tell whether it was Klosyl or not."

"I need to go meet with Majer Zekkarat now."

"To confirm that I knew what I was doing?"

Gustaan grinned. "That . . . and a few other things."

Once Gustaan left, Kaeryla, who had been listening, dropped the concealment. "Akkyld had to know what the Gallosians would do. So why did he send us out on a recon patrol without even another squad?"

"The submarshal and his officers have been very skeptical of our abilities," said Taelya. "It could be that he doesn't want to risk troopers unless he's confident in us." *It could be.* But Taelya had her doubts.

"I don't like it," said Kaeryla tartly.

"Neither do I, but we'll have to deal with it, one way or another." Taelya turned back to Bounder.

Kaeryla returned to finish grooming her mount.

XLI

At the evening meal on threeday and even at breakfast in the officers' mess on fourday, the only officers who questioned Taelya and Kaeryla about their patrol were Sheralt and Valchar. No other officers, except Gustaan, even mentioned it, and that suggested strongly to Taelya that they'd been ordered not to bring the matter up. So why didn't the senior Certan officers want anyone talking to Taelya and Kaeryla? Taelya didn't know enough to narrow all the possibilities.

Immediately after breakfast, Gustaan gathered the four undercaptains together and said, "The submarshal has decided to wait to see what the Gallosians do in response to what Taelya and Kaeryla did before taking any action. That means that Second Squad will not be doing any reconnaissance this morning."

"I thought the idea was to attack and take Passera from the Gallosians so that we could go home and let the Certans take control of the river," said Sheralt.

"We're only here in support of the Certans," replied Gustaan. "We're not supposed to be leading the attack. They're supposed to do the attacking, and we're supposed to protect them from the Prefect's mages."

"That's what we did," said Kaeryla. "What were we supposed to do? Scurry back to the Certan post?"

"I don't think the submarshal realized how effective you two are. In less than a quint the Gallosians lost more than half a company to a single squad, without the loss of a single trooper."

"Pardon me, Captain," said Taelya, "but I'm a little confused. Yesterday, the submarshal was asking why we didn't pursue the Gallosians, and today, he doesn't want anyone leaving the post?"

"I asked Majer Zekkarat almost the same question. He said he'd raised that point with the submarshal. The submarshal said that there were certain strategic concerns. He did not explain those concerns."

Strategic concerns? Like the fact that we're more effective than he thought? That shouldn't have been a problem for any competent officer. And Akkyld was likely competent. So what other concerns could he have? Since Taelya didn't have an immediate answer, she just said, "It might be helpful if we knew those concerns."

"Both Majer Zekkarat and I feel the same way, but there's not much we can do at the moment. I'll let you all know as soon as I know more or when something's been decided."

After Gustaan had left, Sheralt looked to Taelya. "Those exercises the majer developed paid off."

"You could have done the same, and we'll all likely have to use everything we know before this is all over."

Sheralt nodded. "Do you think you were facing one of the stronger whites?"

"He wasn't as strong as Sydon, and Sydon was the strongest white I've encountered, but they withdrew before I could tell more about the mage."

Sheralt shifted his eyes to Kaeryla.

"It all happened so fast. I wasn't thinking about that. I was just trying to throw back those chaos bolts."

"As soon as you did that, didn't they retreat?" asked Valchar. "Do you think they hadn't planned on facing white mages? I mean, what they thought were white mages."

"That was the idea," said Taelya, "to make them think we had two white mages."

"What do you think they'll do now?" asked Valchar.

"About what the Certans have been doing, I'd think," replied Taelya. "They'll stay behind walls. We don't have siege engines. With their two walled posts guarding the river bridge, we'll have a hard time driving them out of Passera." From what she'd seen and heard, the arrival of the Fairhaven mages had essentially re-created the stalemate that existed up to the previous year. She wasn't about to say that because that idea rested on what she'd heard from Sondhyn, and, truthful as he had seemed, there was likely much more he didn't know or hadn't said.

"So what do we do now?" asked Valchar. "Sit and wait until our time is up?"

"Compared to some alternatives," replied Sheralt, "that wouldn't be half bad. I don't think it's going to turn out that way. The Viscount isn't going to pay his men or feed us just for sitting around and waiting. The submarshal has to know that."

"Then what will Akkyld do?" asked Valchar irritatedly.

"I don't know. He could post us downstream of Passera and have us stop every trading boat that's headed for Spidlar. All the traders going that way have to be Gallosians. That might force them out of their walls."

"I don't see the Prefect risking men and mages for a handful of traders," said Kaeryla mildly.

"Well . . ." answered Sheralt, drawing out his words, "then we'll just have to see what Akkyld and Majer Zekkarat come up with."

"While we're waiting, I'm going to check on Bounder," said Taelya.

"I'll come with you," said Kaeryla.

When the two women were away from Sheralt and Valchar, Kaeryla asked, "What do you really think?"

"I don't know what to think, but I do have a question for you. Don't you think it was strange that the Gallosian white didn't try to block or divert the chaos bolts you threw back at his troopers? I know I haven't faced other mages in real fighting before, but I do recall our parents talking about the shields of the Hydlenese mages and how they threw back redirected chaos bolts until Beltur put order inside them."

"He did?"

Taelya nodded. "I've thought about that as well. If I got close enough to a white, I think it might work if I put some order inside my focused chaos bolts, especially if I happened to be facing a strong mage. You might try something like that with a containment holding order." She paused. "I still think it was strange that the Gallosians withdrew so quickly and that the white didn't even try to protect his troopers."

"I hadn't thought about it, but now that you mention it . . . even Valchar would know what to do. Do you think that they just have a few weak whites here?"

Taelya frowned. "That doesn't make sense. Pretty much everyone agrees that they had at least one white strong enough to kill both Certan whites."

"One strong white supervising several lesser whites?"

"That just might be . . . and, if that's so . . ."

"What are you thinking, Taelya?"

"Nothing, yet. Except I need to groom Bounder. I wasn't as thorough as I might have been yesterday."

"Me, either."

By midafternoon, Taelya had heard nothing from Gustaan or anyone else. So far as she'd been able to sense, no one had left or entered the post on horseback or by wagon. She'd climbed to the parapets several times and seen or sensed nothing out of the ordinary. Her thoughts still swirled around the entire situation.

Still . . . for lack of anything better to do, she climbed back up to the top of the west wall. While there was a slight breeze, the white sun beat down, and she was sweating by the time she looked out toward Passera. Then, given that, by the calendar, in five days it would be summer, the heat was scarcely unseasonal.

As before, the vista to the west remained unchanged. She could see wisps of smoke rising from chimneys in the town, no doubt from cookfires or stoves, since she couldn't imagine any other reason to create more heat on an already hot day, except possibly from a smithy or distillery.

As she was about to leave the wall, she sensed someone coming. When she turned and saw Sondhyn, she couldn't have said she was surprised.

"It always looks the same. Most of the time, anyway. Except it's dustier in summer and harvest." He stood perhaps a yard to her left and gazed out for several moments before speaking again. "You and the other woman mage surprised everyone, you know. The officers, that is."

"We're arms-mages. We did what was necessary." She paused, then asked, "Were you and your friend, the one who's been talking to Kaeryla, all that surprised?"

"Khasahm was more surprised than I was. That might be because the other woman undercaptain's younger than you are."

"I don't know that age has much to do with it. It's more a matter of training."

"You were both trained from an early age, weren't you?"

"That's not a question, is it?"

Sondhyn laughed softly. "Not really. How young were you?"

"Seven."

He tried to conceal his surprise, but Taelya saw his eyes widen.

"I thought young, but not that young. And your compatriot?"

"Not quite that young, but close."

"You've killed more than a few men before."

"Any full arms-mage from Fairhaven likely has." That wasn't quite true. Taelya doubted that Valchar had, and Sheralt had killed several pirates and Hydlenese troopers in his escape to Fairhaven, but only two brigands that she knew of. "What do you make of this campaign?"

"What is there to make of it? We're all troopers. We do what's ordered and try to survive."

"Are there that many Gallosian traders who use Passera? Wouldn't most of them use the River Gallos? It's a lot closer to Fenard."

Sondhyn shrugged. "I can't say as I know, but there are some. Gallos is almost twice as wide as Certis, and Fenard is in the far west, just a few days' travel from the foot of the Westhorns."

"It sounds to me like the Viscount wants Passera more to keep the Prefect from levying high tariffs on Certan traders than to gain tariffs from Gallosian traders."

"You've got it all figured out, then." Sondhyn's voice was gently ironic.

Taelya shook her head. "I'm an arms-mage, not a trader. I don't know that much about ruling a large country. I'm just trying to figure out why we're all here."

"That part is simple. We're junior officers. We follow orders as best we can, because the consequences of not following them are worse than following them. Usually, anyway, but I'm not smart enough to know many of those times when it's better not to follow orders. I'm not a mage, either. So . . ." He shrugged again.

"It seems that neither of us has an answer."

"Most people who think they do are wrong, I've found. Is it any different in Fairhaven?"

"It seems better. The Council doesn't have any wealthy merchants on it, and the Duchess mostly leaves us alone."

"Mostly?"

"We're here," replied Taelya wryly.

"Just like the rest of us. In the end, we all answer to power."

"Were you ever attacked by one of their white mages?"

"One destroyed half a squad. We withdrew before he could do worse."

"You didn't try arrows from a distance?"

"He burned most of them out of the air. How did you stop their shafts? I didn't see any shafts burned in midair."

So he was watching. "We can shield a small group like a squad. It doesn't work for a company or a battalion."

"Can all mages do that?"

"I can't speak for all mages. From what I've heard most mages can at least protect themselves from shafts for a time, and some can protect more. It depends on the mage."

"And you?"

"I just told you what we could do."

"That would make a squad as powerful as a company."

"That might be overstating it," replied Taelya dryly. "Possibly quite a bit." She blotted her forehead under her visor cap with her sleeve. "It's getting hot up here. I need to get out of the sun. I appreciate your filling me in on things." She smiled pleasantly before she headed down the narrow stone staircase, feeling his eyes on her back the entire way into the shadows below.

Once she returned to her cramped quarters, Taelya took out her mother's map and studied it. The more she looked at it, the less she understood why the Prefect and the Viscount were spending golds and men over Passera. Both rulers had rivers that flowed to the Northern Ocean. Traders using those rivers still had to pay tariffs to the lands downstream. Those traveling the Passa River or the River Gallos into which the Passa flowed had to pay Spidlarian tariffs. Those traveling the River Jellicor had to pay Sligan tariffs.

In the end, she just shook her head, thinking about what Sondhyn had said, and knowing that she definitely did not have it all figured out.

Is it all just over power and bragging rights?

XLII

Early on fiveday, Gustaan dispatched Squad Two on reconnaissance, but at the last moment, Majer Zekkarat and another majer joined the squad, and Taelya wondered if the majers' timing had been carefully planned, rather than the spontaneous decision that it appeared. As soon as the post gates closed behind the departing squad, she hurried up the narrow stone staircase to the parapets so that she could watch and hopefully sense any oncoming forces. As before, two Certan troopers accompanied the Fairhaven squad, but unlike before, there did not appear to be any Gallosian scouts behind the earthworks. Taelya remained on the wall even when the squad rode beyond her ability to sense either the squad or other forces, but she didn't have even a vague sense of other forces.

As she was pondering all that, she sensed someone else climbing the staircase and turned, half expecting Sondhyn, only to discover Gustaan.

"You can't do much from here," he said genially.

"I'm hoping to learn something."

"Oh? What might that be?"

"I couldn't tell you."

"Do you sense any Gallosians?"

"Not between here and the town, and there's likely not a large force near where Second Squad is now. Beyond that, I can't tell."

"Are there people in the town?"

"There are only a few handfuls east of the earthworks and near the road. There might be more closer to the river."

"Akkyld is thinking of moving troopers out and building up the earthworks on the west side."

"What would be the point of that?"

"We'd be within a kay of the walled post that guards the bridge. With four mages, we should be able to hold that position. Then we could move forward and lay siege to that fort and the bridge. That would force them to attack or withdraw. The submarshal doesn't think that the Prefect has all that many troopers here in Passera any longer. He believes that the Prefect's relying on mages and the walled forts. That's why they immediately withdrew when you and Kaeryla took out close to half a company."

"How does he plan to take a walled fort without siege engines?"

"He says there's a weakness in the gates, but they've never been able to get close enough to use it because of the Gallosian mages. That's really why they wanted us."

"What . . . to shield them while they destroy the gates?"

"That's what he conveyed to Majer Zekkarat."

"That sounds . . . rather hopeful."

"It might be, but why else would they want us, and why would they send three battalions across the Easthorns?"

"Desperation?" suggested Taelya. "Or something else?"

"They could just be using us to weaken the Prefect, possibly to engage his mages. If the Prefect loses too many mages, then the Viscount could take Passera and a good chunk of eastern Gallos."

"That sounds more like what I'd expect," replied Taelya. "I don't see how Passera itself is worth it."

"It's likely not, but holding part of eastern Gallos and the Passa River would possibly allow him to work out an arrangement with Spidlar. As the majer has pointed out, the Spidlarians have no love of the Prefect."

"So all we have to do is get rid of some Gallosian mages and stay in one piece? Even that won't be easy."

"None of us thought it would be easy."

"But why didn't the submarshal just put it that way?" pressed Taelya.

Gustaan laughed, a bitter edge to the sound. "No ruler could say that he was hiring mages to assassinate other mages in order to give his army the edge to take over part of another country. The campaign has to look like it's being waged for a limited objective, with enough men and mages to force the Prefect to keep his mages here and possibly send one or two more."

"So we need to deal with the ones they have before more mages arrive? Possibly even stronger ones?"

"That would be helpful. That might also be why the white you faced was withdrawn so quickly, and why the submarshal has decided to move now. And what

Sheralt and the majers are looking for is some indication about how to proceed . . . and how quickly."

Taelya didn't like the idea that she and the other mage-undercaptains might essentially be used as assassins of other mages. *But then, you're already killing troopers, and why are mages any different?* What bothered her, she realized, was that she was part of an invading force. In the past, she'd been defending her own land . . . and now she was invading another land. *Even if it is the land of the Prefect, who is anything but decent.* Still . . . she couldn't say that she liked being an invader . . . and possibly a hired assassin as well.

"You don't look all that happy," observed Gustaan.

"Realizing that you've been put in the position of being a hired assassin is . . . a little unsettling."

"At times, all troopers are."

"I can't argue with that."

"Is there anything you need?"

Taelya shook her head.

"Then we'll talk later." Gustaan nodded, then turned and headed back down the stone steps.

Taelya returned to surveying the terrain to the west. While the morning sun was strong, there was at least the hint of a breeze on the top of the walls.

Almost two glasses passed before she both saw and sensed Second Squad returning, apparently without pursuit. Once the squad was inside the gates, she hurried down to the stables to wait for Sheralt and Valchar.

Not surprisingly, Sheralt led his mount into the stable before Valchar.

"What did you find out?" asked Taelya.

"There aren't many people left on this side of the river," replied Sheralt, continuing toward a stall.

"Are the houses abandoned?"

"Some are, but more are shuttered or boarded up. It's like people left knowing there would be fighting, but hoping to come back once it's over." The older white shook his head. "They must be used to that by now."

"How close did you get to that river fort?"

"Close enough. Maybe half a kay. They had some archers on the wall, maybe a squad's worth."

"What about the fort?"

"It's not that big. More the size of the Weevett post, and the walls aren't that much higher, if at all. Gates don't look to be that strong. Now . . . the really big post is the one on the west side of the river. It's right on the far side of the bridge. It could hold five battalions, if not more."

"How did you see that?"

"Zekkarat had us ride west and then toward the river."

"What about the bridge?"

"Two stone spans. The middle is like a stone shaft driven deep into the riverbed. Either that or they've built it up on a stone islet or ridge. Couldn't really tell from where we were."

"You didn't try to get closer?"

"There were two majers with us. Zekkarat and a Majer Rembraak. They didn't want us to go any closer. Rembraak especially. I don't think he trusts our shields." Sheralt grinned. "When we got back inside the gates, he asked me if you were as good a mage as everyone said."

"What did you tell him?"

"I told him that I had no way of knowing, but that the Gallosian mage hadn't wanted to stay around after the two of you threw firebolts at him. He didn't look happy. I said it all very politely, with lots of 'ser's and begging his pardon." Sheralt shook his head. "I wouldn't trust him any more than any of the other Certan officers, maybe less."

"Do you know why?"

"Just a feeling. They'd sell us down the river, any river, if it would improve their standing with the submarshal or the Viscount. They won't. Not now. Not until we've delivered Passera to them."

"I've had a feeling like that. We'll have to be very careful."

Sheralt looked back at her. "Even more careful than that, I think."

They both nodded, almost simultaneously.

XLIII

On sixday, the submarshal did not order troopers to occupy or modify the Gallosian earthworks, at least not first thing in the morning. Instead, he ordered another reconnaissance, if in slightly greater force, with Third Squad led by Taelya and Kaeryla, backed by a company from the Eighth Battalion. The reconnaissance force left the post at two quints before seventh glass, an almost leisurely departure time, suggesting to Taelya that the submarshal had no intention of dealing with the earthworks yet. The air already felt uncomfortably warm, with the white sun pouring down through the clear green-blue sky.

Once Third Squad had crossed the bridge over the border stream, Taelya found herself flanked by Zekkarat on her left and Majer Fohvrayt on her right, with Kaeryla and Varais directly behind the three.

"Do you sense any Gallosians nearby?" asked Zekkarat.

"No, ser. Except for an old man working his vineyard to the north of us. I can't quite sense to the river fort from here, though."

"When will you be able to?" asked Fohvrayt.

"Before we reach the earthworks."

"Can all mages sense that far?" pressed the Certan majer.

"Some more, some less. Every mage is different from every other, from what I've seen. But it's hard to tell. There just aren't that many mages." Taelya adjusted her visor cap, then studied the empty road ahead. She hoped that they didn't run into a Gallosian force, because it had been years since Zekkarat had fought with mages, and she doubted that Fohvrayt ever had, and the thought of dealing with superior officers and Gallosians at the same time made her uncomfortable.

"Given that," Fohvrayt said smoothly, "it seems rather odd that a small town such as Fairhaven should have so many."

"That's only because Lord Korsaen made an offer to two families sixteen years ago, and because Duke Halacut and the Dukes of Hydlen made living in their lands uncomfortable for mages, and six mages isn't that many."

"Especially since Montgren only has three others, and two of them are rather elderly," said Zekkarat. "I'm certain that there are more than nine mages in Gallos, as well as in Certis, and I know that Spidlar has close to a score, even if all of those are blacks."

"There is that," replied Fohvrayt cheerfully.

An increased chaotic flow around the Certan majer suggested to Taelya that Fohvrayt was concealing or not saying something. *Perhaps that the Viscount has more mages than that? Or none except for a few protecting him?* But those were questions she didn't think wise or useful to bring up at the moment. So she said nothing and kept searching with both eyes and senses.

A little more than a quint later, as they neared the abandoned earthworks, Fohvrayt again addressed Taelya. "You were rather . . . effective the other day, Undercaptain."

"The two of us were working together."

"Even with two of you, do you think those tactics would work in a larger full-scale battle?"

"They'd work, but they'd likely be just another weapon in a battle that involved battalions rather than squads or companies." Taelya wasn't about to say that Beltur and Jessyla had destroyed a battalion between them . . . or that it had taken an entire day and almost killed them both.

"An effective weapon, it would appear," suggested Fohvrayt.

"Mages can become less effective when larger numbers of troopers are involved on both sides," replied Taelya. "That's unless the commander is experienced in knowing how to use them effectively."

Fohvrayt merely nodded, but Taelya had the feeling that her words might have disconcerted him in some fashion.

Taelya could finally get a sense of the force inside the east river fort, and to her, it seemed as though there might only be two companies there . . . or less . . . and one white mage, whom she sensed as not particularly strong . . . but that might also have been because she was sensing at the edge of her ability to clearly discern.

"Are there any Gallosians near?" asked Fohvrayt.

"The only Gallosian troopers nearby are those in the east river fort."

"Are they mustering to attack?"

"I can't tell that. Only that they're all inside the walls right now."

"That's something," replied the Certan majer not quite dismissively.

"It's a great deal more than anyone else has been able to tell us, especially your scouts," replied Zekkarat, his mild voice concealing more than a little irritation.

Taelya couldn't help but feel a certain pleasure at Zekkarat's reaction, but she said nothing and returned her attention to the Gallosian fort. Nothing had changed.

"We'll move forward, then," declared Zekkarat. "You're to inform us of any possible change in the Gallosian forces or their positions."

"Yes, ser," replied Taelya.

While they rode westward, she continued to let her senses range over the houses and structures on each side of the road ahead, clearly the main street of the east bank of Passera, but could only discern a few individuals, and occasionally couples. As Sheralt had told her the afternoon before, almost all the houses were boarded up or tightly shuttered, which was scarcely surprising, given what Sondhyn had said.

Shortly, Taelya sensed movement along the top of the east wall of the nearer and smaller Gallosian fort. Once she was certain, she said, "They've brought more men to the parapets of the nearer fort, but the gates are still closed."

"Archers, no doubt," said Zekkarat. "They did that yesterday. But their range is less than three hundred yards, and the mages can block volleys from that distance long enough for us to withdraw. Not that we'll approach that close."

After they'd ridden down the deserted main street for around another four hundred yards and were nearing a small and empty square, Fohvrayt said, "And there's still no response from the Gallosians?"

"Aside from a few more archers on the east and north walls, ser, nothing has changed." Taelya turned and looked to Kaeryla. "Do you sense anything different?"

"No, ser."

"We're close to half a kay from the fort," said Fohvrayt. "Shouldn't they be doing more than that?"

Although the majer's voice was calm, Taelya could sense a bit more free chaos swirling around him. "So far they aren't."

"We'll halt in the square. You can get a slightly better view of the fort from there," said Zekkarat. "I'd judge it's just about half a kay from the north wall. Then we'll move north and closer to the river so that you can get a better view of the larger post on the west side of the river."

Fohvrayt frowned. "Is that wise?"

"After what the mages did the other day, do you really think they're going to attack immediately, especially when most of their troopers have to be on the other side of the river? Besides, they couldn't bring that many men to bear that quickly. The bridge isn't that wide."

Zekkarat turned out to be right. The view from the square was better, and from what Taelya could see of the east side of the eastern fort it looked smaller even than she had felt it to be.

Then the Montgren majer turned to Taelya and to Kaeryla. "Do either of you sense any changes in the Gallosian force?"

"No, ser."

"Can you tell how many troopers are in the east fort?" asked Fohvrayt.

"Not exactly, ser, but it feels like no more than two companies at present," replied Taelya.

Fohvrayt looked to Kaeryla. "What do you say?"

"Two companies, ser."

"At least, that's in agreement with what the submarshal thinks." Fohvrayt turned to Zekkarat. "We should move on."

"Then we'll ride west and toward the river so that you can better assess how we might best cross the river and successfully engage the main Gallosian forces." Zekkarat gestured toward a street that angled northwest from the small empty square, at the end of which Taelya could see several low trees, most likely at the bank of the Passa River.

Fohvrayt said nothing.

As Third Squad started down the side street, Taelya checked the main street to the smaller fort, but still sensed no troopers. Then she shifted her focus to the fort positioned on the far side of the river. While she couldn't see it because of the closed or abandoned shops lining the way, she had the immediate feeling that it was far larger than the eastern fort . . . and that it wasn't located immediately adjacent to the river bridge, but at least a good hundred yards north of the bridge causeway, possibly even farther. She could also sense, even without trying, that Sheralt had been understating matters when he had mentioned that the bridge had been reinforced with order. So far as she could determine it was essentially order-locked in place.

But who could have done that . . . and why? The immediate name that came to mind was Relyn, but why would he have poured so much order into a bridge? *But who else could it have been?*

The solidity of the bridge and the difficulty, if not the impossibility, of destroying it likely contributed to the uneasy relations between Gallos and Certis, but, given that, why hadn't the Gallosians simply built their western fort right over the western causeway? That would have provided much greater control over the bridge.

She was still pondering those questions when the combined force reached the end of the street, a small stone-paved area, from which a timber dock extended into the bluish-gray water. The dock was empty, of course, but once everyone had reined up, Taelya turned and looked back southwest across the river at the western Gallosian fort, which resembled a stone square with walls perhaps five or six yards tall. There were no corner towers, and no gates or other entrances on the east or north sides. Taelya couldn't see the south or west sides, but she suspected the main gates were likely on the south wall. Without siege equipment or a means to batter through the main gate, or some method that Taelya hadn't considered, the fort looked close to impregnable.

What are we supposed to do? Destroy their mages and then starve them out? Use magery to break through the gates?

"Don't let the size or the height of the walls fool you," said Fohvrayt. "Only the first three yards above ground are solid. We did bring the critical parts for several trebuchets. Once we take the east fort and hold that side of the city, we can forage for the necessary timbers. After that, with your mages keeping theirs under control, it will be only a matter of time, a few eightdays at most."

What surprised Taelya was that she could detect no deception at all in the majer's words, and that bothered her even more than the deception she expected would have, although she couldn't have said why.

After less than a third of a glass, Fohvrayt nodded to Zekkarat.

The Montgren majer gestured to the street leading east from the paved area. "We'll take that street back."

During the entire ride back to the Certan border post, Taelya sensed no Gallosian forces outside either fort, nor did the Gallosians in the eastern fort put any more archers on the walls, at least not while Taelya was close enough to sense the fort.

Neither she nor Kaeryla said more than a few words to each other until they were back in the stable unsaddling their mounts.

"I don't care for that Majer Fohvrayt," said Kaeryla. "He treated you like you were the lowest of the low, and he totally ignored everyone else except Zekkarat, and he barely tolerated even him."

"That surprises you?"

"No. But it doesn't sit well with me, either. Even when you told him how few troopers there were in the fort, he was condescending, as if he already knew."

"They already know everything, don't you know?"

Kaeryla laughed.

"We could take that fort," said Taelya quietly. "The smaller one, that is."

"How?"

"Use concealments to get close. Then have the Certan troopers form up as if they intended to attack with something that looks like a battering ram. As soon as they get near, Sheralt and I could drop chaos bolts on the walls . . . or into the center of the fort. I need to think about that some." Taelya paused. "But once we have that fort, we're almost on top of the bridge."

"But that fort's too small to hold all three battalions."

"It's big enough to hold us and the Montgren companies. And from there, we could keep Akkyld posted on what the Gallosians are doing. And it would keep us separate from the Certans."

"You really don't like them, do you?"

"Do you? Besides, liking isn't the question. I don't trust them. You can dislike someone and still trust them."

"You don't like them or trust them."

"That's right. But we don't have much choice now, do we?"

Kaeryla just shook her head.

XLIV

After talking her idea over more with Kaeryla on sixday, Taelya was up even earlier on sevenday, waiting for Sheralt in an alcove along the corridor leading to the officers' mess.

He was walking with Valchar when he caught sight of her. "You have that look."

"I need a moment with Sheralt, Valchar. Just a moment." She smiled warmly. "If you'd save us seats next to you?"

Valchar raised his eyebrows, then turned to Sheralt, saying with a grin, "Be careful what you agree to."

Sheralt smiled in return. "That's true about all of us."

"Don't be too long," returned the black mage. "Breakfast is bad enough hot. You don't want it cold."

Sheralt stepped into the alcove and looked at Taelya. "What is it?"

"If you only had to do two or three firebolts," asked Taelya, "how big could you make them?"

Sheralt frowned. "I don't know. I haven't even thought about that in a long time. We were training on how to use less chaos." He paused. "Why do you want to know?"

"I was thinking about how we could take the small fort without going through a siege."

"Firebolts aren't that good against stone. You know that."

"But they're very good against troopers. What if you arched them over the wall and into the center courtyard? Especially if troopers were mustered there getting ready to attack?"

"I'd be surprised if I could manage anything much larger than five yards across. I'd have to be close to do even that."

"We can manage that. We could move close under a concealment. Kaeryla could hold both shields and concealments. You could drop firebolts, taking your time, around the courtyard, and I'd work on the gates."

"Even you can't do anything against iron," Sheralt pointed out.

"I don't intend to. I'd burn away the wood at the sides."

"What about their whites?"

"There's no reason why we couldn't turn back their chaos on the fort."

"What if that didn't work?"

"Then we'd sneak away under shields and concealments."

Frowning, Sheralt fingered his chin. "It *might* work. You ought to talk to Gustaan, though."

"*We* should talk to him. Immediately after breakfast."

"What will you tell Valchar?"

"We'll tell both Kaeryla and Valchar that we're going to meet with Gustaan and that they should be there."

Sheralt nodded. "I'd like to hear what he'll have to say."

After breakfast, Gustaan and the four undercaptains gathered in a corner of the courtyard near the stables.

"Why did you ask to meet with me?" asked the captain.

"To suggest a way to take the eastern fort," said Taelya, going on to explain what she had in mind.

As she explained, Valchar's eyes widened, but Kaeryla only nodded.

When Taelya finished, Gustaan shook his head, not exactly in negation. "The majer said you might have ideas. It might work, but you four mages are taking a certain risk."

"If it looks like it won't work, we can withdraw," Taelya pointed out. "If it does work, the risk is on the troopers who will have to deal with the Gallosians fleeing the fort or remaining inside."

Gustaan smiled wryly. "Wait here. I'll see if Majer Zekkarat has a few moments, not that we're scheduled to do much today."

Once the captain was out of earshot, Valchar snorted, then said, "We're the only ones who've done anything. They should at least be able to use one of those battalions to clean up after we flush the Gallosians out of the fort."

"When you talk to the majer—if we talk to him," added Kaeryla, "say that one of the Montgren companies will be supporting our two squads."

"I wish I'd thought of that before we talked to Gustaan," replied Taelya.

Less than a quint later, Gustaan returned. "I told the majer that you four had a proposal that he should hear, and he agreed. He's waiting in the small conference room."

The four undercaptains exchanged glances.

Gustaan laughed. "Obviously, none of you have been requested to go there. This way." He turned and walked toward the southeast corner of the post, just short of which was a single door, slightly ajar. He rapped once. "Captain Gustaan, with the undercaptains."

"Bring everyone in and close the door."

Zekkarat was seated at the end of the short oblong table. He brushed back a lock of black hair and smiled, gesturing for the junior officers to seat themselves.

"You requested this meeting for the undercaptains, Captain." Although Zekkarat spoke to Gustaan, after he spoke, his black eyes went to Taelya, almost inquisitively, as he asked, "What did you have in mind?"

"Ser," replied Taelya, "we believe there might be a less costly way to take the Gallosian fort on the east side of the river."

"I wasn't aware that the submarshal had revealed any plan to take the eastern fort," replied the majer. "That aside, please explain your plan."

"We'd thought to combine chaos bolts, shields, and concealments to force the Gallosians from the fort . . . or, if necessary to make it easier for our troopers to enter . . ." Taelya went on to explain, but without mentioning concealments, only chaos bolts and shields.

When she finished, Zekkarat offered a wry smile. "A rather cautiously daring idea. It reminds me of Majer Beltur, which I suppose is not surprising. I take it that the request for backup by Certan forces is to make certain that the submarshal has to commit at least some of his forces?"

"Yes, ser . . . but it's also prudent to have a backup."

Zekkarat flashed a grin that briefly illuminated his honey-skinned face. "It's also prudent for me. I'd hate to explain to the majer that I didn't assure backup for his daughter and his niece." The grin faded. "Are you sure you want to do this? I'm asking because it's quite likely the submarshal will agree. His men will likely have an easier time of it this way."

"Easier, but not without risk," replied Taelya. "If this works as planned, it's likely that at least some of the Gallosians will come out of the fort angry and fighting."

"I think I'll refer to that as having his troopers deal with mopping up those who escape. When can you do this?"

"I'd suggest either very early morning or late afternoon," said Taelya. "We'll need some time to do our own reconnaissance—under concealments."

"I'd suggest," interjected Gustaan, "that the recon under concealments not be mentioned to the submarshal."

"So . . . either tomorrow afternoon or oneday morning?"

"Yes, ser," replied Taelya.

"It may be a few glasses before I get back to you, Captain Gustaan. I understand that the submarshal is holding a meeting for his officers." Zekkarat looked to Taelya once more. "Is there anything else I should know?"

"If it works . . . it won't be pleasant for the Gallosians."

"Having seen your family in action, Undercaptain, that would not surprise me." Zekkarat stood. "Until later."

Gustaan led the five Fairhaven officers out of the conference room. Kaeryla was the last and closed the door.

Once they were outside and well away from that corner of the post, Sheralt looked to Taelya. "You thought he'd agree even before you said a word, didn't you?"

"I thought it likely. He's dealt with rulers and arrogant commanders before." Taelya had other reasons for thinking that, but since she had no way of proving them, she kept them to herself. "And Akkyld and his majers are definitely arrogant."

"How do you want to do your reconnaissance?" asked Gustaan, adding, "Not all four of you at once. That's an unnecessary risk."

"Then, just Sheralt and I, and half of Squad Three, with Varais. We're the ones who need to see where we'll be placing chaos bolts."

Kaeryla nodded at that.

"When?"

"This afternoon . . . if the submarshal agrees."

"I tend to agree with Majer Zekkarat," said Gustaan. "Akkyld will agree. Whether he does by this afternoon is another question."

Taelya had the same feeling.

Except that, at a quint past the first glass of the afternoon, Gustaan found Taelya in the stable checking on Bounder. She turned as the captain approached.

"How soon do you want to leave? Akkyld thought it was a splendid plan, according to Zekkarat."

Taelya winced. *If the submarshal liked it so much, there must be something wrong with it.*

"That was my reaction as well. You and Sheralt are going to have to be very careful. I took the liberty of asking Varais and Sheralt to join us, once I heard you'd gone to the stable. They should be here any moment."

Sheralt arrived almost immediately, frowning slightly.

"You didn't think Akkyld would agree?" asked Taelya.

"I thought he would. His *quick* agreement worries me. It's almost as if he doesn't know what to do with us."

"He likely doesn't," replied Gustaan. "They've never worked that well with mages . . . or against them. That's why they've had trouble with the Prefect."

Before either undercaptain could say more, Varais joined them.

"Sers, I hear we have a covert recon mission," said Varais.

"We do," replied Taelya. "We'll need half the squad."

"Good. It's about time we did more than posture."

"You think . . ." began Sheralt.

"Yes, ser. If the Gallosians knew what they were doing, we'd have been attacked more than once." The squad leader turned to Taelya. "How soon do you want to ride out?"

"Within the glass. As soon as we can, carefully. Once we're out of sight from here, at some point we'll be riding under a concealment. So we'll need guide ropes. Don't explain what they're for if any Certan sees them or asks."

"I'll tell them they're in case we take any captives." Varais offered a hard smile.

Preparations took longer than Taelya estimated, and it was two quints past second glass when the post gates closed behind the departing half squad.

"Straight over the bridge and directly to the earthworks. Then we'll enter the town and head south before making our way west to the fort."

As they rode across the stream bridge and into Gallosian territory, Taelya kept sensing for any trace of troopers or mages, but, as before, she felt nothing but the vague presence of troopers and a white mage beyond her ability to discern clearly. But by the time they reached the earthworks, she could sense both clearly, which suggested that, with all the sensing she had been doing, she was slowly extending her range.

They had to ride a hundred yards into the eastern part of Passera before they reached a clear side street heading south, although there were few houses or cots on the street. After a block or so, from the odors coming from a walled area on the west side of the street, Taelya understood why.

A rendering yard.

She glanced directly south and then back to the east, studying the terrain, mostly very low hills, with sparse grass and scattered rocks and boulders, much like the ground near the border, but certainly not impassable. Farther east, the hills leading to the Easthorns looked slightly less rugged, and it appeared to Taelya that a dirt path might afford another way to the border stream. *It might be worth a look on the way back.*

Returning her full attention to the mission at hand, she was more than glad to turn Bounder south on a clay street a block south of the renderer's, and even gladder as the worst of the stench abated with each yard they rode.

"This side of Passera leaves something to be desired," said Varais.

"Just this side?" asked Sheralt.

Taelya couldn't help smiling.

For the next several blocks, the scattered dwellings appeared deserted, but after that most appeared to be only shuttered, and she saw wisps of smoke coming from a few chimneys. When she could sense that they were slightly more than a half kay from the Gallosians' eastern fort, she called a halt, and said, "We'll go under a concealment from here on."

"What if the locals see us vanish?" asked Sheralt.

"It shouldn't matter," replied Taelya. "Even if someone's looking, how many will run to the fort? And even if they did, we won't be anywhere near by the time the Gallosians send anyone, if they even do. After our first encounter, I also doubt that they'd send anyone to look after some thirteen riders."

"Also," added Varais dryly, "after your last encounter, they wouldn't send a small force, and a large force would take time to muster."

"Your logic is impeccable," replied Sheralt. "It's even likely correct."

Meaning that sometimes logic is correct and wrong? Taelya wanted to shake her head. She didn't, but only said, "Prepare for riding under concealment."

In a fraction of a quint, the group was moving westward once more, if more slowly, but since Taelya had only seen a few scattered people, and no riders, it didn't take that long before they reached the cross street that bordered the east side of the fort, where Taelya again ordered a halt, quietly, in order to concentrate on sensing the fort, now only some four blocks to the north.

From what she sensed, there were lookouts on the walls, but the gates were closed, and there were no troopers anywhere near except inside the fort. She hoped that meant reconnoitering the fort would be a little less dangerous.

"Squad forward. Quiet riding."

When they were less than a block away, she called another halt and murmured to Sheralt, "Can you sense the walls and the center courtyard?"

"Roughly."

"Enough to drop a chaos bolt in there while under this kind of concealment?"

"Somewhere in there . . . yes . . . But they'll see where it came from once it leaves the concealment."

"We can start at the south end of the east wall and move north so that we'll be close to the gates when they come out."

"It would help if I could see it."

"I can drop the concealment for a moment if you need it to attack. But not now. We don't want them to suspect what we're planning." Taelya turned, then realized it didn't matter, because Varais couldn't see her. "Squad Leader, we're a block away from the fort. It will be on our left side. When we reach the main street, we'll halt so I can sense the gates. Then I'll order a right turn. We'll be heading east and back toward the border post."

"Yes, ser."

"Now . . . squad forward."

Taelya concentrated carefully on the fort. The walls were not that high, perhaps six yards or a little less from the ground to the top of the wall, but they felt thicker than the way Fohvrayt had described the walls of the main fort on the west side of the river. Also the top of the wall wasn't crenellated to protect archers, which she found strange. But then, she realized, neither had been the walls of the western fort.

She found she was holding her breath as they reached a point on the street opposite the southeast corner of the fortifications and slowly and quietly let it out. There was only one corner tower, and that was on the northeast corner of the walls, and the order/chaos balance of the tower felt slightly different.

Built later?

When they reached a point where she and Sheralt were literally in the middle of the intersection of the cross street and the main street, she called another halt, and concentrated on the gates. As she'd suspected, the iron bands, hinges, and straps on the gates were solid, but there were traces of chaos throughout the wood. Even so, weakening the wood was going to be difficult, possibly more than she'd thought.

But then, if she couldn't do it, and all they could do was drop chaos bolts inside the fort, that would still weaken the Gallosians, possibly significantly, or anger them enough for them to charge out, in which case the four mages and the troopers should be able to deal with them.

If the Gallosians just endured the chaos bolts and stayed put . . .

Then we could do it again.

After Taelya had learned all she thought she could, she turned and murmured, "Squad forward. Right turn."

As the squad walked slowly eastward on the main street, empty as it always seemed to be, or had been on the few times Taelya had ridden it, she concentrated on the fort and especially the gate. After they covered another three blocks, she felt less nervous about being chased. After a few blocks, she removed the concealment.

"Whew!" declared Sheralt. "It's hot riding under a concealment."

"In a little bit, we're going to do some exploring."

The older mage wrinkled his forehead. "I thought we just did that."

"Some more exploring, then. I saw a narrow track beyond that rendering yard, and it looked like it was heading east-southeast. We need to see where it goes."

"Why?"

"I couldn't tell you why." Actually, Taelya could have given a reason, but she had nothing to support it except her feelings. "It shouldn't take that long, and what else are we going to do, except worry about tomorrow?"

"We could drink some of that terrible ale," suggested Sheralt cheerfully.

"We can do that after we explore."

A quint later, the recon squad was riding along a dirt track too wide to be a path and too narrow to be a proper road that had initially angled to the east-southeast, but once it wound through a low place between two rises not tall enough to be called proper hills it turned in a more easterly direction, almost paralleling the road from the border into the west side of Passera.

"This is just going to be a dead end at the border stream," said Sheralt quietly.

Taelya shook her head. "Either it will lead to a border crossing or it will turn south and parallel the stream. It's been traveled enough that it's still being used. That means it goes *somewhere.*"

"Why won't it go north?"

"Because there aren't any trails like this that join the main road in the kay west of the border stream."

Sheralt looked as if he might say something, then shut his mouth.

A quint or so later, on the west side of a low rise, Taelya caught sight of what looked to be the border stream gorge . . . and a narrow defile descending between two low hills. "I'll wager that leads down to a not quite impassable ford over the border stream."

"I'll pass on that wager, thank you," replied Sheralt.

When they reached the top of the defile, really a narrow gorge barely wide enough for a small cart, if that, Taelya reined up. "I can see the trail on the far side. That's all we need to know." She turned to Varais. "None of the troopers are to mention this. To anyone."

"Yes, ser."

"Now we can head back." She turned to Sheralt. "That's what I suspected."

"You wouldn't want to bring a company through here unless you didn't have a choice. It would be too easy to fill a narrow gorge like that with shafts."

Unless you had them under a concealment. But Taelya just nodded.

Once the recon squad was headed back along the path, Sheralt asked, "Why did you suspect that crossing would be there?"

"Because of all the back roads around Fairhaven. Most of them enter the town on less used lanes. Also there were some trails or paths off the main road several kays into the hills east of the border. When there are tariffs, there are always smugglers, and smugglers need paths or trails around the places where tariffs are collected. I hadn't seen any other likely paths. So I thought it was worth looking at."

"You really don't trust Akkyld, do you?"

"So far, he's given me no reason to distrust him. He also hasn't given me any reason to trust him. Besides, it never hurts to have another way out. We'll tell the captain that we looked at side roads and streets leading away from the eastern fort. That's why it took a little longer, and that's certainly true."

"Why aren't you telling him the whole truth?"

"So he doesn't have to lie. He doesn't do it well."

Sheralt's chuckle verged on the bitter.

XLV

In the end, Zekkarat and Akkyld agreed that a late-afternoon attack on eightday made the most sense. At least, that was what Zekkarat told Gustaan, according to the captain, and Taelya wouldn't even have needed to sense his order/chaos levels to know that Gustaan was accurately relaying what Zekkarat had told him. She did anyway.

At third glass of the afternoon on eightday, officers began mustering the attack force, spearheaded by the Fairhaven company, and supported by Konstyn's Montgren company and Seventh Battalion under Majer Rembraak.

At two quints past third glass, Taelya, Gustaan, and Sheralt rode out through the gates of the Certan border post at the head of Squad Three, leading the Fairhaven contingent, followed by Kaeryla and Valchar at the head of Squad Two, and then by Konstyn's company. After a slight interval, Seventh Battalion followed.

Taelya found herself uneasy in the saddle and wondered why, given that she'd certainly fought before. But almost immediately, she realized that wasn't why she worried. *It's your plan, and if it doesn't work . . .*

She couldn't help shivering, more than just slightly, as she thought about those possibilities.

"Worrying about your battle plan?" murmured Gustaan. "That's why officers get gray—or silver—earlier than rankers. The good ones, that is. Most poor officers worry about the wrong things."

"You saw that from the squad leader's side for a long time, didn't you," she replied quietly.

"You know that. Concentrate on what you have to do and what your officers and men have to do. Don't mix their duties and responsibilities . . . or yours."

Taelya stiffened as she realized what Gustaan was saying. *He may be senior, but it's your plan, and it depends on your knowing and sensing what's happening . . . and that means you're responsible.* She swallowed. "Thank you."

"Just trust yourself. You'll do fine."

After the Fairhaven/Montgren force passed the empty earthworks and entered the west side of Passera, Taelya led the way onto the side street past the rendering yard, and then west on the same street the half squad had reconnoitered. Behind them, Seventh Battalion continued down the main street at a measured pace.

When the Fairhaven-led part of the attacking force reached the cross street that fronted the east side of the fort, Taelya turned to Gustaan. "Squad Three will move ahead under a concealment from here. Squad Two will move into position after that, also under a concealment. Have Konstyn wait half a quint before moving up some fifty yards from the southeast corner of the fort. That will give Kaeryla and Valchar enough time to bring up shields if the Gallosians muster archers." She knew she was repeating what they'd discussed, but it was better to make it clear. "When Seventh Battalion's in place, we'll start picking off sentries. At that point, Kaeryla will drop her concealment from Second Squad. You should be able to see that. Then we'll see."

She could only hope that matters would proceed as planned from there. Or that, if her plan failed, it failed with few casualties.

Gustaan nodded to her, then eased his mount away from her and headed back toward Second Squad.

Once Taelya sensed he was behind the last rank of her squad, she took a quiet, deep breath and ordered, "Squad Three. Forward, under concealment."

Third Squad rode north toward the fort, while Taelya concentrated on sensing the troopers on the walls, as well as those inside the courtyard and the position of the gates. The gates were closed, unsurprisingly, and out of perhaps two companies of troopers within the stone barracks or in chambers built into the walls, not that many were in the open, just five troopers on the walls, one at each corner and a lookout on the top level of the single wall tower, on the northeast corner of the walls. Perhaps a score or two of troopers were in various places across the single courtyard within the walls, some standing, some walking, and one group kneeling in a circle in corner.

A bones game, no doubt. She'd only encountered one in her years as a Road Guard, most likely because Beltur had forbidden such games in any buildings involving the Council or the Road Guards, including barracks and quarters, and since mages could sense such activities from a distance, any who wanted to trust their coins on a throw of the bones were inclined to do so elsewhere.

"Do they have a mage in the fort?" asked Sheralt in a low voice from where he rode beside her.

"Just the one, from what I can sense. You can't sense him?"

"There's just a white fuzziness in the middle of the east wall."

"That's him. We'll have to watch him and see what he does. He can't very well throw chaos at us from where he is." Taelya turned her senses to the main street, but Seventh Battalion was still not close to being ready, and neither had Third Squad reached its planned position opposite the northeast corner of the fort, although Taelya and Sheralt were less than a hundred yards from there. "Majer Rembraak is taking his time. His lead company is almost half a kay from the fort."

"We can wait. No one's even discovered the Montgren company yet."

"It won't be that long," predicted Taelya.

"You're going to be surprised," murmured the older white. "Remember. It's eightday afternoon."

Taelya didn't reply, concentrating as she was on checking on the behavior of the trooper on the other side of the street a mere four yards above her head. She was still surprised that no one had raised an alarm when she turned in the saddle and ordered, in a low voice, "Squad, halt."

As she waited, either for an alarm, or for Seventh Battalion to get into position, since the Montgren company already was, she blotted away the perspiration oozing from under her visor cap. Riding under a concealment during the late-afternoon heat was hot, another reminder that tomorrow would be the first day of summer, although, to Taelya, it had seemed like summer for well over an eightday.

Abruptly, a bell clanged from the watchtower, followed by loud shouts that Taelya could not make out.

"Now?" asked Sheralt.

"Not yet. Rembraak's still not in position. We also want to see if they'll muster troopers in the courtyard. I'm wagering they will."

"You said that before."

"We'll see how many." Taelya kept sensing and waiting.

In less than a third of a quint, perhaps two squads were formed up in the middle of the courtyard, and she didn't sense any more troopers arriving. Interestingly enough, the white mage also hadn't moved.

"Chaos bolt now . . . as close as you can to the middle of the courtyard." Taelya kept sensing as the ball of chaos arched over the wall and headed down, then edged it slightly to the west.

There wasn't even time for screams, just the sense of the chill black mists of death.

"Take a good swallow of ale," she said quietly. "It's my turn now." Her first tight chaos bolt took out the trooper in the watchtower, easily enough because he was leaning over the wall to gape at the death below. The second took the trooper below on the northeast corner of the wall. The third took the trooper on the southeast corner. She decided against trying for the two others acting as lookouts on the west corners of the fort because she was more than likely to have missed and wasted the effort . . . and because they couldn't see much from where they were.

More orders were shouted from within the fort, but someone had clearly assessed the threat because Taelya could sense that no one was venturing into the center of the courtyard, but staying as close to the inner walls as they could.

Possibly half a quint passed, and then troopers began to hurry up to the top of the wall. It took several moments for Taelya to sense thoroughly enough to determine that most of them were carrying bows. As soon as the first one drew his bow, Taelya flared him with chaos, then took down the next two.

For more than a few moments, none of the other archers attempted to loose a shaft, then three did all at once. Taelya got one of the three, but two of the shafts flew toward Konstyn's company, where they were doubtless deflected by Kaeryla's shields.

The next time, ten archers stepped back—which they had to, because the walls weren't crenellated—and loosed shafts. Taelya took out one, then took a swallow of ale from her water bottle. She could have done two. *Maybe.* But loosing chaos bolts close together took even more strength.

For another quint, that was the pattern. During that time, Taelya killed another ten archers, in almost leisurely fashion.

"We're picking them off the walls, but they're not forming up inside," said Taelya worriedly. "And there's no point in wearing ourselves out dropping chaos into the courtyard when there's no one there."

"Is it cooler, or am I imagining things?" asked Sheralt.

Taelya paused. "It is." Then she smiled, not that Sheralt could have seen it. "It's late afternoon. Later than I thought. The sun's low enough that we're in the shade of the walls now."

"That's a bit of a help," said Sheralt. "I sense order and chaos near the gate, but not in the courtyard. It's hard for me to tell how many, though."

"You're right. There might be half a company gathered together just inside the gate. From all the iron I sense, they're heavily armed, but they're protected by the walls above."

"So why don't we do it together?" he said, almost wickedly. "I don't have the control you do, and you have trouble gathering huge amounts of chaos. So I loft a big fireball. When it comes down you push it to the side and into the sheltered space behind the gates. That might even help weaken the gates."

"Could you do a couple of them?"

"If I can rest a little between them."

"Let's try one."

Sheralt pulled out his water bottle, uncorked it, and took a long swallow of ale before corking the bottle and replacing it in its holder. "All right. Are you ready?"

"I'm ready."

Sheralt formed and lofted the chaos bolt.

As it sped downward, Taelya chaos-pushed it northward under the overhang of the walls and into the gate area. There were no screams, so sudden had the attack been, only another spreading black mist of death.

Taelya swallowed.

The fort was eerily quiet, but no archers appeared at the walls, firing useless shafts at Second Squad and the Montgren company, and only a few archers had even tried to direct shafts in the direction of Seventh Battalion, positioned as it was some three hundred yards east of the closest corner of the fort.

Another quint passed. Taelya felt as though she'd regained some strength when she sensed that the white mage was moving. "The white's heading toward the watchtower. That's about the only place from which he could launch chaos with some sort of cover."

"Why did he wait so long?" asked Sheralt.

"You'd have to ask him." *Because we're not going away, and because Rembraak has a battalion of troopers that can block the bridge on this side so that the Gallosians aren't going to get reinforcements.*

"I'm going to try something. It might catch him off guard." Taelya kept sensing the mage's progress, well aware that she would need to be quick and accurate. "Just before he reaches a place where he can loose his chaos, I'm going to remove the concealment. As close as he is, he'll be able to sense, even if he is a white. I'm going to need to be very, very accurate."

Thinking about it again, Taelya immediately dropped the concealment. Even in the shadows of the fort, she felt blinded by the light for several moments.

"I thought you'd wait."

"I changed my mind."

Even by the time the blurring had left her vision, the white was still not quite at the lowest level of the watchtower. From what Taelya could sense, he appeared to be climbing an inside staircase. As she studied the tower, she saw a narrow window on the east side of the tower a yard or so above the walls. She didn't see any other openings on the east side, and that meant the white would either use the slit window or loose chaos from the very top of the tower.

You should be able to do it. That opening is wider than the openings in Beltur's infernal device, and it's not that much farther than those distances, just across the street and a few yards up.

What she had in mind would be uncomfortable, but not painful.

As the mage neared the window slit and slowed, confirming her thoughts, Taelya gathered both chaos and as much free order as she could, surrounding the order with chaos. Then, the instant he peered through the window, she fired that narrow order/chaos bolt. Energy flared across the inside of the watchtower, and a single black mist of death wafted over and past Taelya.

She realized something else at that moment—that the white hadn't been that strong, and might not have been much older than her brother . . . and he'd probably been the one with the Gallosian company. *But how could you have known that until it was too late?* And even if she had known, what else could she have done?

A quiet again settled over the fort.

Nearly a quint passed without so much as an archer raising his head above the walls.

Finally, Taelya turned. "We're going to move opposite the main gates. We need to see about bringing them down."

"Yes, ser." Varais's voice was even.

"Squad! Forward."

Taelya halted the squad directly opposite the iron-bound gates, gates that sagged noticeably in the middle, more so than she'd sensed before. Had she missed that, or had Sheralt's firebolt weakened them from the rear?

She was considering how best to attack the gates when Sheralt spoke.

"Why don't you try aiming a tiny chaos bolt at the big hinge strap on the top right side, at the very edge?"

Taelya frowned. "Why? Iron stands against chaos. What would be the point?"

"Have you ever noticed what happens when chaos strikes iron? Iron, not black iron. The iron heats up. I was thinking that might be an easier way to get the wood to burn. Or we could aim at the edge of the straps and see what happens."

"Let's try that, with really tiny chaos bolts at first." Taelya loosed a narrow bolt at the upper iron hinge strap on the right side of the gate. Nothing seemed to happen except for a puff of gray smoke and ashes.

"That will work," said Sheralt. "You're using chaos like a drill. Let me do a couple."

"Go ahead." Taelya was more than willing to let him try.

Sheralt loosed a chaos bolt not quite so narrow as the one Taelya had fired, and the result was a slightly larger puff of smoke and more ashes flying from the impact. He extracted his water bottle and took a long swallow before replacing it. Then he loosed another chaos bolt.

Taelya followed with another right after his. She thought part of the iron strap looked reddish.

Abruptly, the upper corner of the gate turned into flame. Slowly the flames spread across the gate. The two mages watched as the flames began to consume the gate.

"They must have oiled the gate a lot," said Sheralt.

Taelya didn't know what to think.

After a time, the right gate slumped and the remainder crashed forward onto the stone causeway. The left gate, which had also caught fire, continued to burn.

Taelya could tell that before long there would be enough space that she could use shields to widen the opening to allow riders through. "We're going to have to go in . . ."

"Are you crazy? It's still burning," said Sheralt.

"Not yet. In a while. I'll shield us. You flame people." Taelya paused as she sensed the interior of the fort, abruptly realizing that it was essentially empty. She could only sense a handful of men . . . anywhere within the fort. "Never mind."

"Never mind what?"

"Just a moment." She cast her senses to the west of the fort, only to discover that what amounted to half a company of Gallosian troopers were running toward the river bridge. In fact, some of them were already on the bridge. Not only that, but they'd left their mounts, except Taelya had the feeling that the number of horses remaining would barely have sufficed for a single company. She shook her head, then explained, "They fled, and they left their horses. There must have been a rear door or hidden gate or something. You should be able to sense them running to or over the bridge."

Sheralt frowned. "You're right." Then he laughed. "You did it. You terrorized them. After you took out the white, and all those archers, and then the gates started to burn, they were so afraid that they'd all end up ashes that they fled."

That was what had happened, but were the Gallosians that inept? How had they possibly held off the Certans? Or were the more competent mages and forces in the large fort on the west side of the river?

"It has to be a trap of some sort," said Varais. "Real troopers don't flee like that. Not even Gallosians."

"So what do you suggest?" asked Taelya.

"Wait a little. You can't catch many of them. If we did, what would we do with them?"

"Then send a trooper to Gustaan. Have them move up to where we are. Send another to Majer Rembraak. Tell him that the surviving Gallosians have fled, and that I recommend that he watch the bridge just in case the Gallosians are thinking about a counterattack, unlikely as it seems so close to twilight." She paused. "Is there anything else you think I should tell the majer?" Taelya didn't worry so much about what she conveyed to Gustaan. He and Konstyn could sort matters out between them, and Gustaan could certainly tell Taelya what she'd forgotten or could have done. Taelya just didn't want to do anything stupid involving the Certans.

"Tell him you appreciate his guarding your flanks."

Taelya looked to the squad leader. "Should you deliver those messages?"

"That might be best, ser." Varais offered a wry smile.

"Then please do. We don't need any confusion."

"Yes, ser."

As Taelya waited for the gate fires to die out and to see if there were any last attacks, she keep sensing for Gallosians—anywhere—but the only troopers she sensed were what felt like a few severely wounded men inside the fort and those last troopers hurrying across the Passa River.

Less than a third of a quint later, Gustaan and Second Squad arrived, while Konstyn's company positioned itself on the east side of the fort.

The captain looked at the smoldering remnants of the fort gates and then at the two undercaptains. "No siege gear?" His words were gently sarcastic.

"We didn't know that it would work," replied Taelya. "They also weren't very sturdy gates. The survivors fled through some sort of small back gate. I never thought that we needed to surround the entire fort. I honestly thought that if we broke through or got them angry enough they'd attack in force, and the last thing we needed was to be spread out."

"I agreed with that," replied Gustaan. "So did Majer Zekkarat, and so did the submarshal. Frankly, I don't think the submarshal thought your plan would work. He also didn't think it would cost many troopers."

"It didn't cost us any, so far. It might have cost the Gallosians a company. We'll see when we enter the fort."

At that point, Varais returned. "A message from Majer Rembraak, sers."

"Go ahead," said Gustaan.

"The majer appreciates the information," said Varais, her voice even and without emotion. "He will monitor the bridge to make certain the Gallosians on the west side do not attack. Most of those who survived your attack were already beyond practical use of Seventh Battalion before the success of the attack was obvious."

To Taelya, Varais's flat delivery suggested that she was less than impressed with him.

"Thank you, Squad Leader," said Gustaan, adding to Taelya and Sheralt, "There's no point in rushing into the fort, but we do need to dispatch a messenger to Majer Zekkarat informing him of your success."

Success . . . or merely prevention of failure? Taelya was inclined to consider the attack more the latter than the former.

Zekkarat arrived less than a glass later, and immediately directed Konstyn to send in a squad of troopers, after clearing the remnants of the gates. All they found in the early twilight were dead Gallosians and close to fifty mounts, all of which were barely serviceable. Once the two Fairhaven squads moved into the courtyard, the troopers found basic supplies, such as barrels of flour and dried mutton, and Kaeryla sensed that there was no chaos or poison in any of the supplies, although the amounts remaining would only have fed two companies for an eightday or so.

Then Zekkarat gathered the two captains and the four undercaptains to a meeting in the corner of the fort's courtyard.

"I've never heard of magery successfully being used against a walled fortification," Zekkarat said dryly. "The circumstances were unique enough that I doubt it will occur often in the future, if ever, but I'm the last one to argue with success. It would have been better if we could have prevented so many Gallosians from escaping. The structure of the attack proved its success, but that structure made it practically impossible for our forces to deal with fleeing Gallosians. Majer Rembraak didn't know that was happening until most of the survivors were already on the bridge. He saw that before your message, Undercaptain Taelya. He didn't want to have his men trapped on the bridge if the Gallosians attacked in force, especially with archers. He thought that he could have lost a lot of men without protection from you mages. So he didn't follow the ones who fled."

All of that made sense, and Taelya could definitely understand that risking substantial casualties to kill or capture at most a hundred men didn't make sense. What she didn't understand was why the eastern fort wasn't better defended.

Or have the Gallosians relied on a handful of weak mages and greater numbers because the Certans had so few mages and were so reluctant to use them?

That would also explain why the Certans felt they needed mages.

"All this brings up another question," said Zekkarat wryly. "Just what do we do with the fort you've captured? If we leave it, they can regarrison it sooner or later and possibly strengthen it. We can't afford to try to tear it down, because for all of its shortcomings, moving all that solid stone would take time, unless we used most of the Viscount's troopers. That decision, however, has been taken out of our hands.

"I've just received a message from the submarshal requesting that the Montgren forces garrison the fort. He feels that the way you took the fort will keep the Gallosians from mounting any immediate counterattack. He also feels that it's the first step in taking control of all of Passera. To this end, Captain Ferek and his company and three supply wagons will be arriving shortly. The wagons hold provisions and all of your personal gear, gathered by Ferek's men. Seventh Battalion will remain until later this evening when we're more settled."

After a brief pause, Zekkarat offered a lopsided smile. "At least, from here, we'll definitely be able to watch exactly what the Gallosians are doing. And with you mages being right here, the Gallosians won't be able to do to us what you did to them."

Not unless they have a lot more mages than the Certans believe.

XLVI

The first thing Taelya did after Zekkarat dismissed them was to see that her squad was settled. The second was to make sure Bounder was secure in one of the few stalls. The third was to search out the rear gate through which the Gallosians had fled. It turned out that it wasn't a gate at all, but a stone-walled tunnel from a chamber within the walls that went under the street to the west of the wall and came up inside a small square building perched on the embankment overlooking the east side of the Passa River.

No wonder you didn't immediately sense troopers fleeing. Even though that made sense, it still bothered her than she hadn't sensed, or thought to sense, the troopers withdrawing from the fort, possibly because that sort of failure to sense the entire area could be fatal to her troopers under other circumstances.

After that, it was well after eighth glass before matters were settled enough that Taelya and Kaeryla bedded down in a small room that had likely been quarters for junior officers or senior squad leaders. The measured use of order and chaos had mitigated the vermin in the two bed pallets, but with every breath Taelya could smell the faint odor of fire and ashes.

She lay in the acrid darkness on the hard pallet, one of her blankets folded under her head, her thoughts going back over the day. "I still don't see why the Gallosians gave in so easily."

"Sometimes . . . you can be scary. What do you think it was like for them?" asked Kaeryla quietly. "There was chaos-fire scouring the courtyard, and two score died in an instant. Any time that someone tried to fire at us, one of them died in flames. Their only mage tried to strike back and was turned to ashes. Everything they tried failed. Then the gates to the fort went up in flames."

"I didn't think of it quite that way," Taelya admitted.

"They were afraid, really afraid," Kaeryla said, her voice still soft. "I looked at the Gallosians who couldn't leave. There were three of them. There wasn't anything I could do to heal them. Even their lungs were burned. The last one died as I was trying to make it easier for him."

Taelya winced, thinking about every breath hurting . . . until nothing did.

"Have you ever been that scared? Really afraid?" asked Kaeryla.

"Sometimes. I was when the Hydlenese attacked Fairhaven. They cut down people in the streets, even children. I was afraid they'd break into the house. I had nightmares about that for a long time. I've always been afraid that I won't be able to do what I have to."

"You were seven when they attacked Fairhaven. And being afraid that you'll fail isn't the same as fearing for your life . . . or for someone else's. Have you ever trembled, been afraid that, all of a sudden, you'd be dead?"

"I was then. And it could happen any time now . . . I know it could. If we have to face a mage stronger than Uncle Beltur . . ."

"Taelya . . . I was so afraid today. I just knew that there had to be a powerful mage in that fort. I knew he was shielding himself. I knew that at the right moment, he'd shatter my shields . . ."

"There wasn't a mage, and your shields held against all those shafts. You would have held against any mage we've encountered, including Sydon."

"Maybe not Sydon."

"You're stronger than you think."

Kaeryla offered an exasperated sigh.

"You don't think I don't fear things . . . is that it?"

"No . . . you fear or worry about things, people . . . I know that. I've seen it. Maybe . . ." Kaeryla's words trailed off.

"Maybe what?" asked Taelya gently.

"Maybe you were so frightened when the Hydlenese attacked Fairhaven that you'll never be that frightened again . . . because you'll never face anything that terrifying again. I've never faced anything like that."

"Most people who do . . . they don't survive. We survived because your father and mother gave everything they had. I saw that."

"So did your father."

Taelya didn't know what to say. What Kaeryla said was true. Abruptly, she felt her eyes burning in the darkness of the room. She swallowed. After several moments, she spoke. "You said I was scary. What did you mean?"

"You *know* what to do. You always know how to do it. I have to think about it."

"I'm eight years older than you are. That's eight years of training as a Road Guard under your father and Gustaan. You've been trained first as a healer, and second as an arms-mage. You're already stronger than Valchar in everything. By the time you're my age you'll likely know everything I do." *If we both get through this.*

"It's not the training. I've watched you. People defer to you. Gustaan does, and it's not because of Father or Aunt Tulya. Even the Certan officers do."

"People defer to you as well," Taelya pointed out.

Kaeryla yawned, once and then again. "It's not . . . the same thing. It's not. I'm tired. We can talk later. Just think about it."

"You're really tired, aren't you?"

"So are you. You just haven't realized it yet." After another yawn, Kaeryla added, "Good night."

Taelya was still wondering about what Kaeryla had really meant when she finally fell asleep.

XLVII

Oneday morning was the first day of summer, and to Taelya it felt more like midsummer, especially when she woke well before fifth glass with the odor of ashes still in her nose and mouth, and the acrid smell of cookfires in the ancient hearths of the old fort. For several moments, she just lay there, still thinking about Kaeryla's comment about her being scary sometimes.

Then she got up and went looking for water, finally finding a cistern with a hand pump and a bucket that she filled and carried back to the small room. There she used a combination of order and chaos before using some of it to wash, as well as she could, before turning to wake Kaeryla.

"I'm awake. Thank you for getting the water."

"You're welcome. As soon as you're done I need to return the bucket. There didn't seem to be another one."

"With what you did, I think you deserve taking the bucket for a fraction of a quint . . . or even longer."

Since Taelya didn't want to respond to that directly, she said, "This is an old fort. It hasn't been that well cared for, either."

Kaeryla sat up and stretched. "Maybe that's the problem with the Prefect and the Viscount. The more they fight, the fewer the golds either has."

"I don't know. That's quite a palace that the Viscount has, and your father's talked about how large and ornate the Prefect's palace is."

"Exactly," declared Kaeryla. "With all the golds they spend on themselves, there's barely enough left for troopers, mounts, and arms. Father says that it costs us over three hundred golds a year to maintain barely one company, and we pay less than anyone. Twenty battalions would cost thirty thousand golds a year."

"Kaeryla . . . Jellico alone is more than ten times the size of Fairhaven. Rytel is five times our size, and there must be a several score towns, if not a score of scores, the size of Fairhaven. And that doesn't count how many more traders and inns there are to tariff."

"It doesn't matter if the Viscount and the Prefect spend too much on themselves," countered Kaeryla.

Taelya laughed, a touch bitterly. "You're right. So we're here because they don't want to stop spending on themselves and raise and support more troopers."

"Besides," Kaeryla added, "if they both spend more on troopers, nothing changes, and they have less to spend on themselves." She made a gesture toward the courtyard. "I can't talk any more. I need to wash up, and then check the horses, if we can, before we eat."

"I'll start on the horses," replied Taelya.

Less than two quints later, the two undercaptains found the chamber serving the officers, a space containing a long, rickety trestle table, with benches that barely fit all ten officers of the Montgren and Fairhaven forces.

As they seated themselves, Majer Zekkarat declared, "We're going to combine breakfast with a quick officers' meeting."

"No one's going to linger over this slop," muttered Maakym, sitting to Taelya's right.

Taelya looked at what rested in the tin platter—a chunk of barely warm bread that looked to be partly doughy and a browned yellowish mass with chunks of meat, likely mutton, embedded in it. *It's better than hardtack, but not much.* She took a bite. It tasted about the way it looked. Then she sipped the ale in her tin cup—warm, bitter, and slightly sour. Definitely nothing to linger over.

In less than a quint, Zekkarat cleared his throat. "We're not planning any attacks today. The submarshal insists we need time to regroup and plan for the attack on the west side of Passera. I've already posted scouts along the river where they can observe the Gallosian main fort. The Gallosians have closed the iron gates on the span in the middle of the bridge. It appears that they've positioned two squads of troopers there—enough to hold it until reinforcements arrive. With the gate of the main fort less than three hundred yards away, that won't take long."

"Just how are we supposed to break through those gates?" asked Captain Ferek. "And all the troopers that they can jam in there?"

"The jamming factor works against them," replied Zekkarat. "The bridge is almost impossible to destroy. It's built of a stone harder than anything you can imagine, because it's reinforced with order. But the gates are plain iron, and they're not that strong. The troopers defending them can be destroyed by chaos bolts. If they pack them in, that makes it that much easier for us . . ."

As Zekkarat went on, Taelya's stomach tightened at the implications of what the majer had said. At least some, if less than half, of the troopers who had been garrisoned in the eastern fort had the opportunity to flee. Those packed onto the bridge wouldn't have that choice. Some might be able to jump into the river, but most . . . *And we're the attackers for a Viscount who just wants more golds.*

She managed to refrain from shaking her head and tried to concentrate on what else Zekkarat had to say.

". . . Submarshal Akkyld is sending some wagons with supplies and some timbers to rebuild the fort gates, at least enough for our purposes, since we likely won't be here long enough to worry about a siege." After the briefest pause, Zekkarat added sardonically, "One way or another."

Ferek looked at the majer quizzically.

"We either take the main fort and control all of Passera, in which case we don't need this fort, or we don't, in which case we'll either be fleeing or leaving after a season if we're in a stalemate."

"Yes, ser."

"For now, take care of your men and their mounts. Let me know if you come across anything that is unusual or that might help in the attack. That's all." With the last words, Zekkarat stood.

As the majer left the small chamber, Kaeryla immediately looked to Taelya. "Are you all right? Your chaos swirled when the majer was talking."

"Something he said . . . I just need to think about it."

"Are you sure?"

The depth of Kaeryla's obvious concern went through Taelya like cold fire. "I'm fine . . . No, I'm not, but I'll talk to you in just a bit. I have to do something first. It might help. It might not. But it'll be better to talk after I do."

"I'll be in our room then."

"I won't be long." Taelya turned. From the temporary mess, she walked across the courtyard to the northeast corner of the fort. From there, she walked up the narrow staircase that led to the watchtower. When she reached the landing where the Gallosian mage had looked through the slit window, she stopped and studied the landing. She thought there were faint traces of ash, but any metallic items or coins that the white might have had were gone, likely picked up by whatever trooper had been assigned as a lookout from the top of the tower.

Not even a trace. And he was little more than a boy. Possibly not any older than Dorylt. *But what else could you have done?* After several long moments of thought, she shook her head and headed back down to the courtyard.

Kaeryla was waiting in the small room. "Do you want to tell me about it?"

"When the majer was talking about attacking the Gallosians on the bridge . . . it just seemed so . . . strange . . . terrible. It's one thing to kill people who will kill you and destroy your town and family, but we're the invaders here . . . and for a Viscount who wouldn't care in the slightest about Fairhaven, we're going to kill troopers who are protecting their land . . . in hopes that we don't have to fight off the Viscount? I've tried not to think that much about it . . . but . . ."

Taelya just looked at the dusty floor of worn and cracked yellow bricks.

"I thought I was the only one who felt like that," replied Kaeryla. "You never said anything."

"I tried not to even think about it. I just kept telling myself that we don't have much choice."

"That's the problem, Taelya. We don't. We don't have much choice. Not right now. We're trapped between three battalions of Certans and likely some five battalions of Gallosians . . . and however many mages they have. Our only hope is to survive . . . and then see what we can do in the future."

"That's a slim hope," said Taelya bleakly.

"Taelya . . . remember that the Prefect killed my great-uncle and a lot of other innocents. He drove my mother and grandmother from Gallos. He invaded Spidlar and killed thousands. His troopers killed Athaal and almost killed your father. These troopers across the river support that evil man. We *have* to think of it that way. We have to."

Taelya took a deep breath, then smiled wryly. "We at least can try to think that way." She paused. "Thank you."

Kaeryla shook her head. "Thank you for telling me. I worried . . ."

Taelya understood.

XLVIII

By twoday morning, the gates to the eastern fort had been replaced, and Akkyld had recalled Zekkarat and Gustaan to the border post, presumably to discuss the forthcoming attack on the bridge and the Gallosian fort on the west side of the river. But before Gustaan departed Taelya had secured permission for a reconnaissance ride to see what she could sense about the Gallosian fort, since the eastern fort was on the south side of the bridge and its approach causeway, while the western fort was on the north side. By riding to a point on the river embankment north of the western fort and due east of the larger fort, Taelya and Kaeryla would be almost half a kay closer to the fort and able to sense more clearly.

"Don't engage with the Gallosians." That had been Gustaan's sole order.

Taelya had no intention of engaging with anyone.

By eighth glass, the recon force was assembled in the courtyard—Taelya, Kaeryla, and Varais, along with half of Third Squad.

Taelya turned to Varais. "Ready, Squad Leader?"

"Ready, ser."

"Squad. Forward!"

Taelya led the squad directly out the gates, situated on the north side of the fort, and across the main street, which to the left led to the bridge causeway that began less than a hundred yards away. As Bounder carried her across the main street, Taelya looked west at the stone bridge, especially at the closed iron gates set in the middle of the bridge on the massive stone foundation that joined both spans. The gates didn't look that formidable, and Taelya could sense that they were indeed formed of plain iron and not black iron, which would have posed a far greater problem.

But with all the order embedded in the bridge and the spans, why wasn't any put into the gates? The only reason that she could come up with was that whoever built the bridge had wanted it to remain open for use and that the iron gates had been added later.

She still wondered if the bridge had been a creation of Relyn, even though there was no mention of it in *The Wisdom of Relyn,* and she would have known that, given how often she'd read her uncle's copy of the book.

Once they crossed the main street, she turned Bounder onto the road that angled away from the causeway that gently rose to the first span of the bridge and toward the street that ran along the top of the river embankment, not really a river wall. In a few places, lanes ran down to battered piers or docks, none of which seemed to have been recently used. Some two hundred yards farther north, just across the Passa River—whose waters seemed about fifty yards wide and quite deep—from the middle of the of the western Gallosian fort, Taelya ordered, "Squad. Halt!"

Then she turned and concentrated her senses on the structure of the fort, which appeared to be roughly two hundred yards on a side and was set almost two hundred yards back from the west river embankment. There was no way to discern exactly how many troopers the fort held, but she had the definite feeling that the Gallosians had roughly as many troopers as did the Certans, possibly slightly more. She also could sense four white mages, ranging from one who was barely a mage to two that seemed about as strong as Sheralt and one who was definitely stronger, perhaps on the level of Sydon.

After a time, she turned to Kaeryla. "How many mages?"

"Four. One barely a mage, two fairly strong, one very strong."

"All the chaos around them makes it hard to tell exactly how strong they are," said Taelya.

"Father says that swirling chaos usually means they're not quite as strong as they seem."

"Let's hope so. How many troopers?

"More than we have, maybe even a battalion more."

Taelya nodded. "Taking the bridge and that fort is going to be quite an effort."

"Getting across the bridge might be the hardest part. Especially if they bring all their mages up."

"They have more troopers than we do, sers?" asked Varais politely.

"That's what we sense," replied Taelya. "It's hard to tell exactly from this far away, and we have no idea how many are really troopers or how good they are."

"What about the walls?"

"They're thicker and higher than the eastern fort, but not that much," said Kaeryla.

Varais just nodded.

Taelya turned her attention to something else she'd sensed—a concentration of order on the far side of the river, but farther north. She didn't see any structures there, just what looked like the base of a low hill, as if the top and most of the rest of which had been removed or flattened. She looked to Kaeryla. "You see that flattened hill on the other side?"

"That raised area that seems to be filled with order?"

Taelya nodded. "That's it. I think we should look closer at it." She turned to Varais. "There's an unusual concentration of order in that flattened hill on the far side of the river. We need to move closer to sense what it is."

"It's almost a kay north," said Varais.

"The Gallosians still have the bridge gates closed, and we could circle back under a concealment. Besides, there are only two squads on the bridge right now, and there's no mage. If anything changes, we'll head back to the fort immediately."

"Yes, ser."

Taelya could tell that her own last sentence was what the squad leader had sought, and she ordered the squad forward.

A little less than a quint later, after checking to make sure that no more Gallosians had left the fort, Taelya halted the squad across the river from the flattened hill. Except it wasn't a flattened hill. Rather, it was a black stone wall that was oblong, with the long side facing the river, in effect a platform radiating immense and long-standing order.

Taelya had the feeling that, at some time in the past, a significant building had stood there.

But what? After several moments, she realized just what she was observing. *It has to be what's left of Relyn's Temple of Order.*

Taelya remembered reading about it in Relyn's book and Beltur talking about how the Prefect had tried to destroy the temple, but that order still remained. She turned to Kaeryla. "Do you know what that is?"

"No. You sound like you do, though."

"I think it's what's left of Relyn's Temple of Order. The Prefect destroyed the building, but your father once mentioned that the order remaining was too strong even for the Prefect's mages to remove all traces of the temple." A moment later, she added, "I wonder if Relyn was the one responsible for order-binding the bridge together."

"Why would he have done that?"

"To keep the border open between Certis and Gallos, I'd guess."

"What good did that do?" asked Varais. "That was hundreds of years ago, and they're still fighting. It might be better if he hadn't. Then it wouldn't be as easy for them to get at each other. Sometimes borders that are hard to cross make war harder and peace easier."

"That doesn't seem to ever have been possible between Gallos and Spidlar," said Taelya sardonically. "Now that we know what that is, and that it won't be a problem, we need to head back."

"Yes, ser," replied Varais.

Two quints later, the recon squad was back in the eastern fort, and the number of Gallosians protecting the iron gates on the bridge over the Passa River hadn't changed.

As Taelya was unsaddling Bounder, Hassett appeared in the stable.

"Undercaptain, ser, Majer Zekkarat has called a meeting of all the officers for first glass."

"Thank you, Hassett. You can tell Gustaan or the majer that I'll be there."

"Yes, ser."

Once Taelya finished grooming Bounder, she was about to look for Kaeryla when the younger mage appeared.

"You got word about the meeting?" asked Taelya.

Kaeryla nodded. "Do you think it's about attacking the bridge and the Gallosians?"

"You sound doubtful," said Taelya dryly.

"The submarshal hasn't seemed all that eager to attack anything, unless we're doing the attacking."

"So you think we'll somehow be in the fore? Because we have mages and they don't?"

"Do you want to wager on it?" Kaeryla grinned.

Taelya shook her head.

Two quints later, the two entered the small room that served as the officers' mess.

Gustaan and Zekkarat were already there, and Sheralt and Valchar were only moments behind Taelya and Kaeryla. Before long, Konstyn, Ferek, Maakym, and Drakyn followed.

From the head of the table, Zekkarat gestured to Drakyn, who closed the door and took his position at the last place on the right side of the table. The majer cleared his throat, then said, "The submarshal has decided we'll attack tomorrow at first light. The exact plan for that attack depends on certain information." His eyes went to Taelya. "Undercaptain, you've done the most recent reconnaissance. Do the Gallosians have a mage posted on the bridge?"

"No, ser. They haven't had one on or near the bridge. The nearest mages, so far as we can discern, are in the large fort on the west side of the river. There appear to be four mages in the fort."

"Just four?"

"Yes, ser."

"Are they near the main gates to the fort?"

"When we did the recon, they weren't. I can't say where they might be at other times."

"What about the bridge gates?"

"The gates are iron, regular iron, not black iron. There's no additional order in the gates."

"Undercaptain Kaeryla, do you agree with that?"

"Yes, ser."

"Just before the attack, then, you two will make another reconnaissance. If that remains the situation, here is how the attack will proceed. The Fairhaven force will advance up the causeway under a concealment before using chaos bolts to clear the area around the gates. You're only to proceed as close as possible to do that. Then you're to move to one side of the bridge and hold the concealment until a detachment from the first company of Seventh Battalion approaches. You'll remove the concealment so that they can pass. They will have equipment to break open the gates. The Fairhaven force will move up behind the first company detachment and use chaos bolts as necessary until the gates have been opened. Then the first company detachment will remain at the gates—there's enough space for that on the center platform to allow others to pass, while the two Montgren companies will follow the Fairhaven force, followed in turn by the remainder of Seventh Battalion, then Eighth Battalion, and Sixth Battalion. The Fairhaven and Montgren forces will move as far west as possible in order to allow the Certan forces to control the causeway and the space directly before the fort."

Zekkarat paused, then added, "That's if the Gallosians don't bring mages to the bridge. If they do, then the Fairhaven forces will move farther onto the bridge to deal with any mages. If you deal with them successfully, then the attack will proceed. If you are unable to break through their mages, you're to withdraw. The submarshal sees no point in losing mages, since the loss of mages was what created the problems Certis had with Gallos in the first place. That is the overall plan of attack."

The rest of the meeting dealt with spelling out all the various details . . . and took almost two glasses.

By the time it was all over, Taelya wasn't sure what to think. The plan was detailed and seemingly well thought out, with various contingencies spelled out, and it appeared now that the submarshal just wanted to get on with the attack and take over Passera.

As she left the small chamber with Kaeryla and the two stepped into the courtyard, Taelya saw that Sheralt and Valchar had moved into the shade of the wall and were talking.

"I'd like to hear what they think," she said to Kaeryla.

"So would I."

But when they moved to join the two men, Sheralt looked to Taelya. "What do you think about this attack plan?"

"I can't see any other way to get across the bridge," Taelya replied. "We don't have flatboats or anything else with which to cross the river."

"What happens if the Gallosians react immediately and send all four mages against us?" asked Valchar.

Taelya had thought about that, but she still waited for several moments before she responded. "They'd be more exposed there than if they just let us cross and forced us to attack the fort."

"They have to know how we attacked the eastern fort," pointed out Sheralt. "They might not want us to do that again."

"That's true," said Kaeryla. "But do we have any choice?"

"Why are we leading the attack?" pressed Valchar.

"Because, if we attack at all," said Taelya, "that makes the most sense. What doesn't make that much sense to me is why the Viscount and the Prefect have been fighting over Passera for twenty years." She shook her head. "Unfortunately, no one consulted Fairhaven—or us—about fighting this battle. So . . . if we have to fight, we need to fight in the most effective way. Do any of you have a better plan?"

None of the other three spoke.

Taelya laughed, a short and bitter sound. "So we're agreed. The battle plan is the best way to do something that doesn't make much sense in the grand scheme of things, but is necessary to keep the frigging Viscount on our side."

"For how long?" asked Valchar.

"Hopefully, for a few years . . . and maybe by then, Fairhaven will be strong enough so that we won't get dragged into something like this ever again." Taelya had doubts about even that, but she didn't see any better choices, just as their parents hadn't.

"I don't like it," muttered Valchar.

"None of us do," said Sheralt dryly. "We just have to get through it so that we can change things for the better later."

If we can get through it . . . and there is a later. Taelya didn't voice that thought, but just nodded with the others.

XLIX

All three mage-undercaptains were in the temporary mess well before dawn, the room lit only by a single small oil wall lamp that offered so little illumination that Taelya felt she was perceiving the egg scramble more with her senses than with her eyes, which might have been for the best, given that the outside was close to being burned, and the inside underdone. She didn't complain, especially since she knew all the troopers were getting cold rations, although she wasn't so certain she wouldn't have preferred cold rations. The ale helped some in helping her get down what passed for breakfast.

None of the mage-undercaptains spoke much.

What is there to say that we haven't already said?

From the mess, after all four had filled their water bottles with ale, Gustaan led the undercaptains to the stables, where he addressed them. "I can't tell any of you what to do. I will tell you what not to do. I don't want to see heroics. I want you working together, the way you did to take this fort. Don't exhaust yourselves. I had the troopers put bread in all your saddlebags. This could be a long day."

Or a very short one. Taelya tried not to shiver, although the stable was certainly not cool.

"I don't like having all of you so close to the front. With what you have to do, there isn't much choice. Once we get through the gates and on the other side of the river, Kaeryla and Valchar, you need to rejoin your squads, with both squads side by side at the west end of the open area . . ."

Less than a quint later, in the darkness well before dawn, Taelya and Sheralt led the Fairhaven contingent out of the fort and some fifty yards closer to the bridge, where they reined up almost at the foot of the inclined causeway.

"The lead companies of Seventh Battalion are less than a half kay behind us, and they're closing the gap," she said quietly to Sheralt, and to Gustaan, who was right behind them. The fact that the Certans were doing exactly what had been planned was a relief. She hadn't been sure of what to expect, but Seventh Battalion was exactly where it was supposed to be, despite having to move forward in the darkness without mages as guides. While the Fairhaven force could have approached the bridge at dawn or at any other time under a concealment to avoid being seen, concealing the approach of three battalions wasn't possible, not for any length of time.

"We'll hold until they reach the square," replied Gustaan.

Another half quint passed.

"They're at the square," Kaeryla reported.

"They are," confirmed Taelya.

"Put the squads under concealment and move out," ordered Gustaan.

Taelya eased Bounder forward at a slow walk, onto the order-infused stone roadbed of the causeway leading to the first span over the Passa River. The faintest hint of a breeze carried a sour odor she couldn't identify, but at least the wind was out of the west, and that might delay their being smelled, heard, or seen by the Gallosians. She couldn't help but wonder how far they'd get before the troopers guarding the iron gates realized they were under attack.

Each of the stone spans was about forty yards across at the level of the road, and the causeway to the beginning of the first span was about sixty yards long. *A hundred yards in the dark between us and the gates.*

She just hoped that they could get even halfway across the eastern span before the guards noticed, but that was just a hope. Casting her senses behind her, she confirmed that the Certan detachment had moved up in front of the two Montgren companies, while the rest of Seventh Battalion was positioned some fifty yards behind the second Montgren company.

From that moment on, Taelya kept her senses focused on the Gallosian troopers guarding the gates. More than half of them were either seated, propped against the solid side walls that surrounded the platform joining the two spans, or lying down. A handful of troopers stood by the gates, apparently facing into the darkness to the east.

Taelya and Bounder were perhaps ten yards onto the span when she sensed a flurry of chaos around the Gallosian troopers. "They've heard or seen something," she said in a low voice.

"Keep moving at a slow walk," returned Gustaan. "The moment they sound an alarm, move to a fast trot and get as near as you can."

As closely as Taelya could determine, she and Bounder covered another twenty yards so that they were almost within fifteen yards of the gates before a trumpet call echoed from the bridge.

"Forward!" ordered Taelya, dropping the concealment and extending shields across the front of the squad, knowing that without shields, any Gallosian arrows loosed could scarcely miss hitting someone or some mount.

Yet for the few moments that it took for Third Squad to reach a point some ten yards short of the gates, when she called, "Squad! Halt!," she didn't feel a single impact on her shields.

"Chaos bolts now!" ordered Gustaan.

Sheralt loosed the first chaos bolt, arching it over the iron gates, since the gates would absorb much of the chaos if either Sheralt or Taelya tried to throw chaos through the spaces between the bars. The first firebolt landed in the middle of the space between spans, flaring and momentarily illuminating the darkness and the figures of troopers being turned to ashes, as well as those closer to the gates and those farther back who had escaped the chaos.

"They've got chaos mages!" yelled someone, as if that fact weren't instantly known to the troopers who survived the first blast.

Sheralt launched another chaos bolt, this one at the troopers farther from the gates, which took out possibly half a squad. As the light from the firebolt faded, Taelya could sense that the remaining troopers had bolted from the center platform and begun to run across the western span of the bridge.

In moments, the Fairhaven squads were alone just short of the gates.

"To the south side of the bridge!" ordered Gustaan.

As Taelya eased Bounder next to the stone wall, she looked to the east, where the horizon was beginning to show the first signs of greenish gray. Then, almost as soon the Fairhaven officers and troopers had moved, a squad of Certans fast-trotted right up to the gates.

Several brawny troopers dismounted, at least one of whom was carrying a massive sledgehammer.

Even with the efficient used of sledges and cold chisels, it took almost half a quint before the gates swung open.

Taelya wasn't quite sure how they'd managed it, but she was glad that they had. Using chaos on iron was close to futile. She couldn't help but notice that the Certan squad withdrew from the first span of the bridge quickly, clearing the way for the two Montgren companies.

"Fairhaven squads! Forward!" ordered Gustaan.

As the sky turned from greenish purple to grayish green, Taelya and Sheralt led the way through the chaos-fire-blasted area, with its scent of fire and ashes, across the second span, and down the western causeway onto the paved open square that fronted the fort.

She turned her attention to the fort itself, sensing a great deal of movement within. Although the gates had closed behind the handfuls of fleeing troopers and had not reopened, she had no idea whether they even would. *Is this the beginning of a bloody battle or a brutal siege?*

She shook her head. As soon as she and Third Squad cleared the causeway, they needed to get into position just in case the Gallosians did try a quick attack.

Behind her and the Fairhaven squads, she could sense the two Montgren companies, led by Zekkarat, already up the east causeway and moving swiftly across the two spans of the ancient, imposing, and order-bound bridge. Farther behind them, re-forming in some fashion, presumably to accommodate the squad that had broken the gates open, was Seventh Battalion. She could only vaguely sense another battalion, presumably Eighth Battalion, but Sixth Battalion was apparently too far away for her to sense.

A half quint later, Taelya and Kaeryla were at the front of Third Squad, positioned at the west end of the open paved area, with Second Squad just to the east of them, while Konstyn's company was almost formed up farther east, and Ferek's company was coming off the bridge.

Taelya could sense the first company of Seventh Battalion at the foot of the east causeway, but no Certan riders had yet started up the causeway.

"Captain!" Taelya turned to Gustaan. "Seventh Battalion isn't advancing. The bridge is almost clear on the first span, but they're not moving."

"It could be that Rembraak doesn't want to advance until the bridge is completely clear."

Taelya didn't like the delay, even if delays did sometimes happen, and she couldn't help but worry. She could sense the loose swirling chaos fragments within the western fort that suggested preparation for something, and she definitely didn't like the idea of an attack before Seventh Battalion got over the bridge. Her eyes and senses went back to the bridge, where the last of Ferek's troopers were riding down the causeway.

Then she extended her senses farther east.

Her mouth opened, and for an instant, but only an instant, she couldn't say a word. Then she turned back to Gustaan. "Seventh Battalion is withdrawing, and they're moving fast, and it feels like the Gallosians are about to attack."

"Those bastards . . ."

At that instant, Taelya saw the fort gates opening and sensed four mages behind the mounted troopers massed just inside the gates.

"Second and Third Squads!" Taelya shouted. "On me! Center in front of the Montgren companies! Undercaptains! Prepare shields! Now!" She turned to Gustaan. "Get Zekkarat to hold the bridge causeway! We'll hold them off." Even as she finished speaking Taelya urged Bounder forward and to her left.

After the slightest of hesitations, Varais commanded, "On the undercaptain! Move!"

Second Squad had barely settled into position beside Third Squad when the fort gates finished opening as the full light of the just-risen sun poured across both forces. There was no massive rushing charge, but an orderly flow into companies, one company moving at an angle toward the bridge, the other four heading straight toward Taelya and the two Montgren companies behind her. Just outside the gates, behind the advancing force, was a squad that held Gallosian troopers surrounding four mages . . . and one of them was definitely very strong.

Taelya turned to her left. "Sheralt! Throw a tiny chaos bolt at the first rank of the center company of Gallosians."

Without questioning, Sheralt did so.

Taelya was waiting for what she knew would happen when one of the

Gallosian mages intercepted the chaos bolt, strengthened it, and hurled it back toward the flank of Ferek's company. Taelya used the trace of chaos to identify that mage, and, in turn, caught that firebolt and threw it back toward the company moving toward the causeway. The mage again caught the firebolt, and added more chaos to it and this time hurled it at Taelya. She added a touch of chaos, and buried a small chunk of order in it, then fired it directly at the mage who had been redirecting it.

Hsssstt! The mage, the weakest of the four, went up in a flare, largely of chaos, chaos that Taelya hoped concealed the order.

"Did you sense what I did?" she asked Kaeryla, mounted on her left, without looking at the other mage.

"I did."

"Good. I might need a bit of order from you when we deal with the stronger mages." "Might" was an understatement, Taelya knew, given the amount of chaos surrounding the strongest mage.

At that moment, the sound of a gong reverberated from the fort, and the Gallosians, less than fifty yards away already, charged, and at the same moment, archers from the walls loosed shafts. Not only did the archers loose shafts, but they kept loosing them as fast as they could, effectively keeping Valchar and Kaeryla totally involved in using their shields to prevent the Gallosians from cutting down the far smaller Montgren contingent.

Sheralt fired a chaos bolt at the section of the wall that appeared to hold the most of those archers, and one of the remaining mages flung it back toward the Montgren troopers.

Taelya immediately took the bolt and spread it across the center of the charging Gallosians, putting a squad-sized gap in the center of the charge.

Sheralt clearly saw that, because he again targeted the archers on the wall. This time, the strongest Gallosian white redirected the chaos bolt, adding more chaos force to it and firing it barely above the heads of his own troopers toward Taelya, who had been hoping for exactly that.

Although she felt almost ripped from her saddle by the small part of the chaos bolt that somehow escaped her containment and hit her shields, she managed to redirect most of the bolt a little lower than head-high right into the troopers behind the ones she'd taken out with the first bolt. Prepared as she'd been, she realized that she'd almost not been able to return that intensified chaos, so strong had it been.

At the same time, she could sense the pressure of the attacking Gallosians as they angled off Kaeryla's shield and knew that Valchar was feeling the same impact.

She also realized that with the force and numbers of the attack, Valchar and Kaeryla hadn't been able to shield more than their respective squads, and that a good half of the attackers had swept past the two squads and that hand-to-hand fighting was everywhere behind them. Almost disinterestedly, she noticed one good thing: While the area south of the front of the fort had seemed large, it was too small for the Gallosians to bring any more troopers into the attack.

But . . . even if we're successful in killing these troopers, they'll just bring more . . . and even more.

At that moment, another chaos bolt arched over the remaining troopers toward Kaeryla, and Taelya quickly dumped a small coating of order around it and a larger bit inside it and arrowed it at the one of the three remaining Gallosian mages who seemed to be the weakest.

She could feel his shields give, and she followed the first bolt with a narrow bolt of chaos. That resulted in another mist of black death, almost lost in all the death behind her and the two Fairhaven squads.

Immediately another firebolt flew, this time toward Valchar, and Taelya diverted it into the rear of the Gallosian company trying to dislodge Ferek's company from the bridge causeway.

"Valchar won't be able to hold shields over even the squad much longer," Kaeryla said loudly enough for Taelya to hear. As the younger mage finished speaking, another two chaos bolts flew toward Second Squad, both strong bursts of power.

Taelya could only intercept one because of its speed and closeness to the other chaos bolt, and the best she could do was to once more divert it into the Gallosians trying to take the bridge causeway, rather than back at the stronger white mage of the two Gallosian mages remaining. The second flared across Valchar's shields and incinerated several Gallosian troopers in the hand-to-hand fighting to the east of Second Squad.

Taelya looked at the troopers between Third Squad and the mage squad just in front of the fort, then to Kaeryla. "The two of us need to charge the last two mages! It's our only chance. Can you shield me and use your shields like blades?"

"Tell me when!"

"Now!"

"Forward! On the undercaptains!" ordered Varais.

Taelya urged Bounder forward, letting Kaeryla move half a length ahead.

The first line of troopers that Kaeryla cut through didn't even know what struck them. Some of those farther back looked stunned. In what seemed like a quint but was more like moments, Third Squad, led by the two undercaptains, was through the few remaining ranks of Gallosian troopers, and was less than twenty yards from the Gallosian mage squad.

Taelya didn't hesitate. The moment she had a clear line on the slightly weaker strong white mage of the two remaining, she aimed a low, direct, narrow chaos bolt at him, followed by a second, and then a third.

The first bolt flared across his shields, incinerating the nearest troopers. The second bolt surrounded the mage, then faded. The third bolt collapsed his shields, and he went up in a flare of fire. With chaos fire flowing around his shields and then flaring across most of the supporting Gallosian troopers, the remaining white mage threw a massive firebolt at both Taelya and Kaeryla.

Kaeryla somehow managed to turn it back toward the mage, and at that moment, Taelya followed it with another tightly focused chaos bolt, hoping that the combination of two chaos bolts would hamper the other mage—a mage, Taelya realized, who was by far the strongest she'd ever faced.

"Can you give me a little order?" Taelya asked.

"Here . . ."

Taelya added a touch of that order to the next narrow-focused chaos bolt, more to the one that followed, and what remained to the third, each fired off in rapid succession.

As the third bolt hit, she could feel the other mage's shields go, and for an instant she saw his face, just as she strengthened her shields to reinforce Kaeryla's, a face she recognized although she'd only seen it upon one occasion.

Searing white flashed over them.

Taelya couldn't see, but she felt the pressure on their joined shields . . . which held . . . although the force of the chaos explosion against the shields slowed them to little more than a walk. Even before Taelya could see, she ordered, "Third Squad! On me! Back to the bridge!"

She turned Bounder, using her senses to guide her and hoping that she didn't have to use more order or chaos. Her eyes burned, and she was light-headed, but she also knew that the Montgren and Fairhaven forces *had* to cross the bridge before the Gallosians recovered. She *thought* most of Third Squad was behind her and Kaeryla as they headed for the rear of the Gallosian companies.

From what Taelya could see and sense, both Montgren companies, or what was left of them, had joined up and were slowly withdrawing up the causeway, while fending off the attacking Gallosians. Light-headed as she was, Taelya doubted that she could do much more than hold personal shields . . . and she wasn't certain how much longer she could do that.

She let her senses touch Kaeryla. Since the younger mage seemed to have slightly more order/chaos, Taelya asked, "Can you cut through to the bottom of the causeway?"

"If I keep my shields narrow."

"Take the lead and do it. I'll be right behind you." Taelya also sensed that Sheralt and Valchar, and what was left of Second Squad, were following Third Squad, and both still had some shields.

Maybe . . . just maybe . . . we can cut through.

"Mages . . . coming! The mages are coming!"

Taelya had no idea who was shouting that, but she threw out a small firebolt in front of Kaeryla, and for a moment slivery blackness fluttered across her eyes. *You can't do that again.*

The Gallosians there scattered away, trying to escape what likely only would have burned them, but the momentary Gallosian caution or panic gave them access to the causeway.

"To the side, Kaeryla! Let the squad rejoin the others."

Somehow, how Taelya wasn't sure, the four mage-undercaptains formed up as the rear guard of the withdrawing Montgren/Fairhaven force. Sheralt, who had some chaos remaining, used narrow chaos bolts once or twice, holding the Gallosians at bay while the other three linked what shields they had.

Withdrawing just before them and staying close was Varais. Absently, Taelya noted that streaks of blood were splattered across her uniform.

Then . . . just about the time when the four actually reached the beginning of the western span, the gong from the fort sounded, and the Gallosians fell back.

Taelya scanned the paved area, but there were so many bodies that there was no way to count them all, and her eyes were burned.

A voice was talking . . . talking to her, but the words made no sense.

"TAELYA! DRINK SOME ALE!"

Ale . . . ale . . . And it was Kaeryla's voice, she realized.

Finally, as if it took every morsel of strength she had, she fumbled the water bottle from its holder with both hands, finally managing to swallow some of the warm ale, ale that didn't even taste bitter at that moment.

After several swallows, she began to feel slightly less light-headed, and she saw that she and Kaeryla were nearing the iron gates. Gustaan and Zekkarat were waiting there, mounted on the south side.

Taelya's first thought wasn't about the two officers, but about why the Certans hadn't locked or chained the gates, but then she nodded. They would have had to have gotten onto the bridge, and if one of the mages had detected someone fiddling with the gates, that would have alerted Zekkarat much earlier. At least, that was the way it seemed to Taelya, but she wasn't sure she was thinking all that clearly.

"Why aren't they attacking, Undercaptains?" asked Zekkarat.

"Because Undercaptain Taelya and Undercaptain Kaeryla killed all four of their mages, Majer."

It took Taelya a moment to realize that Varais was the one who had spoken.

". . . and that's why all the rest of us survived and got to the bridge, ser." Varais's voice was polite, but barely. "And all four of them demon-near died. They also destroyed at least two companies."

"Thank you, Squad Leader." Zekkarat's tone was weary, more than anything.

"Undercaptains . . ." said Gustaan, "is there any way any of you could make the gates difficult to get through?"

"Taelya can't," said Sheralt. "Neither can Valchar. Maybe, together, Kaeryla and I might be able to do something."

While Valchar and Taelya rode ahead and reined up, Sheralt and Kaeryla dismounted and studied the gates, neither side of which seemed to be damaged. Then Kaeryla lugged a length of chain, one of those whose links had been chiseled apart, back to the center while Sheralt swung the gates closed. In some fashion, using Sheralt's chaos and Kaeryla's order, they wound the chain around the gates and order/chaos-sealed the chain to the gates.

While they did that, Taelya drank more ale and ate most of the stale bread in her saddlebags. By the time Sheralt and Kaeryla had finished, Taelya was less light-headed, but she wasn't likely to be doing much magery for a while.

"I put what order I could in the gates to keep them closed," said Kaeryla to Zekkarat. "It will take a lot to force them open if they don't have a mage."

"They don't," said Taelya wearily.

Sheralt turned to Zekkarat. "For the next few days, they'll have to rip out the gates. After that . . ." He shrugged.

Zekkarat turned his attention to Taelya. "Why do you think the Gallosians aren't following us?"

"Because there's no point in doing so. We've cost them four mages they couldn't afford to lose. What would they get besides losing more troopers? Besides, the Certans are on the other side of the border. We're not about to attack the Gallosians again, and we can't stay here long. The Prefect is likely furious at the Certans, because I suspect the Viscount promised to deliver four junior mages for his mages to destroy in order to allow Duke Maastyn to conquer or weaken Fairhaven. The Prefect's commanders can blame the defeat here—"

"Defeat? We lost almost an entire company," said Zekkarat.

"The Prefect lost four mages and close to three companies today," replied Taelya evenly. "With the two companies in the eastern fort, that's a battalion. So far the only winner is the Viscount." *And not if I can help it.* "We might as well go back to the eastern fort to regroup and rest."

"You think the Certans will let us?" asked Zekkarat.

"They don't have any mages. After a day's rest, we could hold off a siege long enough to destroy a battalion or two, if not more. Even if either Gallos or Certis has more mages to spare, it would take eightdays to get them here."

"Then we should continue to the fort," said Zekkarat, gesturing to the east span of the bridge.

Even order-and-chaos-depleted as she was, Taelya could tell that Zekkarat wasn't exactly pleased. In fact, the seething of his chaos suggested he was furious. At that moment, she couldn't have cared less.

L

Much of the rest of threeday was a blur for Taelya. She did remember Kaeryla insisting she lie down and rest. The next thing she knew it was early fourday morning, dark and well before sunrise. She sat up with a jolt, wondering if the Gallosians had broken through the bridge gates and were laying siege to the small and inadequate eastern fort. Immediately, she tried to sense what was around the fort, but her ability barely reached to the middle of the bridge, far less than a kay away. But she could sense that no one was on the bridge and that the intertwined order and chaos wrought by Sheralt and Kaeryla were still in place. Nor were there any troopers on the streets around the fort.

Kaeryla lay in the other pallet bed, still sleeping.

Taelya was still thinking about whether she should get up when she dropped off to sleep again. When she woke again, to the sound of the door creaking as Kaeryla returned to the room from somewhere, it was light, although Taelya felt it wasn't that late.

"Do you feel better this morning?" asked Kaeryla cheerfully, turning toward the older undercaptain. "Or less tired, at least?"

"Where have you been?"

"I went to look at the wounded. I can do a little healing. I was careful."

"Are you sure?" Taelya sat up. She felt stiff and her back and shoulders ached. She leaned forward gingerly, trying to stretch her back muscles.

"I only did what I could. How about you?"

"How could I not feel less tired? Did you really put me to bed yesterday afternoon?"

"Late afternoon, after I got you to eat some more. Your order/chaos levels were as low as I've ever sensed for someone not dying. You're definitely better this morning. Don't even think about doing any magery. You need to get dressed. We both need to eat, and you especially need more ale."

"What about Third Squad? How many did we lose?"

"Four, according to Varais."

"What about Second Squad?"

"Nine."

"And the Montgren companies?"

"Konstyn was killed, and he lost thirty-five men. Ferek took a slash, but not deep. He lost twenty-three men."

"Half a company, roughly," concluded Taelya. "What about the wounded?"

"Seventeen at last count. Some won't make it. They wouldn't, even if I could do more." Kaeryla took a deep breath.

"If we don't get out of here fairly soon, we won't make it, either," said Taelya wryly. "I can't even sense what the Gallosians are doing, except that there's no one on the bridge."

"I can't sense that much farther, but I can make out the fort, and there doesn't seem to be the sort of swirl of order and chaos that would suggest they're going to do anything today." Kaeryla sighed. "I'm also a little mad at myself."

"Why?"

"Because we really didn't need to have the Certans cut the chains on the bridge gates."

"We didn't?"

"It was a pretty simple lock. Father's been able to manipulate locks for years using order, and he taught both of us. I just didn't think of it in terms of the bridge locks."

"You still would have had to do something on the return," Taelya pointed out, "because the Certans must have had the keys to the locks. And we didn't really lose any time, because the Gallosians were going to wait to attack until we cleared the bridge."

"That's true. I still should have thought about it." Kaeryla paused. "Do you really think the Gallosians won't attack today?"

"They might not want another encounter very soon," said Taelya. "I think we took out close to three companies yesterday." She paused. "There's something else we need to talk about . . ."

"Sydon, you mean?"

"You saw?"

Kaeryla nodded. "When I sensed how strong he was, I thought it might be him."

"You don't think your father . . . ?"

"I don't care what Father thinks," replied Kaeryla sharply. "Sydon either betrayed him or abandoned him . . . and he was a sleazy, greasy lecher. He even leered at me when Father wasn't looking."

"He was almost that bad with me," Taelya admitted. "He was stronger than I am, too. If you hadn't gathered all that order for me, in another chaos bolt or two, he would have broken my shields. In raw power, he's . . . he was . . . almost as strong as Beltur."

Kaeryla smiled. "You had better technique. Father's always said that matters more than strength. Using those narrow-targeted chaos bolts allows you to throw more chaos than most whites. And putting order in the middle of them . . . thinking to do that in the middle of a battle . . ."

"I've done it before," Taelya said, "but I can't gather that much order without weakening myself. That's why I had to ask you."

"If we run across more strong whites, we should work together again."

Taelya nodded.

"We probably ought to get something to eat," ventured Kaeryla.

A quint later, after cleaning up as much as they could, the two made their way to what passed for the mess. Zekkarat, Gustaan, and Ferek were already there. The only other undercaptain present was Maakym. Taelya realized belatedly that she had no idea whether Drakyn had survived the near massacre in front of the Gallosian fort.

"Good morning, Undercaptains," said Zekkarat, "such as it is."

"Good morning, ser," replied Taelya, her words echoed by Kaeryla.

"You two look a great deal better than you did yesterday," said the majer. "I have to admit that, without what you did, none of us would likely be here, although being here is not exactly where any of us would prefer to be."

"No, ser," replied Taelya as she sat down on the slightly wobbly bench across from Gustaan. A trooper immediately set a tin cup filled with ale in front of her and another in front of Kaeryla. Taelya immediately took a long swallow of the ale. It was bitter, again, suggesting that she was at least better enough to notice the difference.

"We've been talking over our limited options," the majer went on, his eyes focusing on Taelya. "What are your thoughts?"

"Collect all the supplies we can fit on any extra horses we can find and immediately move east to get behind the Certans so that we can get to Jellico and across the River Jellicor before the Viscount finds out we survived." Taelya wasn't about to mention her other idea, since she had no idea if it was even feasible. *But if it is . . .*

"How do you propose to do that? They control the stream bridge, and they've got archers. I doubt any of you undercaptains have that much magery left in you."

"I scouted out another way the other day, one that smugglers use. It's too narrow and rough for wagons, but we could ride a company or two through. We'd have to do it one horse at a time. By tomorrow or later today I could go through under a concealment and see if it's guarded. It's almost two kays south of the stream bridge."

Zekkarat frowned.

"There have to be trails that connect with the main road farther east," added Taelya.

"What do you have in mind, Majer?" asked Zekkarat, offering the word "Majer" sardonically.

"As I said, getting behind the Certans and returning home, of course. We can use concealments when necessary." Taelya looked at the scramble and bread on the tin platter that a trooper set before her. It looked and smelled better-cooked than her previous breakfast.

Zekkarat's frown grew stronger. "Did you have any idea that the Viscount would betray us?"

"No, ser. It's just that when I learned that both bridges were narrow and close to forts, I started looking for other ways to get around. With all the smugglers that used to frequent Fairhaven and the side roads they used, I figured that there had to be another way across the border stream."

"What about supplies?" asked Ferek.

"We take what we can from here," replied Taelya. "We forage in a different fashion along the way. The Viscount has to be sending provisions to his own force. If we get behind them, then we can take the provisions wagons on their way west and use what we need and destroy the rest. That will make it harder for them to chase us."

"And make the Viscount even more unhappy," interjected Ferek.

"We tried making him happy, ser," said Maakym dryly. "We saw how that worked out."

A faint trace of a smile crossed Zekkarat's face, but vanished almost instantly. "I don't have a better plan, but I'd like to think over what we'd need. And you two look like you need to eat."

Taelya took the majer's advice and began to eat, slowly at first. She found she was right. The scramble was hot and at least edible. She finished the last morsels of bread before she realized that Zekkarat, Gustaan, Ferek, and Maakym had left. The fact that Maakym had departed with the others suggested strongly that not only had Konstyn been killed, but most likely so had Drakyn.

"What did we miss?" asked Sheralt as he and Valchar entered the mess.

"Only that Taelya told Zekkarat how to get out of here without another battle," replied Kaeryla. "Oh, and how to get more provisions by raiding the Viscount's supply wagons. He still wasn't happy."

"Why? Because she took command of the Montgren and Fairhaven companies and saved his ass?" asked Sheralt, adding, "And ours."

Taelya almost protested, except that was what she'd done. She hadn't thought of it in that way, just that she'd done what was necessary for all of them to survive. After a long silent moment, she said, "We might have lost fewer troopers if I'd understood what the failure of Seventh Battalion to cross the bridge meant. Then we could have withdrawn to the bridge before the attack."

"But you told Gustaan they weren't crossing," Kaeryla pointed out.

"I should have known and insisted," said Taelya.

"By the time you'd insisted and Gustaan had gotten Zekkarat's attention," replied Sheralt as he sat down, "the Gallosians would have been attacking anyway."

"You're likely right about that," conceded Taelya.

Sheralt grinned. "I don't hear that from you very often."

For some reason, Taelya felt herself blushing. "I'm sorry."

Sheralt shook his head. "Don't be. I wouldn't be alive right now if I hadn't followed your advice." Then he grinned again, cheerfully. "But it is nice to hear it."

Taelya couldn't help but smile in return, if briefly.

"What I don't understand," said Valchar, after taking a swallow of ale, "is why the Viscount went to all the trouble of sending three battalions here, just to set us up. Wasn't there an easier way to weaken Montgren and Fairhaven?"

"I think he had more than that in mind," replied Taelya. "He not only double-crossed us, but he also double-crossed the Prefect. He proposed to the Prefect— and I'm only guessing—that he'd make an attack on Passera without directly attacking the Prefect's troopers and mages, and that once we were on the west bank of the Passa River, he'd withdraw his forces so that the Prefect's mages and troopers could eliminate us. The Prefect would agree to losing some troopers in place of fighting the Viscount, and the Viscount could take over Montgren. In turn, with the elimination of half of Fairhaven's mages and the battles between Hydlen and Fairhaven and Montgren, the Prefect could take over a weakened Hydlen, including Fairhaven. They both gain, and they get rid of a troublesome Fairhaven."

She paused and took another swallow of ale, her second cup, before going on. "Except that the Viscount knew, somehow, that we'd at least be able to remove some of the Prefect's mages, and then, that way, he could come back and make a real attack on Passera and take it over."

"You really think the Viscount is that devious?" asked Valchar.

"You might remember," said Sheralt, "that the Viscount didn't get close to any of us during the whole time we were in Jellico."

"But . . . what their majers said . . ." protested Valchar.

"They know we can tell if they lie," said Kaeryla. "I've thought about it. Akkyld never lied. He just didn't tell us everything, and I don't think any of the majers knew what was planned until yesterday morning. Only Akkyld did. That way, he let the majers tell us what they thought was true."

"The Viscount's a truly devious bastard," said Sheralt.

Abruptly, Taelya shook her head, recalling her brief meeting with the fur trader.

"What is it?" asked Kaeryla.

"Jhotyl, the fur trader, he was trying to warn us not to trust the Viscount at all. I just didn't realize how . . ." Taelya let her words trail off.

"You couldn't have guessed from that," Kaeryla said.

"But I should have been more suspicious."

Kaeryla laughed, if softly. "You've been suspicious all along. I don't see how you could have been much more."

Both Sheralt and Valchar smiled and nodded.

After Sheralt and Valchar finished eating, Taelya and Kaeryla headed for the stables, but they'd barely entered the courtyard when Taelya sensed someone approaching.

"Undercaptain?"

Taelya turned at the sound of Varais's voice. "Yes?"

"There's a woman here to see you. She kept pounding on the gate. Breslan came and got me because he heard her pleading with the guards. I persuaded them to let her and her children in. She says that they're mages . . . or could be, and that they'll be killed if they stay in Passera. She might be lying . . . but . . ."

"You don't think so."

"The girl . . . she created a tiny flame . . . on the tip of her finger."

Taelya turned to Kaeryla. "You're a healer. You'd better come, too."

"You think she might be . . . ill in the head?"

"I don't know. Call it more a feeling that you should be there."

The two followed Varais down to an alcove in the courtyard not far from the main gate, where Hassett stood with three others. Varais gestured to the junior guard, and he stepped away, but remained watching, mostly out of earshot.

The woman was red-haired, but her tresses were lighter in shade than Kaeryla's. The two children looked and felt to be the same age, but they were superficially very different, the girl with red hair, the boy with black hair, but both with penetrating blue eyes. They looked to be about ten or so. Taelya could immediately sense higher levels of order and chaos in all three.

"You are mages?" asked the woman. "You're from Fairhaven?"

"We are," said Taelya.

"Both of them are," answered Varais almost simultaneously with Taelya. "Fairhaven is the only place in Candar that has women who are mages and officers."

"My name is Ysabella. They are twins. Their father . . . he was a mage." The redhead blinked back tears, almost as if they were an annoyance. "He said that, if anything happened to him, I was to take them to Fairhaven, especially Annana, but he said it would be better for Sydel, too." She inclined her head toward the daughter. "He said they could learn from a great mage there."

"They're mages?" asked Taelya gently.

"Only a little now." Ysabella nodded to her daughter.

Annana concentrated, and a small ball of chaos appeared above her outstretched hand.

"Sydel . . . he is not . . ."

"A chaos mage," finished Kaeryla. "He'll be a black."

As Ysabella spoke, Taelya sensed the chaos swirling around her, far more than was normal for most people, if not quite so much as usually around a mage. Even more chaos swirled about Annana, but the black of order was settled more on Sydel. Even from her first look at Sydel, Taelya had a good idea of who the father of the twins had been. She managed to keep a pleasant expression on her face.

"How did you get across the river?" asked Kaeryla.

"I stole a boat. I left it tied up. It was the only way."

"How do you know something happened to their father?"

"My cousin is a trooper. He sent word. He said that Sydon had been killed in the battle between Fairhaven and Gallos."

Even though she had guessed at the father of the twins, the name struck Taelya like a chaos bolt, and she struggled to keep her composure. "And after that . . . you want your children to come to Fairhaven?" she asked.

Ysabella nodded. "He said they would have a better life there if he wasn't here to protect them. He said . . . that the great one . . . would not hold grudges against children."

Taelya and Kaeryla exchanged glances.

"Sers . . . the majer might . . ."

Taelya looked at the squad leader. "I'm afraid we *have* to take them. They're an obligation and . . . more." She wasn't about to call it what she thought it might be, an apology or a plea from a dead mage. She turned to Ysabella. "You're coming as well. They'll need their mother."

"I had thought as much. We have packs."

"I left them with Breslan," confirmed Varais.

Taelya took a deep breath. "I'll need to inform the majer." She looked to Kaeryla. "If you'd stay with them and find out what you can about their abilities . . ."

"I can do that."

Taelya turned and went to look for Zekkarat.

She found him in a small chamber off the courtyard. The trooper guarding the door looked at Taelya, as if to question her.

"I need to see him. Now." Then she stepped forward and opened the door, closing it behind her.

Zekkarat sat behind a small table, looking at a map. He looked up without surprise.

"What do you have for me, Taelya?" His tone was worried and weary, also slightly irritated.

"Several matters, ser. First, Undercaptain Kaeryla and I are well enough to do a scouting mission to see if and how the Certans might be guarding the smugglers' notch through the narrow gorge that holds the border stream. If we can do that as soon as possible, then you'll know what choices you have."

"You've left us with few, you know?"

Taelya looked squarely at the majer. "We weren't the ones to limit our choices. We were left with no choices except to undertake this mission. You agreed to the

Certan plan. All we did was keep the Gallosians from totally destroying your force. We're mages. We can tell if someone is telling the truth as they know it. Just why do you think we never were in a position to question the submarshal, and why he never said anything much and nothing that was an untruth around us? Even most of his majers didn't know what he and the Viscount planned."

Zekkarat laughed softly, bitterly. "You're stronger than your father, maybe even stronger than Majer Beltur. You know you offer the only way out. I know it as well. Of course you can go scout. What else?"

"We have to take a woman and two children with us. My troopers will take care of them."

"Have to?"

"They're beginning mages. They're twins, and they're children of a mage we killed. Their mother said that the children's father insisted they go to Fairhaven if anything happened to him. The last thing we need is to hand two more mages over to either the Viscount or the Prefect. And we're not about to kill them to prevent that." *Especially those two, not after what I did.*

Zekkarat actually sighed. "Once again, it seems as though I have little choice here."

"Having more mages is the only way we'll have a chance to hold off the Viscount in the years to come."

"Even if Majer Beltur has been successful, our chances aren't that great. That's why the Duchess agreed to this plan, over my objections and those of Lord Korsaen."

That was something that Taelya hadn't known. "Those chances may be better now, especially once we return to Montgren."

"You think that the Viscount will decide to take advantage of the Prefect's weaknesses?"

"Over the past years, the Prefect has lost more than a few mages. Here in Passera, he lost five." Taelya didn't mention that two hadn't been that strong, but the fact that even weaker whites had been pressed into service suggested that the Prefect didn't have that many strong mages left. As did the fact that Sydon had been posted to Passera enough times to have a relationship with a local woman who'd borne him two children. "He can't have that many left. And we also took out almost a battalion, all told."

"If we get back, that might make a difference." Zekkarat paused, then said, "You'd better do that reconnaissance now. It would be best if we left before dawn tomorrow."

"Yes, ser."

Before she left the small room, Taelya *thought* she glimpsed the slightest trace of a smile.

A quint later, Taelya, Kaeryla, Varais, and eight guards from Third Squad, roughly half of those who remained, rode out from the gates of the Gallosian fort, immediately turning south on the street just east of the fort and riding until they reached the east-west street that led east to the rendering yard and from there toward the winding trail that eventually reached the gorge used by smugglers and others.

Taelya couldn't help but worry about Ysabella and the children, especially when they discovered that she and Kaeryla had killed their father. That was something that should be addressed sooner, rather than later, because it would be devastating to the three, especially the children, any time, but, if much later, it would be both devastating and a betrayal of trust as well.

As before, the streets were empty, although Taelya could sense some people hidden behind closed shutters.

A quint later, when they had ridden through the miasma of near-nauseating odors emanating from the rendering yard and reached the winding path to the southeast, Taelya could not sense anyone within a kay, but wished she had recovered enough to sense farther. She turned to Kaeryla. "It's about two kays from here to the narrow way down and across the stream."

"Did you really think that we'd need another way across the border stream?"

"I didn't know."

"Don't you think the Certans know about it?"

"Some of the ones who are posted here all the time might. But we didn't mention it to anyone, and Varais told the squad not to talk about it. Besides, because it's too narrow for wagons, I'm thinking that there won't be anyone around, or not many, but we'll have to see. That's another reason why we're here now."

Neither spoke for a time as they neared the pair of low hills between which the trail led down to the stream. Just short of the hills, Taelya called a halt and turned to Varais. "If there's anyone on the far side, they'll see us once we pass the hills, and neither of us can sense quite far enough right now. Also, there are only a few places where we can turn our mounts. So . . . wait here while we go ahead a bit."

"Will you be long, sers?"

"Only long enough to sense the other side," replied Taelya.

"I'll do the concealment," said Kaeryla quietly.

Taelya just nodded.

The two had ridden less than fifty yards past where they could have been seen when Kaeryla said, "There are two riders on the far side near where the trail comes out onto the rocky ground."

"Just two?" asked Taelya.

"That's all. They probably think that they can ride back to the post and get reinforcements in the time it takes to get two companies through the notch."

"Then . . . if we take them out, we should be able to get through from here before anyone finds out."

"If they don't post more troopers here," Kaeryla pointed out.

"That's why we'll leave before dawn, and why you and I will be the first through." Taelya tried to sense ahead, but her discernment was getting fuzzy. "How do we turn around now?"

"There's a wider spot a few yards ahead," replied Kaeryla.

While there was a wider place in the narrow trail, it took almost half a quint to get both mounts turned and heading back to rejoin the squad.

When Kaeryla released the concealment and they rejoined the half squad, Varais said quietly, "I was getting worried."

"It's hard to turn a horse there, especially quietly. There are two sentries there, but no larger force." *Not now.*

Once the recon group was riding back toward the rendering yard, Taelya turned to Kaeryla. "We have one other thing we need to do, now. We need to tell Ysabella how Sydon died."

Kaeryla nodded. "I'd thought about that, too. Otherwise, we'd be taking them to Fairhaven under false pretenses."

But the first chore the two had to do when they returned to the post was to find Gustaan and then meet with him and Zekkarat. Locating Gustaan wasn't hard, because he was waiting in the stable.

"The majer said he wanted to see us when you returned. Harrad and Eshlyn will take care of your mounts."

"We'd planned to see him immediately," replied Taelya. *If not that immediately.*

As soon as the three entered the small room, Zekkarat looked up. "What did you discover?"

Taelya told him about the sentries and the narrowness of the defile, and about their plan to deal with it.

"What if they have more men there in the morning?"

"Then we'll deal with them. We may not be at full strength, but there are four of us, and I doubt they're going to have a company out there well before dawn. If they do, we'll have to try something else."

"I'd prefer that not be necessary. When you mages try something else . . . the results aren't always . . . predictable."

"We'd prefer that, too, ser," said Kaeryla warmly, clearly trying to mollify the majer.

Taelya didn't think he was that mollified.

"We'll ride out a glass before dawn," replied Zekkarat. "We have enough extra mounts from the better ones left by the Gallosians to use as packhorses for supplies."

"Yes, ser."

After the three left the small chamber, Gustaan cleared his throat.

"Yes, ser?" asked Taelya.

"There's the matter of the woman and the children."

"Oh . . . I'm sorry," said Taelya. "They're mages . . ." She went on to explain.

When she finished, the captain shook his head. "You're right. We don't have any choice, but . . ." He shook his head again.

The two undercaptains waited for him to explain.

"It's not going to set well with the Duchess . . . or anyone else, once they find out. We'll be accused of stealing mages to build Fairhaven's power."

"We're supposed to leave them behind?" snapped Kaeryla. "Or worse?"

"No. You're doing what's right, and what the majer would want, but it would be best if we didn't say much about it, especially to the other Montgren officers, until we get home."

If we get home. Except Taelya didn't say that, either. "We need to talk to Ysabella again. Right now."

Ysabella and the twins were in the officers' mess, eating bread, likely stale bread, while Hassett sat by the door.

"If you'd step outside for just a few moments, Hassett," said Taelya.

"Yes, ser."

After the ranker left, Kaeryla gently closed the door.

"Ysabella . . . before you go with us, there's something you should know," began Taelya.

"I think I already know, Mages, but please tell me."

Taelya forced herself to speak evenly. "In the battle between us and the Gallosians, Sydon was fighting for them. In the end, it came down to whoever prevailed would ride away, and whoever did not would die. We prevailed. That was how he died. He fought, but we were stronger. I'm sorry it had to be that way, but we both thought you should know."

Ysabella's eyes were bright with unshed tears, but she replied, "I knew that before I came. He said that if you prevailed, you would be strong enough to protect us. He also said that you would tell us that you had bested him. He said that, if you did not tell me, once we reached Fairhaven, we should go elsewhere."

"We hope you would not go elsewhere," said Kaeryla. "The ride back to Fairhaven will not be easy. We may have to fight our way back."

"Sydon said that might be so."

Taelya winced inside. "We will do our best."

"That is all we can ask. If we stay in Gallos, they will be slaves, just as he was, for all his silvers and position." Ysabella paused, then went on. "He said you were honorable. I am grateful he was right."

"We wish it had not happened the way things turned out," said Kaeryla.

"Even mages do not always choose what fate holds. We are in your hands."

Taelya could tell that Ysabella did not want to say more, and that she was having trouble holding herself together. "We will leave very early tomorrow. You will have to ride, but we'll be moving at a walk."

The twins' mother just nodded.

"Would you like a quint or so to yourselves?" asked Taelya gently.

"If you please, Mages."

"Hassett will be here, just outside, if you need anything."

Ysabella barely inclined her head.

The two undercaptains slipped from the room.

Once outside, Taelya said, "Hassett, just keep watch over them, but leave them alone for a bit."

"Yes, ser."

Taelya kept walking until they were away from the mess before saying, "I don't know how she can do this."

"For her children." Kaeryla looked as if she might say something more, but closed her mouth.

For an instant, Taelya wondered why. Then . . . she knew, and she couldn't help it as tears began to flow, and she found herself sobbing.

Kaeryla put her arms around Taelya. "I'm sorry. I shouldn't have . . ."

"You . . . were . . . right . . ."

A bit later, Taelya hugged Kaeryla before letting go. "You think you're over some things . . . and you find you're not."

"We don't ever get over some things, I think. I admire you, Taelya. I don't know that I'd have survived as well as you have."

Taelya blotted her eyes with her sleeve. "I think you'd do just fine." *I hope you never have to find out, though.* She cleared her throat. "I wonder if we'll ever know everything about Sydon."

"We do know two things," replied Kaeryla. "He loved his children and their mother, and he trusted us."

Taelya could agree with the first, but was the second just because Sydon had realized he had no choice if he wanted the twins to be free of the Prefect? *Will you ever know?*

"There's one other thing," said Kaeryla. "I really should look again at the wounded. I might be able to do a little more, but I need you to come with me, to make sure that I don't use too much order."

"Should you—"

"I can do some. How can I not do what I can?"

Taelya unfortunately understood that.

LI

On fiveday morning Taelya woke early out of an uneasy sleep, with visions of Sydon's look of surprise in the instant before he'd vanished in flame and ashes, an image Taelya felt she'd never forget.

Kaeryla looked over and said, "Your order/chaos levels are much better this morning. Much better."

As Taelya sat up, she could tell that she was still stiff, but not nearly so sore as she had been on fourday. After a moment of sensing the order level of the younger mage, she replied, "So are yours."

"Not as strong as I'd like for either of us, but . . ." Kaeryla shrugged.

As she made ready for the day, Taelya could only hope that it wasn't too late, and that they didn't face Certan troopers on the far side of the smugglers' ford, but there was no way that any of the undercaptains had been ready to use magery against even the smallest force on fourday. She could now sense to the west well beyond the western fort, possibly not quite two kays, and that was a great improvement, especially since there didn't seem to be any unusual activity there.

They both dressed quickly and tied their gear up before heading to the mess, arriving there about the same time as Gustaan, who was with Sheralt and Valchar.

Taelya had the feeling that the captain had rousted the other two undercaptains from their beds, because both looked sleepy-eyed, and neither even really looked in her direction.

Three quints later, after cold rations and ale, checking on the surviving wounded, who seemed able to ride, although there was little choice, and saddling their own mounts, Taelya and Kaeryla rode near the front of the diminished Montgren/Fairhaven force, with Gustaan and Zekkarat directly behind them, and Sheralt and Valchar behind them, followed in turn by Varais and the Fairhaven squads and then the two Montgren companies. At Gustaan's suggestion, the cookfires were lit and left burning, with enough wood for several glasses, to give the impression, when the sun rose, that the fort still held occupants. The gates were closed as well to further that impression.

Taelya had also made sure that Varais had plenty of rope, just in case matters actually worked out as planned, and that Ysabella and the twins rode near the rear of the Fairhaven squads. While the three did not look away from her, she could tell that her presence, far more than that of Kaeryla, made them uneasy.

The force followed the same route that Taelya and Kaeryla had used on the previous day, and, as then, no one was out and around, unsurprisingly, given that it was more than a glass before dawn. In the still hot air, the odors from the rendering yard were even more redolent of corruption and decay.

"I can see why smugglers use this route," said Zekkarat, his voice quietly wry. "No dogs could trace them, and no one in his right mind would come this way."

Taelya was thankful that they were riding before dawn, because even with the reduced numbers, their party would have stretched out almost a quarter kay in single file, although that wouldn't happen because the notch extended slightly less than a hundred yards on each side of the stream, and the troopers could proceed two by two until they neared the notch.

Two quints later, when they reached the end of the winding part of the trail, short of the two low hills separated by the path down to the stream, Taelya called a halt and turned to Kaeryla. "There are troopers on the far side. What do you sense?"

"There's a squad on the knoll opposite where the trail reaches the higher ground," replied Kaeryla. "There's no one else within another half kay. Beyond that, I can't sense."

"Are they all mounted?"

"Only two are."

"How far is it from where we could ride at them?"

"Less than fifty yards."

"Then the four of us should be able to take them. We won't be able to do an all-out charge, either. Most likely a fast trot or a little faster, and take out the two who are mounted, and capture the others."

"Even together . . ." began Kaeryla.

"They don't have to know that," said Taelya. "Besides, if necessary, I could use shields the way you do, and Bounder's more than strong enough."

"Are you sure that you can do that?" asked Zekkarat.

"There's no other way to get at them. If some get away, it's still two kays to the border fort. We'll just have to hurry. It shouldn't come to that. Kaeryla will lead, and she'll do the concealment. I'll follow her, then Sheralt and Valchar. Leave a gap of about fifty yards before anyone else follows." As Kaeryla moved forward, Taelya turned to Sheralt, who had moved up past Zekkarat and Gustaan. "We need to take out the two mounted troopers immediately. I'll take whoever is on the right. You take the one on the left. Narrow chaos bolts."

Sheralt nodded just before Kaeryla dropped the concealment over both of them.

Taelya urged Bounder forward toward the notch between the two hills, glad that she could sense the rocky walls on each side. When she reached the fast-flowing stream, although she had judged it was less than a yard deep, she worried that it might be deeper or that someone might splash loudly and alert the

Certans, and she didn't want to be that person. But Bounder walked calmly through the water, which turned out to be not quite a yard deep. Despite it being early summer, Taelya could feel the chill through her boots.

Shifting her concentration to the slope up to the higher ground, Taelya kept track of where Kaeryla was, noting that the younger mage had slowed her mare, likely to move more quietly as she reached the top of the slope. As she eased up beside Kaeryla, she found it momentarily disconcerting to be facing the two mounted riders, who were positioned as if they were looking straight at the two mages.

Then Sheralt eased his mount up on Taelya's left.

"You hear something?" said one of the troopers. "Horses, maybe?"

"Who'd be out this early? Besides, only smugglers use this path."

"Forward. Now," said Taelya quietly. "Drop the concealment." She wasn't about to try to aim chaos bolts by sense alone.

For several moments, the two troopers just gaped, and in that time, the three mages, trailed by Valchar, got within thirty yards, at which point, Taelya fired a narrow chaos bolt at the trooper on the right, hitting him in the chest, but closer to his shoulder than she would have liked. It didn't matter, because it was enough to kill him.

Sheralt's chaos bolt, not quite so tightly focused as Taelya's, spread across the second trooper's chest.

Kaeryla rode almost over the nearest unmounted trooper, who was running toward the mounts on the tie-line, but he took two steps more before pitching forward, trying to survive a crushed throat.

"Do any more of you want to die?" snapped Taelya. "If you move, you will."

A fourth man grabbed for his sabre.

Taelya managed a tight chaos bolt in the middle of his chest. She wasn't sure she'd be able to do much more.

"Don't move," croaked another trooper. "They're all mages."

"That's right," said Taelya. "You behave, and we'll leave you alive."

In a fraction of a quint, Zekkarat, Gustaan, and Varais emerged from the notch.

"Squad Leader! We need those troopers tied up tight," ordered Taelya, before addressing the Certans again. "If any of you cause trouble, we'll start killing the rest of you."

In little more than half a quint the remaining twelve troopers were tied up, and Kaeryla and Valchar were already leading the Fairhaven contingent along the trail to the east and toward, hopefully, the main road through the Easthorns.

Taelya counted the mounts to make sure that a trooper hadn't escaped, but there were sixteen, matching the number of Certan troopers, so there hadn't been a full squad, and no one was unaccounted for. Then she rode back to where Zekkarat had reined up. "Do we need any more mounts?"

"No. They'd just be a hindrance."

"Then once everyone's clear of the notch, we'll shoo them down the gorge. Once they get moving all they can do is come up on the other side. Someone will find them, but it will keep the Certans from getting back to the fort soon, even if they get free in the next quint. Sheralt and I will bring up the rear." *At least for a while.*

"I'll move to the front, then." Zekkarat turned his mount.

Taelya moved Bounder next to Sheralt's mount, where they could watch as the rest of the force emerged from the notch. So far, she couldn't sense anyone coming, either on the Gallosian side of the border stream or from the direction of the Certan border post.

Another quint passed before Maakym reported, "All troopers and pack animals are clear, ser."

"Excellent. You're riding near the rear?"

"Yes, ser. That's what the majer ordered."

"Then we'll ride with you, after we loose the horses."

"Are you just going to leave us here?" asked one of the captives.

"Someone will come and find you," replied Taelya. "That's a lot better than what you left us to face."

"Bitch!"

Taelya rode closer to the trooper who'd spoken. With careful control, she planted the tiniest bit of chaos-fire in the middle of his forehead.

The man screamed, understandably.

"Your submarshal left us to die. You're fortunate I didn't do the same."

"White terror . . ." murmured someone.

Taelya ignored the low-voiced comment and turned Bounder, watching as the last of the packhorses plodded along the trail. Then she rode back to where Maakym and Sheralt waited. "We need to get their mounts moving down the trail to the river."

That took almost a quint, far more time than Taelya had anticipated, and she and Sheralt had to ride at a fast trot to close the distance between them and the rest of the mixed force.

"A couple of Certan officers should count themselves fortunate," murmured Sheralt.

"Somehow . . . I'm not as forbearing as I was a season ago," replied Taelya wryly.

"I can't imagine why," murmured Sheralt sardonically.

LII

Reaching the main road east took longer than Taelya thought it would, and it was well past midmorning before their force finally emerged from the winding side trail through another narrow passage that was effectively concealed from the road by its angle to the road and a stretch of rock that showed neither footprints nor hoofprints.

Toward the east, the road sloped generally upward through rugged redstone hills with occasional cacti and a few scattered low pines. Taelya remembered all too clearly that each incline was followed by a slight decline, and then by a steeper climb. That progression would continue for at least another two days before they reached the boulder-strewn valley, followed by the steep climb up to Middle Pass and the brutal winds that swirled through it.

Once the entire force was back on the road and set in traveling formation, Third Squad became the vanguard, while Second Squad served as rear guard. For the interim, Zekkarat decided to ride at the head of the Montgren forces, rather than with either Fairhaven squad.

Almost a quint went by as Taelya and Kaeryla rode up a long gradual slope, only to reach the top, a swale between two larger hills, and another slight decline before the road began another climb around the side of a larger hill.

Taelya was still pondering what Zekkarat's seeming withdrawal meant and how to deal with it when Gustaan cleared his throat.

"What have we forgotten?" she asked.

"You know," said Gustaan, "Akkyld's going to send dispatch riders. He likely already did once he found out that we were in Certis."

"How else are they going to get to Jellico quickly except on this road?"

"You found side roads around the border stream bridge."

"That's true, but there was a need for them there. From here on the side paths will mostly lead back to the main road. I'm sure there are side roads, but while we're in the Easthorns the odds are that they only go to and from steads or hamlets. Also, we can sense someone coming."

"But not always before they can see us," Gustaan pointed out.

"They'll still have to get past us. We'll just have to do the best we can," replied Taelya. *As always.* She uncorked her water bottle and took a swallow. Not a large one, because the ale would have to last.

As they were approaching another rise in the road between yet one more set of hills, Kaeryla said, "There's a pair of riders to the west. About two kays behind us. They've got spare mounts, and they're moving fairly fast."

"Couriers," said Gustaan almost laconically.

"We should use concealments and capture them so that we can find out what the dispatches say," said Taelya, realizing that Kaeryla could now sense much farther than the younger mage had been able to do even a season ago. *But then, so can you . . .* Or she could before the battle over the western fort. She just hoped she'd get back that ability before too long. "We also need to make sure that the dispatch riders don't get around us."

"How do you propose to do that?" asked the captain.

"Once we head down this next decline, when the rear squad is a hundred yards downhill, we put two mages under a concealment at the side of the rise. There's enough space there. The other two will wait with the rear guard. As the riders approach the crest, we conceal everyone. That way we don't have to do it for long. Once they're within a few yards, we drop the concealment and so do the mages behind them." Taelya paused. "I'll suggest it to Zekkarat."

"That might be a good idea," said Gustaan dryly.

Taelya only had to drop back some twenty yards to where the majer rode.

"Majer . . ." said Taelya politely.

"Yes, Undercaptain."

"Undercaptain Kaeryla has discerned two riders . . ." Taelya went on to explain and then to offer her suggestion.

When she finished, Zekkarat nodded. "I like the idea. I would suggest one addition. If you had another few troopers with your hidden mages, the dispatch riders might be less hasty. That might also lessen the need for magery that could be fatal or destroy any dispatches they might have. That way we might find out more."

"Yes, ser. We should have thought of that."

Zekkarat smiled, almost cheerfully. "There are some benefits to being around for a while, Taelya."

"Majer Beltur thought highly of you even when you were less experienced."

Zekkarat's smile broadened. "You look so young. Sometimes, it's hard to realize that you have more experience than most captains. The only thing you lack is more familiarity with larger groups of officers."

Taelya couldn't quite conceal both the rue she felt and her appreciative amusement at his phrasing. "In other words, more tact, especially when bluntness isn't necessary."

Zekkarat chuckled. "Now . . . we'd better set things up. I'd like to be with the rearguard mages."

"You should be," she replied.

"And it's also a good time to give everyone a rest."

"Yes, ser. I had thought about that."

In less than a quint, the company was in position. Taelya and Sheralt were the mages concealed with four Third Squad troopers on the high north side of the road, led by Senior Guard Khaspar, while Valchar and Kaeryla were with the rear guard.

Taelya listened intently as the two riders rode at a walk up the last yards of the rise in the road.

". . . don't want to get too close . . ."

". . . once we see them . . . we'll hang back, until there's a place where we can ride around them."

". . . might have to wait till night . . ."

". . . if that's what it takes . . ."

". . . tracks still fresh . . . can't be too far ahead . . ."

Taelya forced herself to breathe shallowly, but the two riders stayed to the low side of the road and kept their mounts moving at a walk. So long as the two didn't show any signs of wanting to turn or flee, she wasn't about to release the concealment. The closer they got to the rear guard, the better.

Some thirty yards from the rear guard, one of the two turned his mount.

Taelya dropped the concealment, and the six moved to form a barrier.

The dispatch rider turned back east, only to see the entire force.

"Don't try it!" snapped Zekkarat. "There are mages in front and in back of you. We're not interested in hurting you. Just dismount and keep your hands away from your blades if you don't want a crushed throat or a firebolt in your chest."

"You wouldn't take the submarshal's dispatches . . . to Jellico, sers?"

"The submarshal broke the Viscount's agreement with the Duchess of Montgren. Taking a look at his dispatches hardly compares to that," said Zekkarat.

In moments the two riders were disarmed, their arms bound behind their backs.

Taelya rode down to join Zekkarat, Gustaan, and Kaeryla.

By the time Taelya got there, Zekkarat had the single dispatch pouch. He used a belt knife to cut through the lead seal on the dispatch pouch, from which he extracted a sealed envelope. "Just a single dispatch. Most interesting." Then he used the knife to cut open the envelope, leaving the outside seal intact. After sheathing the knife, he extricated a single sheet and unfolded it. After reading it, he handed it to Gustaan, who read it in turn and passed it to Taelya.

She began to read.

The Highest and Most Honorable Viscount
Rystyn of Certis
Lord of the Fertile Lands

As you ordered, sire, Sixth, Seventh, and Eighth Battalion escorted the
Montgren and Fairhaven forces to Passera. The Fairhaven force succeeded in
taking the Gallosian fort on the eastern side of the Passa River. From there,
the Fairhaven and Montgren forces stormed the stone bridge over the river,
killing most of the bridge defenders. From there, they forced their way onto
the west side. Before Seventh Battalion could cross the bridge and join the
Fairhaven and Montgren forces, the Gallosians attacked. While the
Gallosians were successful in repulsing the invaders, they apparently lost all
their mages and close to a battalion in both battles.

The Montgren and Fairhaven forces regrouped and found a way to leave
Gallos without using the sole bridge across the border stream. This
necessitated their leaving supply wagons behind at the captured eastern fort.
While they will doubtless attempt to return to Montgren, and it is likely
that they will attempt to use the main road between Passera and Jellico, at
this time there is no way of knowing whether in fact they will or exactly
how they will proceed or how quickly.

Sixth, Seventh, and Eighth Battalions will remain at the Passera post, as
previously ordered, awaiting further orders.

The dispatch was signed by Akkyld and sealed. Taelya handed it to Kaeryla,
who read it and returned it to Zekkarat.

"It's close to factually accurate, and it admits nothing," said the majer. "I
wouldn't have expected any less from Akkyld."

"But it makes us the invaders," protested Kaeryla. "That's not quite the way
it was. The Viscount was the one who proposed the plan."

"We *were* the invaders," replied Zekkarat. "We rode into Gallos. We attacked
and took one fort, and then we marched on another and destroyed a battalion and five mages. Admittedly, the majority of that was done by Fairhaven
mages, but Fairhaven is part of Montgren. Even though the whole campaign
was a scheme to destroy Montgren and Fairhaven, the failure of that plan will
allow the Prefect, at least, to claim he was an innocent who was invaded. To
what extent he blames the Viscount will depend on what he decides will benefit
him the most. The Viscount will make some claim, such as that our forces were
escorted on a diplomatic mission, one that we proposed under false pretenses,
and that his forces had no part in the fighting or violence."

"Which they didn't," said Gustaan dryly.

"In any event," continued Zekkarat, "our first priority is to cross the East-horns safely, and our second is to leave Certis without further losses. We can deal with the Viscount's misstatements and lies after that."

Taelya offered a nod with the others, one she didn't feel, or agree with, but there was little point in disagreeing until or unless she could do something.

"I'll keep the dispatch, envelope, and pouch," declared Zekkarat. "The men and mounts have had a break, and we should be moving on."

"What about us?" asked the taller dispatch rider.

"We'll keep your horses," said Zekkarat. "They'll be fine. You're both healthy and unwounded. You can walk back to the post. It's only about ten kays, maybe twelve. We'll give you your water bottles. If you hurry, you might make it before dark. It's mostly downhill. But you'd better start before I change my mind." He paused, then added, "Or the mages do."

Khaspar bent down and cut the bonds of the taller Certan and, while the Certan finished untying himself and the other dispatch rider, he extracted two water bottles from their saddle holders. Then he tossed one to each rider.

"Now," said Zekkarat.

The other three Fairhaven troopers blocking the road to the west moved aside, and the two Certans began to walk back up to the rise. As they moved away and as the Fairhaven and Montgren troopers prepared to move out, Taelya kept sensing the dispatch riders to make sure they kept walking, although she realized, belatedly, that they had no choice.

LIII

By fiveday afternoon, Valchar and Sheralt and Second Squad were riding van-guard, while Third Squad was riding rearguard, just behind the packhorses. Ysabella and the twins followed immediately behind Varais and Khaspar.

Taelya was trying to sense as far as she could behind their force, as well as to both sides, but so far, as she had suspected, the few paths off the main road had seemingly led to abandoned steads, or, in one case, to some sort of disused mine. She couldn't say that she was surprised, given how comparatively dry the hills and lower peaks on the western side of the Easthorns seemed to be.

"Do you think Sydon was training the twins?" asked Kaeryla.

Her question startled Taelya, who was still trying to sense if anyone else might be following the combined force.

"Training them? There wasn't much order . . ." Taelya broke off that thought and added, "He never learned to sort out his own order and chaos. So how would he have trained them?"

"I don't know, but Ysabella seems to know something about order and chaos, and most people who aren't mages don't even consider it that way. And Annana can muster enough chaos to create flames. That could be dangerous, either to her or Sydel. There aren't any Gallosians near right now. I'm going to drop back and talk to them."

"I should have thought about that," admitted Taelya.

"You've had a lot of other things to think about."

"So have you, but you remembered and thought about it."

"You were trying to save our lives. It has to be even more painful for you to even think about training them. Let me talk to them some more."

"I can't avoid her forever."

"You won't. It's only been two days."

Only two days? In some ways it seemed like eightdays ago, and in others, just a few glasses. Finally Taelya said, "Thank you."

When Kaeryla moved to the shoulder of the road and slowed her mare to let Ysabella and the twins catch up with her, Varais eased her mount forward beside Taelya.

"You didn't have any choice, ser."

"I know that. Neither did the mage who attacked my father and forced him to destroy them both. It doesn't make it hurt any less. And that won't make the hurt to the twins any less."

"Doesn't time dull the pain?"

"Some. Mainly, though, I don't feel it as often."

Varais nodded understandingly.

Seeing that gesture, Taelya couldn't help but wonder what trials and pain the squad leader had endured. More than Taelya had, most likely, and Taelya knew that she'd had a lot of people caring for her when her father had been killed. She straightened in the saddle and said, "Thank you. I suspect you've seen much more than I have. I just didn't expect something like this."

"It's always the unexpected that catches you. That's why it hurts the most."

Taelya managed a wry laugh. "That's true. I never would have expected what happened with Sydon. Yet I should have at least realized that he might be one of the mages at Passera. Why else would he have been chosen to accompany the Gallosian envoy? He was likely picked to make sure that he and Klosyl were strong enough to deal with each of us."

"But it turned out he wasn't."

"No. He was. If I'd faced him by myself, he would have broken my shields. What saved us was that Kaeryla and I worked together. He didn't expect that."

"I didn't know mages could do that."

"Most probably can't, but because Kaeryla and I grew up together, and she's black and I'm white, it worked out. She's learned how to deal with chaos, and I've learned enough to handle order." *And that's why Sydon was caught off guard, and why we survived, and why the twins lost their father.*

"Do you think the way you two did that will change magery?" asked the squad leader.

"I don't think so. Not for most mages. You really have to trust another mage for it to work. I asked Kaeryla for help at the last moment, and she gave it without hesitation. Without that . . ." Taelya shook her head.

"Good thing you two could do that . . . for all of us."

"It's taken everyone to get this far," replied Taelya. She just hoped that they all could get back.

Almost a glass passed before Kaeryla rode forward and rejoined Taelya, and Varais slipped back to ride with Khaspar.

"How are they?" asked Taelya.

"They're getting used to riding. I think it's harder on Ysabella than the twins. They're younger."

"And Annana?"

"Sydon encouraged her, but he really didn't train her. I spent a little time trying to get her and Sydel to sense order and chaos. She already could sort of feel it, and I think I made it a little clearer. Sydel can sense order and chaos, but can't do anything with either."

"Both Dorylt and Arthaal were later with that, and I think ordermages are anyway."

"Annana listened, and I think she understood. I'll work more with her later, but I think you should work with her as well before long, maybe in a day or two. You know more about chaos."

Taelya laughed. "I doubt I know that much more. We had exactly the same tutor."

"True. But you likely have a better feel for the nuances of handling chaos. Doing too much with chaos, even surrounded by order, still makes me uneasy. Doesn't handling a lot of order do that to you?"

"I get uncomfortable, and if I try to hold on to it long, I can't do as much. That's why I didn't ask you for order until almost the last moment."

Kaeryla nodded. "That makes sense. If it looks like we have to do something like that again, I can gather order more easily if I don't have to do it quickly, and I can hold it for you."

"I'll try to remember that. Sometimes . . ."

"Sometimes, we haven't had that much time," finished Kaeryla.

"More times than I'd like, it seems."

Neither spoke for a while.

Then Kaeryla asked, "Wouldn't it be better to avoid Jellico on the way back?"

"The way the roads run, it's going to be hard not to be fairly close."

"You're not telling me something," said Kaeryla.

"Later," murmured Taelya, before saying in a normal tone, "I worry about getting too close to Jellico as well. It's just that there may not be any good alternatives." *In more than a few ways.*

For a moment, Kaeryla looked puzzled, then nodded. "I'll have to check the maps and think about it."

"We still have quite a few things we hadn't thought we'd have to worry about, including two more beginning mages." Taelya kept her voice wry.

LIV

Late on sixday, the combined and attenuated force made it to the boulder-strewn valley below Middle Pass. Tired as Taelya was after two long days on the road, and cold rations with a tin cup of ale, she wasn't sleepy, even after the sun had dropped well below the lower peaks to the west. Although it was summer, the higher peaks to the east, those on both sides of the Middle Pass, still glistened white, albeit with a greenish-purple tinge in the last glimmers of light.

While Kaeryla visited the wounded, as she had twice every day since the day after the battle, although her ability to heal had been limited, if less so each day, until fiveday morning, Taelya sat on a boulder that retained some small amount of heat from the sun, despite the chill of the air, not really thinking about much, except that she wasn't looking forward to climbing up and through Middle Pass on the morrow, or how they might have to deal with the Certans at Relugh. Then she sensed someone coming, someone with more chaos than any of the troopers and less than any mage. Immediately, she looked up and watched as Annana walked toward her.

The redhead, taller for her age than most, looked directly at Taelya. "Mage Kaeryla said a mage killed your father when you were younger than me. Is that true?"

"Kaeryla never lies. It is."

"Then why did you kill Father?"

Even as she had understood that Annana would ask that question sooner or later, it still jolted her, and she had to pause a moment before replying. "Because he was trying to kill us. Also, I didn't see his face until I'd already thrown the chaos bolt that killed him. So I didn't know it was Sydon. I didn't know he had children." Taelya paused, then added, "I still would have had to kill him if I wanted to live."

"You're telling the truth." Annana sounded surprised.

"How can you tell?"

"Mage Kaeryla has been helping me. She said she should work with us first. She said I should work with you before long, though."

"That's because you're a beginning white mage. Sydel will work with Kaeryla and other black mages."

"Mage Kaeryla is a healer. Are you a healer, too?"

Taelya shook her head. "I can do some things that healers do. If there's no other healer around, I can do a little healing. More than that would . . . make me sick, because too much order in the wrong places isn't good for whites, just like too much chaos in the wrong places isn't good for blacks."

"That's why healers are black and most war mages are white, Father said."

"Your father was right. Fairhaven and Spidlar are the only lands I know where blacks have been war mages. In the old times, there were also some black war mages. The most famous was Saryn of the black blades. She founded the land of Sarronnyn."

"She was a black war mage and a ruler?"

Taelya nodded. "She was the first Tyrant of Sarronnyn."

"Could I become like her? Except as a white?"

Annana's words expressed more than mere interest. That, Taelya could tell. "If you work, you could be a white war mage. But in Fairhaven there's no one ruler. There is a council of five. One of those councilors is Jessyla. She's a black war mage and a healer. She's also Kaeryla's mother."

"Are there other white mages in Fairhaven?"

"The only other one is Sheralt. He's the undercaptain with the light brown hair."

"There aren't many women mages, are there?"

"No . . . if you work at it, you could be one of the few."

"That would be nice. I should go. Mother said not to stay long."

"I'll walk back with you."

Annana nodded and turned.

Taelya walked the twenty yards or so beside the girl until they reached where Third Squad was bivouacked.

Ysabella turned, a momentary expression of surprise as she looked at the two. Her eyebrows lifted as Taelya approached. "She wanted to ask you why."

"I told her."

"What she said was true, Mother. It was sad."

Taelya swallowed, thinking back to when she'd been younger than Annana.

Unexpectedly, at least to Taelya, Ysabella nodded, then said, "You feel more than you show. That is good."

"She'll need to work with me before long if she wants to be as good as she could be."

Working with Beltur might have been better, Taelya knew, but her uncle was nowhere close, and Taelya could at least start Annana on the right path.

"How young were you when you first started to learn?" asked Ysabella.

"Seven, but that all depends on the mage. Annana should start now or she could hurt herself or others without meaning to."

"Mage Kaeryla said the same thing."

"What about me?" asked Sydel, with a hint of anger.

"You should start, too, but it's different for a black. Blacks take longer to become powerful, and while they're learning they're not as likely to hurt themselves as whites are. Blacks stay powerful longer, and they usually live longer."

"Can blacks become more powerful than whites?" demanded Sydel.

"That depends on the individual black or white and how hard they work . . . and how carefully and how well they work. Raw power isn't enough. You have to learn the best ways to use it."

"You were well taught, then," said Ysabella.

"Why do you say that?"

"You are small and slender, yet you destroyed five strong mages."

"It took the two of us."

"Mage Kaeryla is barely more than a girl, yet she acts far older."

"We were trained by a master mage, from the time we were little."

Ysabella looked to Annana, then to Sydel. "You see. You must learn and work hard."

Taelya knew what Ysabella had to be thinking.

"And now you must rest. Tomorrow will be long." The red-haired woman nodded at Taelya, then half turned to the twins.

Taelya had only taken a few steps away from the three when Valchar beckoned to her. "Yes?"

"You haven't sensed any more dispatch riders, have you? They aren't lurking behind us waiting for a place to get around us, are they?"

"Neither Taelya nor I have sensed any. Have you?" As Taelya answered, she sensed something slightly different about Valchar, but she was distracted by his tart reply.

"I can't sense as far as you can."

"I don't think there will be," replied Taelya.

"Why is that?" asked a third voice.

Taelya half turned to see Zekkarat moving quietly toward them, then said,

"It's more a feeling on my part. I don't think Akkyld would want to fight anyone on a narrow road like this."

"That's true enough," replied the majer. "We also know that he was under orders to leave his forces in Passera. On top of that, the Viscount is known for his tendency to dispose of those who displease him. So staying in Passera would keep Akkyld safer from an immediate attempt to eliminate him." After a pause, Zekkarat added, "There's another possibility. What if Akkyld really didn't want to do what he was apparently ordered to do?"

"You really think that's a possibility, ser?" asked Valchar.

"Think about this," replied Zekkarat. "Never did any Certan troopers lift weapons against us—except for the two troopers at the smugglers' crossing. And only a squad was posted there. An understrength squad as well, possibly even a marginal squad, from what I saw. He also had to know that there was a good chance his dispatch to the Viscount would be intercepted."

"But all that might just be so that he and the Viscount could deny any involvement in our attack on the forts in Passera," said Taelya.

"That's also true," replied Zekkarat. "But given what I've seen of Akkyld, he might well be trying to do both."

"That's like hoarding your ale and drinking it too," said Valchar disgustedly.

"No . . . that's military politics, especially when a commander has doubts about the wisdom of what he's been ordered to do."

Like the way you feel about the Duchess's decisions? Again, as she had before, Taelya kept that thought to herself.

"You think the Viscount's plan was stupid, then?" asked Valchar.

"It was a calculated gamble," replied Zekkarat. "It certainly was well-planned and well thought out. It was even well-executed. But I doubt that Rystyn had any idea that the Fairhaven contingent of four young mages would wreak such damage on the Gallosians. Just as the father of the current Duke of Hydlen had no idea what three young mages could do. Rystyn may fare better than the late Duke, but that remains to be seen, since what you four did will certainly enrage the Prefect. Enraging the ruling power of a neighboring land doesn't always bode well, and the Prefect has a long memory." Zekkarat smiled politely. "I need to check on a few matters. I'm sure I'll see you both in the morning."

Even after the majer departed, Taelya was thinking over part of Zekkarat's phrasing, wondering if it might be anything but accidental. *Or are you hearing what you want to hear?*

LV

When Taelya woke in the gray before dawn on sevenday morning, she was cold and stiff, and it felt more like winter in Fairhaven than the summer it was supposed to be, although she didn't see any frost. *But then it's likely too dry for frost.*

Breakfast consisted of cold trail bread and hard yellow cheese, not quite greasy, with a small tin cup of ale. She was sipping the last of the ale, along with Kaeryla, not even minding the bitterness, when Valchar and Sheralt joined them.

"Enjoying your sumptuous repasts, I see," offered Sheralt cheerfully.

Taelya swallowed the last small mouthful and nodded.

"What about you, Kaeryla?" asked Valchar.

"It's adequate. That's all it has to be. You're cheerful this morning. Is there a reason for that?"

"We're headed home, and that's better than heading into another battle," replied Valchar.

As Taelya turned her eyes and senses on Valchar, she recalled that she'd noticed something slightly different about the black mage the night before . . . and in the early light, or more likely because she wasn't so tired, it was subtly obvious that Valchar had been working to structure his natural order and chaos. He had a ways to go, but the differences were there. She managed to hide her vaguely amused smile . . . *All it took was a huge battle and his shields almost collapsing on him.* Still . . .

"That's if we don't run into any of the Viscount's troopers who have orders to attack us," replied Kaeryla.

"We could just say that we did our job under the agreement, and that we're returning to Montgren," suggested Valchar.

"I sure that Majer Zekkarat will offer that," said Sheralt, "but . . . if the submarshal managed to get messengers around us, they might not accept that."

"For the next few days, at least, maybe even close to an eightday," added Taelya, "that won't be a problem. Not until we get close to Jellico anyway. By the time any messenger even gets to the Viscount, we'll be on the east side of the mountains and close to Jellico. The only place we might have trouble is at Relugh, but the permanent garrison there didn't seem that large."

"They also didn't seem to care that much about anything except getting paid," said Sheralt. "And doing as little as possible."

"Getting paid is good," said Valchar. "I wouldn't mind that."

"You'll get paid when we get back," Sheralt pointed out. "What could you do with the coins now, anyway, except lose them?"

"We didn't even get spoils from any of those battles."

While Taelya realized that was true, she also had to wonder if there had been that much in the way of spoils from the slain troopers in the eastern fort . . . and certainly they'd been fortunate to have been able to withdraw from the west bank of Passera without greater casualties, spoils or no spoils. Rather than comment, she said, "We'd better get ready to pack up and ride out. Today's going to be colder and harder."

"As if we didn't know that," said Valchar sarcastically.

"Sometimes," replied Sheralt cheerfully, "it's necessary to repeat the obvious." Then he grinned at Taelya.

"You whites are both spoilsports," complained Valchar.

"But we have your best interests at heart," returned Taelya, before grinning back at Sheralt.

Kaeryla looked from Sheralt to Taelya, then shook her head, not bothering to hide an amused smile.

LVI

Sevenday was long . . . and tiring. Taelya thought the eastern wind that roared through Middle Pass, especially after the climb even to get through the pass, was stronger than when they had crossed the pass the first time, but that was likely because the wind had been at her back then, and riding into it definitely took effort, even for Bounder. The combined force camped in the same valley as it had on the way to Passera, a valley that seemed every bit as cold as the boulder-strewn valley where Taelya and the others had stopped on sixday evening.

When Taelya woke on eightday, even sorer and stiffer than on sevenday morning, she did notice that there was dew on the few scattered patches of grass, and the air seemed slightly damper. She also noticed that Valchar had made more progress in structuring his order and chaos levels . . . and that the cheese seemed even greasier. She said nothing about her observations and went about getting ready for another long day.

By sunrise, Third Squad was leading the way along the narrow road through the rocky and rugged lower peaks west of Relugh. A quint or two later, once they were well underway, Taelya turned to Kaeryla. "Have you noticed that Valchar has been working on structuring his order and chaos?" While Taelya knew that her cousin had to have noticed, the question was a gentler way of bringing up what she really wanted to know.

"I did notice that," replied Kaeryla. "It's about time. His shields barely held at Passera. You knew that, I'm sure."

"I did, but I never said anything to him. I wondered if you had."

"I did say that his shields might be stronger if he followed Sheralt's example."

"How did you get that across to him? I mentioned it several times, long before we ever left Fairhaven. He ignored me."

Kaeryla did not look directly at Taelya. "I just . . . encouraged him."

Taelya laughed softly.

"It wasn't like that. I just said . . ."

"You just said . . . ?"

"I told him that he was a good person, and that . . . if he didn't do something about his shields . . . that I'd miss him."

Taelya smiled. "You have a softer touch than I do. I never tried that. I should have, but he got so touchy when I suggested it."

"He comes off as crusty, but he's not nearly that way inside."

Taelya raised her eyebrows. "Not to you, apparently."

Kaeryla flushed. "I was just being nice." After a moment, she added, "You scare him, I think."

"Why would I scare him? I'd do anything to keep harm coming to either of them."

"Taelya . . . you're one of the strongest mages in this part of Candar, and you're a woman. Anyone in their right mind would be a little cautious with you."

"You're almost as strong, now . . ." Taelya stopped when she saw the expression of surprise on Kaeryla's face, then went on, "You really are. Everything you've done has strengthened you, and you have more physical strength than I do, and that helps. That was why you could sense farther than I could the other day."

"I never thought . . ."

"It's true. It really is."

"Then . . ." Kaeryla shook her head. "Maybe it's because I'm a healer. People don't think of healers as being as dangerous."

"That's true. Your mother's a very strong war mage, but people who don't know what she's done don't realize it." Taelya decided not to say more. Valchar was very well aware of Kaeryla's power, and if her encouragement was what it took to get him to get better, that was all for the best. *Even if you worry that he sees that encouragement as another possibility.*

But even as she thought that, she realized that Sheralt had been more courteous and not a trace forward in any physical sense . . . and that worried her as well.

Throughout the day, both Taelya and Kaeryla kept sensing for riders, but could discern none. Taelya wondered more than once why they saw no traders or travelers, either, but put that down to the fact that neither group was likely to travel into an area where there was the possibility of battles . . . or of other losses or harm. And in recent years smugglers had definitely preferred the southern route through Fairhaven.

The sun was dropping over Middle Pass, or where Middle Pass would have been if Taelya could have seen it beyond the hills and trees, trees that were far more common on the eastern slopes of the Easthorns, when Second Squad, with Zekkarat at the head of the force, rode through the hundred or so scattered dwellings that comprised the town and then through the open and tired gates at Relugh toward the long and low buildings that looked empty—and were, from what Taelya could sense. As before, the guards barely looked at the troopers, even though there were no Certan troops to be seen.

Taelya was again struck by how different Relugh was from either the unmanned way stations west of Jellico or the manned ones east of the Jellicor River. It was almost as though it had been built for a larger purpose . . . and then half abandoned. *Because former Viscounts needed it as a base to defend Certis from Gallos . . . or for some other reason.*

She wondered if she'd ever find out.

Zekkarat must have asked Valchar or Sheralt if there were other troopers in residence, because, as they neared the barracks, Gustaan rode back and said, "Take the same quarters you did the last time. Zekkarat rode ahead with Sheralt and some troopers and arranged it. Tell your squad not to mention anything except that we accomplished what was expected at Passera and that we're headed home. They weren't expecting us, so it will be two glasses before they'll have anything ready. Use the time to deal with any problems with your gear. The majer wants to leave early in the morning again."

"Yes, ser." For a moment, Taelya felt as though she'd been left out, but then realized it was likely much better for Zekkarat to appear with a male mage. Even after telling herself that, she was still slightly irritated. Then she turned. "Squad Leader, did you hear the captain's orders?"

"Yes, ser. I'll make sure all the men know."

"Thank you."

Once Taelya had Bounder inside the stable, she could see that they certainly hadn't been expected, because one lone ostler and a single youth were scrambling to bring hay into the stall mangers. The ostler paused before passing Taelya and said, "We'll have some grain for the horses in a bit, ser."

"Thank you. It's been a long ride for them."

The quarters were exactly as the two had found them before—stark and bare, although the wooden shutters were closed, which probably accounted for the lack of flies, as well as dusty. Taelya didn't care that much, she realized.

"It's better than either of those valleys . . . or the empty way stations from here to Jellico," said Kaeryla. "Maybe whatever's for dinner will actually be warm."

"It might be. I think all we can count on is enough ale. They will have ale."

Two glasses later, after reorganizing gear and actually washing up, Taelya and Kaeryla joined the two other Fairhaven undercaptains and walked to the so-called officers' mess, where Zekkarat, Ferek, and Gustaan were already waiting.

"We'll all sit at the smaller table," announced Zekkarat. "Informal seating, as the submarshal would say."

Once everyone was seated and the ale had been served, Zekkarat lifted his beaker. "To the submarshal, for allowing us to return home, and to the Viscount for this meal to come after the cold rations of past nights."

"To the submarshal and the Viscount." Gustaan led the response, but after a word or so, the other officers joined in.

Taelya wasn't sure how the majer managed to sound so sincere, but suspected it was a talent he'd learned over serving in three different lands. She also knew that the toast was not for the officers, but for those serving them.

The meal was some form of mutton strips, braised and covered with brown gravy, with potato logs, also fried and covered in gravy, both highly salted. Greasy as both meat and potatoes were, and spicy as the gravy turned out to be, the meal tasted far better than the ones they'd had the last time at Relugh. That might have been because Taelya was far hungrier, but she didn't think so.

"This isn't bad," said Valchar.

"That's because they didn't have to fix as much, and they didn't have time to foul it up," replied Sheralt in a low voice.

Taelya smiled, suspecting that was likely so. She couldn't help worrying about whether other Certan troopers might be arriving, but given that it was almost full night outside, that seemed unlikely.

There was little conversation, except about the road or other trivialities, clearly because no one wanted to reveal, even inadvertently, the circumstances of their return. It would come out later, but hopefully, well after they were on their way.

By the time she finished eating, Taelya was having trouble staying awake, and she could tell that Kaeryla wasn't faring much better. Even a hard pallet bed sounded good.

LVII

Taelya did in fact sleep better, but found it hard to wake up on oneday morning, even with Kaeryla telling her that she needed to get moving. Finally, she struggled into a sitting position on the edge of the pallet bed.

"You were tired," said Kaeryla.

"Weren't you?"

"Not as tired as you are. We need to eat. *You* need to eat."

Taelya offered an amused smile, and before long they had hurried to the mess, eaten a tolerable mutton-egg scramble and some bread that was actually warm, and even managed to fill their water bottles with ale before they left the mess in the company of Sheralt and Valchar.

Taelya did notice that Valchar was continuing to make small progress in structuring his order and chaos. *He is working to undo years of unthinking habits. You were fortunate never to be allowed sloppy habits.* But then, she was coming even more to realize, she'd been fortunate in many ways, especially in those who had loved and cared for her.

As Taelya and Kaeryla were finishing saddling and loading their mounts, Taelya looked over the low stall wall and asked, "Do you plan on working with the twins once we're on the way?"

"I thought that might be for the best."

"Good. Maybe we could work together with them tonight, although it might be cold. As I recall, there's no way station until tomorrow night."

"You think together . . ."

"Annana's still wary of me. I just thought if the two of us worked with her . . ."

"That makes sense."

When they walked their mounts out of the stable, Gustaan rode up. "Second Squad will be vanguard this morning, Third Squad this afternoon."

"Yes, ser."

Moments later, the two joined Varais at the head of Third Squad.

"How was the fare for the men?" Taelya asked.

"Better than last time. That surprised me."

"Maybe the majer was more diplomatic," suggested Kaeryla.

"From what I've seen," added Taelya, "few of the Certan officers are that diplomatic, but then, I've gotten the impression that they feel they don't have to be."

"I just wonder where you got that idea," said Kaeryla.

Taelya mock-glared at Kaeryla, who just grinned.

Almost a quint later, the combined force rode out of Relugh. Taelya hoped it was the last time she'd ever see the dilapidated mountain community.

They rode for close to half a glass before Kaeryla said, "I think it's safe to spend some time working with the twins while we ride. If I sense anything, I'll be back. If you do, let me know." Then she eased the mare over to the side of the road and dropped back to where Ysabella rode with the twins.

Varais moved up to ride beside Taelya, and, after perhaps half a quint, she said quietly, "Am I mistaken, ser, or has Undercaptain Kaeryla become a stronger mage since we left Fairhaven?"

"She's much stronger," replied Taelya. "Undercaptain Sheralt is also stronger, and Valchar is working at strengthening his abilities. You're thinking about something more than that, aren't you?"

"I'm thinking that Fairhaven doesn't need to be so beholden to a Duchess who'd sacrifice all that supports her to keep her lands and title."

"I've worried about that some." Taelya smiled wryly. "But I'm an undercaptain, not a captain or a majer, and not a councilor. It's probably better that I worry about being a good and effective undercaptain and war mage. But . . . if things are to change . . . first . . . we have to get home safely. Second, Beltur and Jessyla have to have fought off whatever the Hydlenese have tried. Third, we may have to deal with an attack by the Certans even after we return. Then, there's always what the Duchess has in mind."

"Begging your pardon, ser, but if you and the other mages succeed, it doesn't much matter what the Duchess has in mind, and Majer Zekkarat knows that. You and Undercaptain Sheralt pretty much destroyed that one fort by yourselves, and you're only two of the strongest six. That doesn't count your brother or Undercaptain Kaeryla's brother."

"You may be right, Varais, but first . . . we do have to get home. I'm not about to taste ale I've never seen."

"You'll get us home, ser."

For all of the squad leader's confidence, Taelya wondered. She also had another question. *Will that really be enough?*

Around first glass of the afternoon, just after Third Squad had taken over being vanguard, Kaeryla turned in the saddle and looked at Taelya. "Do you sense something headed our way?"

"It's indistinct, but I get the feeling that there are both riders and wagons."

The younger mage nodded. "That's about what I sense."

Taelya called out, "Majer! There are riders and wagons headed toward us, a little over three kays away, just beyond that rise at the end of this valley."

"How many riders?"

"We can't tell yet, but it's likely less than a company."

"It could be provisions wagons, but let me know."

"Yes, ser."

Less than half a quint passed before Taelya turned again. "There are five wagons and a squad of troopers."

"Good. Now, let's hope that they don't try to flee."

The Certans didn't flee, but the wagons and troopers had halted, and the entire squad was formed up in front of the wagons when Third Squad rode closer.

"Have the squad halt," ordered Zekkarat.

"Third Squad, halt!" Taelya ordered.

"You two undercaptains accompany me. Shield me, if necessary."

"Yes, ser."

Zekkarat, followed closely by Taelya and Kaeryla, rode up to the older undercaptain at the front of the Certan squad. He smiled pleasantly. "I'm very glad to see you, Undercaptain. I'm Majer Zekkarat of the Montgren forces that supported Submarshal Akkyld in the takeover of Passera."

"Yes, ser." The undercaptain was polite, but plainly confused.

"When we were released to return to Montgren, the submarshal said we could resupply at Relugh. The only problem was that they hadn't been resupplied."

"Majer, ser, we don't have any orders about supplying you."

"Of course you don't," replied Zekkarat in a tone of exasperated patience. "As I just told you, they were supposed to supply us at Relugh, but you hadn't arrived with the supplies, and they had no idea when you would."

"I have to follow procedures, ser."

"We fought the Gallosians on behalf of the Viscount. We lost nearly a whole company, and you're going to quibble over procedures?"

"But who's going to pay—"

"The submarshal will. That is the agreement made between the Duchess and the Viscount." Zekkarat pulled out a rolled-up sheet. "I have it right here. It's even sealed. You can read it for yourself. Certis supplies our provisions. There's not a word about procedures." The majer extended the sheet.

The flustered undercaptain read it. Then he read it again. Finally, he said, "It does say Certis will provision the forces of Montgren . . ."

Taelya could sense both his reluctance and fear.

"Once you provision us," declared Zekkarat, "I'll write and sign a statement that you did so under the agreement. Then you can give that to Submarshal Akkyld. That should provide you with accountability. And who else would have two companies and mages out in the middle of Certis wearing the uniforms of Fairhaven and Montgren? Do you honestly think we'd be this far inside Certis if we weren't supposed to be here?"

"No, ser."

"Excellent. While you're resupplying us, I'll write up that statement for you."

The undercaptain sighed. "Yes, ser. I'd very much appreciate that."

More than a glass passed before various provisions were shifted from the wagons to the packhorses, which included the four mounts taken from the dispatch riders. Most of what Zekkarat requested consisted of trail bread, hardtack, cheese, dried fruit, and salted nuts. Taelya didn't recall ever having gotten either dried fruit or nuts. Absently, she recalled the apple brandy that she'd only had once, and that had been left in Passera.

What a waste . . .

Some goods, such as flour, couldn't be transferred, nor could kegs of ale, but Zekkarat ordered a keg tapped and had the troopers file past and fill their water bottles. Some of the ale was spilled, and that part of the road would likely smell like a brewery for a while, but Taelya was more than happy to have her water bottles full of ale . . . and she was certain that the troopers were more than pleased by that particular resupply.

The additional time spent resupplying resulted in it being near dark by the time the Montgren and Fairhaven force finally reached the slightly shielded vale where they set up camp for the night, and it was full dark before Kaeryla and Taelya met with Ysabella, Annana, and Sydel.

"We can't spend as much time tonight," said Kaeryla, "but you two do need to practice."

"When can we do more than practice?" demanded Sydel.

"For some things," replied Taelya patiently, "it might be years. I practiced throwing chaos bolts for seven years before I had to use one in a skirmish. But if I hadn't practiced all that time, I would have been dead."

Sydel looked puzzled.

Annana swallowed.

"Practicing is how you get better so that you can do things right when the time comes," said Kaeryla.

"Sometimes," added Taelya, "you find that what you learn is useful in other ways." She looked at Annana. "Did you have water in your house . . . where you could just turn a tap and water flowed into a pitcher?"

The girl shook her head. "That only happens in palaces."

"Not even in all palaces," said Kaeryla.

"We both have water like that in our houses, and they're not palaces," said Taelya. "I was only seven when I first used chaos, and I used it to glaze the inside of a cistern in the kitchen so that it wouldn't leak. We have to fill the cistern a few times an eightday, but it makes life much easier. When we're not fighting, Kaeryla uses order every day to help heal people, but it took her six years of practice to learn how."

"Now . . ." began Kaeryla, "I'm going to show you once more how to keep your order and chaos separate . . ."

"Why—" began Sydel.

"Because you'll be stronger and live longer," said Taelya, turning to Annana and adding, "This is especially important for you. Chaos mages—whites—don't live to be much older than your father was if they don't learn to keep order and chaos layered and separate."

"How old are you?" asked Ysabella.

"How old do you think I am?"

"Perhaps eighteen."

"I'm twenty-three. I've been an undercaptain since I was sixteen." Taelya wanted to compare Beltur and Sydon, but since Ysabella had never seen Beltur there wasn't much point in it.

Sydel looked doubtful.

Ysabella turned to her son. "Listen to them. Your father said that the great mage of Fairhaven did not look any older than he had seventeen years ago. She looks years younger than she should. And they destroyed five mages in Passera."

Annana quickly nodded, Sydel more grudgingly.

He's going to be trouble. Thank the demons he's a black. Taelya turned to Kaeryla. "If you'd show them again . . ." Then she fixed her eyes on Sydel and pressed the touch of a containment around him for a moment.

His eyes widened.

"Just concentrate on what she's doing," said Taelya gently. "It really is important."

"Please, Sydel," murmured Ysabella. "I don't want to lose you, too."

Taelya managed to hold a pleasant expression.

LVIII

The next three days on the road were easier, and much warmer. In fact, by midafternoon on fourday, Taelya was definitely feeling the heat of summer, blotting her forehead from the perspiration that oozed continuously from under her visor cap and drinking more water, carefully order/chaos-cleaned, since she'd long since finished the ale she'd gotten from the Certan supply wagons. She was also more than a little tired of explaining to Sydel and beginning to wonder if she ever wanted children . . . and how her parents—and Beltur—had survived her early years as a beginning mage.

The other concern she had was the Viscount. Everyone seemed most concerned about getting back to Montgren, and not about what was likely to happen after that. Taelya couldn't forget that, even if Beltur and Jessyla had been able to deal with Hydlen without losing too many troopers, there were still something like fifteen Certan battalions, and probably half of them could be brought against Montgren—or just against Fairhaven. And Taelya wasn't so sure that the Duchess wouldn't sacrifice Fairhaven to save her position and life. The Viscount certainly wasn't beneath making such an offer, since it was apparent to Taelya that his goal had been to take both Montgren and Fairhaven however he could.

"You've had a worried look on your face for the last glass," Kaeryla said.

"I'm sorry. It's just that we're finishing the easy part of the ride back."

"You think that, even if we can sneak around Jellico, we'll run into troopers on the road to Weevett?"

"That's possible. It's also possible that, somehow, the Viscount will find out once we cross the river, because we won't be able to intercept any dispatch riders. Akkyld will have to send another set of riders. He may have sent them already and told them to stay well behind us until we cross the river."

"That makes sense," Kaeryla agreed.

"That's what I've been worrying about." *And more.* "Think it over, and we'll talk later."

For the next glass or so, Taelya concentrated on the road, as well as the hamlet through which they passed, where none of the men and youths working the fields gave them more than a passing look, despite the fact that the pale blue uniforms of Montgren and the darker blue of Fairhaven were nothing like the brown and green of Certis. *Don't they care . . . or did they remember us riding out?* Either way, it bothered her.

Another glass passed before they rode into yet another way station, this one unmanned, as were all of them west of Jellico except Relugh, raising again the question for Taelya as to why those east of Jellico were manned.

Even before Taelya had a chance to give Varais the order to release the troopers to take care of their mounts, Gustaan rode up.

"A glass from now, after you eat, the majer wants all officers at a meeting in the small side room."

"Do you know why?" asked Taelya.

"He didn't say. I'd guess it has something to do with how we'll approach and get around Jellico. It could be something else, too."

"Thank you," replied Taelya, turning as Gustaan rode toward Second Squad and asking Kaeryla and Varais, "What do you think?"

"How to avoid the Viscount's troopers is the biggest problem," said Varais.

"What else could it be?" asked Kaeryla.

"You're both likely right."

A glass later, after dealing with Bounder, then eating cold rations and drinking a small cup of ale, Taelya and Kaeryla joined the other officers in the small room at the way station. There was one long table with benches on each side.

Zekkarat gestured for them to sit down, but he remained standing as he began to speak.

"Tomorrow afternoon, we'll be stopping at the last way station before we reach Jellico. Because we're . . . unexpected, shall I say, our appearance could prove a problem. I thought we should discuss how to proceed from here. By taking back roads south along the west side of the river, we could avoid getting too close to Jellico and possibly reach the trading road east to Fairhaven. That road goes through Hydlen and comes within twenty kays of Hydolar. Going that way will also take another eightday to get back to Weevett. If we take the way we came, it's the shortest route, but the one most likely to encounter Certan troopers. We'll also have to claim we're on the way home at the way stations, but since none of them hold more than a squad, that shouldn't be insurmountable." Zekkarat looked toward the mage-undercaptains. "You can tell from several kays whether larger forces are already at a way station, I understand."

While his words were almost a rhetorical question, Taelya and Kaeryla both nodded.

"Also, we'd need to ride past Jellico at night or in the early morning well before dawn if we want to avoid a possible armed confrontation with Certan troops. I'd prefer to take the shorter road, but that would mean a very long day, no matter whether it's early morning or late at night, and still runs the risk of more fighting. It's a lower risk, but still a risk. I'd like to hear what any of you have to say."

"We're going to face trouble however we go," said Ferek. "I'd say that we ought to go the shorter route. That way, if they chase us, they'll have less time to catch us, and once we get to the gorge bridge, they just might not want to push farther."

At least not immediately, thought Taelya.

Neither Gustaan nor Maakym offered any comments.

So Taelya decided she had to speak. "I think your plan is the best way to get back to Montgren. I would like to suggest that Third Squad be deployed on the road into Jellico ahead of the main force," said Taelya. "We could wait in the darkness, or under a concealment, to make sure that no scouts or dispatch riders approach the main force while you're crossing the river bridge."

"I'd thought to have some squad do that, but why Third Squad?" asked Zekkarat, his tone casually curious.

"Because Kaeryla and I can sense farther than the other mages, and because we can use containments to restrain pairs of riders without using chaos. Chaos-fire could be easily seen on the road from the city walls in the darkness. Containments also make it impossible for a rider to cry out."

"I hadn't thought of that," said Zekkarat.

"It doesn't mean much in an all-out fight," replied Taelya. "It's more useful in other situations, as we discovered as Road Guards."

"Does anyone else have any comments?"

"That makes sense to me," said Maakym.

When no one else replied, Zekkarat went on, "We'll leave tomorrow as we have before, at sixth glass, but on sixday we'll leave three glasses later so that we'll be nearing Jellico after sunset . . ."

The rest of the meeting wasn't long and dealt with the order of riding and other details.

As the mage-undercaptains walked out of the meeting, Taelya murmured to Kaeryla, "We need to talk with Varais, just the two of us, right now."

Because the two found Varais talking with the two senior guards in Third Squad, Khaspar and Nardaak, they waited until she had finished before moving closer.

"Sers?"

"We need to talk over something with you. You know the majer gathered all the officers together . . ." Taelya went on to summarize what Zekkarat had said.

After Taelya finished, Varais said, "The majer's likely right about the best way. It could take even longer than he said to go south."

"You'd know better than any of us," replied Taelya, pausing before saying, quietly, "What he didn't say is that we have a much bigger problem than just getting home. Much bigger. What's to stop the Viscount from sending ten of his fifteen battalions against Fairhaven and making a side deal with the Duchess?"

Varais immediately nodded. "I've thought about that."

"He's also vindictive," said Kaeryla.

"What are you suggesting, ser?" asked Varais.

"Making sure that the Viscount is never vindictive again. That would at the least buy time and give his successor something to think hard about. It took sixteen years for Hydlen to try again. In sixteen years, Fairhaven could be a lot stronger."

"Is this what you meant by later?" asked Kaeryla, her voice almost amused.

"I meant to bring it up sooner."

Varais nodded slowly. "One way or another we'd have more time. How do you plan to do this?"

"I already got the majer to agree to part of the plan, although he doesn't know the rest, and he shouldn't . . ." Taelya went on to explain.

LIX

The fact that fiveday went exactly as Majer Zekkarat had planned did little to allay Taelya's concerns about what sixday would bring. And the late start to riding on sixday, or the advance past Jellico, as Sheralt ironically termed it, didn't do anything to settle Taelya's concerns. Because of Taelya and Kaeryla's greater range of sensing, Zekkarat had placed Third Squad in the vanguard until the force neared Jellico, when the squad would then move north on the road to Jellico proper, and when Second Squad would lead the way across the bridge and east away from Jellico.

Just past noon on sixday, both Taelya and Kaeryla sensed the same thing.

"Two riders with spare mounts, headed toward us from Jellico," Taelya called out to Zekkarat. "Most likely dispatch riders."

"We'll use the same tactic as before," said the majer, "except I want you to remain under a concealment unless they try to return to Jellico. They can't do any harm to us if they're headed to deliver information or orders to the submarshal. Just move out ahead of us a good thirty yards with four troopers and you two mages. Just before they come into view let me know. We'll call a rest stop, and you move to the side and conceal yourselves. I'll pass the word to Second Squad."

"Yes, ser." Taelya turned. "Squad Leader, if you'd send forward four troopers."

"Yes, ser."

Less than a quint later, Kaeryla said, "They'll be around that curve in a few moments."

"Riders almost in sight, ser!" Then Taelya added, "Detachment to the left shoulder, facing the road, in a single rank."

The moment the six were lined up on the shoulder, Kaeryla concealed them, and the six settled in to wait.

While the riders rode ever closer, because it was even hotter in the darkness of the concealment, or so it seemed to Taelya, she had to keep blotting her forehead to keep the sweat from running into her eyes.

A good hundred yards from Taelya, the riders slowed, but did not stop, possibly because most of the Montgren and Fairhaven force was dismounted and clearly taking a break. The couriers finally reined up just past Taelya's group, clearly puzzled as Zekkarat rode forward to meet them.

"What force . . . oh, you're the Montgren troopers . . ." The dispatch rider frowned. "Why aren't you in Passera?"

"Majer Zekkarat, Montgren battalion. Or what's left of it."

"Ser . . . we didn't expect . . ."

"You should have . . . or someone should have told you. Submarshal Akkyld sent dispatches to the Viscount. We did all we could, and the submarshal's forces now hold the east side of Passera with full access to the river. It wasn't easy. Not at all." Before either rider could reply, Zekkarat went on, "What have you heard about the Hydlenese attacks on southern Montgren?"

"We're just dispatch riders, ser. Just dispatch riders."

"You're more than that," replied Zekkarat in a warm and winning tone. "You know more than anyone except the Viscount and the senior commanders. We've been away from home for a long time. The men would appreciate learning what's happened since we left. Nothing that you shouldn't tell us, of course."

Taelya could sense that the two looked at each other before one finally spoke. "We don't know much, ser. The word is that the Duke of Hydlen didn't attack as planned, and the last we heard there was fighting going on in Hydlen southwest of Fairhaven. No one seems to know more than that."

"Thank you. We appreciate the news." Zekkarat turned his mount and shouted, "Clear a way for the dispatch riders!" Then he turned back to the pair. "We wish you well. The road's dry, but the wind at Middle Pass is stiff. You're fortunate it'll likely be at your back."

Taelya almost didn't want to breathe, but in moments, the dispatch riders were riding along the south side of the road.

Kaeryla didn't drop the concealment until the two Certans had ridden past Second Squad.

"They'll tell Akkyld, of course," said Zekkarat, "but if any message he sends gets here in time to affect us, we'll have far bigger problems. Now, let's get moving."

"You don't think they were suspicious?" asked Kaeryla.

"Of course they were. But they're trained to get the dispatches where they're supposed to go. That means not asking embarrassing questions or upsetting a foreign majer with several companies. They just wanted to get clear of us as quick as they could. And as long as they're headed west, that's all that counts."

Not all that counts. But Taelya wasn't about to say that, especially not when the fighting still might be going on around Fairhaven.

Zekkarat looked to Kaeryla and Taelya. "It's not necessarily bad news that the fighting's still going on, not if it's in Hydlen."

"No, ser," replied Taelya. But while it was promising that the fighting was happening in Hydlen and not closer to Fairhaven, that news had to be days old, and much could have happened since then.

But it's more hopeful than it could have been.

LX

The closer they got to Jellico, the more people they saw, although not many were on the road, and those that were quickly moved aside to let the troopers pass. Few gave the dusty riders more than a passing glance, suggesting to Taelya that troopers riding through Certis were common enough that no one paid that much attention, even to their uniforms.

As the sun dipped lower and touched the Easthorns behind the riders, Taelya had hoped that the hot sticky air would cool, but even when twilight settled on Third Squad, the air turned still and felt even warmer.

The stars had begun to fill the purple-green evening sky when Taelya saw the kaystone ahead, bearing the inscription JELLICO 10K. At that point, Zekkarat called a halt to allow riders and horses a break, then made his way to Taelya.

"I'd thought I'd send you ahead when we're about three kays from the bridge, that is, if you don't sense any large forces there, and I wouldn't expect that this late in the day . . . or this early in the evening."

"That distance will work. We'll let you know if there's some problem before then."

"You think you'll need all of Third Squad?" asked the majer.

"I might . . . and if they're not with us, it's not as though we can just summon reinforcements."

Zekkarat smiled wryly. "That's true. And how would you suggest I use mages in your absence?"

"I'd split Second Squad. Put Valchar in the vanguard to scout the way, and Sheralt in the rear guard to fend off any Certan troopers who may appear."

"I thought you were dealing with them," said Zekkarat dryly.

"We're dealing with those on the west side of the river. Supposedly, the Viscount has another fifteen battalions. There's not that much room at the post adjoining the palace. Some just might be on the east side."

"Then I'll inform Second Squad to split in that fashion when I send word to Undercaptain Sheralt. Do you want a messenger to tell you when we've safely crossed the river?"

Taelya shook her head. "Either of us can sense that far. Just keep moving. We can catch up if we're delayed or engaged. You want the companies and Second Squad as far from Jellico as you can be when you have to stop. Third Squad is small enough that we can use concealments all the time if we run into a much larger force."

"I'd appreciate it if you wouldn't take it upon yourselves to fight such a force. I might not survive Majer Beltur if that occurred."

"We have absolutely no intention of engaging any forces, particularly a much larger force. That I can promise you." Getting involved in an all-out fight was something that neither Taelya nor Kaeryla had any interest in whatsoever. Besides which, destroying an entire battalion, even as Beltur and Jessyla had done, wouldn't shrink that much the number of the Viscount's battalions.

"I'll take your word on that." Zekkarat smiled wryly. "Not that I have much choice. Just be careful."

"We'll be as careful as we can be," Taelya assured him. "Oh . . . and Ysabella and the twins will have to ride with Second Squad. We'll arrange that."

Once Zekkarat had moved back to the head of the Montgren troopers, Kaeryla said very quietly, "Even before you told me, I suspected you had something in mind, and Zekkarat does too. He's just not certain he really wants to know, since he's more than a little wary of you." Kaeryla held up a hand. "Don't even say a word about that."

Taelya smiled wryly, then said, "He sees more than people give him credit for." *And if things go wrong, he doesn't want to have to say that he knew what we were doing.* Taelya knew that they were taking a terrible risk, but neither Montgren nor Fairhaven would stand a chance of surviving except as conquered lands if she and Kaeryla weren't successful. She pushed that thought away and concentrated on what she had to do next . . . and that was to make sure they didn't encounter anyone who might attack them or alert the Viscount.

The next three quints seemed to drag, but when they reached the point where both Kaeryla and Taelya could discern clearly that the roads both across the bridge and to Jellico were clear, Taelya had Varais send word to Zekkarat that the roads were clear and that Third Squad would be moving slowly ahead of the main force.

Once the ranker returned, Taelya turned to Varais. "We'll move up the pace a little now."

"Yes, ser."

In some ways, Taelya felt, riding down the darkened road with the only light being that of the stars and scattered tiny glints and glows from the stead houses and cots they passed and the only sounds those of hooves and insects from the fields and orchards created a sense of the unreal, as if she rode through a dream. At the same time, she knew it was all too real.

A quint later, Taelya sensed the crossroads ahead, where the road to the left led to Jellico, the one to the right ran south along the west bank of the River Jellicor, and the way straight ahead led across the river bridge. She also could sense that, outside of some figures south of the bridge on the river embankment, there was no one near any of the roads.

When they reached the crossroads, Taelya turned toward Jellico and slowed Bounder to a slow walk, but kept the squad moving toward the walled city until they were a good two hundred yards north, when she called a halt. Then she turned to Kaeryla. "You keep sensing the main force and the bridge. I'll keep watch on the side streets and anyone coming from Jellico."

"I can do that."

While they guarded the side road, Taelya concentrated not only on searching for riders or troopers, but on where the best place would be for Third Squad to wait for her and Kaeryla. Less than half a quint passed before Valchar and half of Second Squad led the way onto the bridge causeway and started across the bridge.

Before that long, Kaeryla said, "Sheralt and the remainder of Second Squad are on the last span and almost across the river."

Taelya turned to Varais. "It's time for us to split up. There's a small woodlot or orchard several hundred yards toward the city, and nothing else too close to it, and there's no one hiding in it."

"How long will you be?"

"I don't know. At least two glasses, possibly longer. If we're not back here by dawn, rejoin the main force. There isn't anything you could do."

"You'll be back, sers," said Varais, in a tone that was close to a command.

"That's the plan." Taelya turned Bounder toward the city gates, just about a kay to the north, and Kaeryla turned her mare.

Once they were well away from Third Squad, Kaeryla said quietly, "If we really can't get to him, we need to get away. Not getting him and getting captured or killed would be the worst thing possible."

"I have no intention of getting us killed." *And no intention of failing.* "That would be pointless and stupid. We should be able to do this if we take it step by step and carefully."

Although the city gates were unguarded, when they neared the gates, Taelya said, "Concealments now." That was because the area around the gates was lit by oil lamps, and just in case someone actually might be watching.

Once inside the walls, and away from the lighted area, Taelya and Kaeryla dropped their concealments because they still had to navigate the maze of streets and traveling under a concealment would have slowed them more and taken more of their energy, if only a little, but Taelya didn't want to spend more than necessary. They made their way to the main square, the middle of which was empty, but the edges of which harbored small groups of men. In the darkness, the two mages had a definite advantage in avoiding them, and by staying close to the middle of the streets, minimized contacts, although twice brigands struck at Taelya, who led the way, only to find themselves brushed aside by magely shields.

The next challenge was to get into the palace.

Taelya was glad she'd done some investigating when they had been in Jellico earlier, because she'd found the gate to the stables used by Certan officers quartered in the adjoining post, but, again, when they neared the palace, they used concealments until they neared the quarters building.

Predictably, the stable gate was closed and presumably locked.

"Can you unlock this one?" asked Taelya, knowing that Kaeryla had been taught that skill by her father, one that Taelya had refrained from learning because manipulating cold iron with order quickly got very painful.

For a moment, Kaeryla concentrated. Then she smiled. "It's not locked. It's just barred with an iron bar. I should be able to move it."

There was a sliding sound, and then Kaeryla pushed the door back. "There's no one near."

The two eased their mounts into the stable.

It took only a few moments to find two empty stalls near the door, where the two quietly tied their mounts. Then they made their way to the door from the stable to the quarters proper. That door was closed, but not barred or locked, and there was no guard there. That, Taelya knew, would be the last door without locks or guards, if not both. From the first level, the two climbed the staircase up to the third level, where on the south side of the building was the long corridor that led to the palace, or, at least that section of it where the inside garden and the officers' mess were located.

Before stepping out of the staircase, Taelya said quietly, "Concealments if we sense anyone. Also, remember that there will be at least one guard at the door between the quarters building and the passageway to the palace."

"I'll take care of him, or them," said Kaeryla.

They both knew what that meant.

When, under concealments, the two neared the door to the palace passageway, initially to Taelya's surprise, she could sense that the guard was posted on the quarters side, rather than on the palace side. But it made sense at night. She didn't sense another guard on the other side, which likely meant that there was yet another at the palace end of the passageway.

Taelya had thought that Kaeryla would use a containment to crush the guard's throat, but while Taelya sensed the use of order, it was different, and the guard pitched forward onto the stone floor with a dull thud, and a light clanking sound. The black death mist followed in moments.

"What did you do?" murmured Taelya.

"Blocked his throat from the inside and expanded it enough to squeeze the blood vessels in his neck. A good healer might figure it out, but most will think he died from a burst vessel in his throat."

The doors opened easily enough into a pitch-black passageway, but one, Taelya could sense, that held no one until it reached the next door, the one that opened into the palace. The two undercaptains walked evenly and quietly along the long corridor that seemed even longer than its hundred yards in the darkness. At the far end was yet another set of doors, which appeared to be unlocked, but posted on the other side of the doors, and facing them, was yet another armed guard.

"I'll put a concealment over him," murmured Taelya. "His first thought will be that the lamp went out. I open the door, and you do what you can."

"Tell me when."

"Now."

Taelya dropped the concealment over the hapless guard, who crashed forward with far more noise that Taelya would have liked, but she sensed no one near, and there appeared to be no reaction.

"What next?" asked Kaeryla.

"We climb two flights of steps to the fourth level . . . and then try to find the entrance to the Viscount's private chambers. From where I sensed a mage before, he or they have to be at the back of the palace."

"You didn't mention you didn't know where they were," said Kaeryla dryly, but in a low voice.

"Does it matter?"

"It might take longer."

"You're right."

"So are you," conceded the younger mage, following as Taelya made her way to the staircase she remembered from her previous explorations.

At the top of the steps, Taelya paused to catch her breath, as well as to try to orient herself to the third level, and how to reach the throne room, since she was hoping, if not counting on, the idea that there had to be a moderately direct way from the Viscount's private quarters to the throne room. She could sense a white mage near the rear of the palace and up another flight.

He has to be guarding the Viscount. Why else would he be there?

"We'll have to go by the officers' mess to get to the main corridor leading to the throne room. There's a white mage beyond that."

"I already sensed him."

"He has to be close to the Viscount. But we have to get there first, and I have the feeling that the main corridors are going to be lighted, maybe not brightly, but enough for guards to see us."

"There are several posted along the main corridor," returned Kaeryla.

"We'll have to move slowly . . . and under concealments."

When they reached the square hall off which the mess was located, Taelya could sense all too clearly both the closed double door that led to the main part of the palace and the two guards posted there. She eased closer to Kaeryla and murmured, "I can put a containment around the one on the left so he can't talk or move."

"I'll take care of the rest."

Then one of the guards spoke from some twenty yards away. "You hear anything, Lasskhar?"

"Just your loud voice. You know Gaarhak doesn't like us jawing."

"He's sound asleep."

"It's not that late."

"He's getting rest while he can. I'm not looking forward to tomorrow night."

"Another ball. Last one until fall."

"You said that before. Less than a glass ago."

"So?"

As the two talked, Taelya and Kaeryla edged closer, since the closer they were, the less effort their magery would take.

"There's someone in the hall somewhere."

Even before the guard finished speaking, Taelya had a tight containment around the guard on the left, and almost as quickly, Kaeryla had dispatched the guard on the right. A few moments later, both guards lay on the floor . . . dead. Taelya looked for somewhere to put the bodies, but there were no alcoves or doors nearby. So the bodies would stay where they fell, which might cause more confusion.

You can hope, anyway.

The doors behind the guards were not locked, nor did they have locks, but before opening them, Taelya sensed for how close the next guards happened to be. "The next guards are in the round hall in front of the throne room. That's more than thirty yards. We'll need to slip in quickly under concealments. That way all they'll see is a door opening and closing. They might not see that if they're not looking. We'll do the same thing with the next pair of guards."

Taelya opened the left door and slipped through, followed by Kaeryla, who closed the door quietly. Taelya definitely sensed one of the guards turning to the other, but neither guard moved that much, and they were still talking in low voices as the two mages eased toward them under concealments.

". . . still say that Lasskhar opened the door and looked at us."

"And I'm telling you to forget it. He's not supposed to do that, and he could get in trouble if you say anything. Besides, how do you know?"

"I didn't see him, but I saw the door close. Who else could it be?"

"Just forget it. You can't blame him. Nothing happens here at night if there's not a ball or a big dinner. Not like the old days."

The two guards had barely stopped talking when the two mages struck. This time, when the two men fell, two dull thumps echoed through the hall that formed a semicircle around the throne room. Taelya immediately tried to sense if anyone might be coming. If anyone had heard, they weren't moving.

"Now what?" murmured Kaeryla.

"We look for a staircase to the next level that will lead us to the Viscount's chambers."

"It should be behind the throne room, I'd guess," offered Kaeryla.

The two moved toward the right end of the semicircular hall, where they found another set of double doors.

"They're barred on the other side," said Taelya. "With an iron bar."

"This is going to be harder," declared Kaeryla.

As the younger mage struggled with moving the bar, Taelya sensed beyond the doors, getting a better sense of the rooms beyond . . . and the staircase leading up to the Viscount's extensive personal and family chambers.

Then from beyond the door there was a loud clanking *clunk.*

Kaeryla pushed the door open. "We'd better move faster."

The two stepped into the rear hall, and Taelya closed the door, observing that the rear hall was a mirror match to the one on the other side of the throne room, except that on the right side of the hallway, in the middle, was a wide staircase leading up to a landing. They walked swiftly but quietly toward the wide staircase.

Taelya could sense that, at the landing, the staircase split, and slightly narrower railed staircases headed up at right angles from the landing to the next level. At the top of each staircase was a door of elaborate iron grillwork.

Taelya wanted to shake her head. She'd known getting to the Viscount would be difficult, but it was seeming like a guarded maze. *Which side and door do we take?* Then she realized that the grillwork on the right-hand door was heavier, and far stronger. She was about to say something when she sensed a figure stepping from the doorway at the back of the landing, a white mage almost as powerful as Sydon.

"It will take the two of us," Taelya murmured to Kaeryla, "and we need to get closer quickly."

They edged toward the bottom of the steps.

Abruptly, the white mage declared, "You can't hide from me. Concealments are useless." With that he threw a chaos bolt at Taelya, presumably because he termed her a greater danger than a mere black . . . or because he didn't even sense Kaeryla's ordered form.

Taelya caught the chaos bolt and immediately flung it back, dropping her concealment as she did.

The white mage added more chaos to the fireball and threw it back, saying, "So much power from such a little mage, but it won't be enough, little one."

In turn, Taelya returned it, murmuring to Kaeryla, "Can you spare a little order?"

The chaos bolt came back at Taelya, who took the order Kaeryla had passed her, pressed it into the middle of the chaos, and fired the mass back at the white, following it with a narrow-focused chaos bolt, also infused with order.

The chaos flared around the white, enough so that he could barely hold his shields, as well as enough that the chaos flaring around him turned the tapestries flanking the doorway to the mage's quarters or post into ashes. Taelya followed with two quick chaos bolts, the second of which resulted in a flare of energy that slammed against Taelya's shields and threw her backward across the hall so that she thudded into the wall and could barely keep her feet.

The entire hall was in blackness, the chaos explosions having extinguished if not destroyed the two landing wall lamps.

Taelya immediately reached out with her senses, but was reassured to learn that Kaeryla seemed to be fine. "The iron door at the top of the stairs heading right . . ."

"Let's hope the lock isn't too difficult," replied Kaeryla, who was already heading up the lower staircase in the darkness.

As Taelya walked across the hall, she kept sensing for people moving, for troopers, but there was . . . nothing. She couldn't say she understood . . . unless . . . the Viscount wasn't even in the palace, but why would one of the guards have mentioned the "last ball" if the Viscount weren't around?

When Taelya reached the landing she realized there was a faint glow coming from somewhere, enough that she could barely make out the solid-gold sunburst that filled the center of the green marble flooring the landing. Then she glanced up at the ornate and heavy iron scrollwork of the gate at the top of the steps to the right.

Of course, the white mage to protect him from assassins and the ironwork to protect him from the mage.

"I've already unlocked the gate . . . and the door behind it," said Kaeryla. "Someone's sleeping in the one large bedchamber."

"Let's go and see if it's the Viscount."

Behind the double doors was a large sitting room, with an archway in the wall directly in front of Taelya that seemed to be a library. To her left on the far side of the sitting room were two doors, one open, and one closed. The open one was likely a study, from what Taelya could sense, and behind the closed one was a bedchamber with one person in it.

The sleeping man didn't wake when Taelya opened the bedchamber door, or even when the two walked into the room. Then Taelya used a tiny bit of chaos to light the wall lamp, and he sat up and opened his mouth, but no sound came forth because she'd also clapped a containment across his mouth and body. She could also sense rage. Not fear, but just plain rage, the kind that stirred chaos in a person.

"Does he look like his portrait?" asked Taelya, mentally comparing, as best she could, the older man before her to her recollection of the portrait. The reddish-blond hair was now shot with gray, the green eyes were bloodshot, and the once-thick neck was almost scrawny, but the lopsided squared-off chin was the same.

"They're at least related," said Kaeryla.

For some reason, her words created more chaos and rage, and that was enough for Taelya. She put a narrow-tight chaos bolt through the middle of Rystyn's forehead, then turned to Kaeryla. "Is anyone coming?"

"Not yet."

"Good." Taelya turned and left the bedchamber, moving into the study, where, after a little searching, she found several sheets of paper or parchment, and an inkwell and quill, then wrote a very few words on one of the sheets.

Kaeryla looked at them and read, "'This is the fate of any ruler of Certis who seeks to conquer Fairhaven and Montgren.' That's all?"

"We're short on time, and I don't feel very creative." Taelya turned and hurried back to the bedchamber, where she placed the sheet on Rystyn's now-cool chest.

From there they made their way to the double doors, closing them as they left, before Kaeryla locked them, and then they quickly retraced their path, under concealment, back to the officers' stable.

Then, after they'd removed their concealments and were leading their mounts to the stable door, Taelya turned as a man with a lantern in one hand and a club in the other walked toward them.

"Who are you?" demanded the ostler. "What are you doing here?"

"Leaving," said Taelya. "Right now. You can step back and let us go. Or you can die." She manifested a chaos flame above her hand.

The ostler stepped back. "I'll not stop you."

"Don't tell anyone what you saw," added Kaeryla. "They'll likely kill you if you do."

Still holding shields, Taelya opened the gate and led Bounder out. Kaeryla followed her out into the street, both immediately raising concealments.

Once they mounted, they rode under the concealments until they were well away from the palace and on their way toward the main square. Neither spoke much until after they had ridden, once more under concealment, through the dimly lighted city gates and were several hundred yards south of the walls, and out of the city, where they dropped their concealments.

Belatedly, Taelya realized that while she was a little tired, she wasn't lightheaded, nor were her order/chaos levels more than a shade low.

"You didn't want to kill the ostler," said Kaeryla. "Why not him? We killed all the others."

Taelya knew what the younger mage was really saying. "I killed some and ordered you to kill others. It was the only way we could do it and move fast enough to succeed. At least, I didn't see any other way. The Viscount went back on his word, and more than three score of our troopers have died so far. If he'd ridden into battle, we'd have tried to kill anyone between him and us. Those guards stood between us and the Viscount. Only seven men and the Viscount died. I'd say we were far less bloodthirsty than the Viscount. As for the ostler, he didn't sign up to protect the Viscount. Also, if he's smart enough to keep his mouth shut, there will be more of a mystery as to how we did what we did. Over time, that just might help."

"Why do you think there weren't more guards?"

Taelya laughed softly. "We had to remove guards at four places, as well as a mage. You had to use order skills to unlock or unbolt three sets of doors."

"But there weren't that many people in the Viscount's part of the palace, except a few in the other chambers across from his."

"Those were most likely his consort and her maids." Taelya smiled within the concealment although she knew Kaeryla couldn't see her expression. "With what we know about the Viscount . . . would you want to be near him if you didn't have to be, or if you weren't seeking his favor?"

"There is that. Do you think we were too quiet? I mean, Father created a huge explosion when he killed the old Duke of Hydlen."

"From what he said, he did it the only way he could. Can you think of another way we could have done it?" Taelya paused, then added, "And it did take the two of us. Neither of us could have done it alone. That also might give Rystyn's heir something to think about. Anyway, we did the best we could."

Taelya could sense that Kaeryla wasn't totally happy about the assassination. "What is it that bothers you?"

"Somehow . . . it's . . . so cold." Kaeryla's shudder was perceptible to Taelya even in the darkness.

"It is. It's cold and calculated. You saw hot and raw in Passera. Chaos of a different kind, men wounded and dying, because the Viscount and the Prefect coldly decided that they'd lie and double-cross the Duchess to destroy Montgren and Fairhaven. We didn't kill thousands. We killed an evil ruler and seven men."

"There still might be war," Kaeryla pointed out.

"There still might be," acknowledged Taelya, "but without what we did, there definitely would have been war. There's a better chance for avoiding it now, because the Prefect's lost many of his mages, and because whoever becomes Viscount knows that he's personally vulnerable." She took a deep breath. "What else could we have done?"

After a long silence, Kaeryla finally said, "I don't know. I think that's what bothers me. Partly, anyway."

"It bothers me, too." *But that didn't stop you.*

After another silence, Kaeryla said, "Third Squad is still there."

"Thank you," said Taelya gently.

After they rode another four hundred yards or so and neared the woodlot or orchard, Taelya called out, "Varais . . . we're back."

The squad leader immediately mounted and rode forward. "We were getting worried, sers. It's been almost three glasses."

"We did what we needed to do. Now . . . we need to get across that bridge and catch up with the others . . . but not all at once."

"Yes, ser."

As she led the squad toward the crossroads and the bridge over the river, Taelya couldn't help but think about what Kaeryla had said. Yet, for all that, what else could they have done that would have had any chance of changing things?

She also knew it was going to be a very long night.

LXI

In the darkness some four glasses before dawn, Taelya led Third Squad into the way station in the small town of Eskaard. Everyone in the squad was exhausted, although they hadn't pushed the horses. They'd been careful to stop at regular intervals to water and rest them. Even so, all Taelya wanted to do was sleep, although she and Kaeryla had taken turns leading the squad, and Taelya had certainly semi-dozed in the saddle, as had more than a few in the squad.

"The majer said to wake him the moment you arrived, ser," declared the trooper on sentry duty. "There are rations and ale in the common mess for you and your troopers. The first corral on the right is for your mounts. There aren't any stables."

"Thank you." Taelya tried to keep her voice pleasant.

By the time the squad had dealt with mounts and gear and reached the common mess, Zekkarat was already there, slightly disheveled, accompanied by Gustaan.

Taelya went and got a tin cup of ale before walking to the end of the table where the two more senior officers waited. Then she set her gear on the table, sat down, and took a long swallow of the ale that barely tasted bitter. Then she took a second swallow.

"You took your time catching up, Undercaptain," said Zekkarat, his voice both rough and cool.

"Yes, ser."

"What took so long?"

"The Viscount's palace had quite a few guards and iron-barred doors, ser. Also, a white mage on duty to protect him." She took another swallow of ale.

An expression somewhere between alarm and resignation crossed the majer's face. Interestingly enough, Taelya thought Gustaan was concealing a smile.

"Would you care to explain, Undercaptain?"

Taelya didn't feel like excusing or softening anything. She'd done what she'd thought best. Mostly she just wanted to lie down and go to sleep. "The Viscount lied and double-crossed us. I killed him in his bed with a very small chaos bolt through his forehead. I also left a message saying the same fate would happen to any successor who attacked either Montgren or Fairhaven."

"You killed a sleeping man?"

"No, ser. We woke him so he could see who we were. He was actually angry. Then I killed him. I made the chaos small enough so there would be no doubt who we killed."

"Didn't this create . . . some sort of reaction?"

"Not by the time we left the palace. We were fairly quiet. We did kill six guards . . . oh, and the white mage. By now someone may have found out. But it will likely take them until well after morning to even question people about anything."

"And you don't think anyone's chasing you? Or that an . . . assassination might just provoke a response?"

"Not immediately. I doubt that many people who'd say anything even knew our force rode past Jellico."

"The Certan troopers here at the way station know," Zekkarat pointed out.

"As long as the ones at the way stations ahead don't know, we should be all right," said Gustaan.

"There's also the question of who will be Viscount," Taelya added, "because from what we could tell, none of his sons were in the palace." She took another swallow of ale.

"Don't you think you've made matters worse?"

"They couldn't have been worse. He planned to attack Montgren anyway."

"She's right about that, Majer," said Gustaan.

"It won't make our getting home any easier," said Zekkarat.

"It likely won't make it any harder, either," replied Gustaan.

Zekkarat frowned.

Gustaan smiled cheerfully.

"Do you have any more questions, ser?" asked Taelya. "If not, I'd like to get some sleep. I'm sure we'll be leaving early tomorrow."

"Did anyone see you?"

"Anyone we ran into in the palace is dead." Taelya didn't like explaining about the ostler, and it wouldn't have made any difference in any event. "We were under concealments when we were near the palace and the city gates. It's very unlikely that anyone will know who did it, except from the message I left. And what would have been the point of not leaving the message?" Taelya couldn't stop herself from yawning.

"I think just about everyone would still have known a mage from Fairhaven killed the Viscount, even if you hadn't left a message," said Zekkarat almost sourly. "For the moment, however, I'd appreciate it if you'd keep what you did among the four of us. At least, until we're back in Montgren." He turned to Gustaan. "I'd appreciate your conveying that to Undercaptain Kaeryla."

"I'll take care of that, ser."

Zekkarat returned his attention to Taelya. "Get some sleep. We will be leaving early."

"Do you want anything to eat?" asked Gustaan, standing from the table.

"No, ser. The ale was enough."

"Then I'll show you where the officers are sleeping."

For a moment, Taelya wondered why he was being so solicitous, before she realized he had something to say, something he didn't want Zekkarat to hear. So she said, "I really appreciate that."

Gustaan picked up her gear. "I'll give you a hand with that."

Once they were well away from the common room, Gustaan looked at Taelya. "You've got guts to go with that ability. Your father would be so demon-proud of you. Just screw Zekkarat."

Taelya could feel the tears, but she swallowed and managed to say, "There wasn't any other way."

"No . . . there wasn't. Zekkarat will see that sooner or later. Likely he already does, but doesn't want to admit it. One other thing, the little redheaded mage, she was really worried about both of you. You might want to spend a few moments with her in the morning." Then he pointed to the door ahead. "Go get some sleep. I'll make sure Kaeryla's here shortly, and I'll tell her what the majer said."

Taelya just nodded. She didn't want to try to speak as she and Gustaan walked to the door, and he opened it and handed her the gear. She took it and stepped inside, careful not to wake any of the officers stretched out there.

She didn't even know whether Gustaan closed the door.

LXII

Sometime before dawn, Taelya woke with Kaeryla gently shaking her.

"We need to get up and eat. You especially. Gustaan told me you didn't eat anything last night."

Taelya tried to speak, but found her lips and mouth were so dry that her voice was more like a croak as she said, "I drank some ale last night. I was too tired to eat. I'm not as strong as you."

"You're not as strong as I am?" Kaeryla sounded incredulous. "You're full of . . ."

"Were you going to say 'sowshit'?"

"That's what I thought. Now . . . we do need to eat, and you need to make sure you have ale in all your water bottles."

Regardless of what Kaeryla thought, every muscle in Taelya's body either hurt, ached, or was sore. At least, that was the way she felt as she struggled to her feet and walked with the younger mage toward the common room where everyone was eating. The two sat on a bench at the end of the officers' table, across from Sheralt and Valchar.

"When did you two finally get here?" asked Valchar.

"Late," replied Taelya. "After midnight."

"Why were you so late?" pressed Valchar.

"Because it took longer," said Taelya.

A trace of an amused smile appeared on Sheralt's face.

"What took longer?"

"What we did," replied Taelya, taking a bite of the cheese on the tin platter in front of her, followed by a mouthful of bread. She decided to save the small amount of dried fruit and salted nuts until the end.

Valchar looked in exasperation at Kaeryla. "Can you tell me what it was that took so long?"

"What we did took longer, just as Taelya told you."

Taelya smiled as she saw Sheralt's broad grin.

Valchar looked to Sheralt. "Why are you grinning?"

"Because I told you before that they could answer forever without lying and without telling you anything." Sheralt looked at Taelya. "I take it that you've been ordered to say nothing."

"We have."

"What could you have—"

"That's enough, Valchar," said Sheralt. "All you'll do is make everyone uncomfortable, and we don't need that."

Taelya had to admit that she was relieved that she didn't have to speak first, but she did say, "That's right, unfortunately. Please leave it at that."

Kaeryla looked at Valchar and said warmly, but firmly, "I'd really appreciate that, too."

Abruptly, Valchar shook his head, then smiled and said, "You'll tell us when you can?"

"We will," said Kaeryla.

As she ate, Taelya discovered that she was much hungrier than she'd thought, and she even had more of the strong cheese and the crunchy and stale trail bread, which was still far better than hardtack. She did save the dried fruit, of which there were no extra servings, until the last.

Then, after she'd eaten, gotten her gear, and made sure her water bottles were filled with ale, she and Kaeryla were starting to walk to the corral when she sensed someone hurrying toward them. After turning and seeing Annana, she stopped and waited, as did Kaeryla.

"You're back! You didn't tell us you wouldn't be here last night."

"We couldn't," replied Taelya. "We had to make sure that no one could report to the Viscount that we're riding back to Montgren and Fairhaven. By the time we finished, it was very late, and it took us time to catch up."

Annana looked at her directly. "You're not telling everything."

Taelya glanced to Kaeryla, who was trying to hide a smile, then said, "No, I'm not. The majer asked us not to say anything more. When we get to Fairhaven, I promise you I'll tell you everything."

Annana looked to Kaeryla. "Is she telling the truth?"

"She is."

"Will you tell me anything she leaves out?"

"I will."

"And I'll tell you anything Kaeryla leaves out," added Taelya.

"Good. Will you keep teaching us while we ride?"

"As we can," said Kaeryla. "But now you need to get ready to ride."

"We're already ready. Remember, you promised to keep teaching us."

As Annana hurried toward her mother and Sydel, Taelya turned to the younger mage. "I wonder how long that will last."

"It lasted with you, didn't it?" said Kaeryla gently.

Taelya nodded, not wanting to say more, and the two resumed walking to the corral, where Taelya began to saddle Bounder in the dim light before dawn.

At that moment, Gustaan appeared. "Third Squad will be leading this morning, and Majer Zekkarat will be riding with you."

"Can you tell if he's still angry?"

"More worried, I'd say. I don't think he wants to be the one to tell Korsaen or the Duchess."

"We need to worry about getting out of Certis first. Then we need to worry about Fairhaven and Hydlen. The Duchess can wait."

"I don't know whether you sound more like your mother or Majer Beltur."

"I'll take the compliment," said Taelya tersely, as she tightened the saddle cinches, then mounted. Once in the saddle she looked for and found Varais, then rode toward the squad leader.

"Ser, orders for the day?"

"Third Squad will ride as vanguard, accompanied personally by Majer Zekkarat."

"Sounds like the majer wants us on a tight rein, ser."

"I can't imagine why."

"I still think it was the right thing to do, ser. Everyone in Certis knows he was a complete bastard. Even the Certan rankers were scared to say a word about him." Varais shook her head. "Don't see why the Duchess ever let herself get talked into this mess."

"Fifteen battalions might have something to do with it. Everyone in the squad knows they're not to say anything until we're back in Montgren?"

"Yes, ser. Captain Gustaan told me that as well."

That didn't surprise Taelya.

"We need to form up, ser. I see the majer heading toward the corral."

"Do it."

"Third Squad! Form up!"

Once the squad was formed up, Taelya and Kaeryla led the troopers to the end of the short lane where it joined the main road, in order to allow the Montgren companies and Second Squad to form up behind them.

In less than a third of a quint, Zekkarat rode up. "Move out, Undercaptain." After those words, he eased his mount up beside Taelya and Bounder, and gestured for Kaeryla to fall back.

"Third Squad! Forward!"

Zekkarat said nothing for a good quint.

Taelya could outwait him. She'd learned to wait a long time ago . . . if she thought it necessary.

Finally, the majer spoke. "You must know I'm not pleased with what you did last night. You set matters up so you could do what you planned."

"I did," Taelya admitted. "I did it that way so that I didn't expressly go against any orders."

Zekkarat offered a low and skeptical laugh. "Would orders have stopped you?"

"Most likely not, but this way, you don't have to admit that you couldn't control your officers."

For a moment, Zekkarat didn't speak, and Taelya sensed that her words had definitely angered him. Again, she just waited.

Finally, he said, "Did you ever think about the risk you subjected your squad to?"

"I did, ser. That's why they only guarded the road. Undercaptain Kaeryla and I were the only ones who entered the palace. Squad Leader Varais was ordered to return to your command if we didn't succeed."

"And what if you had been caught and killed? The loss of two mages would have been significant. Did you think about that?"

"I did. But two mages wouldn't make enough of a difference against ten battalions. The Viscount could easily send that many, and still have five or more in reserve. Also, he isn't that well liked. So there's a good possibility that whoever succeeds him would have trouble getting people outraged over his death, especially since the Prefect of Gallos may prove rather difficult after being double-crossed."

"You can't count on that."

"No, ser. But none of us could count on the Viscount not attacking Montgren and Fairhaven after what he's already done." She paused, then added, "Do you really think we could? Honestly?"

"I'm beginning to understand completely why no one wants powerful mages in positions of even limited power."

You mean, in places where we have the ability not to do stupid things or where we can do what needs to be done when no one else wants to admit it? Taelya decided against saying that. Instead, she merely said, "Yes, ser."

"If we get through all this," Zekkarat said thoughtfully, "you'll most likely be the one to succeed Majer Beltur. How would you deal with a niece or nephew who did what you just did?"

While Taelya was stunned by Zekkarat's prediction, and couldn't help but think it was just designed to put her off guard, she only hesitated a moment, if a long moment, before replying, "I think I'd see how matters turned out first."

"As will I," said Zekkarat. "I have my doubts, but I do hope your understanding of the situation is more accurate than mine." Then he nodded. "That's all I had to say. We'll exchange rear guard and vanguard at noon." With those words, he eased his mount toward the shoulder of the road, in order to drop back to the head of the Montgren forces.

Taelya also hoped she'd comprehended the situation accurately. *Because if you haven't . . .* Then she shook her head. It didn't matter. What was done was done.

LXIII

The next three days passed tiringly, but uneventfully, and the Certan squads maintaining the way stations said little and largely stayed out of sight, either because they didn't want to contest the use of the way station or because Zekkarat had been persuasive. Still, by threeday, Taelya was wondering if it might all be an entrapment, if somehow Akkyld or the head marshal in Jellico . . . or someone . . . had sent messengers to inform everyone and to let the Montgren forces reach the gorge—where there was no place else to go, except on a bridge too narrow to allow a quick withdrawal—where they would then attack when the Montgren forces would be essentially trapped.

She kept telling herself that was fanciful, and unlikely, but she still worried. And certainly an alliance between Certis and Gallos, however temporary, had been most unlikely, but it had happened.

One thing that also didn't change was Annana's insistence on being taught, unlike Sydel, who was often slightly sulky about it, at least until Annana pointed out that if he didn't become a strong black she could order him around. Both Taelya and Kaeryla had trouble concealing their amusement when that occurred.

On fourday, they reached the last way station before Orduna, which meant they only had a very long day's ride to the Montgren Gorge, and Kaeryla and Taelya had both assured Zekkarat that only about a squad of Certans were posted there. Unlike their reception at other way stations, the senior squad leader in charge of the station walked out to meet Zekkarat, but before the majer could even speak, the squad leader asked, "Ser, didn't you come through here headed west about a half season back? We heard you'd be in Passera for the summer, maybe longer."

"We thought the same thing," said Zekkarat wryly. "It didn't turn out that way. We took the east half of the town for him and destroyed all the mages who were giving him trouble. That's what we were asked to do, and it's what we did. He didn't have any more use for us, and the Viscount didn't want to feed us any longer. So we headed back home. And we'll be definitely glad to get there."

Taelya admired the way Zekkarat had said it, because every word was factually correct.

"Ser, the two companies that passed through here yesterday didn't say anything about that. The majer just said that, so far as he knew, fighting was still going on around Passera."

"That could be true. Submarshal Akkyld still has three battalions there.

Whether they keep fighting is up to the submarshal and the Viscount. By the way, where did those companies come from?" asked Zekkarat. "The other way stations haven't mentioned them."

"They came from the north. The majer said they'd been there since spring. There were some problems with mountain raiders."

Zekkarat nodded. "That would explain it. I hope you got at least some fodder for our mounts."

"We've got that, ser. Might be tight on some of the rations."

"We'll work it out."

Taelya kept a pleasant expression on her face. Two companies they could handle . . . if they had to, but there was no way of telling how many other companies might be mustered at Orduna, and that suggested that the Viscount might have considered an immediate invasion of Montgren . . . or at least setting up a force if opportunity presented itself.

Once they'd ridden away from the squad leader, Zekkarat asked, "What do you think about two companies headed to Orduna . . . and possibly Montgren?"

"Two companies aren't enough for an attack on Montgren. There either have to be more companies there or the Viscount has just begun to build up forces. He also might have been placing forces there just in case we'd been totally wiped out in Passera. Those companies had to have been dispatched before he could have known what happened."

"So what would you do in my position?"

"Set up an encampment short of Orduna; scout under concealments to determine what Certan forces are where and what side trails we could take to avoid riding past the post; and then rise well before dawn and use those trails and the road to get to the bridge."

"And once we get across . . . then what?"

"Disassemble the bridge . . . or burn it."

"That won't set well with the traders or the Duchess."

"Losing her lands and possibly her life would upset her more, I'd think. But disassembling the bridge would be better, because that way . . ."

"I'd agree with that, but the officer in charge of the bridge detachment might not."

"You have four mages, ser."

"I'm very well aware of that, Undercaptain. Let's just see what we find out. As you pointed out, two companies don't constitute a problem."

"Yes, ser." Taelya doubted that there were only two companies in Orduna, but there was little point in saying more until they knew.

LXIV

By second glass on fiveday, Taelya had the feeling that they were nearing Orduna, a feeling confirmed by a kaystone indicating that the town lay ten kays ahead. Given the low incline a little over a kay away, as she recalled, the poor town could likely be seen from the top of the rise, although there were other dips and rises until they reached a point two or three kays from the outlying houses. She wasn't surprised when the majer called a halt to rest men and mounts and then rode up to her and Kaeryla.

"You two need to go scout and find out what you can, especially how many troopers are there and someplace closer to Orduna where we can camp without being noticed. The two of you, I'm quite certain, can deal with any small groups, but I'd prefer you not be seen."

"We should be able to manage that, ser," replied Taelya.

"And try not to take as long as last time." Zekkarat's words were spoken gently.

"It will take a while, ser. We'll have to get within two or three kays of the Certan post. Doing it under a concealment will take longer."

"I understand. I look forward to hearing what you discover."

After Zekkarat turned his mount and rode back toward the Montgren companies, Taelya turned to Varais. "You have the squad."

"Yes, ser."

Moments later, Taelya and Kaeryla were riding east under the hot afternoon light of the white sun.

"He sent us out alone," said Kaeryla. "He's never done that before."

"He worries about what else we could do."

"We'll have to fight more when we get back to Fairhaven, won't we?"

"I'd be very surprised if it were otherwise. I suspect Beltur attacked the Hydlenese in their own territory. That way he could have taken them more by surprise. Also, that part of Hydlen is barren and doesn't have that many people."

Kaeryla nodded, then asked, "How do you want to scout?"

"Take the road as close to Orduna as we can without running into anyone, but not using concealments except in those places where we could be seen from the town or the post."

A quint later, they neared the rise from which they could most likely see Orduna.

"I don't sense anyone on the road ahead, do you?" asked Taelya.

"Not yet."

"Then we'll keep going on the road. It's faster. Just before we get to the top, we'll do concealments, because that's where anyone who's looking will focus."

As they neared the top of the rise, Taelya concentrated on possible camp sites, but all she could see or sense nearby consisted of rocky outcroppings with scraggly bushes.

Once they reached the top of the rise, as she started down the gentle slope on the other side, Taelya tried to sense anything living within the range of her capabilities—and found various small animals, some goats, but no people. "Now that we're not outlined against the sky, I'm going to drop my concealment for a moment. I'd like to see the post for a little bit, in case something stands out."

She looked at the post, but it didn't appear any different from the last time, and she couldn't make out large numbers of horses or wagons that might indicate a battalion being there, but she was too far away to make out anything clearly enough to be certain. Then she replaced the concealment. "It doesn't look like they've got battalions there, but we'll have to get closer to be sure."

Once they neared the west end of the town, Taelya led the way onto a side street on the north side of the main road, then reined up, well away from any dwellings, but still under a concealment. "See what you can sense."

While Kaeryla concentrated on the Certan post, Taelya focused on the area around them, and then on each side of the town. Especially on the north side of the town, there seemed to be little in the way of promising sites for an encampment. Then she concentrated on the Certan post. When she finished, she said quietly, "What do you think?"

"Three companies, but there are a lot of supply wagons there. Far more than they need for three companies."

"So it looks like they're expecting more companies?"

"Or they plan on those companies staying here for a good long time."

And neither possibility looks that good for Montgren or Fairhaven. "There aren't any suitable encampment sites anywhere to the north. So we'll need to investigate the south side of town. We need to find an encampment site and, if one exists, a side road that will keep us from getting too close to the way station and inns where the Certans are."

Finding a side road was easier than an encampment site. In the end, the best encampment location wasn't all that much closer to Orduna than where Zekkarat had called a halt, just short of the rise in the road and a quarter kay to the south where there was a small stream.

They reported that to Zekkarat first.

"What about the Certans at the post?"

Kaeryla told him.

"Three companies and lots of supply wagons. That sounds like they're setting up for an attack on Montgren over the gorge bridge. There's no other reason. They're also likely keeping those forces at Orduna so that the Montgren bridge guards don't know that they're building up forces."

"Could they be waiting to see if the Hydlenese are successful in invading southern Montgren and Fairhaven?" asked Taelya. "So that they can claim the best remaining parts of Montgren?"

The majer nodded. "That's also possible. I'd like to think that they wouldn't attack immediately, if at all, but we can't count on that, not the way things have gone. It's even more important that we get back without any more fighting, because we'll need every man we can muster. Thank you both."

Another glass passed before the companies and squads were settled into the less than comfortable site, although Taelya had to admit that it was far better than the chilly mountain valleys where they had bivouacked.

Then Taelya and Kaeryla summoned the twins and began their evening instruction. The first thing was the study of how the two were keeping their order and chaos structured.

"You're both doing somewhat better at keeping your order and chaos in the right places," said Kaeryla. "Now, Annana, show me how you're coming with your shields."

"Why are you making us work so hard on shields? Why don't you let me work on chaos?" demanded Annana, turning from Kaeryla to Taelya. "Didn't you work on chaos when you were my age?"

"I did," replied Taelya, "but not much, and I'd been working on shields for three years by then."

"You could work magery when you were seven?" asked Ysabella.

"I had to. There wasn't anyone else to protect my mother when my father, my uncle, and my aunt were all fighting the Hydlenese. My shields weren't that good but they could stop a blade and maybe one chaos bolt. Just like we're teaching you, I had to learn to put order into my shields. Kaeryla, on the other hand, had to learn to include chaos in her shields, the way we're trying to get you to do, Sydel."

"I still don't see what use order is except for defending," said Sydel sulkily.

"When she fought the Hydlenese," said Kaeryla coldly, "my mother destroyed almost an entire company by herself using shields. My father destroyed an entire battalion. They're both blacks."

"Order and chaos are both forces, and they can be tools," said Taelya. "That's what we're trying to teach you. Now . . . Annana, you need to get back to building that small shield, using tiny bits of order to hold the chaos together." *As I've told you at least a score of times.*

"And you, Sydel, need to do the same thing except you use tiny bits of chaos, but let the order hold them," explained Kaeryla.

"When do we get to do more?" asked Annana.

"When your shields are strong enough to protect you from your own mistakes, and, eventually, from other mages," replied Taelya, wondering, far from the first time, at how Beltur had ever managed to put up with her questions.

LXV

Although the ground under her blankets was hard, Taelya had a difficult time waking up and had to force herself to get moving and to eat yet another breakfast of cold rations and water, since they'd long since finished off the limited supplies of ale. Even so, she, Kaeryla, Varais, and Third Squad were ready when Zekkarat gave the order to move out in the darkness before dawn.

The sky was turning from black violet to greenish violet when Taelya led Third Squad off the side road and back onto the main road just east of Orduna. As far as she could sense, there was no change in the order and chaos levels at the Certan way station. Nor was there when she and Kaeryla had ridden far enough east that they could no longer sense the Certans. Before that long, they were riding straight into the rising sun, and, for a time, Taelya was relying on her senses more than sight because if she pulled her visor cap down far enough to block the sun, she couldn't see anything in front of her.

The sun was just high enough that she could see the road ahead when the Certan border post came into view, about two kays ahead—and when Zekkarat rode up beside her.

"Undercaptains . . . we need to get across that bridge quickly. Is anyone following us?"

"Not within three kays, ser," replied Taelya.

"I've given orders to Second Squad to stop, however they can, any messengers from the border post heading toward Orduna. Likewise, if the Certans try to delay or block us, we will take whatever steps necessary to keep our forces moving across the bridge. Once Second Squad is across, have your squad keep moving so that the others aren't slowed, but you two remain in front of the border post gates. Mounted."

"Yes, ser."

"I'll stay in the fore with you. We'll try politeness, first. But be ready to use force if the Certan border guards turn out to be as treacherous as the Viscount . . . or just plain stupidly stubborn. Take out the officers and squad leaders first, and anyone who might run to block the bridge or damage it before we cross. Let me know if you sense anything I should know."

"We can do that."

When Third Squad was a little less than a kay from the border post, Kaeryla said, "There's a certain amount of chaos at the post. They might be mounting up or posting archers on the walls."

"Those walls aren't even three yards high," said Taelya.

"That's high enough to shoot down on us," replied Zekkarat.

As Third Squad approached the border post, some fifty yards west of the narrow timbered bridge that spanned the gorge, Taelya could sense troopers on the walls. Then an officer, a captain, stepped out followed by five men bearing crossbows. The captain stood waiting.

Zekkarat rode a bit forward of Third Squad.

"Ser . . . the bridge isn't open. We need to do some work on it," said the undercaptain.

"He's lying," said Kaeryla.

"One of my mages says you're lying. Do you want to try again, Captain?" asked Zekkarat.

"I have orders not to let any armed force cross the bridge."

"Considering that we're headed home, I'd say that doesn't apply, Captain."

"Those are my orders, ser."

"My orders are for me to get home. Now. If you or your men take a single step to impede us, you will be turned to ashes on the spot, and every single one of your men will be slaughtered. My mages can shield my force against arrows. Do you really want to block the bridge?"

Taelya murmured to Kaeryla. "The post isn't that big. What about dropping a concealment over it? Then his archers couldn't see."

"I could do a shield and a concealment at first, then drop the shield once they're disconcerted," Kaeryla returned in a low voice.

"I'll take out everyone outside the post, if it comes to that," said Zekkarat.

"I have no choice, ser."

"Yes, you do. At the least you could save your men."

"I have my orders, ser."

"Do you really want to die?"

"I have no choice, ser."

"I'm truly sorry for your stupidity, Captain. Mages."

Instantly, the border post seemed to vanish.

At that instant, Taelya fired off a chaos bolt big enough to take out the captain and the five men behind him. Then she turned to Zekkarat. "You lead them across, ser. We need to stay here and make sure the archers don't get anyone." Then she addressed Varais. "One mount at a time, two yards between them. Forward."

Taelya moved to the side of the road closest to the post, ready to use chaos if any Certan trooper was smart and stupid enough to charge out of the post gates, asking Kaeryla, "Can you hold both of them for a while?"

"This is a lot easier than what we did in Passera."

Abruptly a trooper appeared outside the concealment.

Taelya used a narrow chaos bolt to the man's chest. His scream was satisfactory.

Over the course of the glass it took the two companies and two squads to cross, Taelya killed three more Certan troopers.

Then, when Valchar and Sheralt approached, bringing up the rear guard, the two of them the last of the force, Taelya asked, "Did they try to send a messenger?"

"They tried even before you reached the post," said Valchar. "Sheralt took care of him."

"All right," said Taelya. "You and Kaeryla first. Kaeryla, can you hold the concealment and shields until you're on the bridge?"

"If we're leaving now . . . yes." The strain in the younger mage's voice said that she wouldn't be able to hold either much longer.

"Go!" Taelya turned to Sheralt. "Once she lifts the shields and concealment, we need to drop two large chaos bolts into the middle of their post. Then we'll cross the bridge under shields, just in case someone still has shafts or a crossbow."

"Crossbows?"

"There were five of them aimed at the majer. It didn't do any good. Now, let's move a little closer to the bridge."

The two chaos mages were about thirty yards from the bridge when the Certan border post "reappeared." Moments after that Sheralt lofted a large chaos bolt into the middle of the border post. Taelya's chaos bolt was more modest. She had the feeling that they weren't done yet. Then they turned and trotted toward the bridge. As it had been the first time she had crossed the gorge, Taelya had to keep her eyes on the bridge roadway and the far side.

When she and Sheralt reined up outside the Montgren border post, they found Zekkarat looking down from his mount at an undercaptain, presumably the officer in charge of the post and the bridge.

"Can you remove the bridge?" asked the majer.

"Not without orders from the Duchess, ser."

Zekkarat turned to Taelya. "Can you burn it down?"

"I could, but Sheralt could do a better job of it." Taelya looked to the west, impelled by a vague feeling of unease.

Zekkarat turned to the weathered undercaptain. "You either remove it, immediately, or I'll order it burned."

"Ser . . . it'll take glasses . . . maybe days . . ."

"Then you'd better start, and you'd better hurry, because if any Certan troopers arrive before you finish, we'll have to burn it. The mages will take out anyone who tries to interfere."

"It doesn't matter," said Taelya tiredly, turning back to the two. "There's a dust cloud on the road from Orduna."

"Get out the oils!" snapped Zekkarat.

"The oils?"

"The ones you keep just in case Certis tries to invade. They're about to make that attempt."

The undercaptain looked west at the rising trail of dust. "Bridge-burning procedures! Now!"

The Certan column that looked to comprise at least two and possibly three companies was less than a kay away when the last of the oils were spread on the bridge and Taelya and Sheralt sprinkled the bridge with small bits of chaos-fire. By the time the Certans reached the bridge it was an inferno. Even so, a squad started to ride through the flames.

"I'll take the ones on the right! You take the ones on the left!" Taelya called out, following up on her command with tight chaos bolts, one after the other.

After the first riders and mounts went down in chaos flame, the Certans reined up and waited.

So did Taelya and Sheralt, and fortified by the ale Zekkar had brought to them from the border post, more than a glass later, they used chaos to remove the remaining charred timbers. By that time, some of the Certan troopers were dealing with the few survivors of the chaos-fire that Sheralt and Taelya had dropped into the middle of the border post.

As Zekkarat ordered his force to prepare to depart, the still-stunned Montgren undercaptain appeared once more. "Ser . . . how will I explain this?"

"Undercaptain . . . you don't have to. I do. Just report that I overruled you, and considering that I had two companies and four mages, you accepted my orders. You might also point out that we barely rendered the bridge impassable before three companies of Certan troopers arrived."

"Yes, sir. It's just . . . ser . . . that nothing like this has ever happened. I just can't believe that . . ."

"There's a lot that's just happened that hasn't ever happened before. All we can do is our best." Zekkarat looked at the mages. "You all had a little rest. We can still make Weevett by sunset . . . or close enough."

LXVI

Zekkarat had been a shade optimistic. Sheralt and Valchar led Second Squad into the Weevett post half a glass past sunset on sixday. After Taelya dealt with the squad and Bounder, she wanted a decent meal and a chance to wash up. She didn't much care in what order she got them.

She got neither. Zekkarat summoned all officers to the duty room of the post. Valchar was the last to arrive, but only by moments.

Then Zekkarat turned to the Montgren undercaptain, presumably the duty officer. "Tell all the other officers what you just told me. Don't leave anything out. A few more details would also be helpful. Start at the beginning."

"Two eightdays ago, Lord Korsaen died of a wasting illness. There were no healers anywhere near. A little more than an eightday ago, Lady Maeyora was thrown from her horse while riding on her lands and died on the spot—"

"You forgot Commander Raelf," said Zekkarat. "And Duchess Korlyssa."

"Ser, they both died of old age back in late spring."

"It's still part of what happened, and some of that won't make sense without mentioning those deaths. Go on," prodded Zekkarat.

Taelya was afraid she could see exactly where the story was going, and it was absolutely chilling. Although everyone had expected the death of the old Duchess, even earlier than it had occurred, and Commander Raelf had been frail, the other deaths were definitely less than coincidental, particularly Maeyora's demise.

"Fifteen days ago, two eightdays past, Duchess Koralya named Lord Korwaen as her Lord Protector . . ."

Taelya couldn't help but wince. Korwaen was only two years older than she was, and while he'd been perfectly proper around her, that was after she'd put him in his place the first time they'd met. Despite his behavior since then on the two times they'd crossed paths, she'd always felt he was a smarmy bully at heart.

". . . then ten days ago, she sent a dispatch, ordering that the bridge over the Montgren Gorge be kept open at all costs."

"And what did you do, Undercaptain?"

"I . . . kept the dispatch. I didn't show it to anyone. It was against all standing orders. There isn't a single captain left in Montgren, and you're the only majer in all the Montgren forces, and the senior officer." The trooper looked at the mages. "Well . . . excepting Majer Beltur, but he wasn't in Montgren, either."

"You're a very brave man, Undercaptain, and also a very smart one," said Zekkarat. "You just might have saved Montgren. Are there any Montgren companies left in Montgren proper?"

"Only Fifth Company. That's the training company, and it only has two squads because the Duchess cut the pay for recruits. We have two squads here. One is at the gorge bridge and alternates with the squad here. You have two companies, and there are two companies supporting Majer Beltur."

Taelya addressed the duty undercaptain. "What have you heard about the fighting south of Fairhaven?"

"The latest word is that when Majer Beltur defeated the Hydlenese forces in the first battles, the Prefect's forces took over Hydolar and moved in two more battalions to reinforce the Hydlenese. Those battalions hadn't reached Majer Beltur's forces two days ago. That was the last dispatch we received from them. I didn't send that to the palace."

Zekkarat nodded, but he looked anything but happy at that news. "I don't think we have too many choices. Maakym, you have fewer troopers right now. I'm breveting you to captain. You're going to have to go back to the gorge. With the squad that's there and the squad that's here, you'll have more than a company. We'll just have to close the Weevett post for the time being. You should be able to hold off the Certans . . . if we can provide a little help." He turned to Sheralt. "I can't order you, but if you stay with Maakym's company, I think we can hold the gorge. We need a chaos mage who can burn any timbers they could use, and you seem to be good with the larger bursts."

"And Taelya's better in combat," said Sheralt. "It makes sense, and if the Certans cross the gorge now, Fairhaven's trapped."

"Good. And I thank you more than you may know. The rest of us will leave for Fairhaven at dawn." Zekkarat turned to the duty undercaptain. "Do we have any wagons left? Or are there enough stores left here to need wagons?"

"There are provisions here, ser. One old wagon and one cart."

"Then use the cart to supply the gorge post, along with some of our packhorses. We'll take the wagon. It can probably get to Fairhaven. You're now under Captain Maakym's command."

"Yes, ser."

Zekkarat surveyed the officers. "Are there any questions?"

"Ser . . ." began Maakym, "what do I do if I get orders to open the gorge to the Certans?"

Zekkarat grinned, an expression more like that of a hungry mountain cat. "Since no one in the chain of command is going to issue those orders, they could only come from the Duchess or Undercaptain Haaskyn, who's in charge of the training company. You now outrank Haaskyn, but I doubt that he'd be willing to carry such orders to you, especially given his age. Duchess Koralya won't go to the gorge to find you. So that leaves young Lord Korwaen, possibly escorted by some troopers from the training company. You're to ignore any orders to open the gorge unless they're delivered by me or Majer Beltur in person. If Korwaen or anyone else persists and won't leave you alone, lock them up, at least until you find out what happens in the south. Then, with the Weevett post being closed, they might have trouble locating you, and they just might not want to travel to the gorge. And if Lord Korwaen inadvertently got too close to a chaos bolt, that would be just one of those unfortunate misunderstandings that occur in war."

Sheralt nodded.

That might take care of Korwaen, but Taelya still wondered if other toadies now surrounded Koralya.

"Also, with three more mages, two squads, and another company, we just might be able to thwart the Prefect and stop the Hydlenese problem for a while. Think about it. We can talk more at dinner. That's all for now."

Because the joint force's arrival was unexpected, dinner was rather late, and that did finally give Taelya and Kaeryla a chance to wash up thoroughly for the first time in days. There wasn't much they could do about their uniforms except shake out all the dust and use a damp cloth to get rid of the worst of the dirt and stains. Then Taelya rounded up Ysabella and the twins, and all of them joined the others at the small officers' mess.

"Why are we with the officers?" asked Ysabella.

"You're in Montgren," replied Taelya, "and if Annana and Sydel learn to become effective mages, having been around mage-guards and officers will make things easier for them in the future. That's if they behave."

Taelya and Kaeryla put them around the foot of the table, with one mage on each side, but no one, including Zekkarat, said a word. Taelya made sure the ale served to the twins was watered.

As they waited for the servers to bring dinner, Sydel asked, "How much longer will we be riding?"

"One day," replied Kaeryla. "Not even a full day, either."

"Where will we stay?" asked Ysabella.

"We'll have to see," replied Taelya.

"Most likely our house," said Kaeryla. "As I understood it, Arthaal's the only one there. Father said that he and Dorylt could do more good as Road Guards than in combat."

"You two are fighting and men are not?" asked Ysabella.

"Dorylt's fifteen, and his shields weren't strong enough to stand up to an adult white mage. Arthaal is barely fourteen. They're strong enough to deal with brigands, and that leaves Fairhaven protected from those sorts of people."

"They'd just be killed and wasted in that sort of fight," added Kaeryla. "We try to train mages to be as strong as they can be."

"Sometimes," added Sheralt in a warm and humorous tone from where he sat across the table from Taelya, "even if it takes . . . forceful persuasion."

"With some," said Valchar, "gentler persuasion works better." He glanced briefly at Kaeryla, who avoided looking back.

At that moment, Montgren troopers arrived with large platters. The dinner was anything but spectacular, basically a heap of noodles and salted mutton that had been soaked briefly to remove as much salt as possible, with a brown gravy slathered over everything, accompanied by baskets of skillet bread. Even so, it looked to be the best meal Taelya had eaten since the reception at the Viscount's palace. She'd only taken a few bites and a healthy swallow of ale when Ferek spoke.

"The Duchess has to be making a secret deal with the Viscount. Nothing else makes sense. But why?"

Because she's afraid Fairhaven will come to dominate Montgren. Taelya did not offer that thought, but just waited to see what others might say.

"Undercaptain Chaarkyn said she cut the pay of recruits," offered Maakym. "Is Montgren short of golds?" He looked to Zekkarat.

"That, I don't know. I do know that Duchess Korlyssa and Lord Korsaen were concerned for some time that Koralya's . . . tastes . . . were in excess of the tariffs that a land of sheepherders could support. Lord Korsaen and Lady Maeyora never took a single copper from the Duchess, either duchess."

Taelya decided to add one piece of information. "Every year for the last ten years, Fairhaven has increased its tariff payments to the Duchess."

"How do you know that?" asked Ferek.

"My mother is the town treasurer."

"So even with more golds . . ." Maakym shook his head. "But why would she agree to something that would destroy Fairhaven when it's been bringing in more golds. Couldn't she have asked for higher tariffs?"

"So she could have more luxuries?" snapped Kaeryla. "We've had to sweat blood to build Fairhaven. We've had to protect it from brigands and the Hydlenese. No other town in Montgren has to do that."

"Undercaptain Kaeryla makes a very good point," said Zekkarat calmly. "There's also the point that Fairhaven's charter limits tariffs to the same rates as every other town."

"So she'd sell Fairhaven down the river for some more fancy gowns and the like?" said Maakym. "How does trying to let the Prefect take over Fairhaven, and the Viscount take over the rest of Montgren, get her what she wants?"

"The Prefect would likely get at least part of Hydlen and the trade going through Fairhaven, and the Viscount could take over Lydiar from Montgren . . . and Lydiar is a very rich port," replied Zekkarat. "If there is such a hidden agreement, and we have no way of knowing that, it likely stipulates that Koralya would remain the titular ruler of Montgren with an additional stipend from the Viscount. If so, Koralya wouldn't have taken it on faith. She would have had to have received a considerable amount of golds."

"Which the Viscount would have taken back as soon as he was in Vergren," said Kaeryla acidly.

"Of course," said Zekkarat. "For the moment, however, all that is speculation. It would best not be mentioned elsewhere. I'll be *very unhappy* if it is."

Maakym swallowed. "Yes, ser."

"Now," continued Zekkarat, "it might be best to move on to less unpleasant subjects."

For several moments, there was silence at the table.

"You have never said much about Fairhaven," ventured Ysabella. "What is it like?"

"It's smaller than Passera," began Taelya, "but it's been growing every year . . ." The rest of the dinner conversation was similarly innocuous.

After dinner, Taelya walked beside Sheralt and let Kaeryla and Valchar move more and more ahead of them. Then she stopped and looked directly at him. "I'm glad you volunteered. You're protecting all of us."

He smiled. "How could I not after you took all those risks to kill the Viscount?"

"How did you know that? No one ever said a word."

"I know you. You're like Beltur and Jessyla . . . and your mother. If something needs to be done, and you can do it, and no one else can or will, then you'll do it. You were also snooping around the Viscount's palace when we were there."

"I hadn't even thought of that, then. I just wanted to know more about the palace."

"Just in case?" Sheralt raised his eyebrows.

"I thought it couldn't hurt to know more about the palace."

"You have a feel for things, and you were right. You usually are. At first . . . well, it was a little irritating. But I watched you . . . and . . . well . . . that's why I've worked so hard to rebuild my shields."

"But you're so much stronger now. I knew you would be."

"I think I just told you that you're usually right."

"But it mattered to me that you become as strong as you could be. Sometimes . . . you were a little cutting, but you're a good person, and you've become a really strong mage."

Sheralt offered an embarrassed smile. "That's the best compliment I've ever had."

"It's true. I don't think I could crush your shields the way I did before. And you had order/chaos reserves left when we crossed the river back to the east side of Passera."

"That's because Valchar and I didn't have to face the strongest mage I've ever encountered outside of Fairhaven."

"You have to take care of yourself at the gorge," Taelya said. "We need you."

Sheralt raised his eyebrows and said gently, "We?"

"I might need you. I haven't wanted to think about it. Please don't push me. Not now."

"I wouldn't think of it." But a broad smile crossed his face. "I take it back . . . what I said a moment ago. What you said then was the second-best compliment I ever got. What you just said is the best."

For some reason, Taelya didn't know what to say, and she could sense a certain turbulence in her order/chaos balance. Finally, she leaned forward and kissed him on the cheek, then said, "Until later."

Sheralt was still smiling broadly as he repeated, "Until later."

Taelya didn't want to go back to her quarters immediately. So she went to the stable and checked on Bounder, and also got him some more grain. For his sake, she was glad that the next day would be short.

When Taelya walked back into the small room she shared with Kaeryla, the younger mage looked up from where she sat on the edge of the pallet bed.

"Did I sense you kissing Sheralt?"

"Kaeryla!"

"Did you?"

"Only on the cheek."

"He'll expect more now."

"He's going to the gorge, and we're going to fight the Hydlenese and the Gallosians."

"Do you like him . . . really like him?"

"Kaeryla . . ."

"You said that before. You do. You really like him."

"Not another word." Even as she spoke Taelya knew she was blushing. "Not one."

Kaeryla grinned. "I won't say a word." But she kept grinning.

Then Taelya laughed. "I do like him. I just don't know if I like him enough to love him."

"You'll find out."

"What about you and Valchar?"

"I like him as a friend. I'm too young for it to be anything else. I don't even know what I am besides a healer and a war mage."

Taelya couldn't help wondering if Kaeryla's words applied to herself as well, despite the difference in their ages.

LXVII

At breakfast on sevenday, the officers, Ysabella, and the twins sat around the mess table in much the same arrangement as the night before. Breakfast itself was a better than decent egg and cheese scramble and some actual fresh-baked bread.

"Do you think that the Certans will still try to bridge the gorge?" asked Sheralt, looking at Taelya.

Taelya knew what he meant but wasn't saying. "We don't know what the Certans will or won't try. I personally think that they'll try to take over as many lands as they can, as long as it doesn't cost them too much."

"How would you stop them?" asked Ferek.

"Make it costly. We have more mages. They have more troopers. Against Hydlen we took out most of the officers first. You do that for a while, and officers aren't quite so enthusiastic." Except, as Taelya well knew, that hadn't worked so well against the Hydlenese because of the hold the Duke had on the officers' families, which was one reason the carnage had been so great.

"Isn't that . . . a little barbaric?"

"If you want to survive, you do what works," replied Taelya. "Right now, with the gorge bridge gone, the Certans would lose hundreds if not thousands of men trying to rebuild it. If they don't do that, they'll have to move armies north into areas where there aren't many roads and then come across rugged hills. They'd lose a lot of men. If they go south and try to go through Fairhaven they'll get into another conflict with the Prefect, and they'll run into experienced armsmages in Fairhaven. An agreement with the Duchess makes much more sense."

"Much more sense," added Zekkarat, "although we have no proof of anything. So let's leave that alone."

Only for now. Taelya waited to see what others might say.

"Couldn't they be trying to bridge the gorge now?" asked Maakym.

"That would take timbers, and bridgewrights," said Zekkarat. "There aren't many tall trees near the gorge, especially on the Certan side. If you and Sheralt get back there today, I'd guess you'll be there before they're ready to try any bridging."

"Ser . . ." ventured Maakym, "are you going to send a dispatch to the Duchess?"

"That's my decision, Maakym," Zekkarat said gently. "If anyone shows up and asks, just tell them I told you that." After a moment, he added, "I expect everyone to ride out in two quints."

In short, more eating and less talking.

Taelya immediately finished her breakfast, then made sure she filled her water bottles with ale before heading to the stable. After readying Bounder for the day's ride, Taelya left him in the stall and walked to where Sheralt was saddling his horse.

Clearly sensing her approach, he turned.

Taelya looked directly into his hazel eyes. "I just wanted a private moment to wish you well . . . and to tell you to come back safely."

"We have to be successful, or there won't be any safety. You know that."

She smiled ruefully. "Then we'll both have to be successful."

"You and Kaeryla stick together, and no mage can overcome you. Don't get separated in battle. No matter what."

They just looked at each other for another moment.

Then Sheralt took her hands in his and squeezed them gently. "I'll be back. You make sure you come back."

"I will."

"Are you two just going to stand there?" called Gustaan, not harshly, but cheerfully.

"No," Taelya replied, wrapping both arms around Sheralt and holding him tightly for a long moment, then releasing him and stepping back. "Until later."

Sheralt was smiling broadly, if with a slightly stunned expression. "You do know to surprise a man."

"Appreciate it now," said Gustaan in the same cheerful voice as he walked his mount past the two.

Moments later, Taelya and Sheralt were leading their mounts to different parts of the courtyard. While Taelya did not look back, she followed him with her senses until she mounted up and joined Third Squad. She thought she felt his sensing, if at a distance, and she appreciated both the sensing and the distance.

The Fairhaven-bound squads and company left the post first with Third Squad in the lead, followed by Ferek's company, then the single wagon, and finally Valchar and Second Squad. Zekkarat and Gustaan rode ahead of Taelya and Kaeryla, the hooves of the horses clicking on the paving stones of the road that led eastward into Weevett and to the market square.

Although sevenday was usually market day, they reached the square long before vendors usually appeared to set up, but it made Taelya think about what market day might be like in Fairhaven when they arrived. Would the square be as crowded as usual . . . or nearly empty?

By ninth glass, Taelya was all too aware that it was approaching midsummer, and that it would likely be even hotter by afternoon—unless the clouds to the northeast turned into thunderclouds, in which case the chill rain would be brief, and the air would turn even steamier after the storm passed. For better or worse, the clouds passed well to the east of the road to Fairhaven, and the day got even hotter and muggier.

Slightly after second glass, Third Squad was approaching the crossroads with the old trading road to Jellico and Fenard. Taelya nodded to herself, then declared, "There's a black mage with Road Guards, just three of them in all, waiting for us at the west kaystone. Dorylt, I think."

After a moment, Kaeryla nodded.

"You can tell from this far?" asked Zekkarat.

"Only because he's my brother. I would have known if it had been Arthaal as well. I often took care of them when they were young. If it were another mage I didn't know well, all I could say was that it was a black or white mage and how strong he or she was."

"I thought there weren't any more mages in Fairhaven," said Zekkarat.

"I mentioned them last night at dinner. I thought you heard. Dorylt's fifteen. Arthaal's barely fourteen. Their shields aren't strong enough to stand up to any true war mage." *Or they weren't when we left.* "Sending them to fight would have gotten them killed for nothing. Their shields are good enough to deal with a few brigands, and they can sense far enough to warn the town if worse trouble is coming."

"Your father didn't mention them," Zekkarat said mildly.

"You've got every mage who's capable of fighting," replied Taelya. "I wouldn't be here now if the Duchess had insisted that I had to go out and fight the Hydlenese the last time." Taelya was exaggerating, but she was irritated, especially given that Kaeryla had only turned fifteen just before they reached Jellico the first time.

"I just said that he didn't mention them. I'd also agree that he was right not to . . . especially the way things seem to be turning out."

The Duchess would hardly agree with that, since the last thing she wants is more mages in Fairhaven. "I'm sorry," said Taelya with a contriteness she didn't totally feel. "But we've paid heavily, and while Duchess Korlyssa understood that, I have the feeling that her daughter doesn't . . . or doesn't care."

"It is beginning to look that way," conceded Zekkarat, "although I'd like to know more."

"Wouldn't we all?" asked Kaeryla, a touch of acid in her voice.

"We'll find out in time, but there's not much we can do about that now," Zekkarat said. "It won't make any difference if we don't defeat the Hydlenese and the Gallosians convincingly."

And quickly. More drawn-out battles were not to Fairhaven's advantage, Taelya knew.

When Third Squad reached the crossroads and turned east toward Fairhaven, Taelya could sense that Dorylt's shields were definitely much stronger. She still wouldn't have wanted him in battle yet. *But in another year . . .* She just hoped they still weren't fighting in another year.

More than another quint passed, agonizingly slowly to Taelya before she could make out Dorylt's tall and lanky figure, wearing the Fairhaven blue of a Road Guard, and mounted and waiting in the shade on the south side of the main road into Fairhaven. Not until she was within yards of Dorylt and the two others did Taelya slow Bounder. Neither of the other two Road Guards looked all that much older than Dorylt, Taelya had to admit, and that suggested just how desperate the situation might be.

Smiling broadly at his older sister, Dorylt eased his mount forward. "Welcome back! I couldn't believe it was you when I sensed you. You're . . . so much stronger."

"So are you," Taelya replied.

"Some, I'd guess." Belatedly, Dorylt inclined his head to Zekkarat. "Welcome to Fairhaven, Majer. Majer Beltur will certainly be glad to know of your arrival. Since everyone is in Hydlen, except a handful of us, I can escort you straight to headquarters, where there should be enough space. I'll send Swaaltyn ahead to inform the Council of your arrival."

"Thank you," replied Zekkarat. "Do you know if the Gallosian reinforcements have begun an attack?"

"The latest word I heard was that they are several days away, but that was from a dispatch yesterday."

"That's better than we feared," said Taelya.

While Dorylt instructed Swaaltyn, Zekkarat turned to Taelya and said in a low voice, "Just fifteen?"

Taelya nodded.

"What was he doing before he became a Road Guard?"

"He was an apprentice cabinet maker, but we've all been trained in shields, magery, and blades since we were young."

"Somehow . . . that doesn't surprise me."

As they later passed the West Inn, Zekkarat said, "That's new since I was last here. In fact, there's quite a bit that's new. I see why the Prefect is so interested."

"Lord Korsaen and Lady Maeyora knew about all the growth and the increased tariffs to the Duchess," Taelya said evenly. "It apparently means less to her than to the Prefect."

"That's a matter to be addressed later," replied Zekkarat.

And we intend to.

Nearly a glass and a half passed before Ferek's company and the two squads reached headquarters, and since headquarters was west of the square, Taelya could only sense the vendors and customers, who seemed to number less than usual. It was another quint after that when the officers met with the three councilors still present in Fairhaven—Tulya, Taarna, and Claerk. Taelya had left Ysabella and the twins outside the meeting room guarded by two troopers.

The three councilors sat at the Council table, while the officers sat in the chairs facing the table. Tulya's eyes went from Taelya to Kaeryla, then across the rest of the officers. She frowned. "What happened to Sheralt?"

"He's with the company holding the Montgren Gorge against the Certans," replied Taelya. "We had to destroy the bridge—"

"Might I explain the entire messy story?" interjected Zekkarat. "That might save a number of questions and take less time."

"Go ahead." Tulya's voice was cool.

"You may recall that the agreement to support the Viscount against Gallos was considered less than optimal by all of us who have actually fought . . ." That was how Zekkarat began before giving a concise summary of all the events that had occurred through the betrayal by the Certan forces and the subsequent withdrawal from Passera and the approach on the return to Jellico. ". . . when we neared Jellico, Undercaptain Taelya volunteered Third Squad to cover the road from the city to the Jellicor Bridge. Given her accomplishments in essentially saving most of us at Passera and finding a way around the three Certan battalions, I had no hesitations about letting her cover the road. But since I did not witness what happened as a result, I'd prefer that she recount what happened next." Zekkarat nodded to Taelya.

"What happened next was simple, but difficult," said Taelya. "Once the main force was safely across the Jellicor Bridge, Kaeryla and I posted Third Squad where it wouldn't be noticed. Then the two of us used concealments and magery to enter the Viscount's palace. We quietly killed six guards and a white mage. Kaeryla used her order skills with locks to get us through several doors and an iron gate to the Viscount's apartments. We then woke the Viscount, and I put a small chaos bolt through his forehead so that there would be no doubt who we killed. Then I left a note saying that the same thing would happen to any other ruler who tried to attack Montgren or Fairhaven. Then we withdrew. It took us quite a while to rejoin the force."

Although Tulya maintained an even expression, Taelya thought she sensed a certain satisfaction within her mother. But then, that might have just been what she hoped.

"After that," Zekkarat went on, "we continued across Certis until we neared Orduna . . ."

He went on to describe the avoidance of the companies at Orduna and the destruction of the Certan border post, the burning of the gorge bridge, and then the return to Weevett to discover the Duchess's orders to keep the gorge bridge open. ". . . so you see that we've been deceived in quite a number of ways."

"We suspected some of that deception when we heard that Duke Maastyn had died under mysterious circumstances," replied Tulya, "and that the Gallosians declared that northern Hydlen would remain under Gallosian protection until the matter was resolved."

"There's one other matter the Council should know," Taelya said. "After we killed all the Gallosian mages in Passera, a woman fled to us and asked for sanctuary in Fairhaven, not so much for herself, but for her twin children, both of whom are beginning mages, one black, one white. Since, with Kaeryla's help, I killed their father, who would have killed us if we hadn't prevailed, this created a difficult situation. But their father had insisted, if he fell, that his children had to come to Fairhaven. We brought them."

Tulya's mouth opened, just a touch.

"Yes," was all Taelya said, ignoring the lack of comprehension on the faces of Taarna and Claerk. "What else could we do? Leave them there for the Prefect?"

"The irony . . ." Tulya shook her head, then said, "Of course, they're welcome here. Fairhaven has always been a refuge for mages from wherever they have fled so long as they accept our ways and laws." She paused, then added, "From what you two have said, you've been traveling for far too long without rest. Today is sevenday. Beltur and his forces are a day to the southwest, at Eskaad."

"Not Vaarlaan?" asked Taelya.

"No. He picked a town big enough to house and feed all the troopers," replied Tulya. "He doesn't expect the first of the Gallosian and Hydlenese forces until threeday at the earliest. I'd strongly suggest you spend tomorrow and oneday here, unless we get word otherwise. At least tomorrow."

"Some rest for mounts, mages, and men would be very good," said Zekkarat. "We hurried once we heard about the Gallosians moving into Hydlen."

Tulya turned to the other two councilors. "Do you have any questions?"

Taarna immediately asked, "How much will one company and two squads help?"

Zekkarat laughed wryly. "The four undercaptains destroyed almost a battalion of Gallosian troopers without any help from the Montgren companies. We had to leave Undercaptain Sheralt and one company to protect our flank, but the remaining three are quite able."

"You sound as though you might actually defeat the Gallosians," said Taarna.

"Nothing is certain until after the battle, and sometimes not then, but with these three, Majer Beltur, Captain Jessyla, and almost a full battalion of our own, I'd say that our chances are much, much better."

"No more questions," said Taarna.

"Then the Council meeting is over," announced Tulya.

Both Claerk and Taarna slipped out of the room quietly.

Tulya turned to Zekkarat. "I have some women working on the evening meal here at headquarters, helping the single remaining cook. For anything else, Gustaan can tell you what you need to know."

Trust Mother to make sure the food is ready. Taelya just nodded.

"Thank you." Zekkarat inclined his head, then announced, "Officers' meeting tomorrow at eighth glass."

Valchar smiled broadly before following Zekkarat, Gustaan, and the Montgren officers out, leaving Kaeryla and Taelya with Tulya.

Tulya immediately addressed her daughter. "For the moment, we'll put up the woman and her children at our house. They can have your bedroom for now. You can sleep at Jessyla and Beltur's with Kaeryla and Arthaal." She paused. "Dorylt should be able to handle anything from the young mages, shouldn't he?"

"Easily."

"You understand, I hope?"

"I created the problem, and it's also likely that Sydon betrayed Beltur, mostly likely twice, the second time being when the situation forced Kaeryla to go to Passera."

"What are their names?"

"Annana and Sydel. Ysabella is the mother. She's likely only five or six years older than I am, if that."

"Beltur said Sydon liked young women."

"I think he actually cared, at least a little, for her. Sydon told her that the great mage in Fairhaven wouldn't hold grudges against children and that Fairhaven was the only place they could be free."

Tulya shook her head. "We'll work it out. Let's collect them and go home. I already made burhka."

"How did you know?"

"Dorylt told his messenger to let me know first."

LXVIII

In the end, Tulya and Dorylt hurried home to ready dinner, while Taelya and Kaeryla gathered up Ysabella and the twins, and the five rode directly to the stable behind Kaeryla's house. As they reined up outside the stable, Taelya pointed across the street and said to Ysabella, "For right now, you three will be staying there at my mother's house."

Ysabella looked at the brick dwelling and then back at Taelya. "Where will you be staying?"

Taelya gestured to the nearer house. "Right there, with Kaeryla. That's just for the next day or so. Then we'll be leaving to fight the Gallosians and Hydlenese. Right now, though, we need to take care of the horses. After that we'll deal with gear, and get you three settled. Dinner may be a little while, but that will give everyone time to wash up."

When Kaeryla and Taelya finished with the horses, the two carried their gear to Kaeryla's house, where Kaeryla said, "I'll join you all in a bit."

Then Taelya escorted Ysabella and the twins to her house, opening the door, and gesturing for them to enter the front room.

"Just set your packs over on the wall bench," said Taelya, before calling out, "We're finally here!"

Tulya hurried out of the kitchen and immediately offered a warm smile to Ysabella, saying, "I'm Tulya, Taelya's mother," although Taelya could sense something had surprised her mother.

A puzzled expression crossed Ysabella's face. "You are the head councilor?"

"The acting head councilor. Beltur's the head councilor."

"This is a very nice house . . ."

"You expected a grand dwelling?" Tulya laughed. "We've never had the time or the golds for that. It's cool enough in summer and warm enough in winter. We have water in the kitchen and a good stove and more than enough to eat." She turned to the twins.

"This is Annana," said Taelya, "and Sydel. They're ten."

"Just make yourself comfortable here in the front room while I do a few more things in the kitchen. Dorylt will be bringing out some ale in a moment."

No sooner had Tulya departed than Dorylt appeared carrying three beakers, two only half filled. The half-filled beakers went to Annana and Sydel, who sat on each end of the padded-backed bench, and the full one to Ysabella.

"I'll be back with mine and yours," Dorylt said. "Where's Kaeryla?"

"She said she'd be here shortly. Do you know where Arthaal is?"

"He had the east patrol. I sensed him coming in when we left headquarters. He'll probably arrive with Kaeryla . . . or a little later if he had something to report to Dussef or Gustaan."

"You two are doing all the patrols now?"

"Who else is there? Sometimes we get spelled by Dussef or Turlow. None of the recruits are ready to be in charge of patrols."

"Have you run into any brigands?"

"Not in the last three eightdays." Dorylt looked almost sheepish. "Not since I had to take out one from Lydiar. He was threatening poor Bennaryt with a crossbow."

"Containments?"

"For him. It was messy, because I had to shrink the other containment around the brigand and the crossbow. I had to use a sabre on his companion. I can't handle three things at once yet. Not well, anyway." Dorylt turned. "Let me get our ales. I'll be right back."

"Your brother . . . he is only fifteen?" asked Ysabella.

Taelya nodded. "That's when I started riding patrols, but I wasn't an under-captain until I was sixteen."

"Are all of you mages . . . so young?"

"I'm twenty-three . . . didn't I tell you that?"

"You did, but . . ."

Taelya paused, then went on when Ysabella said nothing more. "Sheralt's older than I am. Valchar's a year younger. Majer Beltur and Jessyla are about fifteen years older than I am. And then there's Margrena. She's a healer and much older than any of the other mages and healers."

"You . . . still look much younger," Ysabella finally said.

"I've always been small." Before Taelya could say more, Dorylt returned and handed her a beaker. Then there was a perfunctory rap on the front door, and Kaeryla and Arthaal both hurried in, Arthaal closing the door behind himself.

Arthaal just looked at Taelya, as if stunned.

"I told you," said Kaeryla.

"Told him what?" asked Dorylt.

"How much stronger you are."

"You're almost as strong as Father," said Arthaal.

"I doubt that," replied Taelya.

"Comparisons, especially among family, are distasteful and ill-mannered," declared Tulya as she entered the front room from the kitchen.

"You need to sit down," said Taelya, pointing to the chair they had left empty because it was always Tulya's.

"Thank you. Did I miss anything?"

"Other than distasteful comparisons?" said Kaeryla. "No."

"Good." Tulya turned to the slightly bewildered Ysabella. "You're from Passera, I understand. Did you grow up there?"

Ysabella nodded.

"It's a bit larger than Fairhaven, I'd guess."

"We haven't seen everything here, Lady Tulya—"

"Tulya . . . please. There aren't any lords and ladies in Fairhaven. The only titles are working titles, and we'd like to keep it that way. You were saying about Fairhaven?"

"It looks much nicer than Passera, and there aren't any forts, either."

"No, there aren't, and I think we're happier for that."

"Forts can be traps as well as strongholds," added Kaeryla.

"Do you have any questions I might answer?" asked Tulya.

"Why did you come here?"

"Because we were driven out of Spidlar and then out of Axalt because Taelya was a white mage, even as a small child. We decided that we would make Fairhaven a place where both white and black mages could live. Apparently, this is something that no one but us likes, but, from what I've seen of these younger mages, that just might not be a problem much longer."

"Even against Certis and Gallos?"

"The Prefect of Gallos has lost a great many mages over the last sixteen years, and he will likely lose more. The Viscount lost one of his last mages and his life, I understand. If Annana and Sydel are happy here, we'll have gained more mages and more ability to decide our future. More and more traders are moving here as well. They like the fact that the Council is honest and fair."

"But you must defeat the Hydlenese and the Gallosians."

Tulya nodded. "I've learned never to wager against Beltur and my daughter, and wagering against the two of them . . . that's not a wager I'd take. And that doesn't even include Jessyla."

"I've never heard of women mages who fought."

"There have been some great women mages," said Taelya. "Ryba, Ayrlyn, Saryn of the black blades, and the Westwind Guards are all women, and they've never been defeated."

"I would like to be like that," Annana said.

"You have much to learn if you want that," replied her mother. "Undercaptain Taelya has been training longer than you have lived."

"I will do that. You'll see."

Taelya sensed the iron—or cupridium—behind those words. *She just might.*

"You'll have plenty of chances to learn," said Tulya, rising from her chair. "I think dinner's about ready." She paused and said, "We don't talk about fighting or rulers at dinner. It's not good for the digestion."

Taelya smiled. Usually, that proscription was offered more gently, but she understood that her mother wanted no misunderstandings.

In less than half a quint, everyone was seated around the long table in the kitchen, enjoying burhka and warm bread.

"I've never seen a kitchen like this," marveled Ysabella.

"Neither had any of us until Beltur had it built, and he and Taelya built the kitchen cistern," said Tulya proudly. "She was only seven, but she supplied the chaos to glaze the inside of the cistern."

Annana's eyes widened, which surprised Taelya, because she'd already mentioned it. *Maybe Annana was a little skeptical.*

"Mother doesn't get to tell that story often," said Dorylt with an amused smile, "because the rest of us have all heard it."

"I'm proud of all of you," returned Tulya serenely, "and I hope someday you'll have as much to be grateful for as I do. And I'll stop the family stories."

Taelya didn't get any time alone with her mother until much, much later, when everyone else had retired, either to be alone or to sleep. Then the two sat at the end of the kitchen table in the dim light of a single lamp.

"I must say that I didn't expect you to bring back two young mages."

"Neither did I. I worry some about Sydel. Already, he feels like his father. I'm just glad he's a black."

"Beltur will take care of that, I'm quite certain, if only because both Jessyla and I will insist . . . and I suspect you will as well. Trained willfulness can be an advantage."

Taelya certainly hoped so.

"Ysabella is beautiful, with that striking red hair and green eyes . . . and that skin. How old do you think she is?" Tulya asked, not quite idly.

"I don't know. I never asked."

"I'd be surprised if she's more than a year or two older than you."

"She looks older than that."

"She's not. I understand Sydon always preferred younger women."

"That would mean . . . she would have been . . ." Taelya realized that well might have been why Ysabella had looked so surprised at Taelya's age.

"Exactly, and that was also why Sydon looked more intently at Kaeryla than you."

"He was intent enough when he looked at me," said Taelya dryly.

"That's past. The two of you took care of it, thank goodness. You ladies apparently destroyed quite a number of white mages."

"Five Gallosians and one Certan. It took the two of us to deal with Sydon and the Certan mage. Sheralt, Kaeryla, and I all worked together to destroy the Certan border post at the Montgren Gorge. He's still there so that the Certans can't build another bridge any time soon."

"How is he doing? Didn't you have . . . a bit of an argument . . . before you left?"

"You might say so. I crushed his shields . . . gently . . . and told him that he was an idiot if he didn't start to structure his order and chaos."

"You have been known to be direct. So . . . what happened?" Tulya leaned forward just slightly.

"He spent the entire ride to Passera working on it. He's much, much stronger now. I'm not sure we could have escaped the Gallosians at Passera if he hadn't done that."

"Did you tell him that?"

Taelya found herself blushing. "I told him that he was much stronger . . . and . . . that I was glad. He . . . he said that he'd discovered I was usually right . . ."

"When a man changes for a woman . . . there's a great deal to be said, especially if it makes him a better man or mage." After a silence, Tulya asked, "What are you going to do?"

"I told him to take care of himself . . . he told me the same. We'll see . . . once the fighting's over."

"That's probably for the best . . . right now."

Before long, Taelya said good night and slipped across the street, where Kaeryla had turned down the covers on her parents' bed for Taelya.

LXIX

Eightday and oneday passed quickly for Taelya, possibly because she slept later than she had been, late being all of sometime between sixth and seventh glass, and she did wash all her uniforms, since she had the chance. Both Kaeryla and Taelya spent several glasses each day working with Annana and Sydon, and Ysabella insisted on cleaning the house and the kitchen on oneday, to which Tulya offered no objection.

Although Taelya did enjoy sleeping in a real bed, she worried about the Gallosians and the Hydlenese, even if there was a dispatch from Beltur on oneday that the Gallosians were taking their time, but would likely reach Eskaad by fourday. Given her concerns, she was more than ready to ride out on twoday morning. She had made one change to her gear, as had Kaeryla, and that was a third water bottle. All three bottles were filled with ale, and not watered ale. She needed every bit of nourishment she could get.

Gustaan and Zekkarat had both agreed that Third Squad should be the vanguard, given that Second Squad had but a single mage and that there was a greater possibility of encountering hostilities ahead than from the rear.

Because the combined force rode out before dawn, they encountered neither riders nor shepherds west of Fairhaven, and the sun had just eased over the eastern horizon and the hills to the east of the Hydolar road when Third Squad rode across the border into the lands of Hydlen, heading south.

"What should we expect in the way of hamlets and towns?" Taelya asked Gustaan. While she'd looked over the wall map of Hydlen in headquarters in the past, she now wished she'd studied it more closely, but she hadn't expected to be riding into a battle inside Hydlen.

"This part of Hydlen's never been that prosperous. For the next ten or fifteen kays, pretty much all you'll see are abandoned steads, and one hamlet where all the cots are missing roofs. The first town with people is Vaarlaan. From here it's a hard five-day ride to Hydolar."

Taelya glanced at the hills to the east, one of which had been the site of the first fighting in the last war with Hydlen, and then at the road ahead that slowly curved toward a more westerly direction.

"It is barren," said Kaeryla.

As Gustaan had said, they saw no sign of herders or steads for almost two glasses. Then Taelya saw little more than two handfuls of houses on the north side of the road ahead. The force used the pump and troughs belonging to the small inn in Vaarlaan to water the horses while everyone took a short break. The locals stayed well away from the troopers and mages.

Outside of the town, the ground became more level, and the road shifted direction slightly so that it headed almost due west. Taelya couldn't help but notice that the few trees she saw were short and scraggly, not all that much taller than the head of a rider. By first glass of the afternoon, low bushes, no more than knee-high, began to appear in scattered clumps on each side of the road. The leaves were pale green and thin, and looked prickly.

"What are those bushes?" asked Kaeryla.

"Bitterbush," declared Gustaan. "It grows in salty ground. Nothing eats it. Not even goats."

"Something must eat it," said Taelya.

"Desert rats, maybe," conceded the captain.

Third glass passed, and Taelya didn't see anything growing except bitterbush. She wondered how the ground had gotten so salty when there didn't seem to be any water anywhere, although there might have been some in the low hills to the north of the road.

Then she began to notice streaks of black and gray ash ahead, and several wide patches of chaos radiating away from the road. For several moments, she thought nothing was growing there, except in the chaos-darkened areas, she saw scattered little pale green shoots.

A slight gust of wind brought a different scent, one far more rancid and nauseating. "Someone was fighting here," she said to Kaeryla.

"There are bones along the road ahead," replied the younger mage. "They look like horse bones."

"One of the dispatches the majer sent," said Gustaan, "mentioned fighting east of Eskaad. I wouldn't have thought they'd be fighting in the bitterbush area."

"Maybe that's why the majer attacked here." Taelya studied the terrain ahead. She'd initially thought that the bitterbushes were thinning out ahead of them, but a closer look showed that the thinning had likely been accomplished by chaos—chaos doubtless first thrown by white mages and then returned in force by Beltur and Jessyla.

What bothered Taelya, though, was that for all the ashes and the faint chaos residue everywhere, there weren't any bodies, and no sign of graves or pyres. She tried to sense for . . . something . . . and swallowed as she realized that in the ground beneath the bitterbushes there were more than a few desert rats . . . and some rather large serpents. And more than likely, the carnage had drawn a host of vulcrows.

"What is it, Taelya?" asked Kaeryla.

"I just sensed what's beneath the bitterbushes and the ground."

Kaeryla frowned. After a moment, she grimaced. "No wonder we're not seeing much. And in little more than an eightday."

Over a glass later, past the signs of the battle or ambush, Taelya saw a low rise ahead, then glanced back, only to realize that they had been riding up a gradual slope.

"We're just about at the end of the bitterbush lands," Gustaan announced. "Over the rise ahead, everything changes."

Despite Gustaan's explanation, Taelya was surprised, possibly because, from the top of the rise, she looked out over a collage of fields, orchards, woodlots, and even places that glinted in the afternoon sun and were likely lakes and ponds . . . and there wasn't a single bitterbush in sight to the west.

"How much farther?" asked Kaeryla.

"Another glass," replied Gustaan.

As she rode down the long gradual slope toward Eskaad, Taelya continued to study the terrain, taking in the handfuls of cots set in the middle of fields or orchards, all of them built of wood. She didn't see any that appeared to be abandoned, although there were more than a few that could have used a great deal of repair.

Once they rode into the town proper, which looked to be considerably smaller than Fairhaven, Taelya could see that the dwellings and shops were in slightly better condition than those to the east of the town. The square in the middle of Eskaad was larger than the square in Fairhaven, if somehow dingier, although there were two inns on the square, the Yellow Dog on the south side and the Black Horse on the north side.

The square between the inns was largely empty, except for a pair of older women filling water jugs at the fountain. Both avoided looking at the troopers. Then a rider in Fairhaven blue moved toward the column, reining up short of Third Squad.

"Majer Beltur is using the Yellow Dog as his headquarters. The Fairhaven squads will be quartered there, while the Montgren company has space at the Black Horse. There will be a dinner meeting for all officers at the Yellow Dog at half past fifth glass."

"Thank you," returned Zekkarat.

Third Squad and Second Squad proceeded to the Yellow Dog Inn. Once there, Taelya and Kaeryla had barely dismounted and were walking their mounts into the stable building next to the main building of the Yellow Dog Inn when Beltur appeared, along with Jessyla.

Beltur looked at his daughter and then at his niece with an expression of affection . . . and worry. "I can't say how glad I am that you're both in good health . . . and that you're both much, much stronger. I just wish you didn't have to be here."

"I just wish none of us had to be here," declared Jessyla acerbically. "We didn't get that choice."

Taelya immediately used her senses on her uncle and aunt, but their order/chaos balances were strong and undisturbed. Then she asked, "What do you know about what happened in Gallos and Certis? Did you get a dispatch?"

"Both Gustaan and Zekkarat sent me dispatches. They both explained the treachery of the Prefect and the Viscount, and how you two handled it, including your withdrawal to Montgren and the destruction of the Montgren Gorge bridge. Gustaan said you needed to brief me on what happened specifically with the mages at Passera . . . and what occurred after that." He paused. "That sounds like something neither of the two wanted in a dispatch."

Kaeryla looked to Taelya.

"I'll start. If I leave out anything, Kaeryla can add it. The Gallosians had five mages in Passera. One was in the eastern river fort. He wasn't very strong. I took him out when we captured that fort. When we crossed the Passa River, the Gallosians attacked, and the Certans withdrew. They never even started across the bridge. The Gallosians had three strong mages and one very strong mage. We dealt with all four—"

"No," interrupted Kaeryla. "Taelya took out three of them herself. I helped by throwing their chaos bolts into their troopers."

"The fourth mage was stronger than either of us," Taelya said. "I asked Kaeryla for a lot of order, and then I wrapped chaos around it. It still took several tries before we destroyed him. Neither of us could have done it alone." Taelya paused. "I didn't know it was Sydon until the moment before we overpowered him."

Beltur didn't look particularly surprised. "I wondered if he'd be there. I'd thought it might be possible. I also thought you could work out some way to deal with him, although that was likely as much hope on my part as anything."

"Hope and more worry than you two can imagine," added Jessyla. "You're not telling everything, I don't believe."

"The other problem is that we have the twins. They're Sydon's children . . ." Taelya went on to explain about Ysabella, Annana, and Sydel.

"And he just left her . . . and them?" Jessyla's eyes seemed to flash.

"I don't think he expected us to best him," said Kaeryla. "Ysabella asked him what she should do if something happened to him. That was the answer he gave."

Beltur just shook his head.

"Did Gustaan or Zekkarat write about the Viscount?"

Beltur's smile was one of wry amusement. "They both did. Zekkarat, I think, was somewhat appalled. Gustaan thought the two of you did the right thing. I'd agree, especially after the way the Duchess has behaved. But the Duchess can wait until after we deal with the Gallosians and Hydlenese here. In a way, I can't say what you two did surprises me. Any of it. I have to admit that I didn't consider that you two would be that much stronger together, but I'm very glad that you worked that out."

"We also got Sheralt and Valchar to structure their order and chaos better," added Kaeryla.

"We need to keep working together," said Taelya firmly. "I'd suggest that you consider that before you make any battle plans."

"He will," declared Jessyla. "It makes sense in several ways. Now . . . you two need to deal with your mounts and do whatever you need to do before the officers' dinner. You're sharing a room in the inn."

"We need to talk to Gustaan and Zekkarat before that meeting," said Beltur, "but we wanted to see you two first."

After Jessyla and Beltur left, Taelya looked at Kaeryla. "I would have thought he could have been a little surprised."

"He wasn't that surprised when you used chaos to glaze the cistern when you were seven. Why would he be that surprised that we killed six white mages and a Viscount? Without much help from anyone else?" Kaeryla's voice held more than a little sarcasm.

Taelya couldn't help but laugh.

"We'll just have to destroy a battalion or two this next time, if not more," added Kaeryla, her voice still dripping sarcasm. "Also we ought to look as good as we can for dinner. That way Karlaak and Waandyl can wonder how we did it. That's if they even survived the first battles with the Hydlenese."

After finishing with their mounts, the two found their quarters and cleaned up. Then they waited until all the other junior officers were in the side chamber off the public room in the Yellow Dog before entering. So far as Taelya could tell, Beltur, Zekkarat, Jessyla, and Waandyl were missing. The chamber held one long table, but no one was seated. The murmured conversations paused as the two women undercaptains entered. There was one Montgren undercaptain that Taelya didn't recognize, an older man, most likely a former squad leader.

From where he stood in the far corner of the chamber, Valchar smothered a grin as he looked at Kaeryla. Captain Karlaak avoided looking at either entering undercaptain. The Montgren undercaptain leaned toward Therran and murmured something, to which Therran replied briefly. Whatever Therran said surprised the other undercaptain.

Even before Taelya and Kaeryla reached Valchar and Gustaan, most of the officers turned as Beltur, Zekkarat, and Jessyla entered the chamber.

"Sit where you please," Beltur said pleasantly, taking the seat at the head of the table, with Zekkarat on his right and Jessyla on his left.

Taelya, Kaeryla, Valchar, and Therran sat at the far end of the table, Taelya and Kaeryla side by side across from Valchar and Therran.

Once everyone was seated, Beltur went on. "I'll be giving a brief summary of what happened in Gallos and Certis for the officers who've been here, and then a summary of what happened here for the officers who fought in Gallos and Certis. To begin with, the supposed fight between Gallos and Certis over control of the Passa River was a façade. Once our forces reached the west side of the river, all three Certan battalions withdrew . . ." From there Beltur went on to detail everything after that, including the fact that Fairhaven mages—without naming them—had assassinated the Viscount during the withdrawal across Certis.

When Beltur mentioned the Duchess's order to hold the Montgren bridge open, Karlaak immediately asked, his voice skeptical, "Is there any proof of that? Or is this just another surmise?"

"I have the original order," said Zekkarat coldly. "You can look at it any time you wish."

"But . . . why . . . ?" asked the clearly disconcerted captain.

"We'll have to ask the Duchess," replied Zekkarat. "It might have something to do with Lord Korsaen's death or Lady Maeyora's murder . . . or possibly the sudden appointment of Korwaen as Lord Protector."

The Montgren undercaptain Taelya didn't know nodded slowly.

"Resolving that particular question," said Beltur firmly, "will have to wait until we deal with the Gallosians and Hydlenese. It also means that we will need a decisive victory here. Now . . . as some of you know, but those returning from Certis do not, the Hydlenese sent two battalions and four mages to attack Fairhaven. They believed that would be sufficient, given that we only had two mages and three companies of troopers. Unlike the last time, we decided to move into Hydlen and to attack in the least likely place—the bitterbush lands. We left plenty of bushes between our forces and the road, and when the Hydlenese tried to attack, the bushes and the rodent holes slowed them down and cost them more than a few troopers.

"Their mages also didn't seem to know how to handle attacks by small squads they couldn't see. We just whittled them down, and then finished off the four mages. One effect we didn't consider was how many desert rats have burrows under those bushes. We were fortunate that we didn't have many wounded who were unhorsed. Most likely, half the Hydlenese fallen didn't survive the rats and the serpents."

Taelya didn't wince at that, not after what she'd observed.

"Then we harried the survivors all the way here to Eskaad. There might have been a company remaining, and they fled before we entered the town." Beltur cleared his throat. "I'd rather not try another bitterbush attack. The lands around Eskaad, however, provide a location for a more traditional attack and battle, which is likely what the Gallosians expect. They have slightly more than three battalions, two from Gallos, and an overlarge battalion from Hydlen, with six or seven companies. I'll be going over what I expect from each unit first thing in the morning before we move out. Now . . . enjoy the meal."

Taelya thought about what Beltur had said . . . and what he hadn't, and the fact that everything he had said didn't convey an actual battle plan or even an outline of one. She turned to Kaeryla and said, "He didn't say much except that we'll be moving out in the morning."

Kaeryla nodded. "He has his reasons."

Taelya wondered just how much notice he'd given to the companies before the bitterbush attack . . . and whether there just might be spies within the Montgren or even the Fairhaven forces. *Given what's happened so far, that's definitely possible.*

After that thought, she concentrated on eating the fowl casserole and the warm bread set before her. Tomorrow would be soon enough to learn what her uncle had in mind.

LXX

Both Taelya and Kaeryla woke up in the grayness before dawn on threeday.

"Do you have any idea what your father has in mind?" asked Taelya.

Kaeryla shook her head. "Only that it's likely something that no one else has considered . . . or considered as practical or possible, that it will be hard on everyone, including us, and that Mother agrees with it."

Taelya couldn't but wonder if matters might have turned out differently if her own father had listened more to her mother. *But you can't undo the past.* "We'd better get dressed and get something to eat . . . and bring our water bottles to breakfast."

Surprisingly to Taelya, the two of them were among the first in the small inn chamber serving as the officers' mess, and the first to leave—with filled water bottles. They had just finished saddling their mounts and tying their gear in place when Beltur and Jessyla appeared in the stable and joined them.

"I'm glad you two are here early. I have a question for you," said Beltur. "How would you rate Ferek's company?"

Taelya and Kaeryla exchanged glances.

Finally, Taelya said, "After both Konstyn and Drakyn were killed at Passera, Zekkarat put Ferek's Undercaptain Maakym in charge of the company holding the gorge and breveted him to captain. He trusted Maakym to follow his orders. So long as Zekkarat's in command of Ferek . . ."

"That's what I thought," replied Beltur, "but I wanted your opinion, since the way in which we attack will be determined by the Gallosians' order of march and by the corresponding strength or weaknesses of our force. As for what we'll do today . . . there's a small town a little more than ten kays west of Eskaad. It's called Shaescomb. The Hydlenese stayed there last time. Last night, they stayed at a town some fifteen kays south of Shaescomb. On the ride to Shaescomb, the Fairhaven company will lead, followed by Third Squad and the Montgren company under Zekkarat and Ferek, then the Montgren company led by Captain Karlaak, and last, the company commanded by Undercaptain Vannyk—"

"Is he the replacement for Captain Waandyl?" interrupted Kaeryla.

"Yes. He came up through the ranks. He's solid, if not imaginative. Second Squad will lead Vannyk's company. Valchar's principal task will be to protect Vannyk and those around him. Vannyk's task will be to hold a narrow part of the road just west of Shaescomb. There aren't likely to be many, if any, mages in the lead battalion, which will be Hydlenese."

"How do you know that?" asked Taelya.

"I don't, but that's been their order, and it makes sense, given how the Gallosians think. While Vannyk's company is holding the road at the bridge, Karlaak is to attack the rear of the Hydlenese battalion. If they come up with a different order of advance today, then we'll change our plan of attack. For now, form up Third Squad behind the Fairhaven company. We'll tell Zekkarat the rest of the order." Beltur nodded.

"Remember," added Jessyla, "you two stay together and support each other."

"We will," replied Taelya and Kaeryla almost simultaneously.

Then Beltur and Jessyla strode off.

"He's still not saying much," observed Taelya.

"Would you, after everything that's happened?" countered Kaeryla.

"Not until I had to."

"Exactly."

At that moment, Varais showed up.

Before the squad leader could ask, Taelya said, "We're second in the order, right behind the Fairhaven company. Ferek and Zekkarat will follow us. We're headed toward a town called Shaescomb, some ten kays west. We'll likely get more specific orders once we near the town."

"Who's in charge?" asked Varais warily.

"Majer Beltur, and Captain Jessyla. Zekkarat's effectively commanding Ferek's company."

"Good. The squad's forming up outside."

"We'll follow you out," said Taelya.

Less than a quint later, with the rising sun at their backs, Taelya and Kaeryla rode at the head of Third Squad behind the Fairhaven company as it led the way west out of Eskaad. Taelya did note that the supply wagons and their teamsters remained in the stable yard of the Yellow Dog.

Even well outside of Eskaad, the road was wide enough that Taelya rode flanked by Kaeryla on her right and Varais on her left. None of the three spoke for more than a quint.

"How do you think Majer Beltur plans on surprising the Hydlenese and Gallosians?" Varais finally asked.

"Any way he can," replied Kaeryla.

"And sooner than they expect," added Taelya.

"This afternoon, it sounds like."

"Most likely, but he didn't say," replied Taelya. "We're riding at a moderate pace, and we only have ten kays to cover on a decent road. The supply wagons aren't with us. All he said was that how we attack depends on what order they're riding in. We'll be facing an overlarge Hydlenese battalion and two Gallosian battalions. So far, the Hydlenese battalion has been in the van."

"Two'll get you ten," said Varais, "that the Gallosians have the Hydlenese up front as blade and arrow fodder, and that they'll try to wear us out hacking through the poor Hydlenese bastards."

"I'm sure that the majer's thought of that," said Taelya.

"But he hasn't said *what* he's thought, has he?"

"Not to us." *And likely not to anyone else except Jessyla so far.* Taelya looked westward, taking in the same patchwork of orchards, fields, and woodlots as she'd seen on the ride into Eskaad. In the distance, she could make out low, tree-covered hills.

Even by seventh glass, the white sun shone full on Taelya's back, and she could tell that the day was going to be hot, if not quite as moist as summer usually was in Fairhaven and Montgren, but the road was also dustier, although the dust only rose boot-high on the riders.

It wasn't even midmorning when, as Taelya rode toward a low rise, she sensed, but did not see, riders moving somewhat more quickly westward, over the rise and presumably toward the town, riders composing half a squad following a black mage. *Jessyla.* "Are you sensing what I'm sensing?" she asked Kaeryla in a low voice.

The younger mage nodded. "They're going to stop any couriers from leaving the inn and way station before anyone in the town sights us."

At that moment, the column came to a halt.

More than a quint passed before the column began to move once more, and it was another quint before Taelya rode over the rise and caught sight of a small town nestled in a low and wide valley that narrowed at the far west end where tree-covered hills seemed to stretch for several kays in all directions. The houses and shops that composed Shaescomb were all on the east side of a winding stream crossed by a stone bridge possibly a half kay west of the central part of the town. Beyond the bridge the ground rose gradually into the largely tree-covered hills, where most of the trees appeared to be some type of pine.

Taelya thought she sensed Jessyla and the riders who had accompanied her somewhere near the bridge, but the older black mage was beyond where Taelya could clearly discern her.

Shortly, Beltur rode back and joined Taelya, and a few moments later, Zekkarat rode forward. The four officers continued riding down the gentle incline toward the town.

"You summoned me, Majer?" said Zekkarat.

"I did." Beltur extended a map to Zekkarat. "I've noted the side road to your staging point in the pine hills west of the town. Once you leave the main road, please keep off it so that the Gallosians don't see tracks. Use the terrain and concealments to remain undetected until it is time to attack. Either Taelya or Kaeryla will be able to tell you when we attack. Your task is to attack the middle of the lead Gallosian battalion and to inflict maximum casualties while incurring minimal losses. Third Squad's task is to deal with any mages present and to use the chaos of those mages on the Gallosian officers and troopers, especially on the officers. Third Squad will also attack as the undercaptains see fit." Beltur's words were delivered in a matter-of-fact tone.

"To what end?" asked Zekkarat.

"To destroy any chance for either the Gallosians or the Hydlenese to mount another attack."

"I thought the idea was to win battles, not slaughter troopers," Zekkarat replied.

"Unless we slaughter most of those troopers, we won't win, and we'll have to keep fighting," said Beltur. "We have to get across the point that crossing Montgren is deadly."

"You mean crossing Fairhaven?" suggested Zekkarat.

"Montgren won't exist a year from now if this battle doesn't result in the virtual annihilation of the Gallosian and Hydlenese forces," replied Beltur pleasantly. "Fairhaven is all that will save Montgren. Do you want to save it or not?"

Zekkarat smiled somewhat sadly. "I'm willing to save it on your terms. I don't have to like it."

"Do you think we do?" said Taelya before Beltur could reply. "Especially after being betrayed by Koralya?"

Zekkarat inclined his head. "I wish it were otherwise. I've been betrayed by every ruler I've served."

"We can talk about that later," said Beltur, his voice almost cheerful. "Things just might look up."

"At what price?" asked Zekkarat.

"The price required of those who expected to profit from betrayal."

"Do you really think you can pull this off, Beltur?"

"We have a good chance . . . and no alternatives. So I prefer to think positively. Besides, Jessyla says it will work, and I *never* wager against her." Beltur looked to Taelya and then Kaeryla. "Just stay together and work as you did in Gallos."

"We will," replied Kaeryla.

Beltur nodded, and then rode back toward the rear of the column.

Zekkarat handed the map to Taelya. "Since you're going to be leading the way, you ought to see where you're going." He didn't hide the bitterness in his voice.

Taelya took the map, but did not look at it. "I have no doubt that the troopers moving to attack Fairhaven are under orders to leave no troopers or officers alive. Do you dispute that?"

Zekkarat shook his head. "I just don't like being forced to act the same way."

"Neither do we," replied Taelya. "We'd like to make this the last time . . . for at least another sixteen years until the next idiot ruler gets greedy."

"I think you're even more cynical than Beltur," said Zekkarat.

"I'm a woman," replied Taelya. "My father believed too much that people couldn't be as evil as they often were. Some people will only be good if they see no other alternative. I'm willing to make sure those people have no other alternatives." After a moment, she added, "You should probably ride with us, and we should each take turns studying the map."

Zekkarat nodded.

Over the next quint, the three passed the map back and forth without much conversation.

Finally, Zekkarat asked, "Have you sensed much activity?"

"Captain Jessyla used a concealment to move troopers west of the town before the townspeople could see us. Her squad is likely intercepting any couriers headed west to warn the Gallosians. Right now, she's in a position to sense farther west than we can."

"The Spidlarian councilors were idiots," Zekkarat said quietly. "Absolute and total idiots."

"Because they forced Father out?" asked Kaeryla.

"Not only that, but because he's one of the best field commanders in Candar. That's something that Duchess Koralya doesn't understand, either."

"Does she even care?" asked Kaeryla sarcastically.

"Unfortunately, she doesn't . . . but she likely will. I don't see how we're going to defeat the Gallosians, but given Beltur and you five mages, we at least have a chance."

We have to do better than that. Taelya went back to studying the map before handing it to Kaeryla.

Another quint passed before Third Squad reached the outskirts of Shaescomb, a town with fewer dwellings than Fairhaven, and certainly fewer trees, although Taelya did notice several small orchards of what she thought were apricot trees. She also noted that almost every house was shuttered, and that she saw no one outside, nor any animals, either.

What did surprise her initially was that there were no Fairhaven or Montgren troopers posted as guards or sentries around the inn or the way station. But then, she realized, the inn workers weren't Hydlenese troopers, and the way station wasn't manned, just as the one in Fairhaven wasn't.

Beltur reappeared and pulled his mount in alongside Zekkarat. "The Hydlenese and Gallosians are about three glasses south of here riding toward us. So far, they're not showing any indications that they know we're this close. There's nowhere between where they are and Shaescomb that they could comfortably stop. So . . . it looks like we'll be fighting this afternoon."

Then Beltur rode back along the column, presumably to inform Karlaak, Vannyk, and Valchar.

As Taelya and Kaeryla rode toward the stone bridge, Taelya studied the stream, which looked to be about the same width as the border stream between Certis and Gallos, but with much lower banks and marshy lands and reeds at the edge of the water. The marsh-like terrain extended close to fifteen yards on each side of the water and bordered the stream for at least a kay in each direction from the bridge. The stream itself was slow-moving and perhaps a yard deep and four to five yards wide, enough to slow riders considerably, but certainly not enough to stop a determined assault. The bridge itself was wide enough for a large wagon and two mounts side by side, with stone side walls about a yard high.

Beyond the stone bridge, the road narrowed slightly, to about the same width as the bridge, with slightly sloping shoulders of about two yards. Less than a kay west from the bridge, the ground rose a few yards and the marshy fields gave way to a pine forest. The trees beyond the shoulders on each side of the road were not densely set, but grew with perhaps a yard or two between the lower branches of neighboring trees, enough for a rider, but not for a wagon or for a mounted force to carry out any charge or maneuvers. Jessyla and her half squad were nowhere in sight, but Taelya sensed her close to a kay farther to the northwest in the hills.

Some four hundred yards west of the stone bridge, and shortly after Beltur returned, the Fairhaven company turned northward onto a lane into the woods that consisted mainly of pines that seemed to top out at five or six yards in height.

"The lane we'll be taking to the south is another half kay ahead," said Taelya, "around that curve to the left."

"Is there anyone on the lane?" asked Zekkarat.

"Not for at least three kays," replied Kaeryla, "and we're not taking it any farther than that. There are some deer and one mountain cat in the forest."

Once they turned onto the lane, which allowed barely two mounts side by side, their progress slowed, and it was almost a glass later when Taelya reined up on the south side of a low rise, to the north of which, according to the map, some two hundred yards away, was the main road. The lane veered away to the south, and the map showed it going to a small hamlet some five kays away, with no connection to the main road.

"There's no one near on the road," said Taelya.

Zekkarat immediately turned his mount off the lane and rode up the rise. Taelya and Kaeryla followed. All three stopped at the crest and looked down toward the main road.

The south side of the rise separating the lane and the road was forested with the same low pines as everywhere else along the way, but the pines ended near the top of the rise, and only grasses and low bushes covered the north side of the rise that sloped down to the main road, a drop of perhaps three yards over the sixty yards from the top of the rise to the road. The treeless area on the north side of the rise stretched only about a hundred yards along the south side of the road. On the north side of the road was a shallow, brush-filled depression, beyond which was a steeper and more rugged slope, also more thickly wooded.

After a time, Zekkarat nodded. "We have a way out, if necessary. They don't. The majer must have scouted this thoroughly . . . or he has a very good memory."

Both. But Taelya just nodded in return.

"When you give the signal," said Zekkarat, "the company will loose shafts into the side of the column as quickly as possible. After that, you're going to rake the column with targeted firebolts and one larger one. Are we agreed?"

"We are," replied Taelya. "Then your company will attack the rear of the third company, and Third Squad will attack the fourth company . . . and, if possible, the fifth company as well." *Which will hopefully get the Gallosian mages to throw chaos bolts at us . . . and get the troopers disorganized and panicked.*

"Can you tell how close the Hydlenese are? And how close the majer is to them?"

"The first companies are about two kays west of us. The majer isn't that close to them yet," replied Taelya.

"Shouldn't he be?"

"Not quite yet," said Kaeryla. "Whites can't sense nearly as well as blacks . . . well, except for Taelya and Sheralt, and that's because they were trained differently. But most whites can sense large groups of troopers and mages when they get close."

"The majer wants all the Hydlenese and Gallosians on the narrow forested part of the road before he makes his move," added Taelya.

"How long do you think it will be?"

"I'd judge another glass before the Hydlenese get past us and the first Gallosian battalion arrives." Taelya lifted her water bottle and took a long swallow, then another.

"How long before the Hydlenese reach us?"

"A little more than a half glass."

"Then it's time to move up to near the top of the rise, close enough that we can move into an attack in moments."

Less than two quints later, Zekkarat had Ferek's company in position, and Third Squad was in place at the west end of the formation.

Taelya decided to remain close to Zekkarat until she could discern where the mages were located among the oncoming forces. Almost another quint passed before she turned to the majer. "The Hydlenese battalion has no mages. The first three companies of the first Gallosian battalion also have no mages. There are two moderately strong mages in the fourth company, and none in the fifth company. When Kaeryla removes the concealment will be when the third company is right in front of you."

"And when we loose shafts," confirmed the majer.

Taelya nodded and then eased Bounder back to Third Squad, alongside Kaeryla.

A quint later, just before the riders in the green uniforms of Hydlen appeared, Kaeryla eased a concealment over the Montgren company and Third Squad, even though the force was just below the crest of the rise on the side away from the road. Neither Taelya nor Kaeryla spoke as the battalion rode past. Then there was a gap of close to a hundred yards before the gray-uniformed Gallosians appeared.

While it felt like a glass to Taelya in the hot darkness of the concealment before the first two Gallosian companies rode past, it was likely less than a quint before Kaeryla said quietly, "They've begun the attack on the rear battalion, and the supply wagons are already in flames."

"Just a few moments more," suggested Taelya.

"Now?"

"Now."

The concealment vanished, and, as usual, for an instant or two, Taelya was moving more by her senses than sight while her eyes adjusted to the early-afternoon sunlight. While the sounds of mounts and riders taking the crest of the rise sounded like thunder to Taelya, the Gallosians didn't seem to hear anything at all.

Then, after the first volley, for several moments, the Gallosians didn't even seem to notice the deadly shafts that ripped through the column of riders.

"Bluecoat attack! Bluecoat attack! To the right!"

At that moment, Taelya loosed two quick and small chaos bolts, one at the undercaptain who'd yelled out the order, and a second at shoulder height along the side of the column. More Montgren shafts slammed into the packed column, and Taelya sensed black death mists everywhere.

Time to move . . . before they get organized. "Third Squad! Forward!"

Taelya aimed Bounder at the north side of the road, extending cutting shields a little more than a yard on her left, while Kaeryla aimed her mare at the riders on the south side of the road, with her cutting shields extended on the right.

As Bounder charged down the side of the column, creating gouts of blood and screams cut mercifully short, Taelya arched a small chaos bolt toward the rear of the Gallosian company. The chaos splashed across riders several ranks in front of the two mages, and one of the mages immediately threw a chaos bolt back, a bolt that Kaeryla intercepted and used to decimate much of the squad riding immediately in front of the mages.

Another chaos bolt flared toward Taelya. That one she redirected into the squad she hadn't quite reached. An even larger chaos bolt soared toward Taelya, and almost without thinking she flung it into the squad behind the mages.

"Stay on the undercaptains!" ordered Varais.

Bounder slowed and then angled left to avoid a direct collision with a trooper trying to avoid Taelya, but Taelya's shields on her right were enough to throw trooper and mount into the depression on the north side of the road.

Taelya realized that she and Kaeryla had almost swept through three squads when two more firebolts flared at her, and one at Kaeryla.

Kaeryla redirected the one toward the rear of the fourth company, turning three ranks into flame and ashes.

At the same time, Taelya captured the pair of firebolts, combined them, added a touch of order, and slammed the more massive chaos/order bolt at the stronger mage, strengthening her own shields momentarily as she did so, and closing her eyes.

Searing whiteness flared against her shields, but they held, and the chaos fire flared back across the last two squads in the fourth company, leaving little but ashes.

"We have to take out the next company! Kaeryla! On me! Shields on the out-side! We'll split the middle!"

"On you! Shields to the outside!" replied the younger mage, moving her mare closer to Bounder in the open space between the end of the fourth Gallosian company and the fifth company in the battalion. By the time they crossed the gap, the two had regained their speed, and slammed between the lead riders of the next company.

With only two riders abreast on the road, and the pines flanking the road, the Gallosian companies were strung out and vulnerable to the cutting shields of the two mages, so much so that Taelya could see almost no way or need to use chaos bolts as she and Kaeryla slashed through more than a hundred troopers, leaving the disconcerted survivors as easy targets for Varais and Third Squad.

Yet when the two reined up at where the second Gallosian battalion should have been, all they saw were the advancing blue uniforms of Fairhaven, be-yond which, to the west, Taelya sensed dissipating cold black mists. She also smelled burning flesh, and even the on the southern side of the road to the west seemed to be burning in places, or so it seemed to Taelya.

"There's nothing left of those two companies, sers!" called Varais. "We fin-ished off the few you didn't get."

Taelya immediately tried sensing for Beltur and Jessyla, and took a long deep breath of relief when she sensed them—and most of the Fairhaven company—riding toward them.

"We need to reinforce Zekkarat!" called Beltur. "And then Karlaak."

"Third Squad! Back up the road!" ordered Taelya. After turning Bounder, she let him move at a fast walk, knowing that she might need his full strength once she and Kaeryla reached the fighting.

The ride back east toward the continued fighting seemed to take forever but was likely less than half a quint, during which time Taelya uncorked her water bottle and drank liberally.

The fighting was a confused melee of men and mounts, with the pale blue uniforms of Montgren hard to distinguish from the gray of Gallos, except for the brown belts and patches of the Gallosians.

"Montgren! To the south!" Taelya ordered.

But no one seemed to hear her.

All she and Kaeryla could do, it seemed, was to wade in with Bounder, using their shields to shove Gallosians . . . and some Montgren troopers . . . to the side.

"Keep moving!" Taelya commanded. "We need to get to where there aren't any blue uniforms!"

Taelya thought she and Kaeryla had ridden a kay, but it could only have been several hundred yards before there was a thin line of blue uniforms . . . and gray beyond that.

Once Taelya finally neared the lead Montgren troopers, she threw a tight-targeted chaos bolt over them at the center of the Gallosian line, then a second. It took a third before the Montgren troopers moved to the side. "Now! Charge down the middle! Shields to the outside!"

Taelya could feel the occasional jolts against her shields, but she and Kaeryla kept moving, their edged shields cutting, slicing, and black mists flowing everywhere . . . until, suddenly, there was a gap of several hundred yards between a few remaining graycoats . . . and yet another company of Montgren troopers, troopers that Taelya sensed had been caught between the Gallosians and the Hydlenese.

Taelya charged forward, and the graycoats scattered.

Then she started toward the mass of greencoats bunched up and trying to cross the stone bridge, not even looking back toward the mixed force of Montgren and Fairhaven troopers that followed the two undercaptains.

"Taelya! Stop! Stop!"

Stop? Why now? We're almost done . . .

"Stop! Taelya! Stop!"

The frantic nature of Kaeryla's words finally got through to Taelya, and she slowed Bounder.

Kaeryla rode up beside her. "Your chaos is too low! Let the Fairhaven company finish it. Drink some ale!"

Chaos too low? Not order? That didn't make any sense.

Kaeryla thrust a water bottle at Taelya. "Drink it!"

If it makes her feel better . . .

Taelya took a long swallow . . . and then another . . . and then she began to shiver uncontrollably. The water bottle flew from her hands, and everything began to spin around her.

She leaned forward, her arms around Bounder's neck, just trying to stay in the saddle.

Something touched her, a tiny something, and the spinning slowed.

"Don't do anything," said Kaeryla, her mare almost against Bounder. "I can't do any more. You can't, either."

As if in a daze, Taelya realized that they were surrounded by riders, but in Fairhaven blue.

"Everything's all right, sers. You've done enough. It's almost over."

It took a moment for Taelya to recognize that the voice belonged to Varais.

"It's almost over," Varais repeated. "Poor frigging bastards. Prefect should have been here. And Duke Maastyn."

The thought crossed Taelya's mind that Maastyn couldn't be because he was already dead.

Time passed. At least, Taelya thought it did, although every time she looked up, all her eyes showed her were sparkling flashes. Then another figure rode up. *Jessyla.*

The war mage and healer eased her mount beside Taelya on the side away from Kaeryla, then touched Taelya on the forehead. The spinning sensation faded. "Taelya . . . you can't exhaust yourself that much. If your chaos levels get too low . . . there's no one here who can help. Kaeryla did what she could, and I've given some. Sheralt might be able to, but he's not here."

"Sorry . . . I didn't . . . know . . ."

"You and your uncle." Jessyla's voice was both warm and wry. "Just don't do anything. Drink more ale. Slowly."

"Did it work?" Taelya had to struggle to get the words out.

"You two, and Third Squad, destroyed more than an entire battalion and even a company of Hydlenese."

Taelya had no recollection of fighting Hydlenese.

"Most of the Gallosians are dead. One of them who survived was screaming about the white terror who ripped men apart."

"The Hydlenese battalion?"

"Between Vannyk and the Fairhaven company, not many of them survived, either. Just take it easy. I need to check on some things." Jessyla eased her mount away.

"How many did we lose? Third Squad?" Taelya looked at Varais.

The squad leader looked back evenly, a sardonic smile on her face. "We lost four."

"Just four?" *How . . . could that be?*

"You and Undercaptain Kaeryla shredded a battalion. The few Gallosians who survived that were easy pickings. Any who didn't flee died. The same for the Hydlenese. Majer's orders." Varais shook her head. "He was right to order it. Close to two thousand dead of theirs. Maybe a hundred of ours, most in Ferek's company."

"Zekkarat?"

"Got his arm slashed, but he'll make it."

"Ferek?"

Varais shook her head, not exactly with sadness, but matter-of-factly.

"Take another swallow of ale, Taelya," Kaeryla ordered. "Slowly."

"Your mother said that."

"About healing, she's always right."

And about a lot of other things as well. Taelya groped for her water bottle, then

realized the holder for the first bottle was empty. It took both her hands to ex-
tract the second bottle, and her teeth to pull the cork. Clutching the bottle to
her chest with one arm and hand, she managed to pocket the cork before she
tried to drink. Some of the ale splashed across her face.

"Slowly . . ." said Kaeryla.

"I'm . . . trying . . ."

After a time, Taelya thought her head was clearing some, although Varais
looked over at her and said, "How do you feel, ser?"

"Tired . . . but not so fuzzy in the head."

"She won't be doing any magery for a few days," said Kaeryla.

"Neither will you."

"I didn't plan on it."

Taelya finally could hold the water bottle without her hands shaking and
look around . . . and actually see. There were bodies everywhere, most of them
in green. For a moment, she wondered where the bodies in gray might be,
but then realized all of them were somewhere to the west. She could also see
Montgren and Fairhaven troopers collecting weapons and tools and methodically searching the bodies.

"Sers . . ." ventured Varais, "Third Squad is to go to the local inn here and
take quarters. We won't be leaving Shaescomb until tomorrow morning. The majer has arranged matters."

As she turned Bounder to follow the squad leader, Taelya doubted that much
arranging had been necessary.

LXXI

When Taelya woke, she had no idea where she was, and she glanced around
the small chamber frantically, until she saw Kaeryla's red-haired form sleeping
on the adjoining narrow bed. Slowly, the events of the previous day fell into
place—those that she could remember. Except much of what she recalled she
had little desire to dwell on. Not the screams, the yelling, the gouts of blood
everywhere—except on her, doubtless because of her shields.

She frowned. Had she ever lost her shields? She realized that she was still
holding light shields.

*But then, you wouldn't be alive if Kaeryla hadn't stopped you . . . and given you a
touch of her own natural chaos.*

Taelya winced at the thought of what might have happened to Kaeryla if her cousin had misjudged in the slightest. *She is a healer . . . but she wasn't in much better shape than you were.* At that thought, she sensed Kaeryla, but while the redhead's order and chaos levels were low, they weren't life-threatening.

Several moments later, there was a gentle knock on the door.

Taelya immediately sensed that it was Jessyla, and she sat up and then went to the door and opened it.

"You're definitely better," murmured the healer.

"She's still sleeping," whispered Taelya.

"Not any longer," muttered Kaeryla, turning over and glaring.

"You're both in good enough shape to ride," said Jessyla with a smile, one of relief, Taelya thought. "But you need to hurry and eat. We need to get moving."

"Are the Certans attacking Montgren or Fairhaven?" asked Kaeryla, concern in her voice.

"It's unlikely they're attacking either," replied Jessyla, "but we can't stop them while we're still in Hydlen. Beltur would like for us to get to Fairhaven before night, but that might be pushing it."

Kaeryla immediately sat up. "We'll be ready."

Taelya looked at Jessyla. "How did you destroy that final battalion?"

"We set fire to the supply wagons so that they couldn't withdraw or retreat. Then we picked off the rear guard much the same way as you two did. Then we took out the mages in the next company, and that chaos wiped out most of the company. After that, Beltur and I took turns smashing a few ranks of troopers and let the Fairhaven company move in and clean up that company. Then we'd smash the next rear guard and repeat the process. We didn't have to do much with the last company because all the chaos you two loosed had them so disarrayed that it was even more of a slaughter. We didn't have that much order or chaos left by then. We wouldn't have managed without what you two did. Or what Valchar did to hold the bridge. It took all of us." Jessyla paused, then added, "We doubt that the Prefect has many mages left, and when Duke Maastyn was killed, he left behind only one of his two personal mages. Supposedly, no one knows where the mage went." She paused, then said, "I'll see you two at breakfast."

Once Jessyla had closed the door, Taelya said, "She made it sound so organized . . . as if we hadn't just stumbled through and somehow survived."

Kaeryla laughed. "I'd wager they weren't that much more organized than we were. Maybe a little. They've worked together longer, but they couldn't have done it without us. She said that. And she was telling the truth. We were . . . well, you sounded quite sure of yourself with those orders you were giving. You're like Father, you know?"

"Me?" Taelya couldn't believe what Kaeryla was saying.

"You. Calling out for me to be on your left with shields to the outside . . . you can hold where everyone is in your thoughts, can't you?"

Taelya paused. She'd never thought of it quite that way. "I suppose so. I can just see or sense where everyone is and try to figure out what to do from there."

"It comes naturally to you. I have to think about it. So does Mother. Father doesn't. You don't, either." Kaeryla began pulling on the rest of her uniform.

"That's probably because he had me visualizing things from when I was small."

"He's tried that with Arthaal and me, too. It's not easy for either of us. That's why you'll be the one who follows Father as field commander or whatever it's called."

"What about Gustaan?"

"He's older than Father, and he already defers to you, unless it's something you don't know."

Taelya was still thinking about what Kaeryla had said when the two walked into the officers' mess. Valchar, Therran, and Vannyk were already there, but she didn't see Ferek. Then she recalled Varais's headshake when she'd asked about the captain the afternoon before. She and Kaeryla had just seated themselves when Karlaak walked, or rather hobbled, into the small chamber. His forearm was heavily bandaged.

The captain turned to the two women undercaptains and inclined his head. "Thank you. Your arrival . . . yesterday . . . was more than timely."

"We did what we could," replied Taelya.

Karlaak nodded, then turned and sat down beside Vannyk, who offered a smile before turning to the captain.

"That's as close to praise as you'll get from him," murmured Kaeryla.

In turn, Taelya nodded, then picked up the tin cup and filled it with ale from the pitcher. Even the bitter brew didn't taste that bad. She took several more swallows.

The last three to enter the mess were Beltur, Jessyla, and Zekkarat, whose shoulder was heavily bound.

Beltur remained standing, and all other conversations stopped.

"We'll be leaving in three quints. The riding order will be Third Squad, Second Squad, the Fairhaven company, and then the three Montgren companies in whatever order Majer Zekkarat determines. All of you performed admirably yesterday. With four companies and two squads, we destroyed more than three battalions with four strong mages. It appears that less than two hundred of them survived. We lost almost one hundred troopers, and there are another thirty or so wounded, most of whom will likely survive . . ."

Taelya had the feeling that most of the casualties came from the Montgren companies, although Beltur clearly wasn't going into that.

"At the moment, we don't know if the Certans have tried to bridge the Montgren Gorge, but with a seasoned chaos mage and a full company at the gorge, and with the losses they already suffered at the gorge and the death of the Viscount, I'd be very surprised if they would immediately attempt to invade Montgren. Nor do we know whether other Gallosian battalions are considering additional actions. Based on the number of mages the Gallosians have lost and the casualties taken, I suspect it is highly unlikely that the Gallosians will continue any military activity against Montgren or Fairhaven. What Certis will do is less sure, but since the previous Viscount lost one of his few mages and his successor would face six successful war mages, I think it likely that Certis will not take any immediate action. Since we cannot count on that, however, we will be returning to Montgren as soon as possible. Thank you."

Then Beltur sat down and immediately took a long swallow from his cup.

"What do you think?" asked Valchar, looking to Taelya.

"There were only three Certan companies at the border, and they were awaiting orders. We took out close to a company, and I doubt they've heard anything yet. What Certis does depends on who becomes Viscount, and I'd be surprised if a new ruler is going to start or continue a war until he's more sure of his position." Especially since Taelya had suggested that the position of any Viscount who attacked Fairhaven would not be secure for very long.

"Did you plan that?" asked Valchar.

Taelya just smiled, then took another swallow of ale before starting to eat what might be a fowl and egg scramble.

LXXII

When Taelya and Kaeryla reached the barn behind Beltur and Jessyla's house on fourday, dusk had not quite become full evening. They had no sooner dismounted than Arthaal hurried toward them.

"Aunt Tulya has dinner ready for everyone, as soon as you're all here."

"Mother and Father won't be that long," said Kaeryla.

Arthaal frowned. "Both of you have low order and chaos. When did you last fight?"

"About a day ago. It was all over by late afternoon yesterday. We'll tell you about it at dinner . . . unless you already know."

"All we heard was that you fought the Gallosians and Hydlenese again and beat them badly. Can I help with the horses?"

"Yes!" declared Kaeryla emphatically.

Taelya just smiled.

Less than a quint later, Beltur and Jessyla arrived, and before that long, all seven members of both families were seated around the table in Tulya's house, along with Ysabella, Annana, and Sydel.

"You have no idea how glad I am that you've all returned in generally good health," said Tulya, raising a beaker in a toast. "In thanks for your safe return."

"We're not quite done yet," said Beltur. "We don't know what's happening at the Montgren Gorge, and we have some matters to straighten out with the Duchess. We'll talk about that at the officers' meeting in the morning. Early in the morning."

Matters to straighten out with the Duchess? That was an understatement, as far as Taelya was concerned. Her first thought was that the Duchess deserved the same fate as the Viscount. *But that could have some nasty repercussions for Fairhaven.* Taelya was still thinking about that when Tulya spoke up.

"Didn't you read the message from Sheralt?"

"I did, but . . . he wrote it the day before yesterday," replied Beltur.

"What did he say?" asked Taelya. She hadn't known about the message and couldn't help but feel concern for Sheralt.

"He said that the Certans had made one attempt to bridge the gorge and that he'd successfully destroyed all the timbers. He and Maakym's archers had killed more than a hundred Certans, and the Certans had withdrawn from any positions near the gorge."

"They aren't likely to be back all that soon," declared Taelya. "There were only three companies there when we passed through, and we took out close to a company when we destroyed their border post. If Sheralt and Maakym took out another company . . . it just might be some time before they could bring any timbers or a substantial force to the gorge."

"And that's if the new Viscount wants to take a chance," said Kaeryla.

"What if someone destroyed the message you left?" asked Dorylt.

"I think that's unlikely," said Beltur. "The two of you killed six guards and a white mage, and got through two iron gates or doors without anyone noticing until after you departed. Am I remembering that correctly?"

Taelya nodded.

"Given all the intrigues that surround rulers like the Viscount, it wouldn't be in anyone's interest to destroy that message because it's proof of a sort, along with a chaos bolt through the head, that Fairhaven assassinated the Viscount, rather than one of the heirs . . ."

Taelya saw that Ysabella's eyes had widened as Beltur spoke.

"It serves every possible heir's ambition to have the Viscount's death rest on us, rather than on one of them, because if one of them destroyed the message, then it could trigger more bloodshed."

"There will be intrigues and plotting anyway," said Tulya.

"That's true enough," replied Jessyla, "but it's in their interests for those to proceed slowly. Also . . . if they don't recognize that Fairhaven killed the Viscount, there will be those who will insist on continuing the war with Montgren and Fairhaven . . . and whoever destroyed the message couldn't be certain how many Viscounts might get killed."

"You . . . two . . . killed the Viscount?" asked Ysabella.

"We did," replied Taelya. "He offered an agreement and then went back on it and double-crossed both us and the Prefect." Taelya wasn't about to bring up the matter of the Duchess being part of the double cross. *Not yet, anyway.* "Sydon might still be alive without all that plotting." *And we might not be . . . or it still might have turned out the same.*

"Then he deserved to die," declared Ysabella.

"For many reasons," Beltur agreed. "But we'll still have to be careful with the next Viscount . . . and see what he has in mind."

"What I have in mind," declared Tulya, "is that we all should start eating and stop talking. Until all of you have something solid in your bodies, anyway."

"That's a very good idea," said Jessyla.

Taelya was almost the first to take a bite of the fowl and bean cassoulet, and she couldn't help smiling after that first mouthful. She ate several more bites before she asked, "How did you know we'd be back tonight?"

"I just counted days . . . and I had a feeling," replied Tulya. "Besides, if I'd been a day off, it would have been more of a stew than a cassoulet."

"If Arthaal and Dorylt hadn't eaten it all," replied Kaeryla.

"We would have left some," protested Arthaal.

"Not much," retorted Kaeryla.

"By the way," began Tulya, "you might be interested to know that Johlana has asked Ysabella to help her, and she and the twins just finished moving there. This will be their last regular dinner here, but we'll certainly have them over now and again. I think Johlana's just happy to have young people around again . . . and she could use other hands around her place."

Left unsaid was that Johlana had departed Axalt before any of her grandchildren had been born, and now even the youngest of Tulya's and Jessyla's children were no longer that young.

"She also likes to help people. She always has." Jessyla looked to Ysabella. "She's a very warm and kind woman. You're most fortunate."

"People here are nice," interjected Annana. "Why do they want to fight with you?"

"Because people here are different," said Sydel. "Most people don't like those who are different. No one but Father really liked Mother. You know that."

"Why didn't they like your mother?" asked Arthaal.

Taelya managed not to wince at the question.

"They just didn't. They said her mother was an evil white witch."

Taelya almost nodded. *That* might explain a great deal. She looked to Ysabella. "So your mother could possibly have been a mage here, but not in Gallos?"

"I don't know. She died when I was born. My aunt wouldn't talk about her, and no one else would, either."

"None of that matters now," declared Jessyla. "You're all here, and Annana can be a white, and Sydel a black . . . if you want to work hard enough. If not, you can do other work, and no one will say anything."

But it would be such a waste. Rather than speak, Taelya waited.

"Did you always want to be a mage?" Annana asked Jessyla.

Beltur laughed softly, and Annana looked quizzically at him.

"She wanted to be a mage from the beginning. She just couldn't figure out how," explained Beltur.

"Beltur knew how to teach me. No one else even thought I could."

"You see," said Ysabella, "we are in the right place."

Even Sydel nodded.

LXXIII

When Taelya entered the kitchen at dawn on fiveday morning, Tulya had her breakfast waiting.

"You didn't have to—"

"I wanted to. Besides, you'll need a good breakfast. You and Kaeryla and Third Squad are escorting Beltur to Vergren. I cleaned your least dirty uniform the best I could, and packed your good uniform in your duffel."

"Thank you." Taelya couldn't exactly say she was surprised, either by her mother knowing where she was headed before Taelya herself did . . . or for the thoughtfulness with the uniforms. "Then Jessyla and Valchar are staying here?"

"That makes the most sense, don't you think? She's also the best healer, and there are more than a few wounded. And from what I've heard, together you and Kaeryla may be one of the most powerful magely forces in Candar. You might be needed if the Certans try an invasion . . . or for other reasons. Now . . . eat that ham and egg scramble, or Dorylt will likely be begging some of it from you. You look like you need it more than he does."

"Do I look that bad?"

"You're better this morning. You looked tired last night. So did Kaeryla. I thought you two might be. That was another reason why I had dinner ready as soon as you all could eat it."

"I did like sleeping in my own bed."

"Ysabella thought you would. She's really sweet. So is Annana. Beltur's going to have his hands full with Sydel. It may take the two of you."

"I only met his father once, and once in battle, but Sydel does seem to take after Sydon."

"You two will put him in line." Tulya smiled almost mischievously, then said, "You got Sheralt to do things the right way, I heard."

"Mother . . ."

"Didn't you?"

Taelya shook her head, not because she disagreed, but because she didn't want to discuss Sheralt at that moment.

"He likes you. He more than likes you. Just be careful."

"I know . . . but you were telling me to wait and see."

"From what I've heard, you saw a great deal, and you're older now, in ways that count. You're also not as young as Kaeryla, dear."

"I'm not an old spinster, either."

"You don't have to have children immediately . . . and you shouldn't. But it helps to be close to someone for a time before you have children."

"Mother . . ."

"He just about worships every scrap of chaos you throw his way."

Taelya barely managed not to choke on the ale she had started to drink. Even so, she had to cough several times to clear her throat. "I think . . . you've . . . made . . . your point . . ." She coughed again.

"You're even more stubborn than I am," said Tulya reflectively. "Sometimes, I was too stubborn. I'd hate to see that in you."

"I'll think about it. I likely won't be seeing him too soon."

"You'll be in Weevett tonight."

"He won't be. He'll be almost a day away at the Montgren border post. That's until we know that the Certans won't be trying to invade Montgren."

"Then you'd better finish your breakfast."

Taelya wasn't quite sure what that meant, except that her mother wasn't going to say more about Sheralt for the moment, but she did resume eating.

When she finished, she looked up. "This is the best breakfast I've had in eight-days."

"That was the idea."

"What was the idea?" asked Dorylt as he slouched toward the table.

"That you two get a good breakfast. You need to hurry. Beltur called an all-officers' meeting at sixth glass, and while you're a provisional undercaptain, you're still an officer."

Taelya hid a grin while she took a last swallow of ale before getting up.

"Don't forget your duffel."

"I won't . . . and thank you again for taking care of my uniforms."

"I thought you'd need the good one when you meet with the Duchess. Make sure you're part of that group. If Beltur objects, tell him I said you needed to be there."

"I don't think it will come to that, but I will if it's necessary." Then Taelya hurried to get her duffel and gear.

She and Kaeryla had almost finished saddling their mounts when both Arthaal and Dorylt came running to the barn.

"You two had better hurry," said Taelya. "We're leaving as soon as we can."

"Beltur's having a meeting earlier than usual," grumbled Dorylt.

Arthaal mumbled something Taelya didn't hear clearly.

"Stop complaining," snapped Kaeryla. "He told us last night. You just weren't listening."

"I was tired."

"You don't even know what tired is," returned Kaeryla, taking the mare's reins and turning to lead her horse out of the barn.

Taelya followed with Bounder, and the two mounted, then started toward headquarters.

"We don't have to hurry that much," said Kaeryla. "That way, they might come close to catching up." She paused, then asked, "What do you think will happen with the Duchess?"

"What will happen and what should happen are two different possibilities," replied Taelya, because she'd thought more than a little about Koralya over the past few days.

"How can we trust her after all she did?"

"We can't. But who can remove her . . . besides us? And what would that tell every other ruler in Candar?"

"We don't dare do anything? That's . . . awful."

"There's also the problem that the only document we know about that suggests what she may have had in mind only states that the Montgren Gorge bridge needed to be kept open under all circumstances. Since we've stopped the immediate Certan attacks to take and cross the bridge, that order only shows bad judgment, not a conspiracy with the Viscount."

"You mean . . . she'll get away with it? I can't believe that Father would let that happen."

"I doubt that he will, but the less we talk about it to anyone but each other, the better . . . at least for now. If too many people talk, that will make it harder for your father. Right now, only a few officers know. You might tell Valchar not to say anything yet."

"You could tell him."

"I could . . . but he'd rather hear it from you, and it is your father who will have to deal with the Duchess."

Kaeryla nodded. "I can see that. I'll mention it to him before we leave."

The two undercaptains had tied their horses outside the stable, since the sun had yet to rise and the air wasn't too warm yet, and were walking across the courtyard when Arthaal and Dorylt rode in.

"You could have waited," said Arthaal.

"You could have gotten up when you were supposed to," replied Kaeryla.

Dorylt wisely only said, "We need to take care of the horses and get to the duty room."

As the young men rode away toward the stable, Kaeryla said, "Dorylt's gotten much stronger as a mage."

"So has Arthaal."

"He was stronger than Dorylt when we left. Now they're about the same."

"We're all different," said Taelya.

"Do you think mages should consort other mages or healers?"

"Only if they love and respect each other."

"But if you look at our families, there are more mages among the children."

"I'm not sure I want to be bred like a horse," said Taelya dryly.

"I didn't . . ."

"I know, but the thought bothers me." Taelya opened the door and gestured for Kaeryla to go first. "What if some ruler, like the Prefect, figures that out?"

"Well, it takes a long time for people to have children and their children to have children . . . and it's not good to consort with close relations."

"Keep that thought in mind."

The two made their way to the duty room, where Therran, Gustaan, and Vannyk were already waiting. Before long, Karlaak and Valchar joined them, followed by Dorylt and Arthaal, both breathing faster than usual. Finally, Beltur, Zekkarat, and Jessyla entered the chamber.

"Good morning," said Beltur cheerfully, surveying the room. "We've had a busy summer so far, I'd say. Matters are looking hopeful, but they're not settled yet. Not all of them. I strongly doubt that we'll have to worry about the Prefect or any Duke of Hydlen, if one even emerges from the so-called Gallosian protectorate, for quite some time. Nor will we need to worry about Viscount Rystyn, but since we don't even know who his successor is, that is a loose end that might prove troublesome.

"Even so, at the moment," Beltur went on, "there's absolutely no reason for any Montgren company to remain in Fairhaven. Majer Zekkarat and I agree on that. The first Fairhaven company will be back close to full strength before long, and the second company—that's the one formed out of the Lydian companies—is close to combat-ready. There are certain questions raised by the Duchess's orders regarding the Montgren Gorge bridge, and by the implications of those orders. In order to resolve those questions, Third Squad and I will be accompanying the three Montgren companies on their return to Weevett or Vergren . . . wherever Majer Zekkarat believes those companies should be posted. Third Squad and I will then proceed to Vergren with Majer Zekkarat and whatever companies he feels should return there. Mage-Captain Jessyla will be in command here in my absence. I cannot say how long matters in Vergren will take, but I doubt that resolving them will take more than an eightday, possibly less." He paused. "Do any of you have any questions?"

"Is it possible that the Certans might decide to march south and then take the old road to Fairhaven?" asked Therran.

"Anything is possible, but it would take more than two eightdays for that to occur. First, it will take several days yet for word about the bridge's destruction to get to Jellico. Then it would take several more days to assemble and supply such a force, and almost two eightdays to reach Fairhaven. There's also the likelihood that the new Viscount might not wish to risk his own life or the possibility of an immediate military defeat so soon after becoming Viscount. At the moment, the Prefect can't be too happy with Certis, and if Certis moved a large force against Fairhaven, that might invite retaliation by Gallos."

"In short . . . you don't think it's likely that Certis will move against us soon."

"We need to watch Certis carefully, but I'd say that any Viscount who decides to attack anyone in the near future is likely not to hold his seat. The whole idea behind the hidden alliance between Gallos and Certis was to obtain control of Montgren and destroy Fairhaven without risking that many troopers. Gallos has lost over five battalions and more than ten mages, and Certis at least a battalion, a Viscount, and a white mage. In addition, with the loss of the Montgren Gorge bridge, the traders of Certis will suffer the most."

Taelya nodded at that, knowing that her uncle wasn't pointing out that the loss of the bridge couldn't but help Fairhaven.

"Since there are no more questions, the meeting is over. Third Squad and the Montgren companies will be leaving headquarters in two quints. All Fairhaven officers except those in Third Squad are to remain for daily duty assignments by Captain Jessyla."

Beltur turned and left the duty room, followed by Zekkarat. Jessyla remained. Then the Montgren officers hurried out.

Valchar walked over to Taelya. "There's plenty he's not saying."

"There are reasons for that," replied Taelya, nodding to Kaeryla. "She can explain it better than I might."

Valchar smiled wryly. "Less directly, you mean?"

Taelya smiled pleasantly and said to Kaeryla, "I'll have the squad ready."

Although Varais has already taken care of that. Then she turned and headed for the stable yard and Bounder.

As Taelya knew, Varais had Third Squad formed up and ready.

"Undercaptain Kaeryla is dealing with something. She'll be here shortly."

Varais nodded. "Majer Beltur said we'd lead the way, and that he'd be back here in a few moments. Is it true that we're the only Fairhaven troopers going with the Montgren companies?"

"That's right. I understand that the majer has some matters to discuss with the Duchess. What those are I don't know." And Taelya wasn't about to offer her opinions on what they should be. Not yet, anyway. As she sensed Kaeryla approaching, she turned.

The younger mage wore an amused smile as she reined up beside Taelya. "Valchar knew exactly what you were doing."

"Good. He still enjoyed hearing it from you."

Kaeryla blushed momentarily, then shook her head. "I'm going to have a few words with Sheralt when he returns."

Taelya smiled in return. "I hadn't thought otherwise."

Less than a quint later, Beltur rode up. "We can head out now."

Taelya turned in the saddle and nodded to Varais.

"Third Squad! Forward!"

None of the mages spoke again until Third Squad was on the main street headed west toward the Weevett road.

Then Beltur said, "You'll be the vanguard all the way to Vergren, but I'll be spending most of the time on the way to Weevett going over matters with Zekkarat."

"What matters?" asked Kaeryla, her voice guileless.

"The matters that we're going to discuss, of course," replied Beltur. "You two might have noticed that I understated things at the meeting, but Zekkarat has doubtless figured that out . . . or will. By the end of summer, Fairhaven will have three full combat companies. We already have six fully trained combat mages, and in a year or two, both Arthaal and Dorylt will be much better. Annana will likely follow the example you two have set. Sydel . . . he's going to take some work."

"What that means is that Fairhaven is stronger in terms of troopers and mages than Montgren is," Taelya said.

"Zekkarat knows that already. We need to talk over presenting the facts to the Duchess, as well as a few other things. We'll also get more traders because the gorge bridge won't be rebuilt unless it's designed to be removed in less than a glass. Neither Montgren nor Fairhaven can afford to allow Certis an easy passage into Montgren."

"The Duchess won't like that," said Kaeryla.

"That may be," replied Beltur, "but we won't accept anything else."

"Kaeryla and I will be at that meeting," said Taelya.

"You've decided that on your own?"

"No. The treasurer and justicer of Fairhaven suggested it," said Taelya.

"And so did the head healer," added Kaeryla.

"In that event," replied Beltur, a certain wry amusement in his voice, "I might as well admit that I agree with them."

LXXIV

Taelya had expected to find the Weevett post locked and closed, but there were fresh-faced guards at the gates and a Montgren banner drooping from the flagstaff in the still air of late midafternoon. As Third Squad neared the gates, Zekkarat rode past Taelya and directly up to the guards.

"What company has garrisoned the post? I'd ordered it closed."

"The training company under Undercaptain Haaskyn, ser. We just got here on threeday."

"Where is he?"

"In the duty room, I think, ser." The trooper who had answered looked totally confused, as if he had no idea what Zekkarat wanted.

"We have two companies here, and a squad from Fairhaven. We're headed to Vergren. We'll only be here for the night."

"Ser . . . might I ask?"

"Majer Beltur led our companies to two solid victories over the Gallosians and the Hydlenese. They lost close to six battalions in both battles and at Passera." Zekkarat gestured for Third Squad to follow him into the post.

Taelya thought that the young trooper looked even more bewildered after Zekkarat's brief reply. She wondered what the recruits in the training squads might have been told . . . or not told, as the case might have been.

Third Squad hadn't even reached the stables when a graying undercaptain stepped out into the courtyard. "Majer Zekkarat! Thank the fates you're here. What happened? Why was the post closed?"

"The troopers were needed elsewhere urgently. We'll talk about that at an officers' meeting after we take care of our mounts and arrange for the men. We'll only be here a night. We're headed to Vergren to meet with the Duchess. Oh . . . Majer Beltur led us to two decisive victories in Hydlen."

Undercaptain Haaskyn looked stunned for a moment. "That's . . . wonderful . . . I don't know that anyone expected it."

"We'll go over all of that at the meeting," said Zekkarat firmly in a tone in which Taelya could not only sense, but actually hear a barely concealed displeasure.

The older undercaptain could obviously hear it as well, since he swallowed and said, "Yes, ser."

A good two quints passed before Zekkarat gathered the other six officers together in the small mess. Haaskyn looked particularly dispirited.

"When did you arrive here?" Zekkarat asked Haaskyn without any preamble or explanation.

"On threeday evening, ser. Lord Korwaen dispatched me with the last two squads of the training company to make certain that the Montgren Gorge bridge remained open to traders. I sent two troopers yesterday morning to the border post, but I've had no response."

"That's because I ordered Captain Maakym not to respond."

"Maakym?"

"He was Ferek's undercaptain, but took over Konstyn's company when the Gallosians killed both Konstyn and Drakyn at Passera. That was immediately after the Certans double-crossed us . . ." Zekkarat gave a quick summary of what had happened at Passera and on the return to Montgren, but did not mention the death of the Viscount, ending with, "Given that the Certans were preparing to use the gorge bridge to invade Montgren and given that I had no knowledge about the Duchess's requirement that the bridge remain open, we did what we could to stop the Certans from invading, which included destroying the bridge. The Fairhaven forces were also kind enough to lend us a chaos mage to remain with the company there in order to burn any timbers the Certans might use to try to bridge the gorge."

Haaskyn swallowed several times. "Lord Korwaen did not mention any of that."

"We'll take care of informing Korwaen," said Zekkarat. "In the meantime, you just keep the Weevett post open and operating. Oh . . . and after we blocked the gorge to the Certans, we joined Majer Beltur's forces. Our companies, his company, and the Fairhaven mages destroyed more than three Hydlenese and Gallosian battalions. Then we returned to Fairhaven, and we're now headed to Vergren to report the results to the Duchess."

"I'm sure she'll be pleased, ser."

"Given the possible threat still posed by the Certans, Undercaptain Vannyk's company will also remain here as support for Captain Maakym's force, at least until matters are clearer as to what the Certans may do after what happened at the Montgren Gorge." Zekkarat turned to Vannyk. "You'll need to send two troopers as couriers to Maakym with a dispatch from me, well before dawn tomorrow. We'll go over the details later."

"Yes, ser."

Zekkarat turned back to Haaskyn. "As the commander of an operational combat company, Undercaptain Vannyk outranks you. You're to give him every assistance possible. Is that clear?"

"Yes, ser. What if Lord Korwaen sends any orders?"

"You're to hand them over to Undercaptain Vannyk, who will deal with them and consult as necessary with Captain Maakym."

"But they're from the Lord Protector."

"And they should go to the senior operational officer for action," replied Zekkarat. "That has always been what's required. I'm sure you wouldn't wish to go against the chain of command."

"Oh, no, ser."

"Don't you worry, Haaskyn. We'll make certain Lord Korwaen understands the situation."

"Thank you, ser."

"Now . . . we'll adjourn for a glass, while the cooks see what they can find to feed us." Zekkarat looked to Vannyk. "We have a few details to work out."

Taelya had no doubt that Vannyk would get very specific orders. She also hoped dinner would be palatable.

LXXV

Taelya went to sleep on fiveday night still speculating over what might have happened in Vergren, especially about what the Duchess and Korwaen might have done, but found, when she woke on sixday morning, that she'd actually slept fairly soundly. She sat up on the narrow bunk and stretched.

Kaeryla sat up much more slowly. "I hope breakfast is better than dinner."

"Dinner wasn't that bad."

"How can you say that when your mother's such a good cook?"

"Everyone can't be that good. Besides, I was hungry." Taelya immediately began to get ready for the day and the ride to Vergren.

"I wasn't anywhere near *that* hungry," muttered Kaeryla.

Before that long, the two were in the officers' mess eating. Breakfast was decent—fried eggs in a mild burhka sauce over toasted bread—and by two quints past sixth glass, Third Squad was leading the way out of the Weevett post, leaving behind Vannyk's company as support for what might happen at the Montgren Gorge.

"Majer Zekkarat must have dispatched the messengers to the gorge border post early," Taelya said to Beltur as the squad approached the nearly empty town square in Weevett.

"They left at third glass this morning with spare mounts. Zekkarat wants a response back before we reach Vergren."

"That's pushing it, isn't it?"

"Not too much and not with spare mounts. They'll change couriers and mounts at the border post and then at Weevett on the way back."

"What do you think happened in Vergren with the Duchess and Korwaen?" asked Kaeryla.

"I'd rather not guess," replied Beltur. "We'll hear what the two have to say . . . or what they refuse to say . . . soon enough."

"You're not fond of the new Duchess, are you?" pressed Kaeryla.

"I don't know her well at all. I've only met her a handful of times. It does appear that she's made some unwise decisions and that certain deaths were of a suspicious nature. That's another reason why you two are here. Jessyla would have been ideal, but we needed to leave a strong older mage in Fairhaven."

"So . . . we're strong enough," said Kaeryla, "but not old enough?"

"You've been through enough, but you're not yet seen as old enough," replied Beltur. "What people think and believe, unfortunately, sometimes counts for more than the facts of a situation or person. It took years for people to realize that Jessyla was more than a healer, and years for others to realize that Tulya is incredibly fair as a justicer, and outstanding in managing the town treasury. It will take you two less time to be recognized than it did for them, but it will take time. There are also disadvantages to being seen as strong."

"Is that why Koralya tried to get Certis and Gallos to destroy Fairhaven?" asked Kaeryla. "Because she didn't want Fairhaven to be strong?"

"It's more likely that they enticed her," suggested Taelya, "because she worried about that."

"We don't know any of that, not yet," replied Beltur. "That's one reason why we're headed to Vergren. Now . . . nothing more on the subject. Not until we know more." He eased his mount to the side. "I need to spend more time with Zekkarat. I'll be back in a while."

Almost a glass passed before Beltur returned, and he immediately looked at Kaeryla and said, "Not a word."

Kaeryla frowned, then looked away.

Several quints passed as Third Squad rode northward through the warm and muggy morning air before Kaeryla said, "Two riders headed toward us. They're more than two kays away beyond the two wooded hills."

"I just sensed them," said Beltur. "Most likely dispatch riders. Let's see what they do. We'll have to chase them down if they don't come to us."

"I could throw a concealment around them if they try to ride away," said Taelya.

"Or a containment," added Kaeryla.

"Let's just see," said Beltur. "That might also tell us something."

Another quint went by, and Taelya said, "They're coming around the curve in the road, and they should see us before long."

When the two riders in Montgren blue did come into sight, they were only about five hundred yards from Third Squad and continued to ride for another fifty yards or so as if they hadn't seen the oncoming force. Then the two slowed their mounts but kept riding. Only when they were possibly two hundred yards away did they rein up.

One rider gestured violently to the other, then turned his mount, then stopped abruptly.

"Can you drop a concealment over them from here, Taelya?"

"It's done," replied Taelya, as the two riders vanished from sight.

"We need to ride closer," said Beltur.

Taelya understood, since she'd sensed that Beltur had a containment around the riders, and holding even a comparatively small containment at that distance would get to be a strain very quickly.

Beltur and Taelya, followed closely by Kaeryla, rode quickly to where the two riders were trapped.

". . . can't move, and I can't see anything . . ."

". . . told you we needed to turn back . . ."

When the three mages were within fifty yards, Beltur said, "You can remove the concealment."

Taelya did so.

Both riders blinked, then turned to look at the oncoming mages.

"Ride toward us," Beltur commanded as he reined up. "You'll find you can move that way."

"Now what?" murmured one of the riders.

"You ride toward us, or you'll get very uncomfortable very quickly," said Beltur. "And Majer Zekkarat will soon make it even less comfortable."

The two dispatch riders exchanged glances and then rode forward until they were less than ten yards away.

"Rein up there, and we'll wait for the majer to join us."

Before that long, Third Squad reached the five, and Varais called out, "Squad halt!" Then Zekkarat rode forward to join the three mages.

Beltur said loudly, "I don't think they wanted you to see what they're carrying, Majer Zekkarat."

One of the riders stiffened for a moment.

"I think you're right, Mage-Majer Beltur." Then Zekkarat addressed the riders. "I strongly suggest you don't attempt anything rash. In addition to the majer, the other two officers with him are also mages, and one of them is an extremely powerful chaos mage. Now . . . you can hand over the dispatch pouches peacefully, and everything will be fine . . ."

"But it's from the Lord Protector. It's not for you, ser."

"Since I'm the remaining senior officer in the forces of Montgren, who else would it be for?"

"It's addressed to Undercaptain Haaskyn or Undercaptain Chaarkyn, ser," replied the older-looking trooper.

"Excellent." Zekkarat rode forward.

Taelya could sense when Beltur shifted the containment to a shield behind the riders that would have prevented their fleeing.

The older rider handed a dispatch pouch to Zekkarat.

Having a feeling about that, Taelya asked, "Is that the real dispatch pouch?"

"Yes."

"'Yes, ser'!" snapped Taelya. "And you're lying." She threw the tiniest chaos bolt past the rider's shoulder.

For a moment, the rider who had lied froze. Then he swallowed.

"She's a mage-undercaptain who can tell if you're lying and could kill you if you do again," said Zekkarat. "Now . . . hand over all of the pouches."

Another pouch appeared.

"Is that all?" asked Zekkarat.

"Yes, ser."

"He's telling the truth," said Taelya, who looked to the second rider. "Do you have any pouches or messages?"

"No, ser."

"He doesn't," said Taelya.

"Good," replied Zekkarat. "Now, after we put these two under restraints, we'll see what's in the pouches."

"Squad Leader," Taelya ordered Varais, "please provide an escort for the two couriers back to the first Montgren company and inform the company that they're to be kept under restraints at all times. You can kill them if they try to escape."

Both riders paled.

Even Zekkarat blinked.

Once the riders were led away, Zekkarat looked at Taelya. "You meant that, didn't you?"

"I could be wrong, but when a junior trooper wants to avoid the most senior officer, it smells like treason to me."

"Well," said Zekkarat, "we should see if you're right." He opened the first pouch, took out a document and read for just a bit, then returned it to the pouch with a smile. "Obviously, a dummy message, since it's about the need to maintain discipline." He folded the first pouch and tucked it into his belt, then opened the second, which he began to read, much more intently. Finally, he looked up.

"What does it say?" asked Beltur. "Or do we already know?"

"Pretty much what we feared," replied Zekkarat. "It is to Haaskyn and Chaarkyn. I'll read the guts of it.

"'The Montgren Gorge bridge is to remain open under all circumstances. Failure to comply with this order may result in maximum penalty under courts-martial proceedings. Failure to acknowledge and comply with this order will result in similar and immediate disciplinary action . . .'"

Zekkarat shook his head, then said, "The rest is fancy language emphasizing the need to comply with orders issued by the Lord Protector."

"Signed by Korwaen or the Duchess?" asked Beltur.

"Korwaen as Lord Protector of Montgren."

"He's taking himself rather seriously," said Beltur. "But that might make matters much easier."

Zekkarat nodded. "It might at that, but we'll have to see."

There's far too much we have to see. But that wasn't anything that the two majers didn't already know, and Taelya didn't need to tell them.

Later that afternoon, Third Squad had just ridden past the kaystone proclaiming that Vergren lay five kays ahead when Zekkarat rode forward to join Beltur near the head of Third Squad. "I just got the reply from Captain Maakym. He understands the situation and will comply. The Certans made another attempt to make a crossing on threeday, but took heavy casualties, nearly a company's worth, especially from the chaos-bolts of Undercaptain Sheralt. Maakym only had three men wounded. All Certan forces were withdrawn from the gorge area yesterday. With the bridge gone, he has no way to tell whether those forces were withdrawn just to the post at Orduna or are returning to Jellico. Undercaptain Sheralt could not sense any within two kays."

"That sounds hopeful for the present," said Beltur.

"We've done well on the fighting, but we still have to deal with whatever's happened in Vergren. I have my own ideas, but I'd like to hear yours."

"I think we should just ride up to the palace and see the Duchess. Surprise is often useful."

"What if she seals the palace? It was built as a fortress originally, you know."

"Then we see what we can do about gaining entry." Beltur grinned. "I do believe that we have two mages that managed a similar feat in Jellico. I also suspect you know the weakest gates and the like. And, unless matters have changed, it's not garrisoned as a fortress and hasn't been for years."

"You're right about that," replied Zekkarat. "I also have the feeling that Duchess Koralya might not have wanted to spend additional golds for such garrisoning."

"Sers," said Taelya, "I have a suggestion that might be useful."

"What might that be?" asked Zekkarat.

"Third Squad is experienced in riding as a unit under a concealment. It just might be easier if we rode up under a concealment, used containments as necessary, and then kept the gates open until your two companies arrived."

Zekkarat looked to Beltur.

"If we're detected before we get to the gates," said Beltur, "we're no worse off than we'd have been otherwise."

Zekkarat fingered his chin, then nodded. "We might as well try it."

The road from Weevett ran roughly north-northwest into the center of Vergren until it reached the main square, where only a few vendors remained, unsurprisingly, since it was after fourth glass, and sixday wasn't a market day. At the square, Third Squad, following Beltur's instructions, turned north, following the well-paved road toward the palace. Taelya even remembered the side road to the left that led to Korsaen and Maeyora's estate, the estate that now likely belonged to Korwaen. She wondered how his sister Maenya might be . . . or if some "accident" or "illness" had befallen her as well. She couldn't count on having heard anything about Maenya because, outside of Fairhaven and possibly Westwind or Sarronnyn, no one said anything about younger sisters, particularly if they weren't part of the ruling family. But then, Maenya might just have been conveniently consorted—and that *might* have protected her from Korwaen.

Taelya recalled the palace, if not in detail, but that it was set on a low hill. There was one wall around the base of the hill, with a single set of gates, usually guarded by two men, and then a set of old but sturdy iron-bound doors to the palace proper, with two more guards. The palace itself would have easily fit inside the main courtyard of the palace of the Viscount, although there were outbuildings set on terraced levels of the hill.

"There's too much distance between the wall guards and the palace guards, unless two of us go farther under a concealment," Taelya said.

Beltur smiled. "Who do you suggest?"

"You're stronger with multiple containments. You ought to hold and silence the wall guards and let Kaeryla and me deal with the palace guards."

"I can handle the wall guards without having to remain with them," replied Beltur. "That way, there will be three of us in case we run into trouble at the palace. Also, we won't enter the palace until Zekkarat joins us. Just drop the concealment once we have control of the palace doors. Then the whole squad can watch the smaller doors, while Majer Zekkarat is joining us with the other two companies."

"Did you get that, Squad Leader?" Taelya asked Varais.

"Yes, ser. I'll pass on that we'll be riding under a concealment."

"The road is stone-paved all the way to the walls and then to the palace. That should help keep the men in position."

"Appreciate the information, ser."

Even though Third Squad was far from full strength, Taelya doubted that the palace guards were equipped to deal with battle-tested troopers and three mages. *But you never know.*

Just before Third Squad reached the crest in the road that led down into the vale around the hill holding the palace and its outbuildings, Kaeryla covered the entire squad, which continued at a slow walk toward the wall gate and the two guards. Behind them, the two Montgren companies halted.

Third Squad managed to get within fifty yards of the gates before one of the guards said, "Do you hear horse hooves on the road?"

"They're probably just out of sight."

"Who'd be coming here now? There aren't any troopers in twenty kays. Not so far as I know, and Lord Korwaen hasn't left the palace yet."

At that moment, both guards stopped talking, because Beltur had wrapped them both in containments, and Taelya put a concealment around each.

Once the squad reached a point about five yards from the fallen guards, Taelya said quietly, but firmly, "Squad. Halt." Then she added, "We need to secure the two guards before we proceed."

Beltur was already off his mount with rope in his hands. While it took him longer to tie and gag the two guards using his senses, rather than sight, they were in no shape to resist. Then he dragged both men outside the wall, where they couldn't be seen. After that, he quickly remounted.

"Squad, forward," ordered Taelya. "Slow through the gates. They're wide open, but stay on the pavement."

The troopers managed getting through the gates without scraping themselves or their mounts and proceeded along the stone road. Taelya kept sensing both the road and the area around the palace, just in case some functionary or visitor might be leaving, but all she could sense were three mounts tied outside the main doors to the palace, one of which most likely belonged to Korwaen, at least from what one of the guards had said.

She frowned, then said quietly, "There are four guards by the main doors."

"I thought that might be a possibility," replied Beltur. "When we get closer, I'll take the two flanking the doors. Kaeryla, you take the one on the far left, and Taelya, you the one on the far right. As soon as all four are contained, drop the concealment. It'll be quicker that way because the squad troopers can tie up the guards."

Third Squad reached a point only some twenty yards from the guards when one spoke. "I hear horses. Must be someone coming from the stable . . ."

"Might be the Duchess and her guards . . ."

"She hasn't been riding lately."

"Still hear hooves on the stone . . ."

"Now," said Beltur.

The only sounds that followed the containments were the muffled sounds of falling bodies and a few dull clunks and clanks.

Kaeryla immediately removed the concealment.

"Harrad! Eshlyn!" snapped Varais. "Tie those four up and have gags ready when the mages remove the containments. You'll also have to tighten the bonds once the containments come off."

As usual, it took a moment or two before Taelya could see clearly, but all four guards were sprawled facedown on the stone walk that led to the iron-bound doors. The outer doors were swung open. The inner doors were closed.

Beltur was off his mount and moving to the inner doors even before the troopers finished securing the stunned guards, who were still groggy from the lack of breath. The older one who seemed to recover the soonest looked at the Fairhaven troopers with an expression of total shock, not that he could say anything, gagged as he was.

"I've got the inner doors open, and I've removed the bars," declared Beltur. "You two watch the outside for any other guards. I'll take the entry hallway."

Taelya kept sensing, but she found no one near the outside front of the palace, nor did she sense anyone near Beltur on the inside in the more than half a quint it took for Zekkarat and the two companies to arrive.

Zekkarat had just dismounted when Beltur called out, "Someone's coming to greet us. It might be the Lord Protector. He has two guards with him. Taelya, Kaeryla . . . stand ready to disarm them, if necessary. Taelya, the one on the right. Kaeryla, the one on the left."

The two guards emerged from the palace first, each bearing a small crossbow, ready to fire, and each was pointed at one of the majers.

Neither undercaptain hesitated, and both guards were instantly immobilized.

Following them out into the late-afternoon sunlight was Korwaen, his eyes taking in Third Squad, as well as the two companies formed up in front of the palace. "So what do we have here, a rebellion in the making?" As Korwaen spoke, his tone sneeringly sardonic, he brushed back a lock of foppishly long light brown hair. He didn't seem to recognize that his guards were immobilized within containments.

"No, more like a restoration of the usual order in Montgren," replied Beltur.

"Do you really think you can make whatever you've done stand?" asked Korwaen. "At least a half score of battalions from Hydlen, Gallos, and Certis are making their way here to support the rule of Duchess Koralya. Fairhaven will be reduced to nothing."

"You'll continue as the Lord Protector of the Duchess, I presume?" asked Zekkarat.

"Or possibly in another capacity," replied Korwaen.

At that moment, both guards crashed forward onto the stones.

"Tie them up," ordered Varais, a combination of disgust and resignation in her voice, watching as troopers recovered the crossbows and tied up Korwaen's personal guards.

"I'll have them freed within an eightday, if not sooner," declared the Lord Protector.

"You're assuming several things that may not in fact be true," replied Zekkarat.

"It's time we see the Duchess," said Beltur, turning to Taelya and adding, "We'll need ten troopers, Undercaptain."

Taelya nodded to Varais.

"Harrad and Eshlyn, remain here with me," declared the squad leader. "The rest of you accompany the officers."

Zekkarat turned his mount. "Captain Karlaak, make sure the area remains secure. No one is to leave. Use whatever force is necessary."

"I believe such an order is my prerogative," declared Korwaen.

"It may have been," declared Zekkarat, "but no longer."

By the time all troopers were in position, all the captives fully secured, except Korwaen, and the mounts of those entering the palace tied up, a good third of a quint had passed.

Beltur led the way into the circular entry hall, with Taelya and Kaeryla flanking Zekkarat, their shields extended slightly to protect the majer just in case someone inside had any ideas of violence. Behind them, two troopers escorted Korwaen, his hands tied together at the wrists behind his back.

Taelya could sense his absolute arrogance and certainty. *Is he so self-deluded that he doesn't understand . . . or are we?* Then she shook her head. She'd seen the thousands of bodies, unlike Korwaen, who might have ordered deaths, but likely had never done the deeds or seen the deaths he caused.

Taelya had forgotten just how dark the palace was, with the dark wooden paneling looking almost black. The echo of boots on the stone floor reverberated through the main corridor. Some thirty yards down the main corridor, Beltur stopped outside a door where two guards stood with spears crossed across the door proper.

"The Duchess wishes to be alone, Officers."

Beltur looked inquiringly to Zekkarat.

Zekkarat nodded back, then addressed the guards. "Her wishes are irrel-evant. She needs to hear the latest news of what has happened in the field. As the senior officer remaining in Montgren, I have the right and duty to inform her."

Taelya sensed the chamber beyond the door. There was indeed only one per-son there, seated behind a desk.

"She asked not to be disturbed, sers."

Zekkarat turned. "Undercaptains . . . if you would immobilize them. There's little point in forcing them."

After more than a few moments, the two guards were trussed up and stretched on the floor.

"Khaspar," said Taelya. "Hold the corridor. We're not to be interrupted un-less it's quite urgent."

"Yes, ser."

Abruptly, Korwaen said, "I know you—"

Before he could say more, Taelya clamped a containment across his mouth and turned. "Yes, you do. And you should know that I never liked self-centered indulgent bullies. You will speak only when addressed and only to answer any questions. If you attempt to speak otherwise, I will choke you until you're unconscious . . . unless I do worse."

For the first time, the look and sense of arrogance diminished, but the sense of outrage and anger increased.

Taelya removed the containment. "Is that clear?"

Korwaen's eyes blazed hatred, but he nodded.

Then Zekkarat opened the door and entered the study, followed by Beltur, then by Taelya and Kaeryla.

Koralya looked older than Taelya remembered. Her face was drawn, and the black of her hair was too even and dark to be natural. She wore a gown of silver cloth that, even with her seated behind the wide table desk, showed a feminine figure. Her brown eyes were hard and flat as she looked from Zekkarat to Bel-tur, and quickly and dismissively over Taelya and Kaeryla.

"So what defeats do you report, Majer?"

"I must report," said Zekkarat, his tone ironic, "that, largely due to the efforts of Majer Beltur and Fairhaven, we have twice defeated the Hydlenese and the Gallosians, and that they lost over six battalions in those defeats. Those were dead, not wounded. My forces were betrayed, as you well knew, by the Certans, but, even so, we killed almost another battalion of Gallosians at Passera. The two undercaptain mages here, in response to that betrayal, killed Viscount Rystyn, as well as six of his guards and a white mage, and during and after our withdrawal from Certis, we also destroyed close to a battalion of Certan troopers. Regrettably, we did have to destroy the Montgren Gorge bridge, and it appears that the Certan forces poised to invade Montgren have been withdrawn."

"What have you done, you idiot?" demanded Koralya. "We cannot stand against Certis and Gallos."

"We already have," said Beltur coldly. "Our mages also left a message inside a guarded and sealed palace, after they killed Rystyn, that any Certan ruler who lifted arms against Fairhaven or Montgren would face the same fate."

"You're lying! No one could do that."

"Koralya . . ." said Zekkarat tiredly, "they killed the last Duke of Hydlen, and they killed Rystyn. They entered your palace without anyone being able to stop them. Most of the Gallosian, Certan, and Hydlenese deaths were caused by one Fairhaven company and two squads, and six very good war mages. I forgot to mention that they also killed something like fifteen mages from Hydlen, Gallos, and Certis."

"So . . . are you going to remove me and become Duke of Montgren and Fairhaven?"

Beltur smiled ironically. "No. I think that matters should remain as they are . . . almost. No one in Fairhaven wants much to do with Montgren, and you certainly don't think much of Fairhaven. So . . . we'll let you remain as Duchess, but Fairhaven will no longer pay tariffs to Montgren, since we've been such a burden. And there's one other change that is absolutely necessary."

"I suppose I want to be Lord Protector." Koralya's voice dripped sarcasm.

"Not in the slightest. I don't think you understand. Fairhaven and Montgren are too different to remain in the same land. You will cede the strip of Montgren that comprises the southernmost twenty kays, from east border to west border so that we control the trade road. As for the Lord Protector, the next Lord Protector will be Majer Zekkarat. Not only that, but every Lord Protector of Montgren must be approved by the Council of Fairhaven. And . . . if *anything* happens to Zekkarat, you will be removed as duchess, and Fairhaven will select the next ruler from your family line. Also, if anything strange happens to any other member of your family line, you will also be removed and executed."

Taelya looked at Zekkarat, who appeared stunned.

"What am I supposed to do? Live in poverty?" said Koralya sneeringly.

"Fairhaven contributed nothing to Montgren before we rebuilt it. Your forebears lived well enough. I'm sure you'll manage."

"I'm the Lord Protector," declared Korwaen. "You can't take that. It belongs in *my* family."

"Korwaen," said Taelya, "is Maenya well and alive?"

"Well enough."

"Where is she?"

"At the house."

"Is she healthy and unharmed?"

"Yes."

"But you've kept her confined, haven't you?"

"It's for her own good."

Taelya didn't hesitate. She put a small chaos bolt through Korwaen's forehead. Then she looked at Koralya, even as Korwaen pitched forward, dead. "The position of Lord Protector is now held by Majer Zekkarat. Also, all possessions and lands held by the late Lord Korsaen and Lady Maeyora now reside in Lady Maenya. Any possessions gained by Korwaen revert to the heirs of those dispossessed. Do you have any questions, Duchess?" Taelya looked coldly at the Duchess.

"Who are—"

Taelya slammed a containment around Koralya's mouth. "I'm one of those who killed the Viscount. I'm the one of those who will kill you if you do a single thing that breaks or evades the terms set forth by Majer and Councilor Beltur on behalf of Fairhaven. Do you understand me?" Taelya removed the containment.

"You can't—"

Taelya replaced the containment. "I can . . . and I will. I watched thousands of men die, and I had to kill a great many of them because of your stupidity and greed. I don't like either stupidity or greed. But you can remain duchess so long as you're not too stupid or too greedy. And remember . . . I'm not the only one who can do this. There are at least five others."

At the last words, Koralya paled.

Taelya removed the containment.

Beltur smiled coldly. "Taelya's father was killed in the first Hydlenese invasion. She doesn't have much patience for greed or stupidity. Now . . . do you accept the terms of remaining as duchess?"

"I don't have much choice."

"Not if you want to keep living," said Beltur.

"There's also a certain order about keeping the Montgren Gorge bridge open for Certans," said Zekkarat. "I'm sure you'd prefer that it remain unseen, especially by many of those of means in Vergren. Instead, we can circulate the order by the late Lord Protector demanding the bridge be kept open so that he takes the blame."

"Do we actually have any troopers left to defend the gorge?" asked Koralya.

"We have four companies, some rather shorthanded," replied Zekkarat. "But with the Montgren Gorge bridge gone, anyone who wants to attack Montgren will have to go through Fairhaven. I doubt that any will want to pay that price.

So far, the total deaths suffered from attacking Fairhaven exceed ten battalions, more than twenty mages, and two rulers. So, as long as you behave decorously, Duchess, I believe your position will be secure."

"I can live with that, Lord Protector."

While Koralya's voice was anything but warm, Taelya didn't detect any overt deception. *And there won't be for a while . . . maybe not for years . . . if we keep reminding her.*

"We'll take care of Korwaen's body," said Taelya. "We'll also inform Lady Maenya that she is her brother's heir, and you *will* confirm that in a proclamation, noting only that Korwaen suffered an unfortunate death as a result of unapproved agreements with the late Viscount Rystyn."

"We'll draft those shortly," said Zekkarat, "along with a few others to straighten out the details, such as the proclamations dealing with Korwaen and the one ceding some land to Fairhaven in return for its services blocking invasions by Hydlen, Gallos, and Certis. After we're done, in the meantime, you'll remain here at the palace. That would be for the best in any event."

"I have no intention of going anywhere else," replied Koralya. "Especially at present."

"One company will remain here to guard the palace," declared Zekkarat. "The other will patrol or undertake other duties as necessary."

Another three quints passed before Zekkarat and Beltur were satisfied with the arrangements at the palace, with Karlaak's company moving in residence and taking over palace security, and Koralya had signed the proclamations dealing with Korwaen and Fairhaven.

As the mages and Zekkarat walked from the palace, Kaeryla looked to Taelya. "Why did you place it all on Korwaen? Koralya's just as guilty."

"I doubt that Koralya had much to do with Korsaen's or Maeyora's death, or even her mother's. She was already ruling, and all she had to do was wait for her mother to die. Korwaen never could wait." *Not for anything.*

"But that allows Koralya to place the blame on Korwaen." Kaeryla frowned.

"That's unfortunately better," said Beltur, "than telling the people of Montgren that their duchess made an alliance to turn Montgren into a puppet of the Viscount."

"You'd make a better ruler," said Kaeryla.

Beltur winced. "That would be a very bad idea. It would turn all of Candar against Fairhaven, and everyone would claim we'd planned that all along. If you think we've been fighting wars so far . . . they'd be nothing compared to what we'd face. That would make a family of mages the ruling family of Montgren. That also wouldn't be at all good for you, given who you might have to consort."

Kaeryla winced.

"You're both right," said Zekkarat evenly. "Beltur would make a far better ruler, and his replacing the Duchess would create an alliance of every land in eastern Candar against Fairhaven."

Taelya turned to Zekkarat. "Could we borrow a squad or so to visit Korsaen and Maeyora's estate and free Maenya?"

"Why doesn't the other company accompany you?" replied Zekkarat. "I'd like to see what we might find there."

From the palace, Third Squad, followed by the company commanded temporarily by Zekkarat, rode back past the outer wall and then up the slope and to the side lane on the right, taking it. Behind Third Squad, near the front of the Montgren company, rode Korwaen's guards, their hands tied behind them, with Korwaen's body between their horses and tied over his saddle.

After several hundred yards, the lane curved back to the north, and at the end of the curve were two tall brick gateposts that Taelya remembered and that looked unchanged. The two iron scroll-worked gates were swung open, and Third Squad proceeded on the lane as it ran through a meadow toward a long three-story, stone-walled dwelling situated just below the crest of a rise some five yards higher than the meadow. A low wall enclosed an area three hundred yards on a side, including three outbuildings, one of which was a stable.

Taelya noted that there were still gardens on both ends of the house. Beyond the open gates in the second wall, the stone-paved lane led directly toward the center of the mansion, where it formed an oval around a small garden, with the north side of the oval going under the covered entrance. Off the rightmost curve in the oval another stone-paved lane led to the stable and to the outbuilding behind it.

Beltur led the way to the covered entrance to the mansion, where he reined up less than five yards from where a pair of guards with spears in hand and sabres at their belts waited, one on each side of the closed front doors.

"Summon the Lady Maenya," ordered Zekkarat.

"By whose order?" asked one of the guards.

"By the order of the new Lord Protector, Majer Zekkarat," declared Beltur. "We've brought Korwaen's body back for his sister to burn. He was executed for high treason and conspiring to turn Montgren over to the Viscount of Certis."

The guards looked bewildered.

"But he was Lord Protector," said one.

"I have a proclamation here," said Zekkarat, "signed and sealed by the Duchess of Montgren. It names Lady Maenya as the heir and sole holder of this estate. Do you honestly think that a company of Montgren troopers would be here with such a proclamation if it were not true?"

The two still looked puzzled.

Taelya eased forward slightly. "I'll make this very easy." She gathered a small ball of chaos above her raised hand. "Drop the spears and call for Maenya. If she's confined, open her doors and tell her that she is free, but that she needs to come hear the proclamation. If she is hurt or injured, every one of you will die . . . just like Korwaen."

"Don't fight her, Meerkyl!" called one of Korwaen's guards. "Lord Korwaen is dead. His body's here. Majer Zekkarat's the new Lord Protector, and he's got three mages."

The two guards exchanged looks, then dropped their spears, and looked back to Taelya, almost fearfully.

"Just one of you go and tell her," said Taelya.

The shorter guard opened the door and hurried inside, leaving the door open behind him.

When the silver-haired Maenya stepped out through the doors, almost a third of a quint later, she looked stunned, if but momentarily. Even wearing a simple dark blue shirt and trousers, she was an imposing figure, almost as tall as her father had been. Her dark eyes went to Beltur . . . and then to Taelya. "When I heard a white mage had come to say I was free, I thought it might be you."

"Lady Maenya," said Zekkarat, "you now hold all the lands and golds of your parents, in your own right as Lady. It has been so proclaimed by the Duchess."

"And by Majer Zekkarat, as the new Lord Protector," added Beltur.

"We also have the sad duty," declared Zekkarat, "of returning the body of the traitor, the former Lord Protector Korwaen, who conspired with the Viscount of Certis to betray the forces of Montgren and to turn Montgren over to the Viscount."

Maenya remained clear-eyed. "His body will be burned without ceremony. He betrayed more than Montgren." Then she looked to Beltur. "I can only offer you what hospitality there may be, but I would hope you would avail yourselves of it."

"Lady Maenya," said Zekkarat, "for the present, I will remove all guards employed by your brother and provide a squad to safeguard your estate until you can make other arrangements. Majer Beltur and the Fairhaven Third Squad are free to accept your hospitality . . . if that is acceptable to you and to them."

Maenya looked from Beltur to Taelya. "I hope you will accept. It is the least I can do." Then she looked to Beltur.

"We will accept, provided we can assist where necessary."

Maenya's sad smile was somehow also knowing, Taelya thought, much like that of her mother, almost as if Maenya had foreseen at least some of what had occurred.

LXXVI

More than two glasses later, Korwaen's body was being reduced to ashes in a pyre behind the stables, watched by two troopers and no one else. All of the guards hired by Korwaen had been paid and dismissed immediately, and a squad of Montgren troopers were in residence and patrolling the estate.

Zekkarat, Beltur, Taelya, Kaeryla, and Maenya sat around a small table in the breakfast room of the mansion, while Third Squad was seated around the dining room table. Both had been served the same fare, fowl strips in cream sauce, cheese-lace potatoes, and buttered pole beans.

Before anyone in the breakfast room began to eat, Beltur lifted the crystal beaker before him. "To the Lady Maenya."

"To the Lady Maenya."

For the next small fraction of a quint, the five ate quietly.

Then Zekkarat cleared his throat. "There are a few more details we need to discuss, Lady Maenya. Since you did not wish to retain any of the guards your brother engaged, you will doubtless need to make some arrangements . . ."

"I will do so as quickly as possible, so as not to require the services of your troopers any longer than necessary. If you know of some stipended and reliable troopers who might like work here . . . with some of the loyal former retainers that Korwaen dismissed, we should be fine."

"I just might be able to find a few," replied Zekkarat, with an amused smile, before the smile vanished, and he asked, "Was your father's death due entirely to his illness?"

"Father was truly ill," said Maenya, "but he should have lived longer than he did. Somehow, Korwaen hastened his death. I suggested that to Mother, but she thought I was being unfair, and, although I watched everything, I couldn't prove how he did it. All I had were suspicions, but, then, after Mother's so-called riding accident, I knew. Even then, I couldn't figure it out."

"What happened to your mother, exactly?" asked Kaeryla.

"One of the men reported that someone had been poaching in the woods off the north pasture, but that they'd left and that she ought to take a look. I offered to go with her, but she said she'd be fine with Khamaat. He was the assistant steward. She wanted to look at the damage before Korwaen returned from the palace."

"Why was she in a hurry to do that?" asked Beltur.

"She always talked to him after he'd been to the palace. She'd ask him questions, and even when he wouldn't answer, she could get a good idea of what was happening. She felt that he was manipulating Koralya . . . but I wasn't ever certain who was manipulating who."

"So what happened?" pressed Kaeryla.

"The two of them rode out there. Someone had set a deadfall in the trees with a log, and it came down and hit both of them. When they didn't come back, I rode out there. I found both bodies. Supposedly, the log slashed Khamaat's neck, and he bled to death. There was pine tar on his neck, but it wasn't right. Mother's face . . ." Maenya paused, then swallowed. ". . . was scraped and bruised on one side, but her skull was smashed from behind. There was no way that a log could have caused that kind of damage."

"We hadn't heard those details," said Zekkarat.

"Then, Korwaen accused me of hiring someone to set the deadfall, and he had Koralya order me confined to the house here . . . there's no way I'd do something like that . . . that's something he'd do . . . it was so obvious . . ."

"In short," said Zekkarat, "you didn't do it or set it up, and if you had you wouldn't have been that obvious."

"I didn't. I couldn't *ever* have done anything like that. Why would I? I'd already lost Father. It was all so . . . horrible."

The total truthfulness of that statement washed over Taelya, and she saw Beltur nod as well.

"I think Mother worried, but she wouldn't talk about it. She just kept telling me not to worry, that she *knew* I'd be fine." Maenya shook her head. "I knew that, too. I can't tell you how I knew it, but I worried about her, especially after Father's death. I didn't like how much time Korwaen spent at the palace, and all the new guards he brought in."

"Why did your Mother let him do that?"

"She didn't have a choice, not after Koralya appointed him as Lord Protector and as Father's heir."

Beltur winced.

"You realize, Lady," said Zekkarat almost delicately, "that Duchess Koralya has never consorted and is, at her age, unlikely to have children even if she did consort."

"That's one reason why I felt Korwaen wouldn't do anything to me immediately. There were already too many deaths. In a year or so that would have changed. Possibly even sooner. He had started to consider who might be the best match for him."

For a moment, Zekkarat's comment didn't make any sense at all to Taelya—and then it did, when she recalled that Lord Korsaen had been the nephew and

L. E. Modesitt, Jr.

closest relation, besides Koralya, to Duchess Korlyssa. "But if Korwaen was effectively Koralya's heir, and your father was dying, why did Korwaen murder your parents?"

"I don't *know*," replied Maenya, "but . . . inheritance in Montgren hasn't always gone to the eldest, and Mother and Father were always having to rein Korwaen in." Maenya smiled sadly at Taelya. "Even when we were very young, he tried to bully and browbeat me. You know that. You were there once. Then, once I grew as tall as he was and Father taught me blade skills . . ."

". . . and Korwaen discovered that you could sense what he might do before he did it, the way your mother could," suggested Taelya, "then he grew afraid that you might actually best him with blades . . ."

"I've been better with blades for almost ten years."

"And you worked harder in running the estate and the trading, didn't you?" asked Beltur.

"Korwaen was never interested in what made the family successful. He spent most of his time flattering Koralya."

"Do you think they might have gifted you the estate, or the merchanting, so that you'd be independent?" asked Zekkarat.

"The merchanting was likely. Korwaen had no interest in it, except wanting to take golds from it. He told me more than once that I was the favorite, and that it wasn't fair, because he was the oldest. His friends, those sycophants he called friends, all told him that all inheritances should properly go to the eldest son. I don't think Father and Mother ever played favorites. They just praised what we did well, and told us where we could improve."

"Usually, that works," said Beltur, "but not always. Can you keep the trading going the way it was?"

"I don't see why not," replied Maenya. "After Father got so weak, I was handling most of it so Mother could spend time with him."

"It's all yours now," said Beltur.

"I wish it weren't. I know Father couldn't have lived that much longer, but I'd hoped Mother . . ." Maenya's eyes glistened, and she blotted them. "It's just so . . . wrong. Just as we were getting to where we could really enjoy each other . . ."

"She was quite something," said Beltur. "So was your father. We owe them both a great deal. So does Fairhaven."

"Montgren owes you even more," replied Maenya.

"Indeed, it does," said Zekkarat.

"I think it's a very good idea as well that you're the Lord Protector," Maenya said to Zekkarat. "The land needs what you have to offer." She smiled warmly.

Zekkarat looked as if he didn't know how to respond. Finally, he said, "I didn't ask to be Lord Protector. Majer Beltur insisted on it. I only did what I thought right."

"If everyone did only what they thought right, Candar would be a far better place," replied Maenya. "And Beltur was right to insist on you as Lord Protector."

"He'll also need to be promoted to commander," added Beltur.

"There's no hurry about that," protested Zekkarat. "We need to promote some undercaptains to captain first . . . and restructure the Palace Guard as well."

Taelya smiled and took another mouthful of the creamed fowl, good, but not nearly so good as what her mother cooked. Then she mostly listened for a while, as others filled in Maenya on what had happened over the past season.

Somehow, well after dinner, Taelya and Maenya found themselves alone in the breakfast room, possibly because Maenya kept asking Taelya questions.

". . . what was it like to face other mages . . ."

". . . isn't it strange to be an undercaptain when most officers are men . . ."

"You know . . . I've never forgotten how you stood up to Korwaen. When I saw that, I decided I could do that, too, in my own way."

"You obviously did."

"He never liked it. He'd ask why I wasn't like all the other girls."

"With your mother and father, how could you have been like other young women?"

"That's true," said Maenya, "but compared to you, I was fortunate. I had much more time with my father. He got to see me grow up."

"You lost both your parents. I still have my mother," replied Taelya. "I was fortunate enough to listen to her and learn from her."

"She's still a councilor and treasurer of Fairhaven?"

"She is. She's done a magnificent job of assessing, managing, and handling tariffs, and she's done it in a way that almost everyone thinks is fair."

"I heard, somewhere, that you might have a brother."

"That's Dorylt. He's fifteen, and he's also a beginning mage, but he's a black. He's also been working as an apprentice cabinet maker and as a trainee under-captain. Kaeryla has a younger brother, too. That's Arthaal."

"You're all close, aren't you?"

Taelya offered an amused smile. "We are. In more ways than one. Our houses are across the street from each other, and we share the same barn and stable. We alternate having dinner between the houses."

"I envy you. I never had that with Korwaen."

"It sounds like he never let you be close."

"Only when it suited him. Never for long." Abruptly, Maenya asked, "What can you tell me about Zekkarat?"

"Personally, I don't know much. I have the impression that he never consorted. That might be because he's served in three different lands. He became a Mont-gren officer after the Hydlenese attack on Fairhaven, because he was good, and

Duke Halacut feared competent officers, and because Beltur and Commander Raelf suggested he'd be welcome here. He's solid, but he'll also listen."

"That would be good. Korwaen liked people who flattered him." Maenya tried to stifle a yawn, but failed.

"Oh . . . I've kept you up too long."

"No . . . I'm the one who kept asking you questions. Are you heading back to Fairhaven tomorrow?"

Taelya realized that she had no idea. "I don't know. I don't think we'll be here long, though."

"We can at least talk more in the morning. I'd like that."

Taelya realized that she would as well, and yet, as she walked upstairs to the most luxurious bed in which she would ever sleep, she really wanted to be on her way back home . . . and she hoped it wouldn't be that long before Sheralt would be back in Fairhaven.

Maenya would likely be Duchess of Montgren in years to come, and that was something that didn't appeal to Taelya. *Not in the slightest.* She also realized, belatedly, that she'd never told Maenya that she'd been the one to kill Korwaen, but that, since Maenya had seen Korwaen's body, without shedding a tear, the newly recognized heiress had to have known that Taelya had done the deed . . . if, indeed, she hadn't already sensed it in the way that she seemed to have inherited from her mother.

LXXVII

In the end, Beltur, Taelya, Kaeryla, and Third Squad didn't leave Vergren on sevenday, but early on eightday. They spent eightday night at the Weevett post, then set out again early on oneday morning.

Once they were away from the post and town and headed south on the road to Fairhaven, Kaeryla turned to Taelya. "It's still hard to believe that Maenya will be Duchess of Montgren someday. She's so nice."

"She's nice, and fair . . . and strong in a very quiet way," replied Taelya. "That will likely serve Montgren well."

"She's a little like you."

"You're being kind, and we both know it," replied Taelya. "I don't shout, except in battle, but you really can't say I'm quiet. Sheralt definitely wouldn't think that."

"How long do you think he'll have to stay at the border post?"

"Until we get some indication that the new Viscount isn't going to attack. That could be another eightday . . . or longer."

"Do you really think we'll have to fight again soon?" asked Kaeryla.

"No, sers," said Varais from where she rode behind them and beside Beltur. "Majer Beltur and three companies destroyed over six battalions—and three of them were destroyed with only two mages. You two largely destroyed almost another battalion. Undercaptain Sheralt just destroyed more than a company. Fairhaven and Montgren have only suffered comparatively slight losses. There's little for Certis to gain by attacking us, when they'd just suffer worse losses. Gallos and Hydlen don't have any troopers or mages left. Not many, anyway. Also, no one's even in charge in Hydlen."

"I'd agree with Varais," said Beltur, "but rulers aren't always as bright as they might be."

Nor are some of those who advise rulers. Taelya couldn't help but think about Korwaen . . . and Sydon, each of whom, in his own way, chose shortcuts in hopes of fame and power and ended up paying dearly for that choice.

Then there was Sheralt . . . who'd been stubborn, but not too stubborn, and who'd made the right choice in the end. *With a little encouragement.*

Taelya smiled.

EPILOGUE

The Viscount Rystyr, as the lawful successor to Viscount Rystyn, wishes to remain on the best possible terms with Montgren, as well as with the mages of the independent city of Fairhaven. We would like to assure both the Duchess of Montgren and the Council of Fairhaven that Certis has no intention whatsoever for any use of armed forces in any lands outside the ambit of Certis, and especially not in Montgren or Fairhaven.

At the same time we must protest the use of assassination as a means to wage war and would hope that any differences between our lands could be peacefully discussed before any resort to force is contemplated . . .